## Bound Together

**Adam Cloud,** seeking to find his lost father and to test his new manhood . . . **Jessica Jennings,** trapped in a marriage that was a lie, and unable to deny the truth of her sexual needs . . . **Harry Creekmore,** who had lived by his wits his whole life and now had to prove himself by his deeds . . . **Ishtar Baynes,** whose former sins as a prostitute were nothing compared to the evil she wrought . . . **Promise Jennings,** whose marriage to a stranger was but the first step on her terrifying odyssey . . .

Together they joined on the journey westward. God only knew who would survive.

## Bound for the Promised Land

"Solid, colorful, lively, authentic!"
—*Publishers Weekly*

"The author can write up a storm . . . He is a master!"
—*Philadelphia Inquirer*

*Please turn page
for more critical acclaim*

RICHARD MARIUS'

# Bound for the Promised Land

"HERE IS A WRITER WHO BRINGS UNABASHED, OLD-FASHIONED EXCITEMENT BACK INTO READING . . . Filled with a dozen fully-developed characters, encompassing every disaster from hailstorm to cholera, exploring the psychological wounds of restless men and troubled women, **BOUND FOR THE PROMISED LAND** is impossible to lay down, and haunts the spirit afterwards. . . . A book to remember!"
—*Anniston Star*

"THOROUGHLY ENGAGING . . . Marius is a storyteller with a firm sense of time and place and people."
—*Kirkus Reviews*

"WE NOD OUR HEADS, THINKING 'YES, THIS IS THE WAY IT *REALLY* WAS' . . . Marius is a superb writer from the start of the agonizing journey in Tennessee to its denouement in the Rocky Mountains."
—*Chicago Tribune*

# BOUND FOR THE PROMISED LAND

Richard Marius

A SIGNET BOOK from
**NEW AMERICAN LIBRARY**
TIMES MIRROR

*For Nini, with love*

*All o'er this wide, extended plain*
*Shines on eternal day*
*Where God our King forever reigns*
*And scatters night away.*
*I am bound for the Promised Land*
*I am bound for the Promised Land.*
*Oh who will come and go with me?*
*I am bound for the Promised Land.*

—TRADITIONAL AMERICAN HYMN

# 1

There was a restlessness in the man. Adam knew that, even before Joel Cloud ran away. At times they would sit together in the evening in their windowless cabin lighted only by the blazing fire in the hearth, and they would listen to the wind blowing cold down from the north. And the father would peer up into the gloom gathered against the ceiling, his thin face set in pensive wonder. Once he said dreamily to the child, "I wonder where it all comes from? The wind? Where does it go?"

And in the mellow autumn afternoons when the leaves were changing on the trees and the great sun lay tawny on the land, he would look fixedly up at high formations of birds flying south. He would follow them with his eyes for as long as he could see them. And there was in his face a longing that the boy could feel as a heaviness in his own heart, as though in the midst of the yellow light on the open hillside they were in prison together.

Sometimes Adam thought his father might be a stranger, remote and spellbound in some enchanted realm the boy could never enter. Then Adam was perplexed and troubled that he could not reach his father over that wall of amazed silence that came up around him when he saw some far thing move toward the unimaginable distance. "I wonder where they go?" the father would say, in a voice hardly more than a whisper.

But for all his longing to see far lands, Joel Cloud did not go to the war with Mexico. The other men in Bourbon County went, but Joel Cloud stayed home. "You *can't* go off and leave me and *Adam!*" his wife cried. "Be *sensible*, Joel! You got an obligation to your own folks first. Why, what if you got yourself *kilt* out there!"

Her name was Naomi, and she was a persistent woman. She spoke with a conviction honed on the grindstone of her certainties. Her husband did not argue with her. He worked the red land. He fought the weeds and the forest. He nourished his trusting cows and the squealing little pigs and tended lovingly to his strong brown mules. He patched his harness and saw that the foolish chickens had a dry place to roost, higher than the hungry leap of the nocturnal fox.

And in the evening he sat staring into the fire or else rocking in silence on the porch of the cabin, while Naomi Cloud chattered endlessly about their small world. Joel Cloud stayed home from Buena Vista and Santa Fe, Monterey and Mexico City. He stayed home and did his duty to his own, locked in the order of the farm and the seasons as though he were a wheel in a watch, and the only time he ever smiled was when he looked shyly at his son.

In 1848, when the men who had gone to war trooped home, he went into the village on Saturdays, as farmers always did. In warm weather he sat on this porch or that, or else he hung around the square where the courthouse was. In cold weather he retreated with the rest to the stores where there were stoves and wooden chairs, and he listened to stories. He drank in the treasury of glittering fable and memorable deeds and dazzling romance brought back by his neighbors from that far-off war. In that conflict a strange chemistry had worked; these familiar men had become distant from him and treated him distantly. He had not gone.

Adam went with his father on those Saturdays. And like the father, the son—about fifteen now, tall, rawboned, and quiet—sat enthralled with stories of how it had all been—the wild, desperate charges of the Mexican infantry, the way booming cannon and banging rifles chopped down their gaudy ranks like a scythe working dry wheat in July, the damnable affair of loading a long rifle and working the ramrod in the searing barrel while you were clinging to the rocky ground—being shot at.

They tried to describe the brilliance of the fiery stars in the desert nights, and they whispered about the soft brown skin of Mexican women, their white teeth, their willingness to . . . And here their yarns broke like a swift river on shoals, and they laughed foamy laughter.

Unlike his father, Adam Cloud did not feel the anguish of something lost, trampled forever in the dust by the steady beating of time, a silent drum pounding seconds away. The boy only felt sad because he could detect grief in the high-

2

boned, impassive face of Joel Cloud and also because he had been a reason that had kept his father at home.

Once in the evening, when Joel Cloud had sat all day long listening in rapt and gloomy silence, he took his boy up behind him on the riding mule, and they went home through the dark, all silent except for the steady clippity-clop of the shod mule on the soft dirt road. Finally Joel spoke in bitterness. "I reckon you think I'm pretty worthless, don't ye? I ain't got no stories to tell."

In 1848 the valley came on hard times. It rained too little in July and too much in September, and the harvest barely yielded back the seed. When winter came the cows gave only a trickle of milk because their hay was bad. Pigs came down with a strange disease and died. The chickens did not lay. By December the Cloud family was eating turnips for dinner. By January for supper. Naomi Cloud viewed the disaster with her relentless optimism. "I'm just so *thankful* we have these wonderful turnips to eat! Turnips is so *good* for you. My mamma always said you could eat lots of turnips and keep your hair from falling out. And a turnip don't never sit hard on your belly like ham does." Joel Cloud and his son ate and remained silent.

And that was the year the cholera came. Nobody knew much about cholera except that people said it came from China. It swarmed up the rivers and killed people like bugs. Cholera made its victims burn with fever, then chill. It exploded their guts in diarrhea. Then they vomited. Finally they died in cramps and thirst. Sometimes within a day.

At first it seemed like the scourge of God. Preachers gloated over it for a while. The vengeance of an angry God against people who had not gone to church. But then the plague killed preachers right and left. Finally people were left to die without even the consolation of knowing they were being punished.

The disease flailed Bourbonville as the leaves fell in October. It killed twenty people in a week, including the Methodist preacher, three village drunks, and a lanky young doctor from Knoxville, who tried to tend the sick because he happened to be in town at the time, attending a wedding. They buried him next to the bride and groom, all dead of cholera. For months Naomi Cloud would not let her son or her husband go near town. She made them stay home.

Happy days. Adam was often with his father alone, some-

3

times talking in the languid, rambling way of country people. Sometimes silent together by the fire. Sometimes they used a little of the precious gunpowder to hunt with the dogs in the forest. A bare woodland now, chill and often encrusted with thin ice underfoot even late in the morning.

In January Adam killed his first deer. The happiest thing he had ever done. Happy not only because he fired good and true at the running animal and felt the long rifle bang solidly into his shoulder, but happy, too, because his father let him make the shot, speaking low to him, telling him how to lead the deer with his aim, trusting him even when they were hungry at home, not taking the rifle away to fire himself. And so they had good salt meat for weeks afterwards, and his father was proud of him.

What they talked about most was a newspaper.

Joel Cloud had found the newspaper in the village in the autumn, just before the cholera struck. People gathered around on the steamboat dock one mild Saturday afternoon while a man named Hutchins, with a wool cap pushed back on his head, read aloud a short little item spilled down an inside page in ranks of fine gray print that advertised the wonders on sale in Knoxville up the river.

The short despatch, labeled "Intelligence from Sacramento," announced that there was gold in California.

In some way he never explained to his son, Joel Cloud got possession of that newspaper. Adam was not able to believe that his father would steal. But by some almost magical process, when they rode home on the mule that night, Joel Cloud had the newspaper tucked up under his shirt, next to his skin. It crackled there with the motion of their riding. And in the strained, concentrated silence Adam heard it and asked what it was. The man said, "It's that paper! Now you hush up!"

Joel Cloud could not read. But he had sent his son to school for five grades. A sacrifice it had been for him, doing without the boy's help for hours every day. Now Adam repaid him by reading the story in the newspaper by firelight, slowly, carefully, so Joel Cloud could take it all in at leisure and think about it without having anybody to interrupt him.

Not just once. Adam read it again and again. That winter, when they gathered by the hearth at night after supper, the man would nod at the boy and swallow, and in his laconic

4

way say (as though the thought had newly struck him): "Adam, what about reading me that paper?"

So the boy would gravely and obediently arise to fetch the precious newspaper down from the chink in the log wall over the rope bed where his mother and father slept. He would spread it on his knees, and leaning toward the fire to catch the flickering light, he would read—slowly, laboriously, spelling the sentences out like a mill grinding meal very fine. In time it did not matter if the firelight was so dim that he could scarcely see the words. They were printed on his mind. He could recite them all without fail, just as he could recite the twenty-third Psalm or the Lord's Prayer or the crazy sentence his teacher had taught them to remember how to spell geography—"George Edward's Oldest Girl Rode a Pig Home Yesterday."

At the end his father would sit there, his legs thrown out, entranced and musing and still, as if he expected that there might be more. Finally he would heave a sigh of wonder, his arms folded over one another, and break his silence. "Gold! Think of that! Gold! Just waiting to be fished out!"

Usually that was all he said, though at times he was moved to further reflection of a more philosophical sort. "Think what it'd mean. Some poor fool—like me, for instance—could just walk out there and put his hand down in the right place and pick up a fortune! And he'd be a new man! He'd have *respect!* He could walk through this country with a pocket full of yellow metal that's too soft to make a nail with. That's the real miracle about gold! It ain't good for nothing! But it's worth more than a man's life. And if a man—like me, for instance—if he had himself a pocketful of that yellow gold, why, even ole Will Bourbon would have to take his hat off. Even ole Will Bourbon!"

It was a sublime thought. With it soaring in his mind, Joel Cloud's big, soft eyes glistened, and he licked his lips. His son's fantasies rose, too, as immaterial as the fire. Will Bourbon taking his hat off as they rode by.

Not that Joel Cloud cared what Will Bourbon thought! Will Bourbon owned the larger of the two plantations in the county. Not real plantation country here. Never had been. No cotton. Everybody knew niggers and cotton went together. And when Will Bourbon tried to keep niggers without cotton, everybody knew there was something dishonest about him.

5

He did grow acres and acres of tobacco. Twenty-five slaves lived in the log quarters behind a big house brilliantly white-washed every summer. The big house had calico curtains, no rugs on the wide, softwood floors, and it was sparsely furnished with crude furniture made by unskilled hands. A lot harder to keep warm than Joel Cloud's tight little cabin with its low roof and mud plaster sealing the logs together. But Will Bourbon's house ruled the land around. And he could stand with a haughty expression on his lean, dry, old face, and he could look down on dirt farmers like Joel Cloud who did all their work with their own rough hands. The Bourbons were said to be descended from kings, and they had given their fine soft name to the county and to the town.

Joel Cloud hated Will Bourbon and hated his slaves, because they possessed the curious arrogance that is the property of the servants of the rich, and looked down on Joel Cloud, too.

"Gold!" Joel Cloud said. "All out there! Just waiting to be picked up!"

Naomi Cloud was outraged. "All the gold them fools out there can find is at the end of the rainbow. We got a better life right here on our own little place than any of them poor fools that's going out to California. What's in California anyhow? Just a desert and a lot of old rocks. Only reason folks is going to California is they're just too trifling to make it right here. And if you're trifling here, then you're going to be trifling there, and you're going to get hot besides."

Adam was almost afraid to go back to town in February when his mother finally allowed it. He was scared somebody would bring up the matter of the missing newspaper. Maybe his father would be arrested, put in jail, even hanged. Adam had seen a man hanged once. A ghastly sight with the man screaming when they put the noose over his head, with a neighbor on each side holding to his arms to keep him from collapsing, and when the trap was sprung he kicked his feet with all his might, drawing them up (they were bound at the ankles) in a frantic, hopeless striving to get back onto the scaffold as though the hanging would then be called off, and he would not die. The man had killed a neighbor in an argument over a fence, and if you were hanged for a fence, why not for a newspaper?

But when he got back to Bourbonville, he found nobody worried about an old newspaper. People were burying the

6

horror of cholera in politics. While Joel Cloud had been brooding on his land back up in the hills, Zachary Taylor had been elected President of the United States. Old Rough and Ready was going to show *them* a thing or two. He was a free soil man! No slavery in the new territories opening beyond the Mississippi. In time, the senators from the free states that would be formed would outnumber the senators from the slave states in Congress. The Constitution would be amended; the niggers would go free! And the power of the planters broken forever. Hang the bastards off their fancy porches and teach them a few lessons about law and order.

Politics and gold; talk poured around them both.

A few from the county had already fallen to yellow fever. Gone West. One was a man Joel Cloud knew well. A lanky dirt farmer with a consumptive cough and shoulders so thin they looked like wings folded under his ragged shirt. Abraham Tippet. He lived out near the place where the Methodist church stood amid its graves. His house was a shack and his fields were littered with half-burnt stumps. Abraham Tippet would work awhile on one stump and then on another, looking for an easy one to root out of the ground. He was like that.

"They rode out of here on a couple of spavined mules like somebody had put 'em under a hex. I tell you what's the truth. Their eyes was wild! Him and that slattern woman of hisn! Left everything they had 'cept what they could carry in gunny sacks on them old mules. *Going to Californie!* he said. *Going to get rich!* Crazy!"

A round of laughter at the story. Laughter meant to blow down the foolishness of hope. Yet something forced and worried about that laughter. Like laughter coming suddenly at a funeral when the corpse had complained of a headache before his sudden death, and you have been going around with a headache yourself lately; when the chance comes you laugh to relieve the pressure of terror. What if Abraham Tippet made it? And you stayed here.

Nobody wanted to look like a damned fool, to approve of imbeciles who set out on a couple of rickety old mules for a three-thousand-mile march to the Pacific Ocean. My God! You had to cross the Great American Desert to get to California! Men back from Mexico and Texas knew that. And wild Indians, just waiting to steal everything you had, including your life, your wife, and your hair! Bessie Tippet, Indian

7

squaw! They all laughed and slapped their legs at the thought. But the people who laughed wore doubt in their eyes like the stains of a long drunk. What if Abraham Tippet made it?

For there was gold in California. Real gold, just waiting there to be picked up. Gold like a revelation from a capricious God that could make poor men be born again. Gold, drawing men like a stupendous magnet across the continent. Gold! And even in a rainy February in the backwoods, tall trees leafless and dripping with mist and obscure with fog, there was a sunshine gleaming in the word "Gold!"

For Joel Cloud it was the Mexican War all over again. Other men would go away and come home later with stories to tell. This time with gold to spend. Joel Cloud, having taken no dares from life, keeping his head obediently bowed to soil and hearth, would remain a dirt farmer, worse than nothing.

There was snow in February, the long winter hanging on like a dragon with jaws of ice. Naomi Cloud had sickened in January. In February her ailment sank into her thin chest. She shuffled painfully about, coughing, blowing thick yellow phlegm into rags she carried for handkerchiefs. Her face was gaunt and pale. For a week she had a fever, and her sunken eyes in their dark sockets burned unnaturally bright, like two little candles set back in her thin skull. When the fever finally ebbed, she could not get her strength back. She had to sit down, gasping, her breath scraping in her stiff throat, after the slightest effort. She tried to sweep the puncheon floor one day, and the exertion tired her so much that she fell into bed and slept for hours, as though in a coma.

When she awoke, it was with an undaunted bright smile gleaming in her wasted face like the moon shining in a swamp. "I'm all right!" she said. "I'm going to be just fine! I don't want you all to worry about me, you hear? The good Lord ain't going to let nothing happen to me when I got so much to do in the world—a good boy to raise and a good man to take care of and good land to farm! No sir! I know the Lord's ways, and you can always count on Him!" And she showed her large yellow teeth in that smile, which became a leer of triumph.

Her son watched her raving optimism and was troubled. Her husband looked on entranced, following every motion she made, speechless to her smiles and her glowing assurances, watching, watching, as intently as he might have

8

searched for motion in long grass where he thought a snake might be coiled. Much later on the boy realized that Joel Cloud was hoping that his wife would die. Still later he judged that his mother's loud and persistent claim to ultimate health was really revenge against her husband because she knew he did not love her.

In March spring came in a burst. One morning Adam went outside, and the air stirring in the woodland was mild. It carried a sweet, damp fragrance of wet earth and pine trees, and the ground underfoot was soft. The sun came down strong and bright, and the boy knew that the land would soon dry and that there would be plowing to do, and he was glad. He loved the plow, the sweaty smell of the mules, the damp-dirt smell of the new-turned earth, the cheerful sun, and the hardwood trees in the fringing woods budding with pale green leaf against the somber greens of the pines and red cedars that had kept the winter dark. Plowing was something his father trusted him with now, the man no longer even standing by the mule hames to see that the boy got the harness right, knowing that Adam took no chances. A mule could kill or maim you or make you an idiot with one blow from his quick and deadly hoofs. Manhood was when your father trusted you to harness a mule by yourself.

And Adam, trusted now, was pleased and eager to begin work. After the slack idleness of winter, he could toil; he could be thirsty and slake his thirst from cool water out of a pottery jug, and he could sweat in the afternoon heat and bathe in the creek afterwards—and he could hope again. Hope in spring was like creation, new and unspoiled, to God. Even the big mules sniffed the air with anticipation and twitched their long ears and seemed ready to begin. Like the miracle of spring come back, his mother's good health returned. "I told you all the time!" she said with her tiumphant, whining voice. "I knowed God wouldn't let me die."

And so it was in late March, with the buds on the trees about to unfurl their tender green, that Joel Cloud ran away one night to California to hunt gold.

# 2

Adam woke up to the hound pup whining and scratching to get outside. And when he got up sleepily to open the door, he found that he had to push hard because the door had been chocked on the outside with a stick to keep it shut, and the inside latch had been lifted.

He went barefoot out into the cool yard, uncomprehending, but already feeling a dull alarm in the pale and watery dawn just beginning to light the sky. Everything was dim, colorless; a few morning birds were singing in the gloomy trees. Suspending thought, he made his way down to the barn lot and found that there was only one mule there. Luke, the big blue hound, sire to the lonely, unnamed pup, was gone, too. The pup was running around, sniffing and whimpering, large, felt-soft ears flopping, and Adam could almost smell the emptiness of the place. He went slowly back to the cabin, woke his mother, and told her that her husband was gone.

"Why, what do you reckon happened?" she asked, looking around with her mouth agape under her sharp nose, her eyes darting, watery and afraid. Her skimpy brown hair was tied back under a flannel bandana nigger-fashion, and in her sleep-wild face her furious eyes burned with something akin to panic.

It was the only time she faltered.

The heavy rifle was gone. And an old leather sack his father had made out of deer hide and the powder horn from the hook by the door. His father's few old and shabby clothes were gone, too.

His mother recovered her steely presence of mind like a trap springing shut. "He had a toothache and didn't want to wake us up." She turned to Adam with a bright, false smile. "You go see Mr. Lacy, Adam. Your daddy's going to need help getting home."

10

"He wouldn't take a rifle to go get a tooth pulled, mamma!"

His mother's voice jumped at him like a bobcat in the woods. "Don't you give me no backtalk, Adam Cloud. You go do what I tell you!"

Adam sighed and saddled up the other mule and set out. He felt foolish. The nameless hound loped after him, and Adam rode slowly so the pup could keep up. He felt sorry for the dog.

Jubal Lacy had a farm on the other side of town. He kept a pair of long-handled dental tongs and pulled teeth for his friends. He rubbed salt in the torn and bleeding gum afterwards. "Ain't nothing like salt to keep out infection!" he said with professional cheer. "Salt on a sore is like honey on bread. It belongs there." He had pulled teeth for Joel Cloud. Nothing to do with a bad tooth in Bourbon County but to pull it.

But today Jubal Lacy said, "Why, no, son. I ain't seen your daddy. I'd be glad to yank him a tooth, though. He's a good man, your daddy. Glad to give him the best. And I'm the best around when it comes to teeth. What about you, boy?" He wanted to give a neighborly little peek in Adam's mouth. "I can look, and it won't cost you a penny." But Adam went home, depressed and confused and not wanting to speak to anybody.

"Well, I don't know where he's gone, but he'll be back. You wait and see." His mother's implacable confidence. She cooked meals for three, morning, noon, and night. She set her husband's portion on the back of the stove to keep warm. She flung it out to the pigs only when she was ready to fix the next meal. "He'll be coming back any minute now. He'll have some big surprise for us. Maybe a new cow. Maybe a new dress for me, Adam. A new rifle for you." She babbled. The boy kept silent. Only the hound pup expressed his feelings openly. At night he sat whimpering by the fire for the vanished Luke, until Adam had to take him into his own bed to console him.

Joel Cloud vanished on Monday. It was Saturday before his wife could believe the truth. A farmer named Burl Calloway and his short, plump wife with their motley brood of children came rattling into the yard on a flatbed wagon. The Calloways owned a little place at Varner's Cross Roads. There the twisting road from Bourbonville ran into the broad

11

pike running down from Knoxville on its way to Nashville and to the West beyond. Joel Cloud passed them by at dawn on the morning he left. He made their dogs bark something fierce, and Burl Calloway wanted to talk in soft amazement at how hard it had been to keep Joel's hound separated from his own. But finally he got to the point. "He asked me to come give you a message, Mrs. Cloud. He said he was going to California. He said he'd send for the both of you later on." An embarrassed silence. Burl Calloway looked at the ground and turned red. "He said you better buy another mule in the meantime, Adam. He said you'd need it."

There was more. Joel Cloud had dictated a paper to Eunice Calloway. She took it out carefully and read it aloud to all of them, slowly, in a high, nasal voice, meticulously pronouncing words she had written down like somebody reading the lesson in church. "All I have, my farm, tools and stock, and whatever, I give to my son Adam and to my wife Naomi, and if they have to sell it off to come West and join up with me, it's all right. I give my word to anybody that wants to buy it that it's all right with me to sell it and that Adam's word is my word."

Naomi Cloud listened with a grave and knowing nodding, as if she had expected everything all along. She wiped stiffly at a strand of her lank hair, concentrated with the intensity of an actor on what was said, took the paper at last and officiously handed it over to Adam. She gave not the faintest sign that she was perturbed. "Well, he's been wanting to go. And Joel knows what he's doing; it's just fine with me. But law, law! I sure do hate to think about moving. We've got such a nice little place here. And all my friends at church. But a woman has got to follow her man. It's what the good book says. You all get down and have some coffee."

Burl Calloway and his wife demurred. Courtesy required them to refuse a first invitation. Naomi Cloud insisted. "Now I won't hear to you two good folks going off without a hot cup of coffee. We ain't visited in *such* a long time. I heard about your little Baxter. He was such a sweet boy. I know you miss him. But the Lord gives, and the Lord takes away. I've lost three myself, and I know just how you feel." Baxter Calloway had been carried off by the measles the summer before. Eunice Calloway's eyes filled with tears when his name came up. Her husband looked old and sad. They got down from their wagon and came in to have coffee.

That year the Cloud family had only enough coffee to drink one cup apiece on Sunday mornings. But Naomi Cloud boiled an extravagant pot. And when the Calloways sat down at the crude table near the fire, Naomi insisted that they have two cups apiece. They talked about the good weather and the hard winter just gone. They laughed softly about the new preacher riding circuit for the Methodist Church. He was a young man named Henck, who had been sent down by the bishop with the understanding that he would find himself a respectable wife within a year.

They did not mention Joel Cloud. Nor did they speak of little Baxter again. By silent agreement they held that both of them had passed into a similar cloudy realm. After a decent interval the Calloways rounded up their flock and herded them onto the wagon and left. Naomi Cloud went on chattering to Adam about how nice the Calloways were. She did not mention her husband to her son for the rest of that day. But at supper she fixed only two portions of food.

# 3

It was a year before they heard from him again.

Adam worked the farm and grew big and hard. He was proud of what he had done, but he was lonely, too. He had never talked with his father very much. Silent people, both of them. But they were close; they worked side by side. And sometimes his father said "Look!" and the boy turned just in time to see a brown deer streak through the forest shadows like an illusion of dim light.

Now that his father was gone, Adam's order of things was shaken. The fields seemed empty. Sometimes at night he could not sleep for wondering where his father might be now. Adam had never been outside of Bourbon County. Bourbonville was the only town he knew. He could not even imagine what the West was like in spite of all the tales he had heard

13

about it. His blankness before the word "West" made it seem terrible. And he was afraid his father might die.

Naomi Cloud was undaunted. She began speculating about how they would travel to California. At night her talk was like the ceaseless chatter of chickens. "I think we'll go by steamboat. I don't know how anybody ever makes it in a wagon. All that bouncing up and down would just jolt me to death."

Adam wanted to say something cruel to shake her out of that secure cradle of perverse innocence. He wanted to doubt aloud that Joel Cloud would make it or that, if he did, he would want his family to join him there. California was a new world; why take an old world with you when you went to a new one?

By Christmas he was convinced that his father had died. Typhoid. Smallpox. The dreadful cholera. Indians. Some drunken bully in a saloon somewhere. Starved to death in the desert. Sometimes the fantasies Adam nourished were so real that he had to get up in the middle of the night and walk out into the dark with the no-name hound to shake them off before he could sleep again. Then the slap of the night coolness made him think of the grave. Often when they sang hymns in church his voice broke, and he was glad that everybody was singing so loud that nobody could hear him stumble.

> High in yonder realms of light
> Dwell the raptured saints above
> Far beyond our feeble sight
> Happy in Immanuel's love!
> Pilgrims in this vale of tears,
> Once they knew like us below,
> Gloomy doubts, disturbing fears,
> Torturing pain and heavy woe.

Adam thought he was singing about his father.

# 4

In the springtime of 1850 the letter came.

It got to the village post office four months after it had been sent from California, and the old spinster who picked it out of the canvas mail sack with her shaky hands was amazed. She had never seen a letter from so far away. She sent word to the Clouds by a Negro, who got nothing for his trouble but a cup of buttermilk, a piece of hard cornbread, and a ride back to town in the wagon. The postmistress could have sent the letter by the Negro, but then she might have had to wait for days to know what was in it.

So Naomi Cloud and her son came, the woman dressed in her Sunday best, looking shabby, breathless, and nearly crazy with expectation. Adam had whipped the mules (he had bought another one by now, to replace the one his father had taken with him), wishing that he could explain to them why he was being so mean. The old woman in the post office handed the letter to him when they got there, and he took out his Barlow knife and gravely slit the envelope. He drew out one sheet of cheap foolscap, and in a halting, unnaturally loud voice, he read:

Dear Wife and Adam:

I am getting a friend that can write real good to write you this here letter. He is a good man name of Joe, and he is from Illinois which is a pretty good state, I reckon, and he ain't charging me nothing, and I sure do wish I had something to give him, but I don't. So don't worry none about the letter costing me good money because the only thing I got to pay for is the stamp, and ain't it something how they put pretty stamps on letters like they do now. I got here all right after lots of trials, but I ain't found no gold yet. But things is going to get better because I figure there ain't no way they can get worse.

15

And when things is better, you will be hearing from me again. I promise. Adam, I'm sorry I taken the good mule, but you can plow real good with the other one, and I reckon you know enough to buy you another mule as soon as you got the money. The one I taken got me all the way here to California, and he is still in good health, so you can rest easy about him. You be sure and buy you another mule if you ain't already.
Your loving husband and father,
Joel Cloud.

The signature, done in that strange, flourishing hand, was followed by the scrawled "X" that both Naomi Cloud and her son knew to be Joel Cloud's own mark.

Adam gave the letter to his mother, and he was deeply touched when he saw her take the small rectangle of paper and press it softly to her lips as if it had been her husband's face. It made him almost angry with his father. His mother looked at him with hurt eyes, and Adam gave himself over to brooding. Later he sat hunched over his knees, holding the reins lethargically and watching the dappled light streaking the road in the afternoon sun.

"He don't say nothing about us coming out there to be with him, does he, Adam?" His mother's soft interrogation was hesitant and hollow.

"No, ma'am, he don't," Adam said, and the world seemed huge and sad.

# 5

Work to do. More work than ever before. One man on the place now. Adam. He flung himself into his labor, toiling through the summer heat and reaping his second harvest alone. A little better than the first. He stood in the fields when autumn was aflame on the hills and the air was crisp, and felt the subdued melancholy of the death of the year. He contemplated the way all things died in time. When he sang in church now, his voice rough and strong like the rest of them, he put feeling in the words:

> *Remember, sinful youth, you must die, you must die,*
> *Remember, sinful youth, you must die;*
> *Remember, sinful youth, who hate the way of truth*
> *And in your pleasures boast, you must die, you must*
> *    die;*
> *And in your pleasures boast, you must die.*

There was something almost pleasant in the melancholy, and the colors of October, so mellow and hazy, made him feel oddly at peace with himself and with death. He was satisfied when he counted what he had done. Sometimes he smiled to himself, imagining that his father would come home empty-handed from California. Then it would be Adam's gift to him to show him that the farm had prospered. Adam looked at the dirt road every morning when he went out of the house and every evening when he came in from the fields. If he could have created an image with his eyes, he would have made his father appear in that road, walking home.

Then in the winter his mother died.

Her death stunned him. It was as if the deep serenity building in his own heart reached to the world itself and that nothing out there could change. When she died, the brittle fragility of things impressed itself on him again, and his calm fled.

She took a cold. But she caught cold every winter. Only this time she dragged herself around the house saying nothing, her mind abstracted. The letter had been an end to something. Adam wanted to comfort her, but he could find no words. They were not close enough. Now she was the one who sat gazing into the fire in mute unhappiness. Her skin looked like gray paper, and her shoulders sagged. Defeat.

The cold sank into her chest. She coughed. A rasping, hollow sound, like something grinding in a barrel. She spat the yellow phlegm into rags and threw the rags to boil in lye soap in the great iron kettle out back where she did the washing. Then she got too tired to do the washing. Adam did it for her. Touching her snotty rags was worse to him than putting

17

his hands in a kettle of snakes. But he worked without complaint, and he thought she would get well.

One afternoon in late January she had a seizure of some sort. A wild fluttering of her thin eyelids and a dizziness. The boy helped her into bed, her body like straw. She muttered something about her husband. Then her eyes shut as though she had lost the energy to keep them open. Her lips trembled without a sound under her sharpening nose.

He bent close to her, anxious. "Mamma? Mamma?"

She rallied at his voice. Her eyes opened; her false and habitual smile came back for just a moment. "I want to sleep. Leave me be, Adam. I'll be all right."

He hesitated, then wrapped the quilts around her flimsy body. He was embarrassed at being so close to her. In their physical nearness he was struck by her womanhood—decayed and repulsive—as something added unexpectedly to her motherhood.

So he was happy to leave her to herself. He thought it would be good for her to sleep. He went out into the cold, sunny day. The air made his face burn, but it lifted his heart to be out of the house. He checked his fences and tramped proudly over the land he was beginning to consider his own. He had put his impress on the place. He let the day thicken, and in the weak, red light of the early declining sun, he did the chores. When he was splitting firewood, smelling the good reek of new-cut hickory, he suddenly thought that it was not long until spring. By the time he finished milking, the twilight was oozing like syrup out of the bare woods creaking with cold. High above him like dots of fire the first stars burned through the liquid wintry sky. He felt very happy.

When he entered the house, opening the door softly on its heavy leather hinges, the fire was low in the hearth. The wind was singing a soft song in the chimney. A pleasant sound. He threw wood on the fire and watched the yellow flames leap up and made the no-name dog be quiet. He thought his mother was asleep. She had turned on one side, her face to the wall, buried in folds of quilts pulled over her head. The bed lay in deep shadow. He thought of calling to her, thought better of it. He did not want to talk to her; he enjoyed the peace of the deep silence. He brought more wood in; he and the hound ate supper quietly together and sat looking into the fire afterwards. Finally he went to bed.

Adam awoke in the dark of the very early morning and

found that the no-name dog had gone over to the side of his mother's bed. The dog sat there, sniffing in the way he did when he came on something odd in the fields. Adam got up, pricked by uneasiness now. He went over and pulled the quilts back from his mother's face and touched her cheek with the back of a hand. Her mouth was partly open, and her skin was like ice.

In panic he took her by the shoulders and turned her over on her back. Her thin, bent knees came tenting up under the covers. They were as rigid as oak. He was horrified and let her fall back. Her body tumbled to rest with a gentle rustling of the corn-shucks in the mattress. She was as death had found her—two knife-thin hands folded together under her sharp face, eyes shut, bony knees drawn up toward her sunken chest, her expression slack and empty. In the great silence of the house he heard with uncanny sharpness the breathing of the cold wind at the door.

Suddenly he thought of all the rituals of death, and they were as appalling to him as death itself. He thought of the women of Bourbon County who would come, panting for the drama of grief. Women who would require him to cry and howl for the mother for whom he had scarcely any feeling at all. The women of Bourbon County had already told their gossip about Naomi Cloud. "That husband of hers just run off and *left* the poor thing! And she keeps trying to make out he's going to send for her. But he ain't never going to do it. He's glad to be shut of her." Now they would gossip about Adam if he did not shriek and throw himself sobbing over his mother's rigid corpse, kiss her awful dead flesh. A kiss to the dead the fine one must pay in Bourbon County for remaining alive.

He thought of plump, ruddy, willing Mrs. Hattie Arbuckle. She loved funerals more than she loved to eat or to sleep. The comely, middle-aging, wavy-haired widow Arbuckle, with full ripe lips and eyes that spoke more boldly than her mouth. She invariably came to homes while men did their last solemn watch for the dead. She brought fried chicken. The men sat all night long before the burying to observe the corpse, straining to detect the faintest sign of life. The insurance of the community against the horror of being buried alive.

The men talked drowsily when they were together and told old tales. They smoked and chewed and ruminated about gossip, theology, crops, the long-time dead. Women kept the coffee boiling in the kitchen. And in the slow, languorous darkness, restraints were eroded. In the weird deep of night people found themselves strangely awake, isolated with death in the sleeping earth. Time slowed down then, and they became curiously lonely. And so it was on those occasions when Mrs. Hattie Arbuckle, deprived for so long of her husband's consoling body, learned that other men had bodies to lend.

Adam remembered once when Mrs. Arbuckle brought coffee out to where he stood alone in the fresh night air, removed from the crowd watching over a woman named Black. As he nervously sipped at the hot and bitter brew he had not wanted, she suddenly slid one of her voluptuous arms around his waist and pulled him against her big, soft breasts. She whispered urgently at him, "Adam, honey, I've always had a special feeling about you." He was lucky enough at that moment to drop the tin coffee mug on his shoes, scalding his feet. And while he was dancing about and yelling with pain, Mrs. Arbuckle slid off like a liquid shadow, muttering about the idiocy of "some people."

He looked back at his dead mother, shaking off his terror of Mrs. Arbuckle and the women of Bourbon County. He hated the prospect of touching that lifeless body again. Then it was that the other thought—the one that would take him like a fever later on—came to him for the first time. He could go away. He could ride West. Nothing to hold him here now. Something would happen to her body. He did not like to think of it, but it did not matter what happened to bodies. He would be gone from here forever; everything in Bourbonville, including his mother's corpse, might be as a dream, vanishing at waking.

But he rejected these thoughts and set himself to do his duty. His mother would have to be buried. And the first thing he had to do was get a coffin. He started worrying about the coffin, and he did not worry about Mrs. Hattie Arbuckle so much.

20

# 6

Adam thought of Dothan Weaver. Dothan was a shy, gangling boy nearly five or six years older than Adam. He farmed and did a little carpentry on the side, and people said his work was good. He made coffins. Somebody in the village said he made enough extra money in the cholera epidemic to buy fifty acres of good land; you had to respect a man who could use cholera like that.

So Adam Cloud rode out to find him. The clear, cold sunlight washing the land made every object stand out like something carved from colored ice. Trees, rail fences, fields, houses along with the curling white smoke rising from their chimneys all cut into his vision. And in that still, stupendous brightness, the hard chill of the day was nearly unbearable. A merciless cold that made his breath smoke. The shod hoofs of the mule clattered on the frozen ground. Hard to dig a grave in this weather. Something else to worry about.

*It's warm in California.* He thought it strange that Joel Cloud did not know about his wife's death. Maybe he would be glad. Hard to think that they had been young once. In love. No lines in their faces then. And suddenly Adam reflected that he did not know how his mother and father had met. Their marriage not good enough to make stories about, to preserve the beginnings.

Dothan Weaver was out chopping wood. He kept chopping when Adam rode up. His way of letting Adam know there were things more important in life than visitors. Dothan, lean, hard, with a face like a flat-iron, his chin the point. High cheekbones. A legacy from the Scotch-Irish ancestry his people claimed and did not understand. Like Adam. Pale, watery blue-gray eyes with calculation always in them. He squinted up at Adam finally, holding his axe in both hands. "How do, Adam?"

"My mamma's dead, Dothan."

21

"Ah."

"She died in the night."

"Poor thing. Poor thing."

"I reckon I need me a coffin for her."

Dothan nodded in professional satisfaction. "I reckon."

"You got airy coffins, Dothan?"

"I reckon I always got coffins. The best they is. I reckon if you was to go out to the graveyards and dig 'em up, you'd find that some of my coffins is still holding the water out. I make a good tight coffin."

"You don't have to go on selling it to me, Dothan. I come to buy."

"I just want you to know what you're getting."

There was a short silence. Adam swallowed. "How much does it cost?"

"She ain't a big woman, is she?"

"No. She was always right little."

"How tall you reckon she is?"

"Well, she come up to about my chest when we was standing together barefoot."

"Get down off that mule, and let's take a look." Adam got down. When he departed from the warm back of his mule, the cold cut him like a whip. "Ummmmmm," Dothan said, "I reckon she's about big enough for a dollar and half coffin."

"A dollar and half." Adam was relieved; he thought it would be more.

Dothan looked down and spat with the bashfulness and finality country people always display when they are bargaining. "You can owe me. I don't need it right now."

Adam was annoyed. "I can pay you now. A dollar and a half ain't nothing to me."

"Hah," Dothan said, looking up. "Come on then."

Dothan hitched up his mules to the wagon. He and Adam wrestled a coffin out of the corncrib and onto the wagon. It was a fine coffin; the wood, unpainted and unweathered, was sweet and strong-smelling. Adam complimented Dothan on it and was proud of this last gift to his mother.

It was past noon when at last they got back to the cabin. The sun was high. It shone deceptively in that hard, blue wintry sky, because the air seemed to have become colder. When Adam panted with the effort of lifting the coffin off the wagon, the air burned his lungs all the way to his belly.

22

He had to clean his mother up. A sad, shameful task performed in the dignity of silence. Adam found an old print dress that had been his mother's pride. She had made the dress out of cloth her husband had given her five years before when he went to Knoxville—twenty-six miles away—to sell some cows and brought back presents for his family. Finally with careful tenderness, he combed out her long, gray hair with her wooden comb. She had always worn her hair braided and wrapped in a bun at the back of her head. Now, with her hair down, she seemed vaguely younger, and in the serenity of death she possessed an indescribable quality, perhaps what his father had seen years ago when he loved her.

She would have wanted to lie in the Methodist graveyard toward town. A green and peaceful slope with a view of the river. Friendly neighbors. Her three dead children nearby. But Adam kept thinking about the women of Bourbon County, and panicked at the thought. And there was the cold. Somehow the cold made things different.

Adam decided to get it all over with fast, bury his mother in the yard, under a slender apple tree, now bare of leaves, whose fruit she made into bubbling pies in the autumn. Had made. Her husband had planted the tree just before Adam was born. So Adam thought it was like putting her next to the only living thing she had left of the man who had forsaken her.

"Ah," Dothan said. "it don't seem right to me. But it ain't my mamma. I just make the coffins. It don't matter to me where they're laid."

By the time they got the grave dug, the sun was dipping toward the dark western line of bony trees. Their spades rang on the surface ice like metal against metal. But three inches down they broke into damp clay. And so they dug, breathing hard, feeling the way the chill air taunted their throats, and they had nothing to say to each other. When it was deep enough Adam left Dothan to watch, and he went to find Preacher Clabo.

Preacher Clabo was an old man, a Baptist, cured in the fires of many a revival against the Methodists. Now he was gnarled and feeble, blear-eyed and bewildered by Adam's haste, indeed unable to comprehend exactly who it was that was dead. They stood by the open grave together and sang a feeble and off-key version of the song people in Bourbon County sang at funerals, their voices slow and inharmonious.

*Rock of Ages, cleft for me,*
*Let me hide myself in thee.*
*Let the water and the blood,*
*From thy wounded side which flowed,*
*Be of sin the double cure,*
*Save from wrath and make me pure . . .*

Preacher Clabo's voice was thin and tired. But he got into the rhythm of the song and dipped his head in mournful abnegation to the quavering notes and shut his eyes and looked as though he had been transported somewhere. To youth or to heaven. Adam did not know which.

When the song's sad notes died away, the old man stood by the grave, shoulders thin and bent in the cold gloom of twilight, and prayed. "Oh Lord, we thank Thee for this Thy servant who has lived in the world, and now we give back to Thee the dust that was her body and hope and pray to see her soon in paradise where the sun never sets and the roses never fade." An old man's practiced eloquence, recited over innumerable coffins whose dead he had long since forgot. When his prayer was done, he turned away, and Adam hitched up the wagon and took him home, leading the preacher's old nag behind.

Preacher Clabo had hardly known Naomi Cloud. She was a Methodist. But as they drove along in the awful cold of the early night, the old man rose mechanically to his duty and stumbled through a litany of consolation as habitual as the one sermon he could remember. "We don't know why these things happen, my boy. We only know it's for the best." He faltered and moved his lips, trying to recall what came next in the way some people will fight to remember the name of some familiar person whom they have known since childhood, now absurdly vanished from their tongues.

"The Lord gives, and the Lord takes away," Adam said without feeling. He had read the Bible over and over. It was the only book the Clouds had.

"Yes, yes, that's right," the old man said slowly, bewildered because he had not been able to think of it. He repeated the verse that Adam had quoted, backed up, said it over again. And he was still saying it and trying to make Adam understand the incomprehensible wisdom of God when the youth led him inside the little house, untied his horse, put it snug in the barn, and rode away. He gave the preacher a quarter for coming. Old man Clabo was amazed and thankful. He had not expected anything. By bedtime he had forgotten the funeral, and he would look at the silver quarter shining in his hand and wonder if God had put it there by miracle.

# 7

The winter held on. It snowed, and the wind blew night and day. Thermometers balled up in the bottom of the glass and barely crept into the stem at noon. Old men sat around stoves, cocked their grizzled heads and listened to the wind, chewed their tobacco and tried to recall another winter like this one. The sawing of their unmusical voices was an incantation to conjure up another time when the snow had piled so high, when the river froze solid, when Bourbonville and all the wintry land around were cut off in an isolation as solitary and appalling. A memory to make this winter easier to bear.

Adam kept to himself. People thought he had done wrong to bury his mother in private. So he stayed home and did his chores and looked after his place. Things on the farm had never been better. A good future here. But when he heard the trees crack their mantle of thin ice in the roving wind that stirred through the forest, the sound was so alien to human life that it made him ache with loneliness. And at night, when he slept by the fire with the dog, wrapped in deerskins and quilts, the cold was like a secret enemy creeping in from the dark to lurk there, to seize him should the fire relax its guard and fall into the ashes.

When he slept, he had bad dreams. His mother's dead children standing on their graves in the Methodist graveyard and howling for her. They cried in the senseless, plaintive way children cry when they are tired. All of them had died as infants. An older brother and the two little girls younger than Adam, girls who had bloomed like flowers on snow. He saw them as babies with indistinct faces. He could not remember his brother at all, and the little girls had perished of scarlet

25

fever when he was only six. So they were only shapes to him, expressionless and transparent. But he could hear them cry in his sleep, and when he awoke he strained his ears and thought sometimes that he could still hear them just under the sound of the wind in the chimney.

Sometimes he talked with his mother at night. Strange talks, filled with inner restraint. Even as they spoke, he knew she was dead. He knew she reproached him for burying her in this solitude, this unholy ground. Yet he did not want to act as if he knew the truth—that she was dead—for then she would quit pretending to be alive and go away. And he would be alone.

Very slowly the winter cracked and broke and finally dissolved before the persistent, gentle hammering of spring. The ice melted in the river, and the ground grew soft again. In his fields when he set to the spring plowing, Adam could hear the cheerful salute of the whistles blwoing the big white boats up and down. The trees swelled and came back to life. The world turned from despair to promise, and Adam was astonished in his quiet way that living things standing outside all the hard winter long could find the energy to bloom again and to hold their bright green leaves against the bright sky.

He started going to town again on Saturdays about the middle of March, and he went to church again. He felt the disapproval of the county for the way he had buried his mother. But he kept quiet. People started being civil to him again. For it was spring after a winter such as nobody could remember, and no one could bear a grudge in this season for something as trivial as the way a man buried his mother in that cold.

Adam still felt out of place. He looked around Bourbonville on those crowded Saturdays and felt invisible walls closing on him. He longed for other towns, another life. He thought of his mother, and he began to dread coming to the end of his own life, knowing that this was the only world he had ever had.

People who had gone off to fight against the Mexicans still told their stories. The edge was off them now. Everybody had heard everything. Now men were talking darkly about another war. People had agreed about the Mexican War. But the one that was coming ... people were not agreed on that. In the talk, in sudden and unexpected moments men became very tense. Division. It began to split the town like an axe.

In the summer of 1850, John Wesley Campbell had come home from the West. It was a miracle, people said, for everyone had supposed him dead. They looked out their windows one morning and saw his fine, tall, and youthful form astride a good horse, his young son in the saddle before him, returned home to open his law practice again, to settle down in the town where he and his young wife had come like magic figures from a magic land a few years before the war. She had died. He had left his son in Knoxville with her parents and gone off to fight in Mexico. But when the other fighting men returned, John Wesley Campbell was not among them. People wondered about him for a while, talked about him occasionally, dismissed him as dead. His house on the square remained shut up, and from time to time somebody came down from Knoxville to inspect and clean it. And when anybody asked what news there might be of Mr. Campbell, there was no answer worth anything. He had vanished. When he came back in the summer of 1850, it was as though he had risen from the dead, and they were amazed.

He returned with the smell of space in his fine, black clothes and the look of distance in his eyes. Somehow his tall, austere form was the incarnation of all the enigmas, all the mystery, and all the enchantment, too, that came up in people's minds when they thought about the Great West. He looked like a man with a thousand stories to tell. Yet he did not tell them. He opened up his house again and settled down with his boy and began practicing law.

He was only a little over thirty years old, but there was something indefinable in his face that was already old. He had distant manners. People did business with him because he was a very good lawyer, not because they liked him. He made their wills and wrote out their deeds and settled problems between neighbors like a judge himself, not going to court if he could help it because he did not trust courts. And so the people of Bourbon County gave John Wesley Campbell their respect. Yet respect was never friendship. They left him alone except when they had their business with the law. Then they did call on him, holding their hats nervously and grinning too much and listening to every word he said, for he knew the law to its last sharp tooth and writhing coil.

Mr. Campbell barely knew that Adam existed. He never saw the boy looking after him with craving eyes. Adam saw Mr. Campbell striding down the street, smoking an habitual

27

cigar, looking neither to the right hand nor to the left, and he thought that the man must live still in that world of deeds done under the mighty Western sun. And in the warming spring of 1851 when he saw the lawyer go by in the green square, the boy felt more restless than he had ever felt in his life before. He wanted to run after Mr. Campbell to ask one question: "Why did you come back?"

Still the front part of his brain kept telling Adam Cloud that he would stay here with the rest of them. He even thought briefly that he might marry. He was old enough to marry now, and sometimes at night he felt longings that made him hot and more lonely than ever. People joked with him about girls. And there was a girl.

Her name was Sylvia Roberts—a slender, pretty face, nicely carved, brown eyes, brown hair, long legs that moved energetically under her long cotton skirts, a pert little nose, a smile of intelligence. Sylvia was a name that meant woodland, she told him. She sought him out at the Methodist church after preaching one Sunday morning, almost transgressing the boundary of propriety in her greeting. "Well look, it's Adam Cloud himself! Where've you *been*, Adam?" She laughed, and he could not help but smile.

And the next week, when she was late and he was early, she came in and sat by him, scooting him over on the slatted wooden pew with a silent laugh and a nudge. She shared his hymnbook, holding one side of it while he held the other. He could see how perfectly formed was her small hand next to his big one, and he could smell her and she seemed clean and very nice. Afterwards somebody snickered outside and punched him playfully and said, "I believe Adam's got him a lady friend."

The joke was a part of the ritual of beginning a romance in the county. Something a bent old couple would remember with pleasure years and years later when they recalled their green youth. Adam began to feel a warmth of anticipation when he thought of Sylvia Roberts, and he began to think of her often. He could imagine living with her and children and those other things people imagine when they begin to think about getting married. Settling down.

Mrs. Barkley Roberts invited Adam home to Sunday dinner soon afterwards. "I know you need a good woman's meal, Adam. So Sylvia and me, we got together last night and this morning, and we cooked you one."

A painful moment. Suddenly it seemed that something was being forced on him just before he was ready to make up his mind about it. He had to go home with them. They would take no excuses. Dinner made already; he could not refuse and be polite.

Barkley Roberts was a farmer, a good farmer with good land. He was about the age of Joel Cloud. He was very stiff and self-conscious with Adam—a shy man, lean and stooped with reddish hair going gray on the ends and an oddly delicate mouth, like his daughter's, although not beautiful like hers. He did not laugh as much as she did. Doubtless a man warned by his wife and his daughter to be the sort on this occasion that would make Adam Cloud choose him for a father-in-law. He served Adam with exaggerated, silent courtesy, almost bowing to him, handing him every dish first and embarrassing the boy who had always been taught that ladies were first in everything. Mrs. Barkley Roberts kept up a running chatter about how sad it was that Adam's mother had died, what a good woman she had been, how Adam had done the right thing by burying her at home. She talked so much about that private burial that Adam knew the woman had thought about it, worried over it, wondered if she wanted such a strange young man to marry her daughter, her dear and only child. Sylvia might die, and Adam might bury her without a word to anybody.

But when Adam slowly told them about the apple tree— burying his mother under the living thing that his father had given her—Sylvia looked at him with eyes filled with tears. "Why, that's just the sweetest thing I ever heard of!" she said. And Mrs. Roberts was deeply moved and dabbed at her own eyes with a napkin and said she'd just *known* there was some good reason for what Adam had done—just after she had assured Adam several times that he'd done the right thing, even before he explained.

Adam felt trapped by their care for him. He could tell that now they saw him as a young man with feelings, and they knew he would have compassion for a wife. Without arrogance (with chagrin, in fact) he knew that such men were rare. Sylvia was fine and healthy and pretty, sixteen years old, old enough to assume the duties of a household, to have good babies, to be a woman telling other women about her husband, her house, her family, to go to quilting parties, and to sit up solemnly all night with the dead. "I knowed Adam had feelings, mamma. I told you he did."

Mrs. Barkley Roberts nodded vigorously. "Them was her very words, Adam. This girl sure does believe in you. She's been a real friend when you didn't have many friends. She's took up for you."

Adam looked at the girl, saw her smile at him, and he felt gloomy inside.

There was a moment that afternoon, when he took his leave and rode home, when he thought he just might return in formal courtship and marry Sylvia. He felt, after that good meal and their warm kindness, that he almost owed it to the Roberts family to marry their daughter. He knew it would make them all happy, and he liked to make people happy. He came back to his empty cabin and paced aimlessly up and down the plank porch his father had hammered onto the southern end of it, to please Naomi Cloud. He went to the barn and walked in his fields and looked into the woods, saw the dogwood flourishing in sprays of white, felt the sunlight and felt, too, the pull of his farm, his land, his place in the world. Everybody ought to have a place, and this seemed to be the one God had given Adam Cloud.

He looked at himself in a scrap of mirror treasured by his mother. It was too small to let him see his face all in one piece. He saw broken fragments as he moved the mirror around—his eyes, his chin, his mouth, his cheekbones. He remained a mystery to himself. He wondered how all the pieces fit together, how other people saw him, heard him. And for a time he fell into a trance of speculation, imagining how he looked to other people walking in the street, and from that he passed to wondering how Mrs. Adam Cloud would look on his arm, the two of them going places, living together, having children. He thought of how it would be to hold her against himself in the long night silences . . . He looked around at the cabin and thought it was unspeakably shabby. But he could build a new one. Cut some trees maybe. Have them turned into planks at the sawmill; build a frame house with a porch.

His fantasies became so real and so beguiling that he nearly surrendered to them. He was so entrapped in details that for several hours as the afternoon wore on, he did not think about the bigger things in life—what it should all mean, whether Bourbonville and Bourbon County and an occasional festive trip to Knoxville (where he had never yet been) were

30

really all he wanted out of life. And in the mild twilight of that day he very nearly went down and saddled a mule and rode over to the Robertses' house. He would sit with them on their porch, much better than his, and after a while the mother would look at the father, and Mr. Barkley Roberts would be startled, and then he would consent to the sign. The two of them would withdraw, go to bed, leaving Adam and Sylvia to plan for the future.

*I won't be lonely then!* The thought as soft and entrancing as the moon on a summer night.

Had he gone that day, as he almost did, his whole life would have been different. In the years that followed he always returned to that evening as the moment that determined his destiny. But he did not go. And that night he dreamed of taking a journey, of riding on a rocky path beneath the battlements of castles that flung high turrets into the clouds like the pictures in a book of fairytales he had seen once for a precious hour. He awoke in the morning with the bright sunlight streaming under the crack in the door like release from bondage. He stepped out into the misty dawn of an April morning, looked happily across to the green woods, saw his mother's grave under the apple tree, and it was all somehow strange to him. Something he could leave behind without regret. Even happily.

Now when he thought of Sylvia Roberts, he thought of bondage. Bondage to a world that was not his anymore. So he did not go back to her house, and he did not go to church again. He only saw Sylvia one more time. In town, on a Saturday afternoon, she came up to him in the square with a bright smile, not quite concealing her hurt, to ask him if he had been sick. When he said very uncomfortably that he had not, she nodded mutely as if she had understood something very difficult. And with a quick little jerk she dismissed herself and went away with hardly a word. Adam caught a glimpse of tears in her eyes. Tears made her eyes seem larger and more beautiful. He was cut to the heart, and he nearly called out to her. But he did not. And when she had glided away in the crowd, he did not want her anymore.

For a time at night he returned to his solitary brooding. It became a habit, like drink to some men in the valley. He sat on the porch with the no-name hound and rocked idly until the colors had washed out of the world and the stars came out in their still gleaming over the dark woods. Sometimes he would imagine that he saw his mother's form drifting there among the shadows like a blur on his vision. At other times he recalled his father so vividly that it was like seeing him walk there in the night. And sometimes his neck felt prickly with apprehension, and he could almost feel the ghost of the man beside him, and he thought he might turn suddenly and find the specter of his father there, rocking with him. But when he did turn, the two rocking chairs were empty and still, and Adam wondered if the eerie presentiment meant that his father had died.

His father had filled life; Adam did not understand how much until the man had gone. Protector and sage. Once an Indian had come to the door in the middle of the night. Joel Cloud roused up from the bed at the knock, at the howling of the dog they had then, and went to see who it was, holding a pine knot aloft from the fire as a light. Adam awoke, too, a child, very small and sitting up afraid in his bed. When he saw the Indian's face, plucked out of the dark by the leaping flame, he was terrified. Indians in the middle of the night meant sudden death. So ran the mythology of the valley that even a small child could absorb in the marrow of his bones.

This Indian meant no harm; his wife was about to give birth. And when he understood that, Joel Cloud brought them both inside and helped deliver the human child with the same heatless skill Adam had seen him use when he helped a cow give birth to a calf. Joel Cloud was not a demonstrative man; he only did what had to be done. But when Adam saw his father in charge of everything, doing it well, he felt one of those bursts of confidence in the world that is likely to stay with a boy.

The Indian, a worn representative of a doomed race, mumbled his thanks again and again. He gave to Joel Cloud a necklace of copper beads. The beads still hung on a peg in the wall, blue with corrosion, funny little carvings all over them that Adam wondered about. Indian medicine. Magic. and he wondered, too, what ever had happened to that Indian child who had uttered his first shocked wail of life here, in this house.

That had been 1837. The Cherokees at that moment being shoved off West somewhere by the United States Army. Everybody went West when he had used up the East. The instinct of a continent built into its inhabitants like the secret force of a magnet. "A bird will build a nest; a Yankee will

32

go West!" An old man told Adam that once, a man begging food and lodging and passing on, like the Indian, West.

And so Adam felt the restlessness grow in him, and he doubted that he would be able to face Sylvia Roberts again, and he thought that if he did stay here, somebody else would marry her, and he could not bear that thought. The spring was slowly passing away. Every day he watched the sun set and thought that his father saw the same sun, if indeed his father was still alive. It was May now. The forest was green and the fields were pushing up their crops, and the road in front of his house was dry and blooming at the sides with daisies and goldenrod. A friendly road.

And he began to find a purpose in things, though he could not tell what that purpose was except that it was not to be accomplished here. Old Preacher Clabo, Sylvia Roberts, the decaying body of his mother in her grave, the stories told until they were stale of the war with Mexico—all testified that something in Bourbon County was used up. His thoughts piled up in him like water behind an earthen dam. One Monday morning the thing broke, and Adam got up, milked his cows, did the chores with a liberating finality, saddled a mule, rode into Bourbonville, and sold the farm.

# 8

Five hundred dollars for the farm! It seemed like a fortune to Adam Cloud. Earl Swope, Bourbonville's banker and authentic lord, came out to look at the place, his expression sour and skeptical, the bags under his eyes giving him the look of an extremely sad hound. He took the paper Joel Cloud had left and let John Wesley Campbell read it. The lawyer sat at his desk and studied the "instrument" as he called it, pronounced it legal enough, rode out to talk with Burl Calloway and his wife, rode back again and said Joel Cloud's dictated note was as good as a stock certificate in Earl Swope's bank. Earl Swope looked gravely pained at the comparison, but he named a price. Adam accepted it, thinking all the time that it was strange to trade off a life for five hundred dollars in gold certificates, with no more ceremony than signing his name to a paper. There ought to be speeches, a parade, a voice from heaven . . . Something.

And so on the evening before he left home, Adam felt strange. He had the money folded into a leather pouch that he wore on a belt under his stomach, next to his skin. In his pocket he carried a smaller purse drawn with a string, holding more than fifty dollars—money he had picked up selling things in town. He felt very wealthy. But the farm, no longer his, looked like the Garden of Eden. It was sin and death to leave.

He thought of failure and was afraid. Maybe he would exhaust his money in wasteful wandering in the Great West. He could imagine himself returning here—beggarly, old, ridiculous—only to find some prosperous farmer making use of his good land, maybe married to Sylvia Roberts, children swarming happily around. "You used to own this place, eh? Well, you was silly to sell it, my friend. But I'm glad you was a fool. Yessir!"

He shook off his fantasies and tried to think of happier things. Liberation. He would not be doomed to the dullness of the valley. Year after year of the same thing. The West was freedom. Or so Adam thought in his vision of the green earth rolling to infinity. He had heard tell of the thunder of buffalo across the boundless prairies. And men back from the war spoke of the lonely shriek of wolves in the starry nights. A sound like something beyond the grave. In the boy's mind this West lay at the cloudy border between the world of nature and the supernatural world just beyond. Adam had had no experience that allowed him to understand the tales; he was left groping in confusions of color and sounds and smells, all spinning in and out of each other, all revolving around a great pole star—the West.

One thing he did know. You could be different out there. Free from what you had to be if you stayed East. In Bourbon County.

He had bought a good rifle, a piece worth fourteen gold dollars at the store in Bourbonville. Long, heavy, beautiful, with an oiled walnut stock and an unbreakable steel ramrod and a bore nearly half an inch thick, a look of stunning grace and lethal efficiency. Power.

He cared for his mother's grave for the last time. He was thoughtful over it. The green grass was thickening, but the red clay still showed through like the scaly scalp of a balding Indian. It would take this year and maybe the next to lay a blanket of sod over the gash in the earth where she lay so still. He thought that he would never see her grave again, and the thought made him as sad as if she had been alive and he were leaving her forever. She was a poor woman, forsaken and isolated from her children both dead and alive. He wished that he had loved her.

So on the final night he sat in an odd suspension of feeling on the porch of the cabin. He wished the night would pass away. But there was nothing to do but wait until morning. And while he was waiting, Harry Creekmore walked out of the woods and into Adam's life.

# 9

Harry Creekmore announced himself by a call out of the obscurity where the road descended through the woods. "Joel Cloud! Uncle Joel! Joel Cloud! Are you there, Uncle Joel?"

Adam's hair stood on end. There in the thick dusk glimmered an apparition in ghostly white. The no-name hound went wild with excitement, barking with his hackles up, as if all the vague terrors dreamed in canine nightmares had come to life before him. Adam could hardly hear.

"Uncle Joel! Please help me, Uncle Joel. It's me! Harry!"

"Come on up!" Adam yelled. His throat was tight, and his voice shook.

"Does that dog bite? I am extremely reluctant to be bitten by a dog after all my other tribulations."

The dog was retreating around the corner of the house, barking even more furiously as he backed away.

"He don't bite lessen I tell him to," Adam lied. "Come on."

The apparition approached through the gloom. The closer

it got, the more clearly its blurred outlines organized themselves into a man wearing a white linen suit. The suit was unbelievably dirty, but it was clearly linen, and it was white. Clothing worthy of an aristocrat.

The man also wore a pair of enormous spectacles perched on a very fine nose. Adam had never seen such spectacles in his life. They were as big as cups. They magnified in such a way that the face behind them seemed to recede into two deep and very mysterious pits. At the bottom of each pit gleamed one very sharp blue eye, like a small bead.

"What do you want anyway?"

"I'm searching for my beloved uncle, Joel Cloud."

"Joel Cloud's my daddy; he ain't your uncle."

"My dear young man, there is nothing in nature that says that your father cannot also be my uncle. Please don't be foolish."

"Who are you?"

"I'm Harry Creekmore, from Georgia." The stranger put out his hand with grand affability. "And you must be my cousin Adam. Adam, I'm quite delighted to meet you. Quite delighted indeed. I've waited for this day for years. For years, Adam. I feel that I may weep."

The stranger did not appear close to tears. Adam took the hand that was offered to him and found it to be as soft as biscuit dough.

"Cousin Adam."

"I can see you are a man of few words, Cousin Adam. Yes indeed. I am your cousin, and I am so pleased that we have met at long last. But tell me, where is my dearly beloved uncle? I've come hundreds of miles to see him."

"My daddy ain't here right now."

"Not here? I was sure I'd find him at this time of day. Well now, I'm sure you won't mind if I just sit here and wait for him. And I would appreciate it if you would please make that dog be silent. If he isn't going to bite me, he might as well have the decency not to fracture my eardrums." The stranger sat down, very much at home, in one of the empty rocking chairs and flashed a dazzling smile at Adam. It almost made the twilight glow. He carefully removed his broad, white hat and placed it on his lap, letting his blond hair fall freely to his shoulders. "You're a whole lot bigger than I thought you were, Cousin Adam." He looked around at the cabin and into the woodland beyond, pretending to see. "You

36

have a fine place here. Very fine indeed. Where is my uncle anyway?"

Adam was quieting the hound. He yelled above the dog's barking. "My daddy's in California. Hush, dog! Hush!"

"California! You don't mean it!" The stranger's tone changed considerably.

"I do mean it. He left two years ago. To hunt gold."

"Oh, dear me! Oh, my. California!" The stranger got up from his chair and carefully paced the floor, looking again and again to Adam to be completely sure that Adam had spoken the truth. "California! Good Lord! You mean I've come all the way from Georgia to see my uncle, and he's gone to California!"

"He's been gone two years," Adam said, repeating himself. He eyed the stranger with watchful mistrust.

"Two years! Two years! Oh, me. My dear mother's been dead longer than two years. She didn't know. They were out of touch. Oh, the sorrow of family quarrels. She said to come to my Uncle Joel if I were ever in trouble. And I'm in trouble now. Oh, dear God! Have mercy on me, a miserable offender. Forgive me for those things that I have done and for those things that I have left undone." He bowed his head.

Adam was in an extreme of frustration. "I never heard of you before!"

Harry Creekmore turned a solemn, sad face to him and shook his head. The dim light flashed in those tremendous spectacles, making him look like a creature born unnaturally from the air. "Well, I'm not surprised. You may be surprised, Cousin Adam. But I'm not surprised. Sad. Very sad."

"I don't know what you're talking about! You're sitting there talking about things I don't know nothing about. Nothing!"

"Of course, of course!" Harry spoke in a soothing tone. Like syrup. "It must be a great shock to you. I'll try to explain. You may not believe me, but that's all right. I've suffered so much. I expect anything. Even that my own blood kin might think I'm lying. It's all right. I'll tell you, and I'll go."

Adam sat back down in the rocking chair and took a deep breath. Harry sat down, too. Resigned and gloomy-looking, his large hat held quietly over his long legs, looking out to the darkening woods. Black now in the depths. "You don't

37

know that I won't believe you lessen you tell me what is happening," Adam said.

Harry sighed. "I wish I were crazy, Cousin Adam. I wish I were a liar. Crazy people and liars, they don't have any feelings. I wish now that I had no feelings. But let me tell you about the quarrel. You are my own blood, and you deserve to know. I almost reproach my Uncle Joel for never telling you the truth. You see, your aunt, my dear, departed mother, married my father." A catch came in his voice at the mention of his mother; he seemed almost ready to cry, but he fought down his emotions, letting his chin sink on his chest for a moment.

"Get on with it!" Adam said impatiently. "Go on."

"I'm sure you are surprised to know that your father had a sister."

"He told me he had a sister once. She died of the typhoid before I was born."

"Well, she didn't die," Harry said. "I'm pleased you even knew of her existence. When did your father tell you she had died? How old was he?"

"I don't know. He never did talk much about them days. He never did talk much about nothing."

"Ah, yes. Yes. That is what my mother said. Still water runs deep you know, Cousin Adam. Your father—my beloved uncle—is deep."

"Did you ever know my daddy?"

"Ah, no. No indeed. I never met the gentleman. I know only what my mother told me about him."

"What was your mamma's name?"

"Ah," said Harry Creekmore, turning to face Adam with a knowing look. "Now we will see how much your father told you about my side of the family. Tell me, Adam. What do you think her name was?"

"My daddy said his dead sister was named Melissa!"

Now Harry Creekmore really did look as if he were about to burst into tears. "Melissa!" he spoke the word with a groan. "Melissa! Oh, Adam! Adam!" He put his face in his hands, running his long fingers up over his eyes under his glasses. It was too dark now for Adam to detect tears, but Harry moaned and shook and looked for all the world as if he were sobbing his heart out. "Adam, *Melissa was my mother's name!*"

It made Adam very uncomfortable to see a grown man

cry. "It's all right," he said vaguely. "Don't get upset about it."

Harry lifted his face and stared at Adam through the gloom. "Yes, it's all right now, because my mother is dead; she has ascended to that realm where she does not feel the hurt anymore. But I feel it, Adam. I feel it keenly. The quarrel. The terrible quarrel!"

"I don't know what you're talking about," Adam said, his own frustration beyond endurance.

"My daddy was a planter. When my mamma married him, your daddy disowned her. It was like she'd died. Don't you see? He swore he'd never speak about her as long as he lived. And Adam, that is just what happened! Oh, doesn't it smite you to the heart?"

Adam felt his world collapsing. Had his father deceived him so much? And did his mother know?

"I don't reckon you ever heard tell of my daddy, Hickey Creekmore?"

"Never a word."

Harry sighed again. His sighs were wrenching and theatrical. "Well, it's too bad. Just too bad. I tell you the truth, though, Adam. My mamma and my daddy, they loved each other. He was a planter. But he was a fine man, and he gave your aunt a fine house to live in, and if Uncle Joel hadn't been so proud, my daddy could have helped him."

"My daddy didn't need help from nobody," Adam said fiercely.

"Ah, you're just like him. Chip off the old block." Harry shook his head, a motion quite indistinct in the night that now had crept in on them. The full moon was standing over the woods; in its pale yellow light Harry and all the world around seemed unreal. "I only meant that my daddy was blessed with money, and there might have been times when he could have helped your daddy if only Uncle Joel had been willing. My daddy wrote Uncle Joel a letter years and years ago. Oh, it was before I was even born, and I'm much older than you are, Adam."

"How old are you?"

"I'm thirty. Descending into middle age. Not far from the grave."

"What did the letter say?"

"The letter?"

"The letter your daddy wrote my daddy."

"Ah, yes. Yes. That ill-fated letter. That letter that was the token of affection, taken as a gauntlet thrown down at the foot of a proud gentleman, your father."

"Damn, you sure are hard to get to. I never heard anybody talk like you do. Can't you just say something? Can't you just tell it?"

"Of course, of course. The desire for direct talk is the sign of an honorable man, Cousin Adam. I knew you were honorable, because you are my cousin and we are an honorable family."

"The letter. The letter."

"Yes, the letter. My daddy wrote to Uncle Joel that if there was ever anything Uncle Joel needed, my daddy would be happy to let him have it."

"We didn't need nothing," Adam said.

"Exactly what your daddy wrote to my daddy. And your daddy sent word that if my daddy ever tried to write him again, he would come down into Georgia with a gun and shoot my daddy before his wife and family. Can you imagine that, Adam?" Harry delivered himself of another of those loud, pent-up sighs. "But I don't criticize your daddy. Understand that. I just mean it was sad."

Harry stood up and dusted mechanically at his pants with his large hat. "Well I won't be troubling you anymore. I hope I haven't disturbed your evening. I'll be going." He put his hat on his head. It was like an enormous lily in the moonlight. His glasses shone dully under the brim, like two ghostly lights.

"Where be you going now?"

"Oh, I don't know, Cousin Adam. Somewhere where the wind blows. Somewhere under the sky, where the clouds will cover me. Foxes have holes. I'll find a place. Don't you worry about me. You never knew I existed. You just forget . . ."— his voice caught again—"you ever met me." He put out his hand, and Adam took it. "I'm very glad to have met you. Your warm moment of hospitality has been a kindness that shall glow like a fire in my memory forever and ever, or at least until I lay me beneath the cold sod and the strivings of my woeful heart are taken up by the sighing of the wind."

He made as if to step down off the porch.

"Wait!" Adam cried at him. "You can't just run off."

"Well, I'm not running off, Adam. I'm just leaving. I'm much too tired to run. I've had a difficult time."

"Why? Why?" Adam said. He was nearly beside himself.

Harry only sighed. "My daddy is dead. Uncle Joel predicted a bad end to him, and alas, Cousin Adam, your daddy was right. My daddy had too much pride. He wanted too much. Your daddy had wisdom. A quality lacking in my dear departed parent."

They were standing three feet from each other, Harry with one foot off the porch on the ground, the other still resting on the timber step, knee cocked.

"I don't know what you're talking about!"

"No, no, of course you don't. My daddy died bankrupt, Adam. Can you imagine? Shot himself in the head with a shotgun. It was awful, Cousin Adam. Just awful. I'm glad Uncle Joel doesn't know about it yet. I'm glad I don't have to tell him," Harry whispered, deeply moved.

"Shot himself!" Adam said.

"And of course I have my daddy's blood in my veins, Cousin Adam. I'm no good. No good at all. Don't you ever trust me with anything."

"Why? You don't look so bad to me."

Harry hung his head shamefully. "I'm a gambler, Cousin Adam. Cards and women. They have been my ruin."

Somehow Harry seemed to think that he had been invited to sit down again. He came back up on the porch and collapsed in the rocking chair, slumped forward abjectly, his elbows on his knees. Adam sat down, too. His head was swimming.

"You sure do have a nice place," Harry said. "My sainted mother told me Uncle Joel was one of the best farmers in the country. Everything's got a solid look to it."

"You can't see nothing in the dark."

"My eyesight's so bad I can feel things," Harry said without hesitation. "Those of us who are nearly blind can often perceive things much better than those with keen eyes."

Adam was silent. He did not understand.

"You keep horses?" Harry said.

"Mules!"

"Mules!" Harry said with distaste. "I don't see how you can hunt foxes with mules."

"Never tried," Adam said.

They were silent again, Harry looking off into the dark woods. He made no motion to leave, though he kept his hat on his head. He rubbed his hands together thoughtfully.

41

"I reckon you've got a good life here," Harry said after a while. "Simple. No hypocrisy to a life like this. People don't lie to you, do they?"

"I don't reckon."

"Ah, wonderful. Wonderful. I come from a world where people lie all the time. I think lying is the unpardonable sin. Trying to be something you aren't. It's an affront to God who created us the way He wanted us to be. Don't you agree, Adam?"

"It ain't right to lie."

"Of course! Of course! My sentiments exactly. I'm sure you're planning to spend your life here in this honest, this simple place."

"No," Adam said. "I'm going to California tomorrow morning. I've sold the place."

"Indeed!" Harry said. "Indeed." He sounded very interested.

"Was your mamma older than my daddy or younger?"

"Oh, she was much younger. It's why your daddy got so mad. You know, he treated her almost like she was his daughter."

"But you're older than me."

"A mere detail. My mother married very young. Why, she was hardly fifteen. But older than Juliet. I believe Juliet was only fourteen when she fell in love with Romeo."

"Was she your daddy's kin or your mamma's?"

"Who?"

"Juliet. I didn't get her last name."

"Juliet! Why, Adam, she was a young woman in a play. Have you ever seen a play?"

"You mean like on a stage?"

"Exactly."

"No. We ain't got time for such like in Bourbon County. Only thing I ever seen on a stage was a revival preacher."

Harry clucked his tongue. "You have missed a lot in life, my dear boy. Plays are the finest things on earth."

"That ain't what I heard," Adam said.

Harry changed the subject. "Tell me, cousin. Did I hear you correctly? Did you really say you have sold a fine little place like this?"

"I done it." Adam felt ashamed.

"Well, well, well!" Harry said pensively. "And do I understand that you are about to traverse the continent? You are going to California?"

"I'm going to California."

Harry sighed again. "Well, I reckon the place to go is California. I wouldn't mind going to California myself. I've always said I wanted to go. I have always dreamed of being warm all year long."

There was an extended silence. Adam wrestled with his thoughts. They were like big boxes in his mind. "You can go with me if you want," he said finally.

Harry shook his head. "No, Cousin Adam. You don't want me tagging along with you. You see, I'm a fugitive from justice."

"You mean like a slave?"

"Oh, no! Dear me, no! Not like that, Adam. A different kind of fugitive. You do know the story about Potiphar's wife in the Book of Genesis, do you not, Cousin Adam?"

"Sure," Adam said, at last able to be proud of something before this strange cousin of his. "I know the Bible real good."

"Intelligence runs in our family, Adam. I should have known. Well, you do remember that she became provoked with Joseph because ... because Joseph wouldn't ... Ah, I believe it is unnecessary for me to say what Joseph wouldn't do."

"I reckon I know," Adam said. He felt his face grow red.

Harry sighed like escaping steam. "Well, that very thing happened to me. I was coming upriver from Chattanooga to see my Uncle Joel, and I got mixed up with a woman on the steamboat. She tried to force me, Adam. I resisted. I was born with one inheritance that I shall never surrender, Cousin Adam. Not even in the darkest of times. My honor, Adam. My sacred honor. You do know what I mean."

"No," Adam said.

Harry sounded a little impatient. "Well, you see, she seized me, and I spurned her. But she told her husband that I had seized *her!*"

"Oh," Adam said.

"I had to leave the steamboat rather hastily. Under a cloud, as it were. Fortunately we were right here at Bourbonville. But ..." And here Harry paused again and swallowed, and some real perturbation entered his voice. "I believe I did hear something about dogs ..."

"Dogs?"

"Dogs, Adam. I believe the husband said something about dogs. Going to find dogs to chase after me."

Adam was confused. He could not quite comprehend what Harry was talking about, and the matter was so delicate that Adam did not even know how to ask questions about it. He groped for something. "And you hadn't done nothing?"

"Nothing, Adam. Nothing but defend my own honor. Oh, I understand her husband's wrath. If I were married, and if my wife told me what that woman told him, I would be upset."

"Oh," Adam said.

"I would seek to avenge my wife's tarnished honor."

"Oh. And she was really married." Adam was baffled by it all. He knew about Mrs. Hattie Arbuckle, but he understood her because she did not have a man of her own. It truly shocked him to think that a married woman might be out chasing unmarried men. But his own experience with Mrs. Arbuckle made him sympathize with Harry.

"So what do you figure on doing?" Adam said uneasily.

"That's just it. I don't know. I thought Uncle Joel would take me in, hide me till this thing blew over. Now, now I reckon they'll catch me and hang me. I mean, who's going to believe my word against the word of a woman? You don't have a chance in this world if you're an honest man, Adam. I tell you the truth, I wish now I'd just gone on and done what that woman offered to do with me."

"That wouldn't of been right," Adam said. His voice squeaked unnaturally. He had to clear his throat and start again before he could finish his sentence.

"I am innocent," Harry said in a tone full of abuse. "And look at me." He lifted his arms and made a blurred gesture with his open hands to show his harmless condition.

"Well, you got to go with me," Adam said. "You can't just stay here and be caught like a run-off slave. Come along with me to California."

"Cousin Adam, I have so little money. Twenty dollars at the most. I departed from the steamboat so quickly that I left my baggage behind. It's in Knoxville by now, I'm sure, and I have reservations about going there to claim it."

"Why didn't you have them put your baggage off in Bourbonville?" Adam kept trying to reconstruct Harry's story, to see what had happened. It was very confusing.

"Adam, to tell you the honest truth, I had to jump off the steamboat. You see I was asleep in my stateroom. I haven't been feeling well lately. And I slept right through the stop at Bourbonville. You see, it put me in such a fever to have to tell this woman no, no, no, every day and every night. She pestered me for days and days. We were stuck on a sandbar for a while. I thought that sandbar was going to be the downfall of my honor. I'm sure you understand. I was so tired. So very tired."

Adam was silent, expectant.

"When we were pulling away from the dock at Bourbonville, I realized that I had overslept. I was going to try to get the captain of the boat to put back in, but then that mad husband of the woman I have described came running down the deck, shooting at me. Imagine it, Adam! Shooting at *me!* I, who have never harmed a *bug* in my entire earthly pilgrimage! I tell you it was a shock. I didn't even have time to think. I took a big leap over the side, and the next thing I knew, I was in the water."

"That must of been something," Adam said, awed.

"Yes, it was indeed. You know I was convinced before that moment that I couldn't swim. But once in the water I discovered that swimming came as natural to me as flying to a bird. I am quite disturbed that I have never followed aquatic pursuits before."

"I can't swim neither," Adam said.

"I even managed to cling to my spectacles. My God! If I'd lost them, I don't know *what* I'd have done!" He took his spectacles off, a motion to reassure himself, looked at them, then replaced them on his nose. "Have you ever been troubled with your eyes?"

"Not as I know of."

"Must have got it from my father's side of the family then," Harry said. "People always said I took after him."

"You sure don't look like our side," Adam said.

"I'm sure our kinship lies in the heart," Harry said.

"Well, I got money," Adam said. He made an effort to pull the conversation back to important things. "You can come along with me. I can't leave no kin of mine behind. Not when somebody's trying to hang him."

Harry turned around to face Adam. The moonlight gleamed softly on a wide and grateful smile. "Cousin Adam, let me tell you something. You are a real Christian."

45

"Oh, no, I ain't," Adam said, uneasy again. "I ain't never had no experience. You got to have a experience to be a real Christian. I ain't never shouted."

"Then God has spoken to you in a still, small voice, Cousin Adam. You are a real Christian. I know."

The two of them sat back in their chairs and rocked, feeling the beginnings of the warmth that was to grow between them in the months ahead. Adam wanted to ask more questions, but he was worn out talking to Harry. Harry took off with the conversation like a bird soaring with a string or a worm, and Adam, earthbound, could not follow him. He thought the story would come out later on. There would be time.

# 10

Adam always remembered the morning he left home. He rose from his lumpy bed in the dim light an hour before dawn, and for just a moment as his mind fought up from sleep, he thought it was an ordinary day, his father and mother asleep in their bed in the corner, and the world fixed forever. Then he came to himself quickly, remembered what day it was, and saw Harry asleep in his parents' bed, his glasses laid aside, his long face exquisitely handsome and strange.

He stirred up the fire and set coffee to boiling and looked at Harry's white suit. They had boiled it in soap the night before, boiled it again in clean water in the great iron kettle outside, and left it hanging over the chair to dry. Then he opened the door and went out into the damp, clean air of an April morning blooming with spring. He saw the gray mist hanging in the woods as he had seen it so many times before, and he had to shake his head in the astonishment of knowing that this was the last morning in his life he would be seeing it there.

He fed the stock one last time. He marveled briefly at the murmuring familiarity of the animals, their eagerness for food, their peaceful ignorance of all the morning meant. Mr. Swope had a boy coming out about noon to look after things. The rumor was that the farm had already been sold by the banker to somebody in Knoxville. The animals would be skittish with the new people for a while. But then the new people would feed them, and the animals would become friendly.

Adam grieved. The grief of a young man leaving home for the first time. Leaving home forever, journeying like Abraham into the unknown. He saw his mother's grave, so quiet in the early morning, and he grieved again at her death. But as he did his chores, the sun turned the eastern sky crimson and the day bright and warm, and he knew that it was time to go.

He made biscuits for Harry, and Harry sat happily at the table eating with gusto and praising everything. Harry gave Adam a warm feeling. It was good to be praised. And what language Harry used. Adam had never heard anything like it. The flooding power of Harry's words, the flights of eloquence that Adam could only barely understand. "You know," Adam said all in a rush, trying to express his admiration, "you'd of made a good preacher. A real good preacher."

Harry laughed. Harry laughed often. "I would have been the greatest since the apostle Paul!" he said.

"Then maybe you ought to do it. Maybe," Adam said. He was in awe of preachers. They had touched God, for God had called them.

"We shall see," Harry said off-handedly. "Who can tell what will happen to us in California? Maybe I'll become an evangelist. I've been a sinner, Cousin Adam. But just meeting you makes me feel that life is going to change altogether for me. Ah, I wish my mother were still alive. She believed in God, Adam. She was truly a saint."

"You'll have to tell my daddy about her," Adam said.

"I can hardly wait! Yes, I can hardly wait to meet your daddy, my precious uncle." Harry gorged himself and looked like a cheerful angel, preparing himself for an annunciation of sorts, light beaming from his face like the Holy Spirit.

They set out while the air was still cool. The spring-bursting land was quiet except for the sweet birds. Everything shimmered in the transparent mist that gave strange shapes to ordinary objects. Harry observed that they should avoid the town. Somebody might see them, tell Mr. Bigelow (he was the offended husband) the direction they had gone. So Adam

47

chose a rutted trail that led them in a long loop around Bourbonville, past isolated farms set far apart in the great woodland. They rode in silence because the morning seemed to impose silence upon them, and the tension of escape tightened in them both like drawn wire. The steady tramping of the mules was a muffled sound in the damp earth. Adam marveled that those muley hoofs, rising and falling in the dauntless, stubborn patience of mules, could take them all the way to the Pacific Ocean, to a new life. How strange that it was no more than a mule's strength, this power that would make him be born again!

The dawning world they traversed seemed full of eyes, and the green forest reposing immensely about them brooded like some unimaginable life, watching as they passed by. To Adam, journeying in this moment out of childhood, the morning calm was like a spell, and the tramping of the mules was like an incantation done without words, to appeal to the woodland spirits who would in their capricious way determine the success of their enterprise. All about him in that unique morning, the boy felt an eerie expectancy, and the forest was a hidden realm where at any moment they might hear a voice whispering at them. "Adam? Adam? Where art thou, Adam?"

As it was, his ears played tricks on him. Harry was sure that Horace Bigelow would come. Adam imagined sometimes that in the far, far distance he could hear the faint ringing of voices and barking dogs. But strain though he did, those dangerous sounds remained just beyond the edge of what he could hear distinctly. The voices became only an occasional breeze rustling the leaves high overhead, and when the no-name hound, loping easily along with lolling tongue, did bark, the sound was like a thunderclap and made the sounds Adam imagined seem as nothing. He did hear distinctly the warble of the birds in the forest. A mockingbird. A jay. Sparrows that chirped and sang. And he also heard from time to time the scampering of squirrels in the branches overhead. *They are building their nests! It is time for some to be building nests, and it is time for some to be going. I am glad to be going.*

Steadily the sun rose and burned away the mist so that the day was left rinsed and shining. All the new foliage was green, delicate, and somehow radiant with abounding life. Above them the blue sky arched like some soft fabric of dreams, seen through the tracery of leaves, woven infinitely beyond without a cloud. Bourbonville was behind them now. So was the mounting sun, and their dark shadows astride the shadows of the mules were, in the sunny places, pointing them the way West.

At about nine o'clock they came on two men at the bottom of a hill. They were woodchoppers. Adam heard the clean, steady sound of their axe long before he came to them. They had a flatbed wagon hitched to a team of handsome brown mules. The mules stood stolidly in the traces, flicking their long ears, switching their tails from time to time, and seeming more than half asleep in the drowsy sun. One of the men was wielding the axe. The other sat silently in the wagon, hunched over his own knees, and apparently waiting his turn, for they seemed to have but one axe between them. They had dull faces and looked miserably poor.

Adam did not know them. Their strangeness jarred him. He had always lived in a narrow world where he recognized the people he saw. These men were the first clear sign that he was passing beyond the limits of that familiar world. They exchanged greetings in the laconic way of country folk meeting on the road, and Adam and Harry went on, leaving the woodcutters, their work momentarily suspended, looking impassively after them.

Adam felt their eyes on his neck. In a while he looked surreptitiously back at them. He found them staring still, and to the boy it was as if the mysterious watchfulness of the forest and the great brooding land had now become incarnate. Who could tell about strangers in the road? God had sent three angels to sup with Abraham before Sodom was destroyed. Abraham did not know who they were. And what about these ordinary-looking woodchoppers? *Where are you going, boy? Why? How can you leave this place where God put you down?*

It seemed to Adam that they were smiling at him over the widening distance, though in the confusion of morning sunlight and streaks of shadow he could not be sure. A smile on those dull faces? What could it mean? The more he considered them, the more he was sure that they were more than they seemed. And suddenly the sense of himself in this prodigious world was more intense than he had ever known.

*I will go on! I will not turn back. I will go on.*

And so he kept his back resolutely set against the East, and they came out at last onto the great dusty pike that led to Nashville and the West. There was a lot of traffic on the road. Wagons and carts and horses and mules. A drover herding cows along in languid indolence. Now and then they passed a fine brick tavern with women working around it and clothes hanging in the wind to dry. Taverns of logs, too. Poor and run-down. Farms Adam had never seen before.

But always there was the road.

The road, colored like a streak of rust through the spring land, swarming with motion. Adam felt cast adrift on a great stream alive with humanity. He felt a boundless thrill in his heart.

When Harry reached the pike, he thought he had won deliverance from whatever he feared pursued him. He broke into song, sitting back in ridiculous ease amid the baggage of the mule he rode, his large hat pushed up on his head, his long legs dangling in space (Adam had only one saddle), singing ballads in a tenor voice that was strong and sweet and made people look up at him with surprise and pleasure as he went by.

Sometimes he talked. Snatches of thought tossed down in the bright day like small change glittering in the sun.

"It's a beautiful day! Splendid! Just splendid! Makes you glad to be alive."

"How can you tell?" Adam said doubtfully. "How can you see anything through them glasses?"

"I can't see anything *without* them! Well, that's not true. I see a world. Colors. You'd be surprised how beautiful colors are when you see them all spread out in blurs. Like clouds. You know."

Adam did not know.

"I was nearly six years old before anybody knew I was nearly blind. A lens grinder. He was from Heidelberg, Germany. He came through peddling glasses, and he came to our house, and just like that everybody understood what was wrong with me. I couldn't see! They thought I was dumb! My father had washed his hands of me. Said I wasn't worth anything, and then it turned out I was just blind. It was something. The lens grinder. He kept putting thicker glasses on my nose, and the world kept changing and changing until finally I guess I could see as good as anybody."

"It must have been something."

"Tell you the truth I was disappointed. I mean when you

50

can just *hear* people ... Well, it's better. I didn't know what ugliness was. Everybody was all wrapped up in clouds of color, and everybody was beautiful. But when you can see ... some people are just ugly. You know. My father was ugly. Tell you the truth. That was hard to admit, but he was. Looked like a pig on his hind legs. I never have seen a pig since without thinking about him. That's the truth."

Adam laughed. Harry made him laugh a lot; he had never been with anybody who made him laugh as much as Harry did.

# 11

At night they camped beside the road. They made a fire, and its warmth was good. In early May the nights were still cool, and the fire leaping up threw light above them against the high trees and made the world look strange and full of wonderful things. They pitched the tent Adam had bought from Mr. Mahoney at the hardware store in Bourbonville, Mr. Mahoney, who on the road West seemed as remote as a pyramid. The tent bloomed out like some great flower in the gloom. Others camped around them every night but greetings were restrained. For though at night along the great pike people sought each other for company against the dark, nobody wanted to be too friendly at the first meeting with strangers.

Adam cooked. Salt bacon and hard beans boiled together in a small iron kettle. Spoonbread flung together with cornmeal and water in a pan. Harry perched nearby on a rock or a stump on those evenings, watching as though Adam were concocting magic out of the air.

"Hell, Cousin Adam, you're one good man. So generous. Just like my mamma. You know so many things, too. Think about being able to cook. You're like an alchemist making gold out of lead. I never was any good at cooking. I can't tell you how much I appreciate what you're doing for me. Someday I'll repay you. When we get to San Francisco, I'll take you to the biggest restaurant in town. Hah! But it won't taste this good. My God, Cousin Adam! Nothing I've ever eaten tastes so good as these beans!"

"It's the road," Adam said. "You stay all day on the road, and anything tastes good." Adam was embarrassed and yet flattered. Harry knew how to flatter people so that they believed he was sincere.

When they had eaten, they sprawled by the fire, and they talked. Or rather Harry talked. Adam would always remember Harry's laughing face as he reclined on an elbow, face darkened with dancing shadows, his bright blue eyes shining cheerfully behind his enormous glasses, talking. One tale after another poured out, stories of Harry's life, some of them true, some of them plausible, some of them fantastic. Stories about the future. "I've decided what I'm going to do, Cousin Adam. I'm going to open a theatre in San Francisco. Give a little life to the town. If there's gold in California, then you're going to have people with money enough in their pockets to buy tickets to the theatre. And I'm going to have the biggest theatre in the world."

"I don't see why anybody wants to go spend a night looking at something that ain't true."

"It *is* true, Adam. It's true when you see it. When I lived in Atlanta, there was a theatre where they had plays. I would go in and get lost, Adam. I can't explain it; you have to see it for yourself. The curtains would pull back, and I was on wings."

"I don't reckon I'll ever go," Adam said, sullen before something that seemed so absurd to him, so grand and sublime to Harry.

"Yes, you will, Cousin Adam. Yes, you will, and I'll take you."

"We'll see."

The trip to Nashville took five days. On the third night Adam and Harry were sitting by their fire after supper at a place near where the pike forded a winding, placid river called the Caney Fork. Others were camped on both sides of the river, and fires blazed up and down the bank. The water, like a polished mirror, reflected the dancing light. The night was so clear that upstream, where the river was dark, images of stars shimmered on the surface. Shadowy forms of wagons and carts, animals and lounging human figures filled the night

52

with life. Some children chased each other around the encampment, and from a nearby fireside one small group of men in formless hats passed a jug and talked about the fugitive slave laws. You could chase a slave right into New York City now and bring him back South, back to owners who paid rewards.

Suddenly out of the dark a couple appeared at Adam's side to visit.

The woman was clearly the leader. She was angular and intense, and she moved in a stiffly awkward way as if she had broken something a long time ago. Her hair was tied up in a large bandana, so that her head seemed unusually small and birdlike. But what you would remember about her were the darting little eyes set in that head, eyes like a hawk's eyes, looking for something on the ground to peck at.

Her husband slouched behind her, stolid and gloomy, as though walking in a long-practiced deliberation intended to keep his dignity from being compromised. His long, cadaverous face, once abloom with pimples in some half-forgotten and unnatural youth, now was riddled with scars. A strand or two of slick black hair hung unkempt from a domed and bulbous head going starkly bald. The no-name dog jumped up and barked in alarm when they came near. Adam wondered if the two of them—man and dog—might sniff each other.

"I declare," the woman said, her voice like a saw. "I just said to Clifford here, 'Clifford, that there's bound to be a new tent.' Ain't that right, Clifford? Didn't you just hear me say that was a new tent?" She seemed very pleased with herself.

"You did indeed, my dear. I heard you say so myself. You said it was a new tent."

"Why don't you hush that dog up?" The woman said. "It ain't polite to bark at folks come to visit."

Adam got up, murmuring a confused apology, and tried to make the dog be silent. The dog recoiled, looked at Adam, and kept barking as if trying to convince him of something important.

"You should do all that is possible to discipline that canine in the proper manner," Clifford said. "An ill-trained dog is a reflection on the breeding of its master."

"He ain't but two years old," Adam said. "He ain't hardly more than a pup. Hush up, dog!"

"Then now is the time to train him. Dogs, like young people, are better disciplined in the tender years. Bend a tree

53

when it is a sapling, and it will grow that way. I would beat him if I were you."

"Then he'd bite me," Adam said.

"Mmmm yes. Children do that, too." He held out a lank, dirty hand. "I was bitten to the bone in that hand once by a child in Frederick, Maryland."

"Well, is it a new tent?" the woman asked impatiently, cocking her head back and eyeing the tent with intolerant interest.

"Oh, yes, ma'am! It's brand new!" Adam said. "I mean, we've slept in it twice now, but other than that it ain't been used at all."

The woman shook her head and sighed. Something of the hawkishness momentarily passed out of her face, and she looked tired and sad. "I ain't never had much that's new and nice. I always just like to look at things close up when they're new. Ain't it a nice tent, Clifford?"

"Indeed it is, my love. If I but had the money I would purchase a tent exactly like that for you. It is worthy of your divine soul." Clifford managed what was nearly a smile.

"And I reckon with that there tent, you're going on a long trip?" The woman spoke to Harry. "I mean, I bet you ain't just going to ... to ... What's the next town down the road, Clifford?"

"The next town of any consequence is Nashville, my love."

"Nashville! You ain't just going to Nashville then, are you, mister?"

"Oh, no," Harry said with an easy laugh. "We're going all the way to California. Come September we'll be in San Francisco."

"San Francisco! Maybe we ought to go to California, Clifford. There's gold in California."

"My dear, the infirmities of my back would never allow me to dig gold out of the ground."

"Clifford's got a bad back," the woman said. "He can't lift things."

"Pity," Harry said. "A bad back is an impediment to the exercise that is necessary to keep the bodily juices flowing properly."

"Say, mister, you really do talk good. Don't he talk good, Clifford?"

"Mmmm," Clifford said uneasily. "He does indeed."

"He almost talks better than you do, Clifford."

54

"Now, my dear, you haven't heard him talk enough to make a rash judgment like that."

"I knowed you was going beyond Nashville," she said sternly, giving all her attention to Harry.

"Mrs. Baynes is really very good at this sort of thing," Clifford said.

The two of them sat down by the fire without being asked. Harry and Adam sat down, too. They looked at each other. "I ain't never seen glasses like that before," Mrs. Baynes said, peering at Harry as though he were an object in a circus. "Lord, they look like you could start a bonfire with them."

"You don't use my glasses for that," Harry said with an easy laugh. He thought the Baynes couple should be on stage.

"What do you mean, mister? Anybody knows you can start a bonfire with a magnifying glass. And you got the two biggest magnifying glasses I ever seen hanging on your nose. Just because you're wearing a white suit and talk good, don't think you can fool me! I ain't dumb!"

"If you're nearsighted you don't start a fire with your glasses," Harry said patiently and in good humor. "I'm nearsighted."

"Nearsighted, farsighted! It don't matter. Glasses is glasses, and I think it's cruel of you to be making fun of a poor, honest woman and her husband that's just down a little on their luck."

"My dear madam," Harry said with genuine sympathy, "I would never in the world make fun of you."

"Mrs. Baynes is a very intelligent woman," Clifford said. "On the whole, if she said your glasses would start a bonfire, I'd tend to believe her myself."

Mrs. Baynes kept studying Harry, her little eyes shifting over his face like a couple of sharp fingers pinching tomatoes. "I bet the ladies feels sorry for you," she said in a moment. "I bet them glasses makes women want to give you a little mother-loving. I knowed a feller once name of Potter Lethgo up in Maryland."

"I had no idea you knew Potter Lethgo, my dear," Mr. Baynes said. "The woman is an amazement to me, gentlemen. Life with her is never dull. She is always coming up with surprises."

"Well, Potter, he had thick glasses. And he just about had to fight the women off with a stick. He was a bachelor, and he had a five-hundred-acre farm in Prince George County, and so you could figure women was going to see things in Potter Lethgo they didn't see in just everbody. But I think it was the glasses, you know." She tittered. "They made Potter look like he needed somebody to take care of him." She shook her head. "I bet the ladies just runs up to you on the street and kisses you under them glasses, don't they, mister?"

Harry laughed. "Well now, Mrs. Baynes, I'm a professional man myself. Things like that don't happen to professional men."

"A professional man! You see there, Clifford?"

"Well now, I'm a professional man too," Clifford Baynes said. "Say there, my love, don't you think something hot to drink would taste nice on a chilly night like this?"

"I sure do, Clifford honey. If these folks got any coffee handy, it sure would be nice if they was to offer us some."

"We wouldn't want to impose on your hospitality," Clifford said, looking comfortably at Harry.

"I'll fix some right up," Adam said.

Clifford Baynes hardly looked at Adam. Instead he spoke to Harry. "That is certainly a generous gesture on your part, my dear sir. Coffee is like balm in Gilead when you are fatigued with the ardors of a journey. Coffee warms the spine. It aids in the sleeping process, and has shown itself conducive to pleasant dreams."

"Hey there now, mister," Mrs. Baynes said happily. "You got to go some to talk better than that."

Harry laughed again. He was enjoying these people. "Thank Adam," he said. "Adam's the one who owns the coffee."

Mr. Baynes paid no attention to that piece of incredible information. Harry was the one wearing the white suit. "Now then, just what is your profession anyhow, mister . . . mister . . . ? I don't believe I caught the name."

"Creekmore," Harry said. "Harry Creekmore."

"Pleased to meet you," Clifford Baynes said, without much real enthusiasm. He put out a limp, dry hand, and they shook with each other. "My name is Baynes, Professor Clifford Baynes, Esquire. This is my charming and loving helpmeet, Ishtar."

"Pleased to meet you," Ishtar Baynes said. She delivered herself of a smile that was like an oil slick on water.

"This is Adam Cloud," Harry said.

Ishtar Baynes made a slight noise of doubtful contempt under her breath and scrutinized Adam. Something was distinctly queer here. She prided herself on figuring out queer things.

"I don't believe you responded to my request for information about yourself," Clifford Baynes said carefully. "Just what profession do you belong to, Mr. Deepmore?"

"Creekmore," Harry said. "Well, you might say I'm in the medical profession, Mr. Baynes."

"You mean you're a doctor?" Ishtar Baynes showed a sudden respect. "Well, Doctor, I'd like to get your opinion about Dr. Cristie's Magnetic Fluid. They say it's good for general debility, fits, cramp, paralysis, fistula, palsy, and all them nervous diseases. But what I want to know is this. Is it any good for colds?"

Harry cleared his throat, laughed, and shot a quick glance at Adam. Adam merely looked at him. "Well now, I'm not that kind of doctor, Mrs. Baynes. I've had, ah, some experience . . . some professional experience, I might say, in a field where the object is not to prescribe medicine but to help you locate within yourself those sources of strength that will make you live a successful life."

"Good God, mister," Ishtar Baynes said, shaking her head impatiently. "I fell off at the turn."

Harry laughed again. "I am a phrenologist," he said. "I determine character by a scientific examination of heads."

"Well, well," Mr. Baynes said, nodding his ugly head thoughtfully. "I've heard of phrenologists."

"And now you have seen one," Harry said.

The couple Baynes sat looking intently at him for a moment. They were trying to guess if there were any way on earth they might use Harry to get something they wanted. Anything. But here they were out in the middle of the dark countryside at night, and profit in anything seemed hard to come by.

"I believe I understand that you are a professor," Harry Creekmore said. "That shows in your face. Your nose, you see. It has a little bulge right there. Excuse me, please. But you see, that is an intelligence bump, and most people who have that bump go into teaching."

Clifford Baynes put a hand experimentally to his nose and tried to wiggle it back and forth. "I believe that bump came from a broken nose when I was a child."

Harry shook his head and looked very wise and profes-

57

sional. "It might have been a very lucky accident," Harry said, without flinching. "Your whole career might have been shaped by the sudden development of that protuberance on your nose."

"My husband has taught in some of the finest schools in the East," Ishtar Baynes said, her voice coy and proud. "And if you can teach in the East, you got to be smart. Tell him about it, Clifford."

"Well, I did indeed teach in the George Washington Academy of Frederick, Maryland," Clifford Baynes said comfortably. "You've heard of it, of course?"

"Well, no, I don't believe I have," Harry said. "I've never been out of the South, you see. I don't know much about the East."

"Never been out of the South? Now that is a pity!" Clifford Baynes gravely shook his head, happy to claim an obvious superiority. "Well," he sighed gloomily, "you have missed culture if you have missed the state of Maryland. You have missed civilization, sir. You have missed the George Washington Academy."

"I lived in Boston awhile," Ishtar Baynes said. "Boston has so much civilization it just drips off the trees."

"I think that explains my wife's great natural intelligence," Clifford Baynes said. "She has spent time in both Boston and New Haven. Something does rub off when one is exposed to such citadels of learning."

"My mamma was in the hotel business," Ishtar Baynes said. "We moved around a lot."

"Travel broadens the mind," Clifford Baynes said. "My wife here presents, I think you will agree, a rather unprepossessing exterior. But her mind is as broad as a veritable field. In it rich things grow in profusion."

"Her head shows that, Mr. Baynes."

"Professor Baynes, if you don't mind, Doctor."

"Of course. Professor Baynes," Harry said. "What was it you taught anyway, Professor Baynes?"

"Oh, Latin, writing, spelling, rhetoric, logic, music, natural philosophy, arithmetic. I can teach anything, Dr. Creekmore."

"Mr. Baynes can talk Latin better than anybody you ever seen," Ishtar said. "Talk some Latin to him, Clifford."

"Oh my dear . . ."

"Come on now, Clifford. These folks would appreciate it."

"Well, if you do insist, my dear." Mr. Baynes looked proudly around as though he were perched on a lectern, surveying a vast and speechless audience. He cleared his throat and rolled his eyes toward the heavens as though he felt with deep humility how high he had been raised above the common herd. Then in a loud, slow, dramatic tone he declaimed: "Amo, amas, amat, amamus, amatis, amant."

He stopped at the end and looked off soulfully into space.

"Well, what do you think of *that*?" Ishtar Baynes glowed with pride.

Harry laughed gently. "Excellent! Excellent! You give such a nice, deep sound to the letter 'A' when you pronounce it, Professor Baynes. Truly excellent in a Latinist."

"He can talk Latin all day and all night. That's what drawed me to Clifford in the first place. I don't like him to be with riffraff. You get such a poor class of folks on the road nowadays. I make it my business to keep Clifford here from having to put up with nobody that ain't worthy of him."

"And she does a fine job of it, too, Dr. Creekmore. You will note that I am not associating with all these common people around us." He wrinkled a lip in disdain and made a gesture with his head that seemed to encompass not just the camp spread out on the riverbanks but a world of unwashed people beyond.

"We are deeply flattered that you have chosen to join us, Professor Baynes," Harry said, flashing a cheerful grin at Adam. Adam could not understand why Harry was enjoying these people so much.

"Just last night I set Clifford down next to a real live lawyer from Knoxville. He invited us to coffee, too. He said when we got through drinking coffee with him that he'd never in all his whole life met nobody like Clifford and I. Clifford told him all about the law, and he was so impressed!"

"I'm sure he was," Harry said.

"I'm only sorry that I don't know more about the science of phrenology," Clifford Baynes said. "But I do want you to know that I approve."

"Thank you, Professor Baynes. Thank you very much," Harry said. He inclined his head in a bow.

"And I seen you and your servant here tonight, and I looked at that fancy white suit, and I said to Clifford, I said, 'Now that's quality, honey.'"

"Those were her very words," Clifford Baynes said.

"And I like your glasses, too," Ishtar Baynes said. "The smartest folks I've ever knowed in my life wore glasses. How much did they cost?"

"I really don't know," Harry said. "My father paid for them. And Adam is not my servant, he is my friend and cousin."

"What about that coffee?" Ishtar Baynes said, looking around like a vulture. "My husband wants his coffee."

"It's coming," Adam said.

"We ain't got all night," Ishtar Baynes said.

"Do you find much profit in the phrenology business these days, Dr. Creekmore?"

Harry shook his head sadly. "People are going too fast to learn much about themselves, Professor Baynes. You may have noticed that yourself."

"Yes, yes indeed. The world is filled with foolish people. It is very sad, very sad indeed."

"We ain't got but two cups for the coffee," Adam said. "Maybe you got some cups."

"Oh, that's all right," Ishtar Baynes said. "I reckon you men has had your coffee today. Clifford and me don't mind drinking alone, do we honey?"

"No indeed." Professor Baynes did not take his eyes off the smoky coffee pot. He looked famished. The crust of his dignity seemed ready to dissolve into an interior of ravenous hunger. A terrifying expression in its way. Adam saw it.

Adam looked at Harry, and Harry winked. Adam shrugged and poured out two tin mugs of coffee. He handed them dutifully over to Mr. and Mrs. Baynes. Clifford Baynes took his mug in both hands, and paying no attention to its scalding heat, he held it to his lips and drank it down like cold beer on a hot day.

"That coffee isn't too bad," he said, wiping his mouth on a coat sleeve that was thoroughly filthy. He smacked his lips. "It's a little on the bitter side, and personally I've always liked my coffee with cream in it. But it really isn't too bad. I wouldn't mind having another cup."

"Well, you just take another cup if you want to, honey," Mrs. Baynes said. "If a man's going to be on the road all day long in the hot sun driving a couple of lazy oxen, then personally I figure he's got a right to drink all the coffee he can hold in the evening."

"Well, if you really do think so, my dear," Mr. Baynes said, nodding sagely. He held his cup out to Adam, and his voice took on a surly note. "I'll take another cup of that coffee there, boy."

Adam obediently poured the cup full. This time Mr. Baynes sipped at the brew with a little more leisure and decorum.

"You say you're driving a couple of oxen?" Harry Creekmore said pleasantly. "Where do you reckon on going?"

Mr. Baynes yawned. "Well, sir, I tell you now. It all depends on the situation. We don't exactly know."

"We figure we're going to find someplace where my husband is appreciated for what he is." Mrs. Baynes lifted her sharp little chin and donned a superior expression as if the place where her husband would be properly appreciated had to be very superior indeed.

"You mean you're going somewhere to teach school?"

Professor Baynes shook his head, yawned, and scratched himself. "Well I might have to go back into teaching, but I don't figure on it. I'm tired of wasting my time on ignorant urchins that don't want to learn and don't appreciate my talents."

"Back up there in Frederick, Clifford wasn't appreciated by his students or nobody else. But it's going to be different when we finally do stop and settle down."

"The people of Maryland are of a very low sort," Mr. Baynes said. "Those poor, ignorant, uncivilized souls up there at the George Washington Academy took it amiss when I married my charming wife."

"Well, that sure was mean of them!" Harry said.

"I was just a washerwoman at the school," Mrs. Baynes said. "But Clifford couldn't of got a better wife than me."

"I'm sure that's so," Harry said.

"I took being married to Ishtar here as a challenge," Mr. Baynes said. "You see, I was intrigued by the fact that she was named for the ancient Mesopotamian deity of love, and I knew that a woman with a name like that had to have qualities that could be developed by a person as talented at developing as I am."

Mr. Baynes spoke about himself and his talents for a long time. When the Baynes couple had at last taken leave, the fires all over the campground had burned low; the stars overhead were advancing toward midnight, and the river was a dark streak at their feet.

"That woman's mean," Adam said slowly. "I ain't never seen anybody so mean."

Harry laughed. "She's pitiful, my dear cousin. But you have to take people as they come, I always say. I feel sorry for her."

"I feel sorry for her like I feel sorry for a snake."

Harry laughed again. He did not think the couple Baynes could harm anybody.

"What's this stuff about you and feeling heads?" Adam said. "You didn't tell me nothing about that."

"My dear cousin, there is much about me that I have not told you. Every man ought to preserve something of his past life to reveal slowly. As we know each other better, I shall tell you everything."

They sat for a while. The darkness in the trees by the river was thick. Insects sang there by the thousands. They made the general stillness of the sleeping night even more profound. Harry took his glasses off, folded them carefully into their leather case, and put them in his pocket. He sat staring into a world of swimming blurs that no one but himself could ever enter.

# 12

They came to Nashville. A city of wooden houses and pale pink stores and warehouses perched on a hill and laced with muddy streets. Cows roamed some of the streets, unattended. Dogs barked, and cats slunk through the alleyways. A few trees. A smell of woodsmoke and mud and new-sawn lumber. Adam was excited. He saw women in long dresses walking up and down the board sidewalks. He saw men in stylish woolen suits going about as if they had things to do. He saw things for sale in store windows that he had never even imagined.

Harry was ecstatic. "I like cities. I like to see people. I was made for cities."

"I thought you growed up on a plantation," Adam said.

"I did. I did. But we had a town place in Savannah. And I lived in Atlanta awhile. The theatre ... I wonder if there's a theatre in Nashville."

"I wouldn't know," Adam said. Privately he thought that Nashville had everything, the glitter of Jerusalem and the gold of Ophir.

He saw steamboats at the landing in the green Cumberland River. He had never seen water so green. It wound around the city in a lazy curve, and the boats sat still on the water, all in gleaming white, with two high, thin stacks drawn against the blue sky, speaking silently of wealth and far places.

"I have got to make some money," Harry said, looking around as if Nashville were a box, open for him to put his hands in and take what he found.

"How can you make money?"

"Why, Cousin Adam, I'm going to practice phrenology. I'm going to feel fine heads fondly." He laughed at himself. "Good God! What else can I do!"

Adam was annoyed. He realized Harry was serious. "You can go on with me to California like you're supposed to. I got money. I got more than five hundred dollars."

Harry laughed, perhaps in mockery, though it was hard to tell. "No, I can't go see my Uncle Joel without money of my own. He would only suspect that I had used my relationship with you in an improper way, Cousin Adam. And I cannot throw myself on my uncle with any chance that he might not like me." He put a hand over his heart and looked at Adam with a great deal of sincerity.

"I don't like it," Adam said.

"We need to look for a pharmacy," Harry said. "If you're going to be a quack in this world, you've got to find another quack to get you started, and you can always find a quack in a pharmacy."

They located one on the Broad Way, a wide, rutted street that climbed the hill from the river. The pharmacy was in a frame building with nice glass windows neatly paned and giving onto a dark interior. A large sign spread over the high, false front of the little place. "Dr. Phineas Nelson, Creator

63

and Dispenser of the Famous Nelson's Wild Root Indian Tonic."

"You just follow me, Cousin Adam. And don't look surprised at anything."

Adam went reluctantly. He did not like this at all. Harry's grin had "cheat" written all over it.

Dr. Nelson was a stocky man with very pink cheeks. He wore a very large mustache under a big nose, and he looked both cunning and hopeful. He presented himself when the bell jingled over his door as Harry pushed it open. He was a man in his fifties, dressed sloppily. He came forward through the gloom of the pharmacy with eager gravity, a man who surveyed every situation without committing himself swiftly to any, a man who surveyed Harry now, a man, above all, composed—composed to greet people, composed to be angry or to laugh, composed to contain himself in every gesture, every word, every step, every encounter, composed so that he could never be taken by surprise or overwhelmed or subjected to ridicule or cheated, a man who looked to find the weakness of every man with the sort of defensive malice that allows the fearful to be safe by making them aware of how others may be wounded.

"Yes?" he said, holding his soft hands gently together, speaking in a voice mellow and resonant. "Is there something I can do for you, sir?"

Harry Creekmore boldly put his hand out. "Dr. Nelson, I am Dr. Harry Creekmore from Atlanta, Georgia. Do forgive me for my travel-worn appearance, but I was just passing through town with my assistant here, and I wanted to stop and commend you for your amazing elixir. Your fame has spread to Atlanta, Doctor. I have heard so much about you, and I have been helped so much by you, that I could not pass up this fortunate occasion to meet you for myself."

"Atlanta!" Dr. Nelson wrinkled his smooth, pink brow and looked perplexed. He was a man ready for anything suddenly caught off guard. "Well, that is gratifying to know." He spoke with a false smile, slowly. His quick little eyes shifted from Harry to Adam and back to Harry again. *What do these people want?*

Harry plunged in—voluble, ingratiating, and, above all, profoundly and deeply sincere! Just the right enthusiasm. Just the right expression. Just the right tone. Adam knew Harry was lying but admired him anyway. Harry made lying truly an art.

"I have a personal interest in my visit," Harry said, going on in that smooth, suave voice. "I had a serious catarrh of the nose, and nothing seemed to help me. Nothing! Why, I tried every salve and every tonic anyone could suggest, and since I am a medical man myself, I tell you that my acquaintance in these matters is very large."

"To be sure," Dr. Nelson said, his voice soft and purring like a watching cat's.

"And then a mercantile friend of mine who had passed through your excellent city happened to think of your remedy. He chanced to have a bottle with him that he had brought along for his wife. He urged it upon me because he insisted that my condition was desperate, far more desperate than his wife's."

"A true gentleman I'd say," Dr. Nelson said. He seemed to be melting just a little under Harry's steam, but still his eyes were watchful and very careful.

"Indeed a gentleman he was, sir. But I must confess, Dr. Nelson, that I was skeptical. I didn't believe your tonic could possibly help me."

"Quite right!" Dr. Nelson said.

"I had been disappointed so many times. But my friend persisted when I attempted to demur, and he finally overcame my reservations."

"It is excellent to have a faithful friend," Dr. Nelson said. He rubbed his hands gently together and rolled his eyes over to Adam and came back to Harry.

"So I drank a bottle of your medicine on the spot, Doctor. And within only a day my catarrh was completely gone. I felt no pain whatsoever."

"Amazing!" Dr. Nelson said. He waited.

"I vow that it was indeed amazing to me, Dr. Nelson, and I am here to thank you personally, from the very bottom of my heart, for what you, kind sir, did for me!" Harry put his hand out again and shook Dr. Nelson's hand, and the two men stood there, solemnly exchanging handclasps and waiting behind their smiling faces like two big cats to see which would strike first.

"Well, my assistant and I must be getting on now," Harry said, flashing a bright, dismissing, disinterested smile as he turned to the door. "We're off to California, you know. I am inaugurating a new medical practice in California, in the goldfields!" Harry's determination would have fooled anybody. It fooled Adam. He thought Harry really was going to walk out that door.

It was a very good move, artfully done—like sacrificing a single piece in checkers so you can sweep the board on the next move. Dr. Nelson was suddenly disarmed. "Well!" Dr. Nelson said hastily. "I'm sorry to see you leave so soon, Doctor . . . , Doctor . . ."

He had forgotten Harry's name. Harry smiled at him. "Creekmore, Dr. Nelson! Dr. Harry Creekmore, Ph.D., Phrenologia doctoris!"

"Well, I declare, a phrenologist," Dr. Nelson said, raising his eyebrows. The two men shook hands again. "Ummm, ah, I have a collection of testimonials . . . some of Nashville's leading citizens . . . what my tonic, ah, did for them . . . Perhaps . . ." He raised his pink face in a way that was vaguely imploring.

"I would love to see them, Dr. Nelson."

"And perhaps . . ." The doctor cleared his throat and looked at Adam again. Back to Harry. "Perhaps you might, ah, like to write a, ah, a testimonial yourself . . ."

Harry smiled the kind of smile people use to greet money. "Dr. Nelson, I should be honored sir. Honored indeed. I want the whole world to know how your inestimable tonic blessed me."

Dr. Nelson smiled with the first real warmth that Adam had detected in that rubbery face.

"I keep my testimonials in the desk," Dr. Nelson said. He went to a large oak desk in the rear. Harry and Adam followed him. Harry looked around as if he thought everything was just splendid. Adam thought the place was stuffy. Dr. Nelson had a faint air of spirits about him. It reminded Adam of the way a whiskey barrel smelled empty.

Dr. Nelson fumbled among sheets of paper. He picked on one of them. "My wife's brother has written a fine testimonial. Mr. Hobart Loveday. Very respectable and ambitious young man, Hobart. Spent some time in the earth-moving and construction business. Now, my tonic, ah, cured him of a very serious backache."

Harry read the testimonial and made gushing noises. Dr. Nelson fumbled in the papers again. "And here is a splendid

66

testimonial from my cousin Peter Letsinger." Harry read this one through, nodding his head and moving his lips silently.

"Well, now!" he said finally, in a soft, sincere, marveling drawl that made Adam wince. "I see you cured your cousin of a catarrh like mine. Marvelous, Doctor. Marvelous! With your medicine we ought to be able to banish catarrh from the face of the earth:"

"Well, I'll, ah, tell you something if you'll keep it, ah, strictly confidential " Dr. Nelson said, lowering his voice and very discreetly clearing his throat. "Peter was cured of something a whole lot worse than catarrh! Something very private, doctor. Very private and shameful indeed."

"Do you mean . . . ?"

Dr. Nelson nodded like an undertaker. "You can't, ah, put everything in a letter to be read by the general public in the newspapers. Women and children, you know."

"We must guard their weak and tender morals."

"But Peter had, ah, a very desperate disease. He had a sore on his male organ so big you'd have thought it was a strawberry. But my tonic cured him in three weeks. The sore vanished without a trace." Dr. Nelson drew his last sentence out in a whisper of amazement as if it had been the most astonishing thing he had ever heard.

"I'm sure he was grateful, Doctor," Harry Creekmore said affably. "Tell me, did he drink the tonic, or did he pour it on his gonads?"

"Oh, he drank it. I tell you, Dr. Creekmore, my tonic is pretty stout stuff. It's not something you want to get careless with around your gonads."

"I can tell you are a man worthy of our profession, Dr. Nelson."

Dr. Nelson glowed. "Well, I must confess that you're quite a professional yourself, Dr. Creekmore. To tell the truth I didn't know whether to believe you or not when you came in here claiming to be a doctor. You know now it is. Any charlatan can claim he's a doctor and deceive the unfortunate. When a man's sick, he'll pay anything for medicine, but when I heard you talk about gonads, I knew you was the real thing. It takes a real doctor to know a gonad."

"I spent many long years in medical school in Germany learning the correct terms for everything," Harry said modestly.

"You gentlemens draw you up some chairs and sit down. I think we owe ourselves a little liquid refreshment."

"That's a right hospitable suggestion, Dr. Nelson."

"Just call me Phin," Dr. Nelson said. "Rhymes with thin."

"And I would appreciate it if you would call me Harry."

Dr. Nelson took a bottle of tonic out of a desk drawer and set it on the desk. It was very black tonic. He found three little glasses—none like either of the others—in the same treasury. "I'm fresh out of whiskey," Dr. Nelson said affably, pouring a glass full of his tonic. "But they's one sure thing about a good tonic. You can drink it when you're sick, or you can drink it when you're well. I say a little tonic a day keeps the doctor away. Bottoms up." He allowed himself an abrupt, composed, and somehow eager laugh.

"That is a noble sentiment, Phin," Harry said. "And a noble tonic, too, I might add."

They drank. The tonic was very thick. Adam drank very slowly and cautiously. The taste was not unpleasant. It was very sweet and mixed with spices, cloves, and cinnamon. It burned like fire.

When they had recovered, Harry spoke in a very hoarse whisper. "My goodness, Doctor! That is a very healthy tonic. May I ask what's in it?"

"Well you can ask, Harry, but I ain't going to tell you. It's a secret recipe handed down through generations of noble redskins till I learned it myself from a Cherokee medicine man on his deathbed. And the strangest thing of all is, Harry, that's the truth."

"It tastes a little like molasses to me," Adam said.

Dr. Nelson nodded in appreciation. "Your friend has a very keen sense of taste."

They drank again. Adam was beginning to feel more comfortable. The scalding heat of the tonic spread from his stomach to his extremities in a tide of gentle and soothing warmth.

"Doctor, this tonic is the very elixir of life," Harry Creekmore exclaimed. His face was getting red. "When I had my catarrh, I could scarcely appreciate how good the medicine tasted."

"You can't taste much of anything with a bad catarrh," Dr. Nelson said, pouring them another round. "But my tonic makes you feel good whether you can taste it or not."

"My nose feels hot!" Adam said. He put his finger up to

his nose and missed on the first try. When he found it he rubbed it with immense curiosity as if he had never encountered a nose like it before.

"The heat is precisely what makes my tonic so beneficial," Dr. Nelson said. "It makes you warm all over by increasing the circulation of the blood, thus promoting healing to any part of the body in need of aid. Sickness can't stand heat. Unless of course your sickness happens to be fever, in which case you need something to make you feel cold. Now I've had fever patients tell me that my tonic had precisely that effect on them. They drank a few shots, and they got as cold as ice."

"That is truly amazing," Harry Creekmore said.

Adam giggled and was caught up short by a stupefying hiccup.

"My tonic makes you sleep good at night," Dr. Nelson said. "Two or three glasses and the angel Gabriel's going to have to give you an extra toot to get you out of bed in the morning."

"Ah gentle Morpheus!" Harry said, holding his glass aloft for a moment of contemplation. "How blissful is his silent coming when, tired by the cares of our weary day, we feel ourselves embraced by his soft and soothing arms."

They all drank to Morpheus.

"Doctor, I want to tell you the honest-to-God truth," Dr. Nelson said in a surge of feeling. "I like you! A man that can talk like you has got to be one of the best doctors in the whole damned creation. You talk better than a bank president. I want to shake your hand."

They shook hands; Dr. Nelson poured them another round.

"Phin, I like you, too," Harry said. "I'm sure you're one of the most popular doctors in Nashville. I'm sure you must sell hundreds of bottles of your precious elixir every week."

Dr. Nelson frowned, shook his head, and looked resigned and sad. "Oh, I sell a bottle now and then to women that have the female complaint or bad nerves or headaches or constipation. I mean, I make a living at it, which is pretty good when you think of them that don't in this cruel world. But I've never done as good as I wanted, Doctor. I've never got rich." Dr. Nelson's eyes flashed like burning gas jets in the dark of his soul when he spoke that magic word, "rich."

Harry said, "Phin, if you'll let me say so, what you need here in Nashville, Tennessee, is a new approach."

Much later on Adam was only dimly aware that Harry was helping him out into the sun-blasted street and down to the livery stable where they had left the mules and the baggage. He was relaxed and unmystified when Harry checked them into a hotel. "Be sure you take that dog out in the street when he wants to piss," the hotel clerk said. "This here's a fancy place." And Adam heard Harry's suave drawl assuring the clerk that this excellent pedigreed hound was especially bred with a bladder so large that he only had to urinate every three days.

"No shit!" the clerk said.

"Not exactly that good," Harry said in a rolling, confident, and thoroughly intoxicated voice. "But I will say this for this handsome canine, this marvelous dog. He can go for six days without a bowel movement. So have no fear, my man. When this dog has gone, you will find your room a better place."

Adam wanted to warn the hotel clerk against Harry. But nothing seemed worth the effort. He found himself tumbled into an astonishingly clean bed; the hound licked him in the mouth and whimpered. Adam had heard of how loyal dogs were when their masters lay dying.

He fell into a bad sleep. He dreamed chaotic and fearful dreams. People were threatening him. His stomach blazed. He woke up several times. When he tried to sit, he was blinded by a headache he did not think he could endure. He had never been so sick. The bed itself seemed to spin slowly round and round, and he expected to vomit at any moment. When he did not vomit, he felt sicker than before. The only thing that helped him was his fervent hope that he would soon die.

The next morning Harry seemed completely unaware that Adam was suffering, that anybody in the world could be suffering. He pranced around the room like a dancer. He shaved while Adam lay as still as he could. Harry was singing "Annie Laurie" in a fine, sweet tenor voice. Between bursts of song Harry explained that they would just have to stay on in Nashville for a while.

# 13

It made Adam sick at heart. He wanted to be gone. California pulled at his heart. And May was passing relentlessly on.

But Harry was Adam's cousin, and blood was thicker than water. Adam could not run off and leave Harry in Nashville. Harry needed somebody to look out for him. But then everybody needed to protect himself from Harry, too. Harry had a grin like a fishhook. Now he was looking at himself in the mirror and fixing his bright blond hair and talking about being rich.

He put an advertisement on the front page of the *Nashville Whig*, a very large newspaper with very small type. The ad was paid to run every day except Sunday when, of course, the *Nashville Whig* did not publish in token of the universally accepted dictum that both God and His kinsmen, editors, rested on the Sabbath. Harry's beguiling screed, located almost in the middle of the page, said:

**Dr. Harry S. Creekmore, Ph.D.**
**Now Offers His Own Amazing**
**PROFESSIONAL SERVICES**
**In the Modern Science of**
**PHRENOLOGY**
**To the Fair City of**
**\*\*NASHVILLE, TENNESSEE\*\***

**By Dr. Creekmore's Carefull, Scientific Analysis Of Your True Character and Innate Gifts, A Discovery Amazingly Effected by The Latest Scientific Discoveries In Europe, You Will Be Better Prepared to Make Those Important Decisions About Business, Love, Family Matters, And Both Mental and Physical Health.**

The advertisement further disclosed that the amazing Dr. Creekmore could be seen by the public at Dr. Nelson's Pharmacy on the Broad Way between the hours of nine in the morning and five in the afternoon. In a suggestive and titillating postscript it revealed that he could be seen for private consultation in the evening by appointment and that Dr. Creekmore possessed great wisdom in advising young men about the sweet, sacred mysteries of matrimony.

The advertisement was illustrated by a block print of a young woman's rather melancholy face looking off to one side of the newspaper in the most intimate expectation, as if she were just longing for somebody to come and take her away. Adam thought it was positively indecent.

Then, on the very afternoon that the advertisement appeared, Harry had the good fortune to be consulted by one of Nashville's most eminent preachers. This was the Reverend David J. Packett.

The Reverend David J. Packett had gained considerable reputation by the publication of his book entitled *A Bible Defence of Slavery*. He was the rector of the Southside Episcopal church, and he was noted for his ringing affirmations of the harmony between science and religion. He was the first minister in town known to have preached on the biblical prophecy of the railroad found in the Book of Nahum: "The chariots shall rage in the streets, they shall justle one against another in the broad ways; they shall seem like torches, they shall run like the lightnings." This sermon was so moving that he was asked to repeat it for the members of the board of the new Nashville and Chattanooga Railroad then under construction.

It was this esteemed divine who came rushing to Dr. Nelson's pharmacy to partake of the exciting new science of phrenology as soon as he read about it in the papers. The Reverend David J. Packett was always afraid that somebody else might taste a new style before he did.

Harry Creekmore gravely, carefully, meticulously felt the bumps on the minister's round and rather uninteresting head. He announced his findings in a flat, unemotional voice, in the manner of a very careful scientist. "Yes, um. Much intelligence here. Um. Yes. Very interesting, Reverend. You have the largest intelligence protrusion of any man I have ever examined in Europe or America. Hmmmmmm, yes. You're a firm-speaking man, too. I can see your capacity for courage

72

is represented right here! And you are quite honest too. A man of true integrity. A born leader. You can tell that by this lump here at the base of the medullar region. That is a leadership bump. Now, what's this! Well, well! Very interesting indeed, Reverend. Please don't be offended with me. I have to tell you what my science dictates. You are a man with a decided pineal bulge right here, and that is sure testimony to your attractiveness to the opposite sex. A woman just can't resist the pineal bulge. It is indeed fortunate that you are a minister of the gospel and that right here you have a slight depression behind the left ear denoting a strong will. Otherwise you might be a veritable Casanova, Reverend. Women would fling themselves at your feet. Although, if I may say so, I do not believe you will be troubled with such petty annoyances here. Nashville is a backward town, I'm afraid." Harry delivered himself of one of those theatrical sighs. "I might even say it is primitive. I don't see how a man of your talents can possibly remain here."

"Ah, yes," the Reverend Mr. Packett said softly. "But it is the duty of a Christian to minister to the infirmities of the weak and the backward. I'm sure that if I do my duty here, God and the bishop will eventually promote me to Charleston."

"Ah, yes," Harry said.

Adam watched the performance in gloomy amazement. Harry had decked him out in a greasy white smock. He became Dr. Creekmore's "intern," a title that meant nothing to anybody. From time to time he handed Harry an instrument—a pair of tweezers for the examination of the roots of the hair, a wooden peg for the mysterious feeling of especially difficult heads. Harry's prestige in the eyes of his patients seemed to increase if he had somebody to order around. Adam thought it was all crooked.

The minister wrote a flowery endorsement to be published in the very next morning's edition of the *Nashville Whig*. He also bought three dollars' worth of Dr. Nelson's Famous Tonic. Even considering that Harry gave him a ministerial discount of fifty percent for the consultation, the visit was most profitable for all concerned. The next day Harry had twelve patients.

# 14

Adam begged off. The stuffy air of the pharmacy reeked of tonic. The smell made him sick. And he was sickened too, by the rapacity in Dr. Nelson's eyes and by Harry's almost incredible success at lying. Adam had never seen anything like it.

He consoled himself by walking around Nashville. The spring rains had made the streets muddy. Puddles of brown water shone dully in the sunlight. The air smelled of mud and garbage, new wood and spring flowers.

On the morning of their third day in town he patrolled the swarming docks. Two large, white river steamers were preparing to depart. The *Laura Jane* was bound for New Orleans that very afternoon. The *Braken Post* was off to St. Louis in the morning. The air smelled of pitch pine; the fires were already up around the boilers of the *Laura Jane*. From her slender stacks poured a steady stream of light blue smoke shining with bright sparks that spiraled skyward to melt in the light of the brilliant spring sun.

The docks were alive with important-looking people. Men immaculately dressed and smoking cigars, women clustering around them with billowing skirts. Little children at play, running to and fro. And all around the central actors—the passengers—swirled a host of lesser beings, abominably dressed and hurrying to do things for the people who would go. Shouts, laughter, a sudden explosion of angry cursing. The distinct wailing of a single little baby rising out of the crowd like a bird's harsh song. The heavy grinding of machinery, the trundling of carts and the rolling of loaded freight wagons, the clopping of tired and patient horses and mules, the inevitable thick fragrance of fresh animal dung and new straw, and once Adam heard the clear pealing of a church bell ringing out the hour over the rooftops of the city.

At the fringes of this whirlpool were the idlers like himself—black and white—sitting, standing, whittling, chewing tobacco, otherwise listless and unoccupied, impassive and uncommanded, looking on like stunned children with noses pressed against the unyielding glass of their confinement in time and space.

On the deck of the *Laura Jane* a little brass band was playing "Turkey in the Straw." Adam wanted to tap his feet; he did not. He was not sure he had any right to enjoy music he had not paid for. So he kept very still, trying to be inconspicuous and to stay out of trouble. In this world where he was a stranger, he had no right to anything.

Then the *Laura Jane* let her deep, dual whistle go, and the gigantic sound of it filled all space and vibrated in his head and in his neck and made his very bones throb and lifted him to an ecstasy of longing. He ached to be gone. With Nashville something had been tried, and it had failed. When you failed in building a city, you cast it aside. You took up another city somewhere else and started again. For Adam all the golden-cities-to-be lay somewhere West.

That night he spoke to Harry. "When are we getting out of here?"

It was late. They were eating in the hotel restaurant—steak and potatoes and red wine. Harry insisted on paying, though the meal was more than fifty cents apiece. He could afford to be extravagant now. He had money and the promise of more to come. Much more.

He looked distressed. "*Leaving*, Cousin Adam?" He shook his head. "What on earth do you mean?"

"I mean getting out of here. We've been here too long, Harry. You got money now."

"I'm just getting *started*, Cousin Adam!" Something faintly condescending in his voice, as though Adam were a child saying something terribly silly.

"I want to go to California."

"Adam, I'm doing better than I ever did in my life before. Twenty-four dollars just yesterday! People respect me. Dr. Nelson respects me." He laughed. "Have you seen his eyes get big when people pay me? And when they buy his tonic!" Harry laughed loudly. Dr. Nelson was the silliest man he had ever seen. Adam was silent. Harry felt the silence as rebuke and stopped laughing. Looked earnest and leaned over his plate, his eyes blistering with hope and the candle-light making his glasses look like two translucent yellow

75

moons. "I've got this town by the string, Adam. One pull, and it's mine."

Adam felt tired and impatient. "Harry, you ain't got nothing by the string. You're just fooling a bunch of folks. And you can't keep it up! They're going to find you've been fooling them. They're going to ride you out of town on a rail!"

Harry laughed as if Adam were a ninny. "Oh pooh, Adam. I ain't doing any harm to anybody."

"It ain't right, Harry." Adam was beginning to feel very depressed.

"Adam, if it doesn't hurt anybody, a little lie doesn't matter. The only bad lie is one that hurts people. I don't ever hurt anybody."

"I want to leave here for California in the morning. I want you to go with me."

"Cousin Adam, be reasonable!" Harry's smile was a fire. "I'm being useful to important people. Listen, Adam. A patient told me this very afternoon that he was happy Nashville was getting a railroad. He said Nashville was going to have a railroad, a steamboat dock, and a phrenologist, and all that made it the most progressive town in Tennessee. You see what folks think about me here, Adam?"

"Was that before or after you told him he was going to make a million dollars or have twenty naked women running after him or something else like that?"

"Adam, you wound me to the heart."

"You know something about that pharmacy, Cousin Harry? It smells bad in there. Sweet and stale. You're beginning to smell like it. I can smell the tonic in your clothes right this minute."

"Adam, people pay me good money. People would not pay me good money if they did not think I do them good. I give them confidence. I make them forget their troubles for a little while. It's like being on stage, and my patients are my audience, and I make them believe in themselves, and they go out feeling good. You tell me why it's wrong to make anybody on earth feel good."

"A lie is a lie."

Harry threw his fork onto the plate. It made a clatter in the quiet of the restaurant. "Phrenology is not a lie. It is a science. All right, Cousin Adam. I have not been to Germany. But I have read books by people who have been to

76

Germany. It amounts to the same thing. I have been there in spirit, and the spirit is the true man. Where my spirit has been, there I have been!"

"You believe it, Harry," said Adam, wondering and troubled. "That's the amazing thing. You believe your own lies. You're the one that's being fooled."

"I give people faith," Harry said, hurt and abused. "If we didn't have faith, where would we be?"

"I'd be on the road to California."

Harry looked earnest. Adam thought it was all acting. "Adam, try hard to understand. I sincerely believe Nashville needs me now. People in this town are speaking my name to one another. My business is spreading by word of mouth. One satisfied and happy patient tells somebody who needs me, and so it goes. Right now, while we're sitting here, eating this meal, people all over this great city are speaking with joy about the famous Doctor Harry Creekmore, Ph.D., who has come to bless their town. I could be mayor of Nashville in a year, Adam. And think what that would mean to both of us."

The conversation was getting so silly Adam couldn't stand it. He longed for Harry to burst out laughing. Give some loud and unmistakable sign that he was joking. Then he would clap Adam on the back, agree to leave in the morning, and that would be that. But he didn't.

"You're crazy, Harry. I ain't never known anybody crazy like you."

"People with vision are often called crazy by people who lack it," Harry said. He was very sad and superior. "I am sure many people thought Jesus was crazy."

Adam began to get scared.

Harry was caught by his idea. It was a song to himself. He picked up his wineglass and drank the wine slowly, looking into it as if he looked into the heart of the world. "One must plan ahead," he said slowly. "One must think great thoughts. Listen, Adam, being mayor's just the start. I can feel something in my bones. I feel the heartbeat of history. After all these years, I'm on my way to being something. It's all been building up to this time, this place. And I'm not going to leave here feeling like I do now. What is there in California that we can't have right here? I'm going to stay, Adam! In Nashville." He brought his free hand down on the table with a thump. It made a hard noise in the quiet. Adam stared at him, not knowing what to say.

They looked at each other. Harry made a decision. He said as gently as he could, "I'm sorry, Adam. I guess this is goodbye."

Adam shook his head. "It ain't goodbye. I can't leave my own blood here. I couldn't face my daddy if I was to tell him that I'd left you behind."

"Oh, I can get along, Adam!" Harry laughed.

"No," Adam said slowly, thoughtfully. "You ain't got no sense, Harry. You need somebody to look after you like you was an idiot or something. I reckon I'm all you got."

Harry drew back his head indignantly. "Adam, that's absurd. An insult. I'm a hell of a lot older than you are."

"You're a hell of a lot dumber, too. And you're my blood." It was Adam's turn to sigh. His was involuntary, a deep intake of breath and a silent, baffled curse. "So I got to hang around till you get some sense in your head and come along with me to California."

"Now listen, Adam. I need to tell you something." Harry tried to laugh again, decided against it, searched around in his repertory of expressions and came up with one solemn and stern. "I'm afraid I have to confess something. I have to ask your forgiveness. I've told you a lie."

Adam looked at him keenly. "What lie did you tell me, cousin?"

Harry dropped his eyes and looked at his white plate with a nicely done steak reposing amid brown gravy and white potatoes. "Well, Adam, I'm not your cousin. Not really. I mean in spirit we're cousins. I like you. I like you very much. And I know this sounds very bad, but I just have to own up to it and take the responsibility . . ."

"Did you ever in your life try to say something just straight out?"

Harry scowled. "Why *don't* you give me a chance?" he said. "All right, I'll tell you straight out. I'm not your cousin. I never heard of you before in my life before that day when I had to have help. I got chased off the steamboat in Bourbonville, and I got to talking to some people, and somebody told me that you were going West."

The silence was like the inside of a cave. The door to the hotel restaurant opened and closed. Adam heard it bang, rebound, go silent. He heard voices. They seemed indistinct and very far away. A wagon went by in the street outside.

"Who told you?" Adam said. His voice was like drawn wire.

"I don't know who told me," Harry said impatiently. "I was confused. I had to think fast."

"I'll bet." Adam thought of a cat landing on its feet amid a pack of dogs. Harry scrambling to flee—from something.

"All of it was intended for the good," Harry said solemnly.

"To save your hide."

"I've always considered that a good," Harry said, trying to laugh. His laughter died. Adam looked like the wrath of God.

"You walked all the way out to my house so's you could lie to me. So's you could look me in the face and lie to me." Adam could not reveal to Harry how much the discovery of the lie hurt him; he admired Harry. Now he felt foolish because he felt like crying. Harry had done that to him.

Harry spoke softly. "Adam, it didn't really cost you anything so you're not hurt. Look, I'm going to pay the hotel for the meals we eat here . . ." He reached hastily into his pocket and drew out a fine new leather wallet and opened it and handed a five-dollar gold certificate, crisp and new and folded in half over the table to Adam. "That ought to pay you for your trouble."

Adam sat with arms folded on the table and looked at the money. He did not reach for it. Harry dropped it on the table. "Just feel yourself, Adam," Harry said, laughing again. "You don't have a single broken bone."

"You're a lying bastard, a dirty, no-good lying son of a bitch," Adam said. "I ought to whip the living daylights out of you."

"Now, Adam," Harry said. "Don't raise your voice. People in the restaurant will look at us. I can't bear scenes."

"I wonder if you can bear to have your neck broke."

"Adam, Adam! I wear glasses. Beating me up is something you could easily do, but it would gain you nothing at all. I have never pretended to be a fighter."

They looked at each other. Adam felt his neck get tight, and he knew his face was crimson. He did not know what to do. Harry was protected by his own helplessness.

Just then a joyful voice rang in the late evening quiet. "There he is, Clifford." And advancing on them with her arms outstretched like a playful falcon was Ishtar Baynes.

79

# 15

The Baynes couple fell on Harry and Adam with loud cries of relief and delight. "We've met one of your friends!" Ishtar Baynes said, taking a chair and sitting down without being asked.

Mr. Baynes sat down, too. His dry face was not smiling, but it was aglow with anticipation just the same. "Last night," he said, clearing his throat, "as we were finally drawing near to Nashville . . ."

"We was camping just on the edge of town, and this feller rode in from Knoxville. His name was Gaylord Abernathy. That name mean anything to you, Dr. Creekmore?"

Harry was pale. But he shook his head in genuine ignorance. "No. I don't believe I've heard that name. I don't . . ."

"Well, this Mr. Abernathy sure did know you," Ishtar Baynes said. Her eyes shone. "He went around the campsite where we was, asking folks if they knowed a Mr. Creekmore that wore a white suit."

"He was delighted when we told him that we indeed knew such a gentleman," Clifford Baynes said.

"He practically did a flip," Ishtar Baynes said with a fierce laugh. "He said he just *knowed* you come this way. He went to that town where you're from, Adam."

"Bourbonville," Adam said.

"And he got wind of Dr. Creekmore here in that town, and he just figured that the two of you had gone West together. He said he just *knowed* it!"

"He was very pleased with himself," Clifford Baynes said.

"He must be working . . . Bigelow. Was he working for a man named Bigelow?" Harry's voice trembled, and his eyes behind his enormous glasses danced back and forth like a couple of frightened bugs.

"That's the very name!" Ishtar Baynes cried.

"I believe Mr. Bigelow wants to collect some gambling

debts," Mr. Baynes observed. He did not laugh, for laughter was against his nature. But his face gleamed.

"And he says you made *improper advances* to his wife!" Ishtar Baynes shrieked. "Dr. Creekmore! Dr. Creekmore! Shame! Shame!" She exploded with her hideous laughter, and people in the restaurant were looking at them.

"Shhhhhh, Mrs. Baynes. Shhhhhhh!" Harry said. He looked near-sightedly around, baffled and frightened, his thin hands doing first one thing and then another. He looked as limp as a wet mop hung on a pole of bones.

"Mr. Bigelow seems to think that you, ah, felt his wife's thighs under the table when you were playing cards," Clifford Baynes said. "At least that is the impression Mr. Bigelow seems to have given Mr. Abernathy."

"It's a lie," Harry whispered. He looked hopelessly at Adam.

"Mr. Bigelow intends to fight a duel with you," Mr. Baynes said. "Mr. Abernathy said Mr. Bigelow was the richest man in Knoxville, Tennessee."

"I sure do think it'd be an honor if the richest man in Knoxville, Tennessee, wanted to fight a duel with me, Dr. Creekmore," Ishtar Baynes said.

"Not so, my love," Clifford Baynes said, professorially clearing his throat. "Mr. Abernathy said Mr. Bigelow could put a hole right through the spade on the ace of spades with a pistol at a hundred feet. Are you a good shot, Dr. Creekmore? I tell you! I wouldn't miss it for the world."

"He hates planters!" Mrs. Baynes said. "He's kilt six planters in duels."

"It does appear that planters in, ah, white suits, Dr. Creekmore, have a regrettable proclivity for making indecent advances to Mrs. Bigelow. She must be quite a beautiful woman. I've always appreciated beautiful women myself."

"You can tell that about Clifford!" Ishtar Baynes said, looking very pleased with him and herself.

"But there is a price to be paid sometimes. Naturally a man of honor like Mr. Bigelow must demand satisfaction."

"I bet it gets in all the newspapers," Ishtar Baynes said. "I want Clifford and I to be sure and be there."

"Mr. Abernathy says that every time Mr. Bigelow sees a man in a white suit, he just loads up his pistol," Ishtar Baynes said.

"It wasn't my fault," Harry said, his voice hardly more

81

than a murmur. "She came to my stateroom. She wouldn't leave me alone. I swear it. Every time I turned around . . ."

"We thought you might be willing to give us a little something for telling you all about Mr. Abernathy. He give us a five-dollar gold piece for telling him about you." Ishtar Baynes looked at Harry with the intensity of a vulture.

"Give you something?" Harry murmured.

Adam suddenly took charge. He jumped up from the chair where he had been sitting and grabbed the folded, new five-dollar gold certificate that lay in front of his plate. "Here's your reward," he said scornfully. "We ain't cheap. We're just as good as old man Bigelow."

Ishtar Baynes snatched the money and looked sharply at Adam. She had hardly paid him any attention. Now there was respect in her eyes. "You must be rich, Mr. Adam. Buying that nice tent you got and giving me money like this. I wouldn't of figured you was rich."

"Listen, you go find Mr. Abernathy. That's what you're fixing to do anyway, ain't it? Don't lie to me, you old woman, or I'll knock your teeth down your chicken's neck."

"Sir!" Clifford Baynes said. "That woman is my wife!"

"You shut up!" Adam said. "Or I'll stuff you down her throat and pitch the both of you in the river. What about it, Mrs. Baynes? You're going to run right now and find Mr. Abernathy, ain't you?"

Ishtar Baynes kept her eyes fastened on Adam's face as if they were two lead buttons. "I thought we might go look him up, tell him where you are. Do him a little favor. I ain't rich like you, Mr. Adam. We got to make money anyway we can." Her voice was as cold as cave water.

"Well, I'm telling you to find him right now and bring him back to this hotel in the morning. You ain't going to push us around. You tell him Harry Creekmore is going to fight ole man Bigelow in that there duel, and we aim to shoot Mr. Bigelow in the belly and spread him out from here to Kentucky. You tell him we can't wait."

"Adam . . ." Harry said.

Adam clapped Harry on the shoulder. "This here is the best shot in the whole damn state of Georgia. Tell you what happened two nights after we seen you folks. Three robbers jumped on us while we was camped by the side of the road. Harry killed 'em all three before they could say Jack Robinson."

"Dr. Creekmore did that?" Clifford Baynes looked doubtfully at Harry. Back to Adam.

"It'll be in the Nashville newspapers tomorrow morning. They was a whole gang of 'em. The sheriff didn't want it in the papers till he caught the rest. But he's done it now. You read the papers tomorrow morning. You'll see all about it."

"You telling me the truth, Adam?" Ishtar Baynes looked at him with her thin eyebrows arched. She did not know what to think. She was always busy trying to figure how she could make a profit out of people. When anybody tossed a big lie in her teeth, she had to chew on it awhile, because it upset her calculations.

"I don't tell lies," Adam said.

"Well, well, well," Clifford Baynes said. "I had no idea of the prowess of Dr. Creekmore with firearms." He rubbed his scrawny chin. "I wonder if there might be some way to work up a wager with a few people on the outcome of the contest."

"You go ahead and make your bets," Adam said. "You bet on Harry Creekmore, and you'll have yourselves enough money to buy you a big house in Nashville. I aim to put a little cash on Harry myself. Where's your Mr. Abernathy staying anyhow? I reckon I should go over and see him and work things out."

Clifford Baynes looked at his wife. She looked at him. He cleared his throat. Dry gravel cracking together. "Well, ah, to tell the truth, we are not certain just where Mr. Abernathy can be located at the moment. But I do believe we can find him since we know he's in Nashville."

"Mr. Abernathy's a drunkard," Ishtar Baynes said. "He smelled like a distillery when he talked with us. I bet he come right into town and made for the first saloon he seen."

"We searched for him all over town this afternoon after I happened to notice that newspaper with your very excellent advertisement in it, Dr. Creekmore. Frankly I'm quite surprised that Mr. Abernathy did not see the paper himself."

"He was probably too drunk to read," Ishtar Baynes said. "If they's anything I hate, it's a drunk."

"Nashville is not a friendly town," Clifford Baynes said. He was beginning to be aware of the hostility heating up at him from nearby tables, and he spoke softly.

"They was several hotels that wouldn't even tell us if he was there or not," Ishtar Baynes said. "They practically throwed us out of some places. But you just wait till tomorrow. We're going to go up and down till we find Mr. Aberna-thy, and you can see then how them snotty hotelkeepers is going to tell us how sorry they are they was mean to the friends of Horace Bigelow from Knoxville, Tennessee." She pronounced these last, magical words with special force and threw a vindictive look around the room.

"Since we could not locate Mr. Abernathy, we decided to come in search of you, Dr. Creekmore. We knew where your business establishment was to be found. So we went around awhile ago, and your druggist friend informed us of the hotel you were staying at, Dr. Creekmore."

Harry sat there mute and stricken, looking first at one of them and then the other. Adam punched him in the shoulder and made him get up. Adam was talking. Harry could not understand it. Was Adam gaining revenge against him? Hate-ful revenge against Harry Creekmore, who would never hurt a fly?

"Well, we're going up to bed," Adam said. "Harry has to rest before he fights anybody. It always makes him feel sad when he's got to kill somebody ignorant like your Mr. Bige-low. But me, I like killing. There ain't nothing like a good killing to heat the blood." With that Adam managed his most awful stare at Mr. and Mrs. Baynes and steered Harry by the arm out of the restaurant and up to their room.

Once inside with the door shut, Harry looked at Adam with tears in his eyes. "Is this how much you hate me, Adam? Has the whole world turned against me? I have never shot a gun in my life. Never once."

"Hush your goddamn mouth," Adam said in a furious whisper, looking out into the dark street below and then drawing the curtains. "We don't want to make them think we're going to run. They might tell the sheriff. Get you ar-rested for something. I'm sure if anybody wants to arrest you, some sheriff somewheres would be glad to get his hands on you."

Harry looked at him blankly. "But . . . what are we going to do?"

"We're going to wait till everybody's asleep. Then we're go-ing to get the hell out of here."

"But where are we going, Adam? Where is there to run to?"

"Where the hell do you think? To California!"

84

# 16

It was eleven o'clock before the restaurant was closed, the lobby empty, and the night clerk dozing at the office in front of the door. By then Harry was drunk.

"Adam, I swear, I ain't never going to lie again. Never in my life. From now on I'm going to tell the truth all the time, in everything. How can I thank you? How can I ever thank you? You know, they can arrest me for trying to rape that woman. I didn't try to rape her. That is the honest-to-God truth. But who's going to believe me? Duel or no duel. They can hang me. Oh God!" And the more miserable things seemed to him, the more whiskey Harry drank out of the stone jug.

Adam said nothing. He was still angry with Harry. Deeply and fiercely angry. He did not know why he was bothering to save his skin. Maybe now because it was a game. Mr. Abernathy out there somewhere like a little child being "It" when you played hideyseek at home in the summertime. "It" counted to a hundred and shouted, "Ready or not, here I come!" And you could hear his footsteps running at you in the moonstruck dark, and you had to get the time just right so you could flee home free before he could tag you. Mr. Abernathy was "It." He was coming close, and Adam was crouching to run. Taking Harry with him.

He stood by the window, the room dark behind him, the dog curled at his feet, and looked down into the street. Slowly it grew still. Lucky for them, he thought, that Ishtar Baynes was so greedy. A little less greedy, and she might have waited till morning to resume her hunt for Mr. Abernathy. Harry and Adam had been warned because she did not have patience to wait. She was a bird rather than a cat. He searched the street, trying to see beyond sight. She might be out there in the dark herself, watching. He remained still with his thoughts and his anger.

85

Finally it was time. Adam picked up the sack with his clothes in it, roused the hound, and with great difficulty got Harry to his feet and walking. He saw to it that Harry's precious glasses were folded safely in their case and tucked in Harry's pocket. They slipped out the door and down the wooden steps that creaked so loudly Adam thought they must announce their flight to a waiting world. The dog panted happily. The night clerk roused briefly, looked at them blankly, let his chin fall on his chest again, and slept. They came at last into the open air through the door of the hotel that shut behind them with a soft rattle of wood and glass.

The streets were empty. They gave Adam an eerie feeling. Houses and shops all shut up. A few whale oil lamps threw feeble white lights against the gloom, and the solitude of places accustomed to people was very strange. He half expected to see the cart of the family Baynes looming up in the dark. If they were lurking nearby to sound the alarm, Adam thought he would kill them both. He was sure he could if he had to. But no one disturbed their lonely progress.

The keeper of the livery stable had to be waked up. He was angry about it, a cranky old man with coarse hair and a stubble-strewn face, jaw heavy as an axe, grumbling about the impropriety of waking a hard-working man at this indecent hour. He was wearing long cotton underwear under a pair of baggy cotton pants made with straps and a bib, and his big belly bulged like a woman with child. When he glared at Adam, his wrath was like heat burning in the gloom.

"And drunk, too!" he growled with ultimate self-righteousness as Adam let Harry down in a pile of straw and began hastily to load the mules. "You don't stop to think how a poor man lives, how I have to work all the day long, how I don't get nothing for it, how I need my sleep because I've got the backache and the bile in my liver and the nervous complaint besides. You don't think of nothing but yourself and your bottle!"

Adam was afraid now. The man's voice was like a low, tolling gong threatening to waken something in the night better left asleep. Adam pushed Harry up onto the mule with the saddle, and Harry roused enough to hold on, to look dazedly around, his face wild in the leaping shadows of the small lamp in the livery stable. "My glasses! My God, where are my glasses!"

"In your coat pocket!" Adam said. "Hush up!" He swung

up into the baggage atop the other animal, close enough to Harry's mule to hang onto the bridle, and they went off, riding through the back streets of Nashville for dear life.

They had to cross the Cumberland River. Adam thought that if they could get safely over the river, they could get away for good. He had to rouse a sleeping ferry man, pay him a silver dollar in advance to take them over in the dark. Adam burned inside at the loss of his money. All destined for his father. To see it go like this was to see the farm itself go bit by bit, like sand running through his helpless hands. But there was nothing to do but pay the price.

Even with that outrageous ransom inflicted on helpless travelers in the night, the ferry man cursed them roundly and berated them ceaselessly for waking him. Still the sounds and the sights of the crossing filtered in over Adam's terror and shame of running, and he remembered them when he had forgotten the rest. The vaguely fishy smell of the river, the slosh and foamy gleaming of water rushing against the sides of the boat, the continuous profane grumbling of the ferry man, and Harry's sweet tenor voice rising in drunken song as he leaned on the railing, almost invisible in the dark, utterly indifferent either to the wrath of their pilot or the dangers of their flight.

Something about crossing a river on a ferryboat always reminded Adam of dying. And in the midst of the river they heard the abrupt, slow tolling of a church bell back there in the town somewhere, sounding midnight in twelve solemn strokes carried out over the water and strangely refined to a clarity that seemed unearthly and full of divine mystery.

Finally the ferry crunched to a landing on the north side of the river, and the ferry man dismissed them with one concluding outburst of blasphemy, standing with his feet in the water and telling them that he hoped they would ride into the jaws of hell.

Adam listened to the curse, and suddenly the frustration, the excitement, the fear, the shame all burst free. The ferry man was railing at him, and somewhere back in that town asleep on its hill there lay a man who was running them like rabbits before the dogs, and Adam had paid his good, hard money, part of the price for his father's land and his mother's grave, and still this cantankerous man stood before him, a hulking shadow in the great dark, cursing them as though they were vermin. With a sudden, boiling fury, Adam lashed

87

him in the belly with a knotted fist, flinging all his young strength into the blow.

The cursing stopped abruptly in a violent suck of air. The man's head was flung forward with the blow, and Adam hit him again, this time directly in the mouth. He felt teeth breaking like pieces of dried wood, and he could feel the hot gush of blood on his knuckles, and the man pitched forward and lay silent on the ground.

It was the first time in his life that Adam had ever fought with anybody. He felt a joy that made him want to sing over his victory. But there was no time.

He mounted his mule and took to the road under their feet, winding toward the north star—a beaten track visible to the animals but unseen by the men. The mules were sluggard and sleepy. They wrestled against the bits and snorted in protest at being up at this hour. Adam had to lash at them with the reins until at last they surrendered and plodded steadily on in indignation and resignation and with a strength that made the boy feel affectionate toward them for their dumb and stubborn loyalty. Behind them the nameless hound came loping along, tongue lolling in the dark, panting and happy to be abroad in the night. He sniffed at a thousand scents, glad to be traveling again.

Overhead the stars wheeled slowly across the great sky, and just above the trees a new and golden moon hung in a crescent against the eastern dark. The woods were alive with warbling insects, and there were places where frogs chirruped by the hundreds in marshy lowlands, vibrating choruses that rose to a crescendo of trembling discord and fell away to aching harmony as the two riders passed by. From far away there came the song of a whippoorwill, mellow and eerie and beguiling, and from the hollows of greater distance yet there floated the haunting cry of another in response.

Within the tall forest the darkness was so thick that Adam could not see his hands. In the open spaces, where the cleared land reclined under the faint starlight and moonglow, he had an impression of gently undulating landscape more ghostly than real. And sometimes when they passed by the houses— isolated, sleeping, and shut in the vast night—angry dogs rushed out furiously barking at them. Adam's own hound howled back, and as dogs do, they arrived at a barking stand-off, the house dogs not leaving their own ground and the pilgrim hound bravely howling but discreetly running along with the mules into the dark silence ahead. It was all a ritual as old as dogdom. But Adam was afraid at these exchanges, for every dog seemed to be another messenger of terror, warning of an angry man close behind with a gun, armed to kill any stranger abroad at this unholy hour.

Seeing these other houses, he thought of his own cabin and remembered when he had slept soundly and at peace with his mother and his father in the room with him, when the world was simpler. The memories were keen, and they made him more lonely and homesick and sad than he had ever been.

Adam's fist burned and throbbed where he had hit the ferry man. The joy he had felt slipped away with their journey, and he wondered why he had been so angry. A man had a right to curse, roused in the middle of the night by strangers who would give him no reason for their going. *Maybe I'm bad.* The thought struck him like shot, but he could make no sense of it, and so it settled like the rest of his musings into a hard and ugly mass that lay under his chest like a stone.

Harry's drunkenness turned to sickness with the jouncing of the mule. He groaned with pain, and once Adam heard him gargle and burst with vomit. The keen, fresh air stank suddenly with the putrefaction of Harry's guts, Harry's lying and frightened soul. Harry Creekmore, ready to be mayor of Nashville, vomiting on the dark road, a fugitive in the night.

Adam measured the time they rode by the stars. His mind swam with fantasy and memory as he grew more and more tired. The quiet of his father, the man's bashfulness, the unique, slow, soft way of Joel Cloud when he spoke. And once, long ago, a trivial vision, a light gleaming abruptly and steadily in the far deep of the woods, lingering for a while, then going away and leaving a mystery. His father standing quickly and staring in the direction of the light, wondering aloud if it might be a slave on the loose and dismissing the incident with a sour muttering. Good enough for planter and slave alike when a piece of human property was lost in the dark. "Damn them both!" Joel Cloud said in a voice curiously devoid of passion. Behind the vanishing of the light there remained a mystery in the woods. And what was there in the dark? Maybe the world nobody dreamed of in the day. Adam longed for the kindling of dawn in the east.

Slowly the night did pass away. He realized that he could see the motions of his hands and the outline of the mule's bobbing head, and then Harry's white suit emerged, and finally there was the road—a dull gleaming of beaten earth going, winding, climbing and descending through fields and through corridors of spectral trees—dim shapes on every hand silent and still in the morning haze.

They did not stop to eat or to clean themselves. The two men rode on, through slattern villages waking and stirring to the new spring day, through the rising and warming morning of quickening life and contracting shadows, and as they passed along, Adam thought that all human energy seemed microscopic and petty against the immense stillness of this vast land. *And there's more!* he thought with an awe beyond telling. *All the way to the Pacific Ocean, there's more!*

They saw farmers toiling in the fields, laboring stolidly behind stolid mules, men and beasts alike glistening with sweat and tramping patiently under the sun. *I would be like them if I was home.* A pricking and unwanted thought. *I'm here, going on. I can't never go back. Nothing to go to now.* They saw little children with brown, bare feet, chopping weeds with big hoes, moving down the aisles of faintly green and barely emergent corn in the red-brown fields. *Land's good here. Darker than home. Be proud of land like this. But what's going to come of these folks? Nothing but this. Maybe war after a while. Won't be no war in California.*

They saw an occasional woman boiling her family's wash in front of this cabin or that. Solid figures bending in eternal rhythms over iron kettles, fire kindling under the kettles, the smell of lye soap carried on the air, thick and pungent. Smell of a place in the world. Adam thought wordlessly of the mystery of women. And he wondered that it could be compressed in a shape bending and rising over a black kettle, standing momentarily to shade curious eyes and to stare at them, then bending again as if they had never been. So did their going seem to those who must stay. *They feel sorry for us.* An amazement.

They were hailed and greeted sometimes in the little towns. Curious men looked up, asked questions in the innocent expectancy of country people that they will be told everything if they only ask. *Where you fellers going? Where you come from? How come you ain't got but one saddle for them mules?* Adam made only laconic answers, studying to be neither insolent nor friendly, clutching an aloof detachment around him like a mantle of invisibility. And they rode on.

90

Around noon they came into the single dusty street of a village. A very old man sat on a porch in front of a store. High, unpainted, false front of wood, going dark. Still making a blinding reflection in the great sun. The old man leaned against a wooden post holding up the roof of the porch. The man was whittling, bright chips of wood flaking off a stick like spurts of flame. He sat with his skinny legs dangling in the spring sunlight, making those jerky motions at the wood with a steel knife that seemed much too sharp for an old man. Adam called down, "Hey, mister! Can you tell us what town this is?"

The old man was nearly deaf. He heard a sound, knew it was a human voice, knew also from the inflection that it must be addressed to himself. He got unsteadily to his feet, crying weakly in a creaking voice. "What's that? What's that?"

"What town is this?"

Still the old man could not understand. "What's that? What's that?"

Adam repeated the question yet again, shouting now. He would have kicked the mule on. But a youngish man in shirtsleeves came to the door of the shop and walked out onto the porch. His face as pale as a leaf, hidden from the sun. His skin was almost unnaturally smooth, and he wore sleeve garters, and he was so clean that his fragrant smell was something you could almost see. Adam scorned him. *Woman's work*. The two of them faced each other, filled with contempt and suspicion. "He can't hear you!" the man on the porch said, voice mincing and delicate. "This here's Guthrie. Where you all from that you don't know what town this is?"

*He's looking at my bloody fist. He's scared.* "Guthrie what?" Adam's voice flat, toneless.

"Guthrie, Kentucky! Who are you fellers anyhow? Where you going?"

Adam was so relieved he might have danced. Over the state line. Harry's hunters could not chase them here.

"I reckon we're going to St. Louis. After that, maybe California!"

"California! For gold? You're two years late to be a forty-niner, mister!" He laughed. No humor to the laugh. "What's anybody in his right mind want to do, going to California? Feller I know says all the gold's been scooped out of the ground already. Ain't nothing left out there now for nobody."

Adam did not answer him. He snicked the mules. They

91

moved on down the street. The mules were tired and went slowly. They would find a quiet place in the afternoon. *Kentucky. We'll sleep. We're safe now.*

# 17

"Adam, can you ever forgive me?" Harry's voice, warm and ingratiating, a drawl like syrup. His weak eyes laughed behind his thick glasses, healthy again.. Sober and ready to figure out something else. "I was so frightened, my friend. I had to do something. Thinking up that lie about you being my cousin . . . You see, it was really a compliment to you, Adam. I knew if you cared enough about your daddy to go find him in California, then you just couldn't turn me away if I told you I was your daddy's flesh and blood."

"It's all right."

"Do you forgive me?"

"There ain't nothing to forgive."

"Oh, Adam, there is! There is!"

"No, there ain't . . . We had a hound once. Beagle, somebody said. That hound couldn't help being scared. We come in the house, and that beagle had to go off with his tail dragging the ground, eyes looking at us like we was going to kick it. Wasn't no good for hunting. Every time he heard a gun, he run back home. I wanted to shoot him. But my daddy, he said no. Dog can't help being what he is. We give him to a lady in town. She thought he made a good watch dog."

Harry was bewildered. "I don't see the comparison."

"I mean you're like that beagle. You can't help being what you are. So there ain't nothing to forgive."

"Adam, I resent that deeply. You cut me to the very heart."

"A fact's a fact," Adam said.

"I don't think I ever did anybody any harm," Harry said, sober now. "Maybe I haven't done as much good as some folks, but I don't reckon I hurt anybody."

92

Adam said nothing. He thought of how foolish he had felt when he discovered that Harry had lied to him. Foolish and disappointed. He had enjoyed thinking that he might be kin to Harry.

"Anyway, it's all behind me now," Harry said. "I promise you, I'm never again going to tell a lie."

"Just don't lie to me no more," Adam said.

"Not to you! Not to anybody." Harry put a hand over his chest and looked skyward, his whole face set in an earnest vow. "It's too much trouble anyway," he said, changing his tone to one of believable realism. "You have to work at lying. It takes a lot of effort."

"I reckon it does," Adam said.

"I'm through with the South, too. I'm through trying to pretend I'm some kind of aristocrat. You know, my daddy was a planter, and he did kill himself. That's all the truth. But even that's behind me now. I'm going out West, going to work hard. I'm going to learn how to do something, and I'm not going to lie. You can believe that, Adam. Never again."

They rode on, Harry musing in the soft sunlight, dreamy as a child. "I tell you, I think I could have been mayor of Nashville. But maybe I'll be mayor of San Francisco. I'm young! It's a new world out there. Maybe San Francisco's just waiting for me to ride in, and folks are going to lean off the balconies and out of the windows, and they're going to shout, 'Here's our new mayor.' Maybe somebody's having a dream right now about me, Adam. Maybe they're going to be ready for us when we get there."

Adam laughed. Uneasy laughter. Harry's dreams were like uncaged birds. They soared on the warm currents of the air, and nobody rooted to earth could tell them where to go.

They went on from day to day, through the cleared land and the deep, still forest. So much of the American land was still woodland. It amazed and frightened Adam. Land flattening now. No great hills against the horizon. Marshy sometimes. Mosquitoes buzzed and hummed around their heads. Stung them. Adam knew from what people said that they were drawing near to the great drain of the continent. The Tennessee poured into the Ohio, the Ohio into the Mississippi, the Mississippi sluggishly downhill to the Gulf and the ocean beyond.

Harry talked, told stories, sang. Adam, glad for his company, listened to Harry and thought about his own past. He

93

brought up the pieces of his old life one by one to dismiss them. He did not know exactly what he was doing. His brain worked like a wound clock, ticking off events like seconds to be flung away forever. By the time they had come through the woods of Kentucky, crossed the great Ohio River on a steam ferryboat, and advanced toward Cairo, Illinois, Adam had done the last cleansing of his mind.

He sorted out the memories of his mother. Her bones lay behind him, the last tangible hold on him exercised by the East, where home had been. He began with the earliest recollections of his life—sitting on her warm lap in the rocking chair on a mild evening with the moon hung like a yellow lantern over the woods. The singing night. The regular thump-thump-thump-thump of the rocking chair across the planks.

His mother treasured the porch. Her symbol of an exalted place in a shabby world. When Adam was older and understood how poor they were, it seemed foolish that she exulted in a porch. Now, on his way West, he thought it was pathetic that she had been proud of so little. He knew that she had been good in her way. Content with only a porch. She had loved her husband for giving it to her. Other women would have demanded more.

He thought of how she had stood so proudly in the Methodist church, holding a hymnbook and ostentatiously looking over it, singing in her high, nasal voice, her dark eyes raised in the pride that came because she knew every hymn and never had to look at the words, could devote all her energy to lifting her strong voice into her nose where hymns should be sung. When people praised her for knowing so many hymns, she tried to seem surprised. Poor thing! Standing there in the faded Sunday dress she had sewed herself, her chin cocked back like a hen's beak, singing not only without benefit of the hymnbook but much louder than anybody else, louder almost than everybody else. And now, riding West, Adam was embarrassed and sad at her memory.

He considered the distance that had separated them in life. He had done his duty to her. But they had never been close. She was dead now. Nowhere. Looking down at him? No. Death came and took everything. A card player sweeping chips and deck off the table with a skull's grin and leaving the room with the game in his infinite pocket. Her death a relief to him. It let him go West. No reason to feel guilty about it. *We might get to California in two months.* Forty miles a day on a good mule. Not impossible. Adam felt at peace. He even felt joy.

They rode up through Cairo, Illinois. A dismal place. One wide, muddy street splitting through frame and brick houses. A plague of gnats and the smell of mud suppurating in the heavy air. People in Cairo, Illinois, insolent and dull, eyes burned out like old lamps from longing for the fulfillment of impossible hopes, uncomprehending about their failure, believing in it, not believing in it, hopeful in the midst of their despair, suspicious of strangers who were going on to something better. "We ought to be as big as New York," a man with a thick voice said to them in a big, gaudy, almost empty saloon, resounding with the murmuring of their voices. "I can't understand it. We got all this location, and nothing happens! Look at St. Louis, and look at us!"

"Well, farther West!" Harry said to Adam. Adam saw the hope in Harry's face, the determination. Harry who had only thought about the West a couple of weeks before. Now piling his own dreams like clouds in the direction of the setting sun and bound to follow them. "It's going to be a lot better out there. Adam! You wait and see. We can't even imagine how good it's going to be."

And they rode on.

Up the Mississippi now, on the Illinois side, the land green with forest and field. The river was beside them, below them, running with its almighty power, a giant reclining in the midst of the earth, content to let the world see its brawn. The river shone brown in the sun; it was alive with traffic. The white steamboats went up and down. Side-wheelers and stern-wheelers, pounding at the water, blowing long jets of smoke from their stacks, making the very stones vibrate with their overwhelming whistles. Skiffs poled laboriously along the banks upstream, a flatboat laden with canvas-bundled cargo occasionally drifting with the current, indolent river men holding the rudder, sitting on boxes, watching the river slide by in peaceful lethargy.

At Cape Girardeau they crossed the Mississippi on another steam-driven ferry. Adam looked around at the morning sunlight shining on the houses of the town, on a ruined fort, on the gleaming river, the green trees arching in cool splendor over the water. He saw wildflowers blooming by the million along the banks. He smelled something he could not identify, something of the swift river and space and spring mingled all together, as vivid and as ephemeral as life itself. And he felt in his heart a fullness and a satisfaction, a tremendous sense of self-sufficiency and power and joy he could scarcely restrain.

It was a very simple experience, crossing this river. Or rather it was a conglomeration of simple experiences. And yet that moment would always be so keen in his mind that it became nearly a talisman of memory. He would always entertain the fantasy of going back to that magic river at that place and so reversing all the processes of age and time. Begin life all over again. The nation itself could start again in the good year 1851, and things could be different. So much that should have been different after that sweet and sunny morning.

# 18

That afternoon they came on the Jennings.

When they met, the Jennings were in trouble. Adam and Harry rode out of a shady patch of woodland onto an open space, almost a meadow. And there were the Jennings in three solid wagons with oxen unhitched and grazing and the people who belonged to the wagons scattered about, as if at a picnic in the good sunshine.

Then Adam saw that the lead wagon was awry and that its left rear wheel had been smashed against an outcropping of gray rock in the dirt road. He also saw quickly that the three men in the company were standing about, hands on hips, hats pushed back, staring down at the broken wheel. *They don't know what to do.*

The men were very different. One of them enormous, nearly seven feet tall, great, muscular shoulders like a giant from the Bible. Beside him the others seemed small, though one was smaller than even an average man, so that when he stood beside the huge man he looked like a dwarf.

Two women, two children, and a girl made up the rest of the party.

Adam and Harry reined up. Harry looked around smiling, as if he knew everybody was glad they had got there. Adam looked down. "You got troubles," he said.

"Well, mister, you can see. We got troubles." The little man, smoky eyes strangely still and humorless over a mouth that went too easily to a smile. "We got a broke wheel. What you reckon you do with a broke wheel?"

"I reckon you fix it," Adam said.

"You reckon we fix it! Now that's what I say," the little man said. "But how do you reckon we fix it? That seems to be the trouble."

"I reckon you unload the wagon, and then you jack the wagon up, and then you take the wheel off, and then you fix it."

"Unload the wagon?" another of the men said. He was stockier than the first, nearly six feet tall, stoop-shouldered, older. His hair was sandy, flecked with gray. "You don't think we can fix it without unloading the wagon? We just loaded it up again yesterday. When we got off the steamboat. It was a lot of work."

"Well, you ain't going to rig a jack to get that wagon off the ground. Not lessen you unload it," Adam said.

"We didn't expect anything like this," the older man said. "We came down the Ohio, you see. Didn't have money enough to get us all the way to St. Louis. Had to get off at Cairo." He shook his head helplessly. "I have never driven a big wagon before. None of us knows what to do." He looked up at Adam.

Adam looked at all of them. Brothers. The family resemblance was plain. The same flat faces, thick cheekbones, noses tending to be large. Heavy mouths. The same features differently cast on each face.

"We're foundry men, you see," the little man said. "I mean all except Jason here who's educated! But then he's a foundry man, too. We're good at being foundry men. But we ain't no good at nothing else." He uttered a harsh laugh. A nervous habit, something he had picked up to hide behind. Adam did not like him.

"Ain't you got no spare?" Adam said. He looked in the back of the wagon, under the canvas roof. Heavy boxes made

97

of wood, piled one on top of another. No sign of a spare wheel.

The older brother spoke. "No. We didn't expect . . . I never thought a wheel would *break!* It must not have been made well."

"You got too much stuff in the wagon," Adam said. "You ought to have another wagon if you're going to carry all that stuff."

"We didn't have the money," the older brother said. "We had a certain amount, you see. We had to do the best we could with it. We could only buy three wagons." He looked around, faltering. "It seemed right. One wagon apiece."

"So we got to unload the stuff," the little man said. He cursed. "Jason, it's your fault. You ought to have been looking where you was going."

"I'm sorry," the one called Jason said. "I meant . . ." He stopped and remembered their manners. "I'm Jason Jennings," he said to Adam, putting out his hand. A warm and friendly smile in a face that meant to be sincere and open.

"I'm Adam Cloud. This here's Harry Creekmore."

"Delighted to know you both," Jason said. His voice was warm and glad. Harry slid down off the mule and shook hands. He expressed his very great pleasure at meeting Jason Jennings.

"I'm sorry you've had this trouble," Harry said. "Very sorry. But my friend Adam Cloud here can do anything. I've never met anybody like him. I'm sure he can help." Harry flashed his warmest and most becoming smile at Adam. Harry had seen the girl.

Jason introduced them to the others. He put his hand on Adam's arm to steer him. A very strong and friendly hand. "These are my brothers, Samuel and Asa. This is Asa's wife, Ruth. This is my wife, Jessica. And this is my adopted daughter, Jessica's child, Promise."

"Promise!" Harry was delighted. He smiled like a candidate for county judge. "Promise is a fine name! I never heard it before—I mean, as a name."

The girl smiled and blushed. She had black hair and intelligent eyes. Blue but darker than Harry's eyes. She was very slender, almost small. "My mother gave it to me."

Harry turned to Jessica. "What a wonderful idea, my dear." Jessica was older than Harry was, but he still called her "My dear," like a grandfather. She smiled at his pretensions, amused at him. "I liked the name," she said.

"And I like it, too," Harry said. He took her hand and bowed over it. He captured their fancy like a lord. Harry could open his mouth and sound better than anybody else anywhere.

"Well, we got to get this wheel fixed," Adam said when he had shaken hands with everybody. People did not take to him the way they took to Harry.

"In time! In time!" Harry said. He made much over Ruth, Asa's large-boned wife, and over Henry and Rachael, Asa's children. Rachael was chubby and red-faced and five. "Have you got any candy?" She spoke in a child's voice that flattened the words and leaned on them one by one.

"They ain't got no candy," Henry said in the immemorial tone of older brothers correcting sisters. He was ten, handsome and quiet.

Harry said, "That's right, honey. We don't have any candy. Don't have any place to get it out here. Did anybody ever tell you how pretty you are?"

"People tell me that all the time. I get tired of hearing it."

Ruth spoke sharply to her. "Rachael, you be good now. I don't like hearing you talk like that." Ruth apologized to Harry. "I don't know what I'm going to do with her. She's so spoiled. Where you folks coming from?" Ruth said.

"I'm from Georgia," Harry said. "My father owned a plantation in the neighborhood of Savannah. Adam here is from someplace in Tennessee. What was the name of that town, Adam?"

"Bourbonville."

"Never heard of it," Asa said.

"A fine place," Harry said. "I spent a night there."

"And where you going?" Asa said.

"We are bound for California," Harry said. "Adam to seek his father and I to seek my fortune."

"California!" Ruth said. "Why, we're going to California, too. Ain't that a coincidence?"

"They's lots of folks on the road," Asa said crossly. "Some of 'em's bound to be going to California." He threw a sour look at the disabled wagon. "If we get this busted wheel fixed, we're going to California. If we don't, we're going to stay right here."

"You got to unload the wagon," Adam said. He could not understand their apathy.

"Couldn't we try to jack it up without unloading it?" Jason said.

Adam shook his head. "Be a waste of time."

"I can't imagine a wheel breaking," Jason said, looking hard at the wheel as if he could repair it with his eyes.

"Well, that one sure broke," Asa said. "Come on, Jason. If the man says we got to unload the wagon, we got to unload the wagon." He swore again. "Come on. Let's get to work."

Jason still did not move. His tone was aggrieved and abused. "I went down to the hardware store in Ironton. In Ohio. I told the man I wanted everything I needed to go to California. Everything we needed to have a farm. I don't believe he cheated me. He just didn't sell me a spare wheel for the wagon. I wonder why he didn't?"

"You might take a steamboat and go back and ask him," Asa said dryly. He swore again. "Come on, Jason, Samuel. Let's get to work! My God."

Jason looked apologetically at the newcomers. "Don't pay any attention to Asa here, my friends. He's got a good heart. I wish you wouldn't swear so much in front of your children, Asa. What will they think of you."

Asa laughed his humorless laugh. "I'm raising 'em, and I'm feeding 'em, and I'm putting the clothes on their backs. If they don't think good of me after all that, then they can go straight to hell."

Jason sighed. "You're sure we couldn't try to rig your ... your jack under the wagon just the way it is." He looked with pleading at Adam.

Adam felt exasperated. He was not accustomed to people like Jason. The man was helpless, but he did not talk like a stupid man. His accent was strange. But not stupid. "You got to unload the stuff," Adam said. "Else the wagon's likely to bust the jack, fall. Hurt somebody. You don't want a loaded wagon to fall on you."

Finally Jason agreed, and they unloaded the wagon. It took them a couple of hours. They all sweated with the work, and when the boxes and the furniture were all set out on the ground, Adam wondered how they had got all that stuff in there in the first place. There was a cast-iron stove, in addition to everything else, which they decided to leave in the wagon. "I never seen so much stuff," Adam said, marveling.

"Well, if you're going to start a new life, you need something to begin with," Jason said. He looked doubtfully at Adam, expecting some mockery in return. But Adam did not say anything.

They cut a slender hickory tree and trimmed the branches and rigged a jack, making the fulcrum a pile of stones. They got the wagon up, and Samuel heaped stones under the axle while the others strained with the hickory lever. Adam slipped under the wagon and knocked the pin out that held the wheel on, and then he and Samuel pulled the wheel off. By then it was midafternoon, and shadows were creeping out over the clearing.

"Well, you certainly do know what you're doing," Jason said in admiration.

"You got any blacksmith tools in all this stuff?" Adam said.

Jason shook his head. "I didn't think of anything like that. We bought the plows, you see. And I have some shoes for the oxen. Shoes already made. And whetstones. We have some nice whetstones. But an anvil. And a hammer. I didn't think ..." He looked earnestly at Adam, explaining, begging for forgiveness.

Adam could not understand such ignorance. Such innocence. "Well, I reckon then you got to take that wheel down to the next town. We come through there this morning. Find yourself a wheelwright. Somebody that's got the tools to fix it. Get yourself some spare spokes, maybe some steel tires. Stuff you need to fix it again. You pull all that load, and you're going to bust another wheel."

"Do you really think so?" Jason said. "Surely not. Not if we watch for rocks."

"You'd be a lot better off if you throwed some of that stuff out," Adam said.

Harry spoke up. "Adam, I think it's only right that we help these people. Why don't you take the wheel down to Cape Girardeau and get what they need."

"That would be splendid," Jason said, his face suddenly alight. "If you could take charge of it, Mr. Cloud, we'd be ever so grateful."

Adam felt heavy in the heart. "I got to be getting on. My daddy's waiting for me. In California."

Harry said, "Adam, now be truthful. Your daddy's not waiting for you. He doesn't even know you're coming."

Harry turned his beaming smile on everybody else. "Adam's such a fine person. He doesn't mean to lie. His father's in California, hunting gold. Adam's going out there to look for him."

Adam burned. He was angry with Harry. "If I'm going to find him before cold weather, I got to get out there," he said.

"Cold weather!" Harry laughed and stretched his long arms at the blue spring sky. "You talk about cold weather on a day like this! Adam, be reasonable. There's plenty of time. I was brought up in a tradition that put a great deal of importance on being helpful to neighbors. There are ladies in distress here, and I could never forgive myself if we were to go off and leave these ladies without the aid that we are able to give them."

"We would appreciate your help, Mr. Cloud," Jessica said. She had long, straw-blond hair and a beautifully serene face. Not nervous and shy like her daughter. *How did Jason marry her?* Jason was much older. She looked at Adam with unwavering solicitation, something unusual in a woman in 1851. Adam faltered.

"Indeed we would be so very grateful," Jason said.

"You don't need me," Adam said desperately, already surrendering. Jessica would not release him with her eyes. They were the color of the sky, more clearly blue than any eyes Adam had ever seen.

"Adam can do just anything," Harry said cheerfully. "I have never met anyone more helpful and more able to help. He can rise to any challenge. He is a true gentleman. Don't let his rude exterior deceive you. I have tested him again and again." The flattery was like honey, sticking Adam in Harry's trap.

"Man looks on the outward appearance, but God looks on the heart," Jason said gratefully. "I know Adam is going to help us."

And so before Adam quite understood how it had happened, he had agreed to take the broken wheel back down to Cape Girardeau. He was more than half angry, but Jessica took his hand in her soft one, looked him straight in the eye and said, "I do thank you, Mr. Cloud. I do sincerely thank you." There wasn't any way he could resist her.

# 19

"Samuel can go with you," Jason said. "You can tell him what to do, and he'll do it. I think my own place is here. Samuel's strong as an ox."

"A little smarter," Asa said, grinning scornfully.

Samuel did not notice the insult. He smiled and looked at Adam and nodded his head. "You just tell me what to do, and I'll do it," he said, repeating Jason without even knowing it.

"I guess I'll just stay here and wait," Harry said easily. His voice was like butter. "I don't suppose we need to tire a lot of animals out by riding a troop back down to that town. No sense making a parade out of it." Harry spoke to Promise, addressing his eyes to her, his words to all the rest of them.

"You can tell me all about yourself," she said. "It's so dull just sitting here, not doing anything."

"My dear, I shall tell you stories," Harry said gallantly, bowing to her slightly as though asking for a dance at a great ball mysteriously called in the forest clearing. "I shall tell you stories to make you laugh and to make you cry." He looked around and coughed. "That is, if your family does not object. I would not wish to appear forward. A gentleman is never forward."

Jason laughed wisely, like a patriarch. "We're all one big family here, Mr. Creekmore. We shall be delighted to have you stay." All the women beamed at Harry. He commanded them as if he had been a prince. *It don't matter if they're married or single; they just lap him up!* Adam thought. Yet he was pleased at what Harry had said about him. *He does appreciate me. I can do better than a lot of men. Harry can see that.* Adam thought of people in Bourbonville. They had not flattered him; they seemed dull in comparison to Harry.

"You'll take good care of Rebecca, won't you, Jason?"

Samuel said. He looked worried. He was so big that his worry seemed like a thundercloud when it settled on his face.

"Don't worry about Rebecca," Jessica said. She laid a hand on Samuel's big arm. "We'll take good care of her."

"Sure we will," Ruth said. Ruth was a big woman but not fat. She had big bones, an honest, open face. "Don't give her a thought, Samuel. She'll be all right."

"Why don't you take these gentlemen in and introduce them to Rebecca?" Jason said.

"Sure," Asa said, for once in agreement with Jason. "I bet they ain't never seen nobody like her. She's real interesting, fellers. You ought to go take a look." His expression was reversed from its usual shape. His mouth was straight, but his eyes danced with laughter. Something bad about his laughter.

Samuel looked silently at first one brother and then at the other. "Go ahead," Jason said. "You have to say goodbye to Rebecca, and you know how she likes company." Something too easy about Jason's voice. Something studied and contrived. Maybe frightened, too. Samuel could be a terror if he got angry.

Samuel looked at Jason for a moment longer, his large face as blank as a pumpkin. "All right," he said. "We'll go see her." When he spoke it was a low growl, a machine inside him grinding with pain and difficulty.

Harry fixed a smile on his face. One of those productions meant for the stage. A smile like a piece of tin hammered onto his elegant face.

They went to Samuel's wagon. The back of it was all laced up. Samuel turned around and took a deep breath, expelled it, filled his balloon cheeks for a moment. Asa grinning at him in the background, everyone suddenly still and expectant, watching to see what would happen, and Adam felt their watching. "Look, my wife ... Rebecca." The voice was tortured, slow, and so strained Adam had to strain to catch the words. "She ain't right in the head just now. She don't know that we're on a trip."

"Is that so?" Harry said, as if Samuel had made some pronouncement about the weather, neutral, inconsequential. "Is she unconscious? Oh, no, she can't be unconscious, can she now? She does like company." He looked momentarily flustered, an actor who had muffed his lines. He shot an apologetic look at Adam. Adam remained still and waiting.

Samuel turned crimson: "She thinks she's still home." Eternity passed while he wrestled the sentences out. Adam felt a prickly sensation in his spine. "And I'm begging you. Just go along with what she says. Don't upset her." Canine eyes pleading in Samuel's big head.

Harry's soothing voice poured in on them. "Upset her! Why, Mr. Jennings! We wouldn't upset her for the *world*. We deeply sympathize with your precious wife's unfortunate condition, and as fellow human beings, we only want to help her."

Samuel grinned at Harry with relief and gratitude. *He likes Harry, too.* Adam burned. Said nothing.

Now Samuel revealed an amazing thing. He unlaced the wagon back as if it had been a soft leather shoe. He climbed up, and there before them was a tiny wooden door, the door to a house that had been cut down to fit on the back of a wagon, built into a wooden frame under the canvas top. Samuel hoisted himself up. Stooping so low that he looked absurd, he knocked gently on the little door.

From within a cheery female voice rang out. "Come *in!*" Samuel opened the door, throwing a backward look of caution at them, and went inside, beckoning them to follow.

Harry and Adam clambered up. They both had to bend to get through the door. Once inside Adam looked around in mute astonishment. The canvas top arching over the wooden hoops made it plain that they were in a wagon. Otherwise they seemed to be in a cramped room in a small house. A trundle bed on one side, very narrow. You pulled out the lower bed at night so that both husband and wife had room to sleep. With one bed pushed under the other, there was room for a couple of wooden chairs, a small table with a pitcher and a washbasin of purple crockery, and in one corner, in a diminutive alcove with a yellow curtain, there was a crockery chamberpot. The curtain was pulled to one side. Samuel crept forward as best he could and pulled the curtain to hide the chamberpot. Then he sat down on the edge of the bed. He was so big that he had to bend to keep his head from touching the top of the canvas. There was a very small cupboard with glass doors. It held some fine dishes. Everything had been built to make maximum use of space.

"How completely charming," Harry said, by way of conversation.

Adam looked at the woman, Rebecca. She was sitting comfortably in a rocking chair. A smallish woman, very merry

105

and grandmotherly-looking, with smooth, plump skin, clearly older than Samuel. Maybe much older. She looked unnatural, somehow ageless. She was knitting something from a ball of dull, red yarn.

Samuel cleared his throat, looked hesitantly around. "Rebecca, this here is, uh, Mr. Adam, and this gentleman here is Mr. Harry. They've, um, come to call."

"How nice!" the woman said, laying her knitting primly aside and pulling her dress straight before putting her fat little hands together in her lap. "Won't you gentlemen have some tea? Samuel, go fetch some tea."

Harry was holding his broad white hat, and he sat down in one of the chairs. Adam sat down, too. It was stuffy under the wagon cover, and the air smelled stale. It was hard to breathe. Harry spoke up quickly, "Oh no, ma'am," his voice purring. "We don't care for any tea. Don't want to put you out."

"You ain't putting me out. Samuel makes the tea. In my condition I can't do anything but sit. It's my back, you see. Can't seem to do anything about it. I get so bilious when I walk around. Have you ever been bilious, young man?"

Harry nodded solemnly. "Oh, yes, ma'am. But we don't have time for tea. We're friends of Mr. Jennings here, and we just wanted to call for a few minutes."

"That's real neighborly of you," Rebecca said. Her voice was dipped in sugar, and her coy smile made her mouth look like a little starched rosebud. "Folks ain't as neighborly as they used to be. They don't call anymore, especially on poor lonely women like me with the bilious complaint, but there ain't nothing as good as it used to be."

"There is indeed a decline in the world," Harry said, leaning forward with an elbow on one knee, earnest and troubled. "I have spoken so frequently to my friend Adam here of the decay I have noticed even in my young life."

"When you get to be as old as me, you'll see how bad things really is," Rebecca said. "But law, when you get to be as old as me, then the world's going to be too bad to go on anymore. There ain't nothing going to save us but for Jesus to come back and send the wicked all to hell to burn forever and ever and to take the righteous like me to gloryland."

"Indeed," Harry said. "Exactly what my sainted mother said. She said the world was so bad she expected the Lord to return any day. I tell you, every morning when I get up I listen hard because I know that on one of those mornings I'm going to hear the trumpet, and I know that Jesus will be there when I look up. Jesus and my mother." He brushed a nonexistent tear from one of his eyes.

"She did?" Rebecca's eyes took on an eager squint. "Was your mamma a premillennialist?"

Harry nodded gravely, recognizing one of the old code words. Being a premillennialist meant you thought the world was so awful that only Jesus could save it.

"She must have been a good woman then. She alive?"

"No, ma'am, she's dead. God rest her soul."

"Um," Rebecca said. "Well, I tell you. The Lord's given me the assurance that I ain't going to die myself. The Lord's going to come back and take me home to heaven, and my body ain't never going to see corruption. I know no worm is ever going to touch this flesh of mine. I know Jesus is coming back." She held her little arms out and looked absurdly like a little porcelain angel you might see on a Christmas tree. Harry bowed in contemplation.

"We've had a little trouble with, uh, the foundation of, uh, Jason's house, Rebecca. Mr. Adam and me, we, uh, have got to go get some, uh, stuff to fix it up."

"Mr. Adam!" Rebecca turned her head and impaled Adam on a keen look. "Are you a premillennialist?"

"No, ma'am, I'm a Methodist."

"You don't even know what it is," Rebecca said in disgust. "You can be a Methodist and be a premillennialist at the same time. You watch him, Samuel. Don't let him try to weaken your faith."

"There ain't nothing that could weaken my faith, Rebecca," Samuel said foolishly, solemnly shaking his head to assure he was fixed in his views to the end of time. "Nobody better try. But we got to go see about getting Jason's house fixed."

"I told you when we all stopped living together in the same house that it was a mistake, Samuel."

"You did, honey. You sure did."

"Now you see I'm right, don't you?"

"Honey, I knowed you was right at the time. But it's something Jason wanted. You know Jason. When he gets his mind fixed on something."

"Well, thank God he don't bring them black people around no more. I tell you it was awful! Ever night it was a different

107

bunch, and they was wet and scared out of their wits. You know niggers. They're like dogs. When they get scared they stink."

Harry and Adam looked at each other. They had no idea what the woman was talking about.

"I'm always right," Rebecca said. "I told Jason he was going to get himself in trouble with them niggers, and he wouldn't take my advice. And you know it was the truth."

Samuel looked with extreme apology at Harry and Adam. "They come one night and fired guns into our house. It liked to of scared Rebecca to death."

"I'm a poor, abused woman," she said, her face as fixed as something cut out of soapstone.

"I'm sure your husband loves you," Harry said. "He's said so much about you. I could hardly wait to meet you, Mrs. Jennings." Harry nodded a slight bow, flashing his widest and most agreeable smile.

She gave him an icy look, not figuring him out yet. She looked at her husband. "Where is it you have to go, Samuel?"

"Oh, just down to . . . to . . ." He faltered, working his big and clumsy hands together.

"I reckon you're going down to Portsmouth."

"Yes. Yes, that's right. To Portsmouth, Rebecca." Samuel looked immensely relieved.

Rebecca turned to him. "Samuel, do stop in when you're there and tell poor Nathalia Johnson that I think about her all the time, and I'm so sorry about her little Ned. Tell her I reckon it was just the will of the Good Lord, and she's got to bear up under it as best she can and wait till Jesus comes to understand it all. You tell her Jesus is coming soon."

"All right, Rebecca," Samuel said. "And you try not to worry about me none while I'm gone. You hear?"

She flashed him a smile that would have made a child sick of candy. "I never worry about you, Samuel. My, my! You're big enough to take care of yourself, I reckon." Her rubbery face changed, fell into abysmal sadness, heavy cheeks quivering next to her tiny mouth. "I just worry about poor, helpless me. My heart's hurting me. It makes me feel so uncomfortable sometimes. I just wish Jesus would hurry up and get here."

"Mrs. Jennings," Harry said in a flood of damp warmth, "I'm sure he'll come any day now. Any day."

"Well, if Jesus is going to come back any day, you don't

108

need to worry about Jason's house. It's that Jessica woman, ain't it? She's got notions."

"No, honey. It ain't Jessica. Jessica ain't done nothing."

"Hmmmmmp," Rebecca said. "Mark my words. She's got notions. She thinks she's better than us, and she's just a common woman."

"Rebecca, Rebecca," Samuel said. He shook his big head and did his faltering best to change the subject. "Listen, Jason is going to be right here to look after you. So you'll be all right."

"And I'll be here, too," Harry said with that suffocating good cheer of his.

She gave him a fishy look, as cold as death. "I don't reckon you need to worry about me, mister. We've got our boy to look after us."

"A boy?" Harry said. "I don't believe I saw him as we came up. Was he off somewhere playing, Mrs. Jennings?" Harry looked around in genuine perplexity.

Rebecca grinned with her little triumph. "He's here. You just ain't seen him yet. You didn't look, did you?"

"He's gone off with some friends of hisn," Samuel said. Adam knew he was lying.

"You be careful not to get wet, Samuel. You know how you get cold when you get your feet wet." She looked at Adam; he saw something mean harden in her eyes. He could not understand it, except he knew that she was suspicious of him. He had not played her game.

"My friends used to be here ever afternoon, drinking tea, talking about their trials and their tribulations with their no-good husbands, bringing their snotty little children by so I could brag on them. I used to love it so! But now they don't come. I sit here ever afternoon, and I wait to hear somebody knock on the door, but it ain't nobody but the family. I think Samuel must of drove all my friends away."

"I ain't done no such thing, Rebecca!" Samuel choked the words out, deeply hurt and baffled.

"He ain't very bright," Rebecca said, winking broadly at Harry in a repulsive flirtation. "Ain't nobody likes him. That's why my friends don't come to see me no more. They don't like Samuel."

"Now, Mrs. Jennings," Harry said.

"You wait till Jesus comes back," Rebecca said. "He's going to tell the whole world how I've been abused. You wait and see."

Samuel was grief-stricken. *He's a fool*, Adam thought. The thought filled him with pity, not reproach.

Samuel bent over quickly and kissed his wife on the cheek and got up. For such a big man, his gesture was surprisingly tender. Adam was touched by it. He had seen his father kiss his mother like that. Long ago. *He must of loved her some.* A hope for what had been. He felt how strange it was.

Afterwards, when they were outside in the warm sunshine, Samuel was apologetic. "She's a fine woman. Don't you fellers be taking Rebecca wrong. Don't matter how she is now. She's got good stuff in her. It'll come out when we get to California. You wait and see."

"Of course it will," Harry said affably. He stood very straight next to Samuel and still looked small. "In California we're all going to get a new start. You know what they call California? They call it the golden shore."

"Jason calls it Arcadia," Samuel said, struggling with the last word.

"Indeed! Indeed!" Harry said.

# 20

Adam said to Jason, "Mr. Jennings, it's going to cost some money to get the wheel fixed."

Jason looked at the toes of his shabby boots. "I suppose it will. How much do you think it'll cost, Adam?"

"Oh, maybe a dollar. Maybe two dollars. All the stuff you need to get, it'll cost you five dollars at least."

"Yes," Jason said. He looked up at the sky. "I'm very embarrassed to talk about money. We have so little of it."

"It's hard to come by," Adam said.

"Adam . . . Mr. Cloud, do you have some money?"

Adam was silent. Jason looked at him so earnestly that Adam could not form a lie. "Well, yes, I've got some." They were standing a little apart, and Jason lowered his voice so nobody else would hear.

"Well, listen, Adam. You get it fixed. Pay for it. And I'll pay you what it costs. I have so little ... I mean, *we* have so little. ... We didn't work for six months before we left." He shook his head. "We wanted work, but there wasn't any place for what we could do. Isn't it terrible ... Well, you don't understand. You've never worked in a foundry."

Adam felt that Jason was deliberately steering the discussion away from the unpleasant subject of money, that Jason was assuming that something had already been decided. "I ain't never done nothing but farm."

Jason's face lighted up. "Oh, that's the purest kind of living. Don't say it's nothing. We're going to farm in California. Everybody ought to have a little farm. Be self-sufficient, not beholden to anybody for anything. Don't you agree, Adam?"

"I ain't never thought about it," Adam said.

"Do have a good trip, and we'll settle accounts when you get back," Jason said. He smiled warmly and shook hands with Adam, clasping him on the shoulder with the hand that was free.

So that was all, and Adam found himself going back down the dirt road with Samuel leading an ox and going on foot, the broken wheel strapped on the ox's broad back. Adam led his mule, and in moments the clearing disappeared behind them, blotted out by the great woods. Adam felt frustrated, resentful, and somehow baffled at how he had got himself mixed up with these people.

For an hour he said little to Samuel. The day cooled down as the sun declined. Birds sang around them, briefly warbling light notes. Once Adam heard a crow cawing very far away, a distant, slow, and melancholy sound. It reminded him of home. The dog trotted happily along behind them. Slowly Adam's bitterness seeped away. He was always one to do what had to be done.

Finally Samuel said, "I can explain some things if you want."

"You don't have to explain nothing."

"I reckon you must think we're all crazy."

"I ain't said nothing like that."

"I mean going West and all. Going to make a new start. At our age."

111

"I'm going West, too," Adam said. "My daddy went West. I reckon he's older than you."

"Ah, but he went West to hunt gold. We're going to California to farm. We ain't never farmed. Don't know nothing about it. Jason, he read this book. Said you just put wheat in the ground in California, and it grows up without you even having to put a hoe to it. Says corn grows up as high as a house with six ears to the stalk. Jason says with land like that, even we can learn to farm."

"I ain't never heard of land like that," Adam said. They went along. The sky overhead was darkening with the dying day. Billowing white clouds formed, expanded, moved sedately to the West. Shapes forming in the clouds. A horse's head. A ship. A tall tower. You looked, and they were there; you looked again, and they were gone.

"I figure it this way," Samuel said. "I didn't have nothing to lose by throwing in with my flesh and blood. We're going to learn what we have to learn. And at least they'll be work to do out there. Won't be like the foundry. Wanting to work and not being able to. I went down to the foundry every morning for the last six months, and ever morning the gates was locked, and they wasn't no smoke coming out of the stacks. It's a sad thing to see, that stack up there in the sky and no smoke coming out of it, and you're down at the bottom of it and wanting to work and can't."

Adam laughed. He was liking Samuel. "One thing about farming. You can always work when you have to."

"That's what Jason says," Samuel said. "He says that's why farmers is so good. He says being close to nature makes you strong and good."

"I don't know about that," Adam said. "I've knowed some pretty mean people that worked on the land."

"No, no. It ain't so," Samuel said. "You look at Ruth. Now, Ruth, she's the best one of us. And she loves to plant things. She had a garden in the back yard in Ironton. They was some years she growed enough to keep vegetables on the table all winter long. She likes to can and such like. And look how good she is." Samuel spoke of mysteries he could not comprehend.

"She seems like a real nice lady all right."

"I always wanted Rebecca to like to plant things. But she don't like to get her hands dirty. Says working in the ground makes her sweat."

"It does for a fact," Adam said.

Samuel shook his head. He was a man perpetually bewildered by the world, longing to make something of it. "I always figured if Rebecca planted things, she might get to thinking good thoughts. We had a boy that died of the scarlet fever three years ago. He wasn't but nine years old. His name was Samuel. Just like mine. Folks said we was the spitting image of each other." Samuel grinned in gentle pride, and for just a moment his boy was still alive to him.

"It's mean stuff, the scarlet fever," Adam said. "I had some sisters to die, but they was a lot younger than that. I don't remember them very good." He felt a pang of guilt. He wished he had buried his mother next to his sisters.

"Well, you don't figure a big, strong boy like mine dying of the scarlet fever. But he done it. He was our onliest child, and when he died like that, real sudden, it turned her mind."

"It made my mamma grieve sure enough when my sisters died," Adam said, "She never could talk about my sisters without crying."

"When we come home from the funeral, she set herself down in her rocking chair, and she commenced to knit. She talks like our boy is still alive. And she knits little socks and shirts and such like for little babies. She does real good work. But when she gets finished with something, she looks at it for a minute, and then she'll unravel it and roll the yarn up in a big ball, and she'll start all over again. I've fussed at her about it. Said she ought to give the pretty things she makes to poor folks, maybe send them to the heathen in Afric. But she just sits there and looks at me like she hates me. She used to not unravel things while I was looking, but when I went to sleep at night, she got up, and the next morning the sweetest little shirts and short britches or whatever was just string again. Well, that's the way it used to be. Now, to tell the truth, I've just give up. Hell, I help her unwind it when she wants to do it. It gives us something to do together. We ain't never done much of anything together except have our boy and bury him. I think you ought to do things together in marriage, don't you, Mr. Adam?"

"I ain't never been married. I ain't never thought about it." He thought of Sylvia Roberts. She might have been a dream, barely remembered in the morning.

Samuel fell silent as if some secret reservoir of words was slowly and painfully filling up inside him. Adam heard the

113

squishy plodding of the ox's hoofs, the more rhythmic gait of his mule, the slow, steady tread of Samuel putting one big foot after another in the brown and dusty road.

"We ain't got no chance to have no other children. Rebecca's already passed the change of life. She's older than me. We was lucky to have even him."

Adam was silent. The sun fell in long streaks on the road. It would be deep twilight, maybe dark, before they got to Cape Girardeau.

"And you put a lot into a boy by the time he's nine. I don't mean this in no bad way. But it's like some part of you was wasted and used up for nine years, and when it's all over, you ain't got nothing to show for it. You think back on all the memories you got of a boy that's dead like that, and you say, 'It didn't go nowhere. It was all for nothing.' Do you know what I mean? Maybe it don't make no sense if you ain't never had a child."

"I know what you mean."

"I reckon you're asking yourself why we fixed the wagon up like it is."

"It ain't none of my business."

"We decided we was going to leave. I mean Jason, he decided. We was helping slaves get away, you see. It was Jason's idea. He come back from the North, from Yale, and he was all filled up with this abolition business. I didn't feel one way or the other about it. But Jason, he said we had to help the niggers get free. We run a station on the underground railroad, you know. We'd go out at night and cross the river in boats, and somebody'd meet us with a bunch of niggers, and we'd bring 'em back over to Ohio. They was free when they got to Ohio, you see. We done it for years." He grinned slowly and proudly. "I was shot at more than once. You ever been shot at, Mr. Adams?"

"No," Adam said. He laughed.

"It makes you think," Samuel said.

"But why'd you leave? Why'd you stop?"

"Why, don't you know? Them fugitive slave laws! Now they can chase a nigger into Ohio. They can chase him all the way to Canady. They can get him right in the middle of New York City and take him back to Mississip or Georgia or what the hell. When they passed them fugitive slave laws, mamma died. And Jason, he said it was time to go. They wasn't nothing we could do in Ohio no more. And Asa and me, we don't

114

have no education. We got to do what Jason says. Jason's smart. I reckon he's the smartest man in the world."

"You was talking about your missus."

"Rebecca. You can call her Rebecca, Mr. Adam. Everybody does. Well, she didn't want to go at all. We sold the house. We all lived in the house together. And when we was loading up, she pitched one big fit. She was crazy, I tell you. She cried and cried and took on and wallowed on the floor, and the doctor had to come and give her some opium to make her calm down. He said crazy folks get that way sometimes. They can't stand for nothing to change. He said he seen a woman onct that put her hands in her mouth and jerked her cheeks out. I mean just tore her cheeks out like they wasn't nothing but a sack and her teeth was inside."

"God Almighty!" Adam said.

"So while Rebecca was all doped up, Jason, he got this idea about the wagon. He said we'd fix it up like a little room and tell Rebecca we was still in Ironton."

"Huh," Adam said.

"That room in there, it wouldn't fool me. Hell, anybody can see it's a wagon. But we worked like niggers and got the wagon fixed up in a day, and when Rebecca come out of the opium, she was inside in bed, and we told her it was her room at home, and she believed us, Mr. Adam. I reckon crazy folks can believe anything."

Adam was silent. Something was not right.

"She ain't been out of the wagon since that day, and here we are!" Samuel said. "She ain't hurt herself, and that's the main thing."

"She'll be all right when you get to California," Adam said. His voice was tentative and hopeful. California was where everybody lived happily ever after.

Samuel sighed, a touching gesture full of innocence in such a big man. "Well at least California's going to be different from the iron foundry. Then it was just the same old thing day after day. Nothing ever different except sometimes it was cold in the morning when we got up. And sometimes it was mild, and sometimes it was hot. And sometimes at night I got shot at." He laughed and looked around. The trees were tremendous here. Virgin forest. Never an axe laid to this wood. "I like it like this—seeing the country, meeting new folks. When I was working in the iron foundry, ever day I knowed I was going to blister my face working down next to

115

the furnace. And ever day I knowed I was going to leave when the whistle blowed. And ever night I knowed I wasn't going to sleep enough. We tried to be in bed by nine so we could get up at five to go to work. But sometimes we had to go to the river, and there wasn't no sleeping out there! And now ... Well, now it's something new ever day. It's pretty good to see new places and meet new folks. I never would of come if it hadn't been for Jason. I tell you, Mr. Adam, Jason is the smartest man I've ever knowed."

"You said that," Adam said.

They went along for a while now without a word. The brooding stillness hung around them.

"But truth to tell, I miss the iron foundry sometimes. It was something regular, something you could depend on. Then they shut it down. With that and them slave laws, there wasn't nothing to do but come on out here. Don't you think so, Mr. Adam?"

"I reckon. We're here."

"That's a fact," Samuel said.

# 21

They camped out that night on the outskirts of Cape Girardeau, and Adam watched the mist coming off the river and thought it looked magical. The river entranced him. He thought that if he spent his life in California, he would never see the Mississippi again. The thought made him sad. He had crossed the river with a heart filled with joy that morning. Now the river pouring its way through the twilight and the falling dark made him think of how life ran on and carried people away. He sat by the fire a long time thinking. Then he slept under the open stars, wrapped in his blankets.

They were up early the next morning and into town. There was one blacksmith in Cape Girardeau. His forge was cold, and his shop was vacant. "His wife died of the cholera," somebody said. "You won't be able to get a horse shod around here for at least a week." So they had to leave Cape Girardeau to look for another blacksmith.

They went on down the river on the Missouri side. "Didn't figure it'd be this hard to fix a wheel," Samuel said.

"Jason's wife. How come he married her?" Adam said.

Samuel shook his head. "Ah, me, that's a hard one, Mr. Adam. A real hard one."

"She's younger than he is."

"I reckon so. She ain't thirty-five yet. That girl of hers, she's seventeen. Ah, me, it's It's hard."

"It ain't none of my business," Adam said.

"Rebecca, she said it was a shame. A real terrible shame. Ruth, she said it was good. But Ruth says everything's good."

"If you don't want to tell me, it's all right," Adam said.

"You'll find out. Sooner or later, you'll find out."

"No, I won't. When we get this here wheel fixed, I'm lighting out. I'm going to California. You don't have to tell me nothing. One, two more days, and you won't never see me again."

Adam tried to look indifferent, though he burned with curiosity. When he had shaken hands with Jessica, she had looked at him directly. He thought he had never seen an older woman look at him like that . . . though maybe he had. Maybe Hattie Arbuckle had looked at him with that same shameless and unwavering steadiness. Maybe that was why something inside him stirred when he thought of Jessica. She was beautiful. Hair the color of wheat, bright in the sunlight in waves that looked wind-curled. And those eyes. Women usually managed to look away when they shook hands in 1851. They glanced at a man and looked down and blushed sometimes and always pulled away their hands quickly. Jessica let her hand rest in his for a moment. It was a very warm hand.

"Well, it don't matter," Samuel said. "I wish you'd stay with us myself. We don't know nothing about crossing the plains. Just think." He looked at the wheel still strapped to the back of the patient ox. "We don't know how to fix a wheel."

"You can always get somebody to fix a wheel," Adam said.

"We ain't yet."

"So you don't have to tell me about Jason's wife," Adam said. "It don't matter to me. I ain't going to be with you long."

"Well, there ain't really nothing to tell. She and that girl of hers, they was living down at Portsmouth. They was talk about 'em, you know. She said she'd been married and all. But they was some folks said she wasn't. They was lots that said that girl was a bastard. I don't know myself. I don't care. Rebecca don't like Jessica, but she seems like a nice sort to me."

"But Jason ... Mr. Jennings .... How did Mr. Jennings marry her?" The pair seemed so improbable to Adam. Jessica young and beautiful still. Jason somehow broken. Hard to say exactly how Jason was broken, but he was. Maybe forty-five years old. Not much older than Adam's father but with deep worry lines running up his forehead between his eyebrows and a gaunt expression, hungry for something he had never tasted. Not somebody Adam could imagine Jessica choosing for a husband.

"Oh he just went and asked her. Jason's like that. He decides something, and he goes and does it. We thought he was crazy, but he said he needed him a wife, and he watched her for a while and decided she was the one."

"Watched her? How did he watch her?"

"He watched her. You know. He went down to Portsmouth ever Sunday and hung around. He walked up and down her street. Why, he even hid out in the bushes behind her house to take a look at her. He said he never onct seen her talk to a man on the street. And that's what decided him. So he went right up to the door and knocked and introduced himself and told her he wanted to marry her."

"And she done it? Just like that?"

"Well, not just like that. She taken a week. She thought Jason was fooling. When she found out he really meant it, she said she would."

"Huh," Adam said.

"Ain't Jason the one? I tell you he's smart. He can do anything."

"But he can't fix a wheel."

"Nah, he can't do that," Samuel said. He shook his large head as if he were trying to understand something too much for him. Jason. What the man could do and not do. Jason was a mystery.

# 22

On the third night after they had left, Adam and Samuel, the ox and the no-name hound walked back into the camp where the Jennings party waited for them.

"Well, Adam, you were gone long enough," Harry said, coming out to meet them. The girl Promise walked with him. Adam saw how she looked at Harry. Sick with respect and admiration and wonder at this handsome man in the white suit. *Damn!* Adam thought.

"Don't get me wrong," Harry said, turning a fond look on Promise. "I've had a wonderful time. A simply marvelous time. But we didn't expect you to be so long."

"We had to go a long ways," Adam said. "And it took me a while to find some wheels. That one we carried down with us, it was too busted up to fix."

Jason came out making hearty comments of appreciation. He took Adam by the hand, clapped him on the shoulder and looked him straight in the eye with intense gratitude. "Thank you, thank you, Adam Cloud. You have done well. Very well, indeed."

"You better thank Samuel there, as well," Adam said. "He done pretty good, too. He got us across a river we had to cross, and he carried one of them wheels all the way back."

Jason turned around and looked at Samuel with just a faint trace of displeasure. "Oh, Samuel always does what you tell him to do. He doesn't really deserve the credit that you do."

"That ain't so, Mr. Jennings, but if you want to believe it, it's all right with me." Adam was displeased with the lot of them.

Jason looked at him for a moment, his wide, high forehead crinkled in slight interrogation. But the question remained unasked. Jason's face broke into a wide smile. Too wide, Adam thought. Jason always trying to seem cheerful and full of welcome.

"Adam, Dr. Creekmore has consented to join us in our trip West. And I want to extend to you a personal invitation on behalf of all of us to come along with him. With us, Adam."

"Dr. Creekmore . . ."

Harry looked worried. His smile was confident, but his eyes were full of pleading.

"I didn't mean to tell them, Adam," Harry said, trying to keep his voice steady. "We were talking on the road. The first night. Mr. Jennings and I. And he was asking me what I did for a living, and I told him about being a doctor and all . . ."

Harry looked at Promise and looked back to Adam.

"To think of it," Jason said. "I was so worried. Going all the way across the country. Hostile Indians. Disease. And you never know when sombody's going to break a leg. It's my responsibility, you see." His words were confused, falling over each other with relief. "And when Dr. Creekmore here told me that he had studied in Heidelberg."

"Germany," Adam said. He had never heard of Heidelberg before Harry told him about the lens grinder that came through Georgia making glasses. Harry had told the story to Adam several times, and now Adam remembered that the lens grinder had been from Heidelberg.

"It was difficult in the medical school there," Harry said. His body leaned almost imperceptibly forward, and everything about him begged Adam to go along with the lie.

"Just think of having to learn German," Promise said. "I want you to teach me German."

"My dear, it is a very harsh language," Harry said, taking her soft hand in his very familiarly and patting it. "Your voice is so sweet, so gentle, that it would be a corruption for you to speak a language like German."

There was much more. Adam could not follow it all. It made his head swim to follow Harry, and there was something so intimidating about Jason's bright smile of relief that Adam did not have the courage to try to speak against it. Everybody was happy. Having a doctor among them was like a guarantee of eternal life, security against the long, hard trip ahead. Adam knew it was all wrong, but he was very tired. He had not slept well since the night before they had come on the Jennings party in the meadow. He knew he would have to talk a long time if he exposed Harry's lie, and he was too worn out even to imagine what he should say. It was not

120

worth the trouble, he thought. Tomorrow he would leave them. God knows Harry had given him excuse enough, and Harry would not miss him now that he had Promise and all the rest of them to think he was God in a white suit, come down from heaven to be with them for a little while. *Tomorrow!* Adam thought. *I will go on along.* He thought the words, and when he did they seemed very somber and sad, and he felt very lonely.

They ate a good supper under the sky. And when the meal was over and the dishes had been cleaned up, Jason stood up in the midst of them and solemnly read from the Bible. He had a good voice for reading, mellow, deep, and precise—a man obviously at home with words. He read with a sober and restrained feeling, and the rest of them reclined in a circle around the fire—all but Rebecca. Adam looked at them and saw what the fire did to their faces. Filled them with soft hopes and infinite dreams.

And thou shalt speak and say before the Lord thy God, a Syrian ready to perish was my father, and he went down into Egypt and sojourned there with a few, and became there a nation, great, mighty, and populous. And the Egyptians' evil entreated us, and afflicted us, and laid upon us hard bondage. And when we cried unto the Lord God of our fathers, the Lord heard our voice, and looked on our affliction, and our labour, and our oppression. And the Lord brought us forth out of Egypt with a mighty hand, and with an outstretched arm, and with great terribleness, and with signs, and with wonders. And he hath brought us into this place and hath given us this land, even a land that floweth with milk and honey.

When he was done, Jason deliberately closed the Bible and cast a long and penetrating look around at them all. Adam had been unwillingly entranced by the sound of the voice, treading surely over the regular rhythms of the text, and when Jason stopped Adam heard the droning of evening insects in the trees.

It was as if something invisible had made the leap from mind to mind. And in an uncanny way—perhaps because of his great fatigue—Adam took unto himself the confession of the wandering Jew, and he could see dim, robed forms tramping in the desert heat, and he saw wagons trundling on the

121

long road, and beyond the Jordan lay the blue hills of California, where the land flowed with milk and honey, corn and wine.

The fantasy, striking him more vividly than any other dream of his life, was momentarily painful, as if it had been an invincible light shining in his eyes. But then as swiftly it passed away, and he was in a meadow with ordinary people, and Jason was standing like a very ordinary man in their midst with a Bible he had just shut, and a storm of phantoms was rushing away over the still treetops, leaving the curdled clouds still in the sky and all the world turning blue and purple and dark.

"We should sing something now," Jason said. He flashed his warm and kindly smile at Adam. "We sing every night, Adam. It helps unite us after the toil of the long day."

Adam looked at Harry. Harry's fine and handsome face was filled with a rapture that even Harry could not have pretended. The man had found a home with these people. Harry caught his glance, sensed the wonder in it. "It's good here," he said to Adam. "These people . . ." He waved his slender hand around. "They are the best people I've ever known, Adam."

"I'm sure you've known some wonderful folks in your time, Dr. Creekmore," Ruth said. "A man like you, just naturally meets fine folks."

*She's bought him too.* Adam thought. He was vaguely disappointed. Ruth seemed too good to be taken in by somebody like Harry.

Jason hummed a pitch, as quickly announced a song, hummed again, and the meadowland suddenly rolled with music.

> *Watchman! Tell us of the night*
> *What its signs of promise are?*
> *Trav'ler! o'er yon mountains' height,*
> *See that glory-beaming star.*
> *Watchman! does its beauteous ray*
> *Aught of hope or joy foretell?*
> *Trav'ler! yes, it brings the day,*
> *Promised day of Israel.*

The song ended, and the echoes dwindled away in the great hush of twilight, and all of them sat thinking their own thoughts.

Adam looked up from the grass and found Jessica looking at him. Again she did not look away when their eyes met, and it was finally Adam who broke off their silent touch by averting his face. He felt himself blush and was ashamed, and he could not understand why he felt the way he did.

Jason spoke up in that kindly way. "Dr. Creekmore, your story is so inspiring. I wonder if you would tell it again."

Harry cleared his throat and looked toward Adam. Looked back to Jason. "Oh, yes," Promise said. "It's the most . . . it's the sweetest story I've ever heard."

There was a murmur of laughter around the fire. People seeing how Promise was taken with Harry. Harry took his glasses off and looked perplexed. He found his handkerchief in his coat pocket and began to wipe foolishly at the enormous lenses.

"It really is a sad thing . . . My father . . . Well, you know."

"I know it hurts to tell," Jason said, forcing him gently. "But it does us all so much good."

"I don't believe I've heard this particular story," Adam said. His voice was hard, but only Harry sensed the mockery in it.

"Adam and I don't really know each other very well," Harry said, polishing more furiously at his glasses, the world in his feeble sight become a blur, and Adam was translated into a voice from a realm where nothing could appear to hurt Harry Creekmore, hidden as he was in that soft and private universe where only his imagination could penetrate and nothing could attack him.

"Well, you should hear the story about Dr. Creekmore and slavery," Jason said. "I wish the story could be written in a book to inspire those people who struggle for liberty all over this accursed land."

"I'd sure like to," Adam said.

Harry cleared his throat. The longer he kept his glasses off, the more confident he became. "Well, as I have said again and again, Mr. Jennings, it was nothing very admirable. It began as a matter of principle and ended as a conflict of wills. I didn't do anybody any good." Harry spoke in that self-deprecating humble way that had never in his life failed to set up people—at least new people—for a humdinger of a lie.

"But you do not believe in slavery," Jason said. "That is

the important thing. You, the son of a Georgia planter, do not believe in slavery." Jason spoke as if this were the most wonderful thing he had ever heard.

And Harry was inspired to go on. "Of course not. How could any decent man believe in slavery?"

"We did much good," Jason said. "We helped slaves escape their bondage. But the fugitive slave laws have ruined everything. We have fallen back into barbarism, and the country has consented to it. That's the most terrible thing. The country has consented."

"Husband, we are listening to Dr. Creekmore's story," Jessica chided gently, "We know our story."

Jason looked at her. The fire half-concealed his expression, and the shadows dancing upward over his eyes did not allow Adam to see him clearly. But he had an impression of anger barely contained. Jason paused, then as though remembering himself, said, "Yes. Yes, of course. That's it. We want to hear Dr. Creekmore's story."

"I am very interested in Mr. Jennings' ideas," Harry said grandly. "I find them the most interesting ideas I have ever heard."

"You are too kind, Dr. Creekmore. It is only because you and I agree so much that we like to hear one another. But do go on. Please."

"There is so little to tell," Harry said. "My spirit was all wrong. It started out as a simple thing, you see. I thought slavery was wrong. But my father would not even listen to me when I tried to talk to him about it. And then I said to myself, I am not going to let my own father order me around when I am a man. You see, I was in one sense completely a Southern gentleman. I am proud. I am very proud."

"Pride is a fine thing," Jason said. "Nothing wrong with pride. Arrogance is what is wrong."

"Well, our personal battle became more important than principle. My father could not let a son rebel against his will, you see. And I could not allow my father to take command of my being. If we are not free in our hearts, then where are we free?"

Adam looked up. Jessica was smiling at him as if the two of them were sharing a joke none of the rest understood. Adam dropped his glance, unnerved at meeting Jessica's eyes every time he looked her way.

"Go on," Promise said. "Please go on."

Harry looked around, his glasses still in his hands, his eyes blank and unfocused, and on his face that superior, tragic smile Adam hated because it was false.

"Well, there's not much more to tell. Our conflict became more and more bitter. I deeply loved my father. It grieved me to oppose him. I never in my life wanted to do anything but what he wanted me to do. But then I did want to be a man, my own man, you see." He paused dramatically and shook his head. He seemed about to cry. "It was a very personal thing."

"But you would not have had any disagreement unless you had principles," Jason said with a great deal of approval. "You did a very fine thing."

Harry sighed and shook his head again. "Yes, but you see it had a very evil consequence. My father disinherited me, threw me out of the house without a cent, told me I would have to be on my own from then on. I never saw him after that until he was on his deathbed."

"That's just the saddest thing I ever heard of," Ruth said. Rachael lay asleep against her father's side. Ruth sat with her arms around Henry. He was a large child for his age, with long blond hair, and he loved being loved. He leaned against his mother with a dreamy expression of interest on his face, looking at Harry.

Harry sighed yet again. "He died of a fever," he said.

"A fever?" Jason said. "I thought he died of the smallpox, Dr. Creekmore. I'm sure you told us that he died of the smallpox."

"Well, of course, of course," Harry said, his voice as smooth as butter on a hot day. "But the lethal agent in the smallpox is actually a fever, Mr. Jennings. In my medical practice I have encountered such fevers many times. And they are deadly, sir. Deadly."

"Yes, yes. Do go on."

"So little more to tell," Harry said. Now he did brush his sleeve over one eye and cast his sightless gaze upward to some point where the angels watched over the treetops. "They sent me word in Atlanta. I got home just in time to hold his hand as he died."

"You were reconciled," Promise said. She had already made Harry's story a legend. Part of the fun of listening to it was that she knew what came next.

"Yes, we were reconciled," Harry said, masterfully shrug-

125

ging his shoulders as if he groaned under a weight of immense sorrow. "Completely reconciled. My dear father confessed to me on his deathbed that I had been right all along. He said that slavery was a monstrous evil. A profanity against Almighty God. He could see how it had been destroying the South for decades. I held his hands, and the very last words he spoke to me were a request for forgiveness."

Harry took his handkerchief, held almost forgotten in one hand, and wiped a real tear from his eye. He wished that it had been that way.

"But you did not receive your plantation back again," Jessica said. She was sympathetic, but she was oddly detached. A woman asking a question, probing to see if there would be a different answer from what had come before. *She's smart*, Adam thought. But his musing was hardly more than a reverie. He was so tired; the fire was so good, and Harry's story had something grand to it. He had never known anyone like Harry. The man was a magician.

"No, my dear madam," Harry was saying. "I did not get my plantation back. You see, my father had already made his will, leaving the plantation to a distant cousin. I arrived just as my father lay dying. Naturally in those ultimate circumstances, I could not bring up a subject so . . . so mercenary."

"He didn't change his will," Promise said, feeling the prospect of wealth depart like the death of summer.

"No, he did not change his will. I lost everything." He heaved another long sigh and then, as though striving not to overact, he resumed in a calm, matter-of-fact, and convincing tone, interspersed with an occasional chuckle of whimsy. "So, you see, all my ideals came to nothing. I wasn't able to do the good I wanted to do. If I had kept quiet, I could have had the plantation, and then I could have freed our people, and father could not have done anything about it. The Greeks call it hubris, you see. Insolent pride. I cared more about arguing with my father than I cared about doing real good. I wanted to convert him *and* free the slaves. The result of my pride is that the slaves are still slaves, and my father is dead."

"But you did convince your father," Promise said. "That must have made you very proud."

"On his deathbed," Harry said. "He was a good man except for the slaves. He might as well have died in peace. And I could have done the good in his name. The slaves would be much happier now, I think. I might have converted some other planters before they got to their deathbeds."

It was a stunning performance. Harry's tones were just right. All of them were caught up in Harry the Good ensnared, as all of them were, in the incomprehensible ironies of life.

"I think you're just wonderful," Promise said.

Adam knew it was hopeless then, and Jason who had sat listening with the rest of them, rapt and filled with pleasure, said. "We're so glad you've joined us, Dr. Creekmore. So very glad."

# 23

Later on, in the tent, Adam was nearly asleep when Harry entered. He had been walking with Jason, listening to Jason explaining the woes of the world and agreeing with him in the careful, restrained, and sincere way that Harry could summon up anytime he needed to agree with anybody.

Harry took off his clothes and rolled into his blankets, and for a while there was silence. Out in the woods a screech owl called off in the dark. The sound gave Adam the shivers. The screech owl was the herald of death. Adam had a bad feeling about everything just now. He did not want to hear what name the owl was summoning to the grave. And he did not want to talk to Harry. So he pretended to be asleep.

But Harry was anxious and could not let things rest like that. Harry always had to be probing at things, setting them right, so he could control them. "Adam?"

Adam said nothing.

"Adam, I know you're awake."

"You don't know nothing of the kind," Adam said. "I'm asleep. You don't know what all Samuel and me went through. You wouldn't believe it because it's true."

"Now, Adam, you judge me harshly." Harry cleared his

throat. His voice was tense. "I know you're wanting to know why I lied to Jason."

"No, Harry, you're wrong again. I ain't wanting to know nothing like that. You lied to Jason because you couldn't help it."

"Adam!"

They were silent. Adam could feel Harry's mind working. Harry wanted to be strong and good. He wanted to be a lion of integrity. Adam could sense all that.

"Listen," Harry said, very pained. "We were walking in the dark together. He wanted a doctor so bad. I meant to tell him that I was just a phrenologist . . ."

"Like I said, you just can't help lying, Harry."

"No, no. I didn't mean to lie. I said I'd studied medicine in Heidelberg. And I meant to go on and tell him that the medicine I studied was phrenology. But when I said the word 'medicine,' he started hugging me and blessing God for sending me to be with them."

"God, Harry. You're just a fool. A simple-minded fool."

"I just wanted to make him happy, Adam. I didn't even realize what I'd said until he started jumping up and down. And I couldn't disappoint him. You just can't disappoint folks when they get as happy as Jason got."

"All right, Harry. You made him happy. Now make me happy. Let's get out of here. In the morning."

"You mean leave them behind? Desert them?"

"I mean leave them behind. I want to get on to California. I want to find my daddy."

"We've got all summer to get to California, Adam."

"We're late already. We should have started two months ago. It's almost June. If we ride out on the mules, we can be in California by August. If we stay with these wagons, God knows when we'll be there."

"Adam, listen to me, my friend." Harry sounded grave and solemn. "You *think* your daddy wants you out in California."

Harry's words gave Adam a pain in the bowels. He wondered himself if Joel Cloud really wanted him to come. "He wants me to come. He's my daddy."

Harry laughed. A superior and very adult laugh. Making fun of the silliness of a child. "Look, if he wanted you to come, he'd have written you more than one letter."

"He can't write hisself. It's a lot of trouble for him to write."

Harry laughed again. "Adam, it is the duty of a friend to tell the truth to his friend. I am telling you the truth. You are deceiving yourself. You need to be like me. See the world as it is. Don't lie to yourself."

It was maddening. Harry was the one who ought to be defending himself. But he was attacking Adam.

"Harry, listening to you talk about lying is like listening to a fox in the chickenhouse trying to crow."

"Everyone lies to make his way in the world, Adam. Everyone will lie to save his skin."

"It ain't so." Adam said. He felt no conviction behind his words. He remembered all the lies he had told so that he and Harry could escape from Nashville. Maybe Harry was right. Maybe Adam was no better than any other liar who ever walked the earth.

Harry was feeling wise and philosophical. He lay on his back and ruminated toward the stars, out of sight beyond the canvas above his head. "Adam, my dear friend! This entire country is founded on lying. We hold these truths to be self-evident, that all men are created equal. Who said that, Adam?"

"I don't care. It ain't in the Bible."

"Thomas Jefferson said it when he wrote the Declaration of Indepencence. And when Thomas Jefferson wrote that line, he had more slaves at his place in Virginia than you and me will ever see again, and they did not sit down and eat supper with Mr. Jefferson in his dining room at night."

"I don't know nothing about it."

"Well, I know something about it, and Thomas Jefferson was a liar. And George Washington was a liar, because he fought for freedom and he had slaves, too. And Millard Fillmore is a liar, or he wouldn't be President right now. Hell, Adam, you jump on me for telling a few little white lies that make folks happy. The only difference between me and a hell of a lot of other people in this country is that I can't think up lies big enough to make money and buy votes and be President. But give me time, Adam. Just give me the run of California, and time. A good lie makes folks move, Adam. And I aim to make California move."

"I hope California's going to give us something better than that." Adam sounded wistful even to himself. He had never tried to figure out everything California meant to him. Just his father, he had thought. But now he knew that California was a lot more than Joel Cloud. California was a new world.

"You wait and see," Harry said, laughing and hopeful like Adam himself and filled with good humor. "You just wait. Harry Creekmore is going to be the first President of the United States to call California his home. And a President from California is bound to be the best President this country has ever had, because all our dreams have come to rest in California, Adam. It's as far West as we can go."

"If the dreams are all lies, then the President that comes out of California is bound to be the biggest liar in the world."

Harry laughed. "You just wait and see, Adam. You just wait."

Adam laughed. The conversation was getting so far-fetched that he had to laugh at it. "Well, what are you going to do when you get to be President, Dr. Creekmore?"

Harry got suddenly serious. "Adam, I'm going to shut down all the banks. I'm going to divide up the whole goddamned West in patches. I'm going to give everybody enough land to grow a crop on and feed himself and his wife and his children. And I'm going to free the slaves. I'm going to do all the things Jason says we need to do. He says the small farm is the hope of the world, and I believe him. People cooperating with each other. It's a great dream Adam. A very great dream."

Now it was Adam's turn to laugh and be scornful. "Oh, God, Harry." But he really liked to hear Harry in full run. Better than a circus.

"You'll see," Harry said. He was laughing, too.

They fell into a long silence. Adam dozed, on the verge of sleep. He felt a warm and pleasant darkness enwrapping him, enpty of thought.

"Adam, listen. I've got something very serious to tell you. You're my best friend now. I want you to be the first to know."

"What?"

"I'm in love."

Adam was silent. He knew what was coming. He felt sad, as if he had lost a hope and could not tell anybody about it. A girl like Promise would never love a man like Adam Cloud. Not that he expected this Promise to love him. He was sad because he thought his life was always going to turn out like this. Seeing other people get the things he cound not even admit to wanting.

"You know who I mean. Promise. She's just what I've always wanted in a woman, Adam. She's so pure. I've never known a good woman except my mother. But Promise . . ."

They let the thought of the girl hang. Adam was wide awake now.

"She's had a hard life," Harry said. "Do you know something extraordinary, Adam? Her father and her mother weren't married! She's a . . . Well, you know."

"A bastard."

"Funny, I can't bear to say the word. But yes. Yes. That's what she is. And she knows it. She told me about it. She says Jason must be the best man in the world because he tells everybody to be honest."

"She thinks a right smart of you," Adam said. "You can tell that. Anybody can."

"Do you really think so, Adam? If I could only think . . ."

Adam laughed in irritation. "Harry, don't be an ass. Of course, she thinks a right smart of you. She nearly turns to butter every time you open your mouth."

They were silent again for a while, Harry reflecting with an immense joy on what Adam had said. Adam could feel emotion coming off Harry like heat from a furnace. "Listen, Adam, promise we'll stay with them. It's not late. Not yet."

"It's getting toward June. And we got better than two thousand miles to go. The plains, the desert, the mountains. You don't want to be hanging back."

"All right. It may be close. But we have ages and ages to live. Five months, Adam. That's what Jason's figuring on. October. When the leaves fall at home. It'll be warm then. Please, Adam."

"It ain't going to be like home in the stony mountains."

"We'll cross them."

Adams took a deep breath. He liked Harry. Harry confided in him. Gave Adam a feeling of immense importance. Flattered him, too. And there was something so sincere about the flattery. "Well, he said, "well, we'll see."

In a minute Harry said, "Well, what are you thinking about now?"

"I ain't thinking about nothing."

"You are, too. I can feel it. Something bad."

"Well, I'm just thinking that these folks can't do nothing. Samuel says they can't. And he's right."

"They can do lots of things. Do you know something?

131

Jason Jennings went to Yale. His daddy went broke before the other two could get educated. Jason's older than the others, you see. Ten years older than Asa. Jason can read Latin and Greek."

"They can't do nothing," Adam said. "Take Samuel. He's stronger than a mule. Lord, I ain't never seen nobody so strong. He scares the hell out of me. But listen, he can't hardly yoke an ox. He don't know nothing about animals. He couldn't hitch a horse up to a plow if they was going to shoot him. He walked around behind my mule yesterday and almost got his brains kicked out. I yelled at him just in time. He laughed."

"I can't yoke an ox," Harry said impatiently. "I can't plow. My God, you act like being a farmer is being God on earth."

"I ain't saying being a farmer is anything, Harry. But if you're going out to California to farm, and if you can't farm, then it matters one hell of a lot if you know what you're talking about."

Harry was silent. Very slowly he was beginning to see what Adam was getting at.

"Samuel and none of them brothers of hisn knows how to chop wood with an axe," Adam said. "They can't hammer a nail straight. Samuel says he ain't never in his life shot a gun. And do you know how many guns they got in the bunch?"

"I don't see that that matters. They probably never went fox hunting either."

"They don't have a gun," Adam said doggedly. "Samuel says Jason ain't even sure it's right to eat meat. Says Jason thinks maybe folks ought not to kill nothing."

"Well, that sounds like a noble idea to me," Harry said doubtfully.

"It sounds crazy as hell to me. Listen, Harry, they ain't done nothing but work in an iron foundry, and Jason's gone to school and he's learned to read them tongues. But you can't eat talk, and he ain't fit to do nothing but talk."

Harry was thoughtful. Adam had got to him. He spoke slowly when he resumed. "Adam, look, when we get to St. Louis, I'm going to buy some medical books. I'm going to learn how to be a sure enough doctor."

"Out of books?"

"You can learn anything out of books. Medical books have pictures in them. Pictures of naked men and women. I've seen the pictures."

"Lord," Adam said.

"Listen, I'm going to learn how to do something," Harry said. "I'm not going to go out to California and make a failure out of that, too. I'm going to begin a new life."

"You might begin it by not lying."

"I wasn't born to be on the bottom," Harry said with surprising gravity. "Some folks can take working their way up. But I've got to do better than that. I'm going to be a doctor in California, and I'm going to be governor, and I'm going to be President." He was not laughing now; he was deadly serious. Adam was embarrassed. He could say nothing. He lay there trying to think of something else to talk about, and he became aware that Harry's breathing was deep and regular.

Adam wondered if Harry dreamed as much asleep as he did when he was awake and, while he was pondering this problem, he fell off to sleep, too.

# 24

Adam woke to the faintly paling dawn, the cool air stirring outside the tent. He got up and stepped into the morning. The wagons hulked in still silhouettes against the dim light. The stars were fading. Animals snuffled, and the call of a bird resounded in the woodland—low and mysterious, marvelous and solemn. A good day coming.

The hound followed him, stretching and yawning and cavorting in the way of waking dogs, wanting to play and be loved. Adam stroked the beast, scratched his soft ears. He looked out toward the West, where the darkness still piled like veils hung down from infinity, with the stars settled faintly in them like pearls shining with dull light. He could load up his mules and leave them, telling them all goodbye. No hard feelings.

He sighed at himself. He could not leave them. He began to stir up the fire, setting water on for coffee. In a few moments he was joined by Jason. Jason, astonished with sleep, rubbing his eyes and looking at Adam as if Adam were the strangest thing in the world. Jason's face looked bad. A man his age could look very old when he first woke up in the morning. His eyes puffy, cheeks sagging, and rough lines carved deep around his broad mouth.

"What time is it anyway?" Jason said.

"I don't have no watch."

Jason looked up at the sky and rubbed his big, awkward hand. "It seems awfully early." He looked down at Adam, who did his best to ignore him. "We've been sleeping a little later than this."

"You've been foolish then," Adam said, still without looking at him. "It's time to get moving. You got big loads. You want to rest a long time at noon. That means you got to get started early."

"The oxen have done splendidly," Jason said. He spoke very carefully as if trying to keep his grammar in place. It could slip this early in the morning, when he was tired. Grammar was very important to Jason. Anybody could tell that by how meticulously he framed his sentences. "We used to get up early when we worked in the foundry. That's behind us now."

"It's a good habit," Adam said. He looked up at Jason with a sudden thought. "How'd a man like you come to work in a foundry, Mr. Jennings?"

Jason gave him an acute look. Then laughed. He liked to talk about himself. He felt more friendly to Adam for letting him do that. "Well, it was a strange thing. My brothers were there. Ironton was new, a new city. It was on the Ohio, you know. I was teaching school up in Massachusetts, and people were talking against slavery, but nobody was doing anything about it. Nobody I knew. I thought if I was serious about abolition, I'd come back to Ohio and work in the foundry in the daytime and help slaves get away at night."

"I'd of gone back to school teaching if I'd been you," Adam said. "You couldn't get me to work in no foundry for a hundred dollars."

"Yes. Well, that's right, Adam. But, you see, I *thought* it would be good to work with my hands. Everybody ought to do manual work. Let yourself know you can do it. We all live on somebody's manual labor, you know. And it isn't right to do that and not know what other people do when they put the clothes on our backs or make the iron stoves we cook on or the paper we write with. To tell the truth I didn't like it.

134

Yes. I hated it. The monotony of it. I tried to improve the men I worked with. I talked to them about education, self-help, self-improvement. The spirit of the age." Jason laughed whimsically. No real amusement in the laughter. Jason kept himself too tightly under control ever to give way to real emotions, Adam thought. Jab him in the tail with a knife, and Jason would look carefully around and consider his audience before he cried "ouch." And then it would be with that benign grin on his face, carefully studied. "They laughed at me," he said softly. It was a painful statement. Adam felt sorry for Jason. Life in the foundry must have been hell for him.

"Why did you want to do that anyway?" Adam said.

"What?"

"Make folks better. Make them improve theirselves? Get educated? Why didn't you just leave them alone?"

Jason seemed amazed. "But, Adam, that wouldn't have been right!"

"Why not?"

"It's our duty to help people. To spread the light that we have."

"If they don't want any help, you ought to leave them alone," Adam said.

"But that's just it," Jason said, warming to one of his carefully thought-out and manufactured sermons. "The fact that they don't want help is the very saddest thing about them. And when we see they don't want help, we must show them their ignorance and make them desire to lift their eyes up, to see the stars just over the head of every human being."

"Well, I'm helping *you* now," Adam said. "You better be getting folks on the move. I'm going to be fixing the coffee now. I'm going to yoke up the oxen, too."

Everybody but Harry was as surprised as Jason to get up so early. Jessica came out in a long linen duster, looking around in a feeling akin to fright, to see what was going on. The duster covered her almost completely, but her feet at the bottom were bare and pink. Adam looked at that small nakedness and felt a hot longing. He embarrassed himself. And she looked at him. Again that long, almost meditating look in her eyes. She too seemed older in the morning. It was as if truth stole on them all in the night; then the sun drove it slowly away. Jessica set to frying bacon in a black, cast-iron

135

frying pan. The smell of the bacon mingled with the coffee. The morning wind was sighing through the forest, and Adam set to work with the oxen, thinking the world was very good.

Harry came out with his white suit on and his glasses carefully fixed on his nose. The suit was getting very dirty, but Harry wore it daily. His only memento of his past dignity, his claim to a place reserved for him in the world.

Henry came out and looked hopefully at Adam. "Can I help you, Mr. Adam?"

Adam looked at him. The boy wanted so badly for someone to think he was a man. Adam started to say no, but then he reconsidered. "Sure, Henry, you can help me a lot. When I put the yoke down on a team's neck, you push the hoops up into the yoke. Be careful. Don't tear the critter's necks."

Henry was delighted. He took the bent hickory poles that went under the oxen's necks and fastened them very carefully in the holes bored for them in the heavy wooden yoke that lay across the oxen's necks, binding the beasts together in teams. Adam could have done the job himself, but it gave him pleasure to see Henry so happy to do a man's task. Adam remembered the same happiness when his father had let him help.

The yoking was already done by the time Asa and Samuel came out. Adam could hear Rebecca's harsh voice in her wagon, complaining at Samuel for getting up so early. Her voice inharmonious with the dawn serenity of the clearing. *Why don't he hit her one in the mouth?* Adam thought. But Samuel was afraid of her.

They stood around the fire and ate the biscuits Ruth and Jessica had whipped together, biscuits with hot bacon in them, and they drank coffee. The sun was making the eastern sky red now, and all the stars were gone. The earth waking up, and the sky above like a blue-white eggshell.

Adam looked around and took a deep breath. "We got to throw away some of your stuff. You got too much in your wagons."

Everybody looked at him in surprise. Henry looked anxiously at Adam, then at Asa. Asa's face was red and angry.

"What are you talking about?" Asa said. "That stuff in the wagons. It ain't yours."

"No, it ain't mine," Adam said. "But we're all together now. And if the wagons break down again, we're going to be

136

delayed, and we're all going to have to work to get going again."

"We won't break another wheel, Adam," Jason said, and laughed in his contrived way, trying to let Adam know by the laugh that Adam was talking complete nonsense.

"You can't tell about something like that, Mr. Jennings," Adam said doggedly. "You got all this stuff in there, and you're going to bust wheels. You're going to bust axles. You're going to wear the oxen out."

"I never heard of such a thing," Asa said.

"You better listen to Mr. Adam," Samuel said slowly, painfully. "He knows a lot about stuff." Samuel fell silent because Asa looked at him with an expression of burning disgust.

"What could we throw away, Adam?" Ruth said gently.

"Well, Mr. Jason's got an iron cookstove in his wagon. He's got a plow and a couple of cradle scythes and a big heavy chifferobe. I don't know what all he's got in them boxes."

"Books for one thing," Jessica said. "We have lots and lots of books."

"We can't throw the books away," Promise said, wailing with the thought. "We'd get so *bored* out there without our books."

"You might not get out there if you take your books along," Adam said in a level voice. He enjoyed being harsh with her. She stared at him like a pained child, then looked toward Harry as if Harry could think of some way to save them all.

"Adam," Harry said with great authority, "it does seem to me that we don't have to decide a question like this just now. I always believe that when you have a difficult decision to make, you should think about it for several days."

"I say let's think about it for four months," Asa said. "When we get to California, we can think about what we're going to throw away."

Suddenly the no-name hound began barking. The instant Adam heard the bark, he knew that the day had gone bad, like milk left in the sun. He turned and looked back down the little road that coiled away in the forest toward Cape Girardeau.

At first they all looked on an empty road. Adam heard the sound of wheels before he could see anything. Then, creaking through the long, thin shadows of the early morning, now

137

seeming solid and real and now like a tawny apparition of evil fantasy, there trundled a slowly moving ox cart. The cart dipped and swayed and came on in gyrations of such dangerous inclination that it seemed as if wood and iron might be drunk. The oxen were so unbelievably scrawny that they reminded Adam of the starved cattle in Joseph's dream. And perched above them on the plank that was the driver's seat, with the magnificent aplomb of a hunting vulture, was Ishtar Baynes. Clifford slouched beside her, leaning forward on razor-sharp elbows that rested against his rail-like knees. To Adam he seemed more shabby, more ragged, more gaunt, more calmly arrogant than he had before.

Harry stood up, his long face pale, and for once his mouth hung open in speechless astonishment.

Ishtar Baynes picked him out right away, her needle eyes jabbed at him as though he had been a tender and succulent frog discovered on a social visit to the marsh. "And how are you, Mr. Creekmore?"

Harry tried to answer, but the words turned to glue in his throat. Adam looked at him and nearly laughed. Now they were sure to go on to California. Just the two of them. Ishtar Baynes would tell everything. He had an urge to run at her, shouting and waving his hands to drive her away. He had a terrible fantasy that she might then flap her arms and sprout feathers (black of course), rise screaming above the trees, and fly away. She looked at him.

"We seen you yesterday, Mr. Adam. Coming through that town back there."

"I said to Mrs. Baynes," Clifford said, turning his dry face to Adam as though Adam had been a child ready to be punished, "I said to her, isn't that Mr. Adam?"

"We was pulled up on a side street," Ishtar Baynes said, "I heard you say you was going to St. Louis, Mr. Adam. We figured we'd follow you when you left us in Nashville. But to tell the truth, I didn't figure we'd catch up to you so soon."

"Why'd you figure on following us, Mrs. Baynes?" Adam said.

"Why, because you've been right good luck to us so far, and I figure you're going to keep on being good luck to us."

"Mrs. Baynes here is extremely addicted to a belief in the goddess of fortune," Clifford Baynes said, looking down at his filthy hands.

"You bet your life," Ishtar Baynes said. "My life's been all luck. Sometimes it's been bad. Sometimes it's been good. With you folks we made fifteen dollars. I reckon that's something worth following to California, ain't it, Clifford?"

"Indeed, my love. Indeed."

"Are these people friends of yours, Dr. Creekmore?" Jason looked incredulously at Harry, his carefully constrained face set in an expression of willingness to understand combined with utter disbelief.

"Dr. Creekmore" Ishtar Baynes said. She and her husband looked at each other, and she laughed. "Well, I reckon we know *Dr.* Creekmore, don't we?"

"The gentleman who was looking for you, Mr. Creekmore. Mr. Abernathy? We located him the very next morning. He gave us another five dollars. But unfortunately . . ."

"Unfortunately you'd left town," Ishtar Baynes said. "But I reckon it didn't matter none to us. I figure we'd got all we was going to get out of that Abernathy feller."

"We are very pleased to have a medical man like Dr. Creekmore along with us," Jason said, doing his best to assume his position as the dignified leader of this extraordinary band of pilgrims to the Great West.

"I reckon if you got a bump on your head, he'd fix it right up," Ishtar Baynes said with a screech of laughter.

"Mr. Abernathy was very angry," Clifford Baynes said very gravely. "He tried to get his five dollars back from us."

"But we wouldn't give it to him," Ishtar Baynes said.

"Dr. Creekmore, you might introduce us," Jason said. There was faint irritation in his voice. His restraint just beginning to pull loose.

"Jason Jennings, I'd like you to meet Mr. and Mrs. Baynes." Harry barely managed to get the words out.

"*Professor* Baynes," Clifford said, putting down a limp and filthy paw to take Jason's hand extended to him.

"I have decided to join Mr. Jennings here, and his family. Adam and I . . ." For a moment Harry faltered, and Adam expected him to surrender the whole show. Admit his lying. Ride off then for California and leave the Jennings tribe to their fate. But Harry seemed to inject himself all at once with a narcotic courage. All or nothing. "I have decided to contribute my medical services." He turned his myopic, determined eyes on Jason, removed his glasses in a habitual gesture, again taking that handkerchief from his inside pocket and polishing at the thick lenses while he gaped sightlessly

139

into a confusion of morning colors. "Because of my attitude toward slavery, because of my devotion to abolition," Harry said carefully, "I was forced to flee a steamboat in the Tennessee River in the vicinity of my friend Adam's home. I was pursued by those men who had robbed me of all my possessions on the boat. They pursued me to Nashville, and these kind people were good enough to warn me," Harry said, wheeling slightly to face the general direction of the Baynes cart. "I owe them a great deal. A very great deal, and I only wish that there was some way I might repay them for their great kindness to me."

"Well, any friend of Dr. Creekmore's is certainly a friend of mine," Jason said. He smiled up at the Bayneses, and Adam imagined that Jason had worn just that kind of smile when he entered the iron foundry for the first time, convincing himself for the moment that a detestable job like that was his human duty.

Ishtar Baynes looked from face to face. Adam could almost hear the machinery ticking in her brain, relentlessly calculating how to take an advantage from this situation. Jason, seeing the penetration of her gaze first at one of them and then at another, seemed to falter. "It is a privilege for us to have a medical doctor to go with us on our journey," he said, the words a repetition of sorts, having no sense except in Jason's trying to reassure himself.

Ishtar Baynes was a woman of infinite surprise. She looked Harry up and down and said in a curiously neutral voice now, like a second in a duel asking questions about the ground, "A medical doctor." It was not even a question. Her look was like a long, thin sword plunged smoothly into Harry's bowels, although she spoke only those few words.

Jason said, "We are going to form a farming association in California. We are going to live together in a community apart from the world." He laughed in a careful way. "And maybe—just maybe—the world will finally come to join us." He looked proudly around at Harry. "Dr. Creekmore is going to attend to our medical needs."

There was an uncomfortable silence. The world waiting for Ishtar Baynes. Harry looked at her with desperate pleading and looked at Promise. Promise viewed Mrs. Baynes as a curiosity, a calf with two heads in a circus, something completely unrelated to her world. Ishtar Baynes took it all in.

140

"California. Farming." she said with surprising whimsy. "I've always wanted to farm. It's such a pure life."

"Yes, indeed," Jason said. He smiled at her, glad to find somebody who shared his views. "Banking, trade, they pollute the mind. The source of evil in the world is commerce." He launched into an improving lecture in his eagerly muddled way, and Ishtar Baynes nodded her head, following him with an uncanny intuition, not understanding and not caring about his vision, but understanding Jason in a moment as well as anybody else might have comprehended this strange man in a decade.

Harry took his cue and cleared his throat. "Well, perhaps, I mean ..." He faltered briefly and looked at Jason who had turned politely to hear what Harry had to say. "I was thinking, Mr. Jennings, perhaps Mrs. Baynes, perhaps these two people might accompany us." His frantic eyes flew back to Mrs. Baynes, desperate for her good will. "I mean these people did help me in Nashville. They may have been responsible for saving my life. I do feel that I owe them a debt ..."

"Of course, Dr. Creekmore. Of course," Jason said, his mechanical expression warming like a cool fire to show the emotion of benevolence he felt the occasion demanded. "It is honorable, very honorable to wish to do good to those who have befriended us." He looked around at the rest of them. Asa was leaning against a wagon, looking at the scene with an insolent smile. Jason's eyes fixed on him. "I think ... Well, Asa, I'm sure you will not object ... Of course, you may go with us, share our way, our life ..." He smiled, and it was all settled.

"We thank you, Dr. Creekmore," Ishtar Baynes said. She put a light stress on the word "doctor." Something agreed upon. For the time being.

"Well, Harry, you've done it now," Adam said later on as the little caravan swung out into the road, the wheel on Jason's wagon replaced, the oxen pulling stolidly at the yokes, everything bright in the bright morning.

"It's all right," Harry said nonchalantly. "She's not going to tell on me." He grinned at Adam. Harry was sure that he could charm anybody if he only had the time. Mrs. Baynes had given him time. He would charm her.

"You wait and see," Adam cautioned. "That's what she's doing. Just waiting for her chance."

"Oh, Adam," Harry said laughing. "You shouldn't mistrust

141

people. People are basically good. Even Mrs. Baynes. *You* wait and see. I'll have her eating out of my hands like a little puppy in a week. She's not going to do anything to harm me. Why, there's no reason for anybody to hurt me now. No reason at all."

# 25

But what impressed Adam was not Harry's capacity to charm but the insidious power of Ishtar Baynes to flatter people. At night, when Jason ruminated about the troubles of the world, Ishtar Baynes sat nodding and exclaiming, making such admiring declarations as, "Why, that's what I've always thought. You just put it into words, Mr. Jennings. My, my! You're just the smartest man I ever seen. Ain't it so, Clifford?"

She went to see Rebecca and emerged wiping invisible tears from her sharp little eyes, saying, "Why, that there's just the sweetest woman I ever seen. And she's going to be all right. You wait and see."

To little Henry she said, "My, you're sure handsome, Henry. You got the best looks from your mamma and your daddy. You're strong, too, I bet. You're going to be a big man. I know that."

And to Rachael she cooed and made exclamations of adoration. "I love little girls. And that there is the *prettiest* little girl I ever seen in my life. That mouth. That *beautiful* mouth. And that red hair. I swear it looks like the sunset! Oh, honey, you're just the prettiest thing in the world."

"I know it," Rachael said. Ruth's face darkened when Rachael was insolent. But Ishtar Baynes never paused.

"You hear that? She knows it! Why, honey, you're cute as a *bug!*"

And so with all of them. Except Harry. Ishtar Baynes never complimented Harry for anything. For him she reserved a keen and mocking face, but Harry did not seem to see her malice.

Adam saw both her malice and her cunning, and as he listened to the odious flattery he wondered how anybody could put up with Mrs. Baynes for two minutes. "Flattery to the face is open disgrace." A probverb his mother had often repeated to him. He thought flattery was the mark of bankers and salesmen and other people who had to live off the hides of others, and he thought Mrs. Baynes was a parasite that any healthy person would brush off as though she had been a tick or a fly.

But things did not work that way within the Jennings party. Ishtar Baynes flattered, and people smiled and nodded at her wisdom and told each other how sweet she was. Jason and the others—even Asa—made themselves feel warm and kind by reflecting on how harsh the world had been to Ishtar Baynes. "Of course, the woman has her faults," Jason said, setting his face like a heroic statue made of soapstone. "We all do. But think of the suffering she's endured." Here Jason was as vague as Ishtar Baynes. She had endured great tribulation, but she never did say exactly what. "I think of how any of us might have turned out if we had suffered as much," Jason said. Adam suspected that Jason liked to have Ishtar Baynes around because she was someone so obviously lower than he was in the world. And though he wondered at their delusions, Adam could not deny the power of Ishtar Baynes, for it stood in front of his face every day like the prospect of death.

She left Adam alone after a while. When she flattered him he looked at her with a cold and distant silence, as unmoved and uninterested in her as a stone. Ishtar Baynes left Jessica alone, too. In that mysteriously wise way of hers she perceived that Jessica stood outside the Jennings family, though she was married to Jason. Jason's bearing toward his wife was formal and correct, but it was not really loving, and it did not take anybody long to see that. Even seeing it, some took no notice of it, for many marriages were the same.

Samuel was taken with Ishtar Baynes the way everybody else was, because she praised Rebecca so much and spent so much time with the demented woman as the wagons rolled heavily along. But Samuel retained his loyalty to Adam. They had shared three days together, those days when Adam had treated Samuel with the respect due a grown man, and Samuel relived it again and again.

Sometimes Adam would walk with him, leading his mule

143

to rest the animal, as Samuel tramped along with his lead team of oxen. Samuel would nudge him with an enormous elbow and look down at him from beneath the wide brim of his shabby old hat, and he would smile in a conspiratorial way at Adam. "Hey, Mr. Adam, we really done it, didn't we? We really got them wheels and fixed that wagon."

"We sure did, Samuel. You done it. Without you, we couldn't of done nothing."

Samuel was like a big, dull tiger being led around the country in a cage made of sticks, and if he ever decided to flex his muscles and burst to freedom, no telling what he would do. But Adam liked him. He could not forget how patient and willing Samuel had been on that trip and how he had gotten them across the river when there was no ferry. He felt sorry for the big man because everybody scorned him so much, and Samuel's mind was so slow and thick that he did not understand how people were treating him.

Clifford Baynes followed the lead of his wife, and though Adam did not think Mr. Baynes was smart, the man seemed almost as cunning as his wife. "You see, I am a professor of Latin, Mr. Jennings, and I was terminated from a very fine position at the famous George Washington Academy in Frederick, Maryland, because of my views on that horrid evil of our time, slavery!"

"Just listen to the man lie!" Harry whispered in outrage to Adam. "How can he look you in the face and say things like that!"

Adam stared at Harry and saw Harry's fine lips working furiously under the splendid blond mustache that was sprouting grandly over Harry's mouth. Adam saw that Harry had convinced himself that all his own lies were gospel. He was a medical doctor. He was going to be a help to the Jennings party. He would be governor of California. And he would be President of the United States.

Sometimes everything was so damned confusing that it pleased Adam to ride far ahead of the rest of them, to pretend that he was alone, and to think no thoughts. Then the sun seemed to pour through his body so that he was part heaviness and part light, a creature made of blood and spirit and filled with a radiance that no earthly foolishness could darken.

So it was that they came creaking into St. Louis over the rolling and forested land. Adam saw the oxen labor in their

144

yokes. Agonizing strain. Asa said, "They're fine. Just fine, and what the hell! Ain't nothing but animals. The Lord God made animals to serve man."

St. Louis. An adolescent town getting its growth, sprawled awkwardly at a place where the ground heaved a little, humping out of the marshy land along the giant river. "Don't drink no water out of that river!" A warning somebody spoke almost playfully to Adam when he was standing at the muddy riverfront, looking entranced by the swift motion of the Mississippi. Signs scattered around, sticking out of the mud. "Danger of Typhoid." Nobody knew what caused typhoid, but bad water seemed to have something to do with it, and everybody knew that typhoid made your stomach rot like old rubber. But who would drink out of the Mississippi? The thought made Adam gag!

The river swirled with filth. Rings of oil dropped from the steamboats. Tar. It stank. But in the city packed beyond the river there were good smells. The sweet, clean smell of white-wash on new wood. Fragrance of woodsmoke rising from innumerable fireplaces, wood cut from the inexhaustible supply offered by the great forest stretching beyond. The drift of pitch-pine smoke from the great steamers moored at the crowded docks. Beer brewing sourly in the big, oaken vats in the warehouses near the water.

And something more. Indefinable, fresh and pungent. "You can smell the great plains in St. Louis." An exuberant comment dropped in a saloon where Adam and Harry went for a glass of cool beer, for once alone together, to look, to gape, to lose themselves in the sweaty crowd of happy people who had things to talk about and things to do. Adam was excited—more excited than he had ever been in his life. St. Louis bending West. The nation magnificently swelling toward the incredible Pacific, and Adam was a part of it. Bourbonville seemed remote, petty, dull, a collection of memories that had happened to somebody else, an Adam Cloud lodged in the sunlight like the trunk of a tree blown down by the wind long ago and left to rot in the earth.

He had left Bourbon County! He had had the courage to pick up and depart. And from somewhere nearby now—just out there on the swelling plains—there was a delirious freshness blowing, something grand portending the prodigious future, a vision splendidly vague, rising out of the West.

"I'm so glad I've come!" Adam muttered aloud, nonsensi-

145

cally to himself, unable to contain the exuberant thought in his heart.

"On the way to wrestle with the elephant!" That's what people called going to Califorinia. "The elephant!" Somehow the words conjured up a notion of hard, dangerous work, heavy lifting, exotic power—and gentle friendliness. "Go wrestle the elephant!" People laughed when they said it.

And here on the Mississippi, in the great gut of the nation, was this white city abuilding, singing its lusty songs in a new land and standing as the gateway to all the shining promises out there, and Adam stood with his bursting heart and thrilled to his inner music.

*Bless the Lord, O my soul, and all that is within me, bless His holy name.*

St. Louis! Men with places to go thronged the board sidewalks, making the planks resound with their tramping boots, an irregular drumbeat, tapping, tapping, and the music unheard in the hot spring air all around them. There were men like Adam, like Jason, like Harry, even rodent-faced men like Clifford Baynes slipping through the day with eyes rolling in a perpetually crafty fear, men in homespun and in linsey-woolsey and hand-me-downs who gawked and looked timid or stolid or aloof and carried manifest destiny bulging in their deep pockets and looked toward the smoky Pacific and called it the golden shore.

*Bless the Lord, all His works in all places of His dominion. Bless the Lord, O my soul!*

An endless procession of heavy freight wagons trundling down to the docks, rolling away from the docks, loading the boats, unloading the boats. There were horses and mules and lowing cattle and barking dogs, and there was the reek of sweat and animal shit, and there was the inescapable rhythmic jingle of harness, and the smell of hay.

"It's so filthy!" Harry said, wrinkling his nose. "Sometime you have to see Atlanta, Adam! So green."

"I don't reckon you'll ever see Atlanta again, Harry."

"Do you think so? Well, maybe not. Maybe not." Harry looked solemn and depressed.

But Harry found some comfort in St. Louis. He found a public bath and flourished in the languid heat of an enormous marble tub, and he had his white suit laundered while he waited, his hat cleaned and blocked again, and when he came back to them after the absence of a morning, he looked

146

like a prince out of a book. Adam thought he saw tears in Promise's eyes when she looked at Harry. *She adores him!* The thought a pain in Adam's breast, sudden and lingering.

Jason hated St. Louis. "It's commerce," he said, looking very solemn and shaking his head, his face almost a furious red under the tan that came from his daily march in the open air. "Trade defiles nature. Men are at their best when they are planting their own seed, working their land, taking their harvest, being close to gentle Nature, to Nature's order and harmony."

"Oh, I love the city, husband!" Jessica said with a voice surging with pleasure. "I think I was born for the city."

Jason was annoyed. "My dear, whatever do you mean? Just look at the squalor! The city corrupts the very soul of man. Men do things in the city they would never think of doing in the country."

Jessica could not believe her husband was serious. She tried to joke with him, smiling. "Oh, piddle, husband! The city is glorious!"

"My dear, you should know." Jason's remark, soft and insinuating, like a snake under the door. Jessica only looked at him, but her eyes suddenly clouded with tears. Adam moved quickly away from them.

Adam agreed with Jessica, and in his agreement he felt close to her. Life was beautiful in St. Louis. Not the houses or the stores or the tramping horses or the river. Not the bald, crowded squares where the brown earth was packed down by so many feet, so many hoofs, not the hotels with their thin, tall windows or the shops or the hardware stores or the livery stables. But life! Glorious, moving, dancing life in the hot sunshine. St. Louis was young and hard and on the move, and the country beyond, spread out for thousands of miles, was also on the move, and the motion was everything to Adam, for the opposite of motion was death. And he knew that in the West to come, cities would be even more beautiful than St. Louis.

Harry bought a doctor's bag of shiny black leather. He bought all the tools a doctor was supposed to have, and he bought medicines, too. He did not know what the medicines were. But he bought books, and he told Adam, "I'll read up on everything."

"This bag!" he said jubilantly to Adam. "It makes me feel different."

147

Adam silently marveled. Give Harry clean clothes, a bath, trim his flourishing beard a little, set a black medical bag firmly in one of his fine hands, and Harry did look like a doctor. A transformation as complete as though he had been touched by a magic wand. The wand of the West.

The books were hard to find because St. Louis was not a bookish town, but they finally located a little shop with some works on medicine. Harry bought a large, black-bound tome called *Principles of Surgery*, with strangely dry engravings of the human body deprived of its skin and its hair and showing the muscles in long, lined strips that clung to the bone, and a *Medical Cyclopedia* that listed innumerable subjects in convenient alphabetical order. "To learn how doctors talk, Adam," he said vaguely, "that's the main thing." One little book dazzled him. *Gunn's Domestic Medicine*. Its language was so simple that a schoolboy could understand it, and it was optimistic, too. It gave step-by-step directions on how to handle every ailment, and it always assumed that the patient got well. And a final selection, a book filled with incomprehensible language, called *Diseases of the Nerves*, which held that the sure cure for all nerve diseases was opium.

The books cost eighteen dollars and seventy-seven cents, a scandalous price. After his large outlay for the medical supplies, Harry had to borrow money from Adam. Adam moved very reluctantly to his money belt.

"Write it all down, Adam. I'll pay you back when we get to California."

When Adam said it was all right, Harry insisted. And so Adam wrote down the amount on a scrap of paper, and Harry wrote boldly beneath it "IOU," signing his name in a flowery, aristocratic hand, and for as long as he lived, Adam Cloud kept that little scrap of paper in his purse as the most tangible souvenir he retained of Harry Creekmore.

"Why don't you buy some more pants? And a new shirt?" Adam said, perplexed. But Harry only gave him a prolonged and solemn stare of blank incomprehension.

"Why?"

"Because you can't wear a white suit out where we're going. It'll get filthy."

Harry turned very cool. "No, I have always worn white."

Adam bought a small keg of gunpowder and some more lead for shot. Then he bought another rifle, longer and heavier than the one he had brought with him from Tennessee. On impulse he bought something else that made him tingle. One of Mr. Colt's patented five-shot revolvers.

"This here's the finest handgun that's ever been made!" the hardware salesman said reverently, puffing with self-importance and awe, staring down at the beautiful thing on the counter in a thrall of sweaty, breathless pleasure. "It was made by that there Colt feller in Connecticut. I tell you. They say them Connecticut folks got so gawddamned smart by selling their whole gawddamned state to the devil, women and children thrown in! It makes you think, don't it? How else do you explain how smart they are? They sure ain't godly folks!"

"It was a gentleman from Connecticut who invented the cotton gin," Harry said uneasily. There did seem to be something supernatural and frightening about the intelligence of people from Connecticut.

They took their new possessions back to camp on the fringe of town. "You look like some kind of soldier," Jason said disapprovingly. "Guns make me afraid. I believe in kindness. Kindness does more for history than bullets do."

"Good Lord, Mr. Adam, you must be expecting to be jumped up by the Indians!" Mrs. Baynes said. She put a worried hand up to her thin lips and looked anxious. "Do you think that's likely to happen to us? Are the Indians mean?"

Jason turned to her with lordly superiority. "The Indians are children of nature. They won't hurt us if we don't hurt them."

"I got the guns for hunting," Adam said. "If they's game out there, we can eat some of it."

Jason shook his head. His moral superiority became more and more pronounced if it was not recognized at once, and Adam did not seem to recognize it. "It doesn't seem good to me, going across the plains to a new land, killing things as we go. When we get out West, we're going to conduct a great experiment. You mark my words. In ten years, people all over the country are going to be looking to us as an example. We're going to show the world how to live together in community and peace." His voice rose a little on his vision, and Adam began to see dimly how large that vision was. Like a cloud swelling to cover the sun.

"Well, we'll see, Mr. Jennings," Adam said, not wanting to argue with Jason. Futile to argue with a man who had no feeling.

They all made so much of the guns that nobody stopped to

149

ask why Harry Creekmore had bought all those medical books. Reasonable enough for a doctor to buy medicine and instruments and a bag to replace things he had lost in an accident. But why buy books when he had studied in Germany with the finest teachers in the world? Only Mrs. Baynes looked at the books, looked at Harry with a grin, looked at Adam knowingly. Her expression said very clearly, "Just you don't cross me, Harry Creekmore, or I'll tell everything I know."

Henry was enthralled with the guns. "Real guns!" he said in ecstasy. Adam let him hold the new rifle. The gun was so heavy that Henry could not hold it up for long. Adam took it back with a laugh.

"I'll teach you how to shoot when we get out on the plains," Adam said.

Asa jumped. "No, you ain't going to do no such thing. It's too dangerous. Guns. I don't want this boy fooling around with no guns. He might get hurt. You hear me? You ain't going to do nothing with guns!"

Asa's eyes were greenbrown. Like a cat's. Turned on Adam they were full of fury. *It's just an excuse to get mad at me,* Adam thought. *He don't care about that boy of hisn getting shot. He just don't like me.* The thought was puzzling, but Adam did not care anything about it. All the Jenningses were simpletons. *I'll get them over the plains and the mountains, and then they can go to hell.* He stood, holding the rifle in his hands, and merely looked at Asa.

"If Henry's going to get to shoot the gun, I get to shoot the gun, *too!*" Rachael said. A childish, petulant voice. Five years old.

Asa picked her up in his arms. His harsh face dissolved in a smile of adoration. "Nobody's going to shoot the gun, honey. You might get hurt. I couldn't bear it if anything was to happen to you."

"I get to shoot the gun first!" Rachael said.

"Oh, honey, no," Asa said. "Come on. Take a walk with daddy. Just thinking about you being near a gun makes me sick."

*He loves that girl more than he does his boy,* Adam thought. He looked at Henry. Henry was watching his father and Rachael go off, the chubby little girl toddling along, holding her father's fingers. Adam felt sorry for Henry and told him to come on. They would brush the oxen down.

# 26

Most emigrants bound for California loaded their stock and their wagons and their families on steamboats at St. Louis and went on up the Missouri River to Independence or to Westport Landing or even to Fort Leavenworth or to St. Joseph, where fingers of the Overland Trail began stretching out toward the Platte River. The valley of the Platte was the great flat road to the Rocky Mountains, to South Pass, and to the Great West lying beyond like Eden uncursed.

There were not many emigrants in St. Louis because it was already late to be going to California this year—May, fading toward a hot June, and most of those who were going had already gone. They departed when the grass turned green on the prairies, and that was April. You counted on four, maybe five months to make the journey, and that took you into September. If you delayed a month or two or three, the snow would come down in the stony mountains or in the Sierra Nevada, and you were dead. Or else the living had to eat the dead to survive. The way the Donner Party did. No story was so often told as the Donner story. It cast a shadow of horror over the Western pilgrimage that made men and women hurry before the blade of winter. And most who went West in 1851—a year when the migration fell sharply after two big years—had already gone by the time Adam and the others arrived in St. Louis.

Adam burned to go on. But the rest were so enthralled with St. Louis that they stayed two days. Jason had many chances to tell everybody how bad the city was as he pounded up and down the board sidewalks and took everything in with his cool and reproving eyes. Then on the evening of the second day, he stood up in their midst and read the Bible as he always did. A Psalm. He read it through with great feeling. He repeated one verse at the end. "Com-

151

mit thy way unto the Lord; trust also in Him; and He shall bring it to pass."

Jason cleared his throat then and launched into a little speech. He told them that it was three hundred miles from St. Louis to Westport Landing. In a steamboat they could make it in about a week. Jason had gone down to the docks to talk price with a steamboat captain. The captain was a generous man. All the Jennings party, including the couple Baynes and Adam and Harry and all the wagons and stock, could journey to Westport Landing for one hundred and thirty-five dollars! A great bargain.

But Jason had only fifty dollars.

He explained the situation slowly and methodically. He said that the captain told him that it was already late in the year. If they left on the steamboat tomorrow, they might be just in time to make it through the Sierra Nevada before the snows. If they did not take the boat, they had no chance to make it to California this year.

All the time he was talking, Jason kept his eyes averted from Adam. He explained their predicament very carefully, almost abstractly. But his attitude made it clear that he was talking to Adam, pleading with him. Adam had money to buy new guns; he might have enough to help them onto the jump-off point for the overland trail.

Adam sat in cool silence. It was Harry who spoke up, Harry who was completely swept up now into Jason's vague and exalted vision at a better life, "Adam's got money. Tied to a money belt around his waist! Adam's got nearly five hundred dollars!" Harry was joyful to make the announcement. He turned happily to Adam. "Adam can give us the money to go on the steamboat."

Everybody looked at Adam with relief. Even Asa looked less sour than usual. Jason was solemn; nobody could resist an appeal that was so frank and necessary. Ishtar Baynes muttered that she never would have dreamed that Adam had money. She scrutinized him with the respect an eagle might have had on just learning that snakes are good to eat.

Everybody else was pleased. Promise said with great feeling, "Well, thank heaven!" And she smiled at Adam. Her smile as bright as a summer day.

Adam knew that he was expected to stand up and tell them that he would give them the money. Tell them he was glad to do it because they were all in this together. They were all going to California, all going to a new life, and he would join them in their little community in the green hills, and everything was going to be just grand. Like camp meeting when sinners are converted, and the forest clearing turns warm with peace and fellowship.

Adam wanted to do what they expected. Just for a moment. The easy thing. He thought of how good it would be to have everyone here like him. Samuel was grinning at him. Promise would be grateful. Jessica was leaning forward, her beautiful face set in a cool smile. Jason pleased. And maybe even Asa would not be so hard to get along with. All so vivid that it was like something in the air. The way you feel a thunderstorm building, something you can feel acutely but cannot describe. A surge in your heart.

But Adam was immediately taken with another feeling. The money in that money belt was a farm on a hillside in Tennessee. The land where his mother's bones lay under an apple tree. His father had sweated next to him there, pulling stumps out of the hard ground. A land they had planted and harvested together. A cabin that smelled of wood and charred ash in the clay fireplace and the faint residue of thousands of meals. The sharp smell of mint growing in the shade in the summer. Damp fields turned under in the spring and mellow with color in the fall.

And somewhere out there in California, his father was trying to make a living. Maybe in debt. He might need that money. And if Adam paid their fare to Westport Landing, a lot of that money—the farm, the years of labor, his father's life—would be forever gone.

So he did not look at any of them except Jason. Jason he looked at in the eye. His substitute for a blow. Adam annoyed with himself for the thirst for violence that suddenly came in his throat. He said, "This here money that I've got. It ain't mine to give away. It belongs to my daddy. It was his farm I sold. I can't give you none of it."

Jason composed and almost immoblie face nearly broke for a moment. He drew back, perhaps embarrassed at himself. He looked around, clearing his throat, mumbling something about the sacredness of a son's obligations to his father. A hard, incredulous look passed like a wind over the others.

Harry was outraged. "You've been spending it on foolishness. A rifle. Gunpowder. A pistol you don't need. Something to play with. Why can't you spend some of it for folks that need it?"

"I bought what I bought to get us to California," Adam said. "I bought it to protect all of you."

"Adam, that is ridiculous if you don't mind my saying so. We don't need protection." Jason wrestled with himself. He thrust his face forward, looking very reasonable and sincere.

"All right," Harry said. "Why can't you lend us the money?"

"I can't lend it to you because I don't know if I'll get it back."

"Why, Clifford, this feller don't *trust* us!" Mrs. Baynes at last understood. She cried out like a cat with her tail caught in the door. "Good as Mr. Jennings has been to him. He still don't *trust* us!"

"I didn't say I didn't trust you," Adam said softly. "I just said this here money belongs to my daddy. And I aim to take it to him."

"But we'll pay it *back*, Adam!" Harry said. "It doesn't matter whose money it is! We'll pay it back when we get to California."

"You don't have no money to pay it back," Adam said, even more quietly. "Else you wouldn't have to borrow it."

"Leave Adam alone," Jason said wearily. "I was wrong to bring it up. Please don't quarrel." When they quarreled, Jason looked frightened somewhere behind his stiff face.

Adam was angry, but he spoke very softly. "You got your wagons all loaded up with gear you can't use. You ain't going to get to California with all that stuff because your oxen ain't going to pull it. It don't matter if you want to throw stuff out or not. You're going to have to do it. If it ain't here, it's going to be out there on the prairies somewhere. A thousand miles from nowhere. Right now you can sell your stuff in St. Louis. If you sell it, you'll save your stock, and you'll have the money to get you to Westport Landing."

Adam had never made a speech that went on so long. For a moment there was a weighty silence. Jessica, Ruth, Samuel seemed convinced. Asa looked sullen and hostile; he looked at Jason. Jason looked around. He was wavering.

But just when Adam thought he might win his point, Ishtar Baynes crowed. "So, *that's* it, Mr. Adam! He's mad, Mr. Jennings! He can't admit that he's wrong. He's been telling everybody that our oxen is going to drop in their tracks, and our

154

oxen just keeps on pulling these here wagons like they ain't never going to get tired. He's so mad about it he won't loan you his money. He's bound to do his best to wear them oxen out by making them walk from here to Westport Landing. Don't you all see it? You know him, Dr. Creekmore!" She peered at Harry with a meaningful grin. "You know what he's doing, don't you?"

Harry looked around. Very sober. "I don't think Adam's a bad man." He spoke in a low voice and looked nervously at Promise. She flashed a radiant smile at him as if to say, *What are these silly people talking about? How can they be arguing when you and I have found each other? We should only talk about how good the world is to have brought us together.*

Adam saw the look. Read part of it, Harry fooled everybody. Promise could not see his fear. Adam felt hurt and left out of things in a world where people were fools. He turned on Mrs. Baynes. "The oxen are just about tuckered out. If you don't lighten them wagons, then you ain't never going to get to California. Three hundred miles ain't nothing when you got the stony mountains to cross. Yes, it'd be good if the oxen was to break down between here and Westport Landing. Put some sense into your heads then. But they might make it out there. What's going to happen if they wear out a thousand miles from here? You're going to be lucky then to get to California with the clothes on your back. It don't matter if you do get a free ride to Westport Landing. These here oxen ain't going to make it. You got a choice. Throw a little out now. Sell it. Get some money for it. Or you're going to lose everything you got in the stony mountains."

"He thinks he's *giving* us the money" Mrs. Baynes shrilled. She would not even let anybody think about Adam's argument. She turned on Jason, her voice now like sugar syrup. "You can put some stuff in our cart, Mr. Jennings. We trust you. When we all get there, you can pay us the freight whenever you get the money. It don't matter if it takes you a year to get it, Mr. Jennings. We believe you're a man of your word!" She cast a withering look at Adam. "We ain't like some people."

Jason shook his head. He took a deep breath. "I told you," he said quietly, "I think Adam's right. He's got to take care of his father's money. We can't ask him to do anything else." The words were without feeling.

An Indian caused the final bitterness in St. Louis. They

were riding out at last, on the morning of the third day. The wagons pounded heavily, hard down on their steel springs, an awful burden to the treading oxen that went with downcast heads. Jessica was sitting back in the shade of the wagon top. Adam thought she preferred to separate herself from the rest of them. Something thin and cold between Jessica and Jason, tough, like the film that spreads over milk when it is boiled. Jason plodded at the lead team. He kept his eyes straight ahead, westward, toward Independence and Westport Landing.

Harry walked, leading the pack mule. He stayed near Promise, who sat next to Jessica. They talked and laughed, and Harry told stories.

The other wagons filed slowly behind, beating with the big wheels in the hard ruts, raising gritty dust, and finally came the Baynes cart. Mr. and Mrs. Baynes had taken some boxes from Jason's wagon. Mrs. Baynes looked very happy and kept looking back at the boxes as if they had become new possessions of her own.

Adam rode his mule with one big rifle slung nonchalantly, unloaded, across the saddle and with the gleaming pistol, also unloaded, in his belt. The other rifle was in the baggage of the mule Harry led along. Adam was thinking of nothing, entranced by the town and the motion and their going

The Indian was ancient and gray. He was dressed in leather garb, wet and dried so many times that it clung to him like a thin, second skin. A single feather stuck down in a knot of gray, coarse hair braided in a bun at the base of his skull. A relic from a vanishing West, still alive.

Something about Promise made him curious. He came staggering out to the side of the wagon and put a gnarled red-brown hand on the seat to steady himself and went stumbling along with its slow progress, gazing up at the girl with an intense, unvarying, and wildly hungry stare from deep and shining eyes. Eyes of madness maybe. His long, sharp face was burnished with weather and polished by sunshine and lined with great old age. He croaked out something, something guttural and incomprehensible and somehow rich in his coarse and alien tongue. It sounded like one word repeated over and over again in a tone of wonder. The girl, perceiving him suddenly at her side, jumped in her seat, uttered a sharp little cry of fright, and shrank away. Harry,

156

walking on the side of the wagon opposite to the old man, could not see just what was going on.

Adam's hound, happily trotting along with lolling tongue in the procession, began to bark at the Indian's heels, a loud, deep, melodious cry of canine pleasure at something to bark at. At that moment, a large beefy man stalked off the sidewalk with a curse of fury and struck the old man in the mouth. The Indian flew backward as though he had been made of sticks. He tumbled inert in the street, quivered, and then lay terribly still.

"That'll teach you to pester a white girl, you stinking son of a bitch!" The beefy man was screaming. He kicked the immobile Indian in the ribs. He would have kicked him again except that Promise screamed, jumping to her feet in the swaying wagon seat, with both hands raised to her face.

"Oh, don't! Don't hurt him! Please, please!" Her cry was like an animal shriek. And that was the instant when Jason turned around.

He saw Promise. He saw the big white man savagely kicking at Adam's dog who was playfully jumping back as if the white man was the greatest sport ever invented for dogs. Jason saw the fallen Indian. Harry said, "The Indian said something, and that man there came out and killed him." Jason ran back in confusion.

"Why did you strike that man? He didn't mean any harm. We don't need your help!"

The big stranger was outraged. "What the hell you talking about, you goddamn pissant! You want *Indians* talking to your women? White women? You want her to be a squaw before she's half growed up?" He was yelling.

Jason went white. A crowd was gathering. He had to shout to be heard. "I don't need your help for anything. I don't need any of your cheap advice about how to raise my children!"

The beefy man had taken more than he could bear. With one huge fist he slammed Jason in the jaw. Jason was large and strong. He was not knocked unconscious. But he fell in a daze against the wagon. Suddenly bleeding from the mouth. He put his hands to his face; blood poured through his fingers. Promise screamed again. Jessica stood up in her seat and yelled around the wagon for Adam.

But it was the no-name dog who made the first response. When the big stranger hit Jason, the hound decided things

157

were serious. He jumped at the stranger and sank his young teeth firmly into his right lower leg. The stranger uttered a bloodcurdling yell of pain and began trying to kick the hound off with his other leg. The hound held on and bit down very hard.

Adam came riding up on his mule and saw what was happening. He did not understand it. But he brought his rifle up like a club, and just as the stranger looked up, conscious of a fresh attack, Adam brought the heavy butt of the rifle down with all his might, and hit the white man in the face with it. There was a sound of bone cracking. With cool and methodical skill, Adam came back down with the long steel rifle barrel and beat him across the top of his thick round head. The stranger fell on his face in the dust.

Harry stood still, dumbfounded and helpless. Samuel walked up, looking stupidly around, not knowing what to do until Adam yelled at him.

"Give me a hand with Jason. Get him in the wagon."

Samuel, without a word, picked Jason up and heaved him into the wagon, where Jessica took him in her arms and cradled his bleeding head in her lap.

"Come on, goddammit! Let's move," Adam shouted.

Adam's dog was still barking at the fallen white man. Now Adam called him off. He set the dog on Jason's oxen, as the dog had run the cow in once for milking. He ran happily around the beasts, barking in joy. The oxen rolled frightened eyes at him and moved.

Adam was fiercely proud. He felt not one particle of sympathy for the man he had left broken in the street. He was filled with grim satisfaction because he had proven to all of them—to Promise and to Jessica and to all the rest—that he, Adam Cloud, could do things that they could not do. He could protect them.

But only a mile later Ishtar Baynes looked at him with a cold pleasure. "We could of missed all that if we'd been on the steamboat, Mr. Adam. If you hadn't been so stingy.

# 27

Jason never thanked Adam. Never even mentioned the incident. He sat bleakly on the wagon seat while Adam took over the driving. Jason's face was swollen and blue, and they did not sing or read the Bible at night for a long time.

Jessica spoke to Adam quietly on the first evening after they left St. Louis. "Mr. Cloud, I want you to know that I appreciate what you did for my husband. For us."

"He don't seem to appreciate it none hisself, ma'am."

"It's his way. He doesn't believe in violence."

"Does that mean you believe in it, ma'am? In hitting people? Is that why you're thanking me?"

Jessica remained cool, searching his face for something.

"No, Mr. Cloud. I believe in peace. But I believe in unselfishness, too, and to me you seemed to do a very unselfish thing. You jumped right in there without a thought for your own safety."

Adam turned red. "I wasn't in no danger. I was quicker than he was. I don't reckon I had time to think."

"That was the beauty of it. It was spontaneous, thoughtless, on your part. You saw what had to be done and did it."

Adam laughed, nervous and unsettled by her. "It wasn't beautiful, ma'am. It was kind of messy, if you ask me. I hope my hound don't get sick from biting that feller."

Jessica laughed and tossed her head. Her hair was a dark yellow. It seemed very fine. "Don't be embarrassed, Mr. Cloud. I'm saying I appreciate a selfless act when I see it. You were very unselfish."

She smiled at him. Her teeth were white and even. Adam yearned to kiss her. She seemed so warm, so friendly. He fought off the impulse, told himself sternly that he was an outsider to all these people. Nothing for him here.

"Look, Mrs. Jennings, I don't know what you're talking about. You want to know the truth? I liked what I did. I really did like hitting that feller. I ain't enjoyed nothing so much in ages."

He glared at her and walked away, leaving her looking after him. He knew that he had hurt her. He knew that she would gather her dignity around her like a robe and hide her hurt. And he felt terrible.

The land now was rolling and densely wooded most of the time. Pleasant country. Farms being cleared. Dark soil. Gray rocks outcropping often. Nobody had much to say to Adam. He felt his isolation, cultivated it, was pleased to show them that he needed them for nothing. Maybe in Westport Landing he would leave them. Find somebody else to ride with. Forget everybody here. Forget Harry.

But Harry was the first to make up. He did not apologize. He just began talking as if nothing had happened. "Hell, Adam, you know first thing I'm going to do when we get to Westport Landing? I'm going to take another hot bath. I've got fifty cents laid back. I found it in the pocket where I keep my glasses. I get so tired of being dirty. I never have been this dirty in my whole life before."

"You can wash in the creeks, the way I do. I don't feel so dirty. My clothes don't look too good, I reckon. But I wash something ever night."

"Well, I wash my face, Adam," Harry said delicately. "You know that. But the idea of stripping off all my clothes out here in the open doesn't appeal to me."

"They ain't nobody to look at you."

"Well, what if somebody came up?"

"I don't reckon the world would stop."

"Well, it's the principle of the thing. How would I talk to people if I didn't have my clothes on? And I don't like cold water. What if a snake bit me?"

"Bite him back."

Harry laughed. "I'm terrified of snakes. If I was to see a snake in the water with me, I'd die. You know the thing that horrifies me more than anything else?"

"I couldn't tell you."

"I'm afraid of dying dirty. You know, it's a foolish thing. But I think if I should die dirty, why, then I'd be dirty for all eternity."

"More than likely you'd just be dirt."

"Harry was silent awhile. "That's a sad thought, isn't it? I always thought when I died I'd like to fly up on a cloud some-

160

where and look down at the world and see how it all came out. Don't you think that's possible, Adam? We ought to know how things come out."

"I don't talk about religion," Adam said. "I ain't never had no experience." He thought of what happened to the Indian in St. Louis and the white man he had pounded into the street and the man who brought them across the Cumberland River on the ferry from Nashville. How had all that come out?

Harry laughed. "Well, I never had an experience either, Adam." He turned sober quickly. "I must confess something to you, Adam. I noticed a faintly unpleasant odor around Miss Jennings today, when we were talking. You know, it's amazing. I never in all my life smelled a white woman that smelled, ah, *strong* before today. I must say, it was quite a shock." Harry wrinkled his nose and looked perplexed.

"Everybody shits and everybody sweats," Adam said. "Even Presidents and girls."

Harry suddenly burst into laughter. Something nervous released. "Adam I love your way of plain speaking. I do want you to know that I like you. I sincerely like you."

Adam laughed Harry off. But he was more pleased than he could let on. Harry was peculiar, unlike anybody else Adam had ever known. When Harry was in a good mood, he made all the world shine.

Ishtar Baynes stayed away from them both. Harry spoke to her warmly, lifting his white hat and bowing sometimes and smiling as if she had been a Southern beauty. But she had nothing to get from Harry Creekmore, and she treated him with distant contempt, making little comments about him when Jason was near, comments that Jason could not understand, but that let Harry know that she had not forgotten what she had learned about him far off back down the long road.

Adam treated her with indifference. But then one morning he happened to be riding to the rear of the little procession as the wagons went rolling through a pleasant little village with a church and a schoolhouse, with white fences surrounding neat white houses of frame, not logs, and scrubbed women in long dresses looked at them through glass windows opened to the spring day.

Ishtar Baynes made an abrupt, wistfully cheerful remark.

"This sure is beautiful country, Mr. Adam. And I reckon it must be better yet out in California."

The whimsical tone of her voice struck Adam. "Where you from anyway, Mrs. Baynes?"

"Oh, I'm from a lot of places," she said with a laugh that was not hostile for once. Her husband was asleep, snoring like a very slow bellows in the back of the springless cart. Mrs. Baynes sat in the seat with her arms wrapped around her knees, looking west over the thin, high backs of her lumbering oxen.

"Well, you must of been born somewheres, Mrs. Baynes," Adam said.

"Oh, I was born all right. In a ship on the high seas. The H.M.S. *Royal Pearl!* My mamma told me about it dozens of times."

"On a ship, Mrs. Baynes?"

"My daddy was a ship's captain, Mr. Adam. He was English. So was my mamma. My mamma didn't like for him to leave her home all by herself, and so she got to going with him on the ship, and she taken my sister Irene along. So she was with him in the middle of the Atlantic Ocean when I was born."

"Well, I declare."

Mrs. Baynes laughed that wistful laugh again. "So I don't reckon I'm from anywheres. I'm the gift of the sea to the world. Mamma used to say I was Jonah cast up on dry land by the whale. Only I ain't never figured out where I was supposed to end up. Jonah went to Nineveh, didn't he? And he did some pretty fine things, didn't he?"

"I reckon so, Mrs. Baynes."

"Well, maybe I'll find my Nineveh in California. I sure do hope so, Mr. Adam. I'm tired of all this moving around. I ain't done nothing but move all my life."

Adam laughed warmly in spite of himself. "I hope so, too, Mrs. Baynes. I hope California's good for all of us."

Mrs. Baynes seemed to forget her envy and her malice because she was remembering something else. Old dreams maybe. And for just a few moments there was something in her face that was soft, thoughtful, and unconscious of anybody else in the world.

"You, was telling me about ... about where you come from, Mrs. Baynes." Adam wanted her to go on talking. There was something faintly disturbing in the change he saw

162

in her, looking off into the green countryside as if she had forgotten the kind of person she was.

"Oh, yes. Well, my daddy put me and mamma and my sister Irene ashore in Boston. Massachusetts. I was a sickly child, Mr. Adam. You can't tell that by looking at me now. I'm right tough now. Lord, I've had to be tough to get through all I've got by in my day. But I was sickly when I was born. Couldn't breathe good."

"They's lots of sickly children, I reckon," Adam said solemnly. "I had me a brother and two sisters that died."

"Well, I didn't die," Mrs. Baynes said, and her dark little eyes flashed like electric sparks in her head.

Adam looked off into the silent woods. They had passed through the village so quickly. It lay behind them now. He was full of peace. Nothing mattered except this soft and magical stillness and the creeping of the wagons. Hypnotic. Like a big clock ticking very softly.

Mrs. Baynes talked on. "Of course, now, Mr. Adam, I ain't one to brag. But I've always said that what set me off from other women was what was inside me. What draws men to me is my heart. And I think I got that from my mamma. She was Welsh."

"Welsh, Mrs. Baynes?"

"It's a place in England, Mr. Adam. My daddy was from a place that was called Bristol, and my mamma was Welsh, and my mamma said my daddy married her because she could sing. They all say the Welsh folks has got beautiful voices because they got beautiful souls. And when somebody that's got Welsh blood in her body kisses you, Mr. Adam, you get her soul right there in your mouth." She laughed. The spell of gentle enchantment was shattered. Ishtar Baynes could pour obscenity into anything that had to do with love.

"Well, my daddy put my mamma ashore in Boston with me and my sister, and he give her some money, and he said he'd call back in six months and take us home to England again when I got big enough to travel and got to breathing right." She shook her head in hard and bitter wisdom. "Men, they're all alike. Give 'em ten feet of freedom, and they'll run for the gate like rabbits. That's the last we ever seen of him."

"Oh," Adam said gravely, feigning the sadness men conventionally utter in the presence of death. "You mean he drowned in the sea? I'm sorry to hear it, Mrs. Baynes." A jay

163

called, and the sound died away, and Adam thought of the bird flying on freely through the woods, so green and dense.

"No," Mrs. Baynes said, again uttering that vaguely obscene laugh. "He sailed off to England, and then he shipped out to China. Around the Cape of Good Hope and Africa. And he never did come back for my mamma and me and Irene. He stayed out there. Free like the waves."

"I declare."

"Never sent one red penny to support us. Never even wrote to explain hisself. Never answered a one of her letters to him. Just treated us like we was dead."

"Oh," Adam said. He thought of his own father. In California. California faced on China.

"Mamma, she took on over him something awful. Couldn't stop hating him till the day she died. Wrote to the company in England. Went to see their agent in Boston and all such like that. But it didn't do no good. You know how it is. A man can do just about what he wants in this here world. Especially if he's captain of a sailing boat and can sail off to China any time he takes a notion."

"Couldn't your mamma have gone back to England?"

Ishtar Baynes laughed unpleasantly. The laugh that told Adam he was really very ignorant. "She didn't have no money to buy a ticket, Mr. Adam. The agent for the company, he said it was something personal. He said the company didn't interfere in anything personal. So there we was."

"I declare, Mrs. Baynes."

"So mamma settled down to running a hotel." She laughed knowingly. "We was in the hotel business till mamma died."

"That must have been right interesting."

"Oh, it was real exciting, Mr. Adam. We runned hotels especially for sailors. But for other folks as well. Poor mamma always did have a weakness for sailors. She loved uniforms. That's why she married my daddy in the first place. He had a white captain's suit for summers and a blue captain's suit with brass buttons on it for the winter. They cost plenty, them suits. Mamma used to sit up at night and talk about them uniforms. You get a suit with brass buttons, and it costs plenty, Mr. Adam."

"I wouldn't know, Mrs. Baynes."

She eyed his homespun pants and his shabby shirt. "I don't reckon you would. I bet you ain't never owned a brass button

164

in your life." Mrs. Baynes laughed. The more she talked, the more she found funny about her own story. "Well, ever once in a while mamma would entertain somebody that'd knowed my daddy. Mamma even got to send him a few messages."

"Messages?"

"Well, I reckon you could call 'em that. She sent word that she prayed ever night for his ship to be blowed down to the bottom of the ocean sea so he'd be eat up by little fishes that taken one bite at a time."

Adam laughed. "She sounds like she sure did stay mad at him."

"Well, mamma wasn't one of your folks that can forgive and forget. She couldn't do neither one. But she was pretty good in her way. She taught me and my sister Irene everything we know. And we seen some of the country, too. Mamma was kind of footloose, you know. We had us a hotel in Boston, and then we was in New Haven, Connecticut, for a while, and after that we come down to Baltimore."

"Why'd you get out of the hotel business, Mrs. Baynes?"

Mrs. Baynes laughed in her disagreeable way. "Well I just got too old for it, Mr. Adam. Then mamma died, and we'd moved around so much we just never did get our business on the ground. Always just one step ahead of the bill collectors. Besides, it ain't no pleasure trying to entertain sailors when you ain't got the place for it. You need soft chairs and nice lamps and a pianoforte and a big nigger at the door in a fancy black suit to make them sailors feel like they're worth something when they come to call. You ever been in a hotel like that, Mr. Adam?" Her keen eyes pricked him, and she laughed.

Adam innocently shook his head. "No, ma'am. I ain't never been in but one hotel in my whole life, and that was the one in Nashville, Tennessee, and I didn't see no sailors around."

"It's a pity," Mrs. Baynes said, grinning broadly. "Fine young feller like you. You could have yourself a big time in a hotel like the one my mamma used to run." Ishtar Baynes burst into a peal of laughter. Adam felt like a fool and did not know why.

Harry snickered in a bleak, knowing, and very superior way when Adam told him of the conversation. "Why, Adam, that woman's been a whore! Can't you see it?"

165

Adam blushed, and his face felt as hot as a lantern. "Harry, I don't reckon I know what a whore is. I've read about whores in the Bible. But . . . to tell the truth, I don't know what they do."

Harry laughed warmly and clapped him on the back. "Good God, Adam Cloud, you are the most innocent man I've ever seen. You don't know what a whore is! Oh, Adam, if I could just be like you!" Harry laughed, not harshly. Then he told Adam about whores.

"You mean all you have to do is pay them?"

"Sometimes you don't even have to pay them money," Harry said ruefully. "Sometimes all you have to do is say poetry in their ears."

"She's so ugly!" Adam said, wondering how any man could ever have made love to Ishtar Baynes.

"All cats look gray in the dark," Harry said philosophically. "Old saying. And I reckon it's true enough. You can put your arms around a woman in the dark, do that to her. And you can imagine she's the Queen of England if you want. Anybody. And you get good out of it."

Adam's mind raced from bafflement to danger. "She knows all about you, Harry. A woman like that! You better be careful."

Harry smiled, confident that he knew much more about the world than Adam did. "All you have to do is be kind to her, Adam. Look how I treat her!"

"And she treats you like dirt!"

"The journey's just begun," Harry said. "Give me time. Nobody in my whole life has disliked me who got to know me well. That's all it takes. Just knowing me. I don't understand sometimes. But people like me. You wait and see. She's not going to do anything to hurt me."

The next day the mercurial Harry Creekmore crawled out of his blankets to face the pre-dawn dimness with a dark and harrowed look on his handsome face.

"Adam, I woke up all night long."

"I thought you'd got used to sleeping on the ground."

"No, it's not sleeping on the ground. It's a dream I had all night. About my daddy."

"I dream about my daddy, too," Adam said wistfully.

"I bet your dreams don't keep you waking up all night."

"No."

"Listen, my daddy don't even know he's dead. He keeps

166

coming to me in the night and jumping on me about Promise. He's done it before, but last night was the worst of all."

"What about her?" Adam was mystified.

"Oh, you know. He keeps butting into my sleep and cussing me out for being in love with her. He keeps telling me she's a bastard. And no Creekmore ought to marry a bastard."

"It's just a dream."

"That's the point, dammit! It doesn't seem like a dream, Adam. Really it doesn't. He gets right down in my face and tells me that if I marry that girl, I'm never going to be known in Savannah society again in my life! He says he won't ever let her come to the house. He says he won't remember me in his will."

Adam thought the conversation was foolish. "He didn't remember you in his will. He cut you off without a cent."

"Adam, you have so little imagination. My father is *tormenting* me. When I'm asleep. It's like everything was true that's going to happen in my dream. And it wakes me up, and I'm *afraid* to go back to sleep again. I'm going to be a walking *shadow* of myself." Harry's wail made it seem that he was shocked to offer the world any reduction in his grand presence.

Adam got impatient now. "Well, your daddy's dead. You ain't going to be taking Promise back to your house in Georgia because you don't have no house in Georgia now. And I reckon them snobs in Georgia has forgot all about you anyway. The way I see it, you ain't got nothing to worry about. Just be happy with Promise and forget your daddy."

Harry was not consoled. He looked miserable. "But that's just it, Adam. My daddy came around all night long, yelling at me. Telling me I'm just a goddamned failure. Telling me he always knew I didn't have any sense. Telling me to ... Well, Adam, I can't use the word he uses. But he tells me to do it to Promise if I want, but not to marry her. And when I see her in the daylight, I keep hearing how mad he is at me. And I can't talk to her. I've not had anything to say to her for days."

"She talks when you don't. I don't hear much quiet from you two."

"I feel just awful, Adam. Just awful."

"Well, maybe that's what you want to do, Harry. Use her

167

and throw her away. Maybe your daddy's telling you something you want to hear."

Harry's face, obscured by the faint light, took on an expression of earnest intensity. "No, Adam, no! I swear it. She's so pure. I've never known a woman so pure. I want to marry her, Adam. I don't want to make love to her except to have her adorable children. Just think how beautiful our children are going to be. No, Adam. Believe me this one time. My thoughts about her are all pure. That's why I love her so much. Because of what she's done for me inside. She's purified my soul, Adam."

Adam was embarrassed and impatient. Harry reminded Adam of those people at camp meeting who got saved and gave their testimony whether you wanted to hear it or not. Adam was perplexed; he had never had an experience. He had never been in love.

"Hell, Harry. Hell." He walked away without another word, thinking about the oxen and how they had to be yoked together for another terrible day of pulling. He thought of Promise. The luck Harry had to be loved by her.

# 28

Ruth spent time with Rebecca in that stuffy wagon fitted out like an unbelievable room. Jouncing across Missouri. She listened tirelessly to the twenty-year-old gossip of the person she always called "Poor Rebecca." Ruth imagined that the same madness might come to her. Or some other calamity. Anybody could be struck down. And so she was compassionate because she believed people should share one another's burdens.

Adam liked Ruth. She was large without being fat. Big bones. Clear blue eyes. A monumental quality that made her something to hide behind in a storm. There was not one sharp feature in her face. On the contrary she resembled something molded by the Creator in one of His more jovial moments. A very pleasant face. A look of guileless sincerity to her, and an endless curiosity.

She was curious about everything. "What kind of tree is that? I wonder if that flower would grow in California?" And she was always saying to her childen, "Look!" Look at that chestnut tree, children! Isn't it beautiful? Look at that cloud. The one right up there. Don't it look like a sleeping dog? Look at that cornfield, children. Ain't it pretty and neat? Not a weed."

Sometimes she had the children gathering wildflowers by the road as the wagons creaked along. And sometimes she sat up on the high wagon seat with a child on each side, talking to them, telling them what she knew about the world. Henry listened hungrily. And even Rachael looked around when Ruth pointed to things. A woman with magic about her. She loved to talk about her mother and father. The farm where she had been born back in Ohio. She loved to hand on stories from the great Revolution. Her grandfather had fought against the British, and he had held her on his knee when she was young to tell her stories of Yankee Doodle and General Washington.

Everything in the world was interesting. She yearned for her children to know all of it. And so she talked pleasantly, constantly, except when her husband was around. Respectful then and maybe afraid. Adam liked to ride alongside her wagon when she sat up there on the seat. He liked to listen to her. She never once reproached him for hoarding his money. His father's money. But when he saw her nestling her children in her large arms, he felt guilty. *I should have paid our way.* Too late now, though sometimes when the road bent close to the Missouri River, they saw steamboats on the water, churning effortlessly along.

Ruth was kind and gentle. But she had her prejudices. She did not want to go West. She dreaded California. "We was making it all right in Ironton," she confided to Adam in a soft, wistful voice. "I had me such a pretty garden. You ought to of seen my daffodils. In the spring our yard just turned yellow, I tell you. They smelled so sweet. Don't you like the smell of daffodils, Mr. Adam?"

"Oh yes, ma'am. We had daffodils." Not many. His mother had no talent for growing things.

"I loved my garden. I was at home there." She looked down at her children. A shadow of anxiety. "And I love my children, too. What kind of folks do you reckon we're going to find in California, Mr. Adam?" Her mild voice taut. "Jason says they ain't been spoilt yet. Out there. He says it's a big land. He things we can find us a place real easy. Up in the hills, he says. In a green valley. And we can start farming. But if you ask me, they's lots of folks out there already. And I figure they've mostly been spoilt. Gold. It don't do nobody no good. We're going to have a lot of roughneck gold diggers for neighbors. Ain't no telling what kind of influence they're going to have on our children."

"It won't be so bad," Adam said. "My daddy went out there to hunt gold. He ain't no roughneck. Folks is folks, I reckon." He hoped it was so.

"I ain't meaning to say nothing bad about your daddy, Mr. Adam. I've told my husband again and again that you're the best one for us. You're the only one that ain't being selfish by going to California."

"I don't see how you figure that," Adam said gruffly. He was pleased that Ruth had defended him.

"Well that's what I think. We're selfish, trying to get away from the world. I don't reckon you can do that. Even in California. What do you think. Mr. Adam?"

Adam thought about lying to her. Giving her the assurance he knew Harry could pour out in an instant. But her penetrating gaze went to his heart. She was worried sick, and he could not lie to her. "I don't know, Mrs. Jennings."

"Your friend Dr. Creekmore is a handsome man, Mr. Cloud," Jessica said.

"Harry? Well, I reckon, ma'am. I ain't never thought much about it."

"Of course not," Jessica said with a faint and ironic smile. "He is the sort of man who captivates women. I hope he is honest."

Adam said nothing.

"My daughter is enraptured by him."

"I reckon she likes him all right."

"Likes him!" Jessica snorted. "She glows like a street lamp whenever he looks at her. It's almost scandalous." Jessica patted absent-mindedly at her hair. It was bright in the sunlight.

"Well, he likes her, too, ma'am. Harry's right took with her." Adam cleared his throat and summoned up words he had heard other people use. "His intentions are honorable, ma'am. I know they are."

Jessica gave him a real smile and turned thoughtful. "You know, there was a time and not so long ago when men looked at me before they looked at my daughter. But times change, don't they? People used to tell me life passed quickly. I didn't believe them. Our hearts stay young. I don't feel any different than I did years ago. But our faces wither and grow old."

Jessica's tone was so unexpectedly filled with feeling that Adam rushed awkwardly to defend her against herself. Against time. "Why, you're still beautiful, ma'am. I wouldn't be worrying much about time if I was you!"

She threw him a dazzling smile. "Mr. Cloud, thank you. Thank you so much! It's a wonderful thing for a woman when a man tells her she is beautiful." The smile died. Harry and Promise were ahead, walking arm in arm on the roadside. Jessica looked at them with a longing that pained Adam when he saw it. "But what is happening to me is happening to all of us. We are all growing old. Or else we are dying. My youth is behind me. There isn't much more for me to do but to find a house in California and be a good wife. Do the same thing every day from now on till something takes me into the grave."

Adam could think of nothing to say to her. She sounded bitter and sad. He looked where she looked, to Harry and Promise. They were talking, laughing, so completely enraptured with each other that they forgot everything else, and their love only used the great world itself as a flimsy frame to encircle their dreams.

Adam envied Harry. A hopeless, sad envy mingled with affection. Harry told Adam things Adam wanted to believe about himself. Harry told Promise grand things about the world. He talked about a thousand places with such authority that Adam could swear Harry had been there.

"Harry, it ain't none of my business. But someday she's going to find out. How can you tell her all those stories if they ain't true? What's she going to think when she finds out they're all lies?"

Adam could not imagine a world where lies went undiscovered forever. Buy Harry only laughed in his grand way. "Why should she ever know? Don't be provincial, Adam. The

171

world is what we say it is. I make a better world by talking than anybody's ever seen. What's wrong with that?"

Adam could give no answer. And Promise was in love with Harry. A beautiful thing to see. The girl at that wonderful stage when she had just become a woman. Harry had stepped into her innocence and become her guide. They would share things, intimate things in time, and the more he was with her, the more she would never be able to think of simple memories without thinking of him. He did it all so easily that Adam felt himself to be drab and worthless in comparison.

Adam looked at Promise in the starving way that he had once long ago admired a troop of brightly painted wooden soldiers in a store in Bourbonville near Christmas time. He and his father together, the man's hand on the boy's shoulder, yearning in the hearts of both of them. He knew as he stared at them so hungrily that on the bright, cold morning of Christ's nativity, some child would have those soldiers under one of the green Christmas trees that were becoming so popular in that age, and Adam Cloud would have only an orange.

Every year at Christmas time Joel Cloud did what he could for his only surviving child. What he could do invariably was to buy an orange, brought upriver from far away to the warm south. Adam loved his father for the orange, for the way the tall and stoop-shouldered man would grin in his shy way and not take a single slice of it. "It's your Christmas present, Adam, and you pleasure me more by eating it all yourself than you would if I ate even a little piece of it. You can't understand these things till you have a boy of your own, and then maybe you'll remember and know what I mean."

Now he looked at Promise and yearned for her in the same detached way he had longed for the soldiers, and he reflected with wry amusement at himself that now he did not even have an orange.

"Hey, Adam, I've solved my problem!"

"What's that, Harry?"

"With my daddy, Adam. When he comes to see me at night. In my dreams."

"Harry, he don't come to see you. It ain't nothing, a dream."

"If it happens to you, it's something. But listen, I've fixed him."

172

"How?"

"I've told him I'm a doctor now. If he wants to see me, he's got to have an appointment. And I told my assistant not to give him an appointment. So he doesn't come anymore, Adam."

"You're crazy, Harry. Just crazy." Adam laughed.

Harry laughed, too, and polished his glasses with his handkerchief. He always looked strange without his glasses, like somebody isolated and lifted to a different world, leaving an illusion of body mysteriously behind in his flight. "Well, it worked. I think I'm free of him forever. Adam. Forever."

Harry told Promise great adventure stories. Adam sat by the fire with the rest and listened. He never forgot those moments. The cheerful light blazing against Harry's animated face, the big glasses removed so that the shadows shook their fitful way across his finely carved features and made his words seem true, because in that firelit gloom anything was possible. Harry told good stories, and even if they were lies, in the firelight nothing mattered but the stories themselves.

Harry talked about medical school in Germany. He spoke of his teachers by their German names, and he talked in mocking condescension of how some students had vomited the first time they saw a surgeon dissect a cadaver. He told how cadavers smelled of formaldehyde and how formaldehyde burned his hands and what he thought about the first cadaver he ever cut into. "I wondered what woman he had loved, and I wondered if anybody had ever loved him in return. I wondered about the mother who had rocked him as a baby, and I wondered if a father had planned great things for him and why he had come down to be a pauper who died, selling his pitiful body to be cut up by someone like me." Promise wept openly. Adam felt a lump in his throat. And if Harry Creekmore had never been closer to a cadaver than the definition of the word in his medical dictionary, still somebody had done what he described, and if you took Harry's sentimental thoughts, you could clothe any wasted and naked corpse with them, and you could weep for all those anonymous people who ended up on the cold stone slabs of medical dissection tables.

Adam listened to this and dozens of other yarns in rapt silence. They beguiled the night. But afterwards he was always troubled. Not just by the lies. It was that Harry threw himself into his lies with such terrible warmth that Adam

173

knew Harry Creekmore was believing every word of his own tales when he told them. He took off his glasses. He looked into the swarm of amber shadows dancing out from the hypnotic fire. And he could make the world exactly what he wanted it to be, and the past was but a tissue of insubstantial fantasies that Harry could turn into anything. Something vaguely blasphemous about what Harry was doing. Adam thought Harry was taking the place of God.

They all turned in early so they could get up early now. Adam had got them used to the idea. Jason looked at the oxen and worried silently, though when he spoke he was always full of confidence. But he could not talk away their hoarse huffing when they pulled the weight of those ponderous wagons up the slightest incline. And sometimes to ford an insignificant creek, the wagons had to be double-teamed, and all the men had to get down in the water and labor at the wheels until their backs were nearly broken and they were covered with filth, and even then they only barely made it. Get up early, and they could take more than an hour to rest the oxen at noon, when the sun was beginning to assault them with a terrible power. So they were early to bed, and the camp was silent by the time it was full dark.

But Harry took a whale-oil lamp, and every night he lit the lamp and hung it up in the tent and sat there studying until his weak eyes were about to pop out of his head. Adam dozed, waked up, watched Harry, felt so pained by the spectacle that he shut his own eyes and worried. Harry's eyes screwed up in those enormous glasses by sheer physical effort and the will to endure, and he read slowly, with a concentration intense and full of agony, like looking into the dazzling sun.

He studied anatomy by feeling himself. He begged Adam for kind permission to examine Adam's legs and arms and the joints in his fingers, the position of his ribs. Once Adam was wakened from sound sleep by the white light of the lamp in his face and by the unpleasant smell of whale oil, and it was Harry, down close to him, scrutinizing the lines in his neck and shoulders. "I can't get under my own chin," Harry said, meek, embarrassed, and full of apology. "I thought I could look at yours. I didn't think you'd mind."

Adam sat up in bed, drunk with sleep and wild-eyed. "My God, Harry! You're crazy. You get away from me."

Harry sat soberly, quietly, an expression of infinite gravity making him look very old all of a sudden, like one of the wise men intent on a star. "No, Adam," he said softly, "that's one thing I'm not. Crazy. I'm just trying to learn how to be a doctor. I want to be a doctor. A good doctor. I want to help people, Adam. I want to make up for all the bad things I've done in the world, and I've decided that being a doctor's a good way."

The oxen strained on, toiling in the yokes, their thick tongues hanging out now in the afternoons when they had labored for the sunny day. In the evening Adam could tell that they were bone tired. He had to lead them to the thickest grass and wait awhile before they had the energy to eat. Sometimes a shower blew darkly over the earth and drenched them, plastering shirts to human backs, making Adam lower his head against the driving rain. He was uncomfortable then, but he had always possessed a resigned calm in the face of bad weather, and so when he was being rained on, he let his thoughts sink into him like fire dying into its coals, and he rode along with his mind a carefully drawn blank. But the oxen suffered from the mud the rain made, and they worked harder and were even more tired at night.

Halfway across Missouri they broke another wheel. This one on Asa's wagon. They fixed it. They found a blacksmith who was glad for the business, and he only charged them a dollar. So the wheel was mended, and they still had the extra wheel that Adam and Samuel had brought for a spare. Jason smiled ruefully and cautioned them all that they really must watch where they were going.

"They ain't no blacksmiths out on the plains, Mr. Jennings." Adam said.

Jason looked thoughtful. "Maybe we better buy an anvil and some blacksmithing tools. Maybe you could learn how to do blacksmithing, Adam."

Adam shook his head. "We need to throw things out, Mr. Jennings."

Jason sighed and lifted his eyes heavenward as if he had been destined to suffer much more tribulation than any man should bear in a sporting universe. "Adam, I tell you for the last time. We cannot afford to throw anything away. When we get there we are going to need everything we have." He shook his head. "We'll need more."

Adam looked at new iron plows, at cast-iron stoves, at the extra harness for horses they did not own, at furniture, at heavy wooden crates stocked with clothes, with books, with mementoes, with God knows what. He measured all of it as a weight crushing their chances to make it safely across the plains. And once beyond the plains the mountains were to pass. June was trickling away, dispersing like the slow, red dust swimming in the air when the wheels had ground by in the road. July coming up on them like death.

He felt a crush of terrible sentiment for the plodding oxen. All they could do was to live and to be tired, to sleep, and to toil. He cared for them like a loving father. He bought a stiff brush along the way, and every night when he unyoked them, he and Henry took turns brushing them down. Every night he looked after their hoofs, digging the dirt out of that deeply cloven region that could so easily become impacted and infected, and when the cleaning was done, he rubbed tallow into the hoofs to protect them. And every night he saw that only Henry took note of what he was doing.

Jason kept a journal. "People will look back on our journey as a historic accomplishment someday," he said. "Think how good it would be if Moses had kept a journal." At night, after camp was made, Jason invariably retired to write in his book, a ledger with black leather binding and pages tipped with red. Asa looked on unyoking the oxen as something Adam the servant was supposed to do, and he played with his little girl, held her in his arms, or walked with her. Samuel went inside his wagon to take his nightly dressing down from Rebecca and to see if her chamberpot needed to be emptied. She railed at him as he departed with it as if he had been responsible for the unclean thing her bowels produced.

Adam saw that the oxen had grass to eat, and if five o'clock came—camping hour—and there was not enough grass, Adam would make them go on until they found a meadow for the oxen to graze. He shifted the teams daily. He even cared for the pitiful oxen of Mrs. Baynes. They were old, skin and bones, with big eyes red and worn. Mrs. Baynes refused to let him rotate their two oxen with the rest. She was devoured with the stupid conviction that hers were the best. She did not want to wear them down by letting them carry a load that was not theirs. Or maybe it was that in spite of her protests she knew that the Jennings wagons were too heavy and would finally kill any animal hitched to them.

"You never know about folks, Mr. Adam. I put my oxen in with them others, and something happens. How could I be sure I'd ever get my oxen back?"

"Mrs. Baynes, you was telling me that I ought to trust people when you was wanting me to pay everybody's fare to Westport Landing on the steamboat!"

"Well, now, you didn't do it, did you, Mr. Adam?" She spoke to him with arched eyebrows, and Adam could not think of any answer to give her.

He only looked at the poor oxen toiling along, and he saw them lathering in white foam on the thick amber hair of their gloassy backs, and he heard the dreadful heaviness of the wagons rolling, pounding, rumbling on those good roads in Missouri, and he tried to imagine the plains and the mountains and all that lay out there ahead of them.

# 29

The trees began to give way. The thick forest, still and deep and green, was broken in patches by good farms, and the clumps of woodland grew more and more widely separated, trees lining the courses of little streams and otherwise the great land, heaving in long swells of waving grass.

"It's like the sea!" Harry said with a whisper. They all felt awed and abashed. Here was the edge of the prairie, and they had never seen anything like it before. They had to cross it. No shelter out there. The road would dip into a hollow place, and there was a confining comfort to the landscape. But then it would rise again, and they could see for miles, the land rolling and rolling and shadowed in dark, drifting pools by the sailing clouds.

Harry was more troubled then anybody else by the enlarging vistas. Space seemed to suck the substance out of him. He told Adam quietly, desperately, that he had a peculiar fantasy of drowning in air. He spent a whole morning riding in and out of the swells on the mule, avoiding Promise, avoiding everyone. He did not want to talk or to call attention to himself in any way. Like a frog, perched with beating heart in a marsh, knowing that a snake is slithering somewhere nearby.

Then at noon when they took lunch on one of the elevations and felt the warm wind sweeping at them from the west, Harry quietly took off his glasses and folded them away. He immediately felt better. Space contracted to a hazy blur of bright colors that offered him a pleasant concealment. He talked to Promise then. She told him how handsome he looked without his glasses. But then she said she liked him with his glasses, too. They made him look so intelligent. She was so forward that back in Georgia she would have been considered unladylike. But Harry loved it. It was innocence. She had not learned manners yet. Nor pretense.

"It's so barren out here," she said, looking forward to the grassland with foreboding. "I don't like it when you can't see trees. I like the shade."

"The sun's not hot today," Jessica said with a gentle laugh. "Don't complain."

"Oh, I'm not complaining," Promise said. "I wouldn't think of complaining. But I'll be glad when we see trees again. Lots of trees."

"In California," Jason said. "It is a state rich in timber. You will see." He looked around uneasily. "I sympathize with Promise. It's like the desert."

"Oh, husband, there's grass here," Jessica said, in a good mood. "You don't find grass in the desert. I think it's beautiful here. Look at the space. It makes you feel that the world is still clean."

Adam agreed with Jessica. He had never seen anything so beautiful. He wanted to hold on to the beauty, to keep it so that it would never go away. That would be immortality, he thought. To drift over this green land forever.

At home in Bourbon County, there were moments when he had stood with his father in the late afternoons of wintertime, watching the pale sunshine decline against the blue mountains. He had never been in the mountains. But looking at them on a clear, chilly day in winter gave him the feeling that he could walk only a little way and get to a magic realm. He thought that if he ever went anywhere, he would go there.

But he had come in the opposite direction. The mountains lay to the east and to the south. Here the spaciousness was something he had never dreamed of, something more than the mountain, more than the still calm of the green land in Bourbon County. Here was green, but it was the green of tall grass ceaselessly moving. Here were wildflowers blooming by the million for as far as they could see—an infinite multitude of fragile, brightly painted dots, shining and quivering like intelligent life in the brilliant sunlight.

The wind rippled the tall grass in long waves. There was a tranquillity to the irregular motion and a variation in hue that was hypnotic: the green first pale, then dark again, and pale once more so that the eye could perceive a shimmering of something coming and going but could never precisely describe the way of its passage. In the great silence of noon Adam could hear the swish of the wind's gentle flight as though it had been a still, small voice, and he thought that the voice meant something ahead better than he had ever known.

Rachael and Promise went frolicking in the tall grass and gathered wildflowers, laughing and calling to each other. The little girl's laugh a shrill of pleasure. Henry hesitated a moment, watching them, wondering if a boy almost eleven years old could allow himself such levity. Then he surrendered and picked flowers with them.

At suppertime Jason stood in their midst again, able to read for the first time since St. Louis. The awful bruise on his face had faded. The swelling had gone down, and he seemed to have come out of a cave where he had been buried. He had never mentioned his stiff jaw and seemed to ignore that there had ever been any unpleasantness, that he had taken a blow in the face which had humiliated him, left him dazed and speechless for days. Again the grand old cadences rolled off his practiced tongue.

Whither shall I go from Thy spirit, or whither shall I flee from Thy presence? If I ascend up into heaven, Thou art there; if I make my bed in hell, behold, Thou art there. If I take the wings of the morning and dwell in the uttermost parts of the sea, even there shall Thy hand lead me, and Thy right hand shall hold me. If I say, Surely the darkness shall cover me, even the night shall be light about me. Yea, the darkness hideth not from Thee, but the night shineth as the day. The darkness and the light are both alike to Thee.

Adam knew that part of the moment was Jason's performance, vain and self-conscious in the way that clergymen often are when they try to be humble in public. But it was a splendid show. Listening to Jason out here he felt a serenity beyond all telling, and he thought in a detached way that he had hever jumped and shouted with conversion in any camp meeting revival, and now he did not care anymore. Maybe God lived on the plains, and perhaps here people did not have to strain for Him, and being here might be all the experience with God that anybody required.

They sang buoyantly in the darkening night while the campfire glowed in their midst like a warm star fallen gently to earth.

> All o'er this wide extended plain
> Shines one eternal day,
> Where God our King forever reigns
> And scatters night away.
> I am bound for the Promised Land,
> I am bound for the Promised Land.
> Oh who will come and go with me?
> I am bound for the Promised Land.

They came to Independence, where the red-brick courthouse imposed itself at the top of the treeless hill rising from a grassy land. The large and dusty square was nearly deserted. First day of summer, 1851. The trip from St. Louis had taken a hard month. Now the dead sun burned down on the dun streets, striking everything to stillness except that tiny procession of moving wagons that trundled in, raising the gritty dust.

"You're late," people said, finding much satisfaction in declaring finally that someone had made an error that could not be redeemed. People seemed proud. "Most of this year's emigration left two months ago. Hell, they ain't been nobody going out in the last two weeks except a few riders, some folks bound up to Fort Childs, some fright wagons bound for Santa Fe, some Indian agents, some goddamn missionaries. But they ain't been many for California nohow. Hell, it ain't been nothing but a little trickle compared to what it was last year. Stuff like that gets around to smart folks."

"What happened last year?"

People nearly burst with pleasure, telling a well-known fact to people who did not know it yet. "Well, they was drought on the plains, that's what happened. Grass dried up. You could of walked from here to California on oxen's bones."

"You mean the oxen died?" Jason looked incredulous.

"They ain't no drought this year," Ishtar Baynes shrilled.

"People died, too," the wise men at Independence chortled. "You could just about of walked from here to the Pacific Ocean on the graves of folks that died. Cholera. Goddamn! You don't want to be messing around with the cholera morbus. Them foreigners brung it in. Don't never trust no foreigners. You seen any cholera on the road this year?"

"I am a medical man," Harry said with grave self-importance. "I am of the opinion that the cholera epidemic in this country has now run its terrible course."

Jason looked at him gratefully. But the people in the square of Independence persisted.

"If you get the cholera, you throw the laudanum at it. Block up your bowels. Don't let nothing get out. Your life turns to shit when you get the cholera. Keep your shit inside, and you'll save your life."

"Please!" Harry said. His attempt at dignity did no good. The men in Independence lived far from civilization; they had no reverence for anybody, not even for doctors.

"I know this, folks," one man in a leather vest said. "You're late. Damned late. You might not make it this year. You better get a move on fast, and if you're not by the Sierra Nevada by November, you better stop. Better wait than die."

"It's all your fault, Mr. Adam," Ishtar Baynes crowed. "If you hadn't been so greedy, we could of been here two, three weeks ago. I hope you're satisfied. I hope your money feels good to you now."

"If you wanted to ride the steamboat, you could have sold some of the stuff in these wagons," Adam said. He looked steadily at her, his face afire in the fiery sun.

"There you go again!" Mrs. Baynes shrieked. People looked at her. She was indifferent to them. Jason was looking at Adam. Studying him. Not judging yet. Just looking and feeling that Mrs. Baynes was on his side. If there were sides.

The Missouri River performed a little trick of geography near Independence. The trick turned the fate of the American West. The river came rolling down in a muddy torrent from the North and West, seeming hell-bent to pour right on down to the Gulf of Mexico, a lordly rival to the Mississippi. But

181

then like some great, humbled baron, it bent a knee twelve miles beyond Independence and made a sharp bow toward the East to submit to the Mississippi just above St. Louis. It was one of those arbitrary gestures of the great that determine the lives of underlings who depend on them and have no right to appeal from their almighty whimsy. Far back upstream, the upward fingers of the Missouri touched against the Rocky Mountains, but in rugged high country. No pass there for wagons to cross. And so at some point near the great bend of the river, wagon teams had to strike out across the plains aiming for South Pass—a funnel into the west coast that nature had created herself, so it was said, to assure Americans that their manifest destiny was to expand from shore to shore.

The Jennings party journeyed slowly on from Independence down to a much smaller town called Westport Landing on the malarial flats of the great bend itself. Here the Kaw River paid its own tribute to a mightier river, and you could avoid crossing the dangerous Missouri by going under the great bend and following the sandy Kaw onto a ferry, at the place where a few miserable, slatternly cabins baking in the brown dust were to flower into Topeka, Kansas.

After crossing the Kaw, the westering pilgrims would angle north and west through rolling grasslands to a place called Alcove Springs on the banks of the last river difficult to cross this side of the stony mountains—the Big Blue. From here they would journey up-country, still angling to the north and west and for a time following one of the tributaries of the Big Blue, called, without imagination, the Little Blue. Leaving the Little Blue near its trickling headwaters, they would make a plunge across the dry plains to come up to the valley of the great Platte River at a place traditionally called Fort Childs, though the United States Government had changed the name to Fort Kearny by the year 1851.

Westport Landing was the real jumping-off place to the Great West in 1851. The steamboats stopped here, although a few of them were already braving the tricky sandbars of the Missouri to go on to Fort Leavenworth or St. Joseph. But most discharged their wagons, and the wagon companies raised hell or sang hymns according to taste, or else they simply looked around for a while and said mental goodbyes to the United States and civilization before they moved out. Within an hour they would be beyond the nebulous border of their country and into the Indian Territory, lying mostly vacant and completely unorganized, stretching for thousands and thousands of square miles into the American imagination. Here, beyond the junction of the Kaw and the Missouri, men were beyond the reach of the law. They were on their own. The white man was a pilgrim and a stranger; the prairies were alien to him, for there was nothing in the world like the prairies except perhaps the great Eurasian steppes, and hardly anyone who departed from Westport Landing knew anything about Huns or Mongols or Cossacks.

Jason gaped at a plow in a store at Westport Landing. "Look at that plow!" A low, subdued voice, almost trembling in spite of the tight control Jason always kept on himself. "It looks just like the plows we have in the wagons. But it costs two dollars less than what I paid for my plows." He stopped. His eyes fell on Adam. Looked away. "I wonder if I was cheated."

"You ain't been cheated much, Mr. Jennings. The oxen is the ones that has been cheated. They've hauled them plows of yours all the way."

Something smoldered in Jason. But he kept himself under control. "Adam, I do not want to injure your feelings, but you are becoming tiresome with your litany about the oxen."

Jason's stomach growled: Adam heard it. Jason less formidable when his stomach growled; he colored, and Adam smiled. "The oxen is just getting tired, Mr. Jennings. Me, I'd lot rather be tiresome than tired."

Jason started to say something else, but Adam walked off and left him. *I ought to leave them,* Adam thought. He could not think of one good reason to stay with people who were so unpleasant or else so foolish. But, he thought, leaving them was abandoning children in the snow. They had to have him to help out if they made it across the plains alive. They needed Adam Cloud.

They would have left after a day in Westport Landing. But it rained.

Adam thought they should go on and said so. "Rain always stops sometime," he said

Jason objected. Calmly and dispassionately he reasserted the leadership that Adam was beginning to take on himself. No sense trying to move in weather like this, he said. And Harry, who had had his hot bath, sat carefully in the tent, keeping clean and poring over his medical books, his lips moving, memorizing. Everybody else seemed inclined to sleep.

Adam thought they could make ten miles, but he could not persuade Jason or anybody else. And being shut up with them all made him restless. So in spite of the rain he went out and threw his saddle onto the back of his riding mule and rode splashing off in the downpour to the center of Westport Landing.

He went to the saloon on the hill. It was crowded and dim. Farmers stood around drinking beer with drovers, with freight drivers, a few soldiers, some men in fancy-looking clothes. Westport Landing lunging toward civilization. Laughter and the drone of conversation and the smell of wet clothing—an agreeable place. Adam edged himself in at the bar and drank a cool beer and tried to act as if he belonged there, his fee paid by the five cents he plunked down for his foamy glass. He did not like the taste of beer much. But he liked the fellowship of beer. He liked the light-headedness he got from drinking beer, too. You did not worry about snow in the Sierra Nevada when you had a beer or two.

He hid his nose in his mug, drank deeply, thought he was beginning to like beer a little better, drew the mug away, and was suddenly assaulted by an overpowering smell. Skunk. He looked around in alarm. Had a skunk wandered in out of the rain?

A wiry little man dressed in leather had pushed in beside him. Not young. Maybe not so old as he looked. A very brown face deeply lined, looking like a piece of old tanned leather, worn and supple. Large, bushy white eyebrows. His eyes, the palest blue, were set back in his head under those thundercloud brows. His white hair was stiff and combed straight back and tied at the nape of his neck in a large knot, Indian fashion. He wore a scruffy beard that looked as if it were trimmed from time to time with a hunting knife. But the most noticeable feature of all was a large stained, and badly battered beaver hat that he wore cocked back on his head.

He had been soundly sprayed by a skunk at some recent time. The stink had got into the leather. Now the drenching rain had brought it out in all its glory.

The old man spoke in a high, cracked voice, glancing over at Adam's beer. "Gimme one of them, barkeep!"

The bartender obliged, looking very surly and dark and

moving discreetly away down the bar. In fact, there was a general retreat from the old man, so that in just a moment he and Adam found themselves occupying an arena in the midst of the crowd. The old man grinned at Adam, made a gesture as if to tip that ridiculous hat, and drank his beer down at a long guzzle. He wiped his mouth with a leather sleeve, a big gesture for such a small man. He liked big gestures. "Don't know of nothing you can get for a nickel that's better than beer," he said. He belched.

Conversation stopped in the saloon. people were annoyed and very uncomfortable with the smell of skunk in a closed place. The old man paid no attention to anybody in the place but Adam.

"Sure is good to be back in a saloon again. A saloon means civilization. And I ain't seen no civilization in more than a year."

"Civilization?" Adam said.

"People," The old man said. "I like people. I mean real people. Not Indians. You get tired of Indians. Like living with a bunch of crazy children." He called for another beer.

"Oh," Adam said.

The bartender delivered another beer, slamming the mug down with a thunk. He went away muttering. The smell was terrible; it seemed to get more terrible the longer the old man stayed. Adam had never smelled such a stink. The old man took no notice.

"You from these parts, or be ye a pilgrim?" the old man said.

"I'm from Tennessee."

"Poor feller! Well, I reckon you'll get over it. I knowed a man that had the smallpox onct, and he got over that. There's hope for ye, young feller. Don't give up. Don't ever give up!" He grinned, showing white teeth that were surprisingly fine.

"I'm going to California," Adam said hopefully.

"Going to rassel the elephant!" the old man said with a jubilant cry. He drank off his beer without taking the mug from his lips.

Adam waited until he was through and the old man had wiped his mouth again. "Why do they call it the elephant? Going to California?"

The old man laughed. He seemed peaceful with the world. Easygoing. Always laughing. Adam liked him in spite of the

185

stink. "Well, an elephant, he's big and thick, and he's got tusks large enough and sharp enough to nail you to the ground. Grab him by the tail, and he'll kick your brains out. Grab him by the trunk, and he'll sling you against the first mountain you see. Grab him by the foot, and he'll stomp you to jelly. Ain't but one thing to do to the elephant. Grab him by the neck and hold on for dear life, and he'll tote you all the way to California if you can hang on."

Adam smiled shyly. "Then I reckon I'm going to rassel the elephant."

The old man belched loudly and yelled for another beer, ignoring the condemning silence around him. Adam felt it and was unsettled. "I reckon I might as well go to California myself. Ain't no use going back to the goddamned Oregon Territory. Ain't worth the beaver no more."

"You a trapper?"

"Sure was. Been a trapper for nigh onto thirty years." He sipped thoughtfully at his beer. "But trapping ain't no good now. Folks has stopped wearing beaver hats! They've gone to wearing silk! My God! You know what silk is!"

Adam shook his head.

"It's something that's made by a goddamn worm. Now can you figure that? Goddamn! It makes me sick to think what's happening to this country when folks start wearing worm shit on their heads and calling it a hat." He took his own old beaver hat off his head and set it on the bar and looked at it with the appreciation due an old and trusted friend. "Now that's a hat! That's a hat made for kings."

The old man was about to go on when their conversation was suddenly interrupted. A very large, muscular man had taken all the skunk stink he could stand. He was a man with broad, heavy shoulders, a thick, dull face, and very light blond hair that went back in close waves on his large head.

"Look here, old man," the newcomer said loudly, "what in hell do you mean, coming in a place like this, stinking like that?"

The old trapper looked at him coolly. "I run into a skunk two nights ago. I can't help how I smell. You'll get used to it in a while. I did."

He turned around and started to talk to Adam again. But before he could open his mouth, the man, who knew his rights, grabbed the old man by the shoulders, spun him around like a bag of straw, and picking him up by the front

186

of his old leather jacket flung him away from the bar and toward the door, all as quick and as violent as lightning striking in the trees.

Adam, unaware that the old man had recovered himself like a cat, landing on his springy legs in a crouch, jumped into the fight without a thought. He hit the farmer in the belly with all his might, but before he could draw back to strike again, the farmer was on top of him. Two giant hands closed around Adam's soft neck. Adam felt the blackness coming. He saw the farmer's big, red face with its clenched jaws poised mercilessly above his own.

But suddenly the farmer leaped erect and dropped him. The motion was spastic, like a stick springing from submarine depths to break, shooting upward, the surface of a pond, a gesture frozen with the man's back arching inward, his head thrown wildly back, his tight-clenched mouth suddenly elastic in screamless, incredulous gaping, his popping eyes like huge, unblinking moons, his big hands flung wide and stiff so that Adam was flung back against the bar, choking for breath.

The old man wore a Bowie knife at his belt. It was a heavy knife, razor sharp, and with the farmer's back to him, the old man springing quickly to work as he had so often skinned deer, beaver, and buffalo, plunged the knife-blade through the farmer's legs, edge up, and brought it down hard against the farmer's belly, cutting sharp and true, girding the farmer's bottom as though the man had been a tree, and in the process castrating him with the edge of the knife slightly turned in a motion quick, sure, and eternal.

Adam went down on his knees, sobbing for breath, gurgling, sure his neck was broken, scarcely conscious. For an instant he could not believe his own safety. The old man, so small, so frail-looking just a minute ago, now towered over him, a mountain of fury, waving the bright knife running with blood, shouting an outraged, blasphemous, interminable condemnation to him and all the saloon. Adam thought dimly and without hope that the old man, gone crazy with fury, was now going to cut his heart out.

Only slowly and with stupendous pain in his throat did he understand the words being yelled at him. The old man was pointing at Adam's patent Colt revolver left forgotten in his belt. "You goddamn tin-brained Tennessee pissant! Why the fuckshit didn't you use that there motherfucking-shitass *gun?* Why the fuckshit do you carry the motherfucking-

shitassgodamnjesus thing if you ain't going to *use* it when-
some motherfucking hillbilly is *killing* you? . . ."

The tirade went on and on, a torrent of blue outrage.
Adam had not even thought of the pistol. If the farmer had
choked him to death, Adam would not have thought of it.

The old man cried out, "All right, you boys seen it all. He
started it, didn't he? We was minding our own business, and
he started it, didn't he?

A deathlike silence gave consent.

"Anybody want to dispute that what I done was self-de-
fense? Anybody here care to take me to the law, accuse me
of anything? Anybody here want me to come looking to cut
your balls off?"

Men began to turn away. Somebody vomited. Adam always thought it funny that he smelled the bile spilled out on
the floor in that moment even more sharply than he smelled
the skunk in the old man. Vomit meant deliverance. Nobody
dared touch them.

The old man grabbed Adam by the wrist. He half-dragged
him into the street. The rain was thrundering down. Very
cold. Adam quailed before the chill. He was dumbfounded
and went where he was led.

"You castrated him! Like he wasn't nothing but a hog!"

"I thought it was a pretty good job if you ask me. But then
he was bending over a little, and that let me get the knife under him. Then I just cut. You holpen me a little by letting
yourself be choked." The old man's anger was gone. He
looked at Adam easily and laughed.

"But he's ruint. He ain't nothing but . . . God!"

"Well, I'd be right surprised myself if his prick ever gets
stiff at the sight of a nekkid woman again. Best thing if you
ask me. World don't need kids from the likes of him."

"We never done nothing like that back in Tennessee,"
Adam said.

"Well, you didn't have to," the old man said. They were in
a livery stable, where the old man was loading a fine-looking
mule with his gear. "You do what you have to do, and out
here, you got to do some things you ain't never even thought
of yet."

"I never seen nothing like it," Adam said, nearly crazy
with what he had seen.

The old man shook his head and went on with his work.
"Listen, boy, out in this here country, you don't do nothing

to help your enemy. When a man lets you know he's your enemy, you kill him."

"You didn't kill that feller."

"Oh, he might get infected and die. But if he don't, he's got something to remember me by. If I'd of kilt him, he wouldn't never of knowed it was me. Blink. The light would of been blowed out in his head, and that would of been that. Not no good revenge in that. Why, the feller wouldn't never of knowed he was dead."

"Don't you never get mad at me," Adam said.

"Oh, it ain't likely."

"I'm much obliged."

"Only one thing I wish I could of done for that dirt farmer. Wish I could of cut his prick off and left him his balls. Now that's what I done to the Blackfoot Indian I caught robbing my traps. That Indian's going to spend the rest of his life wanting squaws and not being able to do nothing about his wants, and your average Blackfoot squaw, she's going to be just kind and gentle enough to laugh her head off when she sees a man like that." The old man chuckled. "That kind of thing gets to a Blackfoot."

"Jesus," Adam said. "But didn't you feel like you was trespassing? Don't the land out there belong to them?"

"Hell, no, boy," the old man said jovially. "That land out there, it's too big to belong to Indians. They just live off of it. Like fleas live on a dog or a bear. If you want to own that land, you got to take it. And the Indians ain't enough to do that. It's my land or your land just as much as it's theirs."

Adam shook his head. His neck hurt terribly, and he croaked when he talked. "Just don't get mad at me. You let me know if I do something to make you mad, and I'll stop. By God!"

The old trapper laughed harmlessly. "Well, I don't reckon we're going to get mad at each other. You don't get mad much out here. You know, I went West the first time with Jim Bridger and Bill Ashley in 1822, and I wasn't young then. I've lived with Indians and trappers. And hellfire! I've even eaten with missionaries! Most of the time, it's been one hell of a good life. You meet the best folks in the world out here. And if they ain't good, why, then, most of 'em ain't bad neither. You meet somebody in the woods. And you don't want to kill him first thing! Hell, no! Why, you're so glad to see another human being that first thing you want to do is sit down with him and hear a human voice again. And you want maybe to smoke a pipe with him and maybe drink a little whiskey with him if one of you's got it. And you want to swap lies and maybe just enough truth not to hurt nothing, and after a while you shake hands and turn your back and go on. That's the way it is most of the time. Nearly every time."

The old man looked genial and thoughtful. Like a peaceful God explaining the world he has made.

"But ever so often—just a few times in your whole life— you meet somebody that's going to kill you if you don't kill him first. Maybe he wants your hides. Or your money. Or your squaw if you got one. Maybe he wants your hair to hang up on his door and tell big lies about. Maybe he's just like the poor feller today in the saloon. He gets up feeling mean about something. And he sees you, and he wants to kill you because he thinks killing you will make him feel good again. Maybe he don't even know why he wants to kill you, Just something for him to be doing."

The old man shook his head. His aged and wrinkled face carved with perplexity, the unfathomable foolishness of human beings he could not explain.

"And when you run up on a feller like that, they ain't but one thing to do. Kill him. Don't you pay no attention to that forgive-and-forget shit when you get in a fight with somebody out here. I'd of kilt that farmer if we'd been ten miles west of here on the road, and he was going to California, too. But I figure he's from these parts. I figure he's going to stay right here. So I just cut through his balls, and by the time he can walk straight or sit still on a horse, why, we'll be long gone."

Adam took a deep breath. "What do you reckon his wife will think when they carry him home? His children if he's got children now? What do you reckon?"

"Ah, you can't ask questions like that. You ain't never going to know."

"It seems like you ought to know how things come out. What happens to folks you know." Adam could not go on with the thought. All the half-told stories he had met thus far on his journey were too much for him.

"God's the only one that knows that," the old man said. "And maybe He don't."

Adam changed the subject. He had trouble talking, and he could not hold on to anything difficult for long.

"So you're going to California, too. Sure enough."

"Hell, yes," the old man said. "I just decided. I just floated me three canoeloads of hides down the Missouri. It's took me more than two months, and it ain't worth it going back up there again. Not lessen I want to be an Indian. Besides, I've been getting the rheumatiz pretty bad last few years."

He held his brown hands out and looked at them thoughtfully. "Can't understand it. It gets in my knees. In my ankles. In my hands. Lord, last year my hands swole up so bad I couldn't hardly bend my fingers." He shook his head again. "Then I was scared. I truly was. Scared to let my fire burn down because I thought maybe I couldn't get it lit again."

"Are you afraid to die?"

The old man snorted. "Sure I'm afraid to die. There ain't no good death. I don't never want to die. I want to go to California. I want to be warm all year long. Maybe the rheumatiz won't bother me then. Ain't no good trapping beaver no more. Back there. Well, I said that, didn't I? You get old. You get to repeating yourself."

"It's too bad it's over," Adam said, half-whispering. He talked urgently. He wanted to quit thinking about that farmer back there.

"I reckon I'll prospect for gold or something in California. You know what they say about gold. Ain't no fort so strong that gold won't knock it down. I ain't never made my pile. But I'm going to before I die. All these folks getting rich now ..." He shook his head again as if to clear it of something thick and mysterious. "I figure if I move around enough, I'll get rich someday. I've always wanted to make a fortune and spend it. Die without a dime in a house as big as a palace. Didn't make it trapping. Maybe in California ..." The old man paused, embarrassed at his dreams. Then he spat into the ground. "Well, what about it? Are you going to sit there like a stump? Or are you coming along with me to California?"

"What's your name anyhow?" Adam said.

"My name!" The old man cocked his head and looked dour. He inspected Adam with those sharp, quick eyes. "That's something else about out here, son. Out there in the wilderness, I mean. You don't go asking folks their names like you had a right."

"I'm sorry," Adam whispered. "I don't know the manners out here yet. Forget it."

"Well, I mean, a name's a personal thing." The old man

wrinkled his face, puzzling over something familiar, immense, and strange. "It ain't something you want people to take like nothing, you know. Your name. Give somebody your name, you give him the power to make you turn around any time he calls it. Like you had a string tied onto your nose. And he had a hold of the other end. Maybe a nobody. A little runt with spit for a brain."

"All right," Adam said in forlorn desperation. "Just forget I asked. Please. I don't never want to know your name."

"Give somebody your name, and he's got the power to say bad things about you. You're half-hanged if you got a bad name."

"I won't call you nothing," Adam said. "I don't call my dog nothing. You too. Nothing."

The old man suddenly grinned and clapped Adam firmly on the shoulder, friendly like a big, toothy cat, smelling of skunk. "Well, since you don't want to know, I'm glad to tell you. My name's Joe. Joe McMoultrie. All my friends just calls me Shawnee Joe. It's a name I picked up onct when I had me a Shawnee squaw." He shook his head, puzzling again—a frequent attitude of his, an old man astounded that he was old and that so many things had happened to him and gone.

"Well, I'm right pleased to meet you," Adam said. He put out a hand that had no strength left in it. "My name's Adam. Adam Cloud."

"Well, Adam, when you taken my part in that saloon fight, you made me your friend for life." They shook hands awkwardly, Adam using the unfamiliar gesture of a man and the old man more accustomed to lifting his hand Indian fashion, palm out to show how harmless the hand was, the other resting easily on the butt of his great Bowie knife—just in case. He let his free hand rest there now.

"I didn't do you no good," Adam said, feeling his neck gingerly. It hurt like hell. "You're the one that taken my part. Reckon you're the one that saved my life."

"Reckon I did," the old man said easily. "You should of used your pistol."

"I ain't never even shot the thing."

"Get to shooting it then," the old man said with a wise wink. "Pistol's like your pecker; it ain't no good stuck in your pants."

"All right. I'll shoot it every day. I swear."

The old man finished loading his mule, a yellow mule with thick hams and ears like funnels. "Well, what about it, Adam? You want to go on to California with me? I reckon we're kind of bound to each other now. After this afternoon."

Adam was flattered and relieved. He and the old man could strike out together. Make it to California in two months. He looked at Shawnee Joe and thought that here was a man who said just exactly what he meant. No veil in his words. A good companion for somebody tired of fools.

But then he thought of Ruth. He thought of Jessica. And he thought of Promise. He thought of the children, all so innocent, none of them responsible for the long journey ahead of them, and none of them able to survive without help.

So Adam told Shawnee Joe about the Jennings, and later on he realized that his own life took a turn there in that livery stable with the rain hammering down on the shingle roof, the sweet smell of hay and animal dung inside, spread through the illusory peace of a wet afternoon, the old man looking at him to be sure he got it all right, nodding, laughing a couple of times, clapping Adam on the back, agreeing on what they would do. They were friends now. And a friend did not leave another. "Till death part us!" the old man said. And they laughed together.

# 30

"Look at that man!" Ishtar Baynes said in a loud and outraged voice. "This here's been a respectable group. And look at that man!"

"He looks positively disreputable!" Clifford Baynes said scornfully, his dry rodent's face slick with disgust. But he was cautious enough not to speak so loudly that the old man with the big knife could hear him.

Ishtar Baynes was not so careful. She was a woman, and people did not go around sticking knives into women. It was not considered the mark of a gentleman. "I ain't never heard the like. Mr. Adam met him in a saloon fight" (Adam had given a careful and incomplete account of the brawl in the saloon.) "What kind of folks are we if we got folks coming along with us that somebody meets in a saloon fight?"

Adam thought she was afraid, and he was pleased. She could not rule the old man.

"If he had not been in the saloon, he wouldn't have got in the fight," Clifford Baynes said coldly. "Respectable people stay out of saloons."

Jason was in a dilemma, and his large, flat face was anxious. He spoke a great deal of purity. The world was a cesspool, and they were going to California to breathe clean air. And here was this man who smelled like a skunk and looked lethal, with a knife in his belt, a long rifle in his hand, and an expression that seemed comfortably at home with any sin Jason could think of.

"Mr. McMoultrie," Jason said, clearing his throat and doing his weak best to be firm. "It certainly is very kind of you to want to go along. To help us on the journey. But the truth is, we don't need your help. Look at us." He tried to grin, but failed miserably, swept an uncertain hand around at Samuel and Asa, but then in nervous confusion grinned at Harry Creekmore as if Harry had been the sun, out after a long day of rain.

Shawnee Joe hardly paid any attention to Jason at all. He was pitching his tent. The rain had stopped. The clouds were breaking up in mountains of purple and brilliant white. The clean blue sky was polished and soft behind them, and the sun, dipping far to the west, swelled in the late afternoon air and turned darkly amber. The old man had a bundle of buffalo robes. They looked luxurious and warm and comfortable. Tanned like gloves on the hide side. He piled them on the ground, one on top of the other like a mattress, and began to pitch his small canvas tent over them. "You don't know nothing about the plains, Mr. Jennings," he said in a very matter-of-fact and slightly bored voice. "I can tell that by looking at you. You're going to be almost alone out there. This year's bunch of emigrants has gone when they should of. So I'm going along to help you get there. My friend Adam invited me to go, and it ain't polite for a friend to turn down an invite from a friend."

Jason cleared his throat uneasily and looked around. Things were not going right. He was trying half-heartedly to be firm and strong. Like Moses or George Washington. "Well, now, Mr. McMoultrie, I don't want to be rude. I don't want to seem ungrateful. But facts are facts. Adam here is a, ah, *guest!* We invited him to come along with us. And I, ah, really don't think he has the right to, ah, to ... Well, he can't invite somebody else to join us."

The old man gave Jason a look that was like a clout in the head and laughed. "Jason, you're too much! You mean Adam ain't taking care of them oxen of yours? You mean he's eating your grub and not working his ass off for you in return? You mean he ain't making camp at night and breaking it up in the daylight? Hell, feller, it looks to me like Adam's the one in charge here. You ain't nothing but a passenger, Jason. Poor boob like you. Get out there on the plains, and the Indians would have the lot of you cooking on an open fire!"

"Do the Indians eat people?" Henry said, awed by Shawnee Joe and now afraid.

The old man looked down at him and winked. "They do when they run out of dogs."

Jason was nearly beside himself with humiliation and an anger he could hardly surpress. "No matter how things look to you, Mr. McMoultrie, I am in charge here. Anybody who goes along with us has to accept the fact that I am in charge."

The old man laughed again and clapped Jason familiarly on the back. "You just go right ahead and be in charge then, Jason. It don't make me no mind. You just don't get in my way. And when we go through the country of the Pawnee, when we see the Sioux, don't you get in my way then either. I might have to blow your silly head off."

"I don't mean any harm to the Indians," Jason said frostily. "I am sure that the Indians mean no harm to me."

"Oh, no, Jason? You're just the kind the Pawnee like to see coming. You got some Bibles in your wagons? Read a little Bible when the Pawnee is lifting your hair. Keep your mind off what's happening to you. And if you don't think about it long enough, you'll be dead and won't have to think about nothing."

The old man laughed easily. He flung insults at Jason with the casual and emotionless amusement that a child might feel throwing rocks into a pond.

Jason bit his thick lower lip and looked at the old man in

consternation. "I think the Indians are noble and good. I have read about them. I think kindness and nobility will win kindness and nobility from them in return."

"Godamighty, Jason, I sure do like to hear you talk! Here, hold this rope, will you? I got to peg my tent down tight. Pull it tight now, Jason. Heave!"

Jason did what he was told, embarrassed and annoyed and as helpless as a child.

"I never heard of such a thing," Ishtar Baynes yelped. "I do believe this old man is going to force hisself to go along with us! He's coming where he ain't wanted! He ain't nothing but a savage!" She spoke in a loud and injured voice and looked around for support.

Shawnee Joe pegged his tent down with a big-headed hammer, got up, looked her dead in the eye. "Lady, if I was boss of this here outfit, I'd tell you to shut your mouth. Woman like you's like an ass or a nut tree. You need to be beat to do anybody any good, and I'm pretty good at beating all three of 'em when I need be."

Mrs. Baynes turned red, "Clifford, did you hear what this old man said to me? Are you going to stand there like a coward and let a stranger talk to your wife like this man just talked to me?"

"If Clifford don't like the way I talk, I'll hack his ears off so he won't have to hear me. You ever eat a man's ears, ma'am? They make a right good stew sometimes if you're hungry enough." The old man grinned like a bobcat.

Harry pulled Adam aside. "He isn't like us, Adam. My God, why'd you have to go and bring a man like him back here. You'll spoil the . . . the *fellowship!*"

"What's wrong, Harry? You afraid he's going to find out you're a liar?"

Harry was afraid. Ishtar Baynes was afraid. Clifford Baynes had suddenly discovered a pressing need to go off into the solitude of the thickening light on the plains. *Well, they ought to be afraid,* Adam thought. The old man had something. A power.

He shook Harry off, annoyed and impatient with him, and went to brush down the oxen. Henry moved out spontaneously to help him, smiling shyly in anticipation.

"Look at him!" Asa said, standing nearby and speaking as scornfully as Adam had ever heard a man speak. "Henry's

196

decided to be a groom, and Adam's his boss. I reckon you like Adam better than you like me. Don't you, Henry?"

Henry looked back at his father, hurt to the bone. "Ain't it all right if I help with the oxen?"

"Sure," Asa said, turning away. "You help Adam all you want to, I don't give a damn."

Adam wanted to run after Asa and hit him hard. Knock some sense into his head. But he knew not to get mixed up in a family fight. Asa was strange. Maybe crazy, Adam thought. One of the most hateful men he had ever seen. But Ruth had loved him enough to marry him. Odd.

"Mamma says daddy don't believe nobody loves him," Henry said quietly. "He gets mad so easy. I don't know why."

"It's all right," Adam said, trying to laugh. His throat hurt too much. "Don't you worry about it. He'll be all right in California. Just wait."

"I do love him," Henry said. "He just don't think so. He don't hardly talk to me any more."

The little company went creaking over an imagined line in the muddy earth early the next morning, and when they had made a slight turn to the southwest, Shawnee Joe, riding his mule next to Adam, said, "Well, boy, we've left the United States of America now. This here's the Indian Territory. No law out here but what we make it. Remember that."

Adam looked around and tried to fix the place in his mind. But the ordinary landscape, green and rolling and stretching to infinity, gave no sign of any boundary. And so their passage was undramatic and vaguely disappointing.

The wagons pounded and lurched in the muddy road, and the big wheels turned slowly, as the land rolled in high swells ahead of them. It was empty. The world in the rising morning was lazy and indolent, and the sun rose higher behind them. Their shadows shortened. The day turned hot, and the blue sky became hard. People became drowsy. Nobody was saying much; everyone was uncomfortable with the half-submerged quarrel that had flared up over the old man. Sleep was an escape. Adam dozed on his mule. Large clouds built up in white, thick rolls for as far as they could see. Over everything there hung a prodigious and mysterious silence.

The old man inspected things. He looked at every face and scrutinized every wagon. Every wheel. Every ox. He saw how hard the beasts were laboring in their yokes. At noon he walked around, looking into things, poking here and there, finally gaping in hot astonishment at Jason, who followed him uncomfortably, to show some sign of being the leader.

"You got too goddamn much stuff in these wagons, Jason. You ain't never going to get to California lessen you throw some of this stuff out!"

Jason smiled. "Mr. McMoultrie, I would deeply appreciate it if you would not use profanity around the children. Profanity represents a certain cheapness of vocabulary. I don't mean to hurt your feelings . . ." The smile slipped.

"Oh, you don't hurt my feelings none, Jason. I got feelings like a horseshoe. But you still got too goddamn much stuff in these wagons. You're going to kill your oxen."

Asa came up. "I ain't never seen an ox fall down and die," he said. He was about the same size as Shawnee Joe. Two small men looking at each other, the old man laughing. Always laughing. Holding them in contempt and standing above their reach.

"You probably ain't never in your poor life seen a hell of a lot," the old man said, looking him up and down. Smiling. "But I seen oxen die. And last year, if you'd come along this trail, you'd of seen oxen dying from here to Fort Hall."

"That's because they didn't have grass to eat," Jason said. He tried to affix his smile again. It wobbled. "Somebody told me in the town. It didn't rain last year. The oxen died because of that."

"Well, that's true enough, Jason. You can work oxen to death, or you can starve 'em to death, or you can hit 'em in the head with a rifle butt, and they'll die that way. You're going to work these oxen to death if you don't throw some stuff out. My God on a church steeple. You got enough stuff here to start a store!"

"You ain't in charge of this group," Asa said curtly. "We do what my brother says. He's the boss." Asa wavered a little before the old man's impudent grin. "Like he says."

"Well, what your smart-aleck brother says don't mean nothing to them oxen, Asa. They don't understand no English except for the cusswords. Hey now. Jason here's just like an ox. He's got his mind made up, and he's going straight ahead. I say they's some bends in the road, and only thing I know to do is cuss him like the oxen so he'll bend when the road does."

Jason, deeply injured and feeling put out and sorry for himself, tried to reason with the old man, "Well, you don't have to sound so *superior*. It's not ... Well, it's just not polite. Now I've said it, and I'm glad we've got this out in the open." Jason lifted his chin the way he had seen some professor do long, long ago, and he looked at the old man in civilized triumph.

The old man laughed again and shook his head. "Jason, if you ain't the one. Listen, if your house was burning down, what would you want? Somebody to come tippy-toe to the front door and knock like a preacher come to take collection? Tippy-tippy-tap! Oh, Mister *Jennings?* Your *house* is on fire?"

"We are not in that condition," Jason said frostily.

"No, you ain't." the old man said looking around at the rest of the party gathered uncertainly and peering at the quarrel smoldering there between them like a fire in the bottom of hay. "You're in worse shape. If your house was burning down, the rest of these folks ... That girl there. That little boy. The little girl. These women. All of 'em, they could jump out the windows and be safe. If you wanted to pussyfoot around, that'd be fine. You'd be the only one to burn up. But out there on the plains, Jason, you ain't the only one. All these folks depend on you. And all of you depend on these poor dumb oxen. Now you think about that. I don't give a damn if it's polite or not, Jason. It's true."

Jason ruminated and bit his lip. He looked at the oxen and looked back at the old trapper, looked at Adam standing slightly removed from them, his arms folded, looking on, listening rapt and amazed. Adam had never heard a man talk like Shawnee Joe; he had not thought a man could talk like this to other men and live. Samuel could have crushed him with a single tremendous fist. But Samuel was just as stunned by the old man's presence as the rest of them.

"Mr. McMoultrie," Jason said carefully, "did Adam talk to you about the oxen?"

Asa's red face lighted. "That's *right*, Jason! That's exactly right! It's a *conspiracy!*"

Shawnee Joe's voice was as level as death, "Adam ain't said one word to me about them oxen. He ain't had time. If somebody says me and Adam talked up some story about these oxen, then somebody's calling me a liar. They ain't nobody ever lived long after he called me a liar."

The threat in the old man's words was like something from

another world dropped down among them, as black and heavy and undeniable as a meteorite burning through space to fall at their feet. Asa swallowed and looked at the ground, and his face was scarlet. Henry looked at his father. Silence.

Mrs. Baynes came strutting over. She was immune to death because she was a woman. "Are we talking about them oxen again? Talking about throwing things away?"

"We're talking about the oxen," Asa said gloomily, turning away. "We ain't done nothing but talk about the oxen."

Jason spoke up. "Look, Mr. McMoultrie, I know you don't understand this. We're trying to get to California to make us a living. Something different for our children. For us. We don't want much. A house and some land. Maybe somewheres to look out on the ocean. We've put all we got into what we're carrying with us. If we throw it out, we're going to get to California poor. Maybe like beggars. Maybe then we'll starve to death. With our children too."

Asa looked at Henry. "With our children," he said softly. "You ain't got no children. You don't know what it's like." Asa put his hand on Henry's shoulder, his moods as changeable as the sunlight with clouds passing over it, going and coming again.

But all this sentiment washed off the old man like rain on a slate roof. "You can look at these oxen and see for yourself, folks." He pointed with one wiry hand to what he wanted them to see.

Jason looked worried. "I don't know . . ." He faltered on a dozen thoughts, a weak man challenged and unable to reply. *How did he get slaves across the river?* Maybe because it was dark. Jason could act the man in the dark. He went on, fumbling for words. "What can we throw out? If we throw any of it out now, we might as well have taken the steamboat from St. Louis. We've wasted so much *time* if we're going to throw it out now. If we've carried it this far, we might as well carry it all the way." It was a matter of reason to Jason. He looked to his brother for support. "We put all the money we had in this stuff. All our work for so many years. Our lives. Our hopes." He stopped and looked around, and in the way of weak men from the beginning of time, he took strength from his own strong language. "We're not going to throw it away. I can't do it."

Asa thought that Jason was right about everything, finally.

He said, "I ain't throwing nothing out neither. It's my stuff. These is my oxen."

"I promise," Jason said, retreating slightly before the old man's harsh and contemptuous look. "I promise we'll get to California with everything. I give you my word." His voice became almost a whine. Can't you understand our side of it, Mr. McMoultrie?"

Shawnee Joe spat a stream of tobacco juice into the earth. "I can understand when a man's a fool, Jason. Only thing is, most fools die pretty young. How'd you get to be so old?"

Harry tried to pour medicinal oils upon troubled waters. "Now, Mr. McMoultrie, ah, you shouldn't call Mr. Jennings here a fool. He's been to Yale University."

"Yale University!" Mrs. Baynes perked up as if something she had wondered about had finally fallen precisely in place. "Why, Yale University is in New Haven, Connecticut!"

Jason smiled at her, surprised and pleased to have some recognition of his superiority. "Why, yes, Mrs. Baynes. Yes, indeed. That's just where it is."

"My mamma run a hotel awhile in New Haven, Connecticut. Back about wenty years ago?"

"A hotel?" Jason looked blank.

"Down on Orange Street? You know where Orange Street is, Mr. Jennings?"

"Why, yes . . . Of course, I know . . . A hotel? On Orange Street?"

"The very same. We had a nice big place down there. You might of come down there onct or twice yourself to sing hymns around the pianoforte we had then? Come to think of it, you got a familiar face!" Mrs. Baynes scrutinized him and looked smug. "I think I might know you, Mr. Jennings!"

"No," Jason said. "I'm sure you don't, Mrs. Baynes." It was hard to tell in the intense, hot sun, but Adam thought Jason looked pale.

"If you was just a little thinner, and if your hair was just a shade darker . . ." She cocked her terrible head and looked at him again, and Adam thought, *She's got something on him. Like Harry.* It was like seeing a baby's tender flesh impaled on a large, sharp, and unyielding fishhook.

"I was never at your hotel, Mrs. Baynes," Jason said sternly. "Never in all my life."

"Well, I never was there neither, folks," Shawnee Joe said. "And I reckon what you're saying is you ain't going to lighten your load. Well, too bad. But maybe we can get some good out of it. I say everything has its good side."

Jason, recoiling before the harshness of Ishtar Baynes, turned back to him gratefully. "Well, now, Mr. McMoultrie, that's a surprising statement coming from you. Encouraging. I think a lot of good will come out of it. I think it will help our faith to go on, and what can the world be without faith?" Jason was babbling, his mind someplace else.

"What I meant was that ox steak don't taste too bad. It's a lot better than coyote chops. And when these here oxen dies, then we ought to get a good meal out of 'em at least."

Jason obviously preoccupied, nodded his head dully. Adam wondered if he even heard what the old man was saying.

"You didn't tell me these folks was crazy," the old man said to Adam later.

"I was afraid you wouldn't come if you knew."

"Ah, I like crazy people. They make the world different. Ah, these hands! These hands!" He bent his fingers and winced. "I can't get rid of the rheumatiz! Look how my fingers is swole!" He shook his head, looking down at his gnarled hands as if they were something newly discovered, not truly a part of himself. "Had the rheumatiz winter before last, and it got better in the summer. Had it last winter, and here it is nigh onto July, and my hands still hurt. Ah, I wish we was in California."

"We will be," Adam said. "Just a little while."

"October," the old man said, looking at the sky as if he alone could see some dark and ominous message scrawled there in the blue peacefulness of the afternoon. "October at least. Maybe later than that. Maybe not at all."

The days dragged by. Sunrise, and they were already creaking on the move. Toil and sweat. Rest at noon. Men sprawled silently and worn under the wagons in the black shade. More hard going in the afternoon. The long setting of the sun, swelling toward the undulating western horizon. Camp. Food. Exhausted sleep. Maybe ten miles a day. Sometimes less. The going was harder than it had been before Westport Landing. Creeks to cross without bridges. Slick banks, dropping steeply. The water had a pleasant sound, whispering over round rocks. Hell wrapped in a lullaby. Men got down in the water and dirtied themselves with mud and slime and slaved at the wagon wheels, and afterwards sometimes they had to pick black leeches out of their tender skin, where the vile little worms fastened themselves in their remorseless quest for blood. "Never knowed a leech that wasn't hungry," the old man said philosophically. "Don't let 'em stick to your pecker."

"Mr. McMoultrie, your preoccupation with genitals is disgusting," Jason said with a heat surprising in him. But he went off and examined himself with great care while the old man laughed.

They all stank now. Shawnee Joe's skunk odor faded. They became accustomed to dirt and foulness. They bathed sometimes in the cold running streams. Even Harry. The women went off and washed at themselves as best they could with most of their clothes on. Nothing seemed to do much good. Harry's white suit was ruined. He brushed hard at it every night. But sadly he recognized that he would never get it clean again.

"First thing I'm going to do when we get to Sacramento is to have a hot bath," he said dreamily. "And the second thing is to get me a new white suit."

"Don't know why you wear the stupid thing," Adam said. "It just shows every spot of dirt!"

Harry looked at him with a tired, bored, and patronizing frown. "That's the point, Adam. That's just the point."

Ruth bemoaned the dirt. "I don't believe we'll ever be clean again. It's in my hair! I feel so awful to be walking around with a dirty head."

Henry and Rachael delighted in it. They played in the water when there was a stream to ford. Red cheeks and light hair. Rachael was more active than Henry. Henry one of those children who looked old before their time; even when he played there was a certain gravity in his face. Every gesture of his seemed to say, "I don't want to do anything to make me look silly."

Rachael was sometimes petulant. "It's a bad age," Ruth said, trying to apologize for her daughter. Ruth smiling with painful patience and looking around, begging people with her eyes to see the sweet baby she knew was there. Rachael resented Henry; he was bigger and could do things she could not do. He could wade into running water up to his waist and look back at her with studied detachment. She wailed when the water began to run over her knees. Don't *let* Henry *do* that," she said when her brother proved his superiority. "I

203

don't *like* him to do that." She did not like him to do anything that took the slightest attention away from herself. Rachael the sun with amber hair; worlds revolved around her.

"Needs a good busting, that child does," Shawnee Joe said, shaking his head. "They don't raise children like I was raised anymore. I knowed my place. My daddy would beat me half to death if I'd acted smart like that little girl. The world ain't what it used to be. Going to the dogs."

Adam's hound howled happily. He recognized the name "dog" and leaped and cavorted around the old man when the old man said the magical, canine word. "We can always eat that dog," the old man said, not laughing. "You keep him good and healthy." And he looked at the sky again.

The Kaw River lay north of them, to their right, running like a muddy drain through the flattening land. Sometimes the uncertain road was firm; in other places it was marshy. Then the oxen worked so hard they looked ready to drop on their heads and die. Adam expected their death in the way that he once waited for a drop of water on the end of an icicle to fall. But they went on.

He was exasperated with the work and frazzled by looking at the oxen. "We ought to ride off and leave these folks!" he said to the old man, consoling himself by the expression of an indignation that burned in him like a swallowed penny hot from the forge. "They ain't got no right to hold us back like this, have they? We're going to get caught in the snow, ain't we?"

The old man took a chew of tobacco and squinted into the western light. "You and me would live if we was to get caught in the snow. I've been caught in snow. It didn't kill me, it won't kill me if it happens again. But them folks would die. I reckon that's what comes from going to Yale and working in a iron factory. It don't teach you much how to live in the snow."

"What you got in them jugs?" Adam said. The old man had two bright crockery jugs tied across his mule's back behind the saddle. Two other jugs hung across the back of his pack mule. "Whiskey?"

"You sure do ask a lot of questions. First my name and now about my jugs."

"I was just thinking we'd need whiskey in the snow."

"Well, we might. It helps my rheumatiz. Drink whiskey, and my hands don't hurt so much."

"Let's leave 'em. Go off tomorrow. Why not?" Adam looked fiercely at the old man, thinking of snow. "I don't like snow. I never did like snow."

"We can't leave these folks. You can't do it; I can't do it. Not now."

"A month ago I never heard of 'em."

"Well, we know 'em now." The old man laughed. "We *sure* do. What do you reckon that Baynes woman wants? You reckon she thinks there's some way she's going to get all their stuff? You reckon she's got some scheme?"

"We could be free out there," Adam said wistfully. "Like the wind."

"Tell me something," the old man said. "What about your friend Creekmore? Is he a doctor, or ain't he?"

"How'd you know?"

The old man laughed again. A genial mood. Time endless. The road so slow. "I just knowed, I reckon. He talks too much about it. I knowed a doctor that cut a arrowhead out of my back onct at rendezvous. He give me a pint of whiskey to drink, and he drunk a pint hisself. He stood up and cussed real good to make the air clean. Then he sliced the arrowhead out with a good, sharp knfe. I fainted. When I come to, he was pouring whiskey in my mouth and laughing like hell. I reckon I think all doctors ought to be like him. Be with you someway when you hurt." He sighed. "But then he drunk hisself to death in the end. Funny that doctors die."

Adam chortled. "Well, Harry ain't like that. I don't reckon he ever cut the head of a chicken. He don't like to look at blood."

"Well, he spins a good yarn. All them stories about medical school and them German professors of hisn. Jesus H. Christ! I could of listened all night long. Don't matter if it's lies. I like the way he talks about Germany. God. I can just see the place. Listening to him talk. Hell. You take that man to rendezvous . . ."

"What's a rendezvous? You talk all the time about rendezvous."

"Oh, boy, a rendezvous. That hell and heaven all mixed up together. That's where we used to go down and sell our furs. The company men, they'd come out there and buy. Wouldn't pay us what the furs was worth. Paid us most of the time in watered-down whiskey. But after a while, when we'd drunk a little, and danced a little, and swapped squaws, it didn't matter. I lived for the rendezvous. Funny how it was. Work all year long to make your fortune, and go down to the rendezvous, and you'd lose it in a week or two. But I'd do it over again if I had the chance. And you take that friend of yours to rendezvous, and he'd bring back enough hides to build hisself a hotel in New York like Astor done."

"Why?" Adam felt jealous of Harry. An emotion that came up in him, annoying him. He did not like to be jealous of anybody. But everything was so easy to Harry. Even this old man liked him.

"Why? You say why? Because the man can tell stories. And if they's one thing you want after living out in the woods for a year with not nothing but a squaw and your beaver, why, it's a good story! And him! He can tell stories from here to doomsday!"

"He ain't never been east of Georgia," Adam said sourly. "He's just read a bunch of books. He told me it was all he could do when he was young. Read books. His eyesight was too bad to hunt. Too bad to farm. He's just got his head full of book learning."

"Ah, well," the old man said. "That's his talent. We ain't got it. And what's it matter? Look at that girl."

"Promise." Adam felt heartsick with longing at the very word.

"Promise. That's a pretty name. Yes, my boy. Promise. She's having the time of her life. She ain't never going to forget this. Every day it's going. She can't realize it. What with the mud. And the dust. And the hard work. And mosquitoes. They make it seem like forever. But it's going, and one of these days. Bam! She's going to realize that it's gone, and she's going to realize that this time has been the happiest time of her life. It's good to see something like that. I had my days. Now she's got hers. With that man's stories."

Adam was hurt that the old man did not see his side. "But Harry ain't telling the truth!"

"Ah, don't sound so holy. Pretty soon you're going to try to walk over the Kaw. Like Jesus. And you're going to get all muddy. You live a long time like me, Adam, and you don't know what's true and what ain't for nobody but yourself. You got to do what you got to do. Most of the time, you don't care what other folks do. If they like to scratch, let 'em scratch. Just as long as it ain't your sores they're scratching. If they like to lie, let 'em lie. Just as long as they ain't lying to you about something they're trying to sell you. Listen, I seen a relic of the Virgin Mary onct in a church. Back in St. Louis. It was supposed to be some of the very milk out of her breasts. The priest that showed it to me, he swore up and down by all the saints that it was the real thing. Hell, it was a lie. I knowed it was a lie at the time. But the priest, he believed it. And when I was looking at it. That white, chalky stuff in a little brown bottle made of clay. Why, I believed it myself for a minute. And tell the truth, it made me feel good. Sometimes I still think about it. That milk. And I think about what a good thing it was that the real Virgin Mary did give suck just like your ordinary mother. It ain't bad to think things like that. No matter what makes you do it."

"Are you a Catholic?" Adam asked suspiciously. He gave the old man a sidelong glance, full of dark surprise.

"Hell, yes. What are you?"

Adam swallowed. "I ain't nothing. I ain't never had no experience."

"Well, what the shit is that supposed to mean?"

Adam turned red. He could not look at the old man. He thought the sky was about to swallow him. "I ain't never been touched by the Holy Ghost."

"Good Christ! I hope not!"

"Dammit, if you ain't touched by the Holy Ghost, then you are going to spend forever and ever burning in hell."

"I'll be damned. You don't say!" The old man laughed.

"That's what the Methodists say."

"That's a bunch of shit."

Adam was silent for a minute. He had never run into such blatant unbelief. It was like being doused with ice cold water. "Ever Methodist I ever knowed believed that," he said slowly and very firmly.

"Hell, boy, the Methodists ain't even the true church. Why in hell do you let them scare the shit out of you? If you want to be scared, you come and let the Catholics do it for you. We do it better than anybody."

They came to Papin's ferry over the Kaw. A squalid and dusty little settlement, perched on the south bank precariously, something the prairie wind might blow away. Innumerable wagons and livestock had destroyed the grass in a great, rough semicircle around the crossing. Dust coated everything. A brown and acid dust.

207

A few wigwams with Indian men indolently reclining in the shade. Little dogs yapping about, looking starved. Some ill-looking horses here and there, thin and swaybacked. A few naked children. Greasy-looking squaws with puffy faces and very dark, lined skin. A couple of slatternly houses made of wood with shingle roofs. Grass growing in the shingles.

The Kaw was wide and swift and muddy. Too muddy to see bottom. A bad river. The ferry lay on the near side, against the bank. It was scarcely more than a raft, akin to the ugly houses nearby. A thick rope ran across the river, yellow in the sunshine. It was tied on each side to a stout cottonwood tree. The ferry was tied to the cable with another rope, spliced to make a sliding noose, and in that way it was not swept downstream by the current.

Papin came out to greet them. He was a half-breed, the old man said. Part French and part Indian, a dark and muscular man going to lard in middle age, coarse black hair turning gray, unkempt on his head. His eyes were red and swollen. A man drinking in the cool shade to pass away the long, dull summer.

"You Californians?" he said. A voice thickly accented. Speculative little black dots flashed at them amid the bloodshot whites of his eyes. Darting here and there, measuring their worth. He saw the richly loaded wagons. He saw the way the Jennings men looked. Men out of place. Vaguely afraid.

Shawnee Joe took charge. "We're Californians," the old man said. A Californian was somebody bound for California.

"The gold's all gone," Papin said with a sneer, pleased to deliver bad news. "I ship over folks all summer long. They come back home. No find gold in California."

"We ain't looking for gold."

"You late. Should of go by month now."

"We know what month it is. Reckon we ain't lost track of time like you, Papin. We ain't hiding in no jug. How much be ye charging this year to go acrost on your puny little ferryboat?"

Papin drew out a plug of dirty-looking chewing tobacco. He bit off a hunk; he studied the old man sitting astride his mule and looking down like the reserved wrath of a very old god of the forest. "I reckon I charge six dollars a wagon, a dollar a team, and ten cent a people." Papin chewed. Spat at his feet.

Shawnee Joe took a deep breath. His brown face glowed with fury. "You half-breed thieving son of a bitch! It was four dollars a wagon last year."

Papin looked up innocently. Smiling. "Well, time she is hard. Ain't so much people going west this year. What they is make start from St. Joe. Don't have to cross so many river, so many creek when you leave from St. Joe. If you be smart, you leave from St. Joe, too. If you dumb enough to come this way, you got to pay my price."

"Your mamma was an Indian whore. Your daddy was a frog. You're charging white folks six dollars a wagon."

"Oh, I ain't smart, but I got ferryboat, and I know how to count on fingers," Papin said affably. He held a filthy hand in the air. Stubby fingers spread out. Gesture half obscene. "I count six dollar a team this year. You take it. Or you go back to Westport Landing." He turned around and started to walk off.

"No, wait. I'll pay for it!" Adam said.

Papin whirled on Adam with a beaming grin. "You got *money?* OK, you my friend. You lot smarter than this old man here. Hey, listen. I give you big discount. I show you what nice fella I be no matter what this no good son of whore dog say. I take over all wagon for six dollar apiece. OK? I take dollar apiece for team OK? I take dime for all men everyone. All the women the same. OK? But the kids and you dog? They go free! Free! You hear that? Papin give you something free just because he your friend. And besides! He loves childrens!" Papin looked as benevolent as Judas about to plant a kiss on the world with his big, fat lips.

"The mongrel bastard's trying to tell you he'll save you twenty cents." Shawnee Joe said.

"I'll pay," Adam said wearily.

Shawnee Joe could bear it no longer. He jumped down off his mule and landed facing Papin, his beaver hat clutched in one hand. He shot a furious glance at Adam. "What do you mean, you're going to pay!"

Adam looked at him blankly. "How in hell are we going to get across the goddamned river if we don't pay him?" Adam was exasperated. Yelling.

Jason looked pale and helpless. His big shoulders slumped. "Mr. McMoultrie, if Adam wants to pay, then let him do it. *He has the money!* Better let Adam pay than go through this

209

... this awful scene!" Jason looked at the old man with pleading.

"Shut up, Jason!" the old man said. "Listen, we're going to make our own goddamned ferry. You hear that, Papin? You just lost a chance to make an honest dollar! We'll make our own ferry, and we'll cross this goddamned river by ourselves. And you can go shit in your goddamned hat."

Adam looked at the muddy river rolling only yards away. They heard the heavy rustle of its current. There were places where eddies boiled on the surface and went speeding downstream. Jason looked at the water. Looked up at all of them. Afraid. He was almost sick.

Samuel came up and stood by him. "It's all right, Jason. Look at all the times we crossed the Ohio."

"Hell," Asa said drily, "Jason didn't cross that much. He stood on the bank and left us to go."

"I went sometimes, Asa," Jason said.

"You went onct, I think," Asa said.

"I did go," Jason whispered. "I was brave."

Adam looked at Jason, looked at the river, saw its lethal power gurgling and rushing in the still, hot afternoon, smelled its rank muddiness, and at that moment Adam felt closer to Jason than he was ever to feel again.

Shawnee Joe bossed them to work. They ranged out along the riverbank and cut trees. The Jennings men hitched the oxen to the trees, and when the branches had been stripped away, they hauled the long trunks back to where they would cross. Clifford Baynes followed them around. He suddenly developed a bad limp. He whined. "Oh, my back, my back! Oh, it hurts my back just to see you fine gentlemen straining yourselves like that. I can't do any hard work. I'm truly sorry, gentlemen. If you could just know what a stabbing pain I get in my back when I try to chop wood. But the stabbing pains are not nearly so bad as the shooting pains. Nor the throbbing pains. Gentlemen, I vow to you the throbbing pains are worst of all."

Shawnee Joe leaned on his axe a minute. He looked Clifford Baynes in the eyes. "Why in hell don't you put a plug in that goddamned bunghole you got for a mouth?"

"Sir, are you addressing me?"

"Well, I ain't praying to God."

Clifford Baynes decided to join his wife. She was sitting in Samuel's wagon, visiting with Rebecca.

They worked until their clothes were soaked through and turned dark and the sweat dripped off their hair. The old man was everywhere. Laughing. Shouting. Cussing and laughing at Jason, clapping him familiarly on the back. Commanding. Chopping as expertly as a carpenter with the axe. Tying ropes. Driving the oxen, moving tirelessly like an exuberant gnome taking a little excursion trip along the Kaw River.

They worked until it was too dark to work anymore. They ate a hot supper, and Adam thought the smell of it was the grandest thing he had ever smelled. Jessica made cornbread in the Dutch oven. The little Indian children came swarming around them, drawn by the smell floating softly in the prairie night. Their bellies swollen and hanging like tumors, their thin buttocks, their dull, dark eyes tragic and ravenous as hungry dogs. Jessica gave them some cornbread, fried in bacon grease, savory, soft and yellow, and the little red children gobbled it up until finally she said in exasperation, "There's no end to it! They're eating it as fast as I can make it!"

Shawnee Joe drove them off as though they had been a litter of mongrel puppies. "Git on now. You've had your free bread. We got to eat ourselves."

Ruth and Jessica were upset. "They're hungry," Jessica said in a voice soft and unbelieving.

Jason cleared his throat and read a Psalm:

The wicked borroweth, and payeth not again: but the righteous sheweth mercy, and giveth. For such as be blessed of Him shall inherit the earth; and they that be cursed of Him shall be cut off. The steps of a good man are ordered by the Lord: and He delighteth in his way. Though he fall, he shall not be utterly cast down; for the Lord upholdeth him with His hand. I have been young, and now am old; yet have I not seen the righteous forsaken, nor his seed begging bread.

He put a slight stress on these last words and looked toward the dark where the Indian children were shadows still by their fires. Jessica suddenly spoke up. Her voice was nearly breaking, and she spoke softly. "I don't want to sing tonight, husband. I don't want to sing while those hungry children are watching us."

Jason looked at her gravely. An annoying patience in his

211

face. "Well, my dear, nobody will force you so sing," he said quietly. "I am sorry, but my wife does not want us to sing."

Adam was glad. He did not feel like listening to singing now. Maybe the Indians were cursed. The wicked condemned by God. He could not understand it. Their hungry, resigned, and stolid faces. Jason went to the wagon and drew out his leather-bound diary and began to write in it.

Harry spoke up. "When we get to California, nobody's going to be hungry. You know, Mr. Jennings, when people see what we do ... When they learn the power of love, the whole world's going to follow our example. You wait and see! No hunger there! No bitterness!"

Harry had to call. His voice was a shout in the moving wind, and Jason looked dreamily up from his writing. "Yes," he said, raising his own voice to be heard. "I have always thought ... I am going to California not just for ourselves. That would be selfish. But if the world follows what we do ... There are newspapers now. Telegraphs. What we do can be known by everybody. The age of progress ..." He stopped, his voice dropped, and Adam, stirred uneasily at the ghostly calling of Harry and Jason to one another, did not want them to start again. He slowly relaxed when Harry turned away and went into the tent they had pitched in the dust.

Promise sat on by the fire. Once she looked up at Adam, her face shining in the reflection, something plucked out of the dark. "Do you think we'll make it?" she said.

Adam's heart beat fast when she spoke to him. He felt like a fool. With an effort he mastered the terrible emotion he felt and spoke calmly. "Sure we'll make it. Why, this river—it ain't nothing." He looked over at Samuel. "Is it, Samuel? It ain't nothing, is it?"

"I don't like it out here," Promise said softly. "I really don't like it here. It's so wild. So many things can happen."

"It'll be all right," Adam said gruffly. "We'll get over."

The men took turns watching the stock at night now. Teams of two, watching three hours at a time, tramping and keeping a lookout for any suspicious motion. Jason refused to carry a rifle. "He wants to be better than other folks," Shawnee Joe said. "I've knowed men like him before. Only usually they're missionaries. Usually they're dead when they're his age."

The others were not so squeamish. When Adam walked

212

with one of his heavy rifles cradled in his arms, he thought he would die from fatigue within an hour. He discovered what so many had learned before him, would learn after him. Walking around with the stock in the middle of the night was the loneliest job on earth.

The big dipper rolled in its serene arc around the pole. The stars melted in the pale dawning as the day came, washing the eastern sky first with colorless light and then painting it with a red that made tired hearts rise to meet the rising sun.

Jessica and Ruth made breakfast. Bacon and cornbread, frying on the fresh, cool air. And again the Indian children, empty-eyed and silent, came crowding hungrily around. Jessica gave them cornbread again; the cornbread disappeared as though she had tossed it to dogs. "Why are these children so hungry?"

"Their folks is civilized," Shawnee Joe said dryly. He spoke a few words to the children now in a strange tongue, syllables like rocks knocking together in his throat, and he made a sign with his two hands. The children looked at him with dead, empty surprise. Then slowly, like the night going, they slunk away, leaving the whites to a guilty breakfast, standing, crooking arms to drink the good, strong coffee, listening in silence to the low, deadly murmur of the river sliding nearby.

"It seems so awful to make them go away when they're still hungry," Jessica said. Ruth mutely agreed, her broad face filled with wonder and pity.

"You can feed them all you got, and we'd be here like them, and they'd still be hungry, and we'd be hungry, too," the old man said. His voice was surprisingly soft. "It's the way the world is."

Mrs. Baynes was not disturbed. "I say they's some folks in the world that has things. And they's some others that don't have nothing. If you can get something, then you better do it quick because they's lots of other folks just waiting to get it before you do. And if they get it first, then you ain't got nothing left to get yourself." She was taking huge bites of bacon and hot cornbread, eating like a dog in a crowd. Great, swift gulps. As though she feared another dog might rush up and snatch her meal away.

"Well," Jason said, clearing his throat. "Obviously these people are not representative of the real Indians. I do believe that though it may pain us to see its consequences, justice

213

does rule in the world. People get what they deserve in the long run."

"Just what do you figure is a *real* Indian?" the old man said, eyeing Jason narrowly.

"I have read a great deal about the Indians, Mr. McMoultrie. Frankly I don't believe that anyone has to explain what a real Indian is. We all know that."

The frostily insolent tone to Jason's voice made Adam afraid. He half-expected the old man to whip out his Bowie knife, worn so carelessly at his belt, and cut Jason's throat. Jason could not even imagine the danger he faced, just being near Shawnee Joe McMoultrie, and Adam held his breath.

But the old man just laughed and walked off.

After breakfast Papin came over again, sliding along on his greasy smile. "I see you work damn hard. Listen, it good for old man like you to work hard. You go to heaven faster that way. Work for King Jesus. Amen. But you don't get these other peoples to California faster. You work here maybe two day. And me? I put you on other side of this here damn river in one hour. Look. I tell what I do. I give you big discount now because I see you work. And I like men work. Now, because I like you, young feller, I take you over for only four dollar wagon, one dollar team, ten cent . . ."

"You're wasting your breath and our time, Mr. Papin, sir! We're going to make it all by ourselves." It was Samuel.

The old man laughed. "You heard what he said, Papin. You go fuck yourself with a limber rope."

Shawnee Joe stood with his legs wide apart, one hand on the long handle of his heavy knife. Samuel stood behind him, smiling as if they were enjoying the friendliest conversation in the world. Papin looked at them both. Saw the bright and happily lethal thing in the old man's eyes. He shrugged. Then he laughed. False laughter, like bricks banged together. "You good man, old fellar. You joke one hell of a lot. I like you." And laughing with the same humor that you find in a saw, Papin sauntered off.

The old man spat after him and took charge again.

He got the first wagon down into the river, double-teamed, twelve oxen wading reluctantly into the deep and pointing upstream along the bank. With ludicrous delicacy they slowly drew the wagon after them. Then the men, sweating and groaning and wading in muddy water up to their chests, wrestled the logs alongside and under the wagon bed and roped them in tight, converting the wagon itself into a raft.

The old man looked ecstatic. It was working. He took Jason's leather whip and kicked his mule down into the water, tapping the amber rumps of the reluctant oxen with curious gentleness. It struck Adam that the old man was kinder to animals than he was to people. The oxen responded slowly to his soft blows and turned out into the river, moving with their steady, slow clumsiness against the sweep of the current, and the wagon came lurching heavily behind them. Jason's wagon this time. Jessica and Promise sat up on the seat, bracing themselves with the precarious tipping of the wagon. Adam looked at Promise and saw that she was terrified. But Jessica was in triumph. The brown water came sweeping up over their feet when the wagon plunged in, and the two of them cried out. Promise in terror, Jessica in a thrill of delight. Adam himself nearly cried out The impossibility of things working. But then the wagon settled almost miraculously into the water and floated high, and the old man was swimming his mule and waving his hat in the air, encouraging the oxen with a high, shrill, "Yip-yip-yii-yip-yip!" And the poor, tired beasts were obediently swimming, their heads held up high so that water would not pour into their noses, and the wagon was sweeping after them like a ridiculous ark on the crest of the flood.

Adam rode down into the water himself on his favorite mule, and the no-name hound came prancing joyfully behind, barking furiously, and lunged into the river as though the Kaw had been made for dogs. Adam laughed. He had a long, hemp rope fixed to his saddle horn. The other end of the rope was tied to the back of the wagon. He was to balance the wagon in the river, to keep it from being swept end-around downstream. So he let the rope grow taut, and when he could feel the force of the river, a strength that was like something surging out of the earth itself to drag him down into the darkness, he kicked his mule down into the Kaw, and the river tore at animal and man in a frenzy that he could hardly bear.

The water rolled with relentless might against his knees and washed up his thighs and swept with a swirling, sucking roar around the mule, and Adam was astonished and almost in panic at the unvarying, unyielding power of the current. His confidence was swept away, and he wondered why he had ever left home. The chill and driving power of the river almost took his breath away; he sobbed for air. He wanted to cry out, but he did not have breath. Feeling the steady drive of the torrent against his body, he knew abject helplessness and terror. *If God wanted me to live in California, He would have made me born there!* Again he felt the blasphemy of trying to change the way things were. *We ain't going to make it!* The words shrieked in his heart. The rope pulled at the saddle, at the mule, and the mule's big white eyes rolled back, glazed with the terror Adam felt. He kept thinking almost irately that once the river had tried him and failed, it would decently let him go, leave him in peace. But the river struggled against him, something enormous, vicious, alive, and untiring.

The wagon strained so on the rope that it seemed the rope must fly in pieces or else drag the mule under. But the animal fought the river and swam in powerful, instinctive strokes, and Adam clung with all his might to the saddle. He heard the roar of the river all around him, and the isolation, the danger, and the enmity of nature itself were things he had never before felt, never dreamed of in his worst nightmares.

The river washed hungrily against the oxen. They labored with all their might. Overhead the bright sunshine streamed down. The clouds were as peaceful as sleep. The banks on the other side, so low when they had looked down on them from the southern shore, now seemed to rise like brown cliffs out of the terrible water, and they were more distant than God.

Then wonder of wonders, the oxen touched bottom! Their swimming became a struggling walk, stumbling and forlorn, up the underwater declivity of the riverbed near its banks. Then the wagon tilted upward with a sudden lurch, and the oxen were towing it up and up, and the mule, too, was abruptly not swimming but digging his sharp hoofs into muck, and almost without believing it, Adam was rising out of the water, his mule leaning forward, climbing, winning against the disappointed pull of the river, and the oxen were wrenching the wagon up and going ahead of all of them onto dry land. Adam was thinking then and would think ever afterwards that if in some remote day of doom he should find himself rising from the dank grave, the damp dust he had become turning coherent again into a new body, standing at the resurrection with the multitude of the living dead, he would not be more astonished than he was on that early summer morning when he came up out of the Kaw.

On both sides of the river people broke into cheering. Adam took a deep, sweet breath and expelled it with a shout. Jessica was throwing her blond head back, laughing with joy, her eyes shut against the bright sky. And the old man was waving his hat in the air and chanting some song he had learned from Indians when they had killed their foe. Promise jumped down out of the wagon and cried.

"Everything in the wagon's drenched!" Jessica shouted with a ringing laugh. "The water came in like a flood for a minute! But look!" Adam realized with a shock of delight that she was holding up his two heavy rifles and that they were dry. He had forgotten them.

"I hung the rifles up high, tied them up there against the hoops of the wagon top!" she cried. Adam found himself by her wagon, looking over at her, thanking her, grinning, being foolish and incoherent. He wanted suddenly to hug her. But he was not so bold. So he only admired her, a woman with a beauty at its prime, filled with that radiant glow that is the sum of youth, shining just for a moment before fading into the different light of middle age. "I put the gunpowder up, too," Jessica was saying. She laughed again with pleasure at the surprise she had created in Adam. "Up high, on the top boxes, with the flour barrels. I hope that means fresh meat to go with our bread before this is over."

Adam laughed again. His mind swirled with thoughts as incoherent as the foam in the river. He would get meat for her cooking. He would kill something for her. And behind this silent promise, there was that strange, fresh joy that comes when a man and a woman recognize a bond between them. Adam could not define the invisible knot that suddenly tied him to this woman. A friendship that was out of the ordinary. A human being who let him know that in this crowd, they two shared something that removed them from the others. He could not even begin to describe it. And now there was no time. The river had to be crossed again.

Before it was over Adam and the old man had crossed the river six more times. They shifted the mules. Shifted the oxen. They got everything over including the flimsy cart of the couple Baynes. Mrs. Baynes would not let her precious oxen be used in the rotation.

"These here is our oxen," she said, her head cocked, her

voice wise, "It wouldn't be right to let them be hurt hauling for somebody else. They've been so faithful to us. We just can't let them down."

Harry laughed, trying to be friendly with her. "She's right, Adam. She has the right to do what she wants with her property."

"Don't you mock me, *Doctor* Creekmore," she said in a level and menacing tone. "I know things."

Harry looked hurt and baffled. "I wasn't mocking you, Mrs. Baynes. I was taking your part."

"Ain't nobody ever takes my part," she said.

Adam did not argue, but he felt sorry for Harry. Adam worked until he was half-blind with fatigue, and his arms felt like enormous weights screwed into his shoulders, and his legs were like waterlogged flour sacks. But there was a sweet triumph to it. After they crossed the Kaw, he thought he could do anything—master any terror, cross any river, do any deed. He was different from other men. And in his grand feeling of glory, he believed that he had won some undefined right to Jessica's friendship. His thought did not go further than that; he only recognized that he was a man now.

Maybe the greatest joy was seeing Papin.

When Shawnee Joe got back to the south shore for the second trip, Papin was there, stalking back and forth with a look of conciliation and purpose. He had his boots on; his shirt was buttoned in a very businesslike way; and he wore an oily smile. He was aglow with good will and apology.

"OK, Joe, my friend. You win. You prove you damn good man, by God. Hell, you like Indian, by God! Shit! Amen! Now, I tell you what I do! I take you over for one dollar a wagon. All peoples go *free!* Because why? Because I like you, Joe. You got shit good spirit. Glory hallelujah, by God! And what you going to get better than deal like mine? You tell me, by God!"

The old man only laughed at him. Shawnee Joe not even angry now. He, like Adam, was feeling the glorious triumph of the river. "Sometimes I feel like an old shoe. Worn out. Done. But then I do something like this. And it's different. I'm young again." He held up his hands and looked at them, and his walnut-colored face was renewed in an almost magical way. "I don't even feel the rheumatiz!"

So in the end Papin was left pacing back and forth, ignored, beaten, wringing his big, dirty hands, and wailing.

"You steal food out of these here children mouth. You against Indian! You steal this here country from Indian and not even give Indian way to make living when you go by. You not even Christian! Glory hallelujah. You end up in hell, and you think about poor old Papin when you want water! You remember. You there because you cheat me. An honest man."

The worst trouble crossing was with Rachael. She began to scream when Asa's wagon rolled into the swift river. In the lurching just before the wagon floated, the water came roaring up, swift, muddy, and terrible. She shrieked so horribly that little Indian children on the banks turned and fled. And when they had been safely landed on the northern bank, she screamed on and on. Her face was screwed up, eyes half-shut, and a frozen gaping mouth let her shrieking out like a horn. It was the cry of all children when fire has burned down on top of their heads or animals attacked them or parents beat them. And when they were safe on dry land, she could not take her eyes off the river but stared at it as though it had been an enormous brown snake, holding her entranced by its coiling dance.

Asa took her gently up in his arms and paced patiently back and forth, soothing her. He let her cling to him and weep against his shoulder until she was worn out. Finally she fell off to sleep the way a tired child will do—suddenly and deeply. Her wildly curly, amber hair was against his face and spilled in a tangled wave of dark color down his shirted back. Her little red mouth was open, lips slightly askew, so that she seemed all the more helpless and innocent. And once in her profound sleep, she took a very deep breath and expelled it with a wracking sob as though her body had not yet slowed down from its terror.

Asa walked back and forth and caressed her gently with his hand. Adam was warmed by the sight of him. Peculiar Asa! Adam could forgive him everything when he saw Asa with Rachael on his shoulder. Fathers were always mysterious, Adam thought. And he thought of his own father and wondered just why Joel Cloud left home. Was it only to find gold? And Adam thought of how strange it was that his father's exodus in the middle of the night had brought him— Adam Cloud—out here with this odd assortment of people in the midst of the alien plains.

# 31

They celebrated their victory over the Kaw with a feast. Bread and coffee.

"Let me tell you something," the old man said, looking around sternly at them all. "I learnt something a long time ago. Up on the Platte, where the water's hot and bad, we'll all drink coffee. I learnt if you drink coffee, you don't get sick so much."

"Aha," Asa said, good-humored now but still unable to bury the relentless edge of his sarcasm. "That don't make no sense."

"They's lots of things that don't make no sense, but they're true," the old man said.

"Ah," Asa said and laughed.

They dried their clothes in the sun. Jessica said, laughing and pained at once, "They'll all have to be washed. Everything."

Harry inspected himself with distaste. His white suit was caked with mud. "I'm afraid my suit may be ruined," he said tentatively. "I don't know if I'll ever get it clean again."

Shawnee Joe laughed in his knowing way. "When we get to the stony mountains, you'll find good clear water to wash in. Ain't no good to wash nothing in water out of the Kaw."

Adam was coated with mud up to his shoulders. Thin, sandy mud drying like a heavy skin suit over him in the steady sunlight.

Samuel came out of his wagon looking gloomy. "Everything's a mess. The river has turned everything upside down."

Adam said, "I'll help you fix it up." He felt sorry for Samuel. The big man's desolate and bewildered look.

"I'll go along," Shawnee Joe said. "I'm right interested to meet this lady I've been hearing about so much. Thinks she's still back in Ohio, does she?"

The old man's tone was easy and insolent. He did not have

to veil his feelings around these people. Be easy on them. He was so much better than they were. Samuel looked pained. Hurt. Adam was embarrassed. He had told Shawnee Joe about Rebecca.

"You ought to repair the damage right away," Jason said sternly. Almost blaming Samuel for the river. The mud. Jason accustomed to blaming Samuel for things. And Adam wondered how it had been out in the Ohio. At night, ferrying the niggers over. Jason secure on the Ohio shore, Samuel out doing the work, and if the boat turned over, Jason blamed the stupid brother. Jason went on, gloomily prophesying. "I don't know what would happen if Rebecca were to lose her illusions out here. You know her nervous state . . ." He saw the old man grinning familiarly at him. Shawnee Joe always seemed to be saying, *I wonder what this crazy man is going to say next to make me laugh.* Intransigently insolent. Refusing to take Jason seriously. Jason turned to Harry, his bastion and his shelter. "Do you know anything about diseases of the nerves, doctor?"

"Ha!" Ishtar Baynes cackled, like a pecking hen with mud in her feathers.

Harry shot a worried glance at her, looked at Promise. Then with his easy, syrupy confidence, he said, "Diseases of the nerves are among the most complicated disorders in the entire realm of pathology." The vocabulary of his medical books, studied like magical scriptures every night, was beginning to soak into his own. "I fear I am not well informed on the subject. But then this lack of information is general in my profession. Only a charlatan would presume to tell you things about the mind. For the simple truth is that here our ignorance is as black as the night itself." He finished with his fine head lowered in the proper degree of professional humility, removed his glasses thoughtfully, and began to polish them, the sunlight golden on his blond beard.

Jason was grateful. "Dr. Creekmore, I appreciate an honest man, even when he must tell me an unpleasant truth. An unpleasant truth is still far better than a lie."

"Ha!" Ishtar Baynes cried again. Her head cocked, her eyes malicious and glaring.

"You do agree with me, Dr. Creekmore, that we should avoid everything that might disturb Rebecca? When we get to California we can gradually let her know that she has been moved. But we may induce a state of hysteria in her if we

221

tell her before then." He sighed and clapped big Samuel on the shoulders, shaking his head regretfully. "Samuel knows how much I opposed his marriage to Rebecca. I said she wasn't the woman for him. I argued with him night and day. But to no avail. Now we have to make the best of it. Poor thing, we all have to protect her. I knew she was unstable. Knew it in my bones. But Samuel lacked my experience. And he was in love! Or he thought he was!"

Samuel looked down at Jason with an expression of doglike, trust and gratitude. "I sure do appreciate it, Jason. I sure do. You was right, but she's a good woman. You wait and see. She's going to be all right when we get to California."

"Of course! Of course!" Jason said, patronizing Samuel, mastering the big man in the way a midget can drive a horse by jerking on the bridle or sticking a spurred heel into the beast's helpless flank.

"I am in full agreement," Harry said in splendid vagueness. Very professionally. "We should not disturb the dear woman in the least."

Ishtar Baynes flashed a vulpine smile, drawing her upper lip back over her teeth. "I think Mrs. Rebecca is just the *sweetest* thing."

The inside of the wagon was an unholy mess. The cupboard, fronted with glass, had tipped over. The glass had shattered into a thousand pieces. The river had brought in mud and slime, and Rebecca's full, blue skirt was filthy below the knees. The trundle bed was askew. The blankets were soaked and filthy, and the wagon stank.

But in the midst of the mess sat Rebecca Jennings serenely knitting and rocking in her chair. She greeted them with a rosy smile. "I ain't never seen such a rain. The basement flooded, Samuel. You got to do something about our gutters. Why, they must not be worth nothing."

Samuel looked joyful with relief. He sat down on the wet bed with a dull smile of happiness. He had been nearly beside himself wondering how he was going to explain the flood to Rebecca. Now she had explained it for him. "I'll do it, Rebecca! You bet your life."

"I wouldn't bet my life on you, husband dear," Rebecca said, smiling sweetly. "But do fix the roof."

Samuel turned around with a proud grin to the old man to see if everybody agreed that this was the most wonderful little wife in all the world. Rebecca looked sharply at the old man and smiled, but above the bending of her smile, her eyes filled with wary calculation.

Samuel made introductions. "This here's a new man in the neighborhood, Rebecca. Mr. McMoultrie. His name's Joe."

"Well, I'm so glad to meet you," Rebecca said. Her voice was coated with sugar, but her eyes remained alert and mean. "Are you new at the foundry?"

"I ain't new at anything," the old man said in a tone that was bored and aloof. The two of them looked at each other, and there was something steely and contemptuous in the old man's lined face. "We better be cleaning up this mess," he said finally, looking around.

"Don't you think it was the roof?" Rebecca said.

"Oh, yes, it was the roof," Samuel said nervously.

"I wasn't talking to you. I was talking to that old man there," Rebecca said.

"Mr. McMoultrie thinks it was the roof, too," Samuel said. He looked at the old man frantically. "Don't you, Mr. McMoultrie?"

"Well, don't you?" Rebecca said. Her sharp little eyes were slits in her puffy face, and her smile had faded.

"I think we ought to be cleaning up," the old man said.

Later on Adam said to the old man, "Why couldn't you go along with her, with Rebecca? She won't like you now. And you hurt Samuel's feelings!" Adam was perplexed.

The old man laughed, untroubled. "Ah, you get to be pretty independent out in the Oregon Territory, I reckon. Don't try to make me different just because we're trying to help these folks get across the plains and the mountains. Hell, you don't know it, my boy, but we're doing a good deed. A damn good deed. Now I believe in doing good deeds. But let me tell you something I don't believe. I don't believe you get down and grovel in front of the folks you're helping. I don't know why folks do that. But they do it all the time. But not me. I got too much pride. They either take me like I am, or they don't make it to California."

Adam hardly dared to admonish the old man. He spoke in a murmur of confusion. "Well, but she's crazy. Poor old thing. She thinks she's back there in Ohio. She don't know where she is."

The old man spat a brown jet of tobacco juice into the

grass. "She ain't crazy," he said. "She damn well knows where she is."

Adam was mystified. He thought maybe the old man was right. But he couldn't see the reason for it. Why did Rebecca want to pretend? He had never known people before who had no reasons for what they did.

Breakfast, breaking camp and preparing to move. North now. Dim shapes in the pale dawning. The fire burning up merrily around the coffee pot. The long night behind them and all feelings calm. Everything back in place for the new day's march. Jason drank coffee, sipping at it with the meditation he supposed philosophers used when they drank coffee, and he thought aloud between sips, remembering old discussions from days when he was young and all the world hoped for self-improvement. Then young men talked and planned and sounded wise to themselves.

"There's just one thing that disturbs me profoundly about all this."

Harry said, "What's that, Mr. Jennings?"

"That terrible scene we had with Mr. Papin," Jason shook his head. "Just terrible."

"I'm sorry about it, too," the old man said laconically. He slurped when he drank his coffee, an uncouth sound he delighted in because it pained Jason so much.

"You are?" Jason said. He smiled with surprise and a relief that made his face glow. "Well, I'm pleased to hear that, Mr. McMoultrie." Jason was about to tell himself that he might have been mistaken about the old man.

The old man yawned. "Well, I've just been standing here thinking. I ain't going to pass by here again. I just missed a great chance."

Jason beamed. "Mr. McMoultrie, I'm gratified. I have thought that behind your crude exterior there beats the heart of a gentleman."

"Gentleman!" The old man chortled. "Jason, I'm wishing I'd of broke Papin's back. I'm wishing I'd of kilt him. The world would of been a better place."

"Killed him!" Henry cried in amazement. More clearly than anybody else he saw that the old man meant exactly what he said.

"Hush, child!" Jason said crossly. "Mr. McMoultrie doesn't mean that. He's just expressing himself vigorously."

"Oh, I wish I'd of kilt him vigorously," the old man said almost dreamily. "Cut his heart out with my Bowie knife. Fed his heart to that there dog of Adam's."

Jason looked forlorn. He was a leader whose authority was being mocked, and he resented it, and did not know what to do about it. "I wish you had another spirit, Mr. McMoultrie."

"Well, I don't," the old man said contentedly.

"Mr. Papin is a human being. I will admit that he is very unpleasant. But he still is a man, endowed with reason by the Creator and capable of good if he could only be led."

The old man laughed and folded his arms, looking at Jason with expectant curiosity and waiting to hear what foolish thing he would say next.

Jason was offended but went on. "It is no laughing matter, Mr. McMoultrie. If we only knew what had made Papin what he is, we could understand him. We could lead him to self-improvement."

"We might understand him, but he'd still be Papin, and if he improved hisself, he'd be worse."

"You don't seem to understand. If we could get him to improve, we could get along with him. He could become a part of society."

"I know how to get along with Papin, Jason. Stick a knife in him first chance you get."

"Mr. McMoultrie, that is not a civilized way of looking at human beings."

"Jason, it is the way I look at Papin. I didn't say nothing about human beings."

"He has had experiences. Ever since he was born. The experiences have written themselves on his heart. They have made him what he is. Good experiences would have made him a good man." Jason coughed and looked very wise. "Haven't you ever read John Locke, Mr. McMoultrie?"

"Jason, I ain't never read nothing. But I know this. You take a hog and send him to college, and he is going to come out of college with a diploma in one hoof, and first thing he's going to do is start rooting for acorns in the president's yard. You take Papin and send him to Yale, and first thing he will do is bite the president in the leg, and second thing he will do is pee on the flagpole."

Asa growled. "Can't you see there're ladies present, Mr. McMoultrie? I don't like my wife hearing talk like that."

Ruth laughed. "Don't be silly, husband. If Mr. McMoultrie

wants to talk like that, it ain't going to hurt me none. I don't know if you remember, but I've had me two babies, and I reckon I know what pee is." She laughed good-naturedly, a laugh meant to soothe things. But Asa looked at her and burned.

Jessica laughed, too. "I agree," she said. "It's a sin to talk one way in front of men and another in front of women. Women are people, aren't they?"

Asa glared at her. "That's the way it's always been; that's the way it's always going to be!"

"I hope not," Jessica said coldly.

Adam noticed that Asa could not keep his eyes off Jessica. Whenever he thought no one was looking at him, he stared at her. Something terrible, almost frantic, in the gaze. Adam thought Jessica must know that she was always being watched by those unpleasant eyes. She was usually turned so that she did not have to look at Asa unless she made an effort. And she held her fine chin up in queenly contempt that seemed to be a silent slap. Adam felt a bad premonition of something.

Jason lunged on. He was not accustomed to anybody arguing with him. He looked earnestly at the old man. "If Mr. Papin had had the same experiences I've had, he would be the same person that I am now. And if I had had the experiences that Mr. Papin had had, I would be the person he is now, tending that ferry."

Shawnee Joe swallowed the rest of his coffee. "And if I had wings I'd be a swan, and if I had horns I'd be a billy goat."

"You look like a billy goat anyway," Mrs. Baynes said. "Why don't you never cut your hair, Mr. McMoultrie?"

"Baaaaaaa!" the old man said.

"Isn't it wonderful?" Promise said dreamily. "The dawn! See! The sky's all red. I never dreamed the dawn took up so much room, I never saw the sky so red."

"The dawn is pale compared to your smile, my dear," Harry said reverently, inclining his beautiful blond head toward her beauty, abject and adoring.

"Good God!" the old man said. And in some way they could not quite understand, they were all laughing. All foolishness and pleasure. They had beaten the river and Papin. The road reached out ahead of them into the brightening day, and their hearts lifted. Their arguments were only words. Air. And the road was as solid as earth itself.

# 32

One day's journey on the north side of the Kaw there was a Catholic mission to the Pottawatomie Indians. It was called St. Mary's.

The old man was enthusiastic. "I'll get to hear Mass and confess!" he said. "Last chance between here and California!"

When Jason discovered that they were drawing near to a Catholic mission, he looked tolerant and superior. "There's only one religion," he said. "The transcendental religion of the spirit. All religions point to the same reality. But no religion contains all that reality. That's the only thing I have against the Catholics. They think they have all the truth."

"Say, I'm right glad to hear you be so humble, Jason," the old man said. "Truth to tell, for a while there I thought you was proud."

Jason looked genuinely baffled. "Why, Mr. McMoultrie! I don't see how anyone could ever say I was proud. I have deliberately chosen the path of humility."

The old man laughed, and Jason looked confused.

The mission was a group of little log buildings, newly put together, calked with mud, unpainted, baking and weathering under the blazing prairie sun. The buildings were exposed to the elements without even a sapling to hint of shade. To Adam it all seemed unspeakably dismal. He remembered Bourbonville with affection—the big, green oaks, and the billowing chestnuts growing in such profusion along the streets, trees in yards, trees spreading around the courthouse square, the dense, still forest that reached darkly for miles all around the town. In Bourbon County you won grudging permission from the forest to have a farm, and you kept the license only by ceaseless toil, for the trees would seed themselves and strain to grow as though moved by some dull and malicious intelligence to gain back every little scrap of land they had lost to men in a moment of leafy abstraction.

Until now Adam could not imagine building a house where there were no trees to shade. Only in passing did he ponder the immense labor that had gone into building these houses, hauling logs from great distances to this desolate place. The logs were cottonwood. Cottonwood was soft and split under the axe; it would rot away in a few years, leaving no trace. So the mission looked like so much of the human effort out here—something to be blown away and forgotten after the first storm, when nature aroused herself. Around the little settlement the empty prairies pitched and heaved in long, still, green swells of such enormity that they made the mission seem frail and pitiful. The prairies were like an unspoken prophecy, Adam thought. Human things would be devoured in the end. Space would consume everything. He felt suddenly sad and very homesick, a speck in the immensity of things.

The Indians who lounged about here were the most shiftless they had seen yet. They were wrapped in blankets despite the sultry heat. They were listless and sapped of their last strength, men whose chill was the coolness of death coming. As the wagons lurched in, raising their brown signal of dust, the Indians looked up with the dull, incurious, blank watching they might have turned on dry wisps of grass blowing across vacant land.

*What's wrong with them?* Adam could not speak his question.

The priests came out to meet them. Priests appearing like blackbirds in the heat, sweating over their white collars. "Welcome! Welcome! We have not seen anyone in days and days!" A stocky man, dark, with black hair flecked with gray and benign wrinkles around his mouth.

"I am Jason Jennings." Jason assumed a dignity befitting a leader of men.

"And I am Bishop Miege." He spoke with a heavy European accent.

They shook hands. Jason looked cold and aloof. The bishop hardly noticed. He smiled easily, and he was gentle, and in some vague way he seemed incapable of mustering the dignity you might have expected in a bishop.

Introductions were exchanged, the bishop using both his hands to shake hands with everybody. Adam felt the hands hot and powerful around his own, hands that were callused and hard from manual labor. And then the bishop led them

228

all around, throwing out his arms and waving his hands like a magician to show them his fabulous domain. "You see," he said in that finely cut accent, dark eyes flashing like charcoal aflame, "this insignificant little church is a cathedral because I am a bishop. A cathedral is the church where a bishop sits, you see? The first cathedral in this territory."

The building was in the form of a stubby cross. The bishop stood proudly with them inside and took a deep breath and looked reverently up to the low ceiling. It was surprisingly dark and cool inside, and the bishop swept both his musical hands around and looked with adoring satisfaction to where a rude crucifix was suspended from the plain rafters over a simple wooden altar. "And just by its being here, the power of the Church of God through the ages has been proved once again."

Asa burned to say something to deflate the bishop. "This feller here," he said, pointing to Harry, who stood with Promise on his arm by the bishop, "he's been in the Old Country. He's been in your real cathedrals."

Harry had told them all about Notre Dame, and now the bishop turned happily to him. "Indeed, my friend? You have been in Europe? Where? Have you been in Belgium?"

"Oh, no," Harry said nervously, his face pale in the dimness like a piece of limestone washed in a river. "I haven't been to Belgium. But I was in school in Heidelberg. At the University."

"He's a doctor," Asa said.

"A doctor! Well, well, well! Well, Doctor," the bishop said, shaking hands with him again, "it is an honor to have you here. I have never been to Heidelberg." The bishop shook his head in momentary sorrow. "It is Protestant, you know. I have not traveled much in Europe."

Only Adam could see how immensely relieved Harry was, and only Adam could understand fully the reason for the radiant smile that burst over Harry's face like sunshine. "It is a beautiful city," Harry said. "A very beautiful city."

"Look!" the bishop said again, pointing at the Indians. "These people were once savages. But now they have been baptized." The bishop paused, his silence pregnant with joy and pride. The Indians were slovenly. Jet-black hair clotted with rancid grease, hair hanging to their shoulders. A couple of young ones, with rapaciously quick eyes, crouched in the dust watching every move with terrible calculation. All of them stank. Some of them lay about in the shade, asleep in the dust as though they had been dogs.

That night some of the Indians made a fire in the open air and roasted a fat dog on a spit, the spit run through the dog's rectum to his mouth. When it was done, they tore the charred body off the spit and ate it greedily, stuffing morsels of dog—some of the internal parts raw and bloody still—into their ravenous mouths with suddenly quick hands. They did not disdain the bowels.

Mrs. Baynes was horrified. "Look at that!"

"I see it," Adam said, looking protectively at the no-name hound.

The bishop laughed. "I've tasted dog," he said. "It is quite savory. Quite good." The bishop was a man determined to be at home out here, to say that the creation was good, like God looking at what He had made and pronouncing it good because there was really nothing else to do.

The white people ate in the long, low building that served both as refectory and dormitory for the priests. Five priests in addition to the bishop sat at the table. No Indians there. Adam noticed their absence, turned it over like stones in a bucket in his head, could make nothing of it.

In the very early morning there was Mass, and the old man confessed his sins and took Communion. The dawn was just coming, and the interior of the little cathedral was dim with the residue of night beginning to dissolve. The morning light was just strong enough to make the candles on the rough altar seem pale and weak.

The bishop himself presided over the Mass, singing the ancient service in a powerful and rhythmic Latin, and his sonorous voice boomed in the church. It was a voice filled with confidence and strength, and Adam, sitting silently in the back, could understand its triumphant piety, though the language itself was a mystery.

A few Indians came in to loiter in the cool gloom and to watch. Some of them knelt and took Communion with the old man. The bishop's face, as he dispensed the wafers to their gaping mouths was aglow with celestial joy. Adam saw the Indians and the bishop, and the scene lost all its glory and mystery. Something almost ridiculously incongruous, childish, foolish in the bishop's shining, proud face like a sun beaming down on the vacant, crass faces of the Indians, who gaped up at the altar to receive dumbly the big medicine the bishop gave them. *What do they think?*

But Adam could not laugh at Shawnee Joe. The old man was sternly silent, and his bent form kneeling at the altar rail with his face uplifted in yearning and peace, was so baffling to Adam that he could not even speak to the old man later about it. A puzzle, this gnarled trapper from another world; Adam could not understand him and thought that it would be almost profane to try.

It was Jason who was puzzled by nothing. "Ah, me!" he sighed in a theatrical, patronizing way. "Catholics. So deluded. I don't mean your friend up there, Adam. Why, he's just a simple-minded old man. I don't reproach him. I'm talking about people with intellect. Catholics who know better. They sound so pure and good. But if you don't agree with them, there's always the stake in the background. Ah, me, the Inquisition. How intolerant. Well, there's no hope in the past. We know that, don't we? We must create something new, I tell you. Something completely new. America's the last place, too. The last good land that's not filled up yet. We can do it here. We must . . . Well, it's our last chance, don't you see? If we fail . . ." His voice died away in fantastic musing, his heart uplifted by his own perception of the way things were.

Harry was exuberant. Talk was cheap. They were walking up a grand morning. Talk as free as the air, and Harry could never be around anybody without trying to make that person like him and feel good. "I tell you what I think, Mr. Jennings. I think that when we get to California. When we set up a farming community and live together in peace. When people start seeing what we accomplish by living together, by loving each other, by cooperation . . . Oh, it's certain, certain. The world is going to beat a path to our door. Yes, I believe that. People are reasonable after all. Reason. The glory of humankind, I tell you. When people see something good, they want it for themselves. A good example. It has power to change hearts. More of a sermon in a life than in all the words ever preached from all the pulpits in the world."

"I entirely agree, Dr. Creekmore. Entirely." Jason was caught up in Harry's words. Adam, riding behind the two men who were walking together, listened. He thought of people who were rapt in the flow of sermons at camp meeting. Jason like that. Rapt with Harry Creekmore. And Harry, feeling the appreciation of his audience, was inspired to greater ef-

231

forts. A born orator, soaring on the breath of his hearers to new revelations.

"The only trouble with people is that they haven't seen an example good enough yet. Wars and turmoil. Competition. It's all they've had. But just suppose that we can prosper. I don't mean individually, but collectively. Suppose we make it all for one and one for all. The world is longing to see something like that. People will come, and some will want to stay with us. You're going to have to be ready for that, Mr. Jennings. People are going to try to make you into a new Moses. A Joshua. I know it is going to be hard for you to take. But you must be prepared to have Presidents come, and clergymen, and common laborers. All wanting you to give them the answer."

"But *we* will give them the answer," Jason said. "I can't do it by myself. We must all show them how to live."

Henry was walking along, silently listening. "I want to have a fishpond," he said. "I want to be able to go fishing anytime I feel like it."

"Oh, Henry," Jason said warmly. "We will have the biggest fishpond you've ever seen! I tell you, Dr. Creekmore, children like this are our hope." Jason looked darkly around. The little procession was crawling heavily along, and the sun was getting hotter. "We don't have enough children. That's the trouble. I want to have more children. Our hope for the future, you know. I worry about what will happen to my . . . to *our* dreams when we lie in the dust."

"Well," Harry said confidently, "I don't see that as a problem. We have two children. And you will have families joining, Mr. Jennings. Some sooner than you may think." Harry turned and looked at Jason, plodding by the lead team of oxen, and in Harry's expression was the most perfect happiness Adam had ever seen in anybody. Somehow Harry's happiness made Adam sad. He didn't know why.

Jason gave Harry a knowing smile. "Yes, Dr. Creekmore. Yes. I can see that. It makes me happy. Very happy."

Harry cleared his throat and sounded very medicinal. "And you, sir. You may have children yourself. I see no reason why you should not." Harry's deep Southern accent, thick with confidence and confidentiality, hung in the warming air.

Jason looked at him. Strangely, Adam thought. "Yes," he said. "I always intended to have children. I have not given up hope."

By the hot noon, painfully moving up-country on the dusty trail, it was clear that the oxen were in trouble. The going had been hard since the Kaw. The land north of the river was thick and marshy. Water insects buzzed around animal and human alike, and horseflies stung at the oxen in the moist corners of their eyes, and the pesky little black flies swarmed on their sweaty backs. Adam knew by how they hurt him that they must be deviling the oxen. They crossed some steep-banked creeks, and even double-teaming the oxen did not seem to save their failing strength. After St. Mary's the marshland turned to powdery dust. The trend of the land was up, and the oxen were worn out.

At the nooning Adam, Henry, and the old man unhitched the oxen but did not unyoke them. They could graze together well enough in the yokes and could be speedily hitched up again. The grass was lush here, but the oxen did not eat. They only stood with their great heads hanging and panted for air. Their heaving lungs made a soft chugging in the day.

"They can't go on like this," the old man muttered. He turned around to Jason who stood irresolutely by. "We got to throw stuff out. Else we're going to have dead oxen by night-fall."

Ishtar Baynes had an instinct about possessions. She knew when they were in jeopardy. She came swooping over like a big hawk. "It ain't your stuff! It's easy to talk about throwing stuff out when it ain't yours. When you didn't pay for it."

"You didn't pay for none of this stuff neither, Miz Baynes," the old man said, pushing his ancient hat back and looking at her as if he had been something bizarre left behind by a bankrupt circus. "Why in hell do you worry about it so much?"

"Because it cost good money," she shrieked. "You don't throw away stuff that costs good money."

"We could of sold it back in St. Louis," Adam said dryly. "We could of sold it in Westport Landing."

"You got a simple mind, Mr. Adam," Ishtar Baynes said. "You can't think of but one thing!" She turned to Jason. "They're trying to take over. These two. You're the boss, Mr. Jennings. We do what you tell us to do. We don't do what they say."

"These oxen is dying, Jason," the old man said, his voice like ice in winter, still and cold. "We got to throw stuff out. If we don't you're going to have dead animals by night."

Jason looked absently around, tentatively touching the great and burning prairie with his eyes. He had taken a wool hat out of a box somewhere; it looked like a young man's cap, and Jason's aging and hollow eyes in its shadows looked baffled and afraid. The sky was enormous over their heads. Tremendous clouds, like gigantic rolls of white bread baking in an oven, floated quietly there. "Out here? We can't sell it out here."

"We have talked about this, and we have decided not to throw nothing out!" Ishtar Baynes said. Her words hammered at Jason. "You promised, Mr. Jennings. And a promise is a promise. You promised we'd all make it. With everything."

"So I did," Jason said vaguely. He looked around. The entire company had gathered around. A tense, worried silence of people against the steadily crooning wind, the indifferent sky. Promise shrank against Harry. He put his arm around her, an outrageously intimate gesture, as if she were a child in need of protection. Jason bent his head and ran a hand over the red back of his thick neck, studying the dark shadows foreshortened by the noon, shadows crouching beneath them like goblins at malicious play, hiding from the sun. "I just don't know," he murmured. He squinted around at the brightness and looked vaguely west. "I did promise . . ."

"Mr. Jennings, if you break your promise, nobody will ever believe you again!" Ishtar Baynes could make a pronouncement sound like a knife held at the neck.

Jason turned painfully to Shawnee Joe. "There is something to what she says . . . I promised everybody we would all get through . . . With everything. It's all of a piece, you see. This journey. I got everyone to follow me out of Ohio. Out of Ur of the Chaldees, don't you see? The false gods. No, you don't see. Well, I promised. One piece, you see. If we tear one part of it away, where will it end . . . A clock, you know. If you take one wheel out of the clock, it's all wrecked, it stops. Dr. Creekmore . . . What do you think, Dr. Creekmore?"

"I . . . I don't know," Harry said. He could see the oxen. He could not find any words to charm away their sweat and their weakness.

"I always thought that someday, someone would write . . ." Jason laughed foolishly. Adam felt a chill of presentiment down his back in the great heat of the day. Something was

234

dreadfully wrong. Jason swallowed and stumbled on, his face twitching in that idiotic, apologetic smile of furious embarrassment. "I thought someone would write a book about us. And what that person would say . . . the writer . . . he would say that what kept us going was our faith. Our belief in our purpose when things looked impossible. We would inspire people not even born yet to follow us. It has happened before, Dr. Creekmore. Hasn't it? The Spartans at Thermopylae."

He turned heavily to Harry. Harry looked at him through those enormous glasses, and the sun coming down melted every hope. "They died," Harry whispered, scarcely knowing what he said.

"Oh, yes. Yes, of course," Jason said. "I meant at . . . Well, they beat the Persians *somewhere*. And nobody thought it was possible. People wrote books about what they did." He looked around with a blank, illogical smile.

The old man spoke with unexpected gentleness. "Mr. Jennings, looky here. You got big plans for California. We all do. But your plans is riding on the back of them poor dumb animals, and they're dying. You let them die out here in this sun, and all your plans is going to die with 'em. You look at 'em. Mr. Jennings. You look at their eyes. You look at their tongues. Go ahead. Just look."

Jason looked. He put a hand unconsciously to his chin. His beard was an inch long. He had given up shaving. It was coming out white. Strange to see a beard so different from the sandy color of his hair. Like age straining to leap out of his aging body. "I promised."

"He promised!" Ishtar Baynes said loudly. They all stood there like dolls unbearably suspended on the edge of something dark and terrible, waiting for Jason to decide something. But it was Jessica who suddenly brought them life and motion.

"I know what I'm going to do," she said crisply. "I'm going to throw out my new cookstove. We've learned how to cook on an open fire on this trip. I think we can cook for a while on an open fire in California."

"I bought you that stove," Jason said reproachfully. "I was so proud to buy you that stove."

"We can get along without it, husband. We made a mistake."

"You're disobeying your husband!" Ishtar Baynes shrieked. "That's against the Bible."

Asa grabbed Jason by the arm, stirred out of his own baleful lethargy of heat and expectation. "Them cookstoves costed nearly fifty dollars apiece. They're the best cookstoves I've ever seen."

"I'm going to throw mine out, too," Ruth said calmly, folding her arms across her large bosom. "Jessica's right. We can make do without stoves for a while."

Asa looked at her for just a moment as if he could not believe what she was saying. Then he hammered a declaration at her. "You ain't going to do nothing I don't let you do."

Ruth looked at him with terrible dignity. "I am going to throw out the stove. The good Lord give me eyes to see. And I can see that the oxen are dying. I can see that if they die out here, we may die, too. Not just us, but the children, too. You got a responsibility for the children, husband."

"They're my children, too," Asa cried.

Ruth went stolidly on, barely pausing to let him speak. "You got to protect the children, husband. Just look at them and tell me what's more important. Them stoves or Rachael and Henry."

Jessica spoke imperiously to Adam. "If you and Mr. McMoultrie will help me, Mr. Cloud, we'll throw my stuff out."

"I never seen such a thing!" Ishtar Baynes hopped about in fury. "*Women* taking over the world! I tell you, it's near the end of time when women start bossing their husbands around!"

"I have always been the head of my house," Clifford Baynes said with great satisfaction. He was oblivious to the sun, the oxen, the quarrel, a man just floating like a mote of dust in the air. Adam had never seen anybody like him. "It is the way the world should be," Clifford Baynes concluded, sucking on his thin lower lip with a smack of emphasis and a look of unbearable complacency.

Shawnee Joe took a couple of quick short steps over to Clifford Baynes. "Clifford, if you're the head of your house, you command that bitch of yourn to stop barking."

Clifford Baynes was momentarily jolted. "That ... *Sir!* I *beg* your pardon!" Mr. Baynes turned as red as a radish.

"You can beg all you want to," the old man said in implacable calm. "I'm telling you to make that bitch of yourn

236

hush, or I'm going to cut a hole in your belly, and I'm going to string your guts out like rope through your navel and strike fire to 'em in front of your eyes." The old man put his hand down on his knife, gleaming in his leather belt, and looked hard at Clifford Baynes.

"Sir!" Now Clifford Baynes was as pale as a piece of cheap foolscap. "I am not accustomed to people talking to me in that tone of voice."

"You better get used to it," the old man said. "Long as I'm here, I'm going to talk to you like you need talking to. And if I have to cut your throat to get the rest of these folks to California, then I'll do it, Clifford. There ain't no law out here. Nothing but what we say it is."

"There is always law," Jason said, eager to escape into one of those grand, abstract conversations he remembered from his college days. Sitting around happy fireplaces in the stark Connecticut winter. Debating with others full of hope for what they would do in the wide world. "The law is eternal!"

"The law is what we make it out here, Jason. We're beyond the line where the law is wrote down in books. And the law I make right now says this little rat here keeps his woman still. And if he can't keep you still, ma'am, then I reckon I can." He spoke to Ishtar Baynes in the same calm he might have used to order beer in a saloon. No emotion to his voice.

Ishtar Baynes glared at him. Her words came out of her tight mouth like acid squeezed drop by drop. "I wish I was a man, mister. I wish I was a man. But let me tell you something. Folks don't treat me like you're doing and get away with it. Life is long, mister. Life is long, and I got a long memory."

The old man laughed in her face. A very ugly laugh. Adam cringed at it. Something beyond the bounds. "Woman, all your life, you remember I treated you like you ought to be treated."

Harry was worried. He licked his lips. "I think we, ah, need to understand that we are all hot and tired and a little afraid. And we really do like each other. I know Mrs. Baynes is a good human being. Mr. McMoultrie. I can, ah, *see* her real goodness, And you are good, *too*, sir! A truly fine example of an honest and, ah, *forthright* gentleman! No hypocrisy to *you*, sir!" Harry laughed very badly, a strain that threatened to rupture him.

Jessica spoke quietly. "If you men will come along, we'll get started."

"I'll help, too," Samuel said. "If Mr. Adam's going to help, then I'll help, too."

"Well, now, Miss Jessica," Ishtar Baynes said with sticky sweetness. "You're married to a fine man. A very fine man. I reckon you can't see how you're disgracing him by carrying on with folks like this." She nodded her head in the direction of Adam and Shawnee Joe, looked knowingly at Jason, and smiled.

Jessica only laughed and looked at Ishtar Baynes with cool contempt. "Come along," Jessica said to her crew.

They unloaded boxes from Jason's wagon and got down to the cookstove and wrestled it out. No fire ever built in it. Paper from the stove factory still glued to the shiny black iron. A beautiful thing, better than any stove Adam had ever seen before. A stove belonging in a planter's big, high kitchen. Nigger slaves with heads wrapped up in bright scarves bending over it, bringing out the steaming food. Smell of hickory in the oven, and bacon frying, sputtering in a skillet, and bread baking. No, not for planters. A stove for a house on a green hill looking out to the blue Pacific turning bright in the rising day. Now only a stillborn dream of mornings that would never be.

Ishtar Baynes saw the beautiful stove and scurried up, her face twisted with a new idea. 'Don't just throw it away. Listen, you can load it in our cart. We can tote it to California with all the other stuff."

The old man lost his temper. "Woman, you can't tote this here stove on that cart! Your oxen would die in two hours! Your oxen ain't nothing but skin and bones. What the hell are you talking about?"

Adam agreed silently. The oxen pulling the Baynes cart looked like the starved kine in Joseph's dream.

But Ishtar Baynes was unmoved. "Don't you bother telling me about my oxen, old man! I've drove these oxen all the way down from Frederick, Maryland, thank you very much. And I reckon I'll drive them all the way to the Pacific Ocean!"

The old man opened his mouth to argue. Then he snapped it shut and thought for an instant, a slow smile growing on his face. "Well now, maybe you're right and maybe I'm wrong, Mrs. Baynes. You know your oxen a lot better than me." He looked craftily at Adam. "Let's load this here stove in the cart for her, boys!"

Adam hesitated. He saw the cunning in the old man's face. The oxen would die. Helpless under the sentence of death they stood out there in the sun while their fate was decided, and the old man grinned like a fox in a chickenyard. Adam grieved for the beasts. But Samuel moved to the old man's command, and Adam moved, too. Samuel was as good as a lifting crane. Ishtar Baynes gave them directions they did not need, swooping around them, cackling once with laughter, beside herself with triumph.

Finally she scowled at Jessica. "Now, you do admit before all these witnesses that this here's *my* stove now, don't you?" You could have stuck bricks together with the greed in her voice. Clifford Baynes stood behind the cart, his hands on his hips, his shoulders arched back in proprietary satisfaction as he looked at their new possession.

Jessica smiled. "I give it to you with a free heart, Mrs. Baynes. I sincerely want you to get it to California. I hope you cook good food on it for the rest of your life."

Ishtar Baynes looked at her with blazing doubt. Finally she turned to the rest of them. "You folks here is all my witnesses."

Some of them nodded. Jason, too.

# 33

Jason Jennings.

He hated his own name. The alliteration of it made it vaguely foolish. "Jay-jay," people called him at Yale, laughing. Friendly enough but mocking, too. Jason tried to take it lightly, but even gentle mockery was always a knife twisted silently in his belly. He longed to be taken seriously.

His father had gotten the name out of a book of names. Something vulgar about that, but then his father had been a vulgar man. Rich in the business of selling cloth in the

Western Reserve. Then impoverished and bankrupt in the great panic of 1837 that took dreams down like a sharp axe against the base of a rotten tree. *I am better than he was!* Jason's creed spoken firmly to his own heart. *I have something to live for besides money and the good opinion of worthless people.* He cultivated a dignity and a goodness that would make everyone see that he was not like his greedy, crude father. But he was afraid of the man; and Jason was glad when he died. *Now I can do just what I want!*

But out here he had become confused. Out here in the brilliant sunlight, where heat waves rolled off the swishing grass and nothing would be still. People were yelling contradictions at him; he could not sort out the truth, and he felt his dignity melting. In the crushing emptiness that stretched to infinity all around him, he could not find anything to hold on to to keep himself erect.

He wished they could go back and start the journey all over again. Yes. A new beginning. That is what they needed. They had been so very happy when they had rolled the wagons onto the wooden deck of the Ohio River steamboat at Ironton. Watching the great paddlewheels begin slowly to beat against the water. Watching the black little town recede and vanish and seeing the magical undulations of the riverbanks glide by, gently burying an old life that had gone bad. How beautiful the river had been, shining in the mild sunshine. How green the trees bending over the pearl-colored water. How fine he had felt! A strong leader doing a daring thing! Taking his family West to a new beginning, while others were content to live tarnished lives in a land defiled.

He had returned from the East five years before, when the news came that his father was dead. He came with determination beating in his blood like a sublime drunkenness. Sometimes he was nearly ravished out of his body by the spectacle he could imagine, himself as others would someday see him. Jason Jennings coming home to do something about slavery while others only wrote furiously in their furious papers or else lectured or debated to no account. *I am going to make the world better; I will be better then all those hypocrites who don't know anything but books!*

He was immeasurably pleased to work with his hands in the foundry. *If they could see me now at Yale!* The thought made him grin with satisfaction. *I will write them letters someday. Then they will regret what they did to me!* His heart swelled against his chest at the thought. Going back up there to lecture, to leave them, poor, bookish people, spellbound at the spectacle of a man who did great things! Working with your hands and your strong back kept you pure at heart.

He looked at his fellow toilers in the foundry, and felt as superior to them as he felt to his old acquaintances at Yale. For these workers could not even dream of his role in their town. His nightly comings and goings. Signals and signs and letters left in bottles by his door. Men speaking in the dark in muffled tones and the sound of hoofbeats receding into the gloom. He had a purpose then, and the purpose was renewed every time he took black men and women, and children too, by the hands and led them up out of the river as if out of death, heard them moan and weep with joy, and felt their gratitude.

Sometimes these people hid for days in the cellar of the big house on the hill, where they had lived in Ironton. It was a house bought with the last, dwindling fragments of his mother's estate, money saved back from his father's financial collapse. Providential, Jason thought, that there had been money to buy that house, in just that place, and that it had been for sale when they needed it. His mother adored him. And though she did not like what he did for the slaves, she acquiesced to it. "I never want to lose my Jason again," she said with watery eyes to all the rest of them. "My heart broke when he wouldn't come home." And she bullied the rest of them into doing what Jason wanted too. *I couldn't have persuaded them without her.*

Then came the fugitive slave laws. A slave not free this side of the Canadian border after they were passed. His mother died almost as soon as the laws were published, and Jason, who was always one to look for signs in things, saw that it was time to leave Ohio.

He decided to go West. Something tugged at him from that direction. Had pulled him there for a long time. And now he surrendered to the impulse and dreamed a dream. A fine dream. And when they moved onto the steamboat that day with the fine, new stuff packed in the wagons, everybody was happy. Nothing made people happy like new things bought fresh from the stores.

And when he saw the big rope cables slipped off the docking piles, saw the boat nose out into the great river, he was nearly beside himself with joy. *I have done it!* The very ease

241

of leaving—the house sold for enough money to buy all anybody could think they needed—was a sign. Everything would be good! He walked about on the white decks, his hands folded behind his back like a gentleman, detached and observing. He felt like an admiral of a large ocean vessel.

Now the happy days out of Ironton on the steamboat were like a lost Eden. They were on the burning plains. The oxen were dying. The harsh sunlight of the prairies, a sunshine invincible and consuming, would not allow him to deceive himself about the oxen any longer. He began to doubt not only the strength of the beasts but other things as well. Himself.

He took hold on his resolution. Maybe it was a test. God or destiny favored the daring. Jason racked his heart to find faith and confidence. He had always believed in purpose. He thought that everything in his life had some meaning beyond what it seemed. He looked for auguries in the flights of birds, in the casual things people said to him, in the scraps of paper he found blowing along the street. Everything had a purpose.

Years ago, when he was a child, he met a man who had been to Yale. The man tousled his hair in a friendly fashion and laughed warmly, drawing Jason to him. "You're bright enough, my boy. You ought to go to Yale. Like I did." Jason took it as the voice of God. And so he kept the dream in his heart and went to Yale.

Yale did not turn out well. In fact, nobody but himself knew what a disaster it turned out to be! He nearly died. Nearly killed himself. But he recovered, telling himself. *It was good for me. I learned about them. How contemptible they are.*

And when he came back to Ohio after his father died, he thought to himself, *My father died for a purpose.* Jason knew what the purpose was. To free all the family to follow him in freeing the slaves.

In an inn, where he stopped on the way home, he discovered a book somebody had forgotten, a new book, slender and cheaply bound, by somebody named Lansford W. Hastings and called *An Emigrant's Guide to California.* Jason tucked the book in his pocket and brought it back to Ohio with him, and some nights he took it out and read it. For years he asked himself, "Why did I find this book?" When the fugitive slave laws were passed and his mother died, he

242

understood. "I found the book because I am destined to go to California."

Everything had a purpose.

The same with Jessica. He heard about her living alone down in Portsmouth in suspicious circumstances. Men talked and wondered, and women nodded wisely as if *they* knew about such things. Jason had an absolute loathing for sexual sins! He thought people who committed adultery ought to be stoned to death. And of Jessica he thought, *That is the kind of woman I could never, never marry.*

The power of his own repugnance astonished him. He found himself thinking all the time of this woman he had never seen. And he was drawn to imagining that maybe he was destined to marry a woman just like this. He went to Portsmouth and found where she lived, and he followed her around when she went out on Sunday afternoons. He hid and watched her, and he inquired about her in the town, and he felt a thrill of excitement every time he saw her. Something mysterious and forbidden and so enticing that his heart nearly failed him on those times when he thought that she might have perceived him following her.

Jason had heard of people who resisted going to the South Seas as missionaries, the resistance a part of their divine call. He could not understand why he should feel so strongly about Jessica Marley if she was not destined to play a part in his life. You did not have strong aversion to indifferent things—the grocer on the corner, the man who brought firewood and dumped it in the back yard. He began to dream about Jessica. They were dreams that woke him like nightmares in the dark, sobbing for breath with his hair nearly standing on end . . .

And it had all worked out. Everything had a purpose. You followed your destiny, and you had faith that everything would always work out.

Only now the oxen were dying, and they could not carry the stuff they had bought to California. And if they had to abandon the stuff here in the middle of the plains, why had he bought it in the first place? It was all very puzzling, dispiriting.

He heard himself saying, "It all belongs to you now, Mrs. Baynes." He turned reproachfully to his wife, hoping for some apology from her. "I hope you're satisfied now, Jessica."

But Jessica was not satisfied yet. She hardly paid any attention at all to her husband. "Mrs. Baynes, I have two fine chests of clothing that my daughter and I will be dumping out to lighten the load. Would you like to take them, too?"

"Mamma! My clothes!" Promise was thunderstruck. "You're not throwing out my new clothes! I haven't even *worn* some of them."

Jessica turned and took her daughter in her arms. "Oh, Promise, listen to me. We'll have other clothes in California. Please, my darling. Please don't cry."

Ishtar Baynes, unmoved by any of this, looked at Jessica coldly. "If you want to give 'em away, I reckon we'll be glad enough to take 'em."

Jessica showed Adam where her two chests were. Adam and the old man got them to the back of the wagon, and Samuel took them one by one in his enormous arms over to the cart of Mr. and Mrs. Baynes and stacked them next to the stove.

One of the chests was simple pine, plain and white. The other was fine red cedar, carefully waxed. It had large, brass hinges that gleamed like gold in the bright day. A romantic carving on the dark top of the chest displayed a choir of cherubs singing in the wood.

"My father had this chest made for me when I was a girl," Jessica said softly. "For my twelfth birthday. It is the last thing I have from him. I suppose I should have thrown it out years ago." There was a heavy oak table that belonged to Jessica, too. A monster, black, with thick, claw-footed legs and heavy drop leaves. It also shone with wax and care. "It was a gift from a friend," she said.

"That's all that belongs to me," Jessica said quietly, turning to Ishtar Baynes. "I'm sorry I can't give you any more."

"I *bet* you're sorry," Ishtar Baynes said. She stood stroking the claw-footed table with her greedy hand, her touch as gentle as a mother's against a sleeping baby's cheek.

There was more in the wagon that Adam thought should be thrown away. Furniture. Tools. Wooden crates. But Jason stood in adamantine bafflement when the old man asked him if they could take out anything else. "No," Jason said. "No. That's more than enough."

Now Ruth came up and spoke softly. "You can start dumping my things now."

Asa protested, making a scene. He said terrible things, and

Henry cowered against Ruth as if he expected his father to strike her. But Asa did not hit anybody. The old man stood by Ruth, too, his brown hand almost idly resting on the handle of that huge knife, and Asa's furious eyes danced down to the knife, tested its edge, saw the look in the old man's face, and danced away. Finally, he stalked out into the prairies, away from everybody, and left them alone.

"Asa's going to have a stroke if somebody don't kill him first," the old man said easily.

"He used to be so kind," Ruth said. "All the trouble about money. It turned his head."

"My father lost his money before Asa could get an education," Jason said. "It was too bad."

They unloaded Ruth's possessions, even the potted green plants that she had been carrying across the plains, looking to the garden she would have in California. Ishtar Baynes flapped about them. She made them stack everything onto her cart. Even the second cast-iron stove. It lay twisted up on its side, looking like an animal that had been knocked down, leaving stubby little black feet thrust into the air. "We can sell it!" Ishtar Baynes cried. "We can use one and sell one." The old man looked at Adam and smiled.

Henry walked around with Adam, silent and hurt by the quarrel between his parents. "Daddy used to rock me to sleep at night when I was a baby," he said once. "I remember it."

"My daddy rocked me, too," Adam said, clapping Henry on the back awkwardly, trying to reassure the child.

"Did he get mad at you sometimes?" the boy asked solemnly.

"No. No, he didn't never get mad. But he did run off. He went to California. At least your daddy's taking you with him. That's something."

"That's something," Henry said.

"It'll be all right in California," Adam said. "You'll see."

"Let's go! Let's go!" the old man cried. He made a singing and cheerful sound. The sun was dipping beyond two o'clock. Slowly the oxen began to move. Adam saw with relief that they went along more easily than they had. The wagon wheels did not pound so hard. Jessica and Promise walked. "We don't have to burden those poor beasts with ourselves. It's good to walk. We're going to walk all the way to California."

"I like to walk," Henry said. He looked very manly, very eager, and troubled, too.

Harry gallantly got down and walked along with them, leading his mule along as if it had been a charger on a parade ground. It was a lark to walk. After a while Jessica took off her shoes. They hurt her feet. Promise did the same. The two women went barefoot, laughing about the way the dust squeezed up between their soft toes. Ruth walked, staying well behind Asa. She picked flowers and hummed to herself. Rachael rode in the wagon with Rebecca. Rachael loved to pretend to be back in Ohio.

"Looky there!" Ishtar Baynes screeched when the old man waved his hat in the air and yelled to start. "That Mr. Adam and Mr. McMoultrie, they're just taking *over*. *You're* the boss, Mr. Jason! Ain't you never going to give the *orders*?"

Jason looked at her in helpless appreciation. Adam wondered how Jason could be so deceived by her. Why didn't he tell her to hush? But Jason looked at her as if she were an ally against a conspiracy to deprive him of his birthright.

She went on berating him, berating the old man, berating Adam. Her voice dwindled. Its piercing furor was swallowed by the sunny plains. Clifford Baynes walked at the head of their two miserable oxen. He whipped at them with a short leather whip. They flung themselves into their heavy yoke and strained pitifully, and almost miraculously, short steps at a time, they did move, and the cart, laden until it seemed sure to burst, came trundling after them. Adam could not bear to look. Doomed beasts, helpless and uncomprehending. In only a little while the Baynes cart had become a black spot drifting on the plains behind them. Peace.

Jason cast a worried look over his shoulder. "Don't you think somebody ought to stay back there with them?"

"Oh, they'll be just fine, Jason," the old man said with an easy confidence. And to Adam he murmured, "Now with just a tad of luck, they'll run into the Pawnee or somebody. But hell! I don't know what the Pawnee is going to do with two cast-iron cookstoves."

"What's going to happen to them if the Indians get them?"

The old man spat. "Well, Adam, the fact is the Indians probably ain't going to get 'em. We're still too far south for the Pawnee. But if we're lucky they'll be some young Pawnee bucks that's fooling around down here, and they'll see Ishter and Clifford there and decide that's two easy scalps to hang

246

up on their teepees, and they'll kill 'em. But I don't think that we're going to be that lucky."

Adam felt a twinge of guilt. "Do you think that's right? Leaving them back there like that? To die?"

"Like killing nits." The old man's voice was so indifferent that it made Adam cold. But almost against his will he found himself riding along beside the old man and praying to God fervently that Mr. and Mrs. Baynes would be taken by Indians and killed.

That night the women who had walked were badly sunburned. Bright red faces so hot that they gave off heat. All of them had been gradually tanned by the trip so far. But they had spent the hottest part of the days in the wagons. Now that they were outside all day, the sun went through the flimsy screen of their tans and broiled them. After they camped, they began to experience agony. Their lips swelled up and blistered. Watery knots that looked frightful. Henry looked miserable, sun-smitten and exhausted. The bare feet of Jessica and Promise had been so badly burned that great blisters the size of peas stood out all over them, taut to the bursting.

"It was so much fun at first," Promise wailed. She could not restrain her tears, but she swallowed and did not sob.

Jessica spoke firmly and hugged her daughter. Promise seemed very small. "It will go away. Tomorrow it will be all right."

Harry had some burn ointment in his medicines. He gravely applied it tenderly to the places where the women were burned the worst. It was yellow and sticky and smelled sweetish. It did not do much good.

Ruth shook her head. "Best thing you can use for burns is eggwhite. But law! I ain't seen a chicken since we left Missouri." Her face was alarmingly red. But she did not complain.

The old man looked at their feet and wrinkled his mouth wryly under his beard. "Ah, you folks. Going West with all that stuff. And you didn't bring shoes you could walk in. I'll make you some moccasins. I'll cut off some hide from one of my buffalo robes and make you something to wear. Ah, you folks. Don't know nothing. It's good you got Adam and me to look after you."

Jason winced. Jessica laughed. "We'll learn," Jessica said

cheerfully. "Next time we do this, we shouldn't make any mistakes."

The old man laughed. "That's the spirit, ma'am."

Promise sighed. "Oh, when I get to California I don't *ever* want to do this again."

Jason looked prim. "Your mother's joking, child. Of course, we won't ever do it again."

Harry laughed easily. "We'll just sit and look at the ocean and read books and talk," he said. Adam could see how relieved he was not to have Mrs. Baynes around looking truth at him like knives.

Asa sneered at them all, testy, a smoldering wrath in him all day long, red with more than the sun. "You should of rode in the wagons like white folks. Them oxen is just fine. Look at them. See how good they're eating. You was crazy to throw that good stuff away. You just panicked, Jason. We won't get more stuff like that. We can't afford it. Not for years. How are we going to live in California, Jason? You tell me that, brother!"

"We'll manage," Jason said. His words were fuzzy at the edges. He was tired.

"We'll manage!" Asa mocked him. "We'll manage! You always say, 'We'll manage.' " Asa's tone was mincing with scorn.

"We always have managed," Jason said, trying to keep his dignity but feeling the earth slipping under his feet. "You used to take my word for things. Take it now, Asa. Please."

"Sure, I used to believe you, brother. And look where it's got me! Out *here!*" He flung his hand spitefully out at the empty plains and walked off.

"Don't let him bother you none, Jason," Ruth said patiently. "Asa thinks the world of you. Why, when you come home from the East, he was almost beside hisself. He kept telling me. 'Everything's going to be all right now. Jason's coming home. Jason's coming home.' "

Jason shook his head. "That's the trouble. He expected too much. Too fast. He thought I could change everything. In a single night. Just because I was educated." Jason laughed ironically. "Just because I was educated."

"Well, now," Harry said cheerfully, "it's going to be all right in California! In California, Asa there is going to get the desires of his heart!"

"He never did want much," Ruth said wistfully. "And he ain't never even got that."

"Adam, we better grease the axles of these here wagons," the old man said. "And Henry, you clean out the oxen's hoofs. You got to do a man's work out here. You left your boyhood back in the United States."

Henry was pleased. The old man winked at him. Henry would have died to please him.

The women hobbled around and made supper. A small fire hissed in the scrubwood they had cut from along the creek's banks, wood cut over by people who had camped here and gone on. Ruth and Jessica began laughing at each other for their misery and the ugliness of their blistered faces. They teased Promise into smiling, too.

But nothing could cheer Jason. He walked back and forth, worried about a dozen things, unable to smile. No sign of Clifford and Ishtar Baynes. "What do you think happened to them?" He looked out over the gloomy plains to the south. The sun had gone, and the day had turned to lead. Overhead the stars were beginning to pierce the cloud-strewn sky. The wind blew ceaselessly, rising and falling in irregular moaning and making a sad and lonely whisper in the great world.

From somewhere in the middle distance an animal screeched suddenly, a long, ghostly howl rising unbearably in ever-ascending yelps until it struck a high plateau of sound and held there in a maddening yowl that went on and on and died away finally in a trailing shriek.

"Wolf," the old man said calmly.

It was the first time they had heard a wolf so near, and it made their flesh crawl. The women stopped their laughing and looked anxiously out into the colorless, empty space yawning around them.

The wolf howled again and again, and Adam's hound answered, unnerving them all except the old man. Adam swatted the dog into quiet and the wolf's cry finally subsided.

They ate silently. Afterwards the old man brought out his harmonica. A little thing, shining brightly in the dim firelight like something made out of molten sunlight. He put it to his mouth and played as he played sometimes at night, when it came his turn to watch the stock, when in the drowsy half-awareness of wakeful sleep they heard the clear, fragile notes and knew that nameless sorrow that only solitary music in the night can bring.

Now he played like a man who plays to drive loneliness away from mountain winters. He played as he might play in the midst of his frail canoe in the midst of rivers he had never named. He played as he might play when there was no tobacco to smoke and the motions of his lips and his tongue and his lungs to make the music consoled him and brought him the narcotic peace of thoughtlessness that is the gift of tobacco, and of music too. And all of them sat charmed by the spell he cast. Promise sat with her feet in the spring and with her head against Harry's shoulder, and she drifted off to sleep like a child.

Jason sat with his own thoughts. He tried to summon up the face of Ishtar Baynes, to study it with a leisure he could not dare employ when she was present. A bitterness in his heart, not keen but dull in the way very old and painful things are dull. He felt the ancient shame come flooding in on him with the imponderable and awful power of the tide sweeping in from Long Island Sound in the night when he paced the rocky beach on the Connecticut shore so long ago. He saw the white foaming line swimming violently on the crests of the breaking waves, a line thin and ill-defined and boiling above the blackness of the sea's deep rolling. He thought, then, that he could joyfully plunge into those waves and die and be no more. But he thought of his mother and how she would grieve.

*It was so long ago. We both would have changed by now.*

Jason remembered Mr. Emerson. Youngish and tall and as stately as a sickly prince. Tubercular, people whispered. So Mr. Emerson was endowed with that romance and affection, that breathless, sad admiration the world confers on those who will die young after a prolonged and brilliant boyhood. Mr. Emerson standing in the lecture hall at Yale College, one thin hand poised elegantly on the lectern to his side, and those sharp, aloof, and benign eyes, so full of contained power, nervelessly sweeping the audience of hushed and expectant students and townspeople. Mr. Emerson beginning to speak, that sharp, thin, incredibly clear voice carrying like the firm note of a flute to every corner of the thronged room, an instrument demanding to be heard not by its loudness but for the perfect truth of its tone, and every head bent solemnly forward to hear every syllable. "My topic for this evening is self-reliance . . ."

And Jason remembered walking through the tree-shaded dark of Orange Street afterwards, crushed by an awful feeling of worthlessness and despair. He was failing everything at Yale. He knew that no crowd would ever listen to him the way the multitudes listened to Ralph Waldo Emerson.

All so effortless when other people had ideas and spoke brilliantly and shaped a discourse like the delicate harmonies of a simple tune that everybody could hum when the first singer had gone. But when Jason went into his own mind, he discovered only a dark and empty striving, no thoughts but what others gave him, and the hopeless conviction that the inspirations of life would always blow over his head from someone else. He knew that his mother called him her chosen child. And he knew that his brothers, as young as they were then, waiting back at home, shared his mother's conviction that there was something eternally special about him. But knowing the truth about himself made their hopes in him seem not only absurd but cruel, and he walked the streets angrily and hated them. And was devoured with guilt for his hatred.

He remembered the gaslights burning dimly on Orange Street, making the night world seem spectral, the big, gabled houses with red lanterns beckoning in doorways, and he recalled from a terrible distance his trembling. The distance, so unreal and so akin to death, comforted him after a while as he thought of the way time's slow, patient accumulation covered things; he let himself drift on the cloud of the harmonica's sweet and aching notes. Some things behind him forever; some pains he would never suffer again.

"Trust thyself; every heart vibrates to that iron string." Mr. Emerson. With that voice reverberating in his heart, condemning him to an anonymous life, Jason stood in the dark shadow of an oak laden with new spring foliage and looked at a house where people went in and out.

"What I must do is all that concerns me, not what the people think ... The voyage of the best ship is a zigzag line of a hundred tacks. See the line from a sufficient distance, and it straightens itself to the average tendency. Your genuine action will explain itself, and will explain your other genuine actions. Your conformity explains nothing. Act singly, and what you have already done singly will justify you now. Greatness appeals to the future ..."

Years after, Jason nodded at his memory of the words. *That is true. I am not wicked because of a single act.* He

251

thought the words boldly to himself—and felt how hollow they were.

It had been only a moment. Nothing important.

But now Ishtar Baynes ... Perhaps a relic of his past. No, impossible. Too much chance; coincidences like that did not happen in the real world.

He could not diguise even for himself the relief he felt because she was gone. The campfire burned more brightly. They recovered the almost magical sense of belonging together that had been so sweet before Mrs. Baynes came. Everybody cheerful except Asa. As always with a bone in his throat. He would not be cheerful again until they got to California and things worked out. Jason's heart went out to Asa, touched by the pathetic confidence Asa had placed in him. Brown eyes glowing with relief and trust once. Jason would make things right! Jason chagrined that the truth had been for nothing. At least until now.

*We can go on to California and never see her again! Never think about her anymore.*

*It would be like murder.*

He was stung by the grim thought. His mother had believed ardently in the eternal decrees of God as taught by John Calvin. Jason shook those antiquated old dogmas off when he went to Yale. Mr. Emerson's fine voice a little hammer breaking chains and setting men free to be themselves. The eternal decrees something people laughed at the way they mocked lace collars and camp meetings held by Methodists and Campbellites. But sometimes Jason wondered. Maybe Mr. Emerson had been wrong about the freedom we have ...

The harmonica ceased at last. Time for the old man to go on watch. The women to bed. Jason sat still, ruminating.

*If I do have a destiny, no one can destroy it! Not even that woman. If I do not, then I want to know!* A frantic burst of desperate courage. He knew he was looking his mother's stern old God in the face. It was a familiar meeting, but it never failed to turn his heart to ice and to freeze his bones.

There was a violent thunderstorm in the morning. It blew up from the west just at dawn, a thickening of black clouds boiling across the great sky as if blown by a fury of demons. Lightning crashed and volleyed and made the world swim in wild, electric light. Thunder—the awful thunder of the plains—rumbled above them like something incredibly heavy

252

slid across the thin, hollow floor of the sky. A cascade of icy rain came down in sheets, like a river falling from hell.

In the storm the old man and Adam set out with the hound to find Mr. and Mrs. Baynes. "Somebody has to go back for them," Jason said, his words firm and his eyes set in a terrible resolution. Shawnee Joe and Adam argued. "If you will lend me one of your mules, I will go myself," Jason said. "And if you will not lend me one of your mules, then I will turn the wagons around, and we will go back until we find them."

The old man raised his shoulders in the pouring rain and looked at Adam, and Adam shook his head, resigned and disgusted. They went together because neither of them wanted to stay behind, defenseless before Jason's justification of himself.

As they pulled out, they could hear Rachael shrieking. Her hysterical little voice shrilled in the intervals between the thunderclaps. It was a faint sound, frail in the relentless storm, but as filled with all the terror as any faint sound could be. Adam felt sorry for her, and he understood. The lightning terrified him. On the mule's back he felt high and exposed.

But the storm blew away after an hour. The sky cleared to a pearly blue. It looked washed and pure. Adam was soaked to the skin, and he cursed in his mind in a formal, dispassionate way because it seemed people ought to curse when they were wet on a fool's errand.

Yet the departure of the storm left him happy. The grass shimmered in the sunshine, damp and green for miles. Other colors in his memory had lacquer on them and shone with a deep and waxy brilliance, hard to the touch. But here the colors had been brushed, and the indefinable texture of them was soft and vaguely pale as if the sunlight had rubbed them to tame and make them gentle. The trail was now mud. But after the brown dust of yesterday, the mud was sweet to the smell. The mules moved along slowly, delicately picking their sharp feet up and setting them down, and they were so unhurried in their passage through the vast land that all impatience was drained out of Adam's mind. He surrendered to the irregular motion of his beast and thought of nothing.

At about noon they sighted the cart. In the vivid sunshine, it stood out on a hummock of the green prairie like something misshaped, black, and unnatural. A black tumor portending evil in the midst of the spotless land. "Goddamn," the old man said, spitting with disgust. "They're alive." The hound went rushing ahead. Sometimes Adam was annoyed with the hound for the catholic character of his friendships.

From the distance the cart seemed still. But when they came closer, they could detect motion. When they were closer still, they could see what the motion was.

Ishtar Baynes was standing over the oxen, flailing them with the brown leather whip. She moved in rhythmic, untiring motions, a swinging of her scrawny body so mechanical that she looked like a part of an engine. Again and again she struck them; again and again she drew back her arm, and the whip danced in the air, and her shadow on the ground was as black as the pit of hell. When the two men were close, they could hear the whip making a slapping sound against flesh, and they could tell that the sound was damp with blood.

The oxen were down, sprawled in two bony heaps on the grass, their legs awkwardly askew like something wrecked and destroyed. Ishtar Baynes had cut them with the whip until she had split their hides. The blood was caking and brown, and the skin of the oxen was coming off in strips, exposing a bluish film over their red muscles.

The old man bawled out, "Mrs. Baynes, what in hell are you *doing!*" It was the only time Adam had seen him lose his self-possession.

She drew back and looked blankly at him. She was all out of breath. She sobbed for air, the breath grating in her throat. "I'm showing . . . these oxen . . . who's *boss!*"

"You ain't showing them nothing, Mrs. Baynes! These oxen is *dead!*"

"Oxen ain't supposed to *die!*" she said. Still out of breath she whirled on the fallen oxen and began whipping them again. The whip sloshed in their flesh.

Clifford Baynes got up from where he had been snoozing in the seat of the cart. He always drifted; his wife had not needed him to help whip the oxen. Now he yawned without covering his mouth. "I'm surely pleased that you boys have finally got here," he said affably. "I've been waiting for you."

"We should have left you!" Adam said. He jumped off his mule and went in a couple of big steps to Ishtar Baynes and snatched the whip from her hand.

She whirled on him like a fighting cock. He jumped back. But she only staggered a few steps toward him and stood

254

there swaying in the hot sun, completely done in. She sucked and blew to catch her breath. The motions she made were so spastic and violent that she seemed now like an engine ready to fly apart. Slowly she subsided and sank to her knees. When Adam took the whip away it was as though he had stolen her strength.

"It's her fault," she whispered.

"Whose fault?" Adam said. He flung the whip away. It was caked with drying blood. Ishtar Baynes had blood up to her elbows. "Whose fault, Mrs. Baynes?"

"Jessica Jennings' fault! If she'd just minded her own business, we wouldn't of wore out my oxen. She *upset* things! Now look!" She threw a wild and frustrated arm out at the cart hulking with its heap of goods piled high in the brilliant sun. "We're going to lose all this stuff, and it's all her fault!"

Without another word Ishtar Baynes began to cry. It was a hideous, ugly howling, and Adam was as astonished as he might have been to see a reptile weep. His hound rushed over and began to console her, licking her face. She flung him angrily away and wept on. And in a dreadful way, the sound of her weeping was more terrible than the splash of the whip on the dead oxen had been.

"Now, now, my dear," Clifford Baynes said, not disturbed by the dead oxen, by his wife's sobbing, by the heat, by the loss of anything in the world. "You know what they say. Easy come; easy go. I believe that's a Chinese proverb." He looked around, saw that his wife would not cease her crying, shrugged indifferently and lay back down on the wagon seat, shut his eyes and waited for somebody to do something.

# 34

It was strange to Adam that Ishtar Baynes blamed Jessica and not the old man and him. He supposed later on that she had scorned both of them because they were men. No man could get the best of *her*. And women? She expected women to be easy meat. Among men she could be a woman; among women she could be a tiger. But Jessica was not easy. And that ate at Ishtar Baynes. Jessica had beaten her in something. Outsmarted her.

After she lost her oxen and her loot, she and Clifford began lounging around more and more with Asa. Adam did not know what they talked about; but Ishtar Baynes did most of the talking, and Asa listened. Clifford looked pleased with himself and the world. Sometimes Rachael sat with them, and Ishtar Baynes made over her, feeling her chubby little arms like a witch inspecting a child for eating.

"Don't let 'em worry you," the old man said to Henry while they labored over the oxen at night.

"I ain't worried about nothing," Henry said stoutly. But he was worried, and Adam could see it. Could not understand the way Asa neglected him. Adam wondered if it could be that Henry was old enough to show some signs of independence.

"It'll be all right in California," the old man said.

"You're beginning to sound like the rest of us," Adam said. "Everything's going to be all right in California!"

"It's got to be," the old man said. He looked at Adam and was serious. "There ain't no place for us beyond California. If it ain't all right there, it ain't never going to be all right anywhere."

They crossed a rickety wooden bridge over the Red Vermillion River. A dollar a wagon, and Adam paid it. The old Indian who came out of his neat cabin to take their money was a Pottawatomie. He was dressed like a white man. Adam could see that the black broadcloth suit the Indian wore was rich and elegant. An Indian better dressed than Harry Creekmore when Harry's white suit had been clean and new.

"Lewis!" the Indian said, pronouncing his name with grave, guttural dignity. A white man's name to go with a white man's clothes.

All Adam gained for paying the toll was the reawakened resentment of those who were angry with him for not paying the fare to Westport Landing. "The oxen could have rested up good in the steamboat!" Ishtar Baynes said hatefully. They wouldn't of got all tired then. We'd still have all them nice things."

"Mr. Adam done what he had to do," Samuel said, smiling slowly, shyly. Adam was touched. Their journey with the wheels, something without Jason, had made them friends. Ishtar Baynes looked at Samuel, looked at Adam, put a fresh cipher down in her invisible book: Adam and Samuel were friends.

She and her husband rode with Rebecca, and Ishtar Baynes played Rebecca's game with the devotion of a porcelain image. Sometimes Clifford walked along, clumsily tramping in his hard shoes, wiping his forehead and trying to look at home and in charge. "It's so stuffy in there," he said. "Please don't say I said so."

Adam was grateful for the bridge. The banks of the Red Vermillion plunged straight down to a rough, rocky bed twenty-five feet below. The green water went foaming over the rocks. This river was not deep. But it had an angry sound.

Lewis the Indian led them up along the river and showed them a place where the earth had been dug up. He swept his solemn hands proudly around and looked pleased. "Cholera here. Two years ago," he said. "I bury nearly fifty white folks. I do it with my sons. No get cholera myself." A faintly scornful tone. *You see. I lived, and the white people died.*

And they went on.

The old man had been letting his rifles ride unloaded in the back of Jason's wagon along with Adam's. Now he took them out and loaded them carefully but left them unprimed. They crossed the Black Vermillion, toiling with their shovels and struggling at the ford. Then they came up onto the great prairies again, and the old man kept one rifle in his hand and the other nearby on his pack mule, and he scanned the land in swift rhythms of caution. He made Adam do the same.

They had crossed into the country of the Pawnee.

Late afternoon. They were well up along the Big Blue now. It ran to their left, sometimes near, sometimes distant, lined with cottonwood trees drooping over the swift, dark water pouring to the south. The old man said that within another day they would be at Alcove Springs. There they would make the biggest ford since the Kaw.

"Fellow named Marshal runs a ferry ten miles up the river," the old man said quietly to Adam apart. "But ain't no sense to pay a dollar to cross his ferry when we can ford the river ourselves? What do you think, Adam?"

The old man spoke in questions. Adam knew he was trying

257

to be easy on him about his father's money. He sensed that the old man was telling him that maybe they ought to cross the ferry, not chance the river. But he was still smarting because not a soul had thanked him for paying the toll over the Red Vermillion. Not even Jessica. Everybody too preoccupied to think of him. What he had done for them. He felt abused.

"Let's ford the damned thing," Adam said. "If we lose another one of these here wagons, we can take the oxen that's left and get to California that much faster." "Whatever you say," the old man said with a wink. Adam noticed that the old man did not offer to pay for the ferry himself. The old man was tight with his money. *It's the way to be!* Adam felt strong and confident. He could do anything! He would not let anybody push him around.

He rode ahead slouching in the saddle. Time to make camp. He came to a place where the prairie cupped down in the basin of a sluggish creek. The little hollow made a shelter from the incessant wind.

The mule plunged down through tall reeds and drank eagerly from the slow water. Mosquitoes buzzed and stung. Adam slapped at them. But apart from the mosquitoes a calm ruled over everything. Not the best camp, but good enough.

He rode back to the wagons. "Over here!" he cried. "This way!"

He was so pleased with what he had found that for a moment he did not even perceive what Jason was doing. Jason was making them stop.

Adam came up, puzzled and annoyed. "What's wrong? Why are you stopping? We should camp over there, where there's a spring!"

Jason cleared his throat and looked around. Ishtar Baynes sat up on his wagon seat. Jessica walked, and Ishtar Baynes had taken her place. She wore a grin of terrible pleasure. "Well, Adam," Jason said. "We're going to camp where I say tonight. I'm the leader of this company. We're going to start doing what I say."

Adam dismounted to talk to the old man. "It's that goddamned woman," Shawnee Joe murmured. He shook his venerable head in exasperation, and the wind blew in his white beard, adding vaguely to his expression of frustrated impotence. "She's been out here yammering at Jason, filling the poor man's head with foolishness."

Ishtar Baynes looked down at Adam with a smirk. Harry came up. "What does it matter, Adam? We can walk the stock over to the water. Don't give the silly woman the satisfaction of knowing she's made you mad. Laugh it off." Harry was not laughing. He looked miserable, and afraid to let Mrs. Baynes hear anything that might give her an excuse to be angry with him.

"Godamighty!" Adam said in disgust to all of them. He felt an unbearable and useless fury press up in him, like something choking his lungs. His eyes fell on Jessica. She was standing apart, looking at him in imperial calm. Suddenly Adam remembered what Jessica had said about fresh meat, the easy gaiety of her voice after the conquest of the Kaw pouring on him now like a sunburst, in this dreary and helpless moment when everything seemed fixed in an idiocy he could not manage. "I think I owe you something for keeping my guns dry, ma'am." His voice was tight; but he delighted in speaking to her in public without addressing Jason first. A pleasant breach of manners. Her face was still and inscrutable. "I'm going to hunt something." She smiled, and he thought her own pleasure at breaking the rules was equal to his. A wife smiling at someone her husband had rebuked.

"Be careful out there, Adam," the old man said. "The Pawnee . . ."

He did not finish the sentence. Adam was whistling for the hound.

He rode off, eager to be alone, to cleanse his mind of that look of inane triumph on the face of Mrs. Baynes. He took an odd and secret pleasure from imagining how he must look to Jessica as he went away. Retreat was the only way he knew to save his injured dignity, and he was glad to make it seem that he was going to do something Jessica wanted. The insult to him was so public, so deliberate and foolish, that he hoped wildly that Jason was jealous.

The swelling land, dipping and rising in long and grassy undulations, had a hypnotic effect. He was soon hidden from the wagons in one of those surprising troughs of the prairies. They seemed so flat when he stood looking at them, but when he rode along they heaved in unimaginable ways. He began to think about the illusions of landscape, and peace gradually returned to his heart.

He thought of Jessica with an odd sense of melancholy that had a mysterious pleasure in it. The day before, they had

259

fallen into conversation, and he had told her about home and his father. He told her how he had buried his mother, and he showed her the single letter that had come from California, a letter he folded and unfolded so often that the paper was cracking. She heard him out with solemn attention, asking a few questions, listening in compassionate silence, and finally she said quietly, "I'm sure you'll find him, Adam, and I'm sure that he'll be happy you've come." She looked at him with those nerveless, level eyes, and within his heart he felt something totter and felt danger, too. Something building.

He rode across a swale of land, and the grass swished against his legs and against the belly of the mule, a quiet and irregular whispering like the earth murmuring something to him. The hound came loping behind, tongue lolling, panting with happiness in spite of the hard time he was having in the long grass. The air blew in soft gusts, sometimes dying away altogether, leaving the world immensely still. The wagons were now entirely lost to view. The declining sun was very warm, and he felt a drowsy fatigue from the long day. He held the rifle balanced across the saddle in front of him. It was the rifle with the big bore. Its long and heavy barrel swayed in the sunlight with the motion of the mule and cast sparkling ripples of bright reflected light across the grass, and he was entranced by the dancing images of brilliance. In the great, wombing sameness of the warm land, all his bad feelings dissolved. He rode in the perfect serenity of having no thoughts at all.

But riding out of the swale and onto a long upward heave of the land, he saw something that made his mouth go dry and his heart pound. For there, in the middle distance, was a small herd of buffalo, the first he had ever seen. They were grazing calmly—awkward, shaggy behemoths, black against the spaciousness of grass and oblivious to his presence. He wet his finger and sampled the wind. It was slight and blowing in his direction.

He primed the rifle with a percussion cap. He checked the pistol in his belt and primed it, too. He took up the horn of gunpowder where it dangled from the horn of his saddle, and he dismounted. The grass was up to his knees here. He was glad of that. The hound sniffed the air and whimpered, trembling with excitement. Adam commanded him to silence. The dog shivered and hunkered down on his belly and moved with his master, his wet, black nose twitching with the reek of the buffalo. Adam crept forward, tugging the mule along. The ground dipped and angled generally toward the herd. He stooped down into a defile, and when he came up again he was within sight of the buffalo. They lay about five hundred yards away in a westerly direction.

He tested the wind again. It had changed, blowing across him toward the herd. He cursed and crouched in the grass. Almost at once an old bull raised his shaggy head and looked ponderously around. Adam's heart thudded. He sprawled in the grass in a torment of anxiety, and when the hound whimpered, Adam could have killed him. At some grunt of command from the old bull, inaudible at this distance, the herd began a slow movement away from him. "Oh God!" he muttered—curse and prayer—and lay very still.

The breeze shifted again and died. All the world was locked in a spell of silence. The herd paused lethargically once more to graze. He found another depression, this time almost a ravine, and he led the mule along it out of sight of the buffalo. Judging his distance carefully, he crept up again on an elevation and lay on his belly to look.

Now the herd was only a hundred yards away, so close that he could see moisture glistening on their black muzzles. He could faintly hear their snuffling as they ate. He calculated the distance. A hundred yards was a long shot. If he missed, the herd would run. But if he came closer ... Risky either way. He picked out a smallish bull. Tender meat. The herd seemed oblivious to him still, and the grass here was high. Clinging to the mule's bridle and holding the rifle before him as best he could, he inched forward. He scarcely breathed. His legs ached from his crouching. Seventy-five yards. Hands sweating on the rifle. Slippery. Never in his life had he stalked anything as big as a buffalo.

But then it all went to pieces. A whiff of smell, the slight motion of the grass, the quivering excitement of the dog, a sound he made he could not hear himself. Something made the old lead bull raise his brute head in, alarm and whirl violently about, bellowing a hoarse warning. Adam was amazed to see a beast so heavy move so fast. And then, as if the single members of the herd had been coalesced into a black fluid, the buffalo began to run. In that liquid moment between standing still and full stampede, Adam jumped up, and taking swift aim at his young bull, he fired.

The explosion roared in the quiet air and rang in his ears,

and yet it was curiously single, without echo, the first gunshot he had heard in the great plains. Then the herd was in full gallop away from him, and he felt the ground tremble with their going. Adam cursed and cursed, angry with himself and with the buffalo and with God.

He had dropped the lines of the mule to shoot, and the obstinate creature had jumped back in dumb fright at the loud report and now heeled about and slanted his head to flee. But Adam, lunging and cursing, snatched the bridle line and jerked the mule to a halt with main force. Cursing still in his furious disappointment, he swung himself up into the saddle and rode to where the buffalo had been. The dog was already streaking ahead, barking in the deep, extended musical call of a hound on the hunt.

And here, where the hound ran in circles deliriously sniffing the trampled grass, Adam's black mood was translated to elation. For first in spots and then in an ever heavier track of vermilion, he saw a trail of blood. He reloaded his rifle. He did not curse. but worked the ramrod with cool, dexterous haste, and he felt an excitement that made his fingers tingle. He urged the mule forward. The animal, sniffing the bloody track, reared dangerously, but Adam held the bridle tightly and kicked the mule in the ribs, and they went slowly on.

The land dipped and rose again. Adam could look for miles across the empty prairie, and he could not see a sign of life. Nothing but an eerie and tremendous stillness, and suddenly he felt queer, as if the buffalo might have been phantoms and the blood only an illusion. But the hound picked up the scent quickly and went howling in pursuit, and Adam followed. Finally he heard a faint, weary snorting, a thrashing in the grass, and kicking his obstinate mule to where the hound cavorted and barked, he found his wounded prey, red blood pouring from its nose.

Adam jumped down off the mule and hurried to the fallen buffalo. Throwing the rifle down and working again with cool haste, he drew his knife and deftly cut off the bull's testicles. It was like slaughtering a bull at home. He remembered that a bull calf's meat would taste strong if the testicles were not cut off fast in the slaughter.

Then he cut the bull's throat, finding the same thumb-thick artery that he had so often found on cows or pigs in the slaughter. In a moment it was all over. He stood above his kill, breathing in great sobs of relief. His hands were covered with blood, and his fingers were sticky around the handle of the knife. The dog sat on his haunches, panting and looking around with canine satisfaction.

The buffalo lay still and dead.

Adam felt indescribably proud. He wished that his father could see him. He thought madly of Jessica. He wished that the world could know. And in a fierce, exuberant, brutal bursting of his soul, he went giddy with triumph. Scarcely thinking of what he did, he began to jump up and down, crying in a rhythmic. "Oh, oh, oh, oh, oh, oh!"

The dog began to bark again, not at Adam's commotion, but a bark of warning and alarm, and Adam looked up the long slope he had trailed the buffalo down and saw the Indians.

They were four. They sat very still on their ponies, outlined against the darkening sky. They looked down on him, as motionless as stone, like some two-dimensional illusion sprung from the ground. He saw that one of them held a long rifle, the butt resting against his bronzed and naked thigh, and the thin, straight barrel of the gun looked like a copper spear in the sun that lay now like some semiliquid blazing ball against the steel horizon, turning all the plains to an unmoving, burning fire.

The vision was fleeting. If they held their respective positions for a minute or even for a half-minute, it would have been a miracle. Perhaps they did not stay fixed for even five seconds. But in that intense, surrealistic perception of sunset and danger, there was an eternity, and Adam's mind was forever branded with the sight.

He could remember, too, the sweet smell of the grass, the reek of the slain buffalo, the clean fragrance of the open air. And he could remember how the Indians broke the magic spell by whipping their ponies into a swift gallop down the slope and how he heard their shrill, excited cry, a wildly off-key turbulence of faint notes, and how he understood slowly with gathering amazement that they were riding down on him to kill him.

The hound rushed out a few yards, barking furiously, leaning forward on his long legs. Adam was much calmer than he had been when he had tracked the buffalo. He knew he was going to die. The Indians were perhaps a quarter mile off, coming hard, and he thought briefly that he might yet escape them on his mule. But he instantly understood the folly of his thought—the stubborn, tired lethargy of the mule and how swiftly those Indian ponies were coming. So, stepping behind the uncomprehending mule as though behind a barricade, he leveled the rifle across the saddle, waiting patiently until he could distinctly see the white and black pattern of the single feathers the Indians wore in their hair, and taking a lead aim on the one with the rifle as his father had taught him with the deer, he fired.

It was as though a cord had been suddenly flung around the Indian's neck, jerking him up and back. He flung wild arms skyward, and the rifle went spinning away in a long arc, and the Indian, his head torn back and his mouth furiously agape, careened off the horse and disappeared in the grass, and the riderless pony galloped away in a long and widening curve.

Still the others came on, and Adam, perceiving without heat their deadly rush at him, poured a charge of black powder down the muzzle of his gun, plunged in a patch of cotton after it and then the heavy lead ball, and tamped them down with one hard blow on the ramrod. He primed his weapon no more than a half minute after he had shot the first Indian and dropping this time to one knee because the mule had jumped back in a whinny of terror, he sighted again on the nearest Indian and fired; this one, too, took flight from his pony and tumbled head-over-heels backward into the grass. *He'll be hurt!* Adam's absurd thought when he saw the Indian's moccasined feet go skyward over the rump of his hurtling pony.

The other riders were so close now that they seemed ready to pound him down, and Adam drew his pistol and prepared to fight to the end. But then in a cowardice he could not believe even as he saw it, they wheeled away from him and rode furiously off. In an instant they soared over a rise of ground and left the field to him and to his frantically barking dog.

Only then did he feel how his heart was racing, so hard that it made vision itself shake. Only then did he feel a violent convulsion through his whole body so that he almost fainted. Only then did he think of what it was to die, and he thought that no one would ever have known his fate, and he was filled with a lonely melancholy that crushed his soul flat. All around him, after this storm of noise and motion, the solitude of the plains was almost unbearable.

He knew that he was still in danger. The Indians might find comrades and return from any direction. From all directions. He loaded his rifle again. The dog, quiet now, sat panting by the dead buffalo, and the onslaught of silence became more and more terrifying, like night in the woods when some strange impulse makes the insects stop all at once, and every quaking leaf becomes a terror. He forced himself to listen to the low sighing of the wind in the grass and the buzzing of tiny insects there. He was consoled by the sound.

He started slowly, with terrible caution, toward the nearest fallen Indian, dragging the mule forward, Adam feared a trick. When he had located the Indian, he paused for a long time contemplating the situation with infinite care, looking for the slightest sign of life, holding the rifle forward, ready to fire. But nothing moved. The dog gave the Indian a good, curious sniffing and turned away, uninterested. Adam came on.

The bullet had passed completely through the Indian's body. He lay inhumanly twisted, face down, a hole the size of a fist in his back. The wound was mangled and pulpy, but it did not bleed. In spellbound wonder Adam turned the body over. The touch of the dead man's flesh gave him a creepy feeling, not because it was the skin of a corpse but because it was the skin of an Indian. Alien, remote, and untouchable.

With slowly awakening perception, he saw how scrawny the Indian was, how cordlike and emaciated were the long muscles of the fallen man's arms and legs, every rib showing through the skin in a hard ridge. It was in no way the Indian he had imagined when he pondered those fleet huntsmen of the plains. It was not the imaginary Indian people talked about in Independence or Westport Landing. It was like no picture of an Indian he would ever see.

The Indian was armed only with a knife, and it was still on his leather belt. Adam took it out and looked at it, running his thumb along the blade, finding it dull. He had always imagined that Indians kept their knives razor sharp. It was a very heavy blade with a thick back, and it had a mysterious GR stamped on the metal. A knife made by white men. Adam shook his head and tossed it away. He could not understand. He felt a great flood rising somewhere inside, a darkness that threatened to burst, exploding night all over his mind. He withstood it, resisting thought.

He walked back, still leading the mule, to where the other

Indian lay—the first one he had shot. Here he drew up sharply because, as he came near, he detected an irregular, rasping sound. The dog began to bark again, but Adam shushed him angrily. The Indian was still alive. Adam's heart pounded again. He brought his rifle up and crept close.

The Indian was lying on his back, his head turned to one side, his eyes shut, an expression of excruciating exhaustion on his long face. On one side of his thin chest there was an awful wound. As he breathed the red blood foamed and bubbled around the wound, and Adam understood that the bullet had lodged in a lung. The croaking sound he heard was the Indian's agonized breath passing through the man's throat, an involuntary, agonized strumming on the vocal cords. He also saw that the Indian, like the buffalo, was bleeding from the nostrils and from the mouth, the blood running in time to his labored breathing.

The Indian turned his head and slowly opened his eyes and looked dully at Adam. For a moment the two men stared blankly at one another. Then the Indian's gaze wavered, a bare suggestion of motion, a tiny cringing, but it was eloquent. He was desperately afraid. Adam was shocked. The Indian was afraid of *him!* He had never imagined that Indians could be afraid.

Adam did not know what to do. He could not stay with the Indian. The air seemed to crackle with the silent menace of hidden eyes. If he tried to move him back down to the trail, the man would surely die. And what on earth would the Jennings or any other white person out here do with a wounded Indian?

He walked slowly over to where the Indian's rifle lay and picked it up and got another bitter surprise. It was not a rifle at all. It was a flintlock musket with a smooth bore, very old, good only at short range and almost worthless even then. He laid his own rifle down and cocked the flintlock and experimentally squeezed the trigger. Nothing happened but the stony pop of the flint cracking against the steel pan. The gun did not fire.

He threw the musket down in the grass and walked slowly back to the prostrate Indian. The Indian's eyes were shut now. His red mouth was gaping and bleeding, and the gnats were buzzing around the blood, and sometimes his mouth twitched spastically. The struggling breath went weakly on, always with that hideous bubbling. Adam longed to console

266

him in some way, to take the shot back, to do *something*. But he was helpless before his own act. And finally he crept off almost furtively in some foolish effort to avoid disturbing the wounded man anymore.

The sun was gone now, and the world had turned ashen. The plains were cool, and there was a thickening haze suspended over the horizon. Adam felt an impulse to ride pellmell to the south, back to camp. But the buffalo represented food. And in a dogged will to make this horror count for something good, he resolved not to go back empty-handed. So he set out to butcher the animal and load a quarter on the mule's back.

By the time he was done it was quite dark. The stars were beginning to burn their nightly way down the remote, dark sphere of the sky. There was no moon. Suddenly, from somewhere fearfully close, a wolf howled, ascending notes reaching up to an unearthly and shattering wail. He was quickly answered by another and another until the night was filled with their screeching.

Adam thought of the Indian. He hoped that he was dead by now, but when he went to check, the ragged breath was still stubbornly coming. And Adam realized the wolves would fall on the wounded man and tear him to pieces.

The thing Adam had to do presented itself. His very consciousness reeled before it. But he gathered his courage in the way that a man will gather himself to leap into space. He drew his pistol from his belt, put it swiftly to the Indian's head, and muttering a quick, vague, desperate, unbelieving, "Forgive me, please God!" he fired.

The roar of the gun rang the wolves to silence. The pistol nearly knocked him over with the violent leap in his hand. He stood swaying in utter weariness, exhausted, and sick with self-loathing. He was shocked down to the roots of his hair by how unreal it all was. He held his breath for a moment, listening. In that rapt silence, he perceived that the bubbling breath of the Indian had stopped.

He discovered that he was crying. Once he admitted his tears, he began to sob hysterically. He turned away. Blindly he led the mule along, stumbling, cursing, crying as if his heart would pop open like a bottle in the fire. The dog followed, his long tongue panting now in a rhythm that was ridiculously ordinary. Adam walked with his head down, afraid to look the universe in the face, and he shambled on with a growing and hopeless shame as if his very footsteps across the grassy night were an abomination to God.

In a moment the wolves howled again, first that solitary chief trumpeting his confidence and his victory. Then the rest joined in a loud and infernal shrieking. The noise made his teeth bang together. The mule was skittish and afraid. The dog shivered and barked. But the wolves had no interest in either man or dog. They closed in on their feast. Adam could hear the vicious canine snapping and fighting and yelping going on in the direction of the buffalo. He thought of the dead Indians. With sick revulsion he pondered the knowledge that by morning their bones would be scattered and all their flesh nothing but bile-soaked lumps in the bellies of the predator wolves.

He cried himself out. His mind worked again. He was mortally tired, and his body cried out at him to lie down in the soft grass and sleep. But he was still alive. That was the important thing. He was still alive. He took a sight on the north star and moved south, the direction he had come from. He listened intently to every sound in the night. He could imagine hostile Indians creeping up on him with knives, and every breath of wind through the grass became footsteps drawing stealthily near. The Indians had the right to kill him. And in a just world where sin had its recompense, the Indians must kill him before dawn. But he kept moving, setting one tired foot down in front of the other and going on in the hope that morning would come with a liquid shining to wash away his sins.

# 35

"By God, you killed a buffalo!" The old man was filled with terrible respect. It embarrassed Adam.

"A buffalo! A buffalo!" Rachael danced around and sang. "What is a buffalo?"

"You killed a goddamned buffalo, Adam! First time out."

And in a spontaneous gesture the old man threw his arms around Adam and embraced him and pounded him vigorously on the back. "You're a man now! Godamighty, you're a man!" Adam felt like a chunk of wood.

"Was it difficult, Adam?" Jason said. He was restrained, admiring what Adam had done in spite of himself. Deep in himself Jason wanted Adam to say it was nothing.

Adam was impatient. "I don't know, Mr. Jennings. Hard or easy, I killed the damn thing."

"Well, now, we shouldn't curse, should we, Adam?" Jason said. "Profanity always reveals an impoverished vocabulary."

"Hellfire, Jason, you treat this boy like a slave . . ."

"I have never treated anybody like a slave."

"You treat this boy like a slave, and he goes off and kills a buffalo for you. How many shots?"

"One," Adam said. "I got him in a lung. I cut his throat to finish him off."

"Your hands are still bloody," Jason said dryly.

"Hey, Adam," the old man said. "Wipe your hands off on Jason."

"What does buffalo taste like?" Clifford Baynes asked. He inspected the hind quarter of meat like a dog.

"Better than anything you ever eat in your life, Clifford," the old man said enthusiastically. "Goddamn! You get your first buffalo with your first shot! Adam, you was born to live out here."

"You look so pale, Adam," Jessica said softly. "Are you all right?"

Adam looked at her gratefully. Their eyes touched like fingers in the dark. "I'm tired. That's all."

"We thought you'd left us for good, Adam," Harry said.

Adam gave him a hard look. "I wouldn't of left one of my mules behind if I'd left you for good."

"What did it feel like to kill him, Adam?" Jason's tone, detached, speculative, curious in an unpleasant way.

"I don't know, Mr. Jennings. I can't explain it. I'm tired now. I was all taken up with . . . I felt good when I seen I'd hit him."

"Ah yes," Jason said. "Well, I suppose that's why I've never even killed a chicken in my life. Killing is an intoxication. Something to overcome, I think. It brings out the worst in us."

Jessica laughed. "Adam has brought us fresh meat. We ought to be thankful."

"I told you I'd kill you something, ma'am," Adam said. "I promised. When I killed this buffalo, I was thinking that I was keeping my promise." Adam felt exultant to be so bold with Jason standing right there, not able to do a thing about it.

Jessica looked at him and smiled with surprise, and her eyes were pleased and interrogating. "Why, thank you, Adam. I'm very grateful."

"Hmmmmp," Ishtar Baynes said. She was looking at Jason.

Jason looked stern. "Well, I'm grateful for Adam's thought, my dear. Sincerely grateful. I sincerely like Adam. Adam knows how much I sincerely care for him. But I'm talking about hunting in general. I don't believe we can permit hunting in our community in California. I don't believe a loving community like the one we're going to build can tolerate the spirit hunting creates. It makes a man a beast to kill other beasts."

Jessica laughed dryly. "I've never heard you talk like this before, husband. Is this something new you've decided for us?"

"I believe it is acceptable for a man to have new thoughts," Jason said.

Asa scowled. "It ain't good to laugh when your husband is talking, Jessica."

Jessica tossed her head. The sunlight sparkled in her blond hair. "I have to laugh when anybody talks nonsense, Asa. I'm sorry if the person talking nonsense is my husband."

It was a forward thing for a woman to say, but they were out on the plains and free of the conventional restraints, and Adam had killed a buffalo.

"Well," Clifford Baynes said, "I believe, from an experimental point of view, that we should, ah, sample a steak from that beast before we go any farther."

"Clifford, for onct you and me agrees about something," the old man said with a hoot of laughter. "Let's cook us a steak right now. My mouth's watering."

"Well I don't want any buffalo steak," Jason said, striving to recapture something. His dignity maybe. He did not know what. Things were getting away from him again.

The old man grinned. "That's fine, Jason. Just fine. More for the rest of us that way. Maybe you better see the doctor over there. I always heard if you ain't got a good appetite you're going to die."

"Die!" Jason said. "I'm not going to die." People were not taking him seriously. He swallowed and looked stern. "I have always heard that those who do not control their appetites cannot control their lives."

"I never wanted to control my life, Jason," the old man said, laughing again. "I just want a good ride out of the thing."

*Why are they quarreling?* Adam thought. *Why must these people always quarrel? I could of brung you back the left hind quarter of a man, Jason. What would you say then?*

"I'm going to lie down for a while and sleep," Adam said. "Just over in the grass." He walked away without another word, fleeing that dazzling look of contrived benevolence that Jason poured on him like syrup.

"Don't go too deep to sleep, Adam," the old man called in his cracked and joyful voice. "You kilt the buffalo. You got to take the first bite off his meat."

Another argument broke out. The old man was gathering buffalo chips to make a fire. Ishtar Baynes realized that he was going to cook the steaks over flames rising from dried shit. She screeched like a wounded hawk. "The *ashes* will fly in the *meat!*"

"Just pretend it's spice, ma'am," the old man said cheerfully.

Adam wished he could wake up and find them all gone and himself alone. He was giddy, and in a wakeful confusion that was very nearly a dream he thought of himself and Jessica, left here together.

That night they camped at Alcove Springs near the Big Blue. One spring bubbled up out of the ground, clear, sweet, cold water. The old man said it was all right to drink water like that. Another creek poured over a rock ledge and fell in a torrent, making a music of splashing water ceaselessly through the green vale.

Jason had a mind for a new beginning. "Adam, I'm sorry. Believe me I'm sorry. I've been thinking. I think we've all been selfish. I wanted to have my own way. I apologize. I say we all need to forget ourselves and get on with our journey in harmony! That's what I say! What about it, Adam? Let's forget the past. Let's start all over again."

He smiled hotly around, and Adam was embarrassed.

271

Harry, afraid of silence, took up the thought. "We've all been tired," Harry said. "I tell you what I think! I think we're all just mighty lucky to be together, to be healthy, to be going on so easily to California. I know I'm just thankful I ran into all you folks, and I'm so grateful to you for letting me join up with you." He looked at Promise and smiled with an admiration that touched Adam. Harry was full of pretense and lying. But when he looked at Promise, an innocent little boy, long hidden, seemed to pop out of him.

"On the contrary, Dr. Creekmore," Jason said. "We are grateful to *you!*"

In a way that seemed curiously inevitable Jason had begun a reconciliation with Adam and had ended by exchanging compliments with Harry. Now they sat throwing hope back and forth across the bright firelight as if they were playing a delightful game.

Harry stood up, "I tell you what," he said, looking around through his thick glasses, his face alight with the fire and his happinesss. "Let's just all make a promise to each other that we are not going to say anything unkind. We are not going to quarrel. We are going to try not to hurt people. If we can't speak to each other kindly, then let us resolve not to speak at all."

He looked at Mrs. Baynes, and she looked back at him with her alert little eyes flashing out of a thin face set in a perpetually cheerful superiority and detachment. And without more ado, Harry leaned over and shook hands with Clifford Baynes, who looked startled.

In a moment they were all shaking hands with each other and making professions of their good intentions for the future. "Well, it never would be right for us to want to fuss with each other," Mrs. Baynes said, surprised it seemed that anybody thought any unpleasantness had been going on. "I think everybody ought to be just like me and Clifford. Just trying to get along in a hard world. Live and let live, I always say. Never hurt nobody to be kind."

Mrs. Baynes was so satisfied with herself that Adam knew she had not even been touched by Harry's plea. But everybody did feel better when they had shaken hands all around. Adam even shook with Henry, who drew himself up very solemnly for the moment as if this were some sort of initiation into full manhood. And the old man shook hands and clapped people on the back in a very familiar way and seemed to believe like the others that something new had really come on them. A new spirit. "It ain't good for folks like us to be quarreling," he said in his cracked, tenor voice. "Other times when I've been going West, the country always pushed the people together. It ought to be like that for us."

All of them felt the relief of a tension broken, the release of confession. "I think I may have been unkind to you, Mrs. Baynes," Jessica said. "I'm sorry. Believe me. I'm sorry."

"Oh, that's all right," Ishtar Baynes said in a cloying tone of injury. "They's lots of folks been nasty to me; most folks, in fact. I wasn't born to be fortune's child."

Perhaps only Adam was still sad when all this exchange of pleasantries and promises was over. He rememberd the Indians he had killed. He could not believe he had done it. It had all been a nightmare, and he was awake now. But when he fondled a rescuing thought like that, he looked at the dark-red buffalo quarter the old man was stripping into thin slices to dry in the sun. The Indians had been just as real as the buffalo, and they were just as dead.

"I believe you have grown older today, Mr. Cloud," Jessica said. She seemed to have retreated into a pleasant formalism with him as if things had gone too far before, and now she too was making a new beginning. Adam's heart sank. "You look more serious than you did before." He could only lift his shoulders as if he were tired of talking.

"It's that kill, ma'am," the old man said. "A boy makes his first kill on a buffalo, and he ain't a boy no more."

"Why a buffalo? Mr. McMoultrie? Why not a rabbit or a bird?"

The old man shook his head and laughed as if she could never really understand. "A buffalo because a buffalo's so big, ma'am. So mean. A buffalo can kill you dead if he gets half a chance. You get to be a man by killing something bigger than you. I kilt a grizzly bear onct, and I ain't never been so proud. He was running at me full speed, but I stood there, and I shot him in the head, and he fell dead at my feet." He looked at Adam with appreciation.

Adam turned away and went to take care of the oxen. *I killed two men. Nobody understands. Two men.* He thought that if anyone knew what he had done, the sky would crush him.

Everywhere the debris of previous camps testified to the great emigration that had paused here, wallowed across the

Big Blue, and gone on. Cast-off furniture, wood peeling, empty boxes, metal things rusting away. But there was nobody but themselves in the encampment now. "It's because we're so late," the old man said. To Adam privately he said the emptiness was because the new ferry had started up at Marysville eight miles farther along. "We could still cross over up there if we wanted to," he said, keeping his eyes carefully averted. "But I don't see no need in it myself. We can ford the river."

The trees shivered in the evening cool. Nearby Adam could hear distinctly the strong, low rush of the river running down the great land they had so painfully ascended. Compared to the musical splashing of the spring, the heavy murmur of the river had a sinister sound to it. But Adam paid scarcely any attention. Rivers did not make him afraid anymore. The Big Blue was only an uncomfortable triviality. He thought of the snow drifting silently down in the stony mountains, blocking the passes. July, and they were only at Alcove Springs, going slow, and this year's emigration had long since gone beyond them, leaving them trailing far behind in solitude and danger, too. Adam looked into the dark beyond the magical forms of the trees and wondered what was out there.

They ate well that night. Even Jason ate some of the buffalo steak, smacked his lips and shook his head like some preacher at Sunday dinner, and pronounced everything delicious. "I thank you, Adam. I don't know why I talked so much about being a vegetarian. I suppose I was tired and hot. We can talk about being vegetarians when we don't have anything but vegetables to eat." They laughed in a low, soft pleasure. It was the first time anybody could remember when Jason had said something funny about what might happen to them. In California. In Arcadia.

People laughed often that night, and it seemed that good humor had come back to them.

Jason fell into one of his musings after supper. He sprawled by the fire in negligent serenity, the flames dancing on his broad face and giving his features a dignity they did not possess in ordinary light. He looked a little like a statue or maybe the painted engraving of a President. He rambled on casting a spell of his own soft making, talking while they sat in silent and perfect contentment nearby. They heard the river and the spring splashing like a lullaby in the back-

274

ground and the melodic rise and fall of his deep, full voice, resounding with the conviction that the world could be better than anybody had known. And they were drawn up in his vision because they were mystified at how bad the world had been for them, and none of them could understand why the world had to be bad when it could just as well be good.

Jason fell into an entranced silence at last on that night by Alcove Springs on the Big Blue. They sat and listened to the wind. It was a gentle sound of the great globe swinging in lordly power through the emptiness of space. Henry sat next to his father, his long, blond hair shining in the firelight. Asa held Rachael on his lap. She was sound asleep, and lying there, with her head against his chest, she looked like a cherub with pink, plump checks and long eyelashes, all worn out after a day's singing. The fire rose and fell in the wood with a cheerful sound, and its warmth was friendly, and they were charmed to peace by it.

Then Jason said, "We have not sung in several days. I think we should start singing again. Why did we stop? It was so good with us when we were singing!"

For a moment the notion of singing together again was a sudden embarrassment. But the more they thought of it, the more agreeable the idea became and they all wanted to sing. Jason seizing the moment, struck off a verse:

*Praise ye the Lord, the Almighty, the King of Creation; O my soul praise Him, for He is thy strength and salvation.*

Jason's voice was sonorous, and it was bass when he sang—a fact that always astonished Adam.

Promise joined in at once in her clear, strong contralto, and Harry with his sweet tenor. Asa and Samuel blushed and looked uncertain as they always did when they sang and hummed at first to let themselves slip into song the way large birds will slide down the air to their nests. Their voices were deep and stalwart, throbbing baritones growing stronger as they forgot themselves in the bliss of the music.

Henry sang, his natural soprano rising like faultless chimes and ringing over the rest. Ruth and Jessica sang, and nearby in the canvas-locked tent of Samuel Jennings there suddenly rose the lilting soprano of Rebecca—the poor, mad woman sitting there alone in the stuffy lamp-lit gloom, in her rocking

275

chair endlessly knitting, singing out like a sudden beautiful dream in the velvet night.

Adam, truly and deeply moved, could resist no longer but mingled his strong voice with the rest. He felt cleansed of something, drunk with relief.

> *All ye who hear, Now to His Temple draw near!*
> *Join me in glad adoration.*

Clifford Baynes waited as though attending a moment when he could enter most dramatically. Then he began nodding his head in time to the grand rhythm of the hymn.

> *Praise to the Lord, Who o'er all things so wondrously*
>   *reigneth.*
> *Shelters thee under His wings, yea, so gently sus-*
>   *taineth ...*

He began to hum, quietly at first, but with a gathering power until he was throwing his head back without restraint and striking the notes with a rich and powerful baritone so melodious and fine that Adam was caught up in it with delight.

> *Hast thou not seen How thy desires e'er have been*
> *Granted in what He ordaineth?*
> *Praise to the Lord, Who doth prosper thy work and de-*
>   *fend thee.*
> *Ponder anew, What the Almighty can do,*
> *If with His love He befriend thee ...*

Ishtar Baynes did not sing and seemed vexed with her husband for singing. He seemed to escape her mastery then, for singing was the only thing he did well without her. And in the strange and marvelous singing of Clifford Baynes, Adam perceived one of those fragile visions that men rarely see, a glimpse, as fleeting as the single notes of the song, of what Clifford Baynes might have been if the world—his craven world—had been different. It was something as intangible as the song itself, as hard to pick up as the reflections in a pool and as swiftly gone as an instant of consciousness. But Adam did see it, and he was amazed again by the layers of mystery that descend out of sight in the meanest of men, and the sadness in his heart became a sadness that burned with love for all people.

*I'm wore out. I ain't making no sense.*

They sang on, and the gentle night with its wind sang with them.

When at last they stopped, the quiet rushed in. And everyone else seemed so happy that Adam thought his own misgivings must be a result of his terrible fatigue.

# 36

Adam stood the third watch of the night and saw the clouds thicken and cover the sky. By dawn it was raining and the gray clouds scudded just over the trees, making the air thick. He was annoyed. Hard as hell to harness mules in the rain, clinging to slippery leather. The oxen were temperamental. The men struggled through the difficult work in silence. All of them crotchety and out of sorts.

Jason stood by subdued and silent and cast a long look at the river. Adam was depressed. He had felt so peaceful the night before. But the song and the night had passed, and now this wretched morning. The women brewed coffee and fixed breakfast. Adam looked furtively at Jessica and saw with disappointment that her sunburn was peeling, leaving her face mottled, and her hair was still tangled from the night. Dirt caked her skirts, and she looked untidy. His misery deepened.

Rain spat into the cookfire. The fire cowered in the wood, and an occasional gust of wind threatened to put it out altogether. Adam looked at the river sweeping down, and the confidence he had had about crossing it died away. He thought about the ferry eight miles to the north. He could still lead them up there, pay the fare. Something in keeping with the new beginning they had made the night before. But he thought of his father, the farm back home, the money in the hard leather pouch belted next to his belly. He would ride

277

his mule down into the ford of the river to test the bottom and the current. Then he would decide.

As he went down, the mule shrank back snorting and shook his ugly head in protest. Adam worried. But he kicked the mule down into the stream, and very cautiously and reluctantly the beast descended.

Again as at the Kaw, Adam felt the powerful surge of the river come up, pushing and sucking at both the mule and himself. The water boiled in eddies and swirls and coiled around him like a thousand snakes squeezing at him, and the river roared in his ears. Adam was frightened.

But though the river fought with him, the water came up only a little above his knees. The mule did not even have to swim. He kept his sure sharp hoofs on the bottom, pulling against the river with the slow, stubborn persistence that made mules what they were. The bottom was oozy with mud, and Adam could feel the mud sucking at the mule's feet. But it did not seem deep, and in spite of the power of the current, Adam was sure they could make it.

He crossed and found the old trail on the other side. Then he came splashing back through the river filled with confidence again. He rode back into camp dripping wet. "It's going to be easy," he said.

The old man looked doubtful. "They ain't no time when the Big Blue's easy. We better unload the wagons and take the stuff over trip at a time. The trees around here ain't big enough to float the wagons."

Adam was surprised and annoyed. He did not expect the old man to mistrust his judgment. "I think we could drive right on through myself."

"Look at your mule's feet, Adam."

Adam looked down. The mud came up almost to the mule's knees. It had not seemed that deep in the stream, but the sign was unmistakable. Adam felt ashamed for not noticing it himself. And he was angry. Angry at the old man for knowing so much. Angry because he did not know about the dead Indians.

The old man went on, his voice like a hammer. "That mud's thick enough to get us stuck if we got loads. And we got loads. We're still pulling too much stuff."

"You ain't talking about throwing something else out?" Ishtar Baynes railed at them.

The old man ignored her. "Better unload the stuff and take it over one piece at a time."

"That'll take all day!" Asa said, his voice rough and exasperated.

*Last night we made a new beginning.* Adam thought. Futility. He felt it like cold in his bones.

"Well, now, Mr. Asa," Ishtar Baynes said in a syrupy voice, "maybe that old man is right for a change. We don't want to take any chance of ruining all that stuff." She changed her expression and her tone sharply again without the slightest awareness that she had done so. "Looky here, Mr. McMoultrie. I hope you're telling us the truth. You ain't going to unload the wagons and then tell us to leave all that stuff, too."

"We'll take the stuff first," the old man said patiently. "Won't we, Adam?"

"Whatever you say."

Rachael was clinging to her father. "I don't *want* to cross the river. I don't *want* to get wet." Her amber hair, kinky and damp from the drizzle, was mopped up against her head. She had beautiful hair, so darkly red that its lights showed purple in the curls. Her large, dark eyes peeped around her father and looked to the river, and her face was everything anyone could imagine of childhood terror.

"It's all right, honey," Asa said, very gently. "Ain't nothing going to happen to my Rachael. You're going to be all right."

"I'm scared."

"It ain't going to hurt you." Adam said. He was cross. "It's going to be easy. A lot easier than the Kaw."

Asa said nothing but stroked his little girl's amber hair while she cowered against him and looked fearfully at the river. Adam turned roughly away.

It took all morning long to unload the wagons. The men strained at the work. Adam remained in a bad mood, oppressed by the dirty weather. Still too much stuff being dragged to California by the oxen. He was angry with Jason and the rest of them for not seeing it.

They loaded boxes and furniture and tools on the backs of the oxen and drove the oxen through the river to the other side, undid the ropes and deposited the stuff on the ground, threw canvas over it (though most of it was already soaked) against the rain. And they came back for more.

Adam worked until he thought his arms were going to rip

out of his shoulders. The water pulled at him on every passage, draining him, a fiend drinking his blood. leaving him cold and miserable, stinking of mud and sweat. By a little after noon they had hauled everything over they could carry. A few pieces of heavy furniture stayed in the wagons along with the precious flour barrels and kegs of bacon set up on one of the ponderous oak tables. Adam hoped the furniture would get soaked. Warp and ruin. Then they might abandon it. Save the oxen.

"You should tell poor Rebecca she's going to get wet," Jason said. He was very circumspect sometimes when he spoke to Samuel.

Samuel shook his head dejectedly. "I've done told her."

"What did she say?"

"Aw, she laid into me about fixing the roof again. You know Rebecca, Jason."

"Rebecca is just fine," Ishtar Baynes gushed. "Me and sweet little Rachael spent the whole morning with her. We helped make the time pass."

"I surely do appreciate that," Mrs. Baynes," Jason said. He smiled warmly at her.

"I just want you to know that *some* folks don't run around causing trouble all the time, Mr. Jennings. *Some* folks is on your side."

"We're all on Jason's side," the old man said. He belched in the direction of Ishtar Baynes. "So why don't you haul yourself up in one of them wagons and stop trying to make trouble?"

Ishtar Baynes tossed her head and looked mean. "They's *some* folks that think they're better than everybody else in creation. That's what we call pride, Mr. McMoultrie, and we all know that pride goeth before destruction."

The old man laughed. "Hellfire, Mrs. Baynes. It ain't pride. I'm so much better than you it ain't worth talking about. That's what we call truth. And ye shall know the truth, and the truth shall make you free. Now you hush up and get in that wagon, or we're going to let you paddle across this here river on your tongue."

She got up in Rebecca's wagon and shut the door. Her husband crawled in with Jason. The old man motioned to Adam. "Let's move."

*He ain't human!* Adam thought, so bone-weary he could hardly sit in the saddle.

They double-teamed the oxen. Put twelve onto Jason's wagon at the front. Put two more on the back for balance this time. The old man and Adam rode out to the lead team, and the old man cursed the oxen lovingly and popped the brown leather whip harmlessly in the air above their bony backs. "Move, goddamn ye," he bawled. The oxen lunged forward in the yokes. They went almost sedately down into the swift river. Twelve orange oxen straining in awkward unison in front, two dragged along behind, resisting the way any animal will resist when pulled from the front. The wagon settled into the stream and rocked on the current, and the water foamed up.

Jason perched on the wagon seat with Jessica. His face was tight. She leaned forward, and when the water poured over her feet, she cried out. A thrill of danger and delight, and she looked at her husband and laughed.

*She's pretending not to be afraid. Just to humiliate me!*

Jason was terrified of the water. He had been terrified of water for as long as he could remember. A fear worse than any other fear he had, unreasoning, almost enough to unsettle his mind. Could Moses swim? No need. God parted the waters. Israel passed through on dry land. God, for the mysterious reasons of His Glory, had not parted the waters of the Big Blue. Well, He had not parted the Red Sea waters either. Just a story, symbol of something.

Jason looked enviously down at the old man astride the mule in the roiling water—cavorting, positively *cavorting*—screaming profanely at the oxen, running the shrill encouragement over their hides like a whip. Jason's dream of Arcadia had not included men like this. Shawnee Joe was just like a boss in the iron foundry. Profane and blasphemous. *Why did I do a crazy thing like work in a foundry?* He swallowed. *I did it that black men might be free.*

More than Ralph Waldo Emerson with all his fine words had ever done! Well, it had been hell. A bully of a foreman, always singling him out, screaming at him, hell-bent to humiliate him. Just because Jason was educated. *The foundry was my bondage in Egypt.* The thought seemed grand. But hollow, too. He remembered standing on the banks of the Ohio in the black nights. Seeing a lantern gleam furtively on the other side. Saying to Samuel and Asa, "All right, God help you! Go." And he had stayed behind.

*I was terrified of the river and the night. Of drowning.* His

281

brothers did what he told them to do; he was so much older. He was educated. He was their hope that things would be good again. But in his heart he knew that Asa thought him a coward. And he felt guilty beyond all words for sending his brothers into danger while he remained safe on the northern shore of the great river. *It didn't do any good!* He was almost glad when the fugitive slave laws came; they stopped the nightly terror.

*What is wrong with me!*

Now the people he had led out of bondage, bound for the Promised Land, his own family, were looking to the old man, to Adam, for guidance. Jason looked down at the old man with distaste. What a contrast to Mr. Emerson! But then ... how would Mr. Emerson get oxen over the Big Blue? Jason pondered that one, and he laughed.

Jessica looked suddenly at her husband, pleased to hear him laughing. He did not laugh much. She smiled at him and took his hand. Jason started at her touch, looked and saw the warmth in her eyes, and wanted to go on with it. But the roar of the water was too much to let him talk, and the lurching of the wagon made him afraid as the big wheels cut into the slippery mud below. Clifford Baynes, on the other side of Jessica, with his eyes tightly shut cried out. "Oh, God, help me! Help Thy humble servant. *Amo, amas, amat,* God!" And when they got to the other side, Clifford Baynes jumped down and nearly kissed the ground, hysterical with fear and howling. "I wish I'd never left Frederick, Maryland," In the confusion, the moment of sweet feeling for his wife vanished from Jason, and he and Jessica were again almost strangers on a journey to the same place.

Harry and Promise were to go in Samuel's wagon, sitting up on the seat with Samuel.

Harry drew Adam aside, cleared his throat very gravely, and spoke softly. "Adam, if something should happen to me ..."

Adam could see the romance of the slain young lover growing in Harry's head like a cloud of sugary foolishness. "Oh, for Christ's sake, Harry. Ain't nothing going to happen to anybody. You make me sick!"

Harry looked deeply hurt. But he gathered his old dignity around him and went sternly on. "Adam, if something happens to me, I want you to see to it that Promise remembers me. You be sure she remembers me."

Adam softened before Harry's earnest longing. "Harry, ain't nothing going to happen. Go on now. Get up in that there seat."

"Swear, Adam. Swear you won't let her forget me."

"I swear it! By God, Harry! Now get up there, goddammit. Go on!"

"Thank you, Adam," Harry said, his voice melodious and soft. "You're a gallant friend, Adam. A Christian and a gentleman."

"I ain't never had no experience," Adam said wearily. "Let's go. Let's go!"

The oxen moved down, the old man riding his mule at their head, and the wagon came after, rolling and sliding down the churned black mud into the river. Rebecca and Ishtar Baynes shut off back there together in the magic room that had never left Ironton, Ohio. And when they struck the river, the water poured in, and Adam heard Rebecca cry out. "Samuel! *Samuel!* It's *flooding* in here!" An amazed outrage against the forces of nature she had resolved to ignore and commanded to leave her alone.

Finally it was done, the oxen unhitched and brought back over, and it was the turn of Asa's wagon. When he and the old man brought the oxen up onto the eastern shore of the river again, Rachael began to shriek.

She clung hysterically to her father, like some little animal with claws. He could not comfort her no matter what he did. She fastened herself to his legs and would not let him move. Ruth tried to console her, dropping to her knees in the sodden earth and hugging her to make her be quiet. But nothing worked. Rachael's yowl of terror went on and on all the while Adam and the old man were hitching the oxen, getting them in line, pointing them down toward the river.

Adam was vexed. He went impatiently to Rachael. "Look, Rachael, if you quiet down, I tell you what I'll do. You can come along with me on my mule. You can ride up in the saddle with me. You'll have fun," *I'll settle her down when they can't!* he thought. Something else to be superior about before these people.

Asa looked at him solemnly. An aging face. The lines showing. Green-brown eyes looking perplexed and afraid. "Do you think it's safe, Adam? I'd just as soon have her with me in the wagon if you don't mind."

Adam shrugged and threw up his hands. Nobody trusted

him. He was impatient and cross. "I was just trying to help out. Mr. Jennings. Forget it." He went back to his mule, damning Asa with his back.

"Mr. Adam ..." Ruth tried to speak. She did not want Adam to be angry. She could not finish because of Rachael.

"I want to go with Mr. Adam!" Rachael's shrill, spoiled little whine, wanting to have her own way. A prospect more rewarding than fear.

Ruth spoke softly. "No, honey. You ride with us in the wagon. Where we can hold onto you."

"I don't want to ride in the wagon. I want to ride with Mr. Adam!"

Adam looked at her and squeezed his lips together. He did not like Rachael.

"I want to ride with Mr. Adam. I want to ride with Mr. Adam. I want to ride with Mr. Adam." She turned around and clumsily, wrathfully drew back her little pink fist and hit Asa in the thigh with it. "You let me go with Adam!"

Asa was perplexed. "What about it, Adam? Do you think it's safe?"

Adam was exasperated and worn out. He had mud in his hair. "Why shouldn't it be safe, Mr. Jennings? Look at all the times I've been over today!" He wanted to add, *While you've been sitting on your ass in your wagon!*

"I want to ride with Mr. Adam. I want to ride with Mr. Adam!"

Henry stood close to Adam, looking on gravely at his sister. "Rachael's spoiled," he said softly, shaking his blond head. "She's a girl." Adam again felt sorry for Henry. Rachael was the baby, she was getting most of the love and the attention.

Ruth and Asa argued softly with Rachael to no avail. She pouted, she cried, she hit at both of them. Finally Asa turned around and looked up. Adam astride his mule again. Tired, dripping wet, proud, annoyed, and willing to leave them behind. They could be damned. He had killed two men. They did not even know. Asa spoke slowly, softly, reluctantly as if he had glue in his mouth. "Well, maybe it will be all right. If you don't think it's safe, Mr. Adam. Just leave her here with us. Crying won't hurt her. I don't reckon anything ever happened to a child because she cried." Asa laughed without humor.

"I want to ride with Mr. Adam!"

"It'll be all right," Adam said impatiently. When Asa talked about safety, it seemed to Adam that Asa was condemning him.

"You will be careful with her?"

"I'll be riding the mule, too, Mr. Jennings."

"I want to ride with Mr. Adam. I want to ride with Mr. Adam."

"She's our baby, Adam," Ruth said. Her large, soft face was worried. Adam looked at her and looked at the swift river. For just a moment he considered telling them it was too dangerous.

But before he could lower himself to admit the danger, Asa was doubtfully hoisting Rachael up to Adam on the mule, and the little girl was settling down with her chubby legs astride the saddle, chortling with her little triumph. She had got her own way. She threw back her head and grinned up at Adam in snaggle-toothed pleasure. Not anything attractive about the smile. Not the smile you expected on the face of a sweet little girl.

The old man walked back and took a long, uneasy look at Adam and Rachael. "You be careful," he said quietly.

Adam looked at him and wanted to put the child down. But the old man turned away before Adam could speak. Adam was left with Rachael and his pride. The old man turned to the oxen with almost the same motion that he left Adam. The whip snaked out through the air like something alive and dangerous, and the wagon was yanked ahead. Ruth sat in the back, looking anxiously at Adam and Rachael. "Are you all right, honey?" Anxiety. Adam could not ride after her to hand Rachael up to the wagon. The two oxen hitched to the rear were in his way.

"She's all right, Mrs. Jennings." He told himself everything was fine. Other things he had carried across weighed more than Rachael did. Were harder to hold. With one hand he held the bridle rein of the mule. The other arm was wrapped around Rachael. Her plump little body was hot against him in the chilly rain. Damp child-smell filling his nostrils. Henry came cautiously back to sit next to his mother, holding on to a flap of the canvas to keep his balance against the rocking of the wagon in the stream.

Rachael looked up at Adam. "Do you know what Aunt Ishter and Aunt Becky told me about Aunt Jessie?"

"What?" Adam hardly paid any attention to her. He was

eyeing the wagon. The river had it now. The following oxen were in the water. The oxen in front, the wagon, and the oxen behind made a bow, bent by the current.

"They said she's a whore!"

"What?" Adam's head jerked down. *She don't know what she's saying!* His first, saving thought. But that crafty little face, inches from his own, gave the lie to her innocence. She did not know what "whore" meant. But she knew it was something bad. Adam knew she would have said the word even if she had understood.

She giggled. "I told you. They said she's a whore!"

He tried to keep his voice even. "That is a nasty word," he said, "And it is not true, what they said."

"Aunt Becky and Aunt Ishter said it's true."

"Which one said it first?"

"Aunt Ishter said it first. Aunt Becky said she knowed it was true. They told me special about it." The little girl pleased, expecting Adam to be pleased. A tiny adult sharing in the marvelous conversation of other adults. Adam started his mule down into the water, bitterly angry. *Wait till I get my hands on Ishtar Baynes!* Those two evil women, bending like witches over this little girl to cast their hex, repeating the ugly word, making her repeat it after them, grinning with satisfaction at each other when she got it right. And the little girl formed her sweet mouth and got it exactly right, and when the two older women applauded her and called her the *smartest* thing, she said it again and again.

"I don't want you to talk about it anymore with me. I don't want you to say that word to anybody else."

Rachael's expression changed. She saw Adam suddenly as an enemy.

"I will tell your mamma, and your mamma will whip the stuffing out of you."

"Mamma won't neither whip me. Daddy won't let nobody whip me. I ain't never been whipped. I ain't never going to be whipped."

Adam felt like shaking her. The mule's feet were in the water, the animal stepping gingerly along, feeling the way. "Then I'll whip you myself. And if your daddy tries to stop me, I'll whip him, too."

Rachael began spitting at him, struggling. "I don't want to ride with you. I want to be with mamma!"

Adam clung to her, not caring if he hurt her. "Well, you're

286

going to ride with me," he said fiercely. "They ain't no way for you to get across this river now but to ride with me. And when we get on the other side, I'm going to give your mamma a talking to about you."

She began to shriek, struggling with him, all the harder, throwing a tantrum. She yelled at him. "You're a whore! A whore! A whore!" Ahead of them the wagon was more than halfway over. Ruth was shouting something. Adam could hear her voice, see her on her knees with her hands cupped around her mouth. He could not understand what she said, with Rachael yelling in his ear.

The mule was careful, slow, and tired. Adam was tired, too. More tired than he could ever remember. He could have turned Rachael over his leg and beaten the daylights out of her if there had been time. The boiling river was rising beneath him, and suddenly he felt again the cold strength of the current sweep up to the belly of the mule, up to his knees, to his thighs, sucking and snarling around his body. The river made a deep, hollow, growling sound, angrily tearing at him and the mule. The mule went slowly on, dipping his big head, raising it, picking his way cautiously across the slick, muddy bottom. Little stitching steps. So slow Adam was angry at the mule as he was angry at Rachael, angry at the day.

Rachael saw the green water burst and foam around them, and she heard its roar. She began to screech with terror. She stopped calling Adam a whore. She threw back her head and shut her eyes and with both hands fought to free herself from the tight hold of Adam's arm, as if in freeing herself from him she might escape the river. He felt the wiry texture of her dark-red hair against his neck. He thought his ears and mind would burst like something made of soaked paper. And far ahead, in a hollow somewhere, he heard the remote, faint voice of Ruth yelling at them.

Much later he would accuse himself of the same killing pride that had made Jason and the rest of them think that oxen could not be worked to death. Mules did not fall. And when Adam's mule fell in the Big Blue, he was as unprepared for it as he would have been to meet death walking around a sidewalk somewhere swinging an ivory-headed cane.

Adam experienced the plunge as a sickening lurch and a prodigious splash. Instantly the river was sweeping over his head, and the mule, fighting to regain its balance, was pulling him down. He felt his boots tangled in the stirrups. He felt himself drowning. Then the river simply swept him off the back of the thrashing mule. He felt the frantic little girl in his arms ripped away from his grasp by a million clawing fingers of water. And he was tumbling head over heels and fighting for his life in the great, green dark of the river, trying in vain to scream for help.

He found no breath to cry. No sound at all in his ears but the eerily tranquil, lethal, subriverine gurgling of the current. He thought he would die. But he was flung to the surface, gulping air. Gray sky lowering above him. Gray-green water sweeping him along. The banks rushing by. The sky wheeling round and round with ridiculous lethargy, and he was flailing at the water with all his might and searching for Rachael.

He saw the struggling form of the little girl with auburn hair near him. He lunged for her. The river made his strength puny. She was just beyond his reach. Once she was scarcely a foot from his hand, and he looked into her terror-frozen eyes and just once heard an abbreviated shriek, a pitiful cry, demented with fright, frail as a bird's chirp in the wide river, abruptly choked with water.

Some vagary of the speeding current drove her on just a little more swiftly than himself. He snatched at her and missed. And so she was borne away, and in only an instant the auburn hair and the clutching hand had vanished from the surface of the water, and a little girl named Rachael was no more.

# 37

For as long as he lived, Rachael's death remained burned on his mind. More than a scar. An open wound, perpetually festering, tender, tight with pus. Sometimes his mind would reach gingerly out to it and touch it, and the pain would thrill through him, and he would have to endure it awhile before he could deaden it with other thoughts. Many times he cried out when he was alone, a short, animal sound of frustration and shame that relieved him of a merciless pressure in his chest. At other times he was likely to get up from his chair at home in the evening and begin some sudden, unexpected conversation with his wife. "What's wrong?" she would say, knowing what was wrong by his agitation and by the desperate way he talked to her about nothing.

"I was thinking about Rachael."

"Oh," she would say softly, looking at him with her large and compassionate eyes, glistening with sympathy. "It wasn't your fault."

"Yes, yes. It was my fault."

"No, Adam, it was an accident. And it's all so long ago. It's done, and she is dead." Absolution granted by his wife on behalf of all the human community.

Somehow he got out of the water, swimming, struggling up to his neck in the river bottom, fighting the black ooze of the bank where he emerged. losing a boot in the mire, wildly going back for it, blackly fouling himself from head to toe, pulling the boot back on, rushing up through dense, clinging foliage and running as hard as he could run downstream, breathing so hard, so fast, that his lungs ached. He searched the water in frenzy for any sign of the little girl and desperately counted aloud the seconds, the minutes when she would be without air, the time it would take her to drown. And as he ran, he shouted her name again and again at the top of his voice, and the sound of his screaming was so frail in the vast emptiness that it was like life in eternal space. "Rachael! Rachael! Rachael!"

Somewhere far downstream, exhausted, sick with shame and remorse and lacerated by the underbrush he had fought, he vomited up his breakfast and tasted coffee and bile. And then he seemed to turn loose all his insides, and bowels and bladder went like balloons bursting. Without stopping to cleanse himself, without caring, wishing to punish himself to bring Rachael back, wanting only to die. he started trudging back, his feet like iron, shit and mud scraping at his thighs and grinding in the cheeks of his buttocks, his head giddy, his vision swimming, exhausted and nauseated, and ready to fall to the earth and hope for it to cover him. Somehow he came on the others. And out of the awful confusion, the stink, the foulness, the fatigue, the horror, there was one blazing and terrible instant, cutting like shattered glass in his mouth, that stayed lodged irrevocably in his memory.

That was the sight of Asa's ravaged face as he came running soaking wet and black with mud himself because he had jumped screaming into the river, weeping and crying to know if Adam had found his baby, his Rachael, his darling. Adam had never supposed that a plain face could tell so much. And he had never guessed that a single gesture of his own could make any man look the way Asa looked when Adam dumbly shook his head in negation, unable to speak, unable to look Asa in the eye, able only to weep hysterically like the child Rachael had been.

They searched for three days up and down the river, tramping through the slick underbrush down against the water, muddying themselves from hair to boot, making themselves hoarse with the futile shouting of that single name. *Rachael. Rachael. Rachael.*

They called because all of them prayed that she might still be alive.

They slept in fitful dozing. Jason led them in baffled, halting prayer, interrupted and distracted by Asa's sobs. Ruth stood in stern and silent grief and would not bow when Jason prayed. They gobbled half-cooked food when they were so hungry they could not go on. Food they could not taste somehow restored them. And doggedly they began the search again. Night and day melted together. Another violent storm boiled up out of the western sky, and they were out crying Rachael's name between the thunderclaps, braving the long blue splinters of lightning. And when it cleared and the clouds blew away, the slop of sticky mud and the relentless stinging of mosquitoes and the tearing of thorns and brush became as much a part of life as breath and blood. Light and dark, rain and sun, succeeding one another became the confusion of a nightmare.

Adam taunted himself with fantasies of deliverance. They would hear a faint voice crying. They would find Rachael, bespattered with mud, frightened, half-conscious, thirsty, hungry, her little red dress torn to tatters, her body bruised, only half-alive. But half-alive is not dead! They would nurse her. Adam would warm her with his body. Harry would give her medicines. Rachael would get well. And he would vow to God never to be proud again in his life.

But the river gave back no voice but its own steady rushing

through the great land. The sun came out and flayed the earth with light, and the clouds sailed by overhead, white and huge and insolent with their peaceful indifference.

On the third day, Asa found his baby.

A scrap of dirty red dress caught the smashing sunshine, a tiny signal dully flashed from a brown sandbar far down the river, and Asa splashed heavily over to it, mad with grief, and dug the little body out with his hands, and with his fingernails tried to pick the dirt away from its face.

The body was misshapen and decomposing. It stank of the muddy river and of its own putrefaction. Still Asa dug the horrible thing out and came carrying it back to them in his arms. Adam looked on the remains of a little mouth blankly agape with black mud on little white teeth, and he saw with a final horror that the interior of that tiny mouth was no longer red but a brownish and rotting green.

Asa wept—the terrible, wordless, unblaming weeping of a hopeless soul.

And Adam cursed God in his heart and willed to die.

The old man knew how a corpse was to be buried on the prairies. He cut the thick sod carefully with a spade, making squares that he neatly removed. Hard, sweaty work, but he would not let anyone help him. "It's got to be done just right," he murmured, his face bleak and austere. When the sod was removed and carefully stacked aside, he let them take turns digging a deep grave. "Deep, to keep her from the wolves," the old man said. The little body was wrapped in new canvas and laid gently in the ground, and the grave was filled.

Dark, brown earth spaded over the canvas sack. The stench of the rotting flesh lingered for a little while when the soil had covered it, and then the wind blew it away, and nothing remained but the smell of grass and sweet air and fresh dirt.

They packed the dirt down until it was at the level of the sod. The blocks of sod were replaced on top of the dirt, squares set against each other in the same precise order that they had been cut and removed. The left-over dirt they scattered over the prairies. They carried water and wet down what they could not scatter and poured water on the grave itself, and at last a very keen eye would have had to look carefully to perceive the grave at all. "To keep her from the

Pawnee," the old man said, his face sad and venerable and wise in the way that totems or mysteries are wise.

"Ain't we going to have a marker?" Asa cried. Ain't we never going to be able to come back and put flowers on her grave?"

The old man looked at him. Every line in the old man's face was bent in compassion. He lowered his steely eyes and shook his head, his long, white hair rustling like the shivering of leaves in the cold moonlight. "Mr. Jennings, if you put up a marker, the Pawnee is going to dig up your little girl to see if they's something to rob out of her grave. And when they don't find nothing to rob, they're going to scatter the bones for the wolves to eat. A grave's for lying in, Mr. Jennings. It ain't for flowers. Let your little girl rest in peace."

Asa sobbed, and no one knew how to comfort him. He turned fiercely on Jason. "Wolves! Indians! What kind of land is this?"

Jason's lips moved before he could speak, and when he could say words, his voice was thick and tentative and very slow. "It is the wilderness, and we are passing through it. It is not our destination." Asa glared at him, raised both hands as if to strike him, cried out in frustration, and ran back to his wagon, tearing at his hair and sobbing.

So there was no marker on Rachael's grave, and they went on, and all of them understood a little more keenly how swift and final death is.

# 38

It was Rachael's death that changed things. They had been advancing across the plains, quarreling, singing, eating, marching, no different from a hundred or a thousand or maybe ten thousand other caravans that made the long pilgrimage West. Somehow through it all an invisible net had bound them together, and the net had proven its strength on the night they camped at Alcove Springs on the eastern side of the Big Blue, and all of them were drawn together by Jason's ardent desire for a new beginning. But now that slight, tenuous, fantastic thread that had bound them together in their quest for Arcadia had broken.

Had they not been in the middle of the immense American plains, they might have split apart. But here in this spectral land, the emptiness drove them together, and the wind blowing ceaselessly around them made them all afraid to be alone, to stray too far from the others. So they went on together, their hopes like flags furled and trailing in the dust.

"I hate the wind!" Ruth said bitterly. "You can't never get away from it out here. It don't never stop!" She could not speak of Rachael. But she could relieve the pent-up vehemence in her heart by speaking ill of the wind. She shuddered, her fleshy arms folded across her large bosom, hugging herself, and she looked tense and constrained and hurt, a strong woman not daring to surrender to a broken heart.

"It's so lonely," she said. "So lonely."

And Adam, mute with guilt, heard the voice of the sad wind like a choir singing for a funeral that went on and on.

He said what he had to say to Asa and to Ruth, to all of them. "I'm sorry!" His voice broke over the words, and he wept openly. Weeping not only for Rachael's death but for the futility of his apology.

Jason said, "I don't understand why it happened!" The lines on his face were deeper, and his expression had the baffled and unfocused look of people in shock. His voice was soft, and Adam saw that he was getting gray. His face under the deep tan was ashen and lifeless.

At night by the campfire of dried buffalo chips tentatively burning, he carried on a monologue with them. "Have I ever failed you?" He looked around earnestly as if he honestly did not know the answer to his question. He looked from face to face and met only their baffled silence. Then Harry, speaking like the carefully rehearsed leader of a chorus said, "Of course not, Mr. Jennings. Of course not."

"Rachael's dead," Asa said, his voice low and thick and choked with grief.

"I don't understand," Jason murmured again and again. "I don't understand."

The old man shook his head and stretched his hands to the fire. "It happened because the mule slipped and fell. That's the only reason. Jason."

"No," Jason said. "I promised we would all get there, to California, safe and sound. I promised harmony between ourselves and nature. But nature killed Rachael."

"Ah," the old man said. "Ah."

Ishtar Baynes had an answer. She whispered it around as though she had been blowing on coals to make the flames spurt up. "It was Jessica's fault."

"Jessica's fault? How could it be Jessica's fault? She was in a wagon ahead. She had already gone over!"

The whisper of Ishtar Baynes was like the roar of an empty seashell. "She made you dump things out of the wagons. She made me overload my wagon, kill my oxen. That held us up a whole day. Two nights! Ain't that right?"

"Yes, that's right. But what does that have to do with Rachael?"

"That means if we'd kept the stuff even spread out like we started, we would of got to the river one day early, don't you know?"

"Well . . . Yes. I suppose that's right."

"Now you can't tell me that that mule would of slipped in the water if we'd got here that one day early! That's like saying that the mule is bound to slip in the water ever time he goes across. But I say he just slipped in the water that one day that he done it. And if we'd got here one day early, he'd of got across the water just fine, and little Rachael would be with us right this minute!"

*She was evil, too,* Adam thought. That was the bewildering thing. Rachael was wicked, and in the moment before the mule fell, Adam hated her! *She was just a child!* You don't judge children the way you judge people old enough to know the difference between right and wrong. He convinced himself just enough to increase his guilt. And when he saw people talking and could not hear what they said, he knew they must be condemning him.

"Poor, sweet little Rachael!" Ishtar Baynes said, shaking her head. "She didn't never have a wrong thought. She never done nothing bad. She was an angel, that girl was. I know she's looking down on us from heaven right this very minute."

Always after the Big Blue, Ishtar Baynes seemed to be burrowing into things, like a worm gnawing on soft wood. *She's taking over!* Adam thought dully, watching the way she manipulated Jason. *We can't do nothing about it! She's taking over.*

Why? Adam could not answer that one. What did she want? He was too suffocated with guilt and apathy to care. He rode looking at the plains. A hundred thousand years crept with them over the grasslands. The prairies glistened not only with enormous space but with infinite time. And Adam, riding with scarcely any thought, pondered dully how very long the plains had remained exactly as he saw them now. And after him they would change and never be the same again, never be allowed to rest. His heart, made heavy by all he had experienced, ached for the plains as it grieved for Rachael's death.

"I'm so sorry about the way we busted things up, busted up the way things was going. They was going so *good*, and we tried to change things, and if they's anything you ever want to learn it's not to change things when things is going good." Ishtar Baynes heaved a sigh, like the hiss of a snake. "I ruint my oxen trying to help you people."

"Help *us*, ma'am?" Samuel, huge and powerful with a mind so slow, thoughts in his thick brain dripping at great intervals like water from the roof of a dark cave. Even he had difficulty believing Ishtar Baynes had been trying to help anybody.

She was undaunted. Her eyes were like cut glass. "Sure! Help *you*, Mr. Samuel! You don't think I was really going to keep all that fine stuff for myself, do you?"

Jason, tramping along with the sun on his head, cleared his throat and looked at her. "I believe you gave us that impression, Mrs. Baynes."

"Oh, listen here, Mr. Jennings! I wasn't going to keep *nothing* for myself! I was going to haul it *all* to California for you folks and give it to you when we got there. I was going to show you that they's some folks in this cruel world that don't have a greedy bone in their body. I was going to do it just to show you how much I appreciate what you folks done for me and my darling Clifford here!"

She smiled that melancholy smile of hers, like something chipped out of flint, and cast a pious look around at all of them.

"Well, Mrs. Baynes, you *said* you were going to keep it." Jason wondering, perplexed. Had he misjudged this woman? He was weak enough now to doubt.

"Why, I give you my word as a *lady*, Mr. Jennings. I wasn't going to keep *nothing* for myself!" She hoisted her thin, sharp shoulder blades and cast mournful eyes heavenward and sighed. "But though my spirit was willing, my oxen was weak. God rest their souls!" Her voice descended to that evil whisper again and nearly broke. "They died for you fine folks. And I hate to say it, Mr. Jason. I don't like to say *nothing* bad about nobody. But it was your own wife's fault!"

# 39

Ishtar Baynes.

The first thing she could remember was the reek of strong, cheap perfume and the smell of dank wood in a rambling house in Boston.

She was Ishtar Smith then, a skinny little girl whose dull blond hair had just enough wave in it to be hard to comb and not enough to be beautifully curly. She had very large, brown eyes, and as far back as she could remember there were always other little girls who had things she did not have, and those eyes developed a glint of calculation and inquiry and disdain all together, for she never saw anything she believed was worthily possessed by the flimsy little female nothings who had title to a doll, a house, a toy carriage, a father, or anything else she never had.

The perfume in her house smelled like roses. Such strong roses that the perfume made her gag sometimes. The scent was in the parlor, as thick as powder in the air. It was in the varnished hallway. It was in the brown stairwell that led upstairs. It reeked in the long curtains and in the rugs and in the furniture itself. The only roses in the house were made of faded red paper. But the perfume seemed to saturate life itself.

The only place she could escape the perfume was in the kitchen. There she could smell brown beans cooking and cabbage sometimes and chicken and fish. So she liked cooking smells and washing smells and the smell of cleaning floors and ironing clothes. Laundry seemed like starting all over again, and when she was very young she believed new beginnings were possible.

It was a big house with high ceilings and tall, thin windows. The inside walls were painted white. A bone white that made the curtains seem rich in candlelight. But at night when Ishtar Smith walked through the still rooms, left messy, vacant, and tumbled by the riotous business of the evening, the walls looked stark and ghastly.

Calico curtains done in deep lavender hung down from the windows on thick wooden poles. Her mother bragged on the curtains time and again. "I paid good, hard cash to get the shade of purple I wanted!" But when Ishtar knew the curtains, they had been washed so often in strong lye soap that they had bleached out to a pale and streaked violet, and they looked thin, cheap, and worn.

Her favorite person in the house was not her mother but the girl who worked in the kitchen—a plump, red-cheeked girl from the country named Margaret. Margaret spoke with a Maine twang and said "Ayuh" in two strong syllables and smiled like a good dream when anyone paid her the smallest compliment. Margaret was always stirring around, washing pots, scrubbing floors, cooking, doing things with water, and when she poured water down the pottery drains into the city sewers, they could hear it gurgling and splashing, echoing—and re-echoing until it dwindled to a distant and mysterious silence.

Ishtar and her sister Irene wondered where the water went. And one day Irene said with a long dreamy sigh. "It would be so good to go with the water. Just go out into the world and be free. Never see this place again."

Irene was pretty in a wan, frail way. She had long blond hair, bright blue eyes, and her pale and mottled skin was in the fashion of the day when consumption seemed to be the death most fitting for a lady. Irene's mouth was just a trifle too wide. But when she smiled, good cheer lightened all her features, and as she got older, men were enamored of that generous mouth and wanted to kiss it. Irene was smarter than Ishtar. She thought thoughts that Ishtar could never even imagine, like fleeing this house by pouring herself down the drain.

"I'd run down to the ocean again! I'd be carried all over

the world! And someday I'd float to papa!" Irene was wistfully certain that her father would love her still if she could only find him. "He didn't leave on account of me! He left on account of mamma. And I don't blame him! I wish I could get away from mamma myself!"

Ishtar Smith sat drinking in these fantasies with a rapt and devouring curiosity. And always she thought. *He wouldn't love me!* And when she looked at Irene, saw the remote dreaminess in that thin, too-delicate face, the bitterness and the hurt and the loneliness, Ishtar thought, *She looks down on me! My own sister!* The worst grief of all was to know that Irene had the right.

"Irene's so pretty," the men would say in low, admiring voices, taking every chance to feel her as though she had been a fine young pig at market, letting speculative hands linger and probe. "Irene's so *smart!*" garishly painted women would say, chirping through mouths painted like sweet little rosebuds horribly out of place in their wasted faces. "Irene's so graceful."

And what did they say about Ishtar? "That girl's awful skinny. She don't look too healthy to me. Poor little thing! That tiny mouth. Looks like she's sucked a lemon and can't get unpuckered. Hee! Hee! Hee!" And Ishtar's mother brushed strands of damp hair off her sweaty forehead and inspected her ugly daughter and said in a careworn voice full of pity and foreboding, "My God, Itsy, I don't know how you're going to make it in life. You got to have looks or money to get along in this world, and you ain't got neither one."

Sometimes in these moments of dire prophecy, Isabel Smith would hug poor Ishtar to herself and sigh hopelessly, close to tears. It was a whimsical gesture, the most affectionate her mother ever made toward her. Boundless and despairing pity. Ishtar loved the attention and yet at the same time felt her heart sink like a stone in the bottomless blue of the sea.

"And to think your father named you for some goddamn goddess of love he'd read about somewheres! I always knew the man was a bloody fool!"

The kitchen was little Ishtar's refuge. Margaret was there. The smells were friendlier. And she was unseen by the men who tramped in and out in noisy confusion, cursing, drinking, laughing like pigs, stinking, slamming doors, bawling drunk,

298

quarreling sometimes, sometimes going off singing bawdy songs in the night.

And occasionally in the wee, wee hours of the morning, when the house fell silent, when street lamps glowed weakly against the graying light of the coming dawn, Isabel Smith and Margaret and girls whose names Ishtar had long since forgotten would sit wearily around a common wood table and drink coffee. The girls with their cheap dressing gowns all askew, faces with smeared paint and long hair tangled and with tired, dazed eyes avoiding each other. All of them drunk with fatigue, hardly able to talk. Then the kitchen was a haven and a delight the little girl could never quite explain even to herself. Perhaps it was that weariness was an acid that had eroded away the slick metallic disguises that divided people like armor and because no one could pretend or defend herself or attack, they were very close by default. Sometimes then Isabel Smith would look at her ugly daughter perched there on a high stool with longing, childish eyes, and she would pat the little girl on the head and say, "How you doing, honey? God, what a night! What a night!"

Isabel Smith saw lots of men. She kept a house for sailors on shore briefly from the sea, men troubled and restless like the sea itself, starved for rum and immobile earth, and for a naked female body to hold and, in the foolish way of men, believing that the warm, willing nakedness of a strange woman in bed had some meaning, preserving those masculine delusions of childhood that any woman who would yield to them must love them, at least for that one wild moment of fleshly consummation.

From her mother Ishtar Smith learned what there was to know about men and how to get along in a world where men held the scepter.

"Now you get in that closet, and you listen to the way I handle him!" Isabel Smith commanded her daughters, as soon as they sprouted hair in the crotch, a fine little crop of stiff curls that Isabel Smith attended with the expectation of a farmer looking to harvest his seed. "You got to remember that men are like dogs. And when you get a dog used to getting fed every time he hears you call his name, then he's going to come every time he hears the door slam because he gets used to you pitching food out to him when you open the door. You do what these men expect. It don't matter what you feel. It's best if you feel nothing, my girls. You pretend they're a pack of bloody

299

dogs, and you open the door and throw them your bone, and you remember the rascals have a few shillings to spend, and if you don't get what they have, somebody else will. And money you don't get is money you lose for all your life, for all eternity!"

So Ishtar Smith crouched in the dark closet with her sister, and the two young girls clung to each other in hot fright and devouring curiosity and listened to their mother wallowing in bed with a man just on the other side of the thin wooden door. Her mother groaned and bucked with all the energy she possessed until the cheap bedsprings popped like a broken machine. She panted and snorted. She hissed obscenities in rising excitement, pouring them like jets of steam forced into the pistons of an engine. She groaned like a roar of exhaust. And finally like a safety valve popping off she hissed, "Oh yes! Oh yes! Oh YES!" Bang.

And when the man went reeling out, buckling his belt, in haste to go once he had come, Isabel Smith rested a moment in the dark silence. Then she got up calmly and took a towel and dried herself and opened the closet door and stood there, voluptuous and naked before her daughters, and the voice that had been rent with pretended passion was now as hard as the teeth of a file. "You see? That drunk pig has gone off thinking he's king of the mountain." She turned a gold piece over in her long fingers. "And he threw me this on the bed as he left, don't you know? That much more than the price I charged the bloody bastard at the beginning. He will brag to all his friends about how he knocked me unconscious, and he will likely come back, he will. And they will come to test themselves against him!" She laughed, genuinely amused at how simple men were, how easy to deceive.

"Let me tell you one thing, my girls. You get their bloody money before they get in bed. You pretend to faint when you feel him stop with the juice running into you. That way you don't have to talk to the bloody pigs when they've done. And they will throw more money on the bed to pay you for their guilt. They feel guilty about hurting you, don't you know? And he will come to you again and again!"

She stood there, the tan light of a candle reflecting on the sweat running down her naked body. "You look at me now, my fine little girls, and you see our bank account and our fortune and our future. And don't you dare ever make fun of me for being a whore! You hear me now! My being a whore

300

is what keeps you both alive, keeps you from starving like beggars' brats. And you ain't never going to be better than me!"

After that Ishtar never had a soft feeling again in her life.

It was Irene's turn first because Irene was older. Ishtar watched while her frightened sister was painted up for the occasion. The initiation. That sickening rose perfume was daubed on her in those secret places where Isabel Smith thought a woman needed it. She was dressed in a flimsy red dress that her mother had almost worn out. Ishtar thought Irene looked pale. Still there was something grand about Irene because in a moment she was going to become a complete woman—all like a shot or a fall, utterly unlike the slow, stumbling, ignorant development that made ordinary girls take years and years to grow up.

Irene took her moment with that tense resignation—almost an arrogance— that once numbed virgin victims to walk with their fair heads erect to the bloody altar stone where they would be deflowered with a knife to appease the thirsty harvest gods.

Her god was out of the sea—a young sailor. She sat on his lap in the big living room, grinning as her mother had taught her, showing little white teeth. He laughed in a good-hearted way. And Ishtar (avidly watching through a slit in the cheap draperies hanging in a doorway) gained a sudden understanding of just how vulnerable men were. The sailor's face was somehow boyish and pleasant in spite of the lines burned into his skin by wind and sun. He was hard enough and proud enough and daring enough to spit into the face of the seven seas. But when Irene smiled and stroked his silky beard and tittered in an utterly artificial, glassy way, the hardness melted, and something tender and innocent came out in his face. Ishtar felt sorry for him in the way that a hunter may sometimes feel momentarily sad for the bright bird zinging before his wheeling and shouldered gun.

The sailor gave her mother a gold coin. "It's her first time," Isabel Smith said with a wicked and obscene grin.

The room where Irene and the sailor went smelled of varnish and soap and the inevitable rose perfume. A clean room. Isabel Smith had discovered that men were aroused by the combination of cleanliness and sex, and the bedrooms were scrubbed every day, and the linens were changed and washed. "You get rid of them faster when they think they're fucking something clean," she said. "You don't have to fool around with the bloody beggars to make them get it hard."

There was a profound silence in the rest of the house, broken only when Irene screamed.

Isabel Smith rushed upstairs, red-faced and vexed. A frenzied argument behind the door. The sailor loudly apologetic. Irene's muted sobbing.

But Isabel Smith would tolerate no surrender in her house. She screamed at her daughter, yelled at the sailor. "Are you a man or ain't you?" Then she came tramping back downstairs wearing that eternal, grim, and satisfied expression of mothers who have put their daughters on the path of righteousness by a stern lecture on the facts of life.

In a short while the sailor came back down the stairs looking humble and contrite. In a half hour Irene reappeared, her red dress torn either by the sailor's first eagerness or by her own clumsiness or maybe by her terror. She had put it back on as best she could, striving in a blank way to do what was expected of her. Now the dress seemed to swallow her up, and she looked younger and frailer than ever. The paint on her thin face was smeared, and her long hair that had been so carefully combed was all awry. Her eyes were dazed and red with crying. But she carried herself with cold dignity.

*And she thinks she's better than me!* Ishtar secretly exulted in her sister's humiliation.

A year or so later, Ishtar's turn. She nearly cried out with pain when her mother rubbed the rose perfume down into the cleft between her skinny hips. It burned. Later she understood what had made Irene scream. The man burst into her and hurt worse than anything she could remember. But she gritted her teeth and kept her thin legs spread by sheer willpower, while the man's thing inside her burned back and forth like a pipe heated in fire. She even managed to pant and to speak some obscenity she had learned from her mother. Afterwards, though she felt skinned and raw when she walked, she forced herself to come bouncing down the steps with a grin of triumph.

The man gave her a last hard sqeeze and a silver dollar for a tip, and then remorse sent him slinking quickly off into the dark, scurrying like a rodent afraid to be seen. Ishtar sat in the kitchen afterwards with the others when the business of the night was over. She mimicked his frenzy and made the other girls howl with laughter. And she was proud enough to ignore the bleeding rawness in her crotch where he had been.

And that was the way she began.

Ishtar Smith screwed the future out of her thoughts as though she had been fastening the doors against a hurricane. She never made a plan. She hardly ever used the word "tomorrow." She played her role of pretended passion, and she took a professional pride in her sexual games. She cherished in a perverse, competitive way those foolish men who came to seek her out again and again. Irene was much prettier, but Ishtar had more business.

They had trouble with a policeman in Boston. One night a fight erupted in an upstairs bedroom. The policeman was beating Isabel Smith up. Broke her thin front teeth, of which she had been inordinately proud. (When the men in the parlor downstairs heard the fight, they did what anyone would expect a gentleman to do in such a moment. They fled into the night. No gentleman wanted to be implicated in a fight in a whorehouse.) She was left with two swollen black eyes and bruises on her arms and legs that did not disappear for a month.

The policeman had become enraged at something Isabel Smith said about his manhood. Ishtar never knew what. Her mother hated policemen. He threatened to call the law in on them if they stayed in Boston. Isabel interpreted that to mean that he was going to call in the rest of the police force. She did not think there would be room for that much of a fight in her house. So she got out of town. One lunatic policeman was enough.

They went down to New Haven, a pleasant town on the Connecticut coast with a long tradition of sheltering people cast off from Boston and its environs. At the big house on Orange Street they had an establishment visited not only by sailors but by Yale students and faculty and city politicians and prominent businessmen. Those were the happiest days of Ishtar's life.

One grand thing that Ishtar Smith remembered about the house in New Haven was the big, black pianoforte. (By mid-century smart young blades would be calling it the "piano" for short, a slang word that offended language purists who pointed out that the instrument could be played fortissimo, too.) Isabel Smith played with gusto, her long fingers raised above the ivory keyboard in pouncing motions. It was her heritage as the daughter of a Welsh Methodist preacher. A preacher's girl should have enough music in her to play the pianoforte in church while her father took up the collection. And when they were all in New Haven, the two girls and all the other whores, and often the students and the politicians and the businessmen and sometimes a professor, too, would stand around while Isabel Smith banged out hymns and led them with an acutely sweet soprano. They sang hymns because hymns were the only songs they all knew. They believed the hymns, and one of the more emotional divinity students was persuaded that he had never felt closer to God than when singing by the pianoforte in Isabel Smith's whorehouse.

Ah, they were good times! But they did not last. And in their swift going and loss, she perceived how hollow mere good times can be. Isabel Smith grew suddenly old. She wasted away almost overnight to a lank, thin skeleton. She developed unsightly rashes and had colds all the time. The girls could not get along with her. One of the new houses over on State Street hired a five-piece band and played real drinking songs, and nobody wanted to sing hymns anymore.

Irene ran away. They thought she eloped with one of the students, but they never knew. She vanished into thin air. They never heard from her again.

Things went bad in New Haven. Isabel Smith moved them to Baltimore, looking for sailors in the way that wintering birds will seek the South. There she died. Ishtar could not make it on her own. She began to take in washing, moved by the simple desire not to starve. Baltimore was crowded and impersonal, and the people were unfriendly. On impulse Ishtar went to the town of Frederick to make a new start. And there she found a man to marry her. It was her last chance, and she took it, holding Clifford Baynes like a card in a poker game and waiting for something else to fall to make him good. She had been losing, and she hoped her luck would change.

# 40

They moved slowly and steadily to the northwest and came into the upper reaches of the Little Blue. Thin water whispering through the land and coiling sluggishly around brown sandbars, the water green in the cool shade and blue in the hot open places where it stood in nearly stagnant pools, shining with the reflection of the day. Buzzards flew flapping up, huge black birds ominous against the sky now gone metallic and still with summer. Indian burial amid the cottonwood trees. A corpse tied up there on a wooden platform. For a quarter-mile around the air was thick with the festering stench of rotting flesh.

"Not dead long," the old man murmured. They all thought of Rachael. And they went on in silence.

They flushed an occasional rattlesnake now. Adam shot at one with his rifle.

"Might as well not waste your powder and your lead," the old man said in a level tone, spitting. "Kill snakes all day long out here, and you still got snakes."

They went on.

Boredom. Sunshine lay down on them like a flail. Their faces burned and peeled and burned again. The men bound cloth bands around their foreheads and looked like gypsies. The old man wore his beaver hat with its narrow brim tipped low on his face, and he bound his head with cloth like the rest, but he could not protect his bulbous nose. It stuck defiantly out into the sunshine, swollen and red.

The air was sharp. A tree five miles away by a creek was like something drawn with bright, black ink and very near. The air so uncommonly clear now that it was deceitful. And all of it, the amazing distances, the utter transparency of the atmosphere, the snakes, the dust, the unending trail, the parching thirst—no water for miles at a time since leaving the Little Blue—seemed to build a visible nightmare, a sign of something more terrible lurking just beyond their sight, ominous and dreadful. And all of them felt it.

Only night gave relief, and then the darkness seemed to transport them to another realm, just as strange and just as oppressive as the long and blistering days. The clouds, inwardly afire, burned red when the sun had gone, and slowly they turned to ashes and became blue and then gray as the night wrapped itself around them. And sometimes Adam saw the dark as a devouring thing that might gobble up the earth and at dawn leave them hanging in space while God laughed. He would shake his head to compel such fantasies to depart. He understood then just how slight was the hold of any man on sanity, how distance and space and ceaseless wind and smashing sunlight could make the world seem an illusion.

Rachael's death tormented him. Asa tramped on with a set and determinded anger, speaking to no one. Ruth looked at Adam now and then in silent grief and turned away. And even Henry, helping to brush the oxen down at night, had nothing to say.

Jason was tormented too. He sat by the fire at night, a fire fitfully burning, as he posed the eternal questions, "Why are we going? Why?" And when no one answered him, he said firmly, but with a lack of real conviction, "We are going because we could not stay."

Sometimes Adam found Jessica looking at him. Something illusive and dark in her expression, interrogating him. She was a woman who had learned to search for the intentions of others and to conceal her own. He felt that there was something sympathetic in her expression, and yet he did not know. In the daylight they rarely spoke and shared nothing but those occasional mute glances that Adam found both consoling and mysterious.

Two nights after they left the Little Blue, up on the rising hump of the continent pitching toward the valley of the Platte, Adam stood the first watch with Samuel. They patrolled the camp, and the hound joyfully romped with them, sniffing the air from time to time, pleased with the world. Adam was pleased to have the dog. He would bark at approaching Indians.

The moon was in the last quarter and lay low against the horizon, about to set. The two men had little to say to each other. Rachael's death was in their way. Nothing else seemed worth talking about, and they could not talk about that.

Their measured tread in the swishing grass, the steady, dry stirring of the wind rising and falling were the only sounds, made acute by the silence.

Suddenly Jessica appeared, wrapped in a long, linen duster, a dim and shrouded figure coming up to stand by the desultory leaping and falling of the low-burning fire. Adam saw her first. They were maybe a hundred yards away from her, making a circle around the camp. Samuel said, "It's Jessica. She don't sleep good at nights sometimes."

Adam's heart quickened. He detached himself from Samuel and went to her. "Are you all right, Mrs. Jennings?"

He could not see her expression clearly in the shadows. She stood still and composed, her hands folded gracefully before her, a dark form in the night. She did not answer him for a time but stood gazing into the fire. her face red with the reflected glow and in the shadows thrown over her features looking more beautiful than Adam had thought possible. He repeated the question. "Are you all right?"

"Yes," she said as if she had just heard him. "Yes, I couldn't sleep. My husband grinds his teeth when he sleeps. Something goes on in his dreams now. I can't tell what it is. He keeps me awake."

Adam started to speak but could not. He felt very uncomfortable, guilty, and tense.

"I'm thirsty!" she said suddenly.

"I can make up some coffee right fast."

"Oh, I don't want coffee. I want water for a change. I'm so sick and tired of coffee!"

She went to the water barrel fastened to the front of Jason's wagon, a gloomy hulk in the dim moonlight. She turned the crude wooden tap at the bottom and put her mouth down to it and drank like a man. Adam could scarcely see her. He heard the gentle splatter of water on the ground. It stopped.

"You shouldn't do that, ma'am," he murmured when she came back to the fire.

She sighed impatiently. "I shouldn't drink the water because it will make me sick! I'm about to die for the taste of water, and Mr. McMoultrie says it will kill me to drink. Well, listen, Mr. Cloud, When we get to the mountains I'm going to gorge myself on spring water. I trust that Mr. McMoultrie will give us his consent to drink spring water."

"Yes, ma'am. But if you get sick afore then, you might not make it to the mountains."

"I'm already sick of everybody trying to tell me what I ought to be doing!"

"Yes, ma'am."

They were silent. Jessica burned with something. Adam could not tell what. He felt more and more tense.

It burst out finally. She turned on him. "My husband has been kind enough to tell me this evening what your friend Mrs. Baynes has been saying about me."

"She ain't my friend, ma'am." Adam was alarmed, almost angry with Jessica that she should accuse him of such a thing.

"She came to us because of you, didn't she? She was following you, wasn't she?" He started to protest, but she waved his words away and became more conciliatory. "Oh, I'm sorry. Forgive me, Mr. Cloud. I don't have you to blame. I should blame my husband." She shook her head and folded her arms and looked flustered, and when she spoke, the words stumbled out as if she could not herself believe what she was saying.

"Do you know what he is saying now, Mr. Cloud? He has decided that she is some kind of test. Everything is now a test. Rachael's death. Mrs. Baynes. Your friend Dr. Creekmore has convinced my husband that we are the beginning of a new dispensation."

"Harry just tries to make Mr. Jennings feel good," Adam said uncomfortably. "Harry likes to make folks feel good."

"Oh, yes, yes. I understand. My husband has dreams, and Dr. Creekmore has words. Dr. Creekmore explains my husband's dreams to him." She laughed without humor. "I know Dr. Creekmore thinks it's harmless. Telling Jason people are going to be reading about us in history books! Talking about Arcadia as if it was a new Eden! It sounds so grand, Mr. Cloud. But my husband takes it all so seriously. And now he sees that ... that *awful woman* as a kind of test, something we all must use to prove ourselves before we can be worthy of my husband's plans for us! It's *insane!* You know, Mr. Cloud, this started out to be a ... a *change* to escape slavery, to get a better life for ourselves. My husband says a war's coming, and he says he doesn't believe in violence. He says the war won't come to California. I agree with him on that, I suppose. But now it's all turned out to be a scheme for the salvation of the world! I never agreed to that!"

308

"He didn't tell you what he had in mind, ma'am?"

"*Tell* me! Mr. Cloud, he didn't even tell me he was planning to go West. I found out months after we got married last year that he'd had this idea in the back of his mind. When his mother died, he told me he'd been thinking about it all along. But he didn't say anything about it until then. I can understand why he didn't tell her. She was a terrible bully. I shouldn't say that. But there's no other way to describe her. Talking religion all the time. Predestination. The eternal decrees. Oh, she was painful!

"But when I think of him, just holding the idea in his mind, not sharing it with me, not saying anything about it to *anybody* ... Well, it makes me wonder if I ever did know him. If I ever *can* know him!" She laughed more bitterly. "He told me very politely that I had promised to obey him. And it's true, you know. That's what a woman promises. To obey her husband!"

"Yes, ma'am."

"And now ... Now he's been so upset by Rachael's death. Deranged. Maybe that's too strong. Deeply hurt. He's fallen under the spell of that awful woman. 'If we can't make it work with people like her, then we can't make it work at all,' he says. *His* very words. We could ... Oh, just imagine if he said we had to have *smallpox*. Some awful disease. To see ... To prove we could survive it. To prove that we have the right to live! Can you imagine sleeping in the same bed as somebody with smallpox, Mr. Cloud? Just to test your right to live!"

"Smallpox scares me to death," Adam said.

She laughed, not bitterly this time. "Walk with me, Mr. Cloud. I'm too nervous to sleep. Where's Samuel?"

"He's out there somewheres. I was standing with him when we seen you."

"It's so dark tonight. Everything is a shadow. It's so beautiful in the night, under the stars. We ought to travel in the night. Why don't we do that? Avoid the sun! The sun is so hot in the day."

"Ah, we'd fall in a hole or step on a snake, ma'am. Or maybe the Indians would slip up on us, and we couldn't see to help ourselves. Joe says the snakes is fierce out here at night. They come out to escape the sun, too."

She sighed in frustration and defeat. "I guess it can't be easy. Have you ever thought that nothing is the way it seems,

Adam? May I call you Adam? We don't have anybody out here to call us down for being intimate now, do we?" She laughed again, confidently this time.

Adam grew hot, and his heart pounded. They walked slowly together. not quite touching. She was silent for a time. Then she resumed. "To think ... on a night ... a beautiful night like this ... we could walk along and step on a snake. And die. It looks so beautiful. So calm. Look at the moon! It's like a cup of honey. I don't feel any danger. I just feel peaceful. But we can step on a snake and die."

Adam tramped hard in the grass in his boots. "They try to get out of your way," he said hopefully. "The snakes, if you stomp on the ground, they try to leave you alone."

"We're just not important," Jessica said wistfully. "No one of us. Life's important. But life can be pretty impersonal, can't it? It doesn't matter to nature if a snake lives and a man dies, does it, Adam?"

"I don't know, ma'am. I reckon not."

"The river. I thought it looked so beautiful that day. With all the trees. The rain. I thought the rain was beautiful, too. A relief for our sunburn. And Rachael died. Oh, Adam! It's the most horrible thing I ever saw in my life. Poor Ruth! She's almost insane with grief! I feel so sorry for her! She can't talk to Asa. She can't really talk to anybody."

"It was my fault," Adam said. His voice broke. He choked back a sob, feeling unmanly and terrible. Everything so near and vivid. He could be about to cross the river again, change his mind, and Rachael would still be with them. A terrifying strangeness to the simple fact that she had died so suddenly, so young, when they had known her so well.

Jessica laid a gentle hand on his arm. "Don't blame yourself, Adam. Blame is fruitless. Things happen, and they're done. Just like that. No reason to things, so we can't explain why they happen. We can't do anything to undo what's done. I know something about that!" She took her hand away. Adam felt his arm burn where she had touched him.

"I'll never forget it," he said thickly. "I dream about it at night. Being in the river with her again. Feeling the mule..."

"Hush!" Jessica said sharply. "Hush."

"I wish I'd died myself."

They walked in silence again. The moon was on the horizon now. In a few minutes it would be dark except for the

310

stars. Jessica said, "I've never wanted to die. No matter what I've done, what's happened to me, I never once wanted to die."

Adam heard their footsteps in the grass. He listened for the buzz of a rattlesnake. He wondered where Samuel was. Jessica was so close to him that now her shoulder occasionally bumped against his. She felt soft and warm.

"When I think of Ruth, I know I have no right to complain about anything. I see Mrs. Baynes, and I know it's a waste of time to be angry with her. It lowers us. I've never known anybody like her. And I wish I'd never known her! I could have got on in life without knowing people like her lived. You know why I gave them my things back there? I'm sure Mr. McMoultrie knows. Perhaps you do not, Adam."

"I reckon I do."

"I wanted them to die. I wanted the Indians to get them. It's a terrible thing to find a murderous desire like that in your heart. I had never in my life wanted somebody to die!"

"They say it's hard to kill a snake or a cat," Adam said.

"A snake and a cat! That's just what they are, Adam." Jessica laughed again. The mirthless, explosive little laugh of thwarted people driven to the bare wall to find it twelve feet high and slick as glass. "You know, I hate her for making me hate her. It really is funny!"

"She's a fright, ma'am."

"And when we were standing there, burying little Rachael, I was wondering why God had let Rachael die and that woman live! I wanted to shout, 'O Thou, up there! Thou hast erred! O Lord, Thou hast taken the wrong one.'"

"It ain't for us to say things like that," Adam said uneasily.

"I don't know why not. If God strikes us with disease or with loneliness, if He kills us, why can't we talk back to Him? Do we just have to grovel down here and accept it? I don't see the point. And now that woman has inserted herself into our loss. And she's turning my own husband against me! I am responsible for Rachael's death, because I made us come to that river one day later than we would have come if I had not insisted on giving her my possessions!"

Adam felt miserable. "It's my fault. Nobody knows how much. I reckon the best thing I could do is leave you folks. I ain't brought you nothing but trouble. It's my fault Mrs. Baynes came. And I killed Rachael. I murdered ..." His voice broke, and he could not go on.

"Adam, Adam!" Jessica stopped and spoke to him softly. She stood facing him with both her hands on his arms. He smelled her woman smell, smelled her hair, her breath.

"I was mad," he said with an almost superhuman effort, unable to look at her face in the substantial shadow so painfully near to him. "Mad at everbody! I can't tell you why. It's too awful. I was mad at Joe. At Asa. That's the awful thing. I wanted to prove to him that I could make his little girl stop crying when he couldn't. It was just . . . I don't know what it was. Just spite."

She stroked his arms. "You're not that kind, Adam," she said very softly. "You are not a spiteful man. Our motives are always so mixed up. Good and bad. Somebody told me once that the good and bad in us are as inseparable as fire and smoke. I like to think the good is stronger in most of us. I think it is very strong in you."

He was swept up in her closeness. Her voice was so soft and so near that his skin tingled with her sound. And suddenly he knew that she wanted him, an electric communication jumping between them like the feel of a storm in the air before the first rumble of thunder. He wanted her. He flung down the rifle in the grass and seized her in his arms, and clumsily searching for her mouth with his own, he tried to kiss her.

But she resisted him with all her might. Holding her was like trying to cling to a bear. Her voice, so alluring only an instant before, became as hard and sharp as flint. "Let me go! Let me go! I don't want you to kiss me! I don't want you to kiss me!"

Adam released her, shocked and shamed to his bones. She flung herself backwards away from him, sobbing and breathless with rage. "You animal! You *animal!* I thought *you* were different. You animal! You're just like all the rest of them! Get away from me! Get away! Don't you dare ever touch me again!"

Adam was so stunned that he began to cry like a hurt and startled child. "Oh, please, Miss Jessica, I'm sorry! I'm sorry! Please forgive me! Please, please!"

She spat hate and fury at him. "A man like you thinks if he just puts his arms out, a woman has to jump in like a dog through a hoop in the circus. That's it, isn't it, *Mister* Cloud! You think I'm a slut, a tramp, a piece of trash, a *whore!*"

"Oh, no! No, no, no!"

"You don't care anything about my husband, my reputation, my daughter, my future! Well, let me tell you, Mister Cloud, you keep your filthy hands off me. Don't you dare ever touch me again!"

With that bitter and spiteful imperative, she whirled and almost ran back to her wagon, a blur of motion skimming across the dark grass, the wind going on in soft moaning when the tight hiss of her voice had gone. Adam was left more shattered and humiliated and more guilty than he had ever been in his life.

*I feel worse about Jessica than I feel about killing the Indians. I feel worse about Jessica than I feel about Rachael's death!*

# 41

High along the watershed of the Little Blue, they encountered the Pawnee.

Maybe twenty-five of them marching in indolent resolution across the wide and sunny land. Men mounted on tired, thin ponies, the legs of the men almost touching the ground on each side. Women and children trudging along with stolid faces and downcast heads. Some ponies dragging the inevitable travois of the plains Indians—two long poles, one end of each tied to a leather girth around the pony's belly, the other dragging in the grass behind, baggage tied in the middle. Sometimes a very small child perched precariously on the baggage. Men and women alike naked above the waist. All the children completely naked, children who never laughed and never played. Bones sharp under their copper skins. All of them dark and dusty and weary.

Ruth looked at the approaching Indians and shook her head. Ruth weary and desolate. Still able to have pity because she was Ruth. "Poor things. Poor pitiful things!"

Shawnee Joe spat and checked the charge in his rifles. "Don't waste your time feeling sorry for the Pawnee, ma'am.

313

If you feel sorry for a Pawnee, he's got that much more chance to kill you."

"They're human beings," Ruth said.

"I never said they wasn't, ma'am. If they was wolves, I wouldn't be afraid of 'em."

Jason looked distractedly up at the old man and flashed an unnatural forced smile. "We will receive them as human beings. I am in charge here. When I have let other people take charge, we have come to grief." He looked at Adam. Nothing special in the look.

*Did she tell him what I done? Why don't I pull out now? Leave all of them? Go in the night, by myself?* He looked at the Indians and answered his own question. He was afraid. Terrified of being out here alone now. Space and Indians! He glanced at Jessica. She was watching the Indians come on and seemed to have forgotten that he had ever lived.

"What you don't figure, Mr. Jennings," the old man said calmly, summoning an aloof explanatory courtesy proper for talk with fools, "is that these Indians own this here land, and we're going to take it away from 'em. They ain't room for both us and them, Jason. Not room for Arcadia and Indians. Not room for just plain, simple farming folks and Indians. And the Indians, here lately they're beginning to understand that we ain't going to quit coming. We ain't going to disappear. They're getting right upset about it."

Jason baffled, looked blankly up at the old man on mule-back, terrible in the sun. The old man turned to Adam. "Your guns ready, Adam?"

Adam was holding one rifle balanced across his saddle. He took out a cap and primed the gun so that it was ready to fire. He reached over to the pack mule and took the other rifle out and primed it, too. He handed it over to Harry, who was on foot, hands on hips, squinting at the Indians through his glasses as if they were a collection of the most bizarre objects he had ever seen in his life. When Adam leaned down and handed him the rifle, Harry looked up amazed.

"What in the name of the holy God do you expect me to do with this?"

"Just hold it!" the old man said patiently. "And try to act like you're mean enough to put a bullet through the belly of the first one of them redskins that looks ornery."

Harry laughed jovially. "With these eyes? You think I can

shoot an Indian with these eyes? My God! I'd probably shoot my foot off!"

The old man snorted. Something contagious in this tense moment about Harry's self-mockery. The laughter released tension. Adam's heart lifted to Harry. *Harry is good!* An irrepressible thought, senseless here. No time to ponder it. The old man saying with that perfectly measured calm, "Well, you look at 'em hard as you can and put a goddamned hex on the red bastards and wave that gun around like you're mean as hell."

Jason: "Put up the guns! We've seen enough death. I hate guns."

"I reckon I'll hold on to mine, thank ye," the old man said, polite as a man at a dance. He looked at Adam. Eyes like bullets, words soft as cream. "Kill the first red son of a bitch that makes a bad move."

The Indians came on. The braves, sizing things up, stopped, talking with each other, low voices lost in the wind. Much nodding among themselves and looking darkly toward the whites. Oxen halted now. Still and sweaty and unconscious of danger in the broiling prairie sunshine. Chewing their cuds, thick necks bent.

Then the Indians whipped their ponies into a dusty trot and came riding down on them. Indian ponies spread out on the prairie in a rough crescent with the horns of the crescent forward.

Adam: *They're trying to look grand! They can't.* Vague disappointment, ridiculous when the danger was here. Like this. The Indians had quick, black, expressionless eyes. Eyes darted about, counting men and guns, lingering on the women. Adam hefted his rifle. An unmistakable respect ran through the Indians at the sight of the guns. *Cowards!* Adam remembered the Indian who had been afraid of him. The Indian he had killed. *A man has the right to be afraid of death! I deserve to die. I don't want to die.*

Jason went forward on foot. He wore his large, stiff, ceremonial smile. A man who had seen paintings of William Penn and the Indians under the council tree. Jason posing for the artists who would paint him. *Jason Jennings Meets the Indians and Makes Them His Friends.*

Adam: *Jason's insane.* The thought sudden and sharp.

Jason lifted his right hand. The Indians stopped. Faces set in wooden curiosity. The chief of the band—an old, spare, crooked man with high cheekbones, skin the color of worn horsehide, rapacious eyes, wearing a single black and white feather in the greasy knot of hair at the base of his skull—advanced and raised his own hand. He made a guttural sound. Greeting Jason. Not friendly.

Jason: "Welcome my friends!" His voice boomed. Reduced by space and wind. His smile yawned like a cave stacked with ivory. "Get down. Be welcome." He made gracious, sweeping motions. Urging them to dismount.

Indian eyes picked at Adam and the old man. Eyes hung on Harry. He was as odd to them as they were to him. His glasses made him look like a tremendous owl.

"Look at them, Adam!" Harry said in wonder. "Our poor folks in Georgia got better guns than they do." The Indians had a few old flintlocks. Some bows and arrows. Arrows tipped with sharp yellow stone in the old style. Before white men brought steel.

The old man: "Must be poor bastards. Can't even trade." He spat in the direction of the old chief.

"Whiskey!" the chief said.

Jason's smile died. He frowned. "We do not have whiskey." He was surprised by how clearly that one English word rolled out.

"Whiskey!" The old chief pointed at Shawnee Joe's pack mule. The top of an easily recognizable crockery jug shone out of the fold of a buffalo robe.

The old man moved his riding mule over to his pack mule. As he went, he almost casually swung his long rifle, so that it pointed down at the chief's naked belly. "It's my whiskey," he said slowly, making sign with one hand to translate as he spoke. "And you ain't getting none of it!" He repeated the gesture of refusal and hooked his chin up with a thumb to add insult to what he had said.

The chief stared at the old man. Shawnee Joe glared back. It was a standoff. The chief turned to the others with him and spoke in that harsh and alien voice, the incomprehensible syllables tumbling angrily out to spill like a pile of stones in the grass. The Indian men had edged in closer, inspecting everything cautiously, carefully, like dogs sniffing gingerly at other dogs.

"They want our mules and our whiskey," the old man said. "And our women, too."

316

"I didn't know you carried whiskey," Jason said, sounding injured and betrayed.

"I always have whiskey, Jason."

"Look what's it done for us!"

"It ain't done nothing yet."

Adam was frightened and ashamed of himself for his fright. *I deserve to die!* He tried to make himself mean the thought. But he wanted to live. *Kill three or four of the sons of bitches first. Kill the squaws. Maybe make them think twice. No, these red bastards wouldn't give a damn! Drink whiskey on the dead squaws. Like tables.*

Adam felt in the power of the Indians, and he hated them. *Harry ain't as scared as I am!* Harry was looking at the Indians as if they were strange furry animals made to delight him.

The women and children were drawing up now. The Indian women plodded heavily in bare feet beside the ponies that dragged the travois. Little children lethargic, dull, obscurely frightened. Adam looked at them and felt pity. *My God! They're worse off than pickaninnies!*

The Indians grumbled among themselves. The chief turned back to the whites. He pointed impatiently to the pack mule. "Whiskey!" His voice was loud and urgent.

"He's trying to save his job!" Harry laughed aloud. "That's what the old boy's trying to do."

When Harry said it, they all knew it was true.

Harry was pleased with the world. Henry saw how fearless Harry was and drifted closer to him, standing at his elbow. The boy looked solemnly at the Indians, the sun shining in his thick yellow hair, falling like waves of gold to his shoulders. *He thinks Harry will keep him safe!* Adam was astonished. Harry could charm everybody. *And he didn't even know what trouble we're in!*

"Go to hell!" the old man said to the chief. He made a jerking motion with his hand and spat. The chief threw his head back and opened his black eyes very wide. Insult.

One of the braves had had enough. He kicked his horse and rode insolently over to Jason's wagon. Jessica sat up with Promise on the seat. The young girl, her head all wrapped up in cloth, her face brown and dusty, was stiff with terror. She grinned when she was frightened. Grinned and grinned and grinned. She was grinning now. Her eyes above her stretched mouth were screaming for help.

Jessica stared down at the Indian. She was like flint. He

317

laughed up at her, a sound like a snarl, his face cruel and brazen. He lifted his hands to the seat to climb up.

But in a flash Jessica snatched the whip from its place near her hand. Without hesitating an instant she slapped a coil of it across the Indian's face, aiming ruthlessly at his eyes. There was a hideous crack, infernally loud in the quick, deep silence that fell on them when the Indian moved. The whip tore into his dark flesh. It made a cut to the white bone. The Indian threw hands up and fell back screaming into the dirt, blood spurting. Jason gaped at his wife. "Jessica!" She was standing, her face grim and triumphant, still holding the whip and waiting for the next Indian to come. No one moved.

The Indian was lucky. His life was saved by Harry Creekmore. The moment Harry perceived danger to Promise, he ran toward the women. He forgot all about the rifle he held. He did not know what he would do. But he moved. And he got in the way of the old man who was coolly bringing up his own rifle to kill the Indian. Before Harry had got out of the way, Jessica had laid the brave in the dirt, and the old man was looking up at her with the same unbelief that was in Jason's face.

All the Indians were stunned. Adam spun on the chief, aiming his rifle at the chief's belly. No need. The squaws broke the tension. Burst into a screeching laughter. They pointed at the fallen man and jeered at him. The blood was pouring through his fingers. Bright crimson against his dark skin. The white bone of his skull gleamed once where he dug a finger into the long wound and briefly cleansed the blood away. The squaws thought it was the funniest sight they had ever seen. They must have said obscene things. The braves guffawed. It was the Pawnee way to laugh when one of their number was hopelessly beaten.

The Indian heard the cataract of jeering from his own people. He was humiliated, and he was terrified. Out of this encounter would come a name that would endure for the rest of his life. "Man-Whose-Face-Woman-Cut." Maybe something worse than that. So he did all he knew to do. He shambled to his feet, found his pony, flung himself on the sweaty, saddleless back of the beast, and rode swiftly away. Very quickly he became only a moving speck in the great, windy emptiness of the grasslands.

318

"Poor fellow!" Harry said. "I don't suppose he'll ever be chief now!"

Adam laughed. The old man laughed. And suddenly the whites were looking at each other and laughing almost as hard as the Indians.

No one among the Pawnee band tried to call back the Indian who went away. A defeated Indian had no friends. "They'll never see him again," the old man said. "He'll die like a stray on the plains!" He spat. A prophet pronouncing a curse.

All the whites were more cheerful because of Harry. The old man looked over at Jessica and grinned. "You might as well of kilt him, ma'am. He'll die from what you done. And you done good."

Jessica smiled a terrible smile of satisfaction at the old man. Then she looked after the dwindling speck on the prairies. Her knuckles were white around the handle of the whip, still in her hand.

Adam: *She ain't mad at him because he's an Indian. She's mad at him because he's a man!* Wonder and horror and bewilderment, too.

The old chief turned again to Jason, lifting a hand. Gaunt and imperious. "Hungry! Me big Pawnee chief. You feed!" His way of saving the tatters of reputation left to him when one of his braves had been whipped by a woman. He made stabbing motions with his two hands, pointing to his open mouth.

The old man took a deep and reluctant breath. "I reckon you better give him food, Mr. Jennings. We'll get moving faster that way." He spat again. "Red son of a bitch."

Jason prim and frosty. "I'd already thought of that. You don't have to give me advice." Back to the Indians, smiling his mirthless and glaring smile. He gestured with his hands. "Sit down! All of you. We'll give you food!" His face looked foolishly rapt. Adam remembered the bishop. White men proving something to themselves by cultivating Indians. Trying to make pets out of rattlesnakes when sensible men said it couldn't be done.

The chief made a victorious sign to his braves. A murmur of enthusiasm. They jumped excitedly down from their ponies. They squatted eagerly in a circle, the women and children hovering nearby, stirred out of their great apathy by the prospect of food.

319

The driving envy of the Indians startled Jason. He smiled around at them without conviction. "Your women. Your children! Bring them here. Let them sit down and eat with you. You are all my guests." He made those expansive welcoming gestures again and turned to the women and children, smiling his marble smile. The women and the children stirred uncertainly. About to move. But all at once the scarred old chief understood that women and children were being invited to join men! He jumped up in a blast of fury. He shouldered Jason out of the way and screamed something at the women and children. The children shrank against the women trembling. The women dumbly gave way. They retreated to the safety of distance, hovering in a starved and hopeless expectancy.

Jason fought to keep from falling. He held onto his smile. It was forgotten on his face like a white scar. The chief, grumbling aloud in anger and self-pity, came stalking back to the circle and squatted down. He looked hatefully up at Jason. "Hungry! You *feed!*"

Adam's hands sweated on his rifle. He remained in the saddle, itching to kill one of those Indians. The insolent chief. *She would have to respect me then!* Jessica.

Jason was unnerved. Still grinning like a china doll, he turned around to Jessica. "Mrs. Jennings. Please, my dear, roll down a keg of bacon for our friends here."

Jessica's voice cold and hard. "I can't pick up a keg of bacon by myself, husband. If you cannot order these people away, roll the bacon down yourself."

The old man chuckled. Jason—smiling, smiling, smiling—turned to his brothers. He would not make a scene. "Won't you two help my good wife roll down a keg of salt bacon? For our Indian friends!"

Asa did not move. He stood there like a pole, transfixed by the Indians, his eyes nearly wrenched out of their sockets by terror. But Samuel jumped up into the wagon to obey, smiling like a fool. The keg came down. Samuel, still grinning to please Jason, effortlessly split the barrelhead open with an axe. When the Indians sniffed the fragrance of meat, they flung themselves on the keg like wolves. They crammed raw salt bacon into their mouths with both hands. Within minutes they had devoured the small keg of meat down to the wood. The old chief glowered at Jason. "Hungry! You feed more!"

"I thought we might build a fire. To cook with!" Jason spoke. No heart in his words. The old man laughed. The chief did not understand. Jason looked dumbly around. He gaped up into the jeering face of Shawnee Joe. Looked away as though burned. He spoke to Samuel. Samuel so eager to be helpful. "Hand us down another keg."

It was done. The Indians fell on it as before. They ate this one two-thirds down before they began to fall away from it. The chief, belching, satisfied that he had saved his own skin, turned suddenly to the women and children. He gave a brutal command.

The women and children ate like cowed dogs. They were very quiet. The women took turns digging into the keg and giving meat to the thin little children who crouched silently on their haunches. Sometimes they looked cautiously toward the braves. But the braves slept and paid no attention. The children had big, black eyes.

"What's going to happen to them?" Henry asked, dazed by the sight.

"Same thing that'll happen to us," the old man said. "They'll die." He looked gravely around and spoke softly. "Let's be moving."

Their departure was swiftly accomplished. The oxen pulled forward. The wagons bounced and jostled, making their measured noise of iron tires and steel springs and the low creaking of wood. The Indians were indifferent to their going.

"The Pawnee ain't worth shit," the old man said, his grizzled face venerable and wise like the face of a patriarch explaining the Exodus to children who had never been in Egypt. "They used to be out farther west. But the Sioux chased 'em out. And when they was whipped by the Sioux, the Pawnee just stopped thinking they was worth anything. Now ever Indian on the plains hunts 'em and kills 'em like they was wild pigs. And they kill only them folks they can bully, the Pawnee does! You done real good, ma'am," he said to Jessica. "You showed 'em they couldn't bully us."

"Well, if you ask me, it was a man's job to strike that Indian if anybody had to do it," Ishtar Baynes said. "It's a wonder they didn't kill us all."

"It is that, ma'am," the old man said. "And the wonder is sitting right there on the wagon seat. If Miz Jessica hadn't hit that Indian, he'd of grabbed her or that girl. And if he'd grabbed either one, he might of carried her off, and we'd of had one hell of a time doing anything about it without killing the woman he was carrying. Indians, they're hell on white women! And I don't blame 'em myself. I've lived with a squaw or two." He looked directly at Ishtar Baynes. "And I say a squaw's pretty much like any woman you have to buy. They can do some things for you, but they don't have nothing to say. They just ain't nothing." He grinned. "Know what I mean, Mrs. Baynes?"

Adam thought Mrs. Baynes turned white, but the sun was so bright he could not tell. Jessica laughed. Mrs. Baynes looked around, startled to find herself at bay. "Well, I am not one to criticize. But I will state that I would not have picked a fight with an Indian."

Harry laughed aloud. It was as if his sudden courage with the Indians had made him drunk on something. And he, too, enjoyed blistering Ishtar Baynes. "I really don't think you would have had any problem, Mrs. Baynes."

She glared at him. "And what do you mean by that, *Doctor* Creekmore?"

"Frankly, Mrs. Baynes," Harry said, still laughing. "I cannot imagine a man—even an illiterate Indian—who could *possibly* want to carry you off."

"Hey," the old man said. "That's funny! That's funny!" He doubled over laughing. Jessica laughed, too. Harry looked pleased. Even Promise smiled. She looked tired.

Ishtar Baynes glared at Harry. Her eyes were like ice. "You're right full of yourself, *Doctor* Creekmore! Now me, I remember back in Nashville, Tennessee. You was right glad to hear from me. Maybe we ought to tell these folks all about Nashville, Tennessee."

She tried to sound bold. But Ishtar Baynes was the one who was desperate and frightened now. She had a secret. Sometime, she would use it in a bargain. But there was nothing for her to win now. Nothing! And Harry was slipping out of her grasp.

Incredibly, he only laughed her threat away. "Mrs. Baynes, I will admit that you may have saved my life in Nashville. You allowed me to escape a duel." Harry grinned, almost ecstatic. The wind blew in his hair. "Now the prospect of fighting a duel is funny to me. I can't imagine it without laughing. But there is one thing you did not do for me, Mrs. Baynes. You somehow failed to give me eternal life. Those Indians just then could have killed me. And nothing you did for me in Nashville could have helped. So you just prolonged my life, Mrs. Baynes. I still have to die. And so do you! That's what I just realized, Mrs. Baynes. You have to die, too."

Harry laughed again. He had proven something to himself with the Indians. Adam could not tell what. He was free.

Ishtar Baynes cocked her head back. She looked frightened. "You ain't got no right to talk about me dying!"

"You will die someday, Mrs. Baynes, I promise." Harry looked happily at her.

"I'll outlive you," Mrs. Baynes said. "I promise you that, Doctor Creekmore! I'll outlive you!"

"That doesn't matter, Mrs. Baynes," Harry said softly.

"I want to walk again," Jessica said. "Mr. Cloud, will you give me your hand? Will you help me get down?"

Adam looked up at her startled. He dismounted quickly from his mule. "Yes, ma'am," he said. "Yes, ma'am." He put up his hand to take hers, and she held his and jumped down. For just a moment they were very close. She flashed her cool smile at him.

"Thank you, Adam. Thank you very much," She turned away from him and walked out into the prairie a little way and walked along. Adam thought she looked happy and free, too. Like Harry.


Days of rumination and individual solitude when only Harry and Promise seemed to communicate with each other. All the rest of them seemed locked in a lonely and personal puzzling.

Jason kept his diary, a book of blank pages sewn together in a black leather binding he had bought somewhere back in civilization to fill with the account of their Exodus. He wrote a few lines in it every evening. Nobody asked him about it. A diary seemed personal. He went to the wagon seat when supper was done and opened the book on his knees and wrote with a steel pen he dipped carefully in a large ink bottle unstoppered ceremoniously for the occasion.

Now he wrote more than he had before. His pen flew over the pages. And he spent hours rereading what he had written, poring over the volume sometimes until it was too dark to see, like some ancient holy man of a bookish faith, beseeching the silent text to tell him what God had done.

He decided after a while that he understood Rachael's

death. "There's a harmony to the world," he said with a fierce smile. "Everything in the world has a place. In any piece of music there are bright, high notes you play with one hand and low, dark notes you play with the other to support the melody. Mr. Emerson liked to say, 'There is no object so foul that intense light will not make beautiful.' Rachael's death is beautiful in its own way. I am sure that the time will come when we understand it." Jason looked around and smiled and tried to make them see that everything was all right now that he had understood.

"Ah, he's crazy," the old man muttered, fatigued with everything. "You reckon we're really going to be able to leave him run free when we get to California, Adam? Sometimes I reckon we're going to have to ride up to the first insane asylum we come to in Sacramento and leave him at the door, tied up in a knot so he won't hurt hisself!"

"No," Harry said soberly. "Don't talk that way. He has ideas. Profound ideas. He's a prophet. California's going ... You'll see."

"Prophet, hell!" the old man said. "If he was a prophet he'd lay hands on me and cure my rheumatiz. My hands hurt something awful in the night, standing watch. Can't hardly hold my gun when it gets cold."

"They ain't swole up like they was," Adam said.

"They still hurt like hell," the old man said.

"He isn't that kind of prophet." Harry said. "You two don't understand anything, I swear. You can't figure that things can be different someday. You think the world has to go on like it always has. Listen, Jason can see the future. He ought to be President. He might be President someday. People will be writing books about this. We're in on something great. Like he says."

"Jesus," Adam said wearily. "Harry, I don't mind it too much when you believe your own lies. But when you got to believe the lies of ever crazy man that comes along, it's too much. Too much."

"You'll see. You wait."

"Have to," the old man said with a dry laugh. "We ain't halfway across the plains yet." He laughed again and looked very wise and superior.

Ruth cried when Jason said what he did about Rachael. She would not listen to him anymore. When Jason started to

324

talk like that, she got quietly up and wandered off into the dark. So they went on for a long time.

Asa sat listening to his brother, and his face was like stone.

# 42

They came up onto that great heave of earth that led them into the valley of the Platte. The air was dry and clear, and they could see for miles in the roseate dawnings when they hitched the oxen and broke camp and got under way.

Adam was least troubled when he was most busy. He thrilled when the new day came and there was work to do, and he flung himself into the work and toiled with the strength of ten. Then he was purged of shame and worry, and he did not think of Jessica so much nor of all the other things built up in him like a teetering wall.

So the mornings were good. But the noontide seethed in the heat, and thick waves of syrupy light rolled off the ground, and the inconstant vision and their steady thirst distorted their perceptions so that when the sun was high they moved in a dream world, more terrible and lonely and uncertain because they were so completely alone on the prairies.

Even the old man seemed perturbed. "I come along here last year in the right season. May. When they was folks that knowed what time a wagon was supposed to start out for California. Not like this crowd. Good thing you got me along. You'd die without me. An old man's good for something. I reckon I'm showing you that."

"It ain't our fault we're so late," Ishtar Baynes said. "It's Adam's fault. He wouldn't pay the fare on the steamboat."

"If you'd started out when you was supposed to, you wouldn't never of runned into Adam. You wouldn't never of runned into me. You'd of been most to California by now. And maybe Adam and me, we would of met you on the road somewheres and passed you by, and that would of been the end of that, by God!"

*If we hadn't met them, I never would of met him,* Adam thought. *And if I'd left one day before, I'd never of been mixed up with Harry. What then?* What might have been, how close things came to being different, troubled him, a mystery close and unfathomable, shadows looming in the dark.

"Mamma didn't die till April," Asa said. His eyes were like rocks. "We couldn't of left mamma behind till she was dead."

"We could not have moved her in her condition," Jason said.

"She died of an apoplexy," Jessica explained softly. "She lay in her bed for weeks without saying a word."

"She always liked Jason the best," Asa said. "He couldn't run off and leave her. Not her favorite. I could have left her. I surely could."

"That's not true, Asa. Mother loved you, too," Jason said. "And I know you, brother. You could not have left her to die alone."

"Ha!" Asa said. "You think you're so smart. You think you know everthing just because you went to Yale. You don't know nothing about me, brother. Nothing!"

"Jason deserved to be liked best," Samuel said. "He's got an education. He's smarter than we are, Asa. Leave him alone."

"They wasn't no break in the wagons when I was along here last year," the old man said. "Ah, that was something. Wagons as far as you could look. You could of walked on the wagon tops all the way to California. It looked like that. I wondered if they was anybody left back in the States. But they had a hard time, them folks."

"I don't see how you can say that, Mr. McMoultrie!" Ishtar Baynes said. "We lost that sweet little darling angel Rachael, and you talk about folks that's had a harder time than us. You ought to be ashamed."

"They had a hard time last year, Miz Baynes. Lots of Rachaels died. We're rolling on the graves from here to California. I reckon we roll over somebody's grave ever livelong day. Lots of folks died of the cholera morbus."

Clifford Baynes cleared his scrawny little throat and spoke with great wisdom. "I personally don't believe there's such a thing as cholera."

The old man gave him a grizzled look of inquiry. "Well, it sure fooled a lot of folks that died with it last year, Clifford."

Clifford Baynes was disdainful. "I have never seen anybody die of cholera. And I must say that intelligent people back in Maryland think the entire cholera epidemic was something cooked up by the President to take the mind of the nation off the colored question."

"Slavery," Jason said. "The curse. The mark of the beast in the forehead of the nation."

Their talk a circle, turned endlessly back on itself. Broken sometimes when Jason made sense out of Rachael's death. "God loves those who die young. So Rachael was the most beloved of us all. Death loves a shining mark."

They had no company except an occasional rider who passed them swiftly by, going to or coming from Fort Kearny. The world strange because of its midsummer emptiness, its dazzling light, and the wind which never ceased even when the sun showered down on the still and helpless earth. The old man's eyes searched ahead of them as though there were something final ready to appear out there, something blessed and far more important that the River Platte toward which they made their slow progress through the black and stinging dust. Present and past melted together in that tremendous space and seemed odd and unreal to all of them, as if they were souls floating like gas in the limitless air and nothing had ever really happened. Ahead and behind on every side the great land reached to a yawning and treeless infinity, and the undefined space was more real than anything else, and seeing space on fire with the incandescent light lifted you beyond life and death, beyond sadness or any feeling at all, as though you had been emptied of substance and hung to vanish on the edge of a cloud. To Adam, life had become a speck in a soundless universe. He considered how petty Rachael's death was to the world out here. Here the unending journey made every incident of no account, and death became nothing more than something that happened, robbed of all mystery, as naked as a dried and bleached bone found lying in the waving grass.

He remembered the world where things hung together in a pattern. He and his father had sat in silent communion out on the porch of their cabin every summer evening, listening to the infinite choir of loud insects singing their immemorial song in the woods. And one morning they would waken to hard frost glistening white on the world, and they would find ice riming the buckets and shining in the puddles in the yard

327

and glimmering like tiny snow on every blade of grass and every twig of the forest.

The frost would quickly melt with the vermilion dawn. But that night the forest would be still, for that shifting accident of cold had put a murderous finger into the woods and silenced every singing insect, and the dense forest already tinted here and there with autumn color, was already filled with death. But people had been different in that world. The frost did not kill them by the million. Death was attended with ceremony, with watching and eating and even with laughter of a formal sort, with poor Mrs. Hattie Arbuckle coming to where men sat, to offer them her coffee and her warm, plump, and eager body. Death was something special.

But here Rachael's death in the hot tedium of the plains seemed as trifling as the death of an insect. And the glib confidence of Jason, his moralizing, only made it more certain to Adam that there was no reason at all for it except the lethal pride in his heart that made him want to prove something obscure to Asa. So her death was robbed of any mystery, and her burial in that unmarked grave was no ceremony at all, and Adam discovered that death for human beings was ridiculously commonplace, and that discovery made death more dreadful to him that it had ever been before.

*If she'd just been struck by lightning!*

Adam saw Promise and Harry walking along together, arm in arm, laughing, always laughing, the girl loving Harry with her wondrous eyes and Harry loving her in return, telling her stories. Rachael's death was for them only a momentary distraction from their happiness. They stood apart from everything.

"I'll never forget this, Adam," Harry said sometimes at night, lying with his arms under his head and staring up into the darkness of the tent. "I've never been so happy."

The plains were their playground, a vast stage where the thrilling drama of their love was being played. Adam watched them and felt an envy that was like a worm gnawing far down in soft pine.

# 43

Two mornings after they had left the Pawnee, they were startled by a band of Kansa Indians riding in on them from behind, from the south. The Kansa rode fine ponies and looked intelligent and very proud. Different from the Pawnee. They came swooping down on the slow wagons over a rise in the ground with whoops of triumph. For one heart-jarring moment the whites thought they were doomed.

But the Kansa only wanted an audience.

Waving in their hands, flopping like furs tied over their shoulders, hanging from the leather lines on their ponies, were new scalps—scalps complete with the ears hanging like bloody soft knots of rubber under the coarse, black hair flying in the wind, the scalping operation of the Kansa knives being as expertly done as surgery.

The old man murmured, "Looks like that crowd of Pawnee we met run into a little bad luck."

"Are you certain . . ." Jessica started the question and did not finish it. For suddenly the truth of what the old man said was clear to all of them.

The Kansa rode in a whooping circle around them, cavorting on their ponies like gleeful children, brandishing the bloody scalps and singing their inharmonious song of glory. Jessica and the old man stood together a little apart, the old man holding the bridle of his mule in one hand and a rifle in the other, Jessica with her long, blond hair rippling in the wind, flashing in the sunshine, arms folded studiously before her. Both of them calm and immobile.

Adam could not read their minds. But it struck him that neither Jessica nor the old man cringed before danger. It struck him, too, that both of them were cut out of the same stuff. They were both hard and durable and tough. The rest of them—Adam included—were not so strong.

"Them's Kansa," the old man murmured as Adam hastened to him like a private soldier suddenly under fire and reporting for orders. "The Kansa ain't got no quarrel with us. Later on they'll have quarrel enough, poor devils! But not right now. They think the whites is something that won't last long. Some strange thing just passing through that don't really have nothing to do with them. But the Kansa is kin to the Sioux, and all the Sioux hates the Pawnee. They got just about the right number of scalps to go with that crowd we met. I'd say they massacred them all. Massacred them right down to the last papoose."

They smoked a pipe with the Kansa. White men and red squatting in a circle, the red men loudly boasting of their great victory in the singsong language of the Kansa that only Shawnee Joe could understand, for one of his squaws had been Sioux. But the white men nodded gravely and decorously, and even Jason did not reproach the Kansa to their faces with the fact that some of the hairy scalps were small and that some of them were clearly from the heads of Pawnee women, and only a few were from the heads of men. They passed the long pipe around and smoked in solemn agreement to eternal peace and exhaled the blue smoke to vanish in the clean air. And the Kansa rode on like the wind westward, crying their wild, exuberant song and swinging the Pawnee scalps—trophies, relics, and charms—to the free and limpid sky.


Afternoon.

The old man rose abruptly in his stirrups and pointed ahead, his bent and wiry shape and outflung hand appearing to float in the blue, cupping grandeur of the immense sky. "There she is! The Platte! The Platte!"

They strained and squinted to penetrate that fantasy world of bright afternoon light where everything could be anything. Then they could all see it, a blue-brown streak lying like a gently curving band of enamel along the floor of its immense valley, seeming in the illusion of treeless space to be magically suspended above its banks. And when they saw the Platte, so solemnly motionless in this great light, they felt that other river against their chests calling its cold attention to mortality.

For a whiie they were almost reverently silent. Then the old man broke the spell by singing out: "Good road along the Platte, by damn! Best damn highway in the wide world!

Met an Englishman that told me that onct. We got clear sailing all the way to the stony mountains now. Just don't drink the water. Platte River water's got boogers swimming in it. Make you sick to die! Don't drink nothing but coffee, I tell you. Coffee's the healthiest drink in the world. Beats water by a mile. Hell, coffee even beats *whiskey!*"

"But coffee ain't nothing but water mixed up with a little ground-up *bean!*" Ishtar Baynes protested. Nobody paid any attention to her.

Henry jumped up and down and shouted. Adam thought he was trying to do what he thought a little boy should do when he was glad to see a river. Henry took the joy as an excuse to seize his father's hand and hold it. Asa looked surprised, dropped the hand and walked away without a word.

The Platte meant something tremendous to them. They did not know exactly what. For the whole of what they felt was more than the mere sum of its parts—river, sky, valley, cloud, space. In that still afternoon, the Platte was the Jordan and the Nile, Tigris and Euphrates, Lethe and Styx, a river coming down from the far hills that looked, on the other side, to the blue Pacific.

They were seized in different ways by the spectacle of the river's distant shining. Ruth saw it and cried, almost without sound. Henry, absent-mindedly rejected by his father, comforted her, squeezing her with his strong, brown arms, weeping because she wept. For Ruth the Platte was a shining mark set in the land that measured their distance from Rachael's grave. Like an anniversary of death, the Platte was a sign that Rachael was dead and left behind, never to be recovered again.

Asa, startled from his own dark reveries, saw his wife weeping, and he looked at Jessica, and he despised Jason's wife in his heart.

"We ought to get a big welcome at Fort Kearny!" the old man said. "It's a nice place, Fort Kearny. Supposed to help emigrants out."

"They haven't seen emigrants like us before," Harry said. Harry was now like Jason, bursting into hope almost casually, sipping at his own easy flow of words like a drunk nipping always at a bottle because he has become accustomed to being pleasantly tipsy. "Of all the people going West, we're the ones who are going to leave a mark!"

Jason took up Harry's thought. Harry poured, and Jason

331

drank. "I would like to leave some record of our passing there. A name historians can come back to."

The old man laughed, humoring Jason because the old man was so happy to be at the Platte. "They got a big book there in the fort. Folks passing by sign their name in the book. You can sign, too, Jason."

The women were eager. Civilization meant stores. People. News. Other women to gossip with. Maybe a Protestant church with a parson. A memorial service for little Rachael. Something more like a real funeral than what she had had. A respite from the brooding tedium of the sunburnt plains.

But when they could pick it out in the distance, they were disappointed. Fort Kearny was dismal beyond words.

Sod houses arranged haphazardly. Some of them not yet finished, windows gaping with roofless chambers. A sod wall stood forlornly around a dreary little garden. No palisade. Not a tree in sight. For a while the Platte bordered the trail leading to the fort. And when they drew near to the river, they thought nature herself had played a trick on them. "I wish I could see just one thing in my life that turned out to be what it seemed to be when I first saw it!" Jessica spoke the thought. Disappointment and bitterness squeezed out of her. The Platte was a dozen rivers, all running crazily through brown, sandy gullies that made up its wide bed, and the magic that distance had given the river was blown away like dust in the air. The Platte was disorderly and dirty.

"Craziest river in the world," the old man said softly. "I knowed you wouldn't like it, ma'am. Just don't drink the water." He acted apologetic and terribly let-down, though he had seen the Platte before and knew what to expect.

They arrived at the fort just past noon on the day after their first sight of the Platte. The ground was dusty here. The dust coated all the animals and all the people too. It caked in their hair and stuck to their sweat and curdled in their joints and scraped like grit in the folds of their soft skin. The dust laid a brown patina on the wagons, and in the fort it blew in little eddies around the squalid buildings. Soldiers lounged around in the shade of walls, drained of all energy. Their wide suspenders were awry. Their blue shirttails hung out of their baggy pants. Their faces were sunburnt and grizzled, and their eyes were dull from looking too long at space. In 1851 the most trifling men in America were in the United States Army, and being stationed at Fort Kearny did not help

332

them become better people. Indians loitered about, too. Dissolute, indolent, blank-faced, scrawny. Indians cluttered any white settlement on the plains like slime around a stone in a stagnant pond.

"Tell me something, Mr. McMoultrie," Ishtar Baynes hollered, her voice full of blame, "ain't they no Indians that look good? Do they all look like beggars' brats?"

The old man, solemn and patient: "What about the Kansa? I thought the Kansa looked pretty good myself."

"Awwwwk! Them bloody varmints! With them scalps? They was savages! Ain't none of the Indians civilized?"

"Wait till you see the Sioux, ma'am. I reckon the Sioux will look good enough to you. But the Sioux, they're savages, too. They make the Kansa look like little children at a picnic."

Jason, shaking his head: "The Indians are a disappointment. I must be man enough to admit that. I wish we did not have to look on their shame. The West would be better without them."

Jessica, surprised and ironic: "I thought you were going to love the Indians, husband? You've changed your mind? After all you've said?"

Jason, his voice oddly flat, toneless: "I am man enough to change my mind when I see that circumstances are not what I thought. When the nation proved to me that it would not live up to its ideals, I pronounced a curse on it and led you to freedom. When I see the Indians are savages, I am wise enough not to try to change the dictates of nature. Nature is harsh sometimes. And we are more cruel if we do not accept the harshness."

Adam thought there was something threatening in Jason's voice. Something not there before or at least not discernible. But he could not follow his pondering. The old man spoke up.

"Too bad we couldn't of put it off a hundred years."

"Put what off?"

"Oh, taking this here land away from them Indians. The Indians would of kilt each other off by then. Tell you what I think! In the end it would of come down to the Commanche and the Sioux. One of them would of been left over for us to fight. And that fight would of been a humdinger, I tell you."

"I did not realize that Indians hated each other so much," Jason said. He stalked off a little way from the rest of them, hooking his hands firmly in his beltless pants and looking toward the fort a half-mile or so away. Jason, peeved and subdued: "They ought to be sending somebody out to see us. Who do they think they are anyway? They're supposed to look after us. Why don't they come and tell us hello?"

"Let's make camp," the old man said. "I reckon we're going to stay here a day."

"I want to see the soldiers," Henry said. "I ain't never seen a soldier."

The old man laughing with good humor: "Don't pay to see soldiers up close, boy. Soldiers, they're like rainbows. Lot of color, but ain't nothing to 'em."

Mosquitoes from the river assaulted them. Buzzing swarms. Jabbing little darts in every exposed patch of tender skin. They all grumbled and slapped at the mosquitoes. Promise cried out with the pain, slapped futilely. Tears in her eyes.

"Why *don't* they stop!"

Even Harry could not cheer her up. Lassitude and defeat in her face. Adam was troubled by it. Whenever things did not go well, Promise lost her good humor. Defeated by adversity. *She must be like her father,* Adam thought. *A mysterious thing, descent. Her mother's body; her father's blood. Was he alive somewhere, not knowing what he had given to a daughter that made her unable to bear the great plains?*

But even Adam had to admit that the mosquitoes were terrible. He wondered how the soldiers slept at night with the mosquitoes buzzing around them, lighting on their naked faces, stinging in their sleep-gaping mouths. He thought of Rachael's mouth, hung open in death.

Jason did not help them. He never did. He was born to command others, he thought. He kept looking toward the fort, expecting a welcome. Annoyed and impatient that it was so long in coming.

But suddenly there was a flurry of motion in the compound. Jason's eyes flickered with relief and then pleasure. "They're sending somebody out to welcome us! It's about time!"

He rushed to his wagon and found Jessica's long white comb. He raked it through his hair and through his ragged beard, all the while muttering to himself and glancing excitedly toward the soldiers who were forming now, coming out to greet them. He tugged at his filthy clothing, smoothing himself in the ridiculous expectation that he could make himself neat and clean. He squared his large shoulders and marched out to meet his welcome.

The small company of soldiers riding to meet them looked slothful and bored. Their commander rode just ahead of them, stiffly erect in the saddle. His tatterdemalion troopers made his rigidity stand out in contrast so that there was something nearly comical about him and about them. So Adam thought.

The officer pulled up. Did not dismount. Swept his sharp little eyes around the Jennings party with extreme distaste. He announced himself in a stentorian squeak. His voice pitched higher by nature than anyone would expect in a man who was an officer in the United States Army. "Captain Henry M. Wharton, Sixth United States Infantry, at your service." He looked at Harry.

Harry was laughing. "It was his voice," he said later on. "I never heard a voice like that in a grown man."

Having announced himself, the captain raised a formal hand to the brim of his forage hat in curt salute and showered them with the arid dignity of the United States Army on the plains.

Jason did not understand. He stepped forward. I am Jason Jennings, and this is Mr. Joseph McMoultrie, and this . . ."

It was hot. The afternoon sun was like a hand pressed down on the earth. The captain cut Jason off with an impatient gesture. "I do not have time to listen to your roll call. What are you doing out here this time of year?"

"We're on our way to California."

"California!" The captain crossed his hands on the horn of his saddle and shook his head, a wise man dealing with an imbecile. "Here it is, middle of July, and you're on your way to California. Lord God, mister. Don't you know you can't get through to California this late? Where in hell have you been anyway?"

"We've . . . we've had trouble," Jason said. "One of us . . . We lost a little girl. Drowned in the Big Blue, and . . ."

Captain Wharton was unmoved. "Nearly everybody loses somebody on the way, mister. If you wasn't ready to lose somebody, you should of stayed back East. The fact is, you're damned late. And you can't get through to California this time of year. It don't matter if you lost ten little girls in

335

the Big Blue. That don't change the snow in the Sierra Nevada."

Jason cleared his throat. "I have heard that it does not usually snow in the Sierra Nevada until late October. That ought to be time enough . . ."

The sweat was running down Captain Wharton's face in greasy streaks. The back of his tunic was soaked through. "Hell, mister, who you been talking to about the Sierra Nevada? You got snow there by October 15 most years. And that's in plenty of time to freeze you people to death."

"Sometimes it doesn't snow until later."

"Yep. And sometimes it snows a hell of a lot earlier. Sometimes the passes are shut up by October 1, mister."

Jason took a deep breath. He looked nervously around, clinging to dignity with his fingernails. "Well," he stammered. "Well, we have faith in God."

The captain leaned over his saddle with a terrible leer. "You have faith in God. Well, I'll be damned."

"I do," Jason said, raising his voice.

"Goddamn!" Captain Wharton said, shaking his head. Somebody among the soldiers sniggered.

Adam sat silently on his mule. He had mounted when he saw the soldiers riding to meet them. Some obscure desire on his part to be on a level with them when they came. Adam could see something amusing in the way Jason was taken completely off guard by this soldier's truculence. But something pathetic, too.

Captain Wharton threw a shoulder back at his men, keeping his tanned and leering face toward Jason. "Soldiers, I want you to take a good look at this man. He has faith that Almighty God up there in heaven is going to change the seasons just for him. Gentlemen, I bet this religious feller here is going to find oranges growing in the Sierra Nevada when he goes through to California come this December! These folks here are going to have to travel at night through the passes in winter because they'd get heat stroke from the sun in the daylight."

Captain Wharton's men were amused, and there was a spatter of indolent mirth, giggling, slapping at them like small hands in the immense and terrible heat. Adam wanted to kill them all. The lust for violence came up in him like boiling rock shooting up from the bowels of the earth and pouring out where there had been only brooks and clean air and green

336

grass before. He put his hand on the walnut butt of his pistol.

Captain Wharton did not even glimpse how close he was to death. "Well, it's none of my concern what you and God decide to do about the Sierra Nevada. But it is my concern to get you off the Fort Kearny Military Reservation. You can't camp here, mister. You got to move on."

Jason babbled. "But . . . but *why?*"

The captain's sweaty grin died away in impatience. His face looked like an old piece of soiled granite found long lying in a field of bones. "Because grass is getting scarce out here this time of year, mister. Because we need provender for the stock. Because I said you got to camp somewheres else."

"But you're supposed to *help* us! That's why you're *here!* We're *Americans!*"

The captain spat. Immemorial gesture of contempt. He did not turn his head. The sticky spittle fell in a rolling mud ball at Jason's feet. "First thing I'm supposed to do is help my own men and preserve my post. And I ain't going to risk my stock and my men for every lunatic that comes along here with gold dust in his eyes. Especially this time of year."

Jason was outraged. His face turned red with emotion. "We are not vulgar gold seekers. We are . . ."

The captain cut him off with a weary and contemptuous gesture. "Look, mister. I don't care what you are. I'm telling you something. You got to go ten miles beyond if you want to camp."

"Ten miles!"

"You got good ears, mister. Maybe not good sense, but you hear good. You heard me just right. Ten miles."

The old man stroked his face, knocking his beaver hat back on his head with a tap from the back of his hand. He was sitting on his mule, and he looked directly into the captain's eyes. "You must be a pretty terrible soldier, Captain."

The captain scowled. "What do you mean by that?"

"Well," the old man drawled, spitting carefully into the ground, "if you was any good, you wouldn't be stuck down at no god-forsaken place like Fort Kearny. They'd have you sitting at a desk somewheres in Washington City. Old as you are, and you ain't no more than a *captain?* Maybe you was a coward in the Mexican War. No wonder you got to bully us, Captain. You ain't got many folks in the world you can look down on. Most folks looks down on you. Like they ought to, by God. I reckon you ain't nothing but poor white trash,

Captain. Trash stuffed in that there uniform like straw in a scarecrow!"

The old man's voice was so sedate and mild that its effect was astonishing. The captain's face went like chalk. For just an instant he was speechless, his wrath swelling inside him like gas in a balloon. He was conspicuously aware of the soldiers who looked on, their day enlivened now by the unexpected crude eloquence of the old trapper, who put a period on his insults by spitting emphatically again at the feet of Captain Wharton's horse in the same way that Captain Wharton had spat at the feet of Jason Jennings.

Finally, taking a deep, saving breath, the captain glared at the old man and said, "I have said all I have to say. We will give you a half-hour to move on." His voice was shrill with fury. But he pulled his horse around and rode back to the fort. His departure looked suspiciously like a retreat under fire. Adam called out, "That's telling the son of a bitch, Joe. God, look! If he runs thataway from you, just think how hard he'd run from the first Indian that belched in his face."

The departing troopers looked at Adam and the old man and laughed. Some murmured, grinning to each other. One of them, smiling with pleasure and respect, even tipped his hand up in a salute and said, "Sir!" to the old man. In that mood of faintly rebellious good spirits, the soldiers rode back to the fort.

So the Jennings party did not linger but went on, turning almost due west now, following the great natural road that passed up the wide valley of the Platte toward the stony mountains. The oxen were burdened and thin. They were making less than ten miles on most days. And it was July 12.

# 44

Jason was more deeply shocked by their vile reception at Fort Kearny than anybody could know. He was tired. His legs in the afternoon were like wood. And he was tired not only of the road but of the politely unbelieving silence he found in his own people when he talked to them about the glorious future in California at night. If it had not been for Harry Creekmore, Jason might have given up. Harry believed in him; Harry Creekmore was a doctor, an educated man. If Harry Creekmore believed, then there must be something to Jason's dream.

What could be wrong with the dream? Jason saw the evil of the world and imagined it transfigured. He could not understand why it had not been transfigured already. But though he was often grieved by the evil, he was more often ebulliently grateful that the world had been left for him to transform. Now he felt that his own people had the mark of Cain in their hearts. Unbelief. Humiliating to him, and their doubt made his own heart heavy.

He was more and more detached now from the petty details of the daily march. Rachael's death had stunned him. Using every spiritual resource he possessed, he managed to make sense out of it. When he dreamed of all that could be done in California, Rachael's death became merely an incident. He hypnotized himself with the regular and unending tramping of his feet in the dust, and his mind, cut loose from the earth, soared to purple fantasy. Jason Jennings running for President, when the whole world saw the good he had done. The first President in the history of the country to be elected without a single dissenting vote. The rich and the poor lifting their imploring hands to him. "Help us! Tell us what to do, and we will do it!"

In the brilliant light of these dreams, it was a cold shock when he looked at Asa, saw how haggard he was, saw him talking in low, dull tones apart with Ishtar Baynes, and remembered the reason why. At those times he put his head down and marched, and the dreams came back with their vivid and consoling power.

But Captain Wharton's vicious temper had scattered the dreams almost as irrevocably as soap bubbles bursting. Jason flung back down on his back in a dirty, dusty, stinging world with cruel men leering at him. *I can fail!*

He turned in quiet frenzy to Harry. Always to Harry. "Well, now, Dr. Creekmore, after that warm greeting by our friend Captain Wharton, do you think as much of our enterprise as you did?" He laughed. A forced and artificial effort

339

to be jovial and nonchalant. But he looked at Harry with ravenous and desperate eyes.

Harry, delighted to bring cheer, nodded vigorously. "Why, to be sure, Mr. Jennings. My faith is not shaken by so much as an inch!"

They walked along in a glow of mutual esteem. The side of one of Harry's fine boots was splitting away from the sole. The dust filtered in. He had had to discard his only pair of stockings. One day he put his foot into one of them and split the bottom out of it, and after that it did not seem worth the trouble to wear them. He hated the feel of gritty dirt between his toes. And he walked along dreaming of hot baths in California, paying only enough attention to Jason to remain agreeable.

"So your faith in our venture is still good?" Jason said, giving him a sidelong look of inquiry that seemed pitifully desperate to Harry.

Harry shook his head. "Mr. Jennings, I am committed to your enterprise. Believe me, if I were not so committed, I would not have urged my friend Adam to remain with you. And we would not stay if we did not both agree with you."

"Ah, yes. Adam. He has taken poor Rachael's death very hard."

"Indeed he has."

"He speaks so seldom now."

"His heart is full."

Jason laughed suddenly. A harsh sound in the open day. "Say, that was pretty good what he said to the old man . . ."

"To Mr. McMoultrie."

"Yes, yes. Mr. McMoultrie. In the presence of Captain Wharton. How the captain would run if an Indian belched at him. Very good." Jason laughed again.

Harry laughed, too. Easily, as Harry did everything in public. "Adam is a kind and generous person."

"I take your judgement about him, Dr. Creekmore. You have opened my eyes about about so many things. I must say that your support for my dream of California is gratifying. And if you believe in your friend Adam, then I believe in him, too."

"His heart was broken by poor little Rachael's death."

"Yes, but it was not his fault. It was something bound to happen just because we reached the river on the day we did. Destiny, Dr. Creekmore."

"You sound like a Calvinist, Mr. Jennings." Harry started to laugh. Thought better of it.

"My mother was a Calvinist. Very devout woman, my mother. And I do believe in destiny, Dr. Creekmore. Don't you?"

"I believe in our destiny," Harry said grandly.

"And so do I," Jason said. "I tell you, Dr. Creekmore, in California everything is going to be all right."

Harry dropped back to be with Promise. Jason walked on, and his own gloom came back. He was an ant marching on the cirle of infinity.

*I do believe in destiny.* Everything was a sign of something else. *Captain Wharton is only a test to be passed. Like Rachael's death.*

The sun was merciless. Its heat was a flame on his back, and when he looked out into space, the dazzling light of the plains consumed his sight.

*I will be silent. I will find refuge in silence. Silence is my refuge and my strength, a very present help in trouble.*

He dreamed of green vales in California. Clear water splashing musically over rocks, and cattle grazing. People coming to see what Jason had done. He lost track of what was happening around him. *Let them do what they want.*

"Reckon we'll camp up here ahead, Mr. Jennings."

"Very fine, Mr. McMoultrie. Whatever you say." The sun was in his face, the world melted to a liquid inconstancy.

"Time for your watch, Mr. Jennings. You and Harry tonight. You sure you don't want a rifle?"

"No, Adam. No, I don't want a gun. Is it three o'clock already? Time passes so quickly when you're asleep, doesn't it?"

"It passes awful slow when you're on watch."

"Yes. Yes it does. Strange how we speak of time passing slowly or time passing quickly. Time's always the same. We are the ones who pass. Doesn't it seem unfair that we get older while we sleep?"

"I wouldn't know, Mr. Jennings."

*I will keep on. I will force myself to be pleasant and normal. I will not allow myself to doubt. I cannot look at Asa and Ruth and doubt. If I doubt, I may blame myself for Rachael's death. We could have stayed in Ohio.*

"How was it you met your wife, Mr. Jennings?"

Ishtar Baynes. Jason flinched. He forced himself to sound

341

easy. "Well I heard about her, Mrs. Baynes. She had a reputation for being a fine, strong woman. And I wanted a woman who was strong. Able to get along in a new country. Well, I heard that Jessica was such a woman, you know. So I went over to, ah, to Portsmouth, and I asked her to marry me."

*My wife holds me in contempt. I can't help it! I can't help it.*

"Buffalo! My God, buffalo! Whoopee! Adam get a rifle. Get both your rifles. Buffalo. Fresh meat!"

The buffalo streamed out over the valley, a black tide rumbling along unhurried under the enormous sun, buffalo for miles and miles. A river of buffalo.

"Well, we'll have fresh meat tonight, husband. Look at them go! Don't they look fine! I wish I could go with them. Sometimes I wish I was a man!"

"I don't like hunting! Why do they have to hunt when they know hunting is against my principles."

Jessica laughing in good nature. Unable to take him seriously: "Oh, husband, don't be like that. They are hunting to give us food."

*Why does she put a hand on my arm? Just to mock me! Look at them go. That old man, waving his hat. Riding like a boy. Stronger than I am. How would Mr. Emerson have shot a buffalo?*

Mr. Emerson, standing up in the lyceum in New Haven, beginning to speak amid a vast and attentive silence.

"The future of the American nation must be its own. Europe has given us much, but it has given us already all that it can. What we must now seek is a new civilization that is ours, a civilization that is in perfect harmony with the grand harmonies of nature, a civilization based on the confidence of man in man, or, I should perhaps say, the confidence of man in mankind. My friends, I speak of the courageous independence of brave American souls willing to dare without waiting for the approval of an old and corrupt world. I speak of Americans, a new race of men, who are willing to do what they must do to be worthy of the destiny that God has ordained for this great continent."

*I want to believe in something!* Young Jason Jennings, squeezed between two friends, all leaning intently forward in their hard wooden chairs, rapt with devotion.

"I want to be a buffalo hunter when I grow up!" Henry

cried, ecstatic and shrill with joy. He looked at Harry. "A buffalo hunter or a doctor. Maybe I'll be both."

"I reckon it's all right for them to go chasing buffalo like that. But personally I don't think it's right to be sporting around with poor little Rachael lying dead back there somewheres."

Jessica, bold and cruel: "Mrs. Baynes, I will make a wager with you."

Ishtar Baynes, eyes rolled up in piety: "I don't bet, Mrs. Jennings. I ain't that type of woman."

"All right, you say you don't bet. Then I will make a prophecy, Mrs. Baynes. When Mr. Cloud and Mr. McMoultrie bring back buffalo meat, you are going to sit by the fire and stuff yourself with it. You are going to eat like a pig."

Jason, as though awakened from a deep trance: "Jessica, please! Remember your manners."

Mrs. Baynes: "It's all right, Mr. Jennings. I'm just a poor helpless woman. The world picks on me. It always has."

Mrs. Baynes and her husband gorged themselves on the meat that night, and she only paused in her eating long enough to complain that buffalo tasted strong.

Slowly the land began humping up, crenellating. At the far fringes of the valley they began to see hills rising, sand hills, minute compared to the tree-laden hills they had all known. These hummocks carved by the wind, the winter snows, into every imaginable shape. Jessica looked at the hills, rapt with pleasure.

"Look, look at the hills, husband. Oh, I wondered if we would ever see hills again."

The hills proved that the plains were not eternal and that they were truly moving, making progress against the immensity of the land, winning the right to be in their struggle with infinity.

"These ain't much for hills, Miz Jessica. Just you wait till we see the stony mountains. Then you'll see some hills."

"I know, Mr. McMoultrie, but these hills are higher than the plains. I can't wait to see your stony mountains. The sooner the better!"

"And California, Jessica? Can you wait to see California?"

"Don't frown so at me, husband. Yes, I wait for California with an eager heart. But I want to see the Rocky Mountains, too. I've always read about the mountains in Switzerland. How the snow stays on top of them. Even with hot summers in the valleys. I've seen pictures of the snow and the little villages at the bottoms of the hills."

"You looked forward to seeing the Platte," Jason said reproachfully. "And then when we got close, you said it was ugly. You said nothing was ever what you expected it to be."

"Maybe I did say that," Jessica said, laughing and tossing her long hair in the bright sunshine. "But I always hope. I can't stop hoping. And I hope for California, Jason."

"I suppose you were disappointed in me, Jessica. Isn't that so? Maybe you should have married somebody else. Maybe somebody else would have taken you to Switzerland instead of California."

Jessica, looking at him as if she had just understood a blunder she had made without thinking: "I didn't mean what I said that way, husband. Why do you want to quarrel with me?"

"I don't want to quarrel. I just see that you think I am a fool. I see you're going with me and laughing at my dreams all the way across the continent."

"Do you really mean that every time I laugh you think I am laughing at you? Husband, please! Don't make life so strict that I'm afraid to laugh for fear of making you angry."

"I'm sorry! Believe me, Jessica, I'm sorry."

He felt like a fool.

*If she would not be so cool and distant, even when she is pleading with me! If just one time she would throw her arms around me and cling to me and tell me that she loved me. All would be well then. She comes so far. But then there is a wall between us. I can't get over it. She just married me because there was no one else to have her. She did not marry me for myself.*

It did not occur to Jason that he had not married Jessica for herself; he married her because he thought she would make him a good wife. And her reputation titillated him wildly. The joy of forbidden fruit.

"I don't know why Miz Jessica talks so much about the pretty scenery, Mr. Jennings. What with Rachael dead and all. It just don't seem decent. I don't mean to be saying nothing against your wife. It's just peculiar to me."

"Oh, Mrs. Baynes, don't apologize. I appreciate your concern. I know you don't mean any harm. Sometimes I don't understand my wife."

"Oh, now, listen here, Jason. It's my daughter that's dead.

344

And you don't see me saying that Jessica ain't got the right to look at pretty things. And you, Mrs. Baynes! It ain't for you to be causing trouble ever time you can stick your knife in!"

"Now, Ruth . . ."

"Have you forgotten your baby already, wife? My God! Have you stopped loving her?"

"Oh, Asa, don't talk to me that way. I ain't forgot my love. God knows! But I ain't forgot my life either. We got to keep on living. We got to keep finding pretty things in the world. I agree with Jessica. I think the hills are beautiful. And if Rachael's dead or alive, it don't change how the hills look."

"I will never see anything pretty again, wife. Never again."

"Now come on there, Asa. Seems to me like Henry here's right pretty. If I had me a boy like this here boy, I'd be damned proud."

"I don't recall that anybody was speaking to you, Mr. McMoultrie."

"Well, hellfire, Asa, that don't make no difference. I'm talking to *you!*"

"I always think of Henry with his sister, Mr. McMoultrie. Now when I see Henry, I see something that's half-gone."

"Well, if that don't beat it all! He sure as hell looks like a whole boy to me, Asa. Don't it seem that way to you, Adam? Hellfire, I reckon my eyes ain't no better than Dr. Creekmore's there."

"Your eyes couldn't be as bad as mine, Joe. I have to store something up in my head before I can see it. I look at it hard all day long. Then at midnight I see it!" Harry laughed at himself. The old man laughed, too. Harry always cheerful now, giving them the energy of his laughter.

"I never knowed folks to sit around laughing about a blind man before. It ain't decent."

"There's nothing to do but laugh, Mrs. Baynes. I'm not blind. Not yet. But I will be in time, I reckon. Nothing to do about it but laugh."

"You sure have changed a lot since Nashville, Tennessee, Dr. Creekmore."

"We've come a long way from Nashville, Tennessee, Mrs. Baynes."

"Here comes Miz Jessica, Mr. Jennings. I sure don't want to be talking about her when she walks up. I sure don't want to cause no trouble between you and your wife. Your wife's your own business, Mr. Jennings."

345

"Hey there, Miz Jessica! Glad you come over. This old turkey buzzard here has been laying you out for liking the hills. And Jason here, he ain't got the backbone to stand up for you."

Jason white and breathless. "Mr. McMoultrie. Do you have to cause trouble?"

"I ain't causing trouble, Jason. I'm just saying they's trouble afoot. And you ain't man enough to do nothing about it. Folks like you remind me of poison in sugar. Somebody better give the word about you before there's trouble."

Jason's face was like uncooked dough. "I beg your pardon!"

"Oh, hell. I pardon you, Jason. You can't help what you are. I pardon you, and I feel sorry as hell for you."

"Why don't you leave us? I never wanted you to be with us. You're not our kind."

"Oh, I like being with you, Jason. And I like your good wife here and her daughter. And I like Samuel and Ruth there and Henry. And you couldn't make it without me. You're too dumb. So I'll stay, thankee. And in California, I'll leave you be. Turn you over to Mrs. Baynes there. And to Clifford. What about that, Clifford? You ain't said much lately. Think you can manage in California all by yourself?"

Clifford Baynes, a fish out of water, opened his mouth, gulped, shut it, weakly grinned: "I have always managed. I suppose I shall manage in California, thank you."

Jason, indignant and hurt: "No one has ever talked to me the way you have done, Mr. McMoultrie."

Asa: "Ah, daddy used to talk to you that way all the time, Jason. I remember."

Jason: "Yes, and I left home."

Asa: "Daddy sent you to Yale, and then he went broke. You left home because he told you to go."

Jason, sweating: "But then I didn't come back. I was not bound to him, and I would not come home until he died."

The old man: "Well, you can't leave me, Jason. I'm stuck to you like glue, and you might as well make the best of it."

Clifford Baynes, a slick attempt at a smile: "Now that's a fine idea. Make the best of it. That's what I always say."

The old man: "I thought you always said, 'I'm hungry.'"

Clifford Baynes, injured and muttering and scared of the old man: "Some of us have stomach complaints. I need a good tonic. I can't get tonic out here."

346

Jason, abject and pleading. His world going to pieces around his uncomprehending head: "Please, please! We're quarrelling again. Can't we make another beginning? We must be friends. Please ..." He broke off and looked helplessly around.

Jessica, cool and restrained as if there had been no trouble at all: "Couldn't we ride over to the hills tomorrow? I do so want to see them. A little excursion might make us all feel better."

The old man, grinning: "Them hills is a lot longer off than they look, ma'am."

*Why doesn't she ask me to ride with her into the hills?* Jason brooding, injured, shocked, and defeated.

Jessica, smiling without concern for him: "You will ride with me, Mr. McMoultrie? If I choose to go?"

The old man: "Well, they ain't nothing like your Switzerland mountains, ma'am. They ain't nothing but little old warts when you get close up to them. What do you say, Adam? You want to ride over with Miz Jessica and me to see the hills tomorrow?"

Adam, caught off guard, stammering: "I . . . I don't know." An anxious glance cast tentatively at Jessica, standing there in blond splendor under the noonday sun.

She flashed a bright and somehow mysterious smile at him as though she had made up her mind about something difficult. "Yes, Mr. Cloud will come. We'll make a threesome out of it."

Jason: *She's ignoring me completely.* He nearly burst with jealousy.

Adam, subdued and uneasy: "If you want me to, ma'am."

Jessica: "Why, of course I want you to go. I'm always happy with your company.

The old man, wise and venerable: "Sure Adam's going to go. Might be Indians up there. Never can tell."

Jessica, looking around, a cloud on her face: "Do you think the others will be all right here while we're gone?"

Jason: "We'll be all right. I've always believed, contrary to some, that there was no danger to us as long as we did not provoke trouble. I do not intend to quarrel with Indians. Not now."

Ishtar Baynes: "Seems to me like a woman oughtn't to be

347

running off to the hills with a copule of strange men lessen she's got her husband's permission."

Jason, weakly smiling: "I appreciate your concern for the proper forms, Mrs. Baynes. Indeed I do. But my wife and I trust each other implicitly. She knows she has my permission to do anything she wants."

The old man, nodding and looking to where the hills rose in the brilliant sunlight: "We'll go then. But tomorrow. We'll make a day of it."

Jason, frostily: "Excuse me. I must write awhile in my journal."

The old man, laughing in ungentle mockery: "You writing at noon now, Jason? You was writing just in the evenings."

Asa: "He's always kept a diary. Mamma used to make him." Asa grinning.

*"Jason, my darling, what is this!"*

*"I was just doing what you told me to do, mamma, putting down my thoughts. You said to put them all down."*

*"But thoughts about such things! I never knew you would think about . . . Well, Jason!"*

*"She was peeing in the bushes, and I saw her."*

*"Jason, my precious child. You not only saw her. You watched her!"*

*"Don't cry, mamma. Please don't cry. You know I can't bear to see you cry."*

*It's dirty, dirty dirty! Little girls can be so dirty, Jason! Women can be so dirty. Don't let them pollute your body. Oh, Jason! When thoughts like that come, you must shut the door of your mind to them and lock it!"*

*"I'll try, mamma. Honest, I'll try. Just don't cry. Please don't cry."*

They rested at noon, scattered in clusters clinging to the thin shade of the wagons. "How long do you think it'll take for us to have a good life in California?" Promise spoke, full of whimsy and longing.

"Thirty years maybe," Harry said, himself subdued by the quarrel that had burst up so suddenly a little while before. "Thirty years for real cities to come. Civilization."

"Thirty years! But we'll be old by then!"

Jessica hugged her daughter tenderly. "Promise! Talking about getting old at your age! Wait till you get to be thirty-five! Then you can talk about growing old."

"I don't want to miss life. Waiting for something. I want to have something in life before I get old."

"We have something right now," Harry said. "I think we don't have to wait much longer for the greatest happiness I can imagine."

Ishtar Baynes reclined against a wheel. Her husband was under the wagon, stretched out with the hound, sound asleep.

"Well, I tell you what Clifford's going to have in California."

Jessica sat combing her hair. "What's that, Mrs. Baynes?"

"He's going to have him a whiskey store. I've decided men is always going to drink whiskey, and they got to have somebody to sell it to them. And that's what Clifford's going to do. And me, I'm going to have a hat shoppe."

Jessica, still combing her hair, lifted her brows. "A whiskey store? And a hat shop? My, my, Mrs. Baynes. You talk to my husband all the time about living in a big farm community back up in some green valley in California. Sharing everything. I don't believe I've ever heard you mention a hat shop before."

Ishtar Baynes tossed her head indifferently. "Well, I mean we're going to have a whiskey store and a hat shoppe if something goes wrong. I figure it this way. Folks in California, where they's lots of sunshine, has got to wear hats. Don't you wish we all had hats out here? I'm going to sell hats by the shipload."

Harry laughed, taking off his glasses and polishing them. "That's what we call hedging our bets, Mrs. Baynes."

Jessica sat looking out over the plains and combing her hair in sweeping rhythms that were like music. "It may well be thirty years before I hear a concert again. I don't suppose they will have concerts in California for a long, long time."

Adam sat silently nearby, listening greedily. "Did you use to go to concerts back there . . . where you lived?" He had not spoken to her directly since that night when he had tried to kiss her. But he had heard of concerts in the way she had heard of Switzerland.

She turned a slight smile on him, and looked at him for a long moment, hardly seeing him, as if she were thinking of something completely different. "I only went to a concert once," Jessica said. "But I will never, never forget it."

Ishtar Baynes sniffed. "Well, if you been to one concert, I reckon you don't have to go to another."

"Music isn't like that," Jessica said, laughing suddenly.

*She's beautiful!* Adam thought. When Adam saw Jessica sitting by Promise, he could compare two women and two ages, and he could see the scarcely perceptible signs of age creeping relentlessly across the older woman's face. Yet there shone through them still a radiance softly gleaming, a love of life, restlessness, a vigor, an energy, and a resolve of some sort. All slowly being devoured by time.

"Well, *me*," Ishtar Baynes was saying, "*I* like to think that you do what comes along so's you can say you done it onct if somebody else talks to you about it. I mean, you don't want nobody to say she's done something you ain't. I ain't never been to no concert, but some of these days I reckon I'll go to one. When Clifford and me is rich and folks from all over the place is buying his whiskey and wearing my hats. And I'll know what a concert's like, sure enough. But then I'd want to do something else. Go to the circus maybe. Go to the Catholic church one Sunday. Take a train ride. Do something fancy."

Jessica smiled. "But Mrs. Baynes! Have you never done anything you wanted to do again and again?"

Ishtar Baynes gave her a hostile look. "Not me. Most things I've done, I'd just as soon forget. Look at what we're doing now! Who'd ever want to do *it* again?"

"Oh, I don't know," Jessica said wistfully. "The time may come when we think this is the greatest thing we ever did in our lives."

Ishtar Baynes made a contemptuous sound in her throat. "Only way I'm going to think this trip's any good at all is if it leads us to California and gives us something to eat three times a day, and a place to keep the rain and the cold out, and something to do that we can hold up our heads about. And then I ain't going to moon about how we got there. I'm going to forget ever mile we been hot and thirsty and dirty. And I'm going to enjoy my California. And I'm going to pretend I ain't never been nowheres else."

The sun was falling hotly around them, and the sky showing in great spaces between the peaceful clouds was an astounding and vivid blue. Jessica lifted her face to that brilliant sky and shut her eyes again. "Oh, I could listen to music for the rest of my life. It was Mozart I heard. Wolfgang Amadeus Mozart! A whole evening of Mozart! And I sat there listening to the music, and I thought, 'It can't be this loud! The world will *burst* if music is this loud!' But it only got louder and louder, and I was full of it, positively drunk with it, and it was like something in my heart rushing out to meet what was coming in from the outside. Music within and music without. And there was a harmony when they met in my heart, and . . . Oh, I'm talking foolishness, I know."

"Well, you ain't talking sense," Ishtar Baynes said.

Jessica laughed without malice. "Well, I'm sorry, Mrs. Baynes, sorry that you can't know what I'm talking about. I felt it, and it just carried me away."

"It makes me sick to hear talk like that!" Ishtar Baynes looked at Jessica like a coiled snake.

Jessica was amazed. "But why, Mrs. Baynes?"

"Because the folks that talk like that . . . they think they're *better* than other folks. And they *ain't!*" She stopped; her thin mouth twitched. Then in a little hissing voice she said, "I'm just as good as you are, Mrs. Jennings. I'm just as good as anybody."

Jessica, open-mouthed, was trying to find some courteous response to this dubious proposition when Harry slid easily in before her.

"My dear Mrs. Baynes! You are better than many, many people of my acquaintance! Indeed, madam, you are a *queen!*" Harry spoke with a smile, but the timbre of his voice carried a deep earnestness. For suddenly he was swept away in imagining that Ishtar Baynes could have been different, that his own life might have been something else. He was polishing his glasses, and he could not see the look of hostile interrogation that she flung at him like a knife.

"You, Mrs. Baynes, will indeed have the most successful shoppe in all California! In all the world! Surely our dream has to make room for beauty. And you will give us beauty, Mrs. Baynes. The beauty of art added to nature. They will come from Paris, from Rome, to see your fashions! The President of the French Republic will be there in his red, white, and blue sash. He will invite you to be his guest of honor at a grand ball in Paris. Oh, it will be grand, Mrs. Baynes. And you will be the sun around which the world of beauty and fashion revolves. And we shall bow to you and be grateful for the splendor radiating from your presence to light our poor lives!"

With that Harry leaped to his feet, swept his big, filthy hat around in a flourish of grace, and he bowed low in the direction of Ishtar Baynes—an almost acrobatic motion, his hat in one hand, his glasses catching the light in the other, and he looked so gallant and benign and sincere that Ishtar Baynes actually smiled with the rest of them. She let her smile turn into a foolish, abstracted grin, and she patted her thin brown hair and looked pleased.

Jessica smiled, too. *The poor thing*, she thought.

# 45

Jessica was always impetuous. Once when she was a very little girl, not yet four, she saw a red-winged blackbird skimming through the trees, and she thought how good it must be to fly. She ran around the big house in New York with her young arms outstretched. She leaped up and tried to take flight from the confining earth, even jumping down the carpeted stairway from three steps up, flapping her arms. She imagined herself the companion of birds, soaring beyond the white clouds, dipping above the whitecaps on the sea, speaking to angels, diving and whirling and seeing the beautiful world spread out below her like a carpet of flowers.

She thought that if she could get just a slight start, then the wind might catch her and bear her aloft. So she climbed up to the second floor of the house, to her own little bedroom, and she flung open the big windows that looked down onto the fragrant garden. And before the astonished eyes of a nurse petrified with terror, she jumped onto the windowsill and threw herself into space, her arms outstretched to glide on the cool air. She heard the scream of the nurse all the way along her descent to the soft ground. And as she hit the earth and fell tumbling headlong, the breath knocked out of her but otherwise undamaged, she heard the nurse in the window above screaming and screaming.

That was the first moment she knew fear, for she supposed

that the nurse had had a seizure. And she thought she was to blame, and her father would be angry. About her fall she was only puzzled and disappointed. As she picked herself up, she was smothered by the nurse and by a squadron of other servants who came rushing pellmell into the garden, clamoring, crying, to fall on her, to feel her bones, to demand what on earth possessed the child. Jessica looked up over the anguished servants, curiously detached from them now that she knew the nurse was alive and well enough to be shouting at her, and she saw a robin perched on the low branch of a maple tree in the garden, and she was envious and sad. *Why can't I fly?*

"She's like me!" her father said, nodding his shining bald head, pleased and proud of her for her daring. His pinched face exploded in the wrinkles of a wizened grin. "I was impetuous when I was a boy. It runs in her blood." He laughed. His dry, forced, and somehow humorless laugh that was his habitual attempt to be both at one with the world and superior to it, a division within himself that he could never overcome.

Jessica's mother was young and beautiful, her father's third wife. The first two had meekly deferred to his power and had died, and as they were carried to the tree-shaded graveyard and placed in the huge marble vault he had prepared for himself and for all his family, he turned resolutely to the daily business of living, which included rising, eating, working, calculation, marriage, and the generation of offspring.

Jessica was the last child. Her mother brought her into the world with relief and thanksgiving, able now to hold her lovely head up in the company of those memories that haunted the house—memories of her two predecessors who had done their duty and provided children for a mercantile dynasty.

Jessica's mother had dark eyes and red lips and fair white cheeks. Jessica thought her mother was the most beautiful woman she had ever seen. So soft, so kind. And yet her mother was never at ease, in the house or in the world. Jessica's father was so much older than she. He was not so much husband as master. She served him in fear and trembling, and he seemed hardly to notice except when she failed.

Jessica's father seemed ancient and hard, like a piece of weatherworn granite protruding from the earth, monumental and even handsome in a stern way but unbending and unapproachable, vigorous but still removed from them by his surprising age.

He was proud of Jessica. She knew that. He paraded her out to meet any company who came to visit. There was always company—distinguished company. Once even President John Quincy Adams came to call, and Jessica took his little hand and made a curtsy, and she saw the proud look on her father's face and the way he threw his chest out and his shoulders back and smiled like smooth stone warmed in the sunlight. When she had jumped out the window, her father had been pleased to tell his friends what she had done. She always supposed that the distance between them was because he was so much older than other fathers. But later she supposed that no one had ever been close to him.

When she was thirteen her father bought her a horse. Not a dainty little pony, like the mild things other girls had. But a real horse, a beautiful animal with dark chestnut hair that shone in the sun as if it had been burnished in some magical fire. Jessica rode happily around New York City as if she owned the town, her head held high, her long, blond hair brushed back by the playful wind.

And how she loved to ride! She took the horse across the Hudson, to the wooded, flat land of New Jersey, and there she galloped to her heart's content. At first she took along an awkward groom who did his best to keep up with her. But finally she started leaving the groom behind. It was good to be alone with her horse, with no one to cry caution at her, no one to lag behind and to slow her down.

By the time she was sixteen, she had worn out her fine horse. Her father—shaking his bald head, hissing with laughter at another story to tell—bought her a coal-black stallion so nervous and so spirited that the groom was afraid of him. "I'll turn the two of you loose together and keep the one who comes home," her father roared, pleased that his daughter could master a horse that few men he knew would care to try.

When she was sixteen, she began to go to parties. She circulated through the music among young and old, men and women, freely, enjoying herself, unintimidated by conventions, not wearing her hair in ringlets as others did but straight down her shoulders, an avalanche of gold. Men admired her. She loved the feel of their eyes on her, loved the way men spoke to her. She liked men much better than she did women, but she delighted in becoming a woman herself. Life getting better, richer, happier than it had been in her happy childhood.

If only women were not so dull! Sometimes she looked at her own mother and sighed in distaste and sorrow. How restrained and frightened the poor woman was! Eyes always flashing tensely around to see if she had offended her husband. How intimidated she was, not only by her husband's hard world that seemed to be made of waxy woods so slippery that any but the most cautious must tumble down to destruction merely trying to creep across its polished and untenable surface. And Jessica thought, *What could make a woman be like mamma? I don't want to be like that! Never.* The thought, not unlike her father's contempt for constables and junkmen, was both requiem and hope, a dismissal and a promise. *I am going to be different!*

At one of those gay parties, she fell into conversation with a man with curly dark hair and beautiful eyes. Something vaguely French about him. Something exotic that was as alluring to her as the fine black stallion she rode, a stray spirit tinged with sadness from mysterious hurts and secret disappointments. His dark eyes were luminous, like her mother's. When he looked at her those eyes seemed to melt, and there was such open yearning in them that he seemed famished. She felt warm when he looked at her. And she was elated to see the effect she had on him.

His wife was one of those imperious women who glittered and sparkled when she danced, a woman who looked like a beautiful Dresden figurine, shining coldly in candlelight with a fixed, porcelain smile. Jessica saw her and imagined herself to be a much superior woman. She felt sorry for him. Marriage was so permanent. His name was Lancelot Twilla, and she was as sorry for his ridiculous name as she was for his condition.

He asked her to go to a concert with him. Asked in the way he calculated she might be most likely to accept such a boldly illicit project. "If I were free, Miss Jessica, I don't know what I'd rather do in the world than to take you to the concert this Tuesday night." He shrugged his shoulders and shook his head solemnly as if the thing were totally impossible. "My wife can't go. Or I should say, she won't go. She doesn't like music, you see. But I adore it. It is the stuff of life for me. I might say it is almost my religion. How I wish the world were different! I see you. And I wish the world were fixed so that we might go to the concert together without shame. You know, the Arabs can have four wives! How strange to think that what would be shameful in our society would be the normal practice in Egypt!" Again he rolled his soft eyes heavenward and looked boyish and sad.

Jessica thought the solution to his wish was simple enough. She would go with him. At least she would meet him there, and they would sit together. Something deliciously immoral about the idea, and she could not resist the adventure she saw in it. Later on she could laugh at the girl she had been to enter such a trap so thoughtlessly, with no fear at all. Like jumping out of her bedroom window when she was a child.

She made the simple announcement to her mother that she was going to the concert with a girl friend and with the girl's father. Her mother never asked questions about anything. Her father did not have to know. On most evenings he was not home until late, and even when he was at home, he was nearly always locked in his study. And so it was easy—all so very easy for Jessica Marley to do what she wanted. She went to the concert in one of her father's carriages, and she sat in the dark with the married man who had invited her, and she listened to Mozart and felt her heart nearly explode within her from the power of the music.

In the midst of "A Little Night Music," her secret escort gently put his left hand under his right arm and reached over to her and took her by the hand, and she felt a thrill, a burning in her chest and head that was a combination of emotions, all in turmoil. The music ravished her. She dismissed her restraints. She wanted to do something—anything—to repay him for this glorious evening. He whispered that he must see her again. She mentioned a village and a time on the Jersey side of the Hudson. The music swallowed them up in a universe of sound, and his hand squeezing hers was like a clamp in her lungs causing her to scarcely breathe. Never in her life had she felt anything so intensely. Never in her life had she been so happy.

She awoke the next morning with second thoughts. *It would be better for me to stay home.* But she imagined him waiting for her out there, and she felt sorry for him, and her hesitations seemed cowardly. So she rode out to the designated village.

He was waiting in the churchyard where she had told him

to be. He sat his horse in the round, dark shade of a solitary cedar throwing its tremendous green bulk against the peaceful sky in this peaceful place where the white gravestones rising out of the grass made life seem all the more precious and fleeting than it had ever seemed before. She would always remember that nervous, white figure on horseback in that circle of cook dark so that he was like a cameo carved into her mind.

They rode through the deserted woodland of a summer weekday, seeking solitude, finding it so quickly that she thought God Himself must be blessing them. She believed in God then; she had never had any reason to doubt. They walked in the fragrant woods with the dead leaves crackling underfoot, the residue of green years gone. They sat in the shade, so far from every other human presence, hearing the forest noises like a melody to enchant them. And when he fell on her and began kissing her, moaning at her mouth, she could not resist him, though her dutiful conscience informed her in a formal and remote way that what they were doing was wrong. But who could see? And how much he needed her! The music of the concert still played magically in her ears, and the rapture of that symphony and that darkness was still in her heart.

When he began lifting her long dress up her naked thighs, she struggled briefly. She did not yet know what men and women could do together. No one had ever told her, and she was as ignorant as a child. She was afraid only because she knew that he was about to do something to her that nobody had done to her before, and she did not know what he expected from her. Yet she told herself that she could not simply refuse him, for a refusal would be unfair and ungrateful. Then he was plunging at her, and she cried out involuntarily with surprise and pain.

Just as surprising as that first shock was how short it all was. He worked at her for perhaps thirty seconds. Then it was suddenly over, and he withdrew from her and rolled out of her vision and lay prostrate on his face in the dry leaves. She lay there on her back awhile, looking at how beautiful the sky was through the tracery of leaves high above her head. She was wet between her thighs, and the feel of dry leaves against her naked hips was vaguely painful. But she was sure there must be more, and she was determined to do what he required. It took her a very long time to decide that

357

there would be no more, to make herself sit up and begin the first ineffectual attempts to straighten herself.

She saw then that he was weeping with his face pressed into the ground. He was imploring God to tell him why he had done such a thing to a virgin.

Then, as she sat all disheveled and uncomfortable, she looked at him and slowly understood how weak he was. It took her three months after that to discover that little as they had done together, they had done fully enough to make her pregnant.

"You know, I never have been to a party," Promise said.

"You've never been to a party!" Harry spoke like a jovial doctor listening to incredible, imaginary symptoms. "Why, my dear girl! What a tragedy! What a tragedy for the people who were deprived of your company. I am distressed. Truly distressed."

Harry laughed. They walked along arm in arm. The sun bore down on them, and Harry's feet hurt. But his heart was like a feather. Suddenly, in the midst of his laughter, he felt a not entirely unpleasant sadness.

"I remember parties! The music, the dancing, the reflection of candlelight in the wood of dance floors. An agreeable sight, my dear. Oh, yes! Agreeable!"

Promise said with a very small voice, "And did you go to parties all the time?"

"Why, of course. Of course! All the time. When I was younger." He sighed. "It was a long time ago. A very long time ago."

"Silly! You always talk about being so old."

"I am much older than you, my dear."

"You're *not!*"

"I feel very old sometimes. I hate birthdays. I hate them! I hate them! I hate them!"

Promised laughed. The laughter died to wistfulness. "And did they have much music at your parties?"

"Music! Oh, my dear, yes! Yes, yes, yes! Always music. A little chamber orchestra, you see. Two or three people on the violin. And there was a bass viol, and sometimes, yes, even a pianoforte. Not often. You have to be very rich to afford a pianoforte. And it's so humid in Georgia. Always knocking the pianoforte out of tune. Music out of tune is a pain to me. A genuine physical pain in my ears."

"Oh, it must have been wonderful."

"Well, it was very good. I loved it then. But it's all gone now. Yes. All gone."

"And what did the girls wear?"

"Wear? Oh, well, they wore dresses. You know, ah, *dresses*."

"Silly! I mean what kind of dresses?"

"Oh, ah, satins and silks. I think. Taffeta. Yes, taffeta. They wore petticoats, you see. And when the petticoats were made of taffeta, the girls rustled when they walked. And when they danced . . . when they danced, you could hear the noise of their petticoats almost as loud as the violins. It sounds silly. But it was nice. Very nice."

"Tell me," Promise said, with great hesitation and with more difficulty than Harry had seen in her before. "Could I ask you . . . Do you think . . . Am I pretty?"

"My dear!"

"No, am I as pretty as the girls . . . the girls you danced with in Georgia?"

"Oh, my *dear!* I speak with all the truth of my heart! You are prettier than anyone I *ever* saw in Georgia. You are more beautiful than anybody I have ever known before. My dear! To think that you should ask!"

Harry wanted to hug her, but he remembered himself and held back. It was reckless enough to be walking along with her, arm in arm. But she believed him, and her face glowed with a clear light.

"Jason believes in parties. He's told us so. He says we'll have parties all the time in California. He loves parties."

"Really?" Harry said. "Jason believes in parties?" He was surprised.

"He says there's nothing wrong with a good time."

"Yes. Well, if we have parites in California, I shall escort you, my dear."

"Oh, yes. Yes."

"And I shall ride home again in the dawning."

They looked at each other, caught up in a sudden, rapt silence. If Harry had been in love with her before, he was now filled to the bursting. She formed her mouth to speak, and the soft words came with difficulty. "I hope . . . I hope the time will come when . . . when, Dr. Creekmore, you . . . I . . . we ride home from parties together in the dawn."

So it was that she proposed marriage to him, looking at

359

him with sudden directness and calm. And Harry thought of how good it was that his father had died, that the old world of Georgia was gone, that fate had brought Harry Creekmore out here to the great plains to be with a girl he loved with all his heart.

He had not ever dreamed that life could really be this good. And even as he thought of the goodness, his eyes filled with tears. Perhaps he was only made to dream and never to have, and now that this dream was so good, he must wake up, and waking would be death.

The sight of the hills was a relief. The sand hills to voyagers in the flat and arid plains were a warrant that something was left in the world besides devouring space.

So it was that Jessica experienced that sudden desire so many other travelers felt when they first saw the hills. She yearned to explore them. The old man and Adam went with her, armed with every weapon they had. "This here's getting to be the country of the Sioux, ma'am. And you don't want to be fooling around with no Sioux lessen you can kill them before they kill you. And I warn you now, ma'am. If it looks like the Sioux is going to get you, then I'll have to shoot you."

"Just like a horse with a broken leg," Jessica said with a careless laugh. She never seemed to understand why men believed they had to protect her.

"I mean what I say, ma'am."

"I know you do. And I give you permission to shoot me if only you will ride with me into the hills first."

The old man looked stern. But his brown, lined face gave way to his admiration of her, and he laughed. Adam, looking at him, knew that Shawnee Joe would not hesitate to put a bullet through Jessica's brain if the Sioux were upon them. Nothing the old man did could surprise him. What astonished him on this day was that Jessica wanted him—Adam Cloud—to go with her.

She had forgiven him, he thought. Or perhaps it was something other than forgiveness. She looked at him with her cool blue eyes, and he could not fathom her expression. But it thrilled him and restored him.

The three of them angled off from the main party, leaving Jason looking after them, silent, pensive, abstracted, with Ishtar Baynes perched on the wagon seat just behind where Jason plodded with the oxen.

*She'll make him miserable all the time we're gone,* Adam thought. *Poor bastard.* He nearly laughed.

They rode out to the south where the hills loomed up gray and dun, purple and green, still and compelling and splotched with black shadows of cloud sliding along, and above them the immense sky of thick white clouds against the background of stretching blue. Adam looked up and felt all his burdens roll off his back.

The old man rode in front of them, gradually moving just out of earshot, removed in the venerable dignity of his age from their concerns, and sensing with patient, unjudging intuition that Adam and Jessica had things to say to each other. Adam was embarrassed. He did not want to speak to Jessica alone.

And it was Jessica who spoke first. Her tone was natural and easy, as if nothing bad had ever happened between them, as if indeed they had been only slight acquaintances forced to pass time agreeably together until they could divide.

"When we get to California, do you plan to stay with us, Mr. Cloud?"

"I reckon not, ma'am. I got business of my own in California."

"Of course. Your father. I suppose I thought that both you and he might join us sometime." She smiled faintly, not precisely at him. "I think it would be nice to be going to someone in California. I really don't know what is going to happen to us. My husband started this journey with some modest dreams. Fine vague hopes. And now Dr. Creekmore has convinced him that he is the latter-day Moses and that we are some new Israel in the wilderness. Going to the Promised Land. I don't know what's going to happen when we get there and have to stop dreaming and get to working. Making a life. I want to believe in my husband. I want to believe there can be a better world. We all want that, don't we? It's as he says. It isn't wrong to hope. But sometimes . . . Perhaps it is pride to turn hope into certain expectation. I don't think it is safe to do that. What do you think, Mr. Cloud?"

"I don't know, ma'am. Sure . . . I reckon it's good to hope. I hope to find my daddy. But maybe I won't. Maybe I won't never see him again. California's a big place. Sometimes I feel like a fool for doing this. But I got to do it. I couldn't of stayed home. And I reckon your husband's that way, too. He's got to do what he's got to do. He couldn't stay home, back there where you was. And maybe you'll find what he's looking for. Maybe he won't find everything, but something. But it don't matter if he don't find nothing. He's still got to do it."

Jessica looked at him with appreciation, and he felt his face grow hot with embarrassment at the long speech he had made. She looked away, and her smile turned stiff and ironic.

"Jason thinks we can change things. But sometimes I wonder if anybody can change anything. It's luck if anybody manages to survive, let alone change the way things are. Maybe nobody ever changes anything. I think that sometimes. All the people in the world. All the people who have lived and died ... They make a flood. And which one of them ever managed to turn the flood aside?"

There was something so quietly earnest, so desperate in the undertones of her voice, that Adam spontaneously reached back into his childhood, to a mythology still glowing at the edges, handed down to him at home and in school and in the dusty streets of Bourbonville on languid Saturdays. "Well, there was George Washington."

His response was so unexpected that Jessica laughed. Her long, loose hair seemed to shake like a golden veil in the sunshine. "Yes, there was George Washington, and he had a rich plantation in Virginia, and he was in the right place at the right time, and they made him a general because he was rich, and they say he won the war. But maybe—just maybe, Adam—the war would have been won anyway, without your General George Washington. And if that's so, why he was just a chip on the flood. An imposing chip. Maybe a log or a tree even. But still just going where the waves washed him up. Tell me, Adam," she said, sweeping a fine brown hand around in an encompassing gesture at the great, barren land, "do you really believe that George Washington or anybody else all by himself could be responsible for all this? I mean, could any single person direct what is happening out here, what is going to happen? No. I think there is a tide that sweeps us along, and we go where it directs us. There are some people swept up to the crests of the waves, and everybody can see them, see the wave rolling under them, after them, and we call them 'leaders.' But the tide is pushing them, just the way it pushes all the rest of us, rolling along, out of sight, below." She laughed quietly, dismissing something.

Adam did not know what to say. He felt strangely close to her, this woman who talked about things only men were supposed to think about. He admired her. Perhaps he loved her. Yes, he supposed that he did love her. Well, no harm in that. He was not going to do anything about it. Not now, after what had happened.

"What can Jason do?" she resumed. "All his talk ..." She hesitated, and then the suppressed thing came up like bile. "I tell you what I think, Adam. There is the smell of defeat in Jason. Like smoke in his clothes. I can't explain it. I see you. I see Mr. McMoultrie. I see you getting along out here. And Jason ... He cannot adapt to this land. He is going to fail. We are going to fail. Oh, I don't know."

Her thoughts and her words became confused, and she was silent for a while, regaining her calm. She spoke more quietly then. "I did not know he was planning anthing like this when I married him. He did not tell me anything. He told me about wanting to help slaves to freedom. I knew he was going out to the river, the Ohio, at night. We kept runaways in our cellar. And then the next thing I knew ... Well, I've said all this before, haven't I?"

Adam felt his face grow unbearably hot. They had talked of these things on the night when he had tried to kiss her.

Jessica looked at him; he cast a nervous, sidelong glance at her. She laughed not thinking of his discomfort. "But I have no right to complain. I had to marry somebody, anybody who came along. I had no more resources. When Jason came knocking at my door, why, I thought he was insane. He asked me to marry him. I had never seen him before. And then I thought he was a gift of God. I was grateful to him for taking me. For taking Promise. You know, Adam, when she was born, I held her against my cheek in an old wooden rocking chair, and I sang to her, and I cried, and she was the only warm thing in the world I had to hold. I adore her. And if Jason had told me he was going to be a missionary to Africa or to the South Sea cannibals, I still would have married him if he would take care of my Promise. And so I want you to know that I have no right to complain. We are perverse, Adam. Human beings are perverse. When we are your age, we see the perversity in others. When people are my age, they see it in themselves."

Adam looked at her, and he loved her. He did not dream that his love would lead anywhere. She was so much older than he was. But then her age added immensely to her mystery and to the blind, heavy thing he felt for her. But it also sealed off plans and prospects. She was married. Adam said in a husky voice, "I figure Mr. Jennings was awful lucky to get to you when he did then. He don't know how lucky he is, I reckon."

Jessica looked at him as though she had not heard him aright, as though she had been plucked up from a deep abyss of morose thoughts. Very slowly her face broke into a great smile. She was very brown now, and her eyes were very blue. Adam, his own head wrapped up in a cloth against the sun, felt like a gypsy pirate in her presence.

"How beautiful they are," she said wistfully.

Adam followed her eyes.

"The hills," she said. "I thought we might never see hills again."

"They ain't much."

She laughed happily. "They are everything here. They're the only hills we have." Her smile died, and she became soberly reflective again. In a while she said, "Tell me something, Adam. Do you think things are beautiful because they are rare? Or are they beautiful just because they are familiar?"

Adam shook his head, baffled. He even began to feel peevish because it seemed that she was deliberately ignoring the thing he had blurted out, the thing he felt so powerfully and so hopelessly for her.

She did not wait for him to speak. "I'm trying to say that I think these hills are beautiful because they are new to me. I can imagine all sorts of things about them. The Indians who have been here and gone on. Not just this year or last year but for a thousand years before now. The Frenchmen who saw them when they explored this river. The travelers before us who died within sight of them. Who knows what they have seen? You know, I find all this landscape beautiful. Romantic. I still use the word. There's nothing wrong with being romantic. I did not want to come here. I still resent my husband for bringing me here. It was so unfair. But even while I resent him, I'm so glad I came." She laughed, clear as chimes in the dark. "You see, we are perverse!"

"I reckon I'm glad, too," Adam murmured.

"There are so many things in the world I'm never going to see, Adam. So many things I have seen that I will never see again."

Adam, yearning to rise with her feelings, cleared his throat to hide his emotion, and with a show of carelessness muttered, "You can't never tell what you're going to see."

Jessica laughed again and tossed her head, letting the bright sun ripple in her hair. "I have always loved strange things, Adam. I have always sought new things. I have imagined that adventures were beautiful, and to me a landscape like this is something from a world of strange dreams. To live out here? No, I would despise that. In ten years I would die of boredom. Maybe in ten days. But passing through it ... Then our motion makes these hills something to conjure with. Do you understand that?"

Adam swallowed and felt beaten. "I guess so."

The sand hills were so near now that the old man was turning up a slope some fifty yards ahead of them. His mule hunkered forward in a lethargic, climbing gait. The old man looked utterly impassive on the mule's back, a wiry form become a part of the mule itself, wanting nothing, resisting nothing, perhaps asleep. It was a day for God to doze.

"I will put you a question, Adam. What is the most beautiful thing you have ever seen in all your life?"

Adam, confused, upset at how difficult this conversation was for him, fought back the impulse to tell her that she was the most beautiful thing he had ever seen.

"Tell me," she said, gently coaxing.

What came to him suddenly was the calm of Sunday mornings at home in the spring, when all the world was warm and still and every blade of grass, every green leaf, every bright flower, and the land itself seemed to shine with its own clear light. He got up early with his father on those mornings, and they did the chores. Then they had their coffee. If there was preaching on that Sunday, they hitched up the mules to the springless wagon, and they went off to the Methodist church through the splendid Sabbath calm. Adam always went those mornings expecting the magic glimmering behind the ordinary things suddenly to burst on the world, and there would be no sickness and no separation and no death, and everybody he knew would have everything anyone could possibly want.

Sunday mornings ... Then it seemed that all the world hung softly in a grand expectancy, not for a heaven to come after death but for something tremendous to happen here in the brightness of this sweet life. And Adam walked through those still, glittering mornings silently, in awe, almost on tip-toe lest he disturb the peace of God contentedly presiding over something about to be created anew.

These were the sunny images that came in confusion to Adam Cloud when Jessica Jennings rode serenely with him toward the desolation of sand hills in a yellow world of waving grass and a blue world of sky, where there was no haze to soften the hard edges of land and sky and to paint them with that steamy gentleness that made the world in Bourbon County seem so good to Adam now that he had renounced it forever.

His heart was full of memory, but his tongue seemed thick, and to answer Jessica's question he could only murmur: "Sunday mornings, back home, in the spring. That's the most beautiful thing I ever seen in my life."

As soon as he had spoken the words, he knew that Jessica had misunderstood him. He felt abruptly and sickeningly alone, helpless with the impotency of his tongue. He remembered the way Rachael had slipped just beyond his grasp in the Big Blue. Life seemed to have become a succession of frantic snatches at things just out of his reach, and when he had exerted himself, he was left with empty hands. Maddening.

"You see?" Jessica said softly and almost with reproach. "We are very different."

*No you don't understand!* He wanted to shout at her, to shock her out of her superiority and her complacency. He wanted to tell her of the strangeness and the brooding mystery behind the ordinary things, the alien holiness of land and sky and the great forest that made those lost Sunday mornings so sublime. But he could not find the words. He looked toward the sand hills, shining so keenly in his sight that they cut away all mystery. They were only themselves. His attitude seemed to say that he agreed with her about how little imagination he had and did not consider the matter worth discussing anymore. Surrender. Silent, helpless despair.

They rode up into the hills, and the old man disappeared.

Adam worried. The day was hot, and he was thirsty now. They dismounted and walked because Jessica wanted to walk. Adam kept beside her, awkwardly cradling the two heavy rifles in his arms and seeking the old man, listening for the crunch of another foot against the sandy soil.

"Tell me, Adam, what do you think of Dr. Creekmore?"

"Well, he's my friend."

She paused a long time. They walked. "I like Dr. Creekmore," she said, musing with a curious and distant reverie in her voice. "He reminds me of somebody. I thought he was weak. Now I think he protects us."

"Harry?" Adam nearly laughed.

Jessica cut him off with her seriousness. "I mean it. If it were not for Dr. Creekmore, I think Mrs. Baynes would finally have us in her power. I think the woman is a witch."

Adam felt a chill in the hot sun. He knew there was much about the world he could not explain. Mrs. Baynes a witch? Who could be sure!

Jessica went on, speaking carefully. "She has put a hex on poor Asa. Asa has so much anger burning inside him anyway. He was always angry because he didn't get the chance in life Jason got. Asa thinks Jason failed. And he's convinced that if he'd had the same chance, he would have succeeded. But still he's always done what Jason told him to do."

"He's out here," Adam said.

"Yes. But now Jason has lost his power over Asa. Mrs. Baynes has stolen Asa away, just while we've been watching her. Ruth says Asa was gentle once, that he'll be gentle again. She lays his troubles to not having a job, to being helpless, to losing poor little Rachael. But I think it's more than that. If it wasn't for you, for Mr. McMoultrie, I'd be afraid of Asa out here. I think Asa could be angry enough to kill . . . or maybe something worse. He looks at me sometimes . . . It makes me feel as though I'd walked into a graveyard at midnight and seen a ghost."

"Aw, Asa ain't no danger. Little stumpy man like that! You could swat him like a bug."

"That's always what a man thinks. If he's bigger than his enemy, he doesn't think his enemy can hurt him. Women know better. That woman's put a hex on Asa and on poor Jason, too. Sometimes I think she's wrestling with me to possess his soul."

"She's mean all right."

"But you see, Dr. Creekmore has begun to laugh at her, and my husband respects him. Mrs. Baynes doesn't quite understand what's happening. She's trying to understand. But as long as Dr. Creekmore takes her so lightly, Jason can't take her entirely seriously. And every time he laughs, she seems to fall back a little."

"Yes, ma'am." There was a long silence between them.

"You know, Dr. Creekmore is in love with Promise. I think it is a real love. He is so gentle with her. You do think he's sincere, don't you, Adam? Honorable? He is honorable, isn't he? Oh, yes, of course he is."

"Oh, yes, ma'am. He's right as rain."

"Well, he has a sad, handsome face. A young woman is always likely to be drawn to a sad handsome face. But what do you think about him, Adam? His character? Is he loyal?"

Adam remembered Nashville and decided to lie just a little bit. "He ain't had the chance to be disloyal, and so we've got on right well."

Jessica laughed again. "You are an honest man, Mr. Cloud." She drew in a thoughtful breath, and her brows knitted slightly in worry. "Love always begins in heaven," she said softly. "And it usually ends in hell."

A cloud drifted peacefully over the sun. The black shadows of the hills vanished, and there was one grand, dark shadow over them all, and it was surprisingly cool. Something eerie in the air's becoming cool so quickly when the sun had gone. He thought of snow ahead of them in the Sierra Nevada. Cold wind and ice and deadly silence piling whitely up in the passes they must cross.

"You understand," Jessica said, "I am not asking about Dr. Creekmore with any thought that I could change things if you told me something I did not want to hear. I know I can change nothing. Promise is in love with him—the first real love of her life. I suppose the last she can ever have now. She is madly happy. The way I was happy one time." She paused thoughtfully, and then tossed her head again as if to drive something away. "She's already been happier with a man longer than I was. My own love affair was somewhat abbreviated." She allowed herself a short, faintly bitter laugh.

"Harry says what is to be will be."

"Oh, really? Then he believes what I believe, doesn't he? What Jason's mother believed really. The woman was simply devoured by her faith in predestination. Well, I believe we're

368

just chips on the flood. It's almost the same thing as pre-destination, isn't it? It's a very peaceful thing, you know. Just take what comes, knowing you can't do anything about it anyway. But when your only daughter is in love with a man you scarcely know. . . ! Well, the peace requires a certain effort."

They walked along in a reflective quiet. The cloud above them sailed on, and the sun came flooding back again.

"Tell me, Adam," she said suddenly. "Do you believe in God?"

The question took him by surprise. It released an unpleasant storm of contradictory and half-suppressed thoughts. "I ain't never had an experience," he said grimly. He knew he was not answering the question she had asked.

"An experience?"

"With the Holy Ghost. In church . . . or in camp meeting. You know. Being saved. Shouting and crying, jumping up and down, falling on the ground. You know . . ." He felt helpless and a little foolish. She did not know what he was talking about.

"I think that sort of religion is vulgar beyond words," she said with immense disdain. "But I do wonder sometimes if there might be a God, somebody who can take all the accidents that happen to us and put them together in some pattern that has a purpose."

"I don't know," he murmured. The sun was like an avalanche on his back, smothering him.

"My mother-in-law was sure God had a plan for everything. That is the only religious question, I think. Is the flood that carries us along directed by God? Is it going somewhere? Or is it just moving? And if things were different, would there be any reason for that? I might be back in New York, with my father's inheritance, and I might have a husband I believed in and a house and a place in the world. And maybe I would feel just as strange about everything as I do now. Everything just in motion. Going nowhere."

Adam thought of the ferry over the Big Blue. If they had gone ten miles north, taken the ferry at Marysville, Rachael would still be alive. Why?

"I grew up praying to God," Jessica said. "My father was a very religious man, you see. He was also very old. He commanded all of us to be religious, and we were religious because his age made him a patriarch nobody could talk back

369

to. Now I think he believed that if we were all religious, we might help him when he came down to die."

"Was he some kind of preacher or something?"

Jessica threw back her head and laughed. "Oh, dear, no! He was a merchant. Like my husband's father, but my father was very successful. Very rich. He made a fortune during the American Revolution."

"Way back then!" Adam was amazed.

"He was fifty-eight years old when I was born, Adam. He was a very young man when the Revolution came. He was so proud of me. You see, I proved that he was still a man when he was old. Three wives, seven children, and the last one— me—born when his friends from the old time were dead or dying. He could show me off to people and prove that he had not died already himself."

Adam marveled. "Well, he must of been a pretty stout feller sure enough."

"He was a very strong man with a good constitution. He lived long enough to banish me from his house because his dead friends would have expected as much." She laughed again, this time with keen irony. "His friends were like himself, you know. They worked themselves into the grave making money any way they could. You see, in America, making money any way you can is no crime. The greatest crime you can possibly commit is to be a woman and to have a baby without a legal husband to give the child his sacred name."

Adam turned red and said nothing.

Again silence, feet moving in the sand.

"My father, you see, made his fortune with the Revolution. He sold grain to both sides. Army horses and soldiers eat a lot of grain. And there is always corruption on both sides during any war, and money is the grease that makes corruption work and wars go on.

"But the worst thing about it was the religion. He was an Episcopalian, like Dr. Creekmore. You know Episcopalians are supposed to face the Almighty with a certain dignity. My father looked down on the other varieties of Christianity, but he groveled as much as any Baptist! He was always trying to placate God. He took us all to church every Sunday, and we always sat in one of the richest pews down front. He gave so much money to the church that bishops used to come to our house just to slaver over him. I am serious! They would slaver over him as if he were some succulent morsel of ham and they hungry dogs like your hound there."

Adam winced. "I don't much like preachers."

Jessica made a disgusted noise in her throat as if something were about to come up in her gullet. "Neither do I, and you have to remember that a man gets to be a bishop in the Episcopalian Church by being ten times worse than an ordinary preacher."

She looked so wisely at him that he guffawed. Out here in the sand hills his loud laughter sounded very frail.

"The only real conviction my father was ever able to have came when he banished me from his house. I had disgraced him, you see. And he had lived with all the disgrace he could bear in life. I suppose he thought that if a bastard child had been born under his roof, that would mean the end of everything. He had made a very careful arrangement with God, and he had worked out his arrangement with the country, and he lived in fear and trembling that the whole thing would fall down around his ears. A bastard child was too precarious for him to bear."

"What did he figure was going to happen to you when he throwed you out of his house?" Adam was angry at this man he would never know.

"Well, my father was not the kind to think anything about something like that. He thought he was being strong, I suppose. But it was really because he didn't have any feelings to give him any tenderness at all. He let me pack up a few things in that chest we threw away. The big one. He gave me a thousand dollars. Really a fortune, I suppose. He allowed me to say goodbye to my mother. And he shut the door behind me, and I never saw him and never heard from him again. I am sure that when I walked down the steps into the street and got into a hansom cab that it became as though I had never been born. He simply shut the memory of me out of his mind."

"And your brothers? They didn't do nothing either?" Adam was outraged.

"They were men."

Adam took a deep breath. "Well, if you ask me, you didn't lose much by getting shut of a crowd like that. Your daddy sounds like the worse man I ever heard of."

"Oh, no," she said easily. "I did hate him for a while. I must admit that. I hated my poor, helpless mother, too. But no, he wasn't bad. He couldn't help himself. I decided you cannot blame people for what they can't help." She looked sad and pensive. "He's surely dead by now, dead for a long, long time. At least he's at peace if he's dead. I hope so. I have no feeling about him except that."

Adam was moved. "You should of gone back. You should of kept up with your mamma and gone home when he died."

"Oh my poor mother! She would have died of shame. If I had gone back, my father's ghost would have haunted her into the lunatic asylum! I could not hurt her that much. And I had far too much pride to go back." She drew herself up in the saddle and looked regal and hard.

The sudden change in her was nearly frightening. Adam stammered. "Well, I'm sorry . . . I wish . . . You should of had somebody."

"Well, I had myself, and I had Promise. I'm not bitter. I don't know why I'm not. Maybe it's just because things are pointless and inevitable. And when you feel that, there's no reason to be bitter. I didn't starve. My lover . . . the man who sowed Promise in my womb . . . I sent him word. He had a sister who lived in Ohio, and he sent me to her. Poor man! He wept when he sent me away. My father didn't weep. I was touched. But his sister was something else. She blamed me for seducing her noble brother! You see, she thought that all good men have a right to pursue, and if a woman succumbs, then you forgive the man. She would have agreed with Asa. It's always our fault. I hated living with her. And finally I just moved out on my own, and I'm sure she was relieved."

"Why'd you let him send you away? Why didn't you just stay in New York?"

"It does seem silly now. But that is the way life is, Adam. One silly thing after another. He said I should go to Ohio, and he said he would send me some money, and it seemed to me that since I had got myself pregnant and put him in such a stew that I just owed it to the poor man to do what he wanted and go to Ohio. I suppose in my heart I believed what his sister did, that it was all my fault. And he was terrified to have me in New York. I don't think he trusted himself with me there. He really did care for me, you see. He did the best with us that he could. He was not a strong person. I did not understand how weak he was until it was too late. And I'm not sure it would have made any difference anyway. He and I went to a concert together—that wonderful concert! And the next day he seduced me in a woods in New Jersey! It was absurd. But if I were that age, and I knew all that I know now, I might still do the same thing all over again."

Adam blushed a deep, hot red, and Jessica, seeing his crimson face and his mute embarrassment, smiled gently and laid a light hand on his arm.

"He died young," she said softly. "I grieved when he died. I grieve for him yet."

Adam felt a mysterious double pang of jealousy and relief. "I reckon you did love him after all."

"No, I don't think so. I loved the concert. We made an agreement to see each other the next day, and I loved the adventure of that. It was so beautiful out there ... But I have a husband now. Jason was good to marry me. I really do not waste my time dreaming about the past. That would be futility indeed."

She fell into a thoughtful silence. They came out atop another rise and paused, and they could look for miles across the prairie to where the river lay still like that magic band shining and fixed under the almighty sun, a gleaming stripe of polished silver that made their eyes sting to see. The vista reduced them both to a long silence as if they had talked too much and now needed to rest and regather their strength. By searching the landscape, Adam could discern the wagons crawling far, far away. He was struck by how slowly they went in this enormity of space. Suddenly he felt content with their motion and did not fear the snow that would fall in the stony mountains somewhere far ahead of them. What would come would come. And the creeping wagons were like the hands of a great clock signaling that time itself passed slowly and that life was long.

In his sudden exaltation, Adam wanted to say something comforting to Jessica, so close to him, so quiet after sharing so much. So he said carelessly, "Well, I know Mr. Jason loves you. He ain't like other men, but he's all right in his way, and he'll take care of you now."

She lifted her eyebrows and gave him a quizzical and ironic look. "Oh, do you think so? We are talking about my husband, I believe. That wonderful and kind gentleman who is struggling to convince himself that the opinions of a vagabond washerwoman about his wife may not be entirely true?

373

You do mean that gentleman cares for me, don't you, Adam?"

Her cold vehemence shattered the softness that had enveloped them like a pillow of air. Adam felt rebuked. "I think he cares for you. Yes, ma'am." He stammered; his words sounded helpless and idiotic, the babbling of a very foolish child.

"Well, I really do not know how Jason feels about me," she said dryly, looking frostily away at the distant wagons. "He has never used me as a wife. The only lover I have ever known is the man who gave me my child." She threw an icy look at him the way a very cruel, calm soldier may practice thrusting with a bayonet in a live pig, and then she turned to gaze at the far river and seemed to retreat into her glacial hideaway, impervious either to his confusion or to the broiling sun that silently flailed all sense out of the world.

And while Adam was trying to absorb what she had said, to convince himself that she was bold enough to say what he had heard, the old man came riding from nowhere around one of the nearby hills. He looked at them with a face grizzled, lined, brown, and as impassive as the hard summer sky.

"We better be riding back," he said in a voice unnaturally soft. "We don't want to be out here alone when the sun sets. They's been Indian ponies here in the last day or two. I found their tracks."

# 46

They moved on toward the crossing of the Platte, where the trail would angle sharply to the northwest, toward Fort Laramie. Dry, windy days and spectacular sunsets, filling the sky with flame and smoky cloud, and afterwards the night shone with thousands of stars gleaming like tiny silver lamps hung on invisible pegs across the infinite universe.

"Mr. Emerson said that if we saw the stars only once in a

thousand years that all the world would believe and adore God," Jason said. "He said the memory of that single night's vision would be passed on to generations and generations and that only knowing the vision might come again would make us always devout."

Harry looked blissfully up at the stars, saw them waver like darts of flame in his huge glasses, and he thought that they could not be more constant on enduring or beautiful than his love.

He rode with Promise and Adam on muleback one afternoon and told stories about the Arabian Nights. He showed them castles rising from the sand hills and peopled the magical desolation with strange and exotic names. Promise hung on every word with an enchantment in her eyes that was more magical and beautiful than any picture Adam would ever see. But he thought: *She's so young; she don't know nothing yet. She's got it all to learn.* And so Promise was like a child to him, someone to be protected. Jessica was something more.

Harry walked with Promise alone on the prairies after supper, and the day hung on in that hushed suspense before the first stars came. They were at the Platte crossing now. They did not hold hands or touch each other. They stayed within sight of camp as proper young people were expected to do, so that married and responsible adults could chaperon them with their eyes. But they could talk in private, and Harry, summoning his best eloquence, decided that night to say what was in his heart.

"Miss Jennings, I must speak to you about something that will perhaps pain you to hear. Indeed, it may distress you very much. But when we spoke recently of parties, you expressed sentiments that have emboldened me to speak to you."

She turned on him large eyes filled with wonder and a twinge of fear. "Why, what are you talking about, Dr. Creekmore?"

"You must first swear to me that if I tell you my own sentiments that you will react according to the true feelings of your heart and not according to your generous pity or your charity."

"Why, what on earth are you talking about, Dr. Creekmore? Are you ill? You look suffering!"

"Miss Jennings, I am in love with you. I have never met a

375

woman like you. I never dreamed in all my life that I would be ... that I *could* be fortunate to meet a divine creature who calls forth the feelings in my heart that you awaken in me. I am unworthy of you. But my unworthiness does not govern the way I feel."

"Dr. *Creekmore* ... !"

"Allow me to finish, dear lady. In spite of my profound sense of my own lowly status, your previous gracious words have given me the courage to ask for a declaration, since not to ask would be a crime against my very life in the light of my overpowering, my truly desperate feelings for you!"

"But why me? Why me? You could have any girl in the *world!*"

"Oh, Miss Jennings, you compliment me to the point of utter foolishness. Oh, I don't mean that *you* are foolish, my dear young woman ... But yes, yes, you are foolish if you love me. And I am foolish. The world is foolish. Oh, divine folly!"

"But you *know* I love you. Surely you know I love you. I never dreamed that you could love me!"

"Miss Jennings, it is the quality of innocence not to be conscious of itself. You are the purest, sweetest, most noble, most delightfully artless woman I have ever known. I can think of nothing more ennobling to myself than to spend the rest of my life in your presence, your divine presence."

"Dr. Creekmore, I never thought ..."

"Now please, Miss Jennings, do not cry. Promise! Please don't!"

"Dr. Creekmore! Dr. Creekmore!" Bright laughter, trembling with joy. A face looking at him suffused with adoration. Harry had never felt any emotion so powerfully as he felt his love for her in that moment.

"Harry!" he said. "Please call me Harry! I would be so honored, my dear."

"Harry, I love you!"

"And I love you, too, Promise. More than ever I can tell you. But I must point out some things to you, and you must consider them." Harry wiped his eyes under his glasses with his dirty handkerchief and tried to be grave. He assumed a judicial pose, lifting his chin with authority and imagining how imposing he looked with his carefully combed and cropped beard.

"What can I consider but that I love you?" Promise looked up at him with a tear-bright laugh of happy unbelief.

"You can consider, for example, that I am much, much older than you are, my dear."

"Older?"

"Promise, I am thirty years old!" Again Harry's voice almost broke as he thought of himself at that advanced age, isolated forever from the beauties of youth, from the strength and innocence of his early manhood.

"You don't seem old to me. You seem as young as the morning. I have never liked boys my own age anyway," Promise said very soberly. "They seem so childish. I have always wanted to be married to somebody I could look up to."

"My eyes are very bad, much worse than you know. I am blind without my glasses."

"Poor dear! I will be your eyes for you."

"My voice is so high-pitched. I've always wanted to have a bass voice, to sound like a man with something deep in him."

"The first time I heard you speak, my first thought was how pleasant your voice was. I wouldn't want it any other way."

"I talk too much. That is one of my cardinal sins. I have always yearned to be strong and silent, the kind of man who attracts attention by his composure when he walks into a room. Instead I talk my head off every time I have an audience. I know I make a fool of myself. I know I bore people."

"I have always thought that silent people had nothing to say. Or else I thought they were afraid to say what they really thought about anything. Mamma says gravity is the very essence of imposture. I love you just the way you are! You make everybody happy."

Harry hung his head and looked very shamefully at the ground. He cleared his throat sorrowfully and spoke with painful difficulty. "And there are some things I have done. Terrible things." Now he really did almost break down. "You must understand . . . At least I beg you to try to understand. You see, I was so lonely for so much of my life, and there are always women . . . Well, I never dreamed that you—the girl I dreamed about before I ever met you . . . I never thought you actually existed. And because I did not expect . . . I did not wait . . . Oh, Promise, dear girl! I am so impure that I cannot possibly be worthy of you!" Now the tears came in a flood, and even with his glasses Harry could not see.

But Promise stood looking at him very soberly, with deep

377

compassion. She swept a strand of her long, dark hair back, and the nervous smile that perpetually twitched over her face went away, leaving her large eyes to rule her expression. Only slowly did those eyes show that she was arriving at a vague understanding of just what Harry was talking about. He knew she could not even suspect the memories that were burning in his heart. She hesitated because she did not know just how to answer him. But finally she said, very softly, "I know it must have been very hard. I do not question your past. I do not want to know anything about it—now or ever. It is something behind us, something finished. Now we are together. That is all that matters."

"Can you ever forgive me?"

"Hush. I do not forgive you. There is nothing to forgive. We are going to California. California is a new life. Jason says that everything in the old world is behind us now. We are going to be born again, and there is nothing for a newborn child to regret."

"Please, dear Promise! Please! It would comfort me so much to have your forgiveness. Just tell me that you forgive me."

She gave him a long, inquiring look of puzzlement and compassion. "All right then," she said softly. "I forgive you. I forgive you with all my heart."

And so it was that a great burden fell away from his heart. He had prayed to God for forgiveness, and the skies had been made of brass. He had gazed with yearning at the confessional box at the mission when the old man had drawn aside in the confining dark to confess his sins. But when Promise spoke her simple word, Harry believed. In that moment he stepped out of the last clinging muck at the fringes of the great slough of despond, and the burden of his sins broke away from him. Squinting up through his heavy glasses, he was not surprised to see the first bright stars of the night emerging from the darkening sky. He imagined that their expression was full of grace.

He was a doctor now with a place in the world. The future was going to be brighter than he had ever been able to imagine in the past.

But later that night Harry dreamed, and when Adam came to wake him to go on watch, Harry started up in terror. When he saw it was Adam, and not a phantom, Harry seized his friend by the arm and hurried him out and away from the encampment a little distance apart.

"Harry, what's wrong with you! My God!"

"Adam, I just dreamed a terrible dream. And I know it's true. My father . . ."

"Good God. You told me you'd got shut of your daddy. You told him he had to have an appointment."

"I know. I know. But tonight we were out on a river, and I was on one side, and my father was on the other, and my father yelled at me. I could hear him calling across the water."

"Well, goddamn it, what did he say?"

"He said I was going to die, Adam. He said I was going to come through the cold water to him in a cold land. He laughed at me, Adam. He threw back his head and laughed and laughed, and I could see where he'd shot himself with the shotgun." Harry was close to sobbing; he knew he had seen a ghost.

"I reckon we're all going to die, Harry. But right now I'm going to sleep." Adam made as though to go back to the little tent, but Harry grabbed him roughly by the arm and held him.

"Adam, my father said I would die soon. He said I would never in my life marry Promise."

Adam pulled his arm away. He was annoyed and very tired. "Maybe the world's going to end, Harry. Maybe none of us is going to get married to anybody. Maybe tomorrow morning we'll get up to Judgment Day."

"No, not yet, Adam. I'm the one that's going to die. My father said so. And I believe him."

It was three o'clock in the morning. Nearby Adam could hear the soft mumble of the Platte. It was the South Platte here; they had just passed below the place where the North Platte and the South Platte ran together. The river sang low in the silence, and it was an ominous sound, funeral music in the dead of night, reminding Adam of the Big Blue and Rachael. He wanted to laugh at Harry, to be rid of him for the moment. But Harry's voice was so distressed and urgent, so near to breaking and Harry so close to collapse, that Adam could not bear to laugh.

"It's just a dream, Harry," he said. "My God."

"I want you to swear something, Adam."

"What, for God's sake?"

"Yes, that's right. Before God. For God's sake. If I die ... When I die, I want you to take care of Promise."

"How can I do that?"

"You can marry her."

"Marry her! Harry, you're crazy."

"No, Adam. No I'm not. Yes, marry her, take care of her for as long as she lives. For God's sake. No, for my sake. Swear, Adam."

Adam shook his head. "I've got a hunch she's going to be marrying you, Harry. Let's just let things be."

"Yes, that's what she thinks. We've talked about it. Tonight, Adam. I asked for her hand. She said she'd marry me. We love each other, Adam. But it won't happen. I'm going to die first."

"Harry ..."

"Just swear to me that you will marry her when I am dead."

"Ain't she going to have nothing to say about it?"

"I will leave word for her."

"She don't love me, Harry. She ain't never going to love me."

"She will do what I leave word for her to do because she loves *me*," Harry said quietly. "You will love each other in time. You'll see. You are both good. Good people naturally love each other."

From somewhere in the dark hills beyond the invisible river a coyote screeched in the night. He was answered by another, distant and mournful. Adam was silent. The wind swept and died and moved restlessly again like something unable to sleep.

"Just swear," Harry said.

"All right," Adam said gently. "I'll swear."

"You are serious, aren't you, Adam? You won't forget or make an excuse to leave her?"

"No," Adam said, expelling a deep breath. "I won't forget, Harry. But if she won't marry me, I won't try to force her. I'll marry her if she wants to. That's all I can promise."

"All right. It's enough." Harry fumbled for Adam's hand, found it, and the two of them shook hands clumsily, making a compact. "There's just one more thing."

"Ask."

"Swear that when I die, you'll try to make a coffin for my body. And if you can't make me a coffin, then wrap me up in a stout canvas." Harry laughed uneasily with apology. "I know it doesn't make sense, but I can't bear to be cold and wet. I'll sleep warmer alive if you'll promise me a coffin when I'm dead. Canvas if you can't find wood. But I'd prefer a coffin."

"All right, Harry. I'll do my best."

"Well!" Harry said with obvious relief. "I'm glad that's settled."

Adam at last managed to laugh. "All right, Harry. Now you got to swear something to me."

"Anything you want," Harry said.

"You swear to me that when we get to California, you'll let me kick your ass for keeping me awake at night with a lot of goddamned foolishness about your dying!"

Harry laughed easily, himself again. "If I get to California alive, you can kick me into the Pacific Ocean."

They laughed together. Adam handed Harry the rifle, its steel barrel very chilly in the night air. The coyotes continued their far crying in the northern dark. Adam looked up, scanning the heavens, and saw the stars very near. Uneasily he noticed that the constellation of Orion the Hunter was heaving himself off the eastern horizon. Adam thought fleetingly that Orion was high overhead in the wintertime and walked in snow.

He went back to the tent, crawled inside, and was almost instantly asleep.

Another quarrel burst out in the morning, at the crossing of the river. Asa was sick of drinking coffee, and he made as if to drink from the river, and the old man leveled a rifle at him and threatened to blow him open if he drank the water.

"Drink river water down here, and you're going to be sick. If you get sick, you'll hold us all up, and the snow will catch us in the mountains. I ain't going to let you get sick if it means somebody else amongst us is going to die because of it."

Asa backed down, eyes frozen on the bore of the threatening gun, red-faced, frightened, angry, humiliated before them all. And later Ishtar Baynes set up her coaxing litany of hate again in Asa's ear, consoling him by sharing his boundless and frustrated wrath at the universe.

Everyone was dispirited by the quarrel, not just by the ugly fact of it but by the sign it gave that they simply could not get along. Harry cajoled them and treated it lightly. "It's just nerves," he said happily first to one and then to another, smiling at their sullen or worried faces to show that *he* did not think anything was wrong.

There was no trouble crossing this river. The slow, patient oxen plodded into the shallow stream, dragging the heavy wagons behind them through the swift water like big boxes, flopping on ungainly wheels. The bright day beamed down. The air was clean and fine, and not much got wet. Crossing the South Platte was a picnic compared to the travail of the Big Blue, and their hearts grudgingly lifted, though they did not talk much to each other. The quarrel had brought a silence upon them.

Beyond the South Platte the land humped up into sand hills that made their progress a crucifixion in motion. The oxen strained up and up, and you could hear the roaring of their animal breath in the times they were brought lunging to a halt by wheels mired in the dry sand. The oxen were thin now. The yokes, so heavy and so large, looked cruel on their patient, scrawny necks, and their eyes were hollow and dull.

The men had to shovel the sand out when the wheels were stuck. They wrestled at the wagons, pushing and pulling and sweating in floods. They whipped the oxen forward. Shawnee Joe cursed and struggled and called down the damnation of God on the beasts until in a frenzy of annoyance Jason begged him to stop. Surprisingly enough he did. But then he made fierce and wordless grunts at his labor, and the grunts were more blasphemous than words could ever be.

Adam handled the mules. He hitched the four of them as best he could to the wagon most in trouble at the time. And when they had surmounted a sandy hummock or come up out of a sandy trough or pulled through sand up to the axle trees, there was something else twenty-five yards ahead to mire them down and break their backs again and to torture man and beast.

They had rough sand grinding into their clothing next to their skin. Adam felt sand scraping down in his crotch so that his thick, homespun trousers sawed at him when he walked and rasped unmercifully at him when he worked from the saddle of his riding mule. The sand was in his long hair, beaded up with sweat against his scalp. The sand made burning black lines in his neck. And the sweat pouring down his face sometimes carried sand into his eyes and left him blinking and blind with scalding tears that etched clean streaks down his grimy and sunburned cheeks.

They camped on their first night over the river in a dry and windy desolation. The sandy earth was pocked with clumps of yucca grass; it was hard to find space enough to set up the two tents. Yucca was as tough as hemp; every blade ended in a spike, and when the starved, stupid oxen tried to eat it, they jerked back in pain, for eating yucca was like trying to eat nails and razors.

Every wagon carried a water keg, and the kegs had been filled in the South Platte, and there was water for coffee. But they were all thirsty, and the coffee tasted like tar, and it did not assuage their yearning for water. Only the commanding, obstinate, lethal will of the old man kept them from guzzling water.

The stock had no water at all to drink, and there was nothing for them to eat. The oxen tramped restlessly about and lowered their heads and stretched their necks and bawled piteously. The mules settled into an ominous nervous standing, twitching in their sweaty skin, flicking their long ears, shaking their ugly heads, pathetic and dangerous.

The people ate dried buffalo meat preserved from their encounter with the herd down the Platte.

The old man had gathered buffalo chips down in the valley of the Platte. He heaped them up in a corner of Jason's wagon to use for fuel in this stretch of wasteland where no buffalo ever came. They were enough for a good fire, and the fire was cheerful, and they gathered around it in the declining day and looked into it with their unspoken longings, half-expecting, half-dreading another quarrel. They were all so dispirited, so worn out, that Jason did not read the Bible to them, and they did not sing.

The wind blew fitfully, but the air was heavy and sultry. With the going of the day, sheets of blue heat lightning flickered in a desultory way across the sky as if the heavens themselves were seized by a fit of nerves. As the night deepened, the silent and empty desert of sand all around them seemed to crackle with menace; and in the fitful lightning the air swarmed with portents none of them dared to read.

Gradually the old man lapsed into an easy cheer. He had satisfied himself that they would not drink water. He lounged on the ground at the very fringe of the faint and uncertain light cast by the little fire, a dim form melding with dark, keeping an alert ear trained on the great, unseen land out there, a rifle cradled in one lean arm. He spoke dreamily, eyes half-shut: "This time tomorrow night we'll be down in Ash Holler. Plenty of good water in Ash Holler. Sweet springs gushing up out of the ground. Lord, the springs are ice cold in Ash Holler! This time tomorrow night we'll have so much cold water to drink you'll forget we was ever thirsty. It's like the Garden of Eden, Ash Holler. Plenty of grass for the stock. Wood for fires. They's lots of trees in Ash Holler. And water. Lots of water."

"Ah, I don't see why you got to talk about water. Talk about water, and it makes us think how thirsty we are. Why don't you just hush up, old man?"

"Oh, I just like to talk, Asa," the old man said, unruffled. "And I reckon you got to listen. Lessen you want to turn in."

"What's Ash Holler?" Samuel's voice, curious and intent in the way that dull people are often inquisitive about things. The world so strange. Themselves not threatened but always baffled and struggling to be at home, to understand those mysteries other people find so easy.

"Ash Holler's a canyon," the old man said. "I don't reckon you can call it nothing else. Scooped out place. You know. A holler in the ground. We'll drop down off this high ground into Ash Holler, and you'll see for yourselves. You'll forget all about being miserable. You don't remember misery when you get done with it. Easiest thing in the world to forget."

Jason looked hopefully at the old man. "Trees," he said. "I love trees. I never knew how much I loved trees till we got out here."

"Trees!" Asa said. He was sitting on a wagon tongue. His face looked red in the firelight, a face that seemed to flare up and die away as the flames danced low, as if the fire came from inside him. "I believe all the trees in the whole damned country has been burnt up while we've been wandering around out here. I don't believe they's a single tree left in the wide world. California's a desert just like here. You'll see. Ah, what's this country good for anyway, Jason? You tell us, brother. You got an education. You got the answer to everything up there at Yale. Why did God make a place like this?"

Moody silence. Jason looked miserably into the fire. The wind picking up, dying, being still. Jason brooded, looked timidly at his brother, looked down again and said nothing.

Asa got up and stood over Jason, leering down at him. "I said, Jason, why did God make country like this? What's it for? Or maybe God just forgot this part of it. Maybe he was just playing around. What's the story, brother?"

Jason sighed and shook his head and would not look up. "This country's just to pass through, Asa," he said wearily. "It will make us appreciate what is out there. In California."

"I think this country's pretty in its own way," Ruth said. Another shadow in the dark. She sat in the sand with her heavy knees drawn up in front of her. Henry had sat down by her and leaned against her comforting bulk. "It's so wild. So different. I ain't never seen the like of plants around here. I wish I had somebody to tell me what all the plants are."

"Well, that there prickly devil of a plant is yucca," the old man said. "It ain't fit for nothing but making you cuss. No, I beg your pardon, ma'am. I know ain't nothing going to make *you* cuss. But me? I'm going to cuss ever time I get stung by a spike of yucca grass till the air catches on fire around my head." He chuckled; he liked Ruth.

"Well, just think what this land would be without it," Ruth said. "If it wasn't for the yucca grass, this country would just blow away."

"Then we ought to get out and start yanking all the yucca grass up by the roots," Asa said bitterly.

The old man snorted. "Asa, I swear to God! You're the biggest one bore I ever seen in my life. You won't let nobody be happy."

"Mr. Asa has got deep feelings," Ishtar Baynes said haughtily. "He knows this ain't no time to be happy. What with Rachael dead, that poor little thing!"

The old man turned back to look at her. "You know something, Mrs. Baynes? I ain't never in my whole life kilt a woman."

Ishtar Baynes sniffed. "I'm surprised. I figured you spent your winters killing women, children, old folks, and crippled people."

"Eh, law, woman," the old man said, rolling his eyes heavenward as if for patience. "Well, I tell you something. For once I think Jason's right. This country out here, it's got so much in it. One part of it makes you think another part's pretty. Ash Holler's in just the right place after all this. And you're even right about yucca, Miz Ruth. It's just the kind of grass that ought to be growing out here. It's made for this country. And this country's made for yucca. Like you and your old lady there, Clifford! How do you reckon you'd look if you was going around the country with a quality woman for your wife?"

"Sir!" Clifford Baynes said, mildly aroused.

"I do love things that grow," Ruth said with a sigh. "First thing I'm going to do this fall in California is plant me a big garden when we settle down. In the spring we'll have flowers. I bet we can grow azaleas in California."

Jason said: "I want flowers everywhere. We *will* have flowers. Acres and acres of flowers. Oh, I tell you all California is going to be a better life than any of us dreamed. You wait and see, Asa. I know you feel bad now. But just have patience; have faith."

"Well, I tell you what I think," Ruth said. Her mood was becoming more and more cheerful as she thought of growing things. "I say if we can make a flower garden and have a vegetable garden, too, and if we can make a living in California, it's going to be good enough for me. It don't even have to be better than Ohio. If California's the place for us, then it's going to be a good place. And I'm going to be happy when we get there!"

"We never should of left Ohio!" Asa said. "Ain't nothing going to work out for us. Nothing's ever worked out for us. We're just born to lose out. Daddy lost all his money. We're going to lose everything, too."

Jason flustered: "Now, Asa, really . . ."

Ruth: "We ain't born to lose, husband. We're born to live! And we're born to get along in the world. Of course we should of left Ohio! It was time for us to be going. Time for us to be finding something else!"

Jason, surprised and gratified: "Well, Ruth . . ."

Asa, exploding in fury and shouting: "What are you talking about, woman! You didn't want to go! You and Rebecca! My God! It was the only damn thing you ever agreed on in your life. You wanted to stay put and have your, your *goddamned rose garden!*"

The old man, mild as warm milk: "Asa, I'm going to have to buy you a book of manners and teach you how to talk to a lady. Your mamma sure didn't teach you nothing about being a gentleman!"

Ruth, calm herself: "It's all right, Mr. McMoultrie, Asa's
386

upset. Leave him be. That *was* the way I felt when we was back there, Asa. In Ohio. Maybe I'd still feel that way if we was back there now. But we ain't. We're out here, and I've changed my mind to fit the country. Like Mr. McMoultrie says about the yucca grass. I'm glad to be going to California. I know it's the right thing for us to be doing."

Asa, still furious: "How can you be talking about how good it is to go to California! If we hadn't come out here, to this desert, this, this *goddamned place*, we wouldn't of lost our baby! You're saying you're glad Rachael's dead, wife. *You're glad your daughter drowned!*"

Ruth, breaking now: "Poor little Rachael! Don't reproach me for her, husband. Please don't ..." She wept quietly, trying to control herself, to preserve her dignity in public. Ruth was not one to cry.

Adam understood that he hated Asa. He shot a glance at the old man. The old man was watching, still and tense, and he had that look on his face he had worn at the bar in Westport Landing ... Watching Asa ...

Asa, oblivious to everything but his wife, moving in for the kill against a defeated woman, suddenly his foe: "You said you was glad to be going to California! That must mean you're glad Rachael's dead. If we hadn't been going to California, Rachael would be alive!"

Ruth, controlling herself with all her strength: "You know I am not glad my baby is dead, Asa. But I know you cannot bring back the dead by wishing we'd done something else, something we didn't do. The dead are dead, husband! And life is for the living. And I think that if California cost us the life of our sweet little baby girl, well then, California has got to be the most wonderful place in the world. I'm looking forward to going there, husband, because we paid such a price to have it."

Asa, blazing with victory: "You are cruel and heartless, woman, and you don't have the natural human feeling for your own flesh. I wish I had never seen you. I wish we had never got married. You got a different spirit from me!"

The old man, getting to his feet (painfully, Adam thought) and hefting the rifle almost nonchalantly: "Thank God for that, I say, Asa. Now we've all heard enough out of you. If it wasn't for that good woman there and for your boy, I'd put a bullet in your belly with no more feeling than I'd waste on a mad dog! Now you hush up, or I might do it anyway."

387

Asa opened his mouth to rage at the old man, but the old man shut him off. "One more word out of you, and I'm going to kill you, Asa. I mean what I say."

Asa looked at the rifle pointed at him. A stillness like a caught breath infinitely extended froze them all to silence. Then Asa broke the spell of terror by whirling off into the dark. The pale and bluish lightning flickering mutely in the great distance seemed to be a dancing curtain blown by a supernatural wind to swallow him up. He was like a demonic spirit, Adam thought. And he wished that Asa would step on a rattlesnake and die.

Ruth sat there, clutching her terrified son. She quickly mastered her emotions, and while the rest of them sat in various moods of embarrassment and slowly relieved fear, she did her duty: "Poor Asa. He don't mean no harm. Rachael's death, it's just turned his head. But he'll be all right when we get settled. Don't you folks hold nothing against Asa. He's a good man down deep. The best man in the world. I know him better than anybody, I reckon. He's good, a good man."

Jason cleared his throat. "Asa has been cursed with a quick temper. He was the only one of us who ever tried to fight back against father."

"But daddy whipped him in the end," Samuel said morosely. "Like to of beat him to death with a leather belt. Asa's still got the scars from daddy's belt on his back."

"Asa wouldn't go in the room to see him when he lay dying, when he got to calling for his sons," Ruth said sadly, dully recounting a memory in the way people will repeat terrible stories, telling them over to dilute the horror. "He wouldn't go to the funeral. He wouldn't let any of us tell him about it."

"Well, that's all behind us now," Jason said with forced and unnatural brightness. "We are not going to take the past with us to California. Let the dead bury the dead. In California we're all going to make a new beginning."

It was very much what Ruth had said earlier, and sometimes Adam thought Jason was only an elaborate cavern, picking up the sounds others called to him and throwing them back like an echo of forced exuberance and hollow hope, resounding and resounding to die away at last.

And yet because they were so tense, Jason's bright words now released the bondage of anxiety that had been drawn around their hearts like thin, tight wire. The wire broke, and all of them began to think grand thoughts about California. And Harry was there with his quick tongue, helping them to form the dreams that all of them wanted to come true.

"That's right!" Harry cried. He jumped to his feet and began to walk excitedly back and forth.

"Whatever we were in the past doesn't count now! Whatever bad things we were, whatever sad thoughts we thought ... why, we can forget them all. Just like that!" He snapped his fingers, a sharp, quick sound and threw a hand forward at the emptiness, and a flicker of distant lightning illuminated his wind-blown silhouette with that slimly pointing finger showing like a monument to all the aspirations of humankind for centuries. "Out there is a new world! Out there is hope!" He spoke with genuine rapture and laughed, a cheerful, bubbling laugh, and as had happened so many times before, when Harry laughed, they all felt like laughing.

"I just want to have my garden," Ruth said happily. "That's all I want."

Harry turned toward her and hooked a thumb in his pants, waving his other hand. "You will have your garden. I promise you, Mrs. Jennings! You will have a jubilee of roses. Acres and acres of roses! Plantations of roses! Big white houses with red roses growing in vines up the walls, and yellow roses on the porches. White roses perfuming the windows. You wait and see! When we walk together at night, we will smell the salt smell of the sea, and we will smell the sweet smell of the roses. You may not be able to believe this now, up here in this dry wilderness, my friends, but we will carpet California with roses from the mountains to the ocean!"

Harry's enthusiasm swept through them all, and with him to guide their own blind imaginations, they were all transported to the edge of velvet green fields in California with stalwart houses and roses everywhere and a sweetness in the air that was like their faint conception of paradise.

Jason said, "Dr. Creekmore, you are a wonder! A wonder, sir. A wonder! I bless the day you joined us!"

It was Ishtar Baynes who dissented. "I don't like roses myself. They remind me too much of a house we lived in when I was a little girl. It smelled of roses, and I hated it. I ain't going to have a rose on the place when I get to California."

"Then for you, Mrs. Baynes," Harry shouted, "we'll have

pickles. Vats of brine and cellars filled with pickles and plenty of vinegar. I'm sure you'll like that just fine."

Everybody laughed, even Jason. But Ishtar Baynes did not even catch the joke. "I do like pickles, and that's a fact," she said.

# 47

They came down into Ash Hollow, and it was what the old man had predicted. They found wood and water and rest.

Ash Hollow!

A canyon maybe two hundred fifty feet deep and a mile across, opening off the bleak sand hills into the valley of the North Platte River. Walls of gray rock mottled with blue, crumbling down into the flat green saucer below. Ash Hollow with its ash grove and its dark and pointed cedars and its billowing cottonwoods with their pale foliage. And there were springs gushing their sweet, icy water up out of the ground, and in this time of year—verging on August—abundant grass grew on the canyon floor.

Calm there, too. The wind shut out by the embracing configuration of the hills, and within the canyon the summer heat came down strong and still. Ash Hollow, a blessed relief, something different—astonishingly different—from the barren sand hills they had to cross to get there.

"I'm so glad to be out of the wind!" Ruth said quietly. It was true for all of them.

They came down into Ash Hollow the way most people did. Down the great, steep, brown hill to the south, precipitous desolation descending dustily and perilously into the haven of rest.

They took the wagons down one at a time, lowering them with ropes tied at the rear axles and hitched to the mules, the mules blindfolded, braking the wagons by pulling back with all their might, resisting as mules will always resist when they feel themselves being dragged forward and cannot see where they are going.

Blessed be mules! With the mules braking the heavy wagons, they came slowly and safely down. It took them most of the afternoon.

Only Rebecca gave them trouble in the descent. She in her room in Ohio could not get out and walk down the way the rest of them did. The furniture inside began to shift, and her rocking chair with her in it slid forward to collide with the makeshift toilet, and she screamed that it was a storm striking to carry the house away. Jason said, "Mrs. Baynes, won't you ride inside with Rebecca to keep her company? Maybe you could help ease her mind. She likes you so much."

But Ishtar Baynes looked at the long, dangerous slope and calculated her chances if the wagon should break loose. She decided that she would walk. "Mr. Jennings, I'd rather ride with that poor woman more than anything in the world. I swear I would. But I've noticed that when she's upset like that, company just upsets her more. I don't think it'd be right if I was to ride with her. I think I owe it to the poor dear soul to leave her alone." And before Jason could argue, Ishtar Baynes set off in a cloud of dust down the hill.

Rebecca shrieked at the top of her voice, and the old man, straining with the mules, roared at Samuel. "You got to tell that woman of yours the truth. You got to make her get some sense into her head. Tell her she ain't in Ohio. Tell her she's got to stop making like she is. If she was my woman, I'd go in that wagon right this minute and yank her out of there by the hair and make her look at where we are and hush her up!"

Samuel looked ready to cry. "No," he said stubbornly. "I ain't going to do that."

The old man kept on. "Well if she was my woman, I'd let her know who was running things. I'd slap her across the mouth, slap some sense into her head."

"Don't be talking that way about my Rebecca," Samuel said. The words were an appeal from the heart.

"Ah," the old man said, "ah, you're all crazy! Let her cry. What do I care?"

When they brought the wagon down, Samuel hurried inside. They could hear Rebecca weeping and Samuel trying to comfort her, speaking to her in a low, consoling murmur that even at a distance sounded like abject pleading. But it was a long time before Rebecca was quiet and much longer still before Samuel came out again, looking guiltily at the old man and slinking off to himself full of silence.

The canyon floor was littered with relics of the great emigration. And they grew accustomed to the sight of Ishtar Baynes prowling through ruined possessions and grieving that so many fine things were forever spoiled.

There were graves in Ash Hollow, too. They thought of Rachael's grave back there, and it struck them all with an intolerable strangeness that she was gone forever.

There was a tumbledown shack erected at an unknown time for no reason anybody could think of. In it were dozens of messages pinned up for people who were following on the way West, and some of them were illegible with weather and years old, stained with rain and snow. And there were other letters carefully sealed and addressed to people back East in the empty hope that someone passing in that direction would take the letters along.

For them Ash Hollow was a glory. "It's like paradise!" Promise cried aloud, laughing. She tossed her long black hair and let the light play darkly in it, and she walked around in wonder, cautiously, as shy as a stranger in a magic land that might vanish if she said too much or put her feet down too hard.

Adam watched her and reflected that she had become more beautiful on the trail. Her face was more mature, and she was strong and healthy, and being loved by Harry had made her more confident. She looked directly into Adam's face when they spoke, the way Jessica did with people. Her nervous grin did not make spasms in her mouth as often as it had in the beginning. She was still very quiet, and Adam thought she might be beginning to be wise.

But after talking as much as he had with Jessica, he was mildly disappointed when he talked with Promise. Promise did not think complicated thoughts. Something was beautiful or ugly. She was uncomfortable; she was at ease. Harry loved her; she loved Harry. California would be good. They would be happy there. The trail across the country was something they would forget. She tried to forget it even as it was under their feet. Adam found that it was hard to talk with her just because she insisted on being so happy about what was coming. Still, there was an innocence and a joy in Promise that made Adam long for her in a way that people long for the inaccessible. Promise was unspoiled—and completely beyond his reach. Adam, looking at her, wished things could be different.

They could drink water in Ash Hollow. Jason seized a dipper out of his wagon and filled it with water, and they passed it around. "Our chalice!" he said. They laughed and drank from the dipper, and the tin and the cold made this water better than any water they had ever tasted. And afterwards, for as long as any of them lived, every one of them in being thirsty remembered the water they drank in Ash Hollow.

When they had made camp and savored their triumph over the sand hills and rested in the peacefulness, Jason said, exulting, "This *is* a new beginning! It's not just something we decide now. The land tells us! This land here is a foretaste of what will come in California." It was all airy and just a little nonsensical. But all of them were happy, and they laughed with him and passed the dipper back and forth and humored Jason because they were in such good humor themselves.

"I'm going to take a bath!" Jessica announced.

"A bath!" Ishtar Baynes made a face. "Why, you'd have to take off your *clothes* to take a bath!"

Jessica laughed. She had dimples in her cheeks when she laughed. "I do believe that's right, Mrs. Baynes."

"You'd be *naked!*"

"I believe you are right again, Mrs. Baynes." Jessica flashed her cool smile. "I have never been able to take my clothes off without being naked as a consequence."

"*Naked,* with *men* around!"

"Highly improper and indecent!" Clifford Baynes said, looking at Jessica, measuring her full breasts and fine hips with his eyes.

"We can go over there, to one of the other springs," Jessica said. "If the men stay here where they belong, they will not see our nakedness, Mrs. Baynes. Why don't you come along? You could use a good bath."

"Are you trying to tell me I'm dirty?" Mrs. Baynes cried.

Jessica laughed with a self-possession that was enough to make Ishtar Baynes hate her. "Well, I'm certainly dirty. I suppose you are quite dirty yourself, Mrs. Baynes."

"I never heard of such a thing!" Ishtar Baynes said, as if she had just been insulted in the most shocking way that anyone could imagine. "I mean, when *I* take a bath again, it's going to be in California! And I ain't going to tell no bunch of men about it before I take my clothes off. I'm going to take a bath in private! Like a lady. I ain't going to be sitting there in no tub stark *naked* with men *knowing* I'm naked!" It was the most honest display of emotion anyone had seen in her.

Jessica only laughed and went on, taking Promise with her. Ruth decided that she would go, too. Ishtar Baynes stayed behind, irate and upset. "You see there, Mr. Asa. It's that Jessica woman again. She ain't like the rest of us, honest and God-fearing and modest. She's wicked. And I'm afraid she's going to lead your dear, sweet wife off on the wrong path. Now personally I like Mrs. Ruth. I mean, the real Mrs. Ruth. The one that ain't listening all the time to mischief. But Mrs. Ruth, she just ain't no match for that Jessica woman. Jessica's an *outsider!*"

Adam could not hear the words. He heard only the hiss of her voice, and he saw Mrs. Baynes's long, thin neck bobbing up and down. Asa listened darkly, nodding and looking like a man hearing evil tidings. He was frightening to look at.

Adam had not thus far been able to comprehend Ishtar Baynes. He had supposed that her constant malice had some purpose to it, some malignant plan she had contrived to take over the company—something being carried out with reason and design.

But at Ash Hollow, he began to revise his thoughts about her, and he arrived at a certain simple understanding.

She was a woman without past or future, a woman who might as well go on to California, making that decision in Nashville after an illogical peregrination south and west from Maryland. Her life was as aimless as her origins, a deadweight tumbling through the universe of humankind, through America, in no orbit, having no sun, a fine grain of anarchy grinding in the gears of the world's great clock. And because she was herself without restraint and without destiny, her only consequence was to destroy or at least to jar and disturb the orderly realms she passed through in her accidental progress through space.

She was malicious because that was her nature. She had made chaos because in chaos was the condition where she was at home. She sowed destruction because destruction corresponded to the broken fragments that in their very disorder made up the only soul she possessed. And she had no motives beyond the chaos itself. It was all thoughtless and spontaneous, in the same impersonal, natural way that hawks must fly, that snakes must coil and bite, that mosquitoes must suck blood and bees sting.

Yet there was patience in her aimless malice. And in the calm of Ash Hollow, Adam had time to recognize that Harry was in great danger. *He thinks he's whipped her, but he ain't.* Harry seemed to be in command of the universe, but Ishtar Baynes was waiting . . .

*Somebody ought to kill her!* Adam's sudden thought pricked him like a needle in the interior of his brain, something burning at the point. He looked at her angular form standing against the smooth and serene calm of twilight in Ash Hollow, and Ishtar Baynes glanced back at him with indifferent contempt. She had said her nasty things about the clean women who came leisurely back from their bath, scrubbed and laughing, glowing with pleasure, and combing their long, clean hair. Ishtar Baynes felt no more sense of danger when she looked at Adam than a very large snake might have felt before the gaze of a very tiny mouse. Adam was a servant in her mind; servants were not worth fooling with.

*Somebody ought to kill her.*

The thought had begun in him like a tiny flame, yet it quickly flared to an awful conviction. Adam looked at Harry, so carefree and confident. He looked at Promise, saw how easily she could be hurt, and saw, too, with a biting twinge of jealousy how Harry and Promise loved each other. And he thought, *I will kill that woman before I let her destroy anybody.* He put a hand down to the butt of the steel pistol at his belt. He remembered with a sense of unreality that he had had the courage to kill the Indian. And he believed he could summon the resolution to kill Ishtar Baynes.

*Just wait till she makes her move.* He took pleasure in imagining how startled she would be when he pointed the pistol at her. He experienced such relief at his fantasy that he let Ash Hollow fill him with bliss. Ash Hollow was so fine. Adam had the power to release them all from the curse of Ishtar Baynes. And he believed he could use that power when the time came. His resolution cleansed his mind. He sang under his breath as he brushed the amber oxen down while they fed in the sweet grass.

Adam, Harry, the old man, and Henry took a bath after the women. The old man brought his rifle along. He insisted that he stand guard while the others bathed. He insisted with equal vehemence that Adam hold the rifle and keep a lookout while he dipped himself into the clear water.

Henry laughed and splashed Harry, and Harry laughed back and splashed futilely. Harry without his glasses in the water. Sightless as a mule in a coal mine. But he was happy, his modesty forgotten.

The water was cold. It ran with pleasant strength and massaged tired muscles. Adam shut his eyes and held his breath and clung to the stony bottom and felt the swift current rush through his long hair. They had fatty lye soap that had come from Ohio. It made a gray, smoky-looking lather. But they soaped themselves all over with it and rinsed themselves and did it all over again. Adam lay naked in the water and felt free and good.

"Do you think I can ever be a doctor?" Henry said.

"Sure you can," Harry said, superior as a God. He lay sprawled in the water like some ungainly fish and talked wisely to Henry about what a young man ought to be studying to prepare himself for a medical career.

"You need to learn about medicines. I tell you the truth, my boy. When I look at that bag of medicines I carry, I feel that I have the secrets of the universe in my black bag. It's a wonderful feeling. A feeling akin to magic."

Adam laughed to himself. Harry was fun to see, believing his lies. And Henry was looking at Harry with the rapt delight of a child at Christmas.

All of them had faces and hands burned a deep, walnut brown by the sun. But the rest of them was pink once the dirt had been scoured away. Adam looked at Harry's pale buttocks and thought that he looked very much like a baby. He wondered suddenly at the mystery of men as he had wondered about the mystery of women. Men were something else when they were naked. They assumed poses in their clothing, station, place in the world. But Adam liked them better in the buff. Harry, stripped of all his clothes, was like Henry. A child dreaming.

The old man had Rebecca on his mind. He could not quite understand her. "What's really going on with her?" he asked. "Samuel and that Rebecca woman? Do you reckon Samuel believes she thinks she's back there in Ohio? Me, I don't believe it."

"Ah," Harry said easily, "he pretends because Jason tells

396

him to. Samuel believes Jason's smart, and he loves his wife. I tell you, that is the most amazing thing to me. Samuel loves Rebecca."

"You got to love who you're married to, don't you?" Henry said.

Harry laughed and splashed in the direction of that innocent voice. "Well, it's harder for some than it is for others."

"That wagon ain't no room," the old man said.

"You gentlemen need to see plays," Harry said in an unruffled, affable way. "All you need on a stage is a piece of cardboard that looks like a wall, and you got a wall. Or you need a window painted in the cardboard, and you got a drawing room. That's what Rebecca's wagon is. A stage. And she's an actress. And a good actress always believes the part she's playing."

"I just feel sorry for Samuel," the old man said. "Jason treats him like dirt. Jason's the one," he said ominously. Looking at Henry, he hushed and chewed on his lower lip. Then he said, "Somebody ought to whip the shit out of Jason!"

"Uncle Jason's *good!*" Henry said, looking around as if he could not believe what he had heard.

"Sure he's good," Harry said in a soothing tone. "And he has some profound ideas."

"Ah, bullshit," the old man said. "You ain't with him now. You can talk sense."

Harry laughed. "I always talk sense. Don't you know that? And besides. This boy here . . ."

"Bullshit," the old man said. "Henry here, he's one of us. He ain't one of them. Ain't you, boy?"

Henry was pleased and uncomfortable. "I ain't going to tell nothing."

"Sure you ain't," the old man said. "I don't like Jason. I've decided he's a bad 'un. Looks down on Samuel. Looks down on the world. Thinks he's God Almighty, pope of the prairies! Acts like a simpleton. Full of the milk of human kindness, just because he knows that's the way to get away with murder with some folks. Pretend to be kind. Sincere. Me, I'd like to bust him one in the mouth. Do something to knock that damn fool childishness out of his head. Make him grow up or die."

The old man's cracked voice vibrated with a savory anticipation of violence. But Harry remained unaffected, splashing

397

about in a benign mood. "I just think of his vision. There are not many people with vision in the world."

"Good thing, too, if you ask me," the old man said. "Folks with vision, you can't get them to mind their own business. You can't get them to be real folks. I'd like to kick the shit out of Jason."

Adam said nothing. He was mildly surprised. He lay back on his shoulders in the cold water and looked up at the sky arching above him, marble blue in the late afternoon sun, strings of clouds going pink as the day drew to an end. He was surprised because he nourished the same perverse idea the old man expressed about Jason. The desire to pound him in the head. Hit Jason until the man came up with an honest reaction. Even if it was only to cry for help.

"Well," Harry was saying easily to the old man, "if what you're saying is true—and I'm not saying it is true—maybe it's better the way things are. If Jason's just pretending to be innocent, maybe we'd better let him be. Maybe if he stopped pretending, he'd be so bad nobody could bear him. Now personally I'll tell you what I think about poor old Rebecca." He laughed again in that free and joking way of his. "I just don't think I could bear to have her and Mrs. Baynes out in the open together. I just wish we could find some way to make Mrs. Baynes think she was back in Maryland where she belongs."

"I seen a broom in the back of Jason's wagon," Adam said. "Maybe we could give it to her and let her ride back home."

They all laughed, even the old man. Then it was his turn to bathe.

Jessica made bread in the Dutch oven and fixed brown beans, boiling them in the pure water, and the bacon was delicious that night. They drank the water like wine, passing it around in Jason's dipper. They forgot that they had ever been dry and thirsty and filthy with sand and sweat. They reclined in the lush grass after they had eaten, and they were satisfied.

"I don't believe I have ever felt such peace," Jessica said. And that was the way all of them felt until the Indians rode in.

Harry—of all people—saw them first.

He thought they must be a figment of his tortuous sight. But they inserted themselves across his vision with an undeniable finality that convinced him that they existed in the same world he did. He jumped up speechless. He knew that this was the moment he was to die. He had not expected death to come when the world was so sweet.

Adam, looking idly at him, did not comprehend. He was alarmed, not by the advancing Indians, whom he did not see, but by the furious transformation in Harry's face. Layers and layers of carefully plastered and gaudily painted illusion had all at once cracked and crumbled and washed away in an unseen storm.

Yet with equal abruptness Harry's jaw set again under his blond beard. His weak eyes hardened. It was Harry, acting now with that courage of the hero he willed to be, who ran to the back of Jason's wagon and brought out Adam's two rifles. He handed one over to Adam and took the other one himself. And he stationed himself before the campfire ready to die without shame.

By the time Harry moved, the rest of them had seen the Indians, too. They were riding in from the mouth of the canyon in purposeful single file and drawing near deliberately and self-confidently on their shining ponies.

The old man moved as swiftly as a great cat crouching to pounce. He snatched up his rifles and primed them and handed one over to Samuel. So they had four guns at the ready as a troop of thirty Indian braves rode in on them, braves so handsome and so sinewy and so finely made that Adam had never seen any humanity like them.

Adam perceived at once how desperate the predicament of the whites was. It was not just when he counted the Indians and read the strength in their bodies and the calm in their bearing; it was when he saw how tense the old man was, when he thought of how isolated they were here in this place, that he knew they could die.

"Why, they're beautiful!" Promise cried. She jumped up by the fire and stood gaping at them, filled with terror and admiration. She went spontaneously to Harry, coming to him naturally as though some powerful magnetism drew them together in danger. And just as spontaneously Harry put an arm around her, to protect her as best he could. He stood there leaning forward in his determined courage, awkwardly clutching the rifle (useless to him) with one hand, embracing her, nearsightedly and doggedly peering at the coming Indians with an expression of worried and baffled concentration.

At that moment Adam's heart melted with affection for

399

Harry. Harry was like a violet, improbably growing in the scalding sun. But Harry willed with all his might to be a tree in the wasteland, and Promise came to him, and Adam loved them both and was ready to die for them.

But there was no time for sentiment. "They're Sioux," the old man said in a low voice, solemn, reverent, and perhaps resigned. "And we're damn lucky. They're coming back from a good hunt! But you don't never know about the Sioux. Good hunt might give 'em ambition. Make 'em decide to carry off a few scalps and some white women to boot. Damn!" His voice, soft and tense, vibrated like a spring.

Adam could see the ponies bearing travois now. Every travois carried a burden of dark red meat tied with thongs, or else the black, hairy hides of the buffalo.

*They won't be wanting to eat our oxen.*

Relief, momentary and thin, quickly gone. He saw Jessica; he saw Promise. His imagination swirled with terror. And like a tremendous hand squeezing his heart and his bowels, hatred for these Indians clamped down hard on his insides. He and the rest of the whites were helpless. These Indians could molest them and go unpunished. Adam impotent even with a gun in his hands. One bullet! Then the pistol. Then ... He felt the malicious injustice of a universe that could bring him to death, and Jessica and Promise ... He muttered under his breath. "Shit." His word was an obscenity he hoped God could hear.

Yet even in his bitterness, he knew what Promise meant when she called them beautiful. He had never imagined that any men could look like these Sioux. Tall and straight. They sat their rugged little ponies with the indifferent and masterly calm of men who had been born to horses, who had ridden on horseback before they walked on their own two legs, who fought on horseback, hunted on horseback, slept there, took their pleasure on horseback, riding like the wind, their horses strong appendages to their own strong bodies ...

But their faces were more striking than anything else about them. They were smoky red and regally calm, set in an arrogance that was both innocent and unself-conscious, finding in themselves such complete confidence that not one of these Indians could ever suspect or imagine that anyone else on earth could be his equal.

The chief of the band was cautious and scornful. He looked over the four white men holding the rifles. He inspected with obvious admiration Samuel's huge bulk bent over the rifle like a giant holding a pencil. And in the great silence suddenly enthralling the cool evening, a silence deepened by the quiet, rhythmic tattoo of hoofbeats, Adam could almost hear an electric sparking in this chief's heart. His face, taking in the four frail rifles, was the face of a warrior whose life had been a hard school for courage, survival the daily diploma for success and death the duncecap for failure. And now he was pleased with the rifles because they offered him the chance of death, and the chance of death was a chance to live and perhaps to die like a chief before his braves, for to him death was that great sea that granted a beautiful coast to life.

The chief led his riders in a great circle around the solitary white encampment. Adam gazed at the stolid faces staring back at him, curious and proud eyes flashing over the whites, lingering sensually on the women. But having circled them in leisurely speculation, the Indians seemed to dismiss them. They took their ponies to the spring across the canyon and assembled in maddening calm to take counsel, talking and looking occasionally over at the whites, who stood in a ragged bunch, waiting to react to the next gesture that the Indians would make.

"What are they going to do?" Jessica. Her voice as steady as a fine clock ticking, a woman with wound steel springs in her heart. Adam admired her, and he was more ashamed of his own heart pounding in fear.

"They're deciding if they're going to kill us," the old man said laconically. "You women better get in them wagons."

Jessica laughed. "You said once you would kill us before you let us fall into the hands of the Indians, Mr. McMoultrie."

Adam was stunned at her laughter. The calm of it. The old man did not take his eyes off the Indians. "Adam," he said flatly. "Give Jessica here your pistol."

"My pistol . . ." Adam babbled.

"Give it to her. I think she'll know what to do with it if the time comes."

Mechanically Adam removed the pistol from his belt and primed it with five little copper caps. Jessica, smiling still, glided to him, her hand outstretched.

Adam looked at her. Their eyes touched like fingertips. He wanted to cry. His voice quavered and embarrassed him.

"You pull the hammer back. Like this, ma'am. Then you pull the trigger."

Jessica was cool. "Thank you, Adam. I'll remember." She took the gun in her hand. "Promise. Come along."

"Oh, I hate Indians!" Ruth cried in exasperation. "I hope when we get to California we won't never see an Indian again! I hope we can sit out on our porch in the evening and watch our neighbors go by like civilized folks."

"Well, personally, if you ask me, Indians is just men!" Ishtar Baynes cried, looking at Jessica, looking at the pistol. "And I'm going to see Rebecca, and I don't want nobody with no guns around me!" Her voice was nearly hysterical.

"I think I'd better accompany my wife," Clifford Baynes said.

The old man swung his gun around. "You stay right here, Clifford. You ain't much, but you're a man! We need men to make a show."

"Sir, I will go where I please!" Clifford Baynes turned pale.

"You'll go to the devil sooner than you think if you don't stand still."

Clifford Baynes wavered, and then his knees seemed to collapse and he sat down cross-legged by the fire, gaping at the Indians across the canyon, hypnotized by terror.

*He's more afraid than I am!* Adam felt a foolish satisfaction.

"This is madness ..." Jason started off in indignation, looked at Jessica, glanced back at the Indians and lost the thread of his discourse and fixed his eyes on them as if they were something he had never even considered before.

"Go on, get in the wagon!" the old man commanded Jessica, who still stood by, thinking something none of them could read. "Tie the ends down and keep out of sight!" he called softly, as she moved off. "And take that young 'un with you." He nodded toward Henry.

"No! I don't want to go," Henry cried. "I want to stay out here. With the other men."

"You heard what the man said!" Asa yelled. He jumped up. Trembling with terror himself, he could not tolerate courage in his son. "I mean for you to get the hell in that there wagon, or I'm going to slap your head off."

"I said I want to stay here!" Henry suddenly bold and unflinching before his father.

402

*By God!* Adam's heart swelled.

Asa rushed toward his son screaming in outrage. "You get in that goddamned wagon!"

"Hush!" the old man said. "Let him be. Boy's got to be a man sometime. If he don't want to go inside, that means he's old enough not to go."

"I *told* you to get inside!" Asa advanced on his son, a hand backthrown to strike. Henry ducked his head to take the blow, but he did not move his feet to run.

The old man raised his voice just a note. "You leave that boy alone, Asa. You hit him, and I swear by God above, I'll kill you dead."

Asa stopped and dissolved suddenly. An awful look of hatred thrown against the old man. The old man looked back at him with contempt. Asa not big enough to make him afraid.

Henry stayed, moving close to Adam, away from his father. The women disappeared into the wagons.

And the Sioux, finished with their palaver, mounted again.

"It's now," the old man said.

"I didn't tell Promise I love her!" Harry said suddenly.

"She knows," the old man said. "Don't worry."

The Sioux came suddenly wheeling their ponies around and galloping back across the canyon floor, crying and shouting and pumping their guns in the air in time to their thundering charge, their racing ponies raising a storm of sandy dust.

Harry sighed and shook his head. "I sure as hell would feel better if they were chasing a fox!"

The old man turned around and shot him a look of complete mystification, and Adam laughed in spite of his terror. "Don't shoot till you see one of 'em point a gun at us!" the old man yelled. "I got a hunch they're just playing!"

He was right. Like children in a schoolyard game, the Indians came pounding down almost atop the little band of whites—and veered away, laughing with heads thrown back to the sky. They swung around and came back, galloping and yelling. This time they passed so close that Adam could have reached out and slapped one copper leg as a pony flew by. Now, thirty feet away, the band pulled back on their ponies and stopped. They dismounted, sliding off the butts of their mounts and coming to a stand all in a row, holding their weapons triumphantly aloft, laughing still, proud of their horsemanship, proud of their agility, proud of the fear they had plastered on white faces.

Only the chief remained mounted.

*Goddamn them to the pit of hell!* Adam's heart thudded so hard that he saw double. He could not see to aim. *Couldn't shoot if I wanted to. Goddamn! Goddamn! Goddamn!*

Now the chief, straight as a knife on his pony, grave and sure and scornful, kicked his mount and came riding down on the old man. Chief to chief. Adam thought again of the schoolyard. Recess. One boy challenged another. A game before spectators. *Shoot him off his horse!* End of all games.

Adam longed to shoot; his big hands knotted and ached around his rifle. But he did not dare. Not with some thirty armed warriors standing nearby, eyes as hard as granite chips. Almost on top of the old man, the chief leaped yelling off his pony and came to an astonishing standing halt, crouching forward, fighting on tiptoe for balance, not five feet from the old man's face. The chief held a musket and wore an eager, expectant grin. *What do you think of that, old man?*

Shawnee Joe did not flinch. Even his eyes did not blink. He spat a jet of tobacco juice into the grass at the chief's widely spread feet.

*Old man, whatever it is, you've got it!*

It was the chief whose expression was marvelous to watch. His finely carved face all joyful and wild, like a child in frolic. Behind him the braves set up a cry, a rude cacophony of chanting notes, a ritual and guttural chorus to the chief's triumph. And Adam perceived something about Sioux society that he was never to forget. It was all game and spectacle. To act so that others of one's own good kind applauded. Take away the spectacle, and the Sioux might as well disappear, too.

The chief unleashed a cataract of words. He held his musket up like a great baton, giving metallic force to his oration, gesturing with it in time to his speech.

"He looks very like a barbarian shaking his spear at the Romans," Harry said cheerfully. He was not afraid. Adam saw how calm he was. More truly calm than the old man. *Harry!*

With his free hand the chief made a fist and pounded his chest. His braves murmured their enthusiasm for what he was saying, resonating like a symphony of drums. He flung words

404

at the whites, and Adam felt the violent and nightmarish terror that comes when frightened people feel themselves swept away by a flood they cannot understand, unable to find a hold for their hands, every syllable spoken to him a slippery stone that he might grasp only in vain.

And so he was relieved almost to wild tears when the old man spoke up, at home and fluent in the same dissonant tongue that the chief spoke.

*He had a Sioux squaw. Maybe more than one.*

And now the two of them, white chief and red, spoke quietly for a few minutes, with appalling dignity, feeling each other out. The Sioux braves looked on this strange white man who knew the language of the people and granted him the grudging admiration of magicians who have come upon one not of their guild who is nonetheless practicing their lore.

Jason came striding up by the old man, foolishly grinning, waiting to be introduced, resenting the respect and attention mistakenly given to a subordinate.

*He don't want nobody to forget that he's chief around here.*

The old man turned somberly to Jason, to them all, and spoke with measured gravity. "His name is Little Thunder. He is their chief. They're on their way home from the hunt. It's been a good hunt. Be careful, Jason. They're cocky as hell."

"Well make them welcome!" Jason spoke in his most contrived voice. The one that boomed out hearty welcomes. The one that came ringing out of his chest, deep as a drum. The one he had used to greet Adam and Harry so many miles back. Ingratiating, superior, and false. "Ask them if we can give them anything to eat."

The old man half-smiled. The smile collapsed in wonder at Jason's stupidity. "I'll be damned, Jason."

"So you may be," Jason said haughtily, tired of the old man, tired of being pushed around. "Just tell him what I said please!" Jason's chin went up, and he half-shut his eyes. The old man took a deep breath and translated.

A river of words crashing over rocks now, breaking up into shards, showering syllables against one another. The old man saying much more than Jason had said. Maybe apologizing. The Indians listened with deep attention, bent forward, heads cocked.

*Like the Egyptians listening to Moses when he stood before Pharaoh!*

Then they burst into a raucous shout of laughter. Jason looked around indignantly, unable to understand. A man slapped by inferiors. His skin pale and glossy with sweat, high forhead shining in the gloom.

Little Thunder let the laughter die into grinning insolence. He spoke again, a harsh flailing of insults. You did not have to know his language to understand how his eyes flashed with contempt. He frowned mightily, slapped his naked thigh, pointed at Jason with a scornful hand, threw that hand back, palm open, to show the whites something, and all the other Sioux screamed with laughter. Jason humiliated, crimson, angry, his eyes twisting about in amazed fury.

"He says they got plenty buffalo to eat," the old man said calmly. "He wants to know if you need anything. He says you don't look too good to him. He says you look like bleached buffalo shit."

*Kill all the damn buffalo!* Adam thought fiercely. *Then see how proud these red sons of bitches will be.*

He hated himself instantly for the thought. Pure malice. The Indians had beaten him in a game. Change the rules then. Kill the buffalo. Steal their goddamned pride. Put them in their place. Copper bastards. Listen to them laugh then. Ha-ha!

Little Thunder spoke to his braves, and the Sioux howled with laughter. Baiting the white men with their scorn. White men inferior. Lost the game. Must look up to the Sioux. Like every other creature inferior to the Sioux on the green face of the sweet land.

Jason blushed a deeper red, angry now. His face dark in the deepening twilight. Jason clinging to his dignity. "Ask them if they'd like some coffee." His mouth tight, puckered with styptic words, vinegar thoughts.

The old man translated. Little Thunder flung his beautiful dark head back, looked disdainfully down his long nose with complete contempt. He delivered himself of another rush of words. And from it they all could hear one word distinctly, the English word every Indian on the plains seemed to know. Whiskey.

The old man resolutely shook his head. Lied with a lawyer's legal lying. Jason Jennings had no whiskey. Every night when he made his shelter of canvas and buffalo robes, the old man stowed away his four crockery jugs with the precious liquid in them. He nipped at one of the jugs. "Just to help the hurting in my hands." he told Adam and Harry. And sometimes Harry had a taste, too. But now, the vital liquid hidden, the old man stared at the Sioux with the steadfast and innocent gaze of a professional liar, a lawyer, a judge, or even a President. No whiskey.

Little Thunder, accustomed to liars, frowned on him, spoke words of outraged, furious, and contemptuous disappointment. Behind him the braves broke into murmurings of discontent. An ugliness to the sound. Like white water in a swift river over jagged rocks.

In the end the old man placated the Sioux with an offering of tobacco. He produced his ancient clay pipe and an old and very worn leather sack of Virginia's finest. The Sioux crowded around, squatting down in a circle, jabbering now like children. And Adam enjoyed the childish enthusiasm, the crafty joy, the triumphant excitement of Indians about to be given a treat for nothing.

Jason did not smoke, although he sat with them. He burned because the Sioux had settled on the old man as the chief. "It is a filthy weed," Jason grumbled, though he had never mentioned an aversion to tobacco before. "I will not compromise every principle I have."

The old man tried to explain why Jason would not smoke. But Little Thunder explained in one word. "Mormon!" The chief spat into the fire. Samuel and Asa smoked as they had smoked with the Kansa. Adam smoked, taking a whiff and holding it in his mouth. He had never used tobacco. But now he decided that he liked to smoke. He sat with his rifle across his legs, and the night air was cool, and both fire and smoke were easeful to him.

Young Henry sat in the circle with them and smoked like the rest. It was a strange sight. The grave, blond child holding the long clay pipe with astonishing expertise, copying the Indians without a hitch and taking the smoke in his mouth without a sign of aversion or being sick.

Little Thunder was enchanted with Henry. He put out a hand and rubbed it through the boy's tousled blond hair, felt the muscles of Henry's strong arms, and when Henry smiled bravely up at him, Little Thunder made a loud exclamation of pleasure and spoke hurriedly with obvious admiration. The old man looked stern and grim. "Little Thunder says he

would like to have this boy here as his own son. He says giv
him to the Sioux and in ten years Henry will be a big chie
like Little Thunder."

Asa looked astonished. Anger flamed up in his face. "No
You tell that red son of a bitch to keep his filthy paws off m
son!"

The old man fixed Asa with a cold stare and turned slowl
to Little Thunder and spoke in Sioux. Little Thunder nodde
gravely and looked at Asa and nodded again and said some
thing full of meaning and regret. "What did you say!" As
hissed.

"I told him you were proud of your boy. I told him yo
were happy Little Thunder liked your boy, but I told him yo
wanted to make Henry a big chief with the white man. And
tell you, Asa, to shut your goddamned mouth now and kee
still because I ain't good at making up lies. And if I tell Littl
Thunder what you really say, he will take your hair and you
prick and your boy in five minutes, and you ain't going to
have nothing left to be proud about, and you ain't going to
be able to be mad at anybody in the world."

The old man's voice was mild and conversational. But i
was enough. Asa subsided, throwing the old man a look fille
with such hate that Adam cringed. All that emotio
compressed in Asa, ready to explode, and the old man indifferent to it. Asa less to Shawnee Joe than the bite of a
mosquito, for the old man would have flicked a mosquito
away.

Little Thunder presided in regal nonchalance next to the
old man. Shawnee Joe held his rifle almost idly, the long barrel straight up like a lance. But Adam saw that the old man's
gnarled right hand never left the trigger. Little Thunder knew
Shawnee Joe would kill him first if trouble came. The chief
was honored. Part of the great game.

Very slowly Little Thunder understood that Jason had
some authority here. The expression in his eyes was unbelieving at first. He expostulated with the old man, speculating,
searching Jason with his sharp eyes, not finding what he
sought—the secret to this white man's medicine that made
him a chief.

"He thinks you own some kind of magic," Shawnee Joe
said, with just a hint of that ironic smile. "It's the only way
he can explain you being a chief."

"Tell him I have the magical gift of civilized intelligence,"

408

Jason said darkly. "Tell him I'm sorry he can never know what that means."

The old man translated, and the Sioux nodded with satisfaction at each other, and Adam knew that the old man had lied again but knew also that he could not keep it up. Jason would get them killed yet.

It was Little Thunder, not Jason, who knew what the manners of the plains required. One chief must recount his coups to another, those blows struck in brave violence that had raised him to be a chieftain. It was his solemn duty to make this petty alien chief all the more honored and grateful that someone with the heroic reputation of Chief Little Thunder had stooped so low as to smoke the pipe with a band as miserable as this.

So Little Thunder talked in a curiously hypnotic singsong, making gestures with his hands, pumping, stabbing, pointing, and the old man sat next to him in stolid lassitude and translated Little Thunder's tales in a mood of timeless endurance appropriate to Indian stories.

"He says to tell you that when he was a very little boy, he kilt a brown bear single-handed in the Black Hills with not nothing but a spear. He crawled into the bear's cave and jammed the spear down the bear's gullet, and that bear's skin is still the one Little Thunder sits on to judge his people."

"Well," Jason said, frowning more deeply, "tell him I suppose he ought to be glad he came out alive. Tell him I hope he didn't go around doing foolish things like that all the time. I'd say that was a very childish story."

"He also says that when he was a very small boy, he kilt a running wolf with a shot from a bow. He tells you that was before the people had guns like they do now."

"The people? What people?"

"The people is the Sioux, Mr. Jennings."

Jason managed a fastidious little laugh. "Tell him he has a very narrow conception of humanity, Mr. McMoultrie. Tell him there is much more to humanity than the Sioux. The Sioux are insignificant in the history of the world."

"I can't tell him that, Jason." It was obviously difficult for the old man to control himself before Jason's willful stupidity.

"Why not? You afraid of insulting something as ridiculous as this, this preposterous savage?"

"I am afraid of insulting him, Jason. I am afraid of getting

409

us kilt, Jason. I'm afraid of getting your wife and all the other women in there kilt or worse. Yes, I'm afraid."

"I do think you should be reasonable, Mr. Jennings," Clifford Baynes said. His face was pasty, and his words were unnaturally shrill and hurried, and he even managed a wax little smile. "Personally I think Mr. Thunder there is an expert narrator of fascinating stories I'm just dying to hear."

Jason glared at him. The old man went on in that calm and measured voice. "And even if I was not afraid of Little Thunder, I still could not tell him what you want me to, Jason."

"And why not?"

"The Sioux don't have no word for humanity, Jason. To them they's just the people and the others. The others don't count for nothing. You and me, we ain't even got the right to be called people."

"Oh, now, that's preposterous, Mr. McMoultrie. This is really going too far. Really. Tell them . . ." Jason was struck by inspiration. "Tell them they ought to love the Pawnee."

The old man looked coolly at Jason and almost imperceptibly shook his head. There was a tense and expectant silence. Little Thunder leaned forward, curious and intent. The old man had run out of the capacity to lie. He translated, and Adam could see the way the old man's knuckles whitened around the stock of his rifle. Prepared to kill. Little Thunder nodded slowly as if something unfamiliar were being opened to him. Finally he jerked back his head and gaped at the old man and then at Jason. He was incredulous and angry and responded with a furious outrage that nobody could mistake.

Shawnee Joe took a deep breath and spoke again. Resigned, explanatory, apologetic, dispassionate murmur. Little Thunder began to laugh. The laughter jumped from Indian to Indian like lightning skipping through tall trees. Little Thunder howled something at them. Some of them flung themselves on their backs and wallowed in the grass. They looked at Jason as though he were a terrific clown, telling them the greatest joke they had ever heard. And the joke made them forgive him for insulting the people by denying that they were unique.

"I told them what you said, Jason. I'm tired of lying for you, you petty little son of a mother-fucking bitch," the old man said in that heatless calm. "I told them you said they ought to love the Pawnee."

410

"It isn't funny," Jason said miserably.

"Tell *them* that," the old man answered. He nodded his head toward the laughing braves.

Little Thunder spoke again, sovereign to slave.

"He says to tell you he got his first scalp when he was fifteen years old. It was a Pawnee brave."

"Tell him I don't want to hear about his murders," Jason said. "He should know that civilized people do not respect his bloodiness."

Shawnee Joe spoke in the Sioux tongue. Little Thunder nodded vigorously. He leaned over with a wild grin and pounded Jason on the back. Jason jumped back. His face was swept with fear and astonishment.

"What did you tell him this time?"

"I told him you said he was the bravest goddamned warrior you'd ever seen. I told him you'd be proud to call Chief Little Thunder your son."

"That's a lie!" Jason looked on the Indian chief with loathing. A finely wrought wrapping stripped away, revealing something naked and terrible underneath Jason's pretensions. He turned on Little Thunder and spoke in a loud, clear, exceedingly careful voice that resounded over the twilight deepening on the canyon floor. "I think you are a savage! A hopeless barbarian! I do not even think you have the right to be called a man. You don't even have a soul. You are worse than a dog!" He ran out of words. His face was scarlet. He was breathless and weary, a man whose mind had been addled.

Little Thunder's smile died. He could hear the angry tone in Jason's voice. He looked at the old man in blank inquiry, his head drawn back. Adam thought: *Well, this is it. They're going to scalp the lot of us.* He looked up and saw high amber threads of fiery clouds streaking the sky far above the walls of the canyon. *How beautiful it is!* He shifted his rifle minutely in his hands and chose a brave to kill.

The old man spoke again. Hesitantly, making something up. The Indian listened, an ear cocked, and nodded his head in slow, compassionate understanding. He put out a rough hand at the last. Jason found himself shaking hands with Little Thunder without having the least notion why.

"What did you tell him this time?" Jason was nearly weeping. Helpless and frustrated.

"I told him that your only son had been drowned on this

411

trip. I told him now you were very sad because you did n[ot]
have a son. I told him you begged Chief Little Thunder t[o]
join us and go all the way to the big waters with us and liv[e]
with us and be your son and our brother. I told him you wer[e]
yelling because you wanted your son to hear us over in th[e]
spirit world, and when your son saw Little Thunder, he'd b[e]
content that you had such a son to take his place. And I'[m]
begging you, Jason. For the love of God! Hush your mouth!"

Little Thunder nodded sagely. Jason was furious. "I'm go[-]
ing to leave. I'm not going to sit here and be party to thi[s]
mockery of everything I believe in." He made as if to get up[.]
But the old man grabbed him roughly, and with irresistibl[e]
force Shawnee Joe slammed Jason down again so abruptl[y]
that Jason's teeth must have been jarred up to the sockets o[f]
his eyes.

The old man, still holding Jason by the arm, looked over a[t]
Samuel, hulking stupidly in the firelight, silent and entrance[d]
by the drama being played out before him. "Samuel, Jason'[s]
out of his head. If you think a right smart of your woman, i[f]
you think something of them other women and of yourself
and us, you slap your brother unconscious if he moves to ge[t]
up. I don't care if you kill him. Give him a backhand and[d]
slap him down. If you let him insult this here chief, then we
are all going to die, and them women is going to die, too. Or
else they're going to be squaws. They're going to put up tents
and take down tents, and they are going to work like slaves,
and they are going to be used any way them Indians want to
use 'em."

Samuel looked over at Adam. "Mr. Adam?"

Adam nodded.

Samuel smiled with a terrifying stupidity, his slowly
growing grin spreading like spilled acid on his smooth face.
"All right, Jason. You sit still, you hear? If you move, I'll kill
you before the Indians get the chance!"

Jason, amazed, looked hard at his brother, and his eyes got
as big as cups. "What are you talking about, Samuel?"

Clifford Baynes whined: "Oh, Mr. Jennings! Please be still.
I do feel so terrible. Oh, God! What possessed me to come
West? Why did I ever leave the sacred precincts of the
George Washington Academy of Frederick, Maryland? Oh,
God, help me! *Amo, amas, amat ...*" He babbled incoher-
ently, his eyes rolled first heavenward and then toward Little

'hunder and then to heaven again. His thin hands twisted to-
ether, and his shoulders trembled.

Asa pleaded: "Jason, for Christ's sake! Get hold of your-
elf! Remember the rest of us! For Christ's sake, don't get us
:illed."

Jason sneered at him. "When am I going to stop living my
ife for you, Asa? When is it going to be over? I am a man
ung on a cross, and that cross is my worthless family. When
are you all going to be able to stand on your own feet! I've
given you everything I am. All my substance. When is it gong to be enough, Asa?"

Adam had never seen Jason like this. But he was astonished at Asa, too. Asa quailed like a dog being whipped with
a belt. Asa, perpetually seeming about to overpower Jason,
now lost heart all at once when Jason attacked him. He could
only mutter: "I'm sorry, Jason. Please don't let them kill us.
I'm afraid to die, Jason. Oh, please don't make them kill us!"

And Adam could see that Asa's habitual bad humor was
only a pretension of manhood. Now, faced with death and
the rebuke of a brother he knew was superior to himself, he
became only a fearsome little man, clutching at a soul too
full of holes to hold any courage at all.

For just a moment there was a tense, terrible expectancy,
and none of the whites seemed to know what to do or say.
But then Harry broke in. Always Harry with the right word
for any crisis.

Harry looked with stern dignity at Little Thunder. Little
Thunder was watching this babbling commotion among the
whites with a deepening scowl. Harry drew himself up and
said in a loud voice, "Tell them, Mr. McMoultrie, that we
have come all this way just to see the Sioux. Tell them that in
our country all men speak of the Sioux, their bravery, their
beauty, their victories in war, their strength, their mighty
hunts. Tell them that we are too humble to be brothers to the
Sioux. But we would desire to be their loyal servants, their
friends, their confederates. Tell them we wish to make their
friends our friends and their enemies our enemies."

Jason whirled around and looked at Harry aghast. But the
old man showed tremendous relief. He nodded in grave approval. He turned to Little Thunder and translated. The
Sioux bent forward like enchanted children. At the end they
exploded with a grand chorus of enthusiasm that sounded like

413

"How! How! How!" repeated again and again. And as the cried, they pounded their fists on the ground.

It was all the applause Harry could wish for. His audience stretched away from him in the dark, breathless and innume able. He took his glasses off and carelessly folded them in the inside pocket of his filthy white coat. And he went o swept up on the power of their approval and on the wings his own daring. "And tell them that everywhere in the Ea where the white men gather, people speak in reverence an wonder of the brave Chief Little Thunder. Tell him there no place among the white men where the renown of his dee has not been heard."

"Lies, lies, lies!" Jason cried.

"Tell them our chief here fervently agrees with what I sa and that all of us say with him, Lies, lies, lies, because that the way the white people express their agreement and the admiration for the great Chief Little Thunder."

Shawnee Joe allowed himself a faint and ironic grin of d light and translated. And like a music master waving sli hands to direct an orchestra, Harry gestured to the white and all of them but Jason (who looked around like a ma completely bereft of his senses) cried with all their migh "Lies, lies, lies!" They flung themselves into their lou charade with abandon. Adam cried lustily, taking pleasure the release from tension the yelling gave him, hugely enjoyin the spectacle, enjoying the look of utter bafflement on Jason face, very dim now in the gloom, and Adam began to believ that they might live through this night. Henry shouted with laugh on his eager young face. And Samuel and Asa thre back their heads and bellowed and laughed and bellowe some more.

Jason sat still and stunned. The old man translated wit the invariable calm of a great machine softly running. Littl Thunder sat sternly, his copper face suffused with grim d light. He received homage like a man who has been reco nized to be exactly what he thinks he is. And he lifted his chi to another degree of grave pride when his braves, swayin rhythmically from the waist and drumming their flat hand on the ground, took up the chant: "Lies! Lies! Lies!"

Jason glared furiously at them, but the Indians now too his expression to be only the properly grim look of a pett chief addressing their own grand leader. And Harry said "Tell him that our chief has taken a vow to the evening sta not to smile or laugh until we have passed through the land of the Sioux and have departed to the great blue waters and left them all in peace."

The old man translated. Little Thunder nodded his approval. To the Indians whites were all bizarre. Poor, bleached, worthless things. To come from a land where the Sioux had never been and to journey to a land where the Sioux would never go. A cold, shadow race with no spirit.

Little Thunder talked now. All the night long he recounted his coups—the men he had slain in single combat, the animals he had killed in the hunt, the pains he had endured without crying out, the perils he had faced without faltering. He showed them his scars. He beat his chest. And the old man sat there, tireless, speaking in a quick monotone that was still clear and strong eight hours after they had begun, fueled occasionally by smoke from the long pipe, which he refilled through the long night with his own supply of choice tobacco.

And it was Harry who remained the chorus, boundlessly energetic, responding at appropriate times with amazed admiration, with vicarious terror, with elegant abnegation to everything Little Thunder said. The rest of them nodded with sleep and started awake again. Harry pulled them along, smiling with his bright teeth reflecting the firelight, slapping them with the flail of his tongue. And they did the motions his grand words required them to do, moving like dead men twitching to galvanic shock, and Little Thunder was content.

At last when dawn was beginning to pale the eastern dark over the canyon wall, Little Thunder arose and yawned. There were loquacious goodbyes, and Little Thunder gave Harry a stiff hug and was hugged enthusiastically in return. Little Thunder tousled Henry's hair again and admired him. Then the Indians melted into the gray gloom of the coming dawn. The canyon rumbled briefly with the dimishing hoofbeats of their ponies. The silence came back. From far away in the canyon they could hear the solitary, disembodied screech of a wolf, and nearby in the trees they could hear the soft twittering of waking birds and the whisper of the dawn wind blowing gently through the foliage.

The old man got up looking stiff and venerable and tired, somehow shrunken by the long ordeal of the night, his lined face gray in the early light, and his steely eyes dull. He rubbed his hands for a moment, massaging the pain away

415

from his joints, and then he looked at Harry with slow, admiring deliberation and put one of his hands out. The two men shook hands, Harry nervous and weak and somehow both embarrassed and frightened as though he had just now begun to understand the danger they had been in and what he had accomplished through the long, long night.

"Dr. Creekmore, you done good. You might of saved our lives. Hell, I reckon you *did* save our lives. You made them Indians friends. You can talk better than any chief I ever knowed. I'm right proud to make your acquaintance."

Harry actually blushed before the old man's scattered praise. He put on his glasses again and seemed awash with relief and happiness. He beamed down at the wiry old man whose head came up only to Harry's bearded chin. And Harry said in wonder, "I thought we were all going to die. Not just me. But all of you. I was sure of it." He turned a joyful and weary face rapturously toward the place where the new day was coming over the sheer bluffs. "Now this morning is like a free gift. Something added on I never dreamed of having. I don't think I've ever seen a morning more beautiful."

Promise came running to him out of the wagon where she had been asleep. Samuel told her, "Your friend Dr. Creekmore saved us all." She hugged Harry shamelessly, and Harry hugged her in return. The old man grinned at them both and clapped Harry familiarly on the back. Even Asa seemed cheerful this morning. But Jason got up, silent and isolated, distracted by all that had happened. He gave Harry a keen, questioning look and walked away into the mist, and Adam knew that Jason believed Harry had betrayed him, and all that kept Jason civil was the belief that Harry was, after all, a medical doctor.

# 48

They moved up the valley of the North Platte now. Slowly, very slowly, trundling their ten hours a day. Another wheel broke on Jason's wagon. Just splintered and fell apart, and they replaced it with the spare Adam and Samuel had brought across the river way back in Missouri.

The river lay on their right, running swiftly over its shallow, sandy bed. The trail came close to it, veered away, swung near again. And one day in the dead stillness of a hot, dusty afternoon, Adam looked ahead of them and saw blocks heaped up low against the horizon as though a child had left a playhouse there, a blue, curious spectacle. He showed them to the old man. The old man shaded his eyes, squinted and nodded and spat in the earth. "It's the Courthouse," he said. "They call that there Courthouse Rock."

The vision was uncanny. It rose slowly, imperially, gigantically, and as they crawled heavily toward it, the rock became a great, hulking fortress of stone asserting itself in celestial calm against the enormous sky, claiming dominion over the vast and level plain. As they came on and on, its very bulk, its peerless eminence, commanded their silent concentration. Adam looked at Courthouse Rock and fell to musing. Their slow pace and the great rock drinking the sun and rising out of the flat plain captivated his sight and hypnotized him.

Jason, too, brooded at Courthouse Rock. He plunged along by his lead oxen, all alone in a world where he had found refuge from the deceit and injury of his companions in Ash Hollow. He did not even talk to Harry anymore. His eyes were fixed on the great shimmering rock, and he hardly looked where his feet were stepping.

The rock came nearer and grew bigger. There was an odd and terrifying threat in its almost imperceptibly swelling grandeur. They saw it all one night and all the next day, and on the second night it was large enough to block out the stars

417

behind it. On the next morning it was there, emerging from the soft iridescence of dawn as they silently broke camp and moved on, the rock slowly taking the brightening sunshine and the rising heat like something huge, feeding on light and warmth and still growing. On the next night it was grander still, still ahead of them, off to the south and west, and Jason watched it with fixed, silent fascination, as if he were waiting for the rock to move or do *something*, and he did not dare take his eyes off it lest it quiver while he was looking away.

On the next morning he could bear the suspense no longer. He spoke to the old man. "Mr. McMoultrie, why don't we ride over there and see it up close?" His voice was tense and thin, and the smile he flashed was like grease on his face.

The old man shook his head and spat. "It's a whole lot farther off than it looks, Jason."

Jason laughed recklessly. "Oh, it's not far off at all. We could be over there and back in an hour."

"More like a day, Jason."

Jason's broad face turned blood-red. "Mr. McMoultrie, you are asking me not to believe the testimony of my own eyes. Am I so childish in your estimation that you think you can convince me that black is white and white is black?"

The old man heaved a resigned sigh. "I'm just saying the air up here is awful clear, Mr. Jennings. You ain't used to air like this. And the ground is flat as a plate. You ain't used to that neither. You lose your judgment about distances out here."

"I can see, Mr. McMoultrie."

The peevishness was hot in Jason. In his voice, in his broad, angry mouth, in his puckered eyebrows. In his heavy arms folded belligerently across his chest. In the testy angle of his head. People were not believing in him.

His appearance was troubling to the rest of them. They had all seen something new emerging in his personality when they sat with the Sioux in Ash Hollow. They thought it would go away with change or rest. But now his pride was hinged to Courthouse Rock, he was determined to ride over to inspect it. "I'm tired of being held in contempt by everybody!" he fumed.

To keep the peace, the old man agreed to ride along with him. Jason could not see that the old man's surrender was the greatest contempt of all.

"I'll go, too," Adam said. He did not want to go.

418

The old man shook his head. "No, you stay here. Keep to the trail, along the river. We'll ride to the rock and join you up ahead somewheres. For Christ's sake don't shoot us when we come in. It'll be dark. I'll whistle like this when we see your fire."

"We're not going to be gone that long!" Jason said angrily. But the old man ignored him and whistled, fingers in his mouth, a shrill, warbling tremolo that lingered and lingered and then died in the soft morning. Like a bird Adam had never heard before. It made chill bumps run down his spine.

"Well, you take my riding mule. Mr. Jennings there can ride on it. I'll drive his oxen."

Jason looked around at all of them and flashed a pasty smile. "We'll be back in the early afternoon."

So the two of them rode off. The company moved sluggishly on, and the departing riders became steadily more minute in the morning distance.

Adam drove the lead team. The other oxen moved lethargically, and Jason's wagon creaked as it rolled, making its rhythmic *eek-eek-ka-BAM* in the hard earth. The other wagons were strung out behind him at great intervals, so the powdery dust raised by one wagon had time to settle before the next one came along.

Jessica insisted on leading the two pack mules. She walked near Adam in moccasins the old man had made for her out of buffalo hide. They felt wonderfully free together. Adam was glad to be with her, and she talked lightly and happily. Jason's presence was a burden they realized most when they were relieved of it. They could laugh together and talk. Adam could look at her all he liked. There was nobody nearby to reproach them.

They talked only of inconsequential things. But as the day waxed, Adam understood how important those inconsequential things had been in his own life. The soft leather hinges on the cabin door. The heavy chestnut mantelpiece his father had so laboriously hewn out with an axe to put over the fireplace in the hope that someday they would have a clock. They had never been able to buy the clock. Clocks were expensive. He remembered the flitting little bird that nested in a tree near the cabin using a whitened, flimsy, snakeskin to frighten away other birds.

Jessica spoke of the furniture in her room when she was a child. She talked of some things in the chests abandoned on the trail. A blue velvet gown she had worn once to a party when she was twelve. A crystalline goblet her father had given her with delicate black flowers etched on it, and how she had imagined that if flowers grew in ice, they would be like these.

And Adam, talking listening, talking again more easily than he had ever talked in his life, was shown a mystery—how life is an intangible web woven invisibly between simple objects that mean little in themselves. But when the objects are gone, life must be built again, changing with irrevocable finality in the process.

And so the plains again became for him much more than mere land and space. They were the substance of an invisible magic that would make all of them into new creatures. Not necessarily better. But new. Old things passed away. Adam felt sad, nostalgic, vaguely troubled and even guilty. For what would they become out there? But he knew as they talked that Jessica was content, for she spoke of the little things, those foundation objects, with serene detachment. No wonder she had been the first one willing to throw her stuff out of the wagon! She did not need possessions, which, removed from their accustomed place and shifted an unbelievable distance to the Great West, could never again be what they had been in that other life, now strange, dead, and lost forever behind them.

The sun burned up the morning sky to their backs. It stood grandly over their nooning and then sank slowly down its tremendous western arc before them like a fiery balloon swelling and settling to rest. Courthouse Rock, still off in the distance, came up parallel to them, and then almost imperceptibly began to recede. They made camp in a good place by the river in the late afternoon, heard the water with its liquid whispering over the sand bars, heard the insects humming in the tall grass, listened to the rise and fall of the wind, smelled the clean air.

Still no trace of the departed men, And as the sun continued its grand retirement, the clouds turned smoky dark, glowing at the edges as though aflame with molten iron within. The night came on, full and dark and filled with stars.

Still no sign of the old man and Jason. The camp settled to rest. Adam took the first watch with only his hound. He was too worried to sleep. And there was a special pleasure to the first watch. When you did lie down, you knew you could sleep without interruption until time to move in the morning.

He tried to keep the fire burning brightly to act as a beacon, heaping it up with scrub brush cut from along the riverbank. He tramped dutifully out to look after the mules and the oxen. He kept looking toward the place where the bulk of Courthouse Rock thrust itself up very black against the richly starry sky.

"I couldn't sleep, Adam."

Jessica's voice, spoken softly to him in the night, made him jump. He had been dreamily reliving his wonderful day with her. Now the suggestion in her voice startled him more than her sudden appearance. She stood with a shawl wrapped around her, scarcely more than a silhouette standing in statuesque calm very close beside him.

"Ain't no sign of them yet. I reckon the old man was right." His mouth was dry, and his words were clumsy.

Jessica, too, seemed tense. They were both mutely aware that Jason was somewhere out there, too far away to look after his wife. Adam thought suddenly, recklessly, that Jason deserved whatever happened to his wife. "It's like Mr. McMoultrie said," Adam said in a husky voice. "It's a lot farther than it looks."

"You can't tell Jason anything," Jessica said. She laughed fitfully; it was as if an agreement had been struck between them to blame Jason.

"I hope they ain't lamed one of the mules." Adam began to stroll almost casually off into the dark, away from the campfire. His heart was hammering. The prospect of being humiliated again gave him a moment of fear and revulsion.

Jessica did not give him time to think. "I have never seen the stars as beautiful as they are out here," she said, throwing her head back to consider the sky.

Adam walked slowly along and was silent. He threw a sidelong glance at her, looking at her shadow in the clear night.

"They are so still," she said. "So calm. They never seem troubled by anything. I look at them sometimes and think: they will be just the same long after everything in the world that troubles me has been forgotten. I find that a comforting feeling." She laughed softly. "It makes me feel very unimportant. And there is great freedom in being unimportant. Then nothing you do has any consequence worth thinking about."

They were silent. They were quite removed from the campfire now. It was dark all around them. Heat lightning began to flicker in the distance, mute and magical.

Jessica said: "There are so many more stars out here than at home. I was not prepared for a sky like this." Forced words. Something to say. To relieve the pain of silence.

"The air's so dry," Adam said. "Back home in summer, the air's all thick and heavy and damp. You can't see the stars so good when the air's like that." His voice solemn and husky.

Jessica laughed again. Artificially. Tension relaxing just a bit. Her laughter in the dark like the soft tinkling of gentle chimes. "Don't you think that means something, Adam? The stars are up there, back in the East. But we can't see them. Out here we can see them." She laughed again, more genuinely. "My husband could make a long sermon out of that. Alas! He does not have the imagination to think of such a thing by himself."

Adam felt his arms tightening, his throat stiff. "Well, I reckon it does mean something."

"It's a richer land out here, I think. Everything is more free. Even the power to see. Just tonight I feel liberated from something. I don't even know what. But being out here like this, seeing the stars, smelling the fresh air, I feel more free than I have felt since I was a child."

Adam was silent, pondering her, wondering what she meant. Her soft arm brushed against his. Lingered. Went away. The place she had touched burned.

"Have you ever felt really free, Adam?" she said softly.

Adam laughed. Weak, forced laughter. He made words come. "Well, I don't know. I don't reckon I've ever been really free. Always had to look out for somebody. Or something. Don't know if I'd want it any other way. Maybe I'm free now. I don't know."

"But you're not free now," Jessica said. "You have to look after us."

"Oh, you folks don't need me. I reckon I could go on if I wanted to. You'd be all right."

"You do really want to go on. But you can't. You have to stay with us. It's your nature to look after people." She sighed and paused. "I'm am very thankful that you are like that. And I beg your forgiveness for anything I have done to hurt you, Adam."

Adam's face burned. He tried to go on talking normally.

'Well, when we get to California, I reckon I'll be free enough then."

Jessica laughed gently. "No, not even then. You're not made that way, Adam. You will always have somebody to look after. People who need looking after will come to you. There will always be somebody."

Adam was again silent. He could feel something swelling between them. Something like a violent storm in an impossibly small space, a soundless wind blowing something irrevocably away. His head was light.

She resumed in a moment. They were walking very slowly now. "I mean that you are the sort who takes up obligations, Adam. You do not run away. Your kind makes the world hold together. I really do mean that as a compliment. The greatest compliment I can give."

Her arm brushed his again and now her shoulder, too. Soft and warm. She lingered next to him. And suddenly she laced her arm through his, and they walked together. Their hips were touching now, touching and not touching and touching again. She was dressed only in her cotton nightgown with her linen duster wrapped around her. Heat lightning danced against Courthouse Rock. Adam hoped wildly that Jason had been lost out there. Scalped maybe by Indians. But what about the old man! Adam tasted regret. He loved the old man.

Jessica went steadily on, speaking softly in his ear. "I think I feel very sorry for you, Adam Cloud. There will always be people to take advantage of your strength. Like Dr. Creekmore. My husband. Myself."

They stopped as though at a prearranged signal. She turned to him, her face directly under his, her mouth inches from his own. All around him the dry lightning danced and quivered, and the magical quiet held him on a feathery balance.

"Adam, it is very cool. I wonder if you would put your arms around me."

He obeyed her in a jerky and staggering silence, letting the rifle fall in the grass, putting his arms awkwardly around her waist, discovering that she was larger than he had thought but deliciously soft. And so he pulled her to himself, feeling her warmth the length of his body.

He did not fully understand her, and he could hardly believe what was happening even while it was bursting in him

like fire. He went on with motion without ever telling hims
until the last instant just where it would end.

It was a madness. Later one of the things he regretted m
was that he had not seen her nakedness. He could form
clear impression of her body. For the entire episode was on
visual in those fitful illuminations of the blue lightning. It w
all full of feeling—her warmth, her rounded hips, that su
prising solidity of her soft body, the cleft in her buttocks, h
strong thighs entwining him.

"Please go slowly, Give me peace. Peace."

He did not know what she meant. They were wallowing c
the ground, and the night was full of smells—the grass, h
skin, her hair, the damp earth, full of the taste of her w
mouth pressed against his, the muffled, swishing sound c
their two naked bodies roiling in the cool grass together.

When he entered her, guided and instructed by her hand
she heaved and groaned beneath him, her head back, he
mouth agape, and once she wrapped her legs so tight
around him that his body was momentarily held as though i
a vise, and he was forced to stop his own motion. For a me
ment they lay rigidly pressed against each other, sobbing, an
then she released him and let him continue and drew he
knees up on each side of him, letting her now bare fee
dangle in the air. He could see her naked legs dimly in th
coming and going of the far lightning, and he remembere
that those legs were unusually slender in spite of all tha
strength he had felt in them. Later he thought it was foolis
to have glanced behind him at those suspended legs, t
remember that sight above all others, but it happened tha
way, and he never forgot it.

It was all over very quickly, and Adam had only a vagu
sense of time. Sometimes it seemed that the experience wa
all memory and no happening at all. A mystery. He lay spen
atop her, their soft wetness sticky between them, and he
kissed her in a fumbling, clumsy, childishly tender way, no
even knowing how to fix his mouth to hers. She lay quietl
beneath him awhile, her strong legs apart, stroking his hair
delicately and almost absentmindedly with her hand, ap
parently lost in thoughts she did not wish to share with him
or perhaps could not speak.

"I love you," he sobbed at last, unable to contain his
feelings or control his words. "I love you! I love you!"

"Oh, Adam," she said quietly on a note of pain. "You can't love me. It's too late. Too late for me."

"You can run away with me," he said in a vehement whisper. "When we get to California, nobody will know you've been married to Jason. You ain't really been married to him. You told me yourself. I love you. We can go in the morning. Hellfire! We can go right now! To hell with all of 'em."

His heart leaped to joy with the idea, and he raised himself, looking wildly up to the stars sprinkled by the thousand overhead. Everything seeemed possible.

But she only lay there in a terrible calm, stroking his hair with that soft hand, and when he fell into an exhausted silence she said quietly again, "It's too late, Adam. I am almost thrity-five years old. It is far too late for us."

"It don't matter. It don't matter." He was crying.

"It does matter. It will matter very soon."

He argued with her. But she rolled away and pushed him gently aside. "I have peace now, Adam." She picked herself up and let her disheveled clothes fall softly back into place. She kissed him swiftly, holding his face in her two tender hands. And then she was gone.

He was left alone with the night and his dog, hardly able to imagine that it had all really happened and more confused and upset than he had ever been in his life. "I will kill Jason," he muttered fiercely to himself. "If I kill him and make it look like an accident, she will have to marry me. I will not let her go."

In his resolution he felt all life slipping away from him as if it had just been announced that he would die this evening. He was so distraught that he had to keep pacing back and forth. He did not call for anyone to relieve him of the watch at midnight, because he knew he could not sleep, and he could not explain himself to anybody on earth—except perhaps to Jessica.

The Big Dipper wheeled around the pole star, a giant timepiece in the sky with a single crooked hand longly marking the silent hours. Adam tried to make plans. He remembered how he had killed the Indians. And he told himself that he could do exactly the same to Jason. But when he tried to imagine killing Jason, his massacre of the Indians became unreal. Finally he was lost in a turmoil of fantasy that threatened to crush him like an avalanche of snow. He paced back and forth until his legs felt like wood. Still he could not stop walking. The night bore on him, and his heart wa squeezed dry of emotion.

The dawn was coming in a glaze of liquid pearl when th old man and Jason finally rode into camp. The old ma whistled. But there was no need. Adam saw their blurre shapes from afar, and the hound, asleep on his paws, wok and ran howling happily and cavorting on his hind feet meet them. The two men were mortally tired. In the colorles light the old man's face was worn, and his pale eyes wer sunk to tiny points of fire blazing in hollows of dark fatigue His hands were red and swollen, and he held painfully to th reins of his mule.

But greater weariness showed in Jason. His cheeks sagged The lines in his face were cruel carvings made with a blun knife, and his eyes were sunken and amazed.

"We rode all day long before we got to it," he said ver slowly, perplexed, in a lassitude that made Adam think o stagnant pools with green scum caking the surface of the stil water. "And when we got there, I wanted to climb up to loo around, but it was already getting dark. Too dark to take th time to climb the thing. Indians lurking around maybe. Yo know. We couldn't see what was up there. In the dark. We just came on. Didn't even try to climb it. After all that ride Nice little stream behind it. We drank. An illusion. The whole thing was an illusion. Mr. McMoultrie was . . . Well, owe him an apology. I am man enough to apologize to any one when I've been wrong. I never saw anything like it. We haven't had anything to eat . . . Strange . . . I . . . I was wrong!"

"But we're back safe," the old man said with surprising gentleness, as though he were speaking to a child.

"Yes, you're back," Adam said flatly, looking at Jason. These were the first words he spoke to anyone after he and Jessica made love. And it was hours afterwards before he began to believe that everybody was so concerned for Jason that nobody thought of accusing Adam of anything. No one even suspected, and Jessica looked at him with a cool half-smile as if they had been the most distant of acquaintances.

So they went on. A creaking procession under the great sun. Oxen weary, patient, the mouth of July nearly gone. August near. Everybody quiet. But when Adam looked at Jessica, he remembered her soft moan in his ear when he entered her. *I have made love to her!* It seemed as unreal as the dead Indians he had left for the wolves so many miles before.

Chimney Rock came up ahead of them now. A slim point of still stone, a spire ramming the enamel blue sky, seeming near in the illusory way that Courthouse Rock had seemed near. But where Courthouse Rock had amazed them with its bulk, Chimney Rock astounded them with its high, spooky delicacy. They came on it for three days, seeing it always like the pillar that had guided Israel through the wildnerness. A sign of something. They could not tell what.

The trail was not entirely empty. They met freight wagons coming back from Fort Laramie on ahead. They met riders trotting by, carrying government despatches and looking grim and tired. And sometimes there was a company of wagons retreating from the grand adventure.

"We got out there to Fort Laramie," a hale, bluff man with abnormally pink cheeks said. He was sweating, his grin a fire blazing in his face. "And then we heard that the hardest part of the whole danged trip was still ahead of us. We got to feeling kind of uneasy, you know. The hardest part ... You can't never tell. And we decided all at once we hadn't lost nothing in California. We decided to turn around and go home. Where we belong."

"You could have made it," Jason said.

"Maybe so. Maybe not. That's a matter of opinion, brother." The man laughed in the forced way that salesmen meet each other. He spoke confidently, eager to convert Jason to his despair. "You really think you can make it out there?" he said, cocking his head and looking sideways as though they both knew that Jason was joking.

"I have faith," Jason said slowly. His voice was thick and dull and very weary. But the other man had not heard Jason Jennings filled with zeal and dreams. And so he only laughed like a sensible person listening to a child's babblings. "Well, we got that good, brown dirt back in Illinois, and I got faith in that."

"Every man has to make his own choice," Jason said.

"It ain't that we're cowards now," the man said. "You wasn't *thinking* we was cowards, was you, brother?"

Jason allowed himself a gentle and tranquil smile and looked at the high sun, measuring the angle to locate himself in the tremendous day. "I was just thinking how far we've got

to go before we camp tonight. We have to be moving alon
now. I suppose you gentlemen have to be moving, too."

For hours afterwards the Jennings party could see the slug
gish dust of that forlorn and defeated crowd of men risin
and receding in the shimmering heat waves of the plains.

They moved up toward Mitchell Pass at Scott's Bluff. "Fel
ler named Scott, he was a trapper for the Astor folks. H
taken sick here, and his friends left him to die. Didn't war
to fool with him. Found his skeleton next year, picked clear
down there by the river. Foot of the bluffs. Don't never trus
your friends when you get sick out here," the old man said
"You might get a rock named after you, but you got to di
for the name, and I'd rather live myself and not have nothin
named for me except maybe a son."

Here the crenellations in the rocks, the shades of purple
blue, gray, green, and yellow, the black shadows, the wall o
tan stone hundreds of feet high were spectral and forbidding
The carven shapes of marl made all the formations look lik
ruins of a dead city looking down on them from a millio
years of time. Broken temples, fallen spires, streets hig
above them choked with debris, all still and solemn in the af
ternoon air.

"It's the most romantic place I've ever seen!" Promise
cried. But Adam looked at her and thought how childish she
seemed next to the stately calm of her mother. He glanced a
Jessica, remembering the warm solidity of her body behind
her clothes.

Harry was plunged into gloom. "I don't know what it is,
but it makes me sad," he said privately to Adam. "You
remember what you swore, Adam. You will take care of
Promise when I die."

"You ain't going to die!" Adam said fiercely. When he
thought of marrying Promise now, he was aghast. An ancient
taboo. "You're going to live forever, Harry. You're going to
bury me! It's your luck. Your goddamned *luck!* You'll stand
by my grave and preach the sermon—ashes to ashes and dust
to dust. I reckon you'll be a preacher for the day. My God, is
there *anything* you can't be, Harry?" He kicked his mule
sharply and rode on through the pass. Harry was left staring
bleakly after him, injured and bewildered.

Adam rode through the pass and started down the long,
rocky incline on the other side. Instantly he became aware of
a change in the atmosphere, an electric suspension that made

his skin tingle, and he stopped brooding about his troubles. Looking up to the western horizon, he saw black clouds building swiftly, cloud piling on top of cloud. He had never seen clouds so dark. And he was struck with terror.

Terror that grinds every other emotion to powder and obliterates thought. Clouds boiling and coalescing, the soft violet of the common prairie clouds festering to purple and almost instantly to that violent black. Lightning was flashing out of the belly of the storm, and below the clouds the light was queer and green.

Adam drew the mule to a halt. "It's going to storm!" The cry was as futile as naming death. "Unhitch the oxen!" the old man yelled just behind him. Equally futile. The storm came on so swiftly that no human effort could cope with it. It fell on them with a wild and terrifying shriek, and the thunder cannonaded off the high stone bluff with a roar that went on and on. The great towers flashed blue and white in the lighting, and the rumble of the wind was like the passing of gods to war. In the brief intervals between lightning flashes, the blackness was a hood pulled down over the face of the world.

The rain struck them like a flail of cold and driving violence, and Adam was soaked through to the skin in an instant. The mule went into a frisky pirouetting, trying vainly to turn in some direction to escape the stinging punishment of the rain. The revolving world, dimly seen, became uncertain and full of nightmares. The power of the storm was so great that it dissolved the sturdy shapes of things. The wagons, the oxen, the mules, and everything else caught out in this terrible pounding were translated into vague, gray shadows, only swimming suggestions of themselves.

Within the tumult of the storm there were human screams, voices shouting unintelligible and nonsensical commands, consolations, terror. Adam could not shake off his panic. It clamped around his skin like the rain itself. He shuddered and felt sick at his stomach. Yet he managed his mule, and he began to think coherent thoughts, and he saw that Samuel had managed to free his oxen and let them go, and he tried to get back himself to help Jason, who was ineffectually fumbling at his.

Then the hail struck.

The first icy stones clattered down so unexpectedly and powerfully that Adam thought briefly that they might have

been swept with gunfire. Only the old man recognized t
hail instantly for what it was. He flung a buffalo robe ov
himself for protection, and Adam saw him turn, beastlik
with his back to the wind, slouching low over his jumpin
and kicking mule. But the rest of them, locked in their ow
separate prison cells of terror, could not defend themselves.
was as if some alien and malign force had decided to destro
them all from ambush.

Adam heard an animal bellow, a ragged, horrid chorus c
bellows, a clatter of wagons. He looked back up the lor
road descending out of the pass, saw the huge hailstone
bounding off the rocks, saw Samuel's teams go hurtling by
saw two wagons careening down on top of him, and kne
that the oxen had stampeded.

He heard a scream and another and another. He manage
to jerk his mule out of the way as the wagons shot by, th
oxen galloping madly into the teeth of the storm, damagin
each other, blinded and battered by the hail, running head
long to escape.

Adam was dazed. The hail pounded him. He could tast
blood in his mouth. The blows on his back took his breatl
away. Yet he wrestled his mule after the wagons by mair
force. He chose the one he thought carried Jessica an
Promise. And he made his mule run, keeping his eyes fixe
on that bouncing and tormented shape, blurring and comin₂
clear again in the awful rain.

They came plunging out of the pass and off the trail, anc
the oxen, galloping straight ahead, carried the wagon wildl
careening, looking as if it must break to smithereens at an
moment. Adam came pounding in pursuit. Slowly, slowly h
gained ground. He drew abreast of the wagon seat, the mule
itself stampeding now, the oxen galloping with all their might
His face was sticky with the flying mud kicked up by beas
and wheel, but almost as quickly as he was pounded by a
blob of sodden earth, the beating rain washed it away. He
felt the mud oozing down inside his shirt, and he had a furi
ous memory of how he had dirtied himself in the Big Blue
with Rachael. Finally he could lift his eyes to the wagon seat.
And he saw a vision that turned his heart to stone.

There sat Ruth—strong, stolid, frozen with terror—on that
hideously bounding plank seat with nothing to cling to but
the seat itself. Her large body was slapping up and down with
the flight of the wagon. Her long, brownish hair, usually done

up neatly in a bun at the back of her head, had come loose and flew like a soggy banner in the wind. The hailstones pounding against her soft flesh made her flinch and duck, and yet she bore them without letting go the seat. She was fixed in a thrall, and Adam galloping alongside, separated from her by less than ten yards—the distance they rode on a normal day when they talked of simple things—might have been in another world.

He did something then for the very last time in his life. He prayed.

The futility of his prayer overpowered him. The gods were dead. Jehovah had perished. Ruth would be granted no miracle. All the world too swift and solid for miracle. She would live or she would die, and God had nothing to do with it.

He heard the first wheel break in a loud, sharp, sudden *cr-a-a-a-a-ck* different from the roar of thunder. He saw the wagon shudder and pitch away from him, and he heard the second wheel break and then a third, and he saw the wagon collapse. The tongue splintered, and the oxen in their headlong panic dragged the tangled wreckage on for perhaps fifty yards before they became hopelessly ensnarled in the lines and yokes. The wagon veered up and slammed down on its side with an awful, splintering crash. There was no sound except for the driving rain, the incessant thunder, and the hoarse, feeble cries and heavy thrashing of the wounded and dying oxen.

Adam jumped from his mule into the melee, changing worlds. In the wreckage of the wagon he found Henry. The boy was buried in sodden blankets. He was bruised and so hysterical with fear that he could not say anything for a moment. He could only gape at the world with wide, wild eyes, his mouth trembling violently. Then he began to cry, and Adam knew that the boy was all right.

But where was Ruth? Adam climbed out of the wreckage, raced back, and found her where she had been flung onto a bed of rocks when the first wheel broke. She was unconscious. Her clothing was torn, and she was caked with mud. One large, pink breast hung through a rent in her dress. She was all cuts and bruises, and the blood oozed out of her, diluted from red to pink in the pouring rain.

But what made Adam sick was her arm. Her right arm—the arm she used to hug her son, to tend her flowers. It had been broken. Not simply broken but shattered, crushed.

Bloody pulp below her elbow, skin scraped away, red muscles flayed and mangled, broken white rods thrust through the mess in jagged needles of bone.

Henry came running up, sobbing. But when he saw his mother, he became completely calm. That was what Adam always remembered about Henry. Henry knew when there was something too much for tears.

He stared at his mother with a sucking breath. "Is she dead?"

"No. She's breathing!" They had to yell to be heard.

"What are we going to do?" Henry shouted again. Dreadfully calm now. Bending for instructions. Adam wanted to hug the boy. So proud of him. No time.

Adam tried to stretch Ruth out carefully so that if there were any other broken bones in her she would not suffer. He hurried back to the wagon's rubble to fetch canvas, something to shelter her from the raging storm.

But even as he wrestled canvas out of the wreck, the rain ceased. It was like a spigot that had been turned off. The low, violent clouds cracked and broke up, showing great patches of high, waxed blue, immaculately smooth. And as swiftly as it had come, the storm blew away, leaving the world dripping and serene. The sun came pouring down, splendid and smiling in that impersonal mockery of a universe that made changes on its own whim and let humankind be damned.

Ruth groaned, a deep and heavy sound, harsh against the gentle dripping of water all around. Adam looked at her with resignation and felt the tears in his eyes. She was going to die. The day turned so bright that now Ruth needed shelter from the sun. He set himself to a rig a soggy canvas over her for shade. As he moved about he realized how fearfully he had been battered by the hail. He ached to move. Gingerly he felt himself on the face and the shoulders and on his ribs and hips. Everywhere he touched throbbed with pain. And yet the day was so beautiful now!

In a near daze he kept thinking that it might all have been a nightmare, come to him as he sat dozing on the mule. But the wagon lay a wreck of broken wood and rent canvas, scattered baggage, and pitifully dying oxen. His mule was cut by the hail and stood with his large head lowered. Ruth lay there covered with filth and blood, her arm crushed, unconscious, groaning with every breath.

So it was no dream.

# 49

"Dr. Creekmore, it's up to you now." Jason speaking, a man drugged by events too much for him. A slow and solemn voice, very thick. He had hardly spoken to Harry since Ash Hollow. Hardly spoken to anyone.

Adam gave Harry a stunned look. Harry no doctor, Harry a fraudulent feeler of heads for profit, lying his way to California. And here was Jason Jennings, gray and lined and very, very old, looking dependently at Harry with a dead expression, muttering, "Dr. Creekmore, it's up to you now."

"You're going to have to cut that arm off, and that's a fact," the old man said, his voice low and level. The certainty of daylight and the seasons.

"Yes," Harry muttered. His angular face was bloodless and gaunt. He stared at Ruth's arm.

"Gangrene if you don't take it off right now. She'll die pretty horrible if you let gangrene take her." The old man spoke very low. Reverent in the way of the old toward death.

"But he ain't no *doctor!*" Ishtar Baynes screamed. "He can't do that poor woman no good at all!"

She put her hands to her mouth. She had hoarded her secret, polishing it with her fantasies of how she would use it in the end, but knowing that it could only be used once. And now she had spilled it out, and she was as shocked as Harry. Ishtar Baynes had been moved despite all her calculation by Ruth's plight. And she had revealed Harry's secret out here where it could do her no good, like a woman dropping eggs on the floor when she had intended to use them in a cake. Now her face was askew with the sight of Ruth's mangled arm and with the knowledge of what she had done.

"What?" Jason mumbled, looking dazedly at her. "What did you say, Mrs. Baynes?"

Mrs. Baynes could not stop herself. "He ain't no *real* doctor! He ain't no *real* doctor! In Nashville! We seen him in

Nashville when he was feeling heads. He ain't no real doctor."

Jason gaped at her. At Harry. Harry pale, adjusting his glasses on his nose, looking at Ruth, looking as if he wanted to take his glasses off.

And Ruth lay numb with shock and barely conscious on the tailgate of Jason's wagon. Jason's wagon and its occupants spared. The oxen had simply run till they could go no farther, and the wagon had held together. The canvas cover rent in a hundred places where the hail had smashed through. The Bayneses in Rebecca's wagon, not stampeded because Samuel had loosed the oxen, slow Samuel understanding danger more quickly than anyone else. Ishtar Baynes was hardly bruised.

*Why couldn't she of been killed?* Adam Cloud savagely cursed the universe; the universe yawned above him. The sunshine showered down.

Ruth was wrapped in soggy blankets. Her crippled arm lay askew beside her, exposed to the air, pulpy with gore. She was pale, dirty, bruised, bloody, and her breath was swift and shallow. "Don't worry none about me," she said. "Is Henry all right?"

"I'm just fine, mamma."

Ruth smiled weakly. "Poor thing! It ain't been a good trip for you, Henry," she whispered. "You must of been scared to death. Don't you worry none about me. I'm going to be all right."

All Asa's oxen had to be killed. Adam shot them one by one with a rifle. They drove Jason's wagon near Ruth to give her an elevated place to lie on, unhitched his tired oxen, and rounded up Samuel's easily enough. The oxen were placidly grazing now, switching their tails as if there had never been a storm.

And Harry Creekmore, M.D., the renowned doctor who had studied surgery under the most eloquent and learned professors of Heidelberg, Germany, had himself a wooden operating table on the tailgate of a wagon in the open air where he could see to cut off Ruth's mangled right arm. The afternoon cool and clean. A light wind stirring their damp hair, whipping gently through their wet clothes, drying the world. All of them disheveled, filthy, weary, hollowed-eyed.

"He ain't no real doctor! He ain't nothing but a hypocrite." Ishtar Baynes swallowed, looked wildly around, sensed an advantage, and plunged recklessly on. "I didn't want to say nothing, Mr. Jennings. I knowed you wasn't ready to believe me. I knowed you'd just get mad at me for telling you the truth when I couldn't prove it. But this is *serious!* He ain't no real doctor."

They all looked at Harry. Every face registered a different set of emotions. Asa's face puffy and stained with drying blood, his body fearfully bruised by the hail. "Are you a doctor, or ain't you, Dr. Creekmore? If you ain't no doctor, and if you hurt my Ruth, then I'm going to kill you."

"He'd have the right," the old man said, murmuring at the obvious justice inherent in the nature of things. If Harry did any harm, the old man would stand aside while Asa killed him. Executed him.

"Ask Clifford!" Mrs. Baynes shrieked. The expression of dazzling joy spreading on her face was unbearable to watch. Adam wanted to kill her. But he could not. She had justice on her side. Justice made a wall around her. Around *her!* Clifford knows!" she cried. "Clifford knows what was going on in Nashville, Tennessee."

Clifford seemed mildly surprised. He wiped a paw over his sallow face. "Indeed, ah, I do know. We met this man on the road before Nashville. We, ah, shared some coffee with him one night. He told us then he wasn't a real doctor. My wife, ah, had a complaint. He could not help her. He just felt heads. A phrenologist, I believe, is the name applied to those fraudulent persons who, ah, do such things to deceive a gullible public. Ah, yes, a *phrenologist!*"

Harry looked at Mrs. Baynes, saw the victory in her glittering eyes, looked at Promise who was confounded, expectant, deeply puzzled, and hurt. He saw the waiting, murderous silence in all of them. His feeble eyes met Adam's face and flicked away.

And Harry laughed.

His sudden laughter was like an electric shock pricking all of them, making every head jump. He shrugged his slender shoulders under his filthy jacket. "You know this woman," he said carelessly, throwing a nonchalant hand in the direction of Ishtar Baynes. "And you know me. We have been together every day for weeks. Now one of us is lying. But I will tell you all something. You don't have any choice. If you believe this evil woman here, Mrs. Ruth will certainly die. Die horribly. If you trust me, I *may* be able to save her life. It is not certain that I can save her. Doctors sometimes lose their own children." He paused magnificently.

Ishtar Baynes had expected Harry to collapse. She *knew* he would not try to amputate an arm. But now she saw Harry laughing at her. And she saw doubt in their faces. Not doubt of Harry now, but doubt about her. She screamed again: "He ain't no real doctor. He's a head-feeler."

Harry drew himself up. "And you, madam, are a used-up old whore! *You* are the fraud, madam. You have had your time in the brothels of God-knows-how-many cities. And you dare to come out here on the plains where the very sun that looked on your whoredoms condemns you, and *you* dare to lecture *me* about telling the truth."

Ishtar Baynes went white. She seemed to dry up before their eyes. She put a thin, pale, trembling hand to her thin, pale mouth.

It was Clifford Baynes who yelled now. A squeak. "A ... A ... Why, here now, sir! What ever do you mean?" He wiped a hand frantically through his sticky black hair. He looked at his scrawny wife. "I demand an explanation for that horrid name!" He was not asking Harry. He was asking Ishtar Baynes.

"Honey!" she said desperately.

"Don't stick your honey to me, woman!"

Harry laughed cruelly and put his hands on his hips, rearing back. His face glowed like the sun. "A whore, Mr. Baynes. A woman who has had hundreds of lovers for pay. Not much pay, I'd say. A woman who is probably diseased this minute."

Jason, nearly beside himself: "I don't want us to talk about these things around women."

Jessica, cool and calm: "I don't know why not, husband. You have been willing to talk about many such things with this woman in secret. I don't know why we can't hear publicly what she is."

"No," Ishtar Baynes said.

Harry, laughing still: "And why did she stop selling herself, Mr. Baynes? Why did she come to Frederick, Maryland, and seduce you? Oh, you poor fool! She stopped for the same reason that finally stops every whore. She got old. And nobody would pay to have her anymore. She took you on for nothing because better men could not pay her anything. And

436

now I must stop this foolish conversation. I have an operation to perform!"

Clifford Baynes, his head bobbling like a rubber ball: "I thought she was a virgin! A virgin!"

Ishtar Baynes, looking like a wild bird with a broken wing: "Don't listen to him, honey. It's a lie. It's a lie. A damnable lie. I was a virgin. I swear to God. I was a virgin."

Clifford Baynes, grasping at straws, his eyes rolling with humiliation: "I personally can *attest* to her virginity!"

Harry, jovially: "You can do a lot with blackberry juice, Mr. Baynes. My father always said that. And how do you know anyway? How many virgins have you had in your life? How many women?"

"Sir!" Clifford Baynes said.

"Oh, honey, I never done you wrong," Ishtar Baynes said.

"She's all you deserve, Mr. Baynes," Harry said.

*He's going too far!* Alarmed at the reckless way Harry jumped the last human restraint, Adam remembered how Harry had talked about being mayor of Nashville. How Harry talked about being President. Too much pride. *Pride goeth before destruction.*

"I ain't done nothing to you. Don't talk like that about me." Ishtar Baynes.

Adam: *She's pitiful.* Her eyes rolled like a cowed dog's.

Jason, white and sick: "Dr. Creekmore, please. There are women present."

Harry laughed.

Clifford Baynes stuttered abominably. "I . . . I have t-t-t-t-to think! Think!" He turned away from them in a daze and stumbled off, his hands up to his head, his shoulders hunched under his old black coat.

Ishtar Baynes ran after him. "Let me help you, honey. You don't want to be thinking without me to help you. Honey, wait for me. Please wait."

He turned on her, one thin hand thrown back. "Get away from me, woman. Don't touch me. Don't you dare touch me."

He turned again and shambled on, Ishtar still following. Their noise receded with them.

Jason looked like death. "Please! Please! Enough of this. Whatever is true about Mrs. Baynes . . ." He stopped and turned back to Harry, making a feeble and meaningless gesture. "I do not believe Dr. Creekmore would tell us he is a doctor if he were not a doctor." And then, as if admitting that his own assurance was a lie, he turned on Adam. "What do you say, Adam? Is he a doctor or isn't he?"

Adam looked over at Ruth, who seemed to have lost consciousness again. The sight of her arm made him flinch, and his mouth felt as dry as sand. He looked at Harry. Harry smiled with terrible pride and irony. "Tell them what you think, Adam."

"I believe Harry ... Dr. Creekmore!" Promise cried out before Adam could make up his mind to lie. She recovered herself, and her voice became cool and crisp. As if she had aged ten years. "We are not going to get anywhere if we stand around here fighting like this. We must let him get on with it."

Silence. The wind moaned and sighed around the high rocks overhead. The sun beat down.

Harry swept his eyes over all of them. "I will now operate," he said.

Adam, swept up in admiration and terror: *By God! He's really going to do it.*

Harry set to his work in grand calm. He brought out his fancy black bag full of medical tools and medicines. "We need to have her sit up." Harry turned to Asa, who looked drained and helpless. "Mr. Jennings, you will have to hold your wife around the body. You will have to hold her very tight."

"I can't. I can't."

"What do you mean, you *can't!* She's your *wife*, goddamn you!"

Jason: "Dr. Creekmore ..."

Asa, beginning to cry: "I can't! I can't! I can't!"

Harry, his smile sardonic and terrible: "Just like I thought, Mr. Jennings. You're a goddamned coward. All bluster and fakery and no courage."

Jason, hands outstretched like a blind man: "Please, Dr. Creekmore, please ..."

Henry looked at his father and said not a word.

"I'll hold her good," Samuel said. Samuel hulking over them all, sad and silent, gaping on conflicts he could not understand, possessing not exactly courage but that bovine patience that will go where it is led. Harry was satisfied and nodded.

"You'll do better anyway. I just thought I'd give your brother there the chance to be a man."

Adam thinking: *Too far, damn you Harry! Too far.*

Back to Ruth. Harry had no time for lesser things. He spoke gently in her ear. "Mrs. Jennings, I am going to have to amputate your arm. Cut it off. It's the only way to save your life. I want to save your life so you can live to be an old woman. A mother to your son. A good wife. I want you to have your garden, Mrs. Jennings. I want you to have roses and grandchildren. But you have to trust me. I can't do it if you don't trust me. Do you trust me?"

Ruth's eyelids fluttered: she could barely whisper. "Yes." Much softer than the soft winds around them.

Asa sobbed. Harry ignored him. "All right, Samuel. Lift her up."

Her lips moved. Harry bent his ear to her mouth. "What is it, Mrs. Jennings?"

"I never dreamed I'd have a part of me cut off. It's something I never worried about."

Harry smiled. "Think how much time you've saved by not worrying," he said. She smiled back at him.

He took a deep breath. "Now Ruth—I'm going to call you Ruth now—I have a little bottle here with a new drug in it. We call the drug chloroform. I am going to put a little chloroform on my handkerchief, and I am going to put my handkerchief on your face, and you will breathe very deeply in and out, and in just a minute you'll go to sleep. A very deep sleep. Do you understand?"

"Yes."

"And while you are asleep, you will feel no pain at all. I will cut away that arm, and you will not feel any pain. It will not hurt you. Are you afraid?"

A slight hesitation. Ruth did not speak. She only managed to shake her head in negation, a motion so slight that she scarcely moved at all.

"Ruth!" Jessica said. "I'm here, Ruth. I can't think of anything to do. But I want you to know I love you." Jessica's voice broke.

Ruth opened her eyes and looked at Jessica and whispered something. Too faint to be heard. There were tears in her eyes; tears in Jessica's eyes, too. Ruth looked up at Samuel holding her, his brawny arms locked around her thick waist. "Good Samuel . . ." She mustered all her force to pronounce those two words distinctly and aloud. Beyond that she could not go. Samuel smiled foolishly down on her and was proud and embarrassed.

"All right," Harry said with authority. "Let's get on with it."

Harry brought the chloroform from the black bag. The bottle was nearly black. He removed the cork. It came out with a faint pop. A strong, sweet odor floated in the air. Harry poured some of the chloroform on his dingy handkerchief and put it gently to Ruth's face, holding it over her nose and mouth. He nodded to Promise to stopper the bottle again.

"Breathe in," he commanded. Ruth breathed. "Again," Harry said. She took another deep breath. Her eyes were shut. "Again," She breathed. "Again," he said gently. She breathed, and her headed nodded. In only a moment it had fallen over.

"All right, we have to work fast, before the chloroform wears off." He took off his coat and threw it aside. He rolled up his sleeves. His arms above his wrists pink like a baby's skin.

He hesitated just a moment. Took a deep breath. Steeled himself. And got to work. He took a long, sharp, thin knife from his bag and made a straight cut around Ruth's large arm a few inches above the elbow, slicing neatly and without hesitation through the skin and the fatty layer under it. It made the blood gush out. Jason, staring fixedly, silently, astonished by it all, turned a paler white. But it was not much blood. Harry let it pour out over his slender hands as if it were nothing. Almost instantly the rest of them thought it was nothing, too.

Harry took a smaller knife now and deftly cut back under the skin, separating skin from muscle in a band around the arm above the cut. Then he made two slits in the skin and peeled it back a couple of inches.

"Promise! Hold it there!"

Anybody had to obey Harry when he spoke like that. The girl moved swiftly, took the bloody skin and held it so that it was like a short sleeve, folded back.

Ruth sat with her eyes shut, breathing regularly, snoring slightly. Harry put some more chloroform on his handkerchief and held it to her face briefly.

Then he took up the large knife again. He put it close

440

against the place where the flap of skin was folded back. He bore down strongly, making a vigorous sawing motion, slicing through the muscles of the arm as if he had been carving a ham, until they heard distinctly the faint *tock* of the knife striking solid bone, and in a smooth sweep of his hand, he cut around the bone, neatly severing the muscles.

Now there was much blood. It came flooding out in a vivid scarlet spurting from the big artery that runs down the inside of the arm. Adam felt sick. But Harry moved with utter, precise calm and stanched the flow by squeezing the arm with his left hand. With his right he laid the knife quickly aside and took up a large piece of linen that he had set out. It was clean, so clean that it seemed impossible for it to be out here, where everything was so filthy. It was a large square with a slit cut to the middle on one side. Moving with incredible and precise speed, Harry pulled the linen roughly into the cut he had made, letting the bone slide through the slit. Then he pressed it up against the muscles and checked the flow of blood so that he could stop squeezing the artery with his other hand.

"Jessica!" he said quietly. "I need you to hold this in place." Jessica crowded in beside Samuel, by Promise, her face set, calm.

Now Harry took out a fine little hacksaw, sharper and finer than any they had ever seen. With it he cut down through the bone, moving with nerveless, quick energy, the sound of the saw making a soft rasp in the quiet afternoon. *Bzzzzz-bzzzzz, bzzzzz-bzzzzz, bzzzzz-bzzzzz*—like a jarfly droning off somewhere in a tree. And Harry, calmly holding the bottom part of the arm at the shattered place where bones and pulp and dirt all clotted together in the bloody wreckage, went on sawing until the fine saw broke through, and he held the severed arm in a grotesque handclasp before setting it down with unusual tenderness on the rocky ground.

Next he drew out a small set of pincers, and motioning to Jessica to lift the linen away, he quickly seized and closed the big artery. He drew it out and held it, shifted the shiny pincers to his left hand, and taking a long needle threaded with waxen thread, sewed the bluish, severed end of the artery shut. Working still with that fantastic confidence, he pulled out the smaller vessels one by one, sewed them shut until the bleeding stopped, except for the ooze of blood from those very small vessels that he could not close.

441

"Now we need some hot water to clean it up!" For the first time Harry looked around with the old Creekmore bafflement on his face. He had memorized all he needed to know about amputations from *Gunn's Domestic Medicine.* But he had forgotten the water for cleaning up. However, the old man had seen the need. The fire was made and the water was hot before the arm was off. And when Harry looked around, momentarily annoyed with himself, the old man said quietly, "I got the water ready, Doc. I seen Dr. Whitman out in the Oregon country take an arm off once. God rest his soul. He didn't do it no better than you done."

Harry smiled absentmindedly. He scrubbed the dirt and the gore off his own hands. Working with compassionate gentleness, he took another piece of clean linen from his bag, wet it, and delicately cleaned the wound. He inspected the sewn vessels one more time, and very carefully he drew down the flap of skin that Promise had been holding folded back on that upper arm. He set the flap carefully over the end of the stump, pulling the sewn arteries and veins down so that the ligatures he had made hung out of the flap, where later they would fall off of their own accord. He put a sticking plaster over the flap so that it would hold together. Then he bandaged the arm with clean linen bandages, being careful not to get the wrappings too tight. Afterwards Jessica very carefully cleaned Ruth up as best she could, bathing her all over with warm water. And they put her gently to bed in Jason's hail-rent wagon.

By then the sun was red, and the day was about to go.

# 50

---

Years and years later, when people understood about germs and infections, when Joseph Lister was in all the medical books and doctors washed their hands before they operated and boiled their instruments to sterilize them before they ever pricked human flesh, Adam was even more amazed at what Harry had done.

In 1851 nobody had ever heard of those destructive little microorganisms called "germs" except as a laboratory curiosity, and the notion that they might cause disease was undreamed of. Infection was called "proud flesh," because it insisted on being different from ordinary flesh and calling attention to itself, and nobody knew what to do about it.

Ruth's arm did not get infected.

Even so she almost died. She went into a burning fever, and Jessica sat up all night with her and bathed her face and her body, and Ruth cried out in delirium, moaning unintelligible names and sounds, sometimes calling for Henry, sometimes for Rachael. Never once for Asa.

Asa brooded and looked on. He was an outsider now. An exile who could not leave them. Nobody had much to say to him. People were embarrassed and struck silent by his uncomfortable presence.

Harry felt all over Ruth's ribs, moving expertly around her breasts so that he would not touch her immodestly. He thought she had broken two or three of them, but there was nothing to do for broken ribs except to let them heal. In the meantime you endured the pain. "She may have something else broken inside her," Harry said sternly, professionally. "We'll have to wait her out." Everybody deferred to Harry now because he was in charge. He was a doctor.

Harry proclaimed his superiority with graceful nods and waving hands, and Adam could see the strange confidence written in his face. "I did it, Adam. You did not believe me. Nobody believed me. But I did it." And Adam had no answer but silent awe to return to him. Harry had done it. How could anybody doubt him now? They all praised Harry. And Harry smiled and nodded and tried to be as gracious to them as he could, feeling genuinely humble and genuinely proud.

They waited that night and the hot day afterwards and the night again and the day after that, and August came drifting in on them, and the old man muttered that he could smell autumn in the night air now. Just a breath. But if the breath was here, the body of winter was not far behind.

Jessica sat up that third night with Ruth till deep in the dark morning. Then giddy with fatigue she came out of the wagon, leaving Promise to watch. Jason was wrapped up in his blankets, apparently asleep. Adam stood guard over the stock, and Jessica asked him to walk a few minutes with her so that she might clear her head.

They walked out of sight and out of sound of camp and sat in the grass and held each other. Adam felt her hair against his face. He put his arms over her breasts and squeezed her to him. "Run away with me," he whispered. "Please God! Let's leave this. Tomorrow morning. You can ride one of my mules. Please, please!"

"No," she said. "I have told you. It is too late. This will pass. We will get to California. And when we do, we will never see each other again. I want it that way. I don't want you to see me get old."

"I love you. I love you so much. I'll always love you."

She was quiet for a long time, and Adam felt how distant she was even when her head lay on his shoulder and he had his arms around her. She was as far away as the stars she watched overhead. Finally she said, "Once I thought I knew what love was. I wanted to be in love. I thought I was in love. Now I don't even know what love is. To love a man. I think being in love with a man is a risk and a burden. I know what age is. I know what time is. And I know that my time for love has gone."

Adam could not think of anything to say to her. He felt helpless despair, and it was in that mood that he made love to her again, she giving him a mute signal by sliding down into the grass and pulling him down on top of her. She was hungry and straining for him, and when he entered her, she begged him to go slowly, but he was so maddened by her warmth, her soft nakedness, her urgent giving, that it was all over before he wanted it to be.

He lay with his face in the sweet grass, wanting to tell her again how much he loved her. But he could not bring himself to say words she did not want to hear. So he could only whisper a blundering apology for how quickly he had finished, knowing that she had yearned for him to go on and on.

She stroked his head and laughed gently in the dark. "It's not an endurance contest," she said. He laughed nervously, not understanding what she meant, laughing because he felt too stupid to talk to her. He believed she was forgiving him for something, perhaps for the foolishness of his desperate love. And a sadness came up in him, huge and immortal, that he could not fend off.

He was terrified of discovery. He thought everybody must

know that Jessica had gone with him into the dark and that they had committed adultery. He supposed that the hound, which had lain slumbering nearby while they strained and pushed at each other, would surely find a voice and tell the world.

But no one seemed to notice anything out of order. People were too preoccupied with Ruth and their own loss and the fate that awaited them in California. It did not seem possible to Adam that he could do what he was doing and not be found out, for he thought the eyes of God must be on him and all the creatures God had made must know.

From somewhere Ishtar Baynes had acquired a black eye and a thick, bruised lip. Her husband would not sleep in the tent with her now but rather rolled himself up in tattered blankets under Jason's wagon at night. He was silent, withdrawn, and deeply injured. Ishtar Baynes was silent, too, sitting aside with scrawny legs drawn up like poles under her filthy dress, arms wrapped around her thin knees, looking at them with baleful eyes and at Harry with hatred.

Finally Ruth stirred and came to herself. She awoke crying weakly. She whispered that she had dreamed Henry had drowned. And when she saw her only son still alive, she put her good arm up and the bandaged stump, too, and wept without sobbing, the salt tears running out of her eyes and down the sides of her face, her expression full of joy. Henry stood nearby and hugged her cautiously, afraid lest he hurt her. When Ruth dropped off to sleep again, he stroked her hair, and the boy looked wiser than Adam had thought a child could be.

Asa had nothing to say. He watched and looked at his son. His son hardly ever looked at him.

The covers of the two serviceable wagons had been badly cut by the hail. Holes all through them. The wind whistled through the holes and made an unpleasant dull howling.

While they waited for Ruth to get better, Samuel and Adam set to work sewing patches on Samuel's wagon cover. "That sure was a storm," Rebecca said in genuine awe. She looked up with the recollection of honest terror through the gaping holes in her artificial ceiling, where the blue sky glowed high overhead.

"I ain't never seen no storm like that one before. Maybe Jesus is fixing to come back to judge the quick and the dead.

445

Are you ready for King Jesus, young man? Have you ever had an experience?"

Adam worked inside with a large needle while Samuel worked outside. He shook his head, bored with her. "No, ma'am, I ain't never had no experience."

"Oh, lordy!" Rebecca cried in false alarm. "That means you're going to burn forever in *hell!*"

"I reckon it does all right."

"Well, ain't you *worried* about it?"

"No, ma'am. I don't reckon so. What is to be will be."

"You mean you think if I was to pick up a rattlesnake, and if it was to bite me, I wouldn't die if it wasn't my time to die?" She turned to one of her favorite doctrinal arguments and looked craftily at him as if she had served up a perfect stew of entrapment.

Adam said flatly, "You couldn't pick up no rattlesnake here, ma'am."

She sat back indignantly. "I'd like to know why I couldn't pick up a rattlesnake if I took a notion I wanted to!"

"They ain't no rattlesnakes in Ohio, ma'am," Adam said. "If you're going to find you a rattlesnake to pick up, you got to go West."

Unexpected counterattack. She fell back to rocking swiftly again and thought for a few moments. "Well, I sure ain't never going to go West. I'm going to stay right here in Ironton, Ohio, where I belong, right here in my own house. And since they ain't no rattlesnakes in Ohio, they ain't no reason to talk about rattlesnakes."

"You was the one that brung it up, ma'am."

"The only reason I was talking about it was to show you how miserable that stupid doctrine is. What is to be will be! The very idea! It means I could pick up a rattlesnake, and if it wasn't my time to die, God wouldn't let the snake kill me."

"That's right, ma'am. And it means that you can be sitting right here in your own little house, and if it comes your time to die, then you can't do nothing about it. You'll just keel over dead as a rock."

Rebecca laughed in her most scornful tone. "That *sure* ain't going to happen to me, young man. I'm fit as a fiddle."

"Ah, you don't know, ma'am. God's awful tricky sometimes. I've knowed folks to be fit as a fiddle one day, and next morning all their strings was broke."

"Young man, the God *I* believe in is a God I can trust to do the right thing. And if there is anything that is *not* the

446

right thing, it is to strike some poor old abused woman dead when she's sitting in her own rocking chair, minding her own business."

"Yes, ma'am." Adam went on working with his needle.

Rebecca watched him tentatively for a while. She rocked furiously. Then she suddenly looked around as if she had been struck by an important and secret idea. She stopped rocking and gestured to him furtively, making a sign for him to bend down.

Adam bent, looking at her cautiously. "What is it, ma'am?"

"Young man, tell me the truth. Your secret will be safe with me," she whispered, her little eyes darting toward the outside. "Don't you think they're *all* crazy? I mean *all* of them? Jason and Asa and Samuel, too? And you should of knowed their mamma! Lordy! I ain't never seen such a crazy bunch!"

"How do you reckon she keeps it up?" Adam asked Harry later. "Living in that wagon, pretending she's sitting in her house back there in Ohio? How can she keep a straight face and do that?"

"I told you," Harry said with a comfortable yawn, elegantly stretching with the boredom of his own habitual wisdom. "It's theatre."

"Then I ain't never going to no theatre," Adam said.

"Adam, my dear and faithful friend, you are backward. Please do not be offended if I tell you how backward you are."

*He ain't no doctor!* Adam kept thinking. The knowledge was like a stone in his belly. *He's going to go too far.* Sometimes the thought was not completely worrisome. Harry Creekmore riding for a fall. Just a little fall. To let Adam know that the world had an order to it, where there were some things you could count on.

For Adam knew that there was something ineluctable about Harry's pride. It drove him to struggle against being ordinary. And the simple power of Harry's will made him not only succeed but look for higher ground, for greater triumphs, and for an imperishable glory. Harry was an actor, too—a magnificent actor, sweeping elegantly across his stage from applause to applause.

*It can't last,* Adam thought.

"I'm so thankful poor Rebecca wasn't hurt," Samuel said to Adam afterwards. "I got the oxen loose just in time." The big man had tears standing deep in his eyes.

"You done good, Samuel. You always do good," Adam said.

"Rebecca likes you, Adam. She said you and her talked. I told her I like you, too. I'd appreciate it if you'd go talk to her some more. I've told her you was my best friend."

Samuel looked like the incarnation of confused emotions. Big and hulking, his eyes filled with tears because he had been thinking of how his dear wife might have been killed, a smile of pride on his moon-face, because he was talking like a man worthy of having a best friend. It was a sign of adulthood and independence.

Adam did reluctantly go visit Rebecca again. He found her cross, knitting with complete concentration. Her skin was sallow and puffy, and her hair was tangled, dull, lifeless, and streaked with a gray that was an unhealthy yellow, hair and complexion alike showing the effects of being too long away from the sun.

*She ain't well!* thought Adam, but the reflection was casual because he did not see her much. And when they finally got under way again he scarcely thought about Rebecca, except to puzzle occasionally at how much Samuel loved her.

Ruth was slung in a canvas hammock that the old man rigged for her in Jason's wagon. Jessica and Promise took care of her. Asa walked along with nothing to do. He shook hands with Harry once and tried to apologize to him, and Harry accepted the apology grandly.

They made twelve hours a day now. The old man was anxious. "The snow's going to get us in the Sierra Nevada sure enough if we don't get a move on. Maybe we ought to put up with the Mormons for the winter, Jason. Better get to California in the spring than freeze to death in the Sierra Nevada."

"Mormons!" Jason was incredulous. "Those wicked, lustful, heathen people. Them and their so-called wives ... I couldn't bear the thought!" Jason's loathing for the Mormons was the strongest emotion Adam had seen in him yet.

"They got plans for the West," the old man said mildly. "Same as you, Jason. Maybe you'd find out that you and them had a lot in common."

"There is no comparison between me and them," Jason said.

"It's August," the old man said patiently. "We ain't half-

448

way. We got to put up somewheres. The Mormons would keep us."

"I won't discuss the subject anymore," Jason said with a visible shudder. "It is warm now. We can make it if we push on."

The old man gave up for the time being. Adam looked at Jason and hated him and yearned to kill him. He thought of ways he might make it seem that Jason had died by accident. *Shoot him when we're standing watch some night. I could say I thought he was an Indian in the dark.*

The plan was plausible; it rattled chains of fantasy in Adam's brain, especially when he tried to sleep. He did not do anything about it.

Now they were up like machines in the early dark, before the first dim gray of morning, the fire bursting cheerily around the soot-blackened coffeepot, the crackling sound of bacon frying in iron skillets, the savory smell hanging in the cool air. And by the time the east turned to wine with the approaching sun, they were on their way, shouting at the oxen, hearing the lurching grumble of the two wagons, a sound that was their daylight symphony. And so they traveled until the sun sank in front of them and turned crimson above the horizon so that they could look it in the face without blinking their eyes. Then only did they camp quietly, hardly talking to each other because the sense of urgency in them was so great. They did the evening chores, put the oxen out to graze and fed the mules from the dwindling supply of oats. The mules were getting thin. Like the oxen. Adam grieved for them.

All of them sensed winter in the cool nights now. The old man's hands swelled up more and turned an angry red, and his silences were longer than they had been. In the daylight hours the trail was almost always empty except for themselves. And they were all weary of the journey.

Yet Jason was buoyed by Ruth's steady recovery. To him the world was gradually turning rosy again. One night he said, "Everything's happened to us that's going to happen now. If Ruth had died, then I would have known that we were defeated. But she did not die, and that is a sign to me that we have been through the fire. We have been proved like fine gold. We have passed our tests. And now we are bound for the Promised Land."

"Yes," Harry said, as if he had long been a student of the seasons in human life, "I am sure that nothing will stop us

449

now." He clucked his tongue and looked solemn, a prophet delivering himself of his message for the day.

Ishtar Baynes was nothing now. She huddled on the edges of the firelight, always on the opposite side from her husband at night, and neither of them had anything to say to anybody. Jason, believing that she was a whore, was scarcely civil to her, and both she and her husband were like strays, hanging on the fringes of things to receive what scraps of food might be handed over to them.

"As soon as we reach civilization, Mrs. Baynes, I hope that we shall never see you again," Jason said. And Adam, seeing her so completely defeated, found himself feeling sorry for her, and Jason's prim, stern condemnation gave Adam no pleasure at all.

Ruth's recovery did seem to be a gift. "I'll have to learn to garden with my left hand," she said with a laugh. "But I reckon I learned how to use my right hand once, and now I can learn with my left if I take my time at it. We'll have our roses yet in California. You wait and see."

Adam realized years later that they had all been living a story. In good stories there was always something wrong somewhere. There were drama and conflict, a slide into disaster, and finally a climax where everything seemed ready to fall apart. But then, in the climax itself, things suddenly turned around. The conflicts were resolved, and good came out on top. And everything rolled smoothly to a happy ending, where everyone who deserved good luck lived happily ever after. Ruth's recovery became the sign of victory for all of them. Jason said things would be good now. Harry agreed. And who could any longer dispute Harry's word?

They passed Fort Laramie, and they saw the blue pyramid of Laramie Peak rising solidly against the other blue of the sky. It was the first outpost of the stony mountains.

There was a doctor at Fort Laramie. He was a pudgy, balding man with the bearing of a man who drinks too much whiskey in solitude and does not want anyone to suspect. Yet everyone knew just because the doctor spoke so carefully and carried himself so stiffly. He inspected Ruth's arm, because Harry off-handedly expressed the opinion that it might be good to consult with another doctor. Harry was that confident.

The military doctor, discovering that Harry had studied at the famous University of Heidelberg, was abashed. "I just studied for a year," he said in a slow sigh of alcoholic fumes.

450

"Back in Philadelphia. My teachers weren't no good." He shook his head.

He examined Ruth's stump. He had a hard time of it to focus his eyes. But when he finally got them fixed, his head farsightedly reared back, he achieved a certain distinction and looked stern and knowing. He pronounced Harry's work to be one of the finest amputations he had ever seen. And he congratulated everybody gravely and excessively on the good fortune of having such a splendid surgeon as Harry Creekmore in their company. "I'm sure I've heard your name, Dr. Creekmore! It rings a bell in my head. Did you ever write any medical books?"

"Just one," Harry said modestly. "It's out of print now. I did a little treatise on diseases of the head." He looked significantly at Jason.

"That's it!" the blear-eyed doctor said. "I've read your book!" And so the doctor at Fort Laramie became, like to many others Adam was to know, eager to build a golden legend about somebody else, and desperately determined to believe in that legend himself.

At Fort Laramie the officers in charge shook their heads soberly and spat and looked as forbidding as Laramie Peak rising ahead of them. "It's too late to make it to California this year," they said. "Middle of August already! That means you got two good months on the trail if everything goes right. And you can't bank on things going right out here. Let's see. That puts you maybe October 11 at the earliest through the Sierra Nevada. Planning to get through that late is like pointing a pistol at your head with three bullets in it, twirling the cylinder, snapping the trigger and hoping not to get your brains blown out! Better find you a place up ahead and lay by. You don't want to be like the Donners!"

Jason only smiled. He stood with his arms folded across his chest and looked as superior as a statue. "But there is a chance for us to get through."

"Oh, sure, there's a chance. But listen, mister, out here you figure your chances pretty careful. When you lose, you're dead."

"I'm sure we'll manage," Jason said.

On the day the officers, lounging around on the broad, green parade ground, sang their dirge of snow, the sun was hot and beaming down, and the sky was an incredible blue. Laramie Peak rose up against the horizon, still and tremen-

451

dous. And to Jason the mountains ahead marked the end of troubles.

On that day Ruth was up walking around for the first time since her accident. She was still weak and dizzy but getting stronger every day. She helped fix breakfast, laughing good-naturedly and insisting, when Promise and Jessica tried to make her lie down, "No, Jessica honey, I got to learn how to use this left arm. You don't do me no favor by doing everything for me. I ain't never going to have my right arm back again. And I ain't going to spend the rest of my life having folks wait on me!"

The wife of one of the officers had the women in for tea. "I don't believe Mrs. Baynes will care to associate with women who are her superiors," Jason said. So Ishtar Baynes sat in the wagon with Rebecca. But Promise and Ruth and Jessica went and had real tea with sugar and napkins under regular crockery cups, and they talked and laughed with the women at the fort, and when Jessica told about Rachael they all cried.

They stayed overnight at Fort Laramie. Adam and the old man got oats for their mules, and the mules ate until they stopped eating because they were full. Adam felt good to see his animals content.

In the morning they pushed on, and the old man rode ahead on his mule, playing the harmonica, holding it carefully in his stiff hands. They came to a rise, moving now through sandy and rocky country. The thin river below them was blue, the sky was blue, the mountains were blue, and Adam felt a surge of joy in spite of all his foreboding. It was all right! Everything was going to be all right! He caught Jessica's eye and grinned at her. She smiled with open pleasure at him in return, and Adam put aside fantasies of murder. He rode close to her, dismounted and walked awhile by her side.

"You told me once," he murmured, "that when we die it's too late to see how foolish our fears have been. It's foolish to worry about being old. Age, it's just something wrote down in a family Bible somewheres. It don't mean nothing more than that."

She laughed happily, in a mood to believe, and he took her laughter as assent. When they got to California, he would take Jessica away. He would confess everything in front of Jason, and she could not stay with her legal husband then. In California the petty laws that bound people back East could be abandoned, just as all of them had abandoned a past that had proven itself unsuitable. Adam looked on Jessica and counted her as his own, and he was more happy than he had ever been in his life.

They camped that night at Register Rock, where hundreds before them had carved their names. The low, domed hill with its sheer limestone cliff was like a teacher's big slate set against a meadow where there was good grass. The river splashing over its marshy and sandy bed nearby gave them good water, which the old man said they could drink because it was so cold.

They sat in a circle eating bread Jessica had baked for them, and they passed the dipper around and drank and felt more serene together than they had since Rachael died. Mr. and Mrs. Baynes remained apart, silent and isolated from each other and from the company at large by their separate humiliations. Their withdrawal made the communion among the rest of them all the better, and Adam reflected that if it had not been for the couple Baynes, this whole trip might have been joy. Well, it would be better now. He knew things would be better.

He talked easily to Jessica, and she talked to him and laughed and tossed her head and looked pleased to be admired. No one—not even Jason—seemed suspicious that anything might be wrong. And Adam knew that things would work out, that life would be good.

He carved his name among all the others at Register Rock, and it is there to this day, the way that he made it. It was a sign of the confidence he felt.

Only the old man was glum that night. He sat flexing his hands, rubbing them together to massage the pain out of them, and looked out to the mountains ahead of them and kept his thoughts to himself.

# 51

And now the country was more hostile than it had been. No buffalo were to be seen. No trace of them in dried buffalo chips for fire. They had to find scrub timber here and there, and it was hard to ignite and hard to keep burning. The rocky foothills of the mountains rose around them, and at night it began to get cold. Adam awoke one morning and crawled out of his buffalo robes to stand the last watch of the night with Samuel, and the wind was so sharp that he decided on the luxury of coffee in the blowing dark. When he took down the water pail, he found a thin crust of ice on the water. Only that once was the ice there. But ice in August was a fearsome thing, and Adam pondered it and mentioned it in a low voice to the old man, and the old man puckered his wrinkled face and shook his head.

So now when they walked the night watch they drew buffalo robes around them and tramped clumsily about, replenishing the fire, muttering about the cold. Their days—long days inclining always upward—passed in toil and in silence. Everybody but Rebecca walked, and at night they were all exhausted and fell to sleep like dying men.

At night, too, the old man calculated the march of the stars. He and Adam watched the upward march of the winter constellations, and they saw that Orion was all the way up in the sky before the dawn now. "When the sisters come at twilight, they carry snow in their hair," the old man muttered. His hands were swollen so badly now that he gave up trying to carry a rifle. He caught cold and could not shake it off and snuffled and coughed and doctored himself with whiskey and fell into long, gloomy meditations.

Adam remembered his mother's last sickness and felt a different kind of chill. The old man was mortal. It seemed hardly possible.

"We'll be all right!" Jason said brightly. "It's not cold enough to hurt anything yet. We'll warm up in the desert.

454

Think how bad it was in the hills, before Ash Hollow. Think how good we felt when we got to cold water." They had the desert to cross before the Sierra Nevada. Jason had never been in the desert.

One afternoon Adam killed an antelope. A fantastic shot, at long distance, made by a ruse. He crouched behind a stone and waved a cloth on the end of a long stick, and the antelope, devoured by curiosity, came slowly close to see what it was, sniffing and looking, until Adam fired and killed it with a single shot through the heart. So they ate well that night, and the old man showed Adam how to make jerky, and Adam did it. The old man nodded in stern satisfaction. They had buffalo jerky yet, and they had kegs of bacon and three kegs of flour, and now they had antelope, and if snow caught them, they could kill the oxen, too, and they would not have to eat each other until maybe February. So the old man said, looking as grim as Elijah.

But Jason laughed and swore they would not be caught by the snow.

They waded the North Platte—three feet deep and running without vengeance—hardly more than a branch, by the red buttes. Sandstone cliffs rising above them over the river, catching the fiery afternoon sun and the wind. An eagle rose, flapping into the air above them, screaming a harsh, indignant cry.

Wood was abundant now, and the rocky ridges towering on each side of them were black with conifers. Somebody at the fort had told them about a big Indian meeting with the whites that was going to be held soon. "Watch out for the Blackfeet," an officer said. And the old man said the Blackfeet were the most cruel Indians in these parts, and when they looked at the dark trees in the middle distance, they all wondered if secret eyes watched them. But they had big fires at night, and the fires drove back the solitude and made danger seem remote. They were happy at night.

They made an unpleasant discovery. The flour had gone bad. The kegs were not waterproof after all. Jessica opened a keg one night and found it swarming with little white worms and smelling vaguely rancid. They dumped it out. But opening the remaining kegs one by one, they found them all reeking and twitching. So they would eat no more bread, and meat and beans without bread began to be unbearably tiresome. Adam got to hating the taste of salt, and he thought of apples and hot biscuits. Once in the night he began to hunger

455

for turnips, and then he laughed to himself and thought he was truly mad.

But Jason was undaunted, and Harry spoke easily in the firelight, when anything was possible, about how easy life was going to be in California.

As Jason grew in strength and confidence after his ordeal of doubt, the old man seemed to decline. Adam puzzled and worried over it and did not know what to say, because there seemed to be nothing to do.

The cold seemed to be the final blow. "I ain't never had the rheumatiz as bad as I got it now," the old man said, his voice choked with the phlegm in his throat. He held up his stiff and swollen hands to Adam. Adam saddled the mules every morning and fed them at night, and he insisted that the old man ride even when the rest of them walked to spare the stock. He helped the old man up in the saddle and tried to manage things so that the old man would not have to humiliate himself by asking.

"I need your help now, Henry. More than before," Adam said to the boy. And Henry threw himself with more energy into work and brushed the oxen and helped grease their hoofs and greased the wheels of the wagons himself and did the work of a man, while Asa stood musing and aloof from all work and Jason preached to Harry and heard Harry preaching in return and Samuel took care of Rebecca and talked to her about Ironton, Ohio.

The old man was gloomy. "Look at Mrs. Ruth. She lost her arm, and she gets around better than me now. What's going to happen to me?" And he fell into a fit of coughing that left him red-eyed and breathless.

"You'd already be in California if it hadn't been for me," Adam said remorsefully. He was full of guilt every time he looked at the old man.

"Ah, you're good company, Adam. I don't regret nothing. Honest I don't."

"You'll be all right when we get down in the desert. It's going to be warm down there. You don't get the rheumatiz when it's warm like in the desert."

"Warm! Oh, Jesus, I hope it's warm. If I hadn't run into you, Adam, I might of gone back to Oregon. Just out of habit. I ain't never had the rheumatiz like this. I couldn't of lived through the winter up there. I couldn't of held my gun to hunt. I'd of died." The words were slow and cautious, as if the old man had just missed a terrific danger in something ordinary and could not understand it.

"You'll be all right. Just wait to the desert. And in California, you won't never have the rheumatiz in California."

"Ah, let me tell you something, Adam Cloud. Be glad you ain't as old as me. And I don't say that because if you was my age you'd be close to dying. That's part of it, I reckon. I ain't going to live as long as I have lived. But I mean you'd better be glad you didn't go West when you was young. Like me. Now of course you're younger than I was when I went the first time. A lot younger. But back then the West was ten million square miles of woods and the woods was full of beavers, and they was folks back East that was wearing beaver hats the way God meant for folks to cover their heads. And they was Indians moving like a bunch of ghosts in the trees, and when I went out there for the first time it was before the Indians figured out that whiskey and white men and furs all went together, and they was good to live with. Back then you looked up at a hill or a mountain or a single goddamned tree and knowed there wasn't another white man in the whole history of the world that'd ever seed what you was seeing right then.

"I learnt stuff you could of learnt real easy, Adam. You're damn smart. And hell, I was smart too back then. How to make a big fire in the rain. How to keep dry. How to keep warm. How to kill supper. How to trap beaver. How to hide from the goddamned Blackfeet. Hell, I learned everything they was to know about how to live in country like that. I learned it like I was borned to it, and I thought I was, and I was happy. Lord, I thought I was in heaven out there.

"But you know something? Ain't nothing I learnt out there no good no more. I spent my whole damn life learning it, and I learnt it better than anybody I ever knowed, and ain't none of it worth passing on to nobody, because where it was useful is all gone. That way of life. Gone like the snow in summer. I've outlived my time and seen it pass away, and if you'd been my age back then, you'd of learnt it, too, and you'd of lost the place where you could use it. Like me. But I tell you, boy! Who'd of ever thought that this country out here could be used up? That we could lose it like it was?"

"You lose everything if you live long enough," he said. He was thinking of Jessica.

The old man shook his head. "No, what you're going to find in Californie, that's going to be around awhile. That's going to be the real life, whatever the hell it is. And you'll have it because you're young, and you're going to have somebody to hand it on to. Me, I ain't never going to have it. It's like this summer. Time's running out on me. And the devil got in me way back there and ruint me. The devil that hides in the springs and the river and blows through the trees. He eat me up and made me give my life to the West, and then he took the West away from me. The West I was used to. Think of that! He taught me to live in a magic land, and then he waved his hand, and it all went away."

The old man crossed himself and looked skyward where the moon, coming off the full now, glared down at him like an unblinking silver eye.

"And I didn't even know it was the devil that done it till it was too late. I thought it was God that taken me out there and showed me the blue skies and the rivers and the mountains. Now I look at it, at the mountains, and I can see up there where I ain't never going to climb again, and I know how close I am to dying. I thought it was God took me out there, and it was the devil all along. Lord have mercy on us!"

# 52

He made love to Jessica again beyond the red buttes, where they had crossed the North Platte and left it behind. It was an accident, something no one could have predicted.

Samuel was to stand the middle watch with Adam that night, the worst watch of all. The one that stretched from midnight till three in the morning. But after supper, Samuel took sick. Something wrong with his stomach. He vomited and lay down in sudden exhaustion to sleep, groaning slightly when he breathed. Asa helped him to bed and came back looking bleak and frightened. "What if it's cholera?" he murmured.

"Could be," the old man said. "We'll know in the morning, I reckon."

They were swept by a flurry of fear, but Harry calmed

them. "I believe I can assure you that Samuel does not have cholera. And if he does, do not fear. I am sure that I can cure him."

"I ain't never knowed no doctor that can fix the cholera," the old man said.

So Adam volunteered to stand the middle watch alone. As she was going to bed Jessica spoke to him in a low, quick voice—the sort of furtive communication guilty lovers have exchanged since the beginning of adultery. "So you will be out there alone tonight?" She moved swiftly away, gathering her dress around her and giving no sign that she had even spoken to him, leaving Adam to know what she meant.

His lusts puzzled him. When he saw Jessica by day, when there was no chance for them to touch, when he looked at her modestly skirted legs and knew that they had been naked to him and wrapped around his naked thighs, when he thought of her voluptuous body moving in rhythm to his own, when he heard her voice calmly speaking of inconsequential things and remembered its urgency in his ear, her breath on his face, he was driven nearly mad by desire.

But when the moment came for him to love her again, when he must count on a certain time and a certain place and the possibility of discovery, he was devoured by a guilt and a sadness that was hell to bear. Jessica was married to somebody else. She slept beside Jason every night. And when he turned in his sleep, he moved against her body. No matter how much he might assume gallant poses in his fantasies, things like marriage made a difference to Adam Cloud.

He tried to sleep, but he could not. The minutes marched by on leaden feet. And at midnight when Harry came prancing in to awaken him, Adam had to pretend to be startled from slumber. He took a rifle and wrapped himself in one of the buffalo robes, and all the world was cold and very still. Adam walked, every sense painfully acute. His heart thudded in his neck. It seemed hours before Jessica's dim form fluttered into view and came to him. He led her out into the night and wrapped them both in the buffalo robe, and they loved each other.

It was an accident that had given them this night, and it was another accident that made Samuel call to Adam and call softly, letting them know he was coming before he stumbled on them. Samuel alerted to the direction because the friendly hound went bounding to him. Samuel following

459

the damnable, gyrating dog, calling, "Adam? Adam? Where are you, Adam?"

Adam felt blue terror. Never in his life had he moved so swiftly. He cursed the moonlight. He frantically fixed his shirt, remembered his pants and jumped to his feet, still pulling at his shirt. All with the furtive and desperate haste of a jackal streaking into the night when he hears the lion roar.

"Here, Samuel. I'm here!" He heard how breathless he was, how his voice trembled. And Samuel, who had come out into the dark expecting only Adam, suddenly perceived not one but two dim forms detaching themselves from the night and appearing almost magically before him. And as he drew up short in puzzlement, his slow wit wondering and hesitating, Jessica spoke with the easy greeting of Sunday morning.

"Hello, Samuel! I'm so glad you're feeling better. You know, Asa was afraid you might have the cholera." She laughed lightly as if they were all dismissing preposterous thoughts. "I couldn't sleep. I came out for a walk. Adam and I were talking about the beautiful night. Have you ever seen so many stars?"

A moment ago she was groaning in passion, and her voice seemed to come from deep in her throat. Now her voice was as smooth as sweet milk. Adam was dumbfounded at the transformation in her.

Samuel was silent for a moment. When he did speak Adam could hear the timbre of doubt in his voice. "Oh, hello, Jessica. Hello. What are you doing ... Adam ... I got to feeling better. I felt bad about Adam, being out here all by hisself. I knowed he was ... I thought he was alone."

"Well, I think that's wonderful, Samuel. We're so glad to see you. I wonder if you got sick because of something you ate. I do hope it wasn't my cooking."

"Oh, no. No, Jessica. I mean, there ain't nobody sick but me, and you cooked for all of us. I don't know what it was. I ain't never been sick. It wasn't nothing. See, I'm better now."

"Well, I couldn't bear to make you sick, Samuel. Not after all you've done for us."

"I ain't done nothing for you."

"Oh, you know what I was just saying to Adam here?" She went on, not giving Samuel a chance to think. "I was saying I can't wait to eat vegetables again. Corn! Wouldn't you just love to have some good white corn again, Samuel? And green beans! Oh, how I'd love to have a taste of good green beans with some hog fatback swimming in the brew."

460

Samuel, with longing: "That sure would taste good."

"And greens! I wish I knew what things are good to eat out here. I was just telling Adam we might pick some wild greens if we knew what we ate wouldn't poison us!" She laughed again, swabbing away at any impossible fantasy of danger.

The suspicion in Samuel's slow mind would go away as slowly as it came. "You two was just out here . . . talking?"

"Oh, yes," Jessica said with another laugh. "I kept turning over and over in our blankets, and I was afraid of waking Ruth up. Poor thing. It's so cramped in our wagon now."

"And Jason don't know you're out here?" Samuel said.

"Oh, dear! I hope not. I wouldn't have waked him up for the world," Jessica said. "Isn't Dr. Creekmore wonderful! What he did for Ruth! But poor thing! Having to go through the rest of life without her right arm. She can do it if anybody can. Why, she has more strength than I'll ever have. We should all be thankful it was not much worse than it was."

Adam did not like Jessica now. She was being too false. Like Harry. Beneath her forced and light-hearted banter he could feel her calculation that Samuel was too stupid to catch her in a lie.

"You got to be careful about walking out here in the dark," Samuel said, still slowly, his mind tramping determinedly through a morass. "Indians. They sneak up on you in the dark."

"Oh, I know!" Jessica said. "That's why I called to Adam and asked him to keep me company. I was sure he could protect me." She laughed again. This time a distinct note of revulsion in the laughter. "I would not be happy to be carried off by Indians. Not after what we've seen of Indians." She shuddered. "And poor Jason! It would be such a burden to him if anything happened to anybody else."

"Jason seems right happy here lately," Samuel said.

"Oh, yes, he's happy. But you don't know the worries the poor man carries around in his heart. I'm not sure I know all of them. He talks to me about some of them, and I know he has more on his mind than any of you can realize."

It made Adam sick. Jessica's voice, bright as a piece of polished nickel, rolling on and on, full of sympathy for everybody, covering their deed with a performance of elegant informality and natural pleasantry. And Adam knew, if Jessica did not, that Samuel was not fully deceived. For underneath her flow of glittering artificiality, Samuel's own voice remained puzzled, slow, pondering, and Adam could feel his wariness like something tangible in the dark.

Adam had a sudden, powerful impulse to declare their adultery, force Jessica to be honest, load his mules in the morning, and go off with her, leaving the rest of them and deceit itself behind. He could not understand what on earth it was that Jessica was afraid of losing. Promise? Promise was nearly grown, and Jessica was going to lose her to Harry soon. But Adam did not respond to his impulses now; he kept still, guilty and afraid.

Finally Jessica yawned with elaborately feigned sleepiness and said, "Well, now, I guess I did what I wanted to do. I'm ready to go back to bed. To get some sleep. You gentlemen must excuse me. Don't tell Jason you saw me out here, Samuel. I wouldn't want to worry him anymore. He thinks I can't take care of myself."

"All right," Samuel said, still slowly, and Adam felt himself turn red in the dark.

Jessica was dressed only in her nightgown and her duster, and Adam knew she must be cold. But she was as nonchalant as if they were standing in the summer sunshine. Adam, wrapped up in the buffalo robe, shivered violently. And he was glad to see her go.

He paced back and forth with Samuel, frustrated and embarrassed and silent. He and Samuel had nothing to say to each other, and Adam wondered if they would ever be friends again.

# 53

He rode on ahead now during the days, feeling uneasy when he looked at Jessica's cool smile, ill at ease with Jason's babbling optimism, jealous of Harry and Promise, confused with what had happened to him, with what would happen, and all out of sorts. He felt better alone.

The sun was sliding into the long afternoon. It was maybe

three o'clock. A steady, strong pleasant heat poured down on him. The night before had not been so chilly, and this day was fine. For several hours now they had been seeing Independence Rock rising in the distance. It was a black and oddly reptilian shape humping out of the level ground like a giant sleeping turtle.

They were crawling up along the Sweetwater River, a gentle little stream that ran with a quiet lapping over its pebbly bed. Adam would have called it a "creek" back home. Very slowly, a company of wagons became visible to him. The wagons were in camp just under the great, dark protuberance of stone. Adam felt suddenly cheerful. They had not seen wagons in days. Wagons meant people and cheer. Visiting and gossip. A crowd of happy faces swapping tales around a campfire in the night. Some relief from the monotony of the same faces, the same talk, the same delirious hopes. And perhaps company and relief for the long trail ahead. Adam's heart soared.

Yet as he rode slowly in on the camp, it began to seem strange. It was odd to see wagons already in camp this early in the afternoon. But something else was wrong. And when he realized what it was, he felt an eerie prickling at the roots of his hair. No animals grazing nearby. Not an ox or a mule or a horse. *Their stock's run off!* The explanation did not satisfy him. He could see no human forms either. A spooky air of desertion and vacancy hung over the place. Nothing but the wagons. Dead still. Their canvas bleached white. Ominous in the brilliant sunshine streaming down.

A man appeared suddenly. He jumped down out of a wagon and ran toward Adam, holding up both hands and waving them. He lurched and staggered and nearly fell, but recovered himself and came on. As he drew near, Adam, reining back on his mule, looked down at the man's face, perceived horror and sickness, protruding cheekbones and gaunt cheeks. He was so taken by astonishment and fright for a moment that he did not understand the dull, dreadful word spoken again and again, a hoarse croaking like the clapping of a large, broken bell.

"Cholera! Cholera!"

When he did understand, Adam was seized with fear. Cholera! He backed the mule away in terror.

The man from the wagons was emaciated and more than half-mad. He came lunging toward Adam like the vision of death, pronouncing the word over and over again.

463

"Cholera! Cholera! Cholera!"

Adam, backing the mule, yelled down at the man. "Don't get near me. How bad is it? What's your story?"

The man stopped, stood still, and grinned! "It hit us three weeks ago. Eighteen of us dead already. Three left. We can't bury the dead. Won't nobody help us. Won't nobody stop. All our stock stole by the Indians. By somebody. Maybe by whites. People passing by just go around. Like we wasn't even human beings no more. Like we was sick animals. Ride like hell to get away from us. You will, too, I reckon." The grin crafty and mysterious. His shouted words vibrating with a curious satisfaction.

When the man spoke, it was like a command to the wind, which picked up again and swept softly in Adam's direction, bringing him the sweet, insidious, and unmistakable reek of rotting flesh. People said the wind carried pestilence. Adam felt the fresh, dry breeze with its stench blowing in his face. It was like being touched by the fingers of death. He wheeled the mule around and fled back toward the others.

"Go on!" shouted the man. "Run off from us like the rest of them done."

"They's cholera up there!" Adam cried, all out of breath with fear. "We've got to go 'round. Cholera! Cholera!" Adam felt panic. Could not resist it.

The old man drew up on his mule. Looked around in stuporous dread and fixed his pale eyes on those distant and desolate wagons. Jason and Samuel stopped their oxen. Asa came wandering up, heard the news, looked blankly toward the ghostly wagons, and spoke the thought of all of them. "I didn't think we was going to have any more trouble." He looked cuttingly at Jason.

The old man sat his mule and looked grim. "We'll go around," he said quietly. "To the north." He nodded his head in that direction. "We ain't going to fool with no cholera. He didn't touch you, did he, Adam?"

Adam shook his head, and the first time he tried he could not speak. Finally he got the words out. "No. He didn't touch me. But the wind. The wind blew on me, and I smelled death."

"All right," the old man said. "We might be lucky. We might not get it."

They were agreed. And then it was that Harry Creekmore was taken with an attack of overweening pride.

Harry had been walking comfortably with Promise. They

464

were leading the two pack mules along, engrossed in a very agreeable conversation. Promise was admiring Harry, and Harry was spinning out detailed plans for their life together in California. The same old plans. Maybe Harry was bored with them.

For now he came hurrying up with the inquisitive air of a very important man who expects to be informed about serious things. When he heard that it was cholera, he stood with his feet wide apart, his hands on his hips, and he squinted confidently through his imposing spectacles at the grim wagons drawn up in the distance.

"Cholera, is it?" Voice nerveless and flat.

"It's too bad we have to abandon them like that," Jason was saying, shaking his head sorrowfully.

The old man was not troubled by such sentiments. "Better go around than to die with them folks. When you can help somebody, you go do it. But when a man's got cholera, then there ain't nothing anybody can do. You leave him to die. And you go on by, and you live."

Jason heaved a very pious sigh. "I am in agreement with you, Mr. McMoultrie. That may surprise you. But we have so much at stake. So much depending on us. The future. We have to look after our own."

"No," Harry said.

They looked at him in annoyance. He stood imperially straight and looked fixedly at that forlorn and distant encampment.

"What the hell are you talking about?" the old man said.

"I'm a doctor. I took an oath."

"You ain't going to swear at the cholera and make it go away." he old man spat and looked at Harry with contempt.

"No, I swore to help people when they need me. I took the oath of Hippocrates, the oath every doctor has to swear before he can be a doctor. I swore that oath."

Adam was thinking, *He ain't never taken no oath. He ain't never been inside no medicine school!*

The old man looked alarmed. "Listen to me, Doc. I don't know if you've noticed lately, but doctors die just like plain folks. And a right smart of doctors has died of cholera."

Harry looked around with a superior air and said very calmly, "You don't have to go with me. I wouldn't think of asking anybody to do that. I have to go. You can keep on. I can catch up with you later. In a few days. But it is my duty

465

to heal the sick." He paused deliberately. "Or at least to comfort them when they are dying."

"It ain't your duty to kill yourself," the old man said, angry and exasperated now. "It ain't our duty to let you bring cholera back to us in your clothes. In your hair. My God!"

"All of you doubted when I had to operate on Mrs. Ruth. I saved her life. You should know not to doubt me now. I know I can help those people."

He turned as if there were nothing more to be said and got his black medical bag down from Jason's wagon. He went over to the pack mule, to the same ungainly beast he had ridden saddleless that morning so long ago, when he and Adam had departed together for the Great West. And he began taking down the baggage.

*It's my mule,* Adam thought. *I ought to tell him to get his hands off my mule!* But he said nothing. He knew that if Harry did not ride the mule, he would walk.

Adam had no saddle for the mule, but Harry did not require a saddle now. He did not ask to take the mule Adam rode, saddled, because he did not want to break the rhythm of the stately show he was making; he did not want to be an actor who stumbled over an unessential property just as he was leading a breathless audience through the silent storm of the magnificent suspense he was creating for them. So he threw himself awkwardly up on the mule's back. (Even when he was playing the role of Great Medical Hero, Harry could not mount a saddleless mule gracefully.) He adjusted himself, clutched his bag, managed noble composure, and looked gravely down at them.

There was something comical about it, though nobody laughed. There sat Harry in his imposing gravity, his long, slender legs sticking out like elbows of pipe on each side of the gaunt mule, his clothing unspeakably filthy, the white of his suit a mockery and a foolishness now.

"Isn't anybody going to go *with* him?" Promise cried suddenly. She was nearly hysterical.

Harry looked down at her like an actor gaping blindly into an audience beyond the footlights when some member of that audience unexpectedly rises from her chair to utter a solitary scream in the dark.

"If he wants to go, then it's his lookout," the old man said implacably. Like an oracle. His voice cracked and solemn, like a rumbling from the center of the earth. "He's got the choice ever man has. He can shoot hisself or go hang hisself or eat poison or pick up snakes. He can go over there and play like the Lord God. But I can do what I want because I got the same choice he's got, and I'm choosing to stay right here."

"You're a *coward!*" Promise cried.

Adam winced. The old man turned his pale eyes on her. "I ain't no coward, ma'am. But I ain't no fool either."

Promise looked at him, and it was like gentle water splashing over a granite wall. She spun around, raking them all. "You're *all* cowards! You're *all* cowards! You're going to let him go alone!"

"It ain't your business to be calling *us* names," Asa hissed at her. "You're along with us on charity. You ain't got no right to call your betters names. Beggars can't be choosers."

"I beg your pardon!" Jessica wheeled on Asa with fire in her eyes, her whole body arched in indignation.

But Promise had flung herself on the stage with Harry now, and she was determined to take the scene. "If you are going to go, then I am going to go with you."

Harry was shocked and undone. "No! You can't!" Suddenly, against all his expectations, it was beginning to get more serious than he had dreamed.

"I am not going to let you go over there alone!" Promise cried. She rushed for Adam's mule, and there was a sternness in her face that would not be contradicted.

And that was when Adam surrendered. Spoke up with a sigh of hopelessness and resignation, terror growling inside him. "All right. All right. I'll go along, Harry. Goddammit! Goddamn you."

"No!" Promise cried again, wrestling with Adam for the mule. "I'm going to go with him. You're too much of a coward to go with him. He deserves better than you!"

"You're going to stay right here!" Adam said. He flung her aside with one arm and hurled himself up into the saddle, and because he caught her off balance, she went reeling back, and Jessica caught her daughter just before she fell and held her. When she felt her mother's arms tightly around her, Promise dissolved in tears.

"You're crazy!" the old man said quietly to Adam. "If missy there wants to go, then you let her go. It's her choice. Don't you be going because she's making the choice for you, Adam. That ain't right. Everbody's got the right to make the choice for hisself."

Adam looked at the old man; the old man looked at him.

467

There was nothing more to say. Adam turned to Harry and spoke softly. "Let's go."

So they rode off together, and behind them the silence of the day fell on those who were left behind, and no one could find a word to speak in farewell.

Adam went with Harry simply because the conventions of the time demanded that he do so. He was angry with Promise, blaming her because he had to go. And he was afraid.

But Harry rode along like some major general inspecting invisible troops. From time to time he whipped his head sharply to the right or to the left. Showing his profile. But even the wind had died. No applause anywhere. Nothing but silence grasping at the slow, steady clopping of the mules. Finally, the same man came stumbling out, crying, "Cholera! Cholera! Cholera!"

Harry turned around to Adam and said calmly, "I know I can help these poor people, Adam."

They rode up with the man running beside them, and Harry got off the mule. He clutched his black medical bag with ridiculous authority. A talisman. For just a moment he seemed uncertain, as though he had forgotten his lines and waited to be prompted. The man was screaming at him. "Go on off like the rest of them. Go to hell! Leave us to die!"

"I am a doctor," Harry said. "I have come to help."

The words had their effect. The man drew back and stopped screaming. A crafty expression rose in his face. "A doctor, are ye? Then what do ye charge?"

"What?"

The stink of death was thick around them. Not a breath of wind. A heavy, unbearably sweet smell, like a weight pushing down, shutting off the good air. Adam wanted to vomit.

The stranger was leering at Harry. "I asked you a question, Doctor. What do ye charge?"

"I don't charge anything!" Harry was exasperated. "I told you. I am a doctor. I help people." He looked up at Adam, deeply perplexed. His performance not going well.

"Everybody always charges something. Like the little boy said, you don't get something for nothing in this world."

Harry was baffled. He threw a desperate glance back to the Jennings wagons, two white spots in the sunshine. "Well, I promise. I'm not going to charge you anything."

"How do I know you ain't going to send me a bill when you get done? When you fix these folks up? I ain't going to be paying for *their* cholera. I ain't got no cholera."

"I'm not going to send you a bill. I don't even know your *name*! My God, man!" Harry was losing all his composure. He looked around to Adam for help. Found none. "I can't send you a bill if I don't know your name!"

"Puddentame. Ask me again and I'll tell you the same."

Harry took a deep breath. Nearly choked on it. He was pale under his tan. The real world closing in on him. "I think we better look at the sick, mister."

The man's eyes burned. "It ain't right to charge me for 'em. I ain't nothing but a driver. They ain't even kin to me. Spent their time looking down on me. Like I was some kind of white nigger. Wouldn't even let me eat with 'em." He looked at the wagons. "You see what they got for being so proud, don't ye?"

Adam and Harry looked around. Another man was clambering unsteadily down out of the back of one of the wagons. He looked to be a very old man, his hair snowy white and bushed around his head as though it had been uncombed for weeks. He tottered toward them, shielding his eyes clumsily against the brightness. The driver yelled at him. "You ain't going to pay me nothing, are ye, old man? You're going to cheat me out of my wages." The screech was like a file drawn over tender flesh.

The old man paid him no attention. He came up to Harry, putting out weak, frail arms in a beseeching gesture. "Habe ich recht gehört? Sie sind Arzt?"

Harry's handsome face, already troubled, now took on an expression of utter confusion. "What?"

"Oh, you can't understand nothing he says, the old fool. He's *German!* Come all the way from the Old Country to hunt gold in California. That's the way it is with all them foreigners. Greedy as a bunch of pigs! I say the only folks that ought to be in this country are good Americans."

"German!" Harry said.

"Ich bin aus Berlin," the old man said.

"What?" Harry looked up at Adam confounded and met only Adam's relentless and unhelpful stare. He looked like a child about to weep before some unattainable prize. He shook his head slowly. "I don't understand. I don't understand."

"Ain't nobody understands them. Speaking that foreign gibberish all the time."

"Don't you speak any *English?*" Harry yelled at the old man, speaking slowly and distinctly.

"Aus Berlin!" the old man said, slowly. "I come from Ber-

469

lin. Now all sick. All dead but me and frau. Magenkrankheit! Schrecklich! You know the Magenkrankheit? You doctor?" A dazed and hopeful scrutiny of Harry's blank face.

"Berlin," Harry murmured. "These folks come from Berlin, Adam. What about that?"

"Maybe they know some of your old professors at the medicine school," Adam said dryly.

Harry looked up at him and nodded, hardly knowing what he said, where they were. "I was at Heidelberg; they are from Berlin."

"You ought to be able to talk his language real good since you was in school over there for so long," Adam said.

"Hilfe! Kannst du . . . Can you help us?"

Harry puckered his lips, looked up again at Adam for encouragement, found none, gaped at the old man, looked down haplessly at his medical bag as though it had been a thin railing over an abyss. He steeled himself. "Yes, yes. I can help you. I am a doctor."

"Gott sei Dank!" the old man cried. He flung himself forward to embrace Harry, nearly fell, and knocked Harry's glasses awry. Harry dropped his medical bag in panic and, shoving the old man back, seized his glasses with both trembling hands. Without them he was blind. "My wife. Sick. We sell everything to come." The old man turned on his unsteady feet and started back to his wagon.

Adam dismounted. He felt curiously at peace. They all walked toward the wagon, but when they got near the rear the stench of death poured invisibly out of it like a sewer in flood. Adam gagged. The old man turned, made the short, courtly little bow polite people in Europe make to welcome visitors across their threshold, remembered himself, and climbed up, awkwardly eager.

Harry came after him, sweating profusely. The sweat had poured through his filthy white coat and stood across his back as a dark, wide stain. Adam followed reluctantly. And finally came the driver, sedately swearing, puffing with the effort, determined not to miss anything.

Under the canvas the air was hot and stifling. They might have camped in the shade of the rock, but they had not done so. The smell was so foul that Adam's stomach heaved. He had never experienced anything like this. Not even Rachael's decomposed body. He held himself in the wagon with Harry by sheer resolution.

The wagon was well packed with new goods. These people

470

had been well off in Berlin. Enough money to come across the sea and to buy these things they would never use. There was a bunk in the very back of the wagon. In the bunk, lying on the filthy blankets, was a rotting corpse.

The old man looked down at the corpse and made a clucking noise with his tongue. "Joseph," he said dully. He did not explain who Joseph had been. Nor did he seem to notice the stench. And he was not struck by any horror at the thing lying there that had once been a man. He led the way forward around boxes to another bunk. There in blankets that were of fine wool, brightly dyed red and black, lay the body of a woman.

Adam could tell she was dead as soon as he saw her. But Harry looked skeptically at the body. He knew something was wrong. Did not understand that it was death until he put his hand gingerly on the woman's forehead, then on her neck, and felt how cold and stiff was her skin. He turned around, vexed, baffled. He looked at the old man who stood crooked forward with age and anxiety, clasping his hands, gaping at Harry with interrogation in his red and unfocused eyes.

"She's dead!" Harry whispered. He could not speak aloud. Witlessly he added, "Don't you know?"

"Dead." The old man's voice was flat. No surprise left in him. He hobbled a step closer and stared down at his wife. Her lips were blue.

"Todt!" He very tenderly and carefully put out a hand and laid it on his wife's forehead as Harry had done. The old man's hand was splotched with age, and it trembled. "I tenk she is become better. No fever." His voice quavered.

"No fever!" Harry was exasperated now. Adam could tell he was frightened. "Of *course* there's no fever. The woman's dead!"

"She will not . . ." The old man gave up his stumbling English and fell into German again and began to cry, his hand still pressing on his wife's forehead. He put his head down to his hand, and they were head to head, wife and husband, corpse and life.

"Let's get outside," Harry said thickly.

"I could of told you she was dead," the driver said with infinite superiority and insolence, grinning at Harry.

"Why didn't you then?"

"I ain't paid for being no doctor. You're the one that's going to send the bill."

"Why don't you shut your goddamned mouth!" Adam said.

He turned around to the old man. "Come on, old man. Come on. You can't do no good here!"

Two left alive out of twenty-one. All the wagons held corpses. Men, women, children. Every imaginable state of decomposition. Maggoty and black. Bodies contorted into relics of every agony. The stink enough to choke a healthy man, destroy a man sick in mind or body. Something so strong that you wondered how it could go on and on because it seemed that anything with so much force must burn itself out. But it went on.

The magnitude of the disaster these people had met slowly imposed itself on Adam as he looked into wagon after wagon. Drained him of feeling. You did not have great emotions about disaster when it came. You did what had to be done. Emotions came later on. Did that horror actually happen? Yes. How did I endure it? I do not know. One does what one must. I did not see it all at the beginning. You only live each moment, and if there is something to endure in that moment, well, then, you carry it like a load on your back.

"Maybe we ought to go on," Harry said in a low, tense voice.

"I reckon we ought to dig a grave for the dead."

"A grave! Why? Why should *we* do it?" Harry was losing his nerve. An avalanche of fear coming down on him.

Adam took a deep breath. "I don't know, Harry. I reckon just because we've come over here. Somebody's got to do it. We can't leave these folks above ground. It ain't decent. They stink. Folks ought to be buried when they die."

"We don't have to bury folks we don't even know. My God, Adam! They don't care."

"You're the one who said we had to come over here, Harry. Do our duty. You're the fancy doctor. Now I'm saying we got a duty to do. It ain't the one you was thinking about, but it's here. We got to bury the dead."

"Doctors don't have anything to do with the dead. A doctor is for the living. We ought to go. Not take any more risks." Harry looked around and shuddered. "I don't like it here."

"What about the old man and the driver? Don't you think we ought to take them two along with us, Harry?"

"No! No, of course not! Don't be a fool, Adam! What good can we do them? They're both crazy."

"Are you afraid the old man's going to tell the truth on you? Is that why you want to leave him behind, Harry?"

"Truth! What truth could he tell on me? He's crazy!"
Harry laughed, scornful and nervous at once. "Can you understand a word he says?"

"That's it, Harry. He could tell folks you don't talk German. Just because you can't understand him. Is that why you don't want him to go along? Is that why you're willing to let him stay here and die?"

Harry looked pained and frightened. He took off his glasses and polished them vigorously. "I amputated Ruth's arm, and she got better. You saw me, Adam. It doesn't matter what anybody says. It doesn't matter where I've been and where I've not been. I am a doctor. I have become a doctor."

"Well, your doctoring got us into this fix. It got me to come along with you when I knowed better."

"I didn't ask you to come."

"I had to come because your lady friend got all hung up in your act, Harry. The old man said you couldn't do nothing. But he was wrong. You can do something. You can help me bury the dead."

"If I want to go back, you can't stop me, Adam. I'll just get on that mule and ride off. You can't stop me."

"I wouldn't even try to stop you. But tomorrow I'd come along with that old man slung up here on the back of my mule, and he'll talk German all the way to California."

"Adam, why do you hate me? I had no idea that you hated me!" Harry was wounded and puzzled. Adam was puzzled, too. *Why am I doing this to him?*

"I don't hate you, Harry," Adam said. "But maybe if you help me bury these folks, it'll knock some sense into your head. Maybe, just maybe, you'll quit thinking that you're first cousin to the Lord God. That might be good for you, Harry."

Later on Adam blamed himself for everything that came afterwards. He was angry with Harry for Harry's boundless pride. But then Adam was the one with the truly annihilating pride. He wanted to rub Harry's nose in something. Harry had luck. Promise. The future. Praise and admiration. Everything Adam did not have. And just one time Adam wanted to be on top. To humiliate Harry. Get back at him for contriving all those preposterous lies. For getting away with the lies. Teach him a lesson.

"Can you handle a spade or not?"

Harry gave him a dazed look. "A spade?"

"To dig a grave with. A spade!"

Harry sighed and shook his head in surrender. "Yes. I
473

guess. I have calluses on my hands now, remember? Me! Harry Creekmore with calluses on his hands." Homeric laughter. Loud and false. Harry was afraid.

Adam only looked at him. Then left him standing subdued and silent by the worthless medical bag and went to rummage around the wagons for spades and returned with three long-handled ones. He spoke to the driver. "You come along and give us a hand."

The driver lounged insolently against a wagon wheel. Made no sign of obedience. "I ain't going to give you no hand with nothing. I ain't paid to dig graves for folks. I'm paid to drive oxen."

Adam looked at the man for a moment, despising his grin. He tried to think up some way to force him to help. The driver leered at him as if to dare him. Adam decided the man would be dangerous working nearby with a spade in his hand. Let the thing drop.

"When you get done with them spades, you be sure and put 'em back," the driver said. "They don't belong to you."

"They don't belong to you neither," Adam said.

"They will," the driver said. He looked down at the old man, squatting on the ground and babbling.

Adam and Harry moved on over near the river and went upstream until the stink died. There, where the air was clear, they set to digging.

Adam yearned for somebody else to come to help. Samuel maybe. He felt lonely and miserable. The earth was like concrete. When he dug his spade into it the first time, he was tempted to fling the thing aside and give up. Tell Harry to come along. Excuse them both. Ride back to their own crowd. Forget these people. Let the buzzards take care of their corruption. And maybe if Jessica should come over—doing the bold and singular thing that was her nature to do—that would be an excuse. Ride away to spare Jessica the horror. He envied Harry. Promise willing to stake her life to be with Harry. Maybe Jessica would stake her life to be with Adam Cloud. Her lover.

But no one came. Adam felt loss widening inside him. A pit opening. No one to care for him. Jessica had never told him that she loved him. He threw himself onto the spade to fight off the fear of death and the terror of his unimportance before the world.

The earth was softer when they had hacked their way through the thick sod. The digging went faster, and Adam's gloomy thoughts dissolved in his work. His muscles grew tired, then numb, and he kept on like a machine, finally mindless.

At last the sun fell in blood-red silence behind a stony ridge to the west.

Adam felt a horror of darkness, an isolation in the universe. He wrestled against the black feeling of exile this job imposed on him. He was bitter with Harry, who toiled silently, patiently, without complaint, accepting the punishment Adam had meted out. And because Harry did accept it, there was no satisfaction in the punishment for Adam. Only a sense of futility.

Harry worked hard. Clumsily. He handled a spade as awkwardly as a child will handle a spoon when he is first learning to feed himself. But he worked with all his strength. He wanted to make something up to Adam. The glistening sweat poured down his face in great gouts and soaked his wavy blond beard and made his face slick. Slick so that his precious glasses kept sliding down his nose. Finally, to protect them, he took them off. He folded them with meticulous caution and put them carefully away in their case in the inside pocket of his filthy coat. He took the coat off, and groping for the edge of the grave, laid it gently aside, asking Adam in a low voice to keep an eye on it. Then his spading was even less effectual than it had been.

When the twilight had coagulated into dark, they were so tired that their arms hung. They went back into the death camp to see what had become of the old man and the driver. They ridiculously expected that someone might have cooked supper for them.

But the two survivors had not even built a fire. Adam gathered fuel and struck it to flame. The two men came and sat down by the fire. The old man sat gingerly and unsteadily, babbling incessantly in German. The driver found a chunk of raw bacon somewhere and squatted on his haunches, holding it in both hands and gnawing greedily at it like a cannibal. Adam and Harry had no desire to eat anything out of any of these wagons. They would rest until dawn. Bury the dead. Move on. Try to forget. Take baths in the Sweetwater upstream. Soap themselves down to the bone. Burn their clothes. Even Harry's white suit. Harry was willing now. An offering to Adam. Anything to make Adam forgive him for his lying, for getting them into this awful predicament where nothing had worked out right.

"I helped Ruth," Harry murmured in a daze. "I thought . . . I *really* thought I could help these people. It doesn't matter what I used to be. Where I went to school. If I heal the sick, if people believe in me, then I'm a *doctor!*"

The more Harry wanted to be forgiven, the more guilty Adam felt. Burying these pitiful corpses seemed more and more foolish. Even diabolical. A stupid revenge against Harry. And yet Adam could not quite force himself to say, *Harry, let's quit. Let's go back. I was just jealous of you. Come on. Let's get out of here. We're even now.*

Like coming to the Big Blue when he was hostile to all of them. He could not say then: "There's a ferry ten miles on up the river. Let's go to it. I'll pay." Some perverse reluctance blockaded his tongue. To tell Harry, "I was jealous of you for your luck," would open too many doors to his own heart.

Harry brought his medical bag to the fire and set it behind his head like a pillow to recline on. An official presence to support him. So the four of them sat, no one speaking but the old man and he continuously. Time creeping as slow as ice swelling. Off in the starry dark Adam could see a dot of firelight in the camp, where the others waited. The distant sight made him very sad.

*They ought to go on!*

At least, Adam thought, they should remove themselves until there was time enough to see if the pestilence might strike Adam or Harry. Shawnee Joe should have thought of that. Made them go on. Adam and Harry could trail behind until days had passed.

When the driver finished his meal he began to stare at Harry like some stupid and inquisitive animal. "Them's the thickest glasses I ever seen in my life," he said after a long while, hunching closer, sneering and curious at once.

Harry turned and looked at him with a start, wakened from fantasies dancing in the fire. "I'm nearly blind. If I didn't wear glasses, I couldn't see anything."

"You sure do look prissy with glasses like that. Like some kind of big owl."

"I can't help the way I look," Harry said with injured dignity. "It's better than being blind."

The driver scooted himself over more familiarly to Harry and scanned his face. "Your face looks warped. It looks too little behind your glasses!"

Harry shot a quick and annoyed look at him and wished

he would go away. The driver inched closer, leering and intense. Harry tried to ignore him.

"I want to peek through them glasses."

Harry looked around in quick panic. "No!"

"I ain't going to hurt them none," the driver said in a nasty, wheedling tone. "I just want to see what it looks like through them glasses."

"No!" Harry put both hands up to his face to hold the glasses by their earpieces. "You might break them!" Harry's voice was shrill.

"Leave him alone!" Adam said. "He ain't bothering you none. Don't you be bothering him."

The driver looked around in an affectation of innocence. "I ain't doing nothing to hurt him. I just want to see through them glasses."

"They ain't your glasses. I'm warning you!"

"Please!" the driver said, turning back to Harry. "I ain't never seen glasses like them before. It ain't fair for you to hog 'em all to yourself. Just give me *one* look!"

Adam stood wearily up. He put his hand down to the pistol in his belt.

"I said for you to leave him alone!"

The driver threw him a surly and defiant look. "Well, I reckon I'll peek through them glasses if I *want* to!" And as he spoke, the driver whirled and lunged forward and snatched Harry's glasses away and leaped back, holding them triumphantly aloft in one hand. "See!" The two thick lenses glimmered like tiny red lamps with the reflections of firelight.

Harry was stricken with fear. He leaped up in torment and cried, "No, no! Give them back to me! Give them back to me!"

The driver danced heavily out of range. Like a bully on the playground playing the game of steal-the-cap with a small child. The old German raised his voice slightly, as though annoyed at this rude interruption—and talked on. Adam yanked his pistol out and aimed it at the driver's belly. "You give him them glasses back, or I'll kill you!"

"Please! Please! My glasses! My glasses!" Harry was standing and groping at the blindness that had suddenly enveloped him. He was sobbing.

The driver looked down at the pistol in Adam's hand and grinned, untouched by fear. He looked with insane confidence at Adam's face, Adam trembling with anger and the unreality of everything, clutching the pistol, shaking—remembering

477

suddenly that the pistol was not primed, that it would not fire, that it would take moments to draw an explosive cap from his shirt pocket and insert it into the revolver, that they were momentarily helpless before this loutish man's evil whimsy.

"You ain't going to shoot me just because I want to peek through this feller's *glasses!*" the driver chortled. And as he spoke, he jammed the glasses onto his nose, cruelly twisting the flimsy earpieces to fit around his large cabbage ears.

Adam jammed the worthless pistol back in his belt and snatched up one of the long-handled spades, stacked nearby. "You give them glasses back, or I'll slam you in the head with this spade!"

Harry shrieked. "Adam, don't break the glasses. Please, mister, *please!* For the love of God, don't hurt my glasses!"

The driver did not hear them at all. The glasses had clamped a hideous world of dizzy distortion over his eyes. He swayed drunkenly about, gaping wildly through the huge lenses as if he were looking into the pit of hell and seeing himself tortured there. His hands waved flatly before his face as though he were fending something horrible off. His face was so frozen in terror that he could neither breathe nor speak.

Then in a choking struggle, yelling to release himself from the awful thrall of loathsome things, he put both his big hands to his face, and exerting all his might, he clawed the glasses away and flung them into the fire.

When the glasses hit the fire, there were two sharp, shattering little *plinks* as the thick lenses burst in the heat.

Harry heard the terrible little sound. "What happened! Adam? Adam? Tell me what happened." But he knew the answer to his own question. He collapsed on the ground and began to cry, his head buried in his slender fingers.

Adam paused with the spade upraised. He was petrified by the scene. The driver looked stupidly around like a dull man foolishly coming to himself after a nightmare. Both Adam and the driver gaped for an instant into the fire, where the shining steel rims of the broken glasses turned black, where splinters of glass simmered red in the flames. Adam's anger boiled suddenly in him. He yelled, "You *bastard!*" He swung the spade, meaning to split the driver's head in two. But the driver's reflexes saved him. He ducked and fled headlong off into the dark, and the swishing spade cut the empty air.

Now Adam primed his pistol. Thinking dismally that he

478

should have done so when they first came back from digging the grave. Thinking that he and Harry should have made their own fire back up there where the grave was, leaving the driver and the old German to be cold and dark together. Regretting with all his heavy heart that he had set out to punish Harry by burying these dead.

So he came back to the fire and found Harry sprawled there disconsolate, his body wracked with sobs, big, oily tears pouring down his fine face, muttering again and again: "They're broken, aren't they? They're broken, aren't they?" His drawling voice was as soft as the wind on a summer twilight.

"Yes, they're broken."

"You sure they're not just cracked? Can we stick them back together with something?"

"No, they're pure busted, Harry. Ain't no way to get them back together now."

"Why did he do that? Why?"

Adam could give him no answer and no comfort. The night ahead of them stretched for a thousand years. And when he was sure there was no hope, Harry fell to crying again, and his weeping went on and on.

In the first faint light of dawn, Adam began transporting corpses to the grave. Burying the dead had now become a thing he did to punish himself. Harry could be of no help to him. Harry was in a daze, nearly comatose, staring speechless into space, dried out and exhausted from his weeping.

Adam found a piece of big canvas to drag the bodies in. One by one he hauled them to the grave and dumped them down as though they had been loads of manure. He dirtied his hands in corruption. He did things he never could have imagined he could do. He did them out of the impulsions of guilt, for it was to bury the dead that he had made Harry stay where Harry's insolent pride had led them, where Adam's vengeful pride had kept them.

Once he glanced up at Independence Rock, and on the dome he saw the driver standing. The man had evidently climbed up there in the night and now stood darkly shaped in black against the delicate sky. An ominous, eerie sentinel, too far away for Adam to take a shot at him with the Colt pistol. And what did it matter? Adam looked up, felt apathy instead of revenge, and worked on.

It took Adam three hours to deposit the last corpse in the grave. The bodies and the fragments of bodies lay heaped indecently on each other. The sun was beaming hotly down. The stench was something beyond imagination. Above him buzzards wheeled in the sky. *Where were they yesterday? Why didn't we see them then?* Another mystery with terror at the heart of it, and Adam forcibly dismissed it from his mind.

He set about covering the bodies with dirt, working steadily, breathing hard. And as the reek of rotting flesh was absorbed by the clean soil, Adam began to feel expiation and victory.

Finally he was done.

Adam said softly to Harry, "Well, we better go back now. It's all done."

"Yes. Done."

"You can get yourself some new glasses in California."

"No, this is the end."

"Shit on that!" Adam said.

"It's the end. You'll see. My father told me I would die."

"That was a dream, Harry! My God." Adam felt spooky, tired, and deeply frustrated. "You can't put no stock in dreams!"

"It's the end of me."

"Look, it's going to be fine in California. We're going to be in California before you know it. You want to take the old man or leave him here?"

"Oh, take him if you want. I've been found out."

"Harry, that's foolish! You ain't been found out. You couldn't do nothing about the cholera. Nobody could. Them folks was already dead."

"I've been found out."

Adam was feeling sick. "Don't talk foolish, Harry. It's bad enough without you talking foolish." Adam shook his head to clear it. "Come on, dammit! What are we going to do about the old man!"

"Do what you want."

Adam shot a glance up the rock to the grim shadow of the driver standing so high above them against the sky. "I reckon it's the right thing. To take him."

"Take him then."

Adam spoke harshly to the old man. "Old man! Come on with us. You can't stay here. You can go with us to California."

The old man looked up and was annoyed. The look of a

480

concentrating mind incredibly distracted. His face seemed to say, "Why are you bothering me?"

Adam spoke again, sick and weary. "Come on now. You got to go with us. If you stay here, you'll die!"

The old man jerked his head away, determined to ignore Adam.

Adam put his hands down under the old man's armpits and tried to hoist him to his feet from behind. The old man resisted him, squirmed out of his grasp throwing his arms straight up the way a child will do who does not want to be held. So Adam could not pick him up. And when he was free, the old man sat defiantly back down again.

"Old man, listen to me! If you stay here, that crazy driver up there will come down and kill you. So he can have all this stuff!"

But nothing could budge the old man. Adam looked helplessly at Harry. Harry showed no interest in anything. Adam took a deep breath and turned away. Left the German there in a world remote from all other worlds.

"Come on!" Adam commanded Harry. "It's time we was getting out of here!"

As they rode away, Adam looked back over his shoulder at Independence Rock. The driver was gone from his lofty perch. Adam supposed that he was already scampering down the slick slope of the rock to get at the old man and to loot the wagons.

Then what? Adam wiped the sweat out of his eyes. His head felt swollen inside from trying to put everything together, make sense out of things.

When they got back to the Jennings camp, Promise came running to meet them, followed by Adam's gamboling hound. *My own dog didn't go with me. He stayed back here with them.* He had forgotten about the hound. *He had more sense than we did.*

When Promise saw Harry, saw his blindness and the abjection in his face, when Adam told them briefly what had happened, she took Harry's face in her slender arms and consoled him with tears in her eyes. And Harry, unable to see the faces looking at him, unable to be ashamed now in a world that had hidden itself behind the swimming blur of his sight, wept like a child.

# 54

"You ain't so smart-looking without them fancy glasses of yourn, Mr. Creekmore." Ishtar Baynes, speaking up from the side of Jason's trundling wagon. Harry and Promise sat above her on the seat, and Ishtar Baynes walked.

Jason was annoyed with Harry for trying to take care of cholera. And without his glasses, groping in the dimness, Harry had lost his authority. He was helpless, and Jason, no longer dazzled by him, could speak harshly.

"That was foolhardy, Dr. Creekmore. I am sorry for the loss of your glasses. But I must tell you frankly. You brought it on yourself."

And so Ishtar Baynes came out of her lair to assault Harry once again, and Adam—weary with himself and all of them and with this interminable journey—could see that the victory over her had been temporary and that she was ascending among them like a buzzard catching one of those invisible currents of air and soaring aloft to spy out the helplessness of its prey.

Promise sat with an arm laced through Harry's arm. He looked straight ahead, over the oxen, over Jason plodding by the lead team, and he saw nothing but a wave of color and a liquid swirl of shape. The Rattlesnake Range now passing by in sharp pinnacles and needles of bare rock off to their right was to him only a streak of darkly radiant brown. And beside him, striding along like a skeletal harvester, Ishtar Baynes imposed herself on him and Promise and chortled with vengeance and satisfaction.

"Have you ever thought that folks get exactly what they deserve in life, Mr. Creekmore?"

"Yes, Mrs. Baynes. I have pondered that fact many times. I do not believe people do get what they deserve."

"I never once did nothing against you. You told these folks you was a doctor, and I knowed you wasn't no doctor. But out of the goodness of my heart, Mr. Creekmore, I didn't say nothing about it."

Harry was silent. Promise clung to him, protecting, seeking protection.

"And then you said that awful thing about me. Told that awful lie. In public, you said it. In front of a child. My husband. My husband won't speak to me, Mr. Creekmore. He won't have nothing to do with me. What do you think of that?"

Some thin residue of Harry's old irony remained. "I'd say your husband was lucky, Mrs. Baynes. I wish we didn't have anything to do with you. I wish you'd go away and leave us alone."

"You see what you got for telling stories on me, Mr. Creekmore. God busted your glasses. That's what he done! You told the kind of lie God don't forget. And he punished you for it. You notice God ain't done nothing to me, Mr. Creekmore."

"He probably doesn't want to dirty his hands, Mrs. Baynes," Harry said softly.

"Ain't you got no pity, Mr. Creekmore? Can't you say you're sorry? I'm willing to be your friend if you tell me you're sorry and if you admit the truth to these folks. That you ain't no doctor. You tell folks you ain't no doctor, and I ain't never going to say another mumbling word against you, Mr. Creekmore. I swear."

Harry was silent.

"My hat shoppe. How'm I going to run a respectable hat shoppe when my husband thinks bad thoughts about me and won't even talk to me? You tell me that, Mr. Creekmore!" There was an edge of panic in her voice. "Maybe he ain't even going to stay with me when we get to California. Maybe he's going to get shut of me like I was an old sock, all because of what you said, Mr. Creekmore. And what am I going to do in California without no husband to take care of me?"

"Maybe you can go back to your old profession, Mrs. Baynes," Harry drawled softly. "I hear California's hard up for women. Somebody might be so hard up that he'd be willing to take you."

"You're still pretending that lie about me was true!" Ishtar Baynes did not scream; she hissed at him. "Well, you listen to me, mister fancy-pants liar that ain't fancy no more. I know it's all your fault what happened. You told that awful lie on me just because I told the truth about you. How you ain't nothing but a head-feeler. You ain't even that! You ain't nothing at all. And I'm going to keep right on telling it till you admit it, Mr. Creekmore. I'm going to see you get what you deserve?"

Harry sighed. "Mrs. Ruth is out there walking somewhere, Mrs. Baynes. I heard her talking awhile ago. With her boy. I amputated her arm. I saved her life. You go ask Mrs. Ruth if I'm a doctor."

"You just memorized a book," Ishtar Baynes said with a malicious understanding Harry could feel like slivers of glass broken in his skin.

He was silent.

"And what about them folks with the cholera? You didn't do them no good, did you, Mr. Creekmore?"

"I didn't do them any good at all, Mrs. Baynes. They were dead. I am not God. I cannot resurrect the dead."

"You rode off like a God, thinking you was going to help folks that can't be helped. You thought you could help folks God didn't want to let live. You thought you was better than God."

Harry sighed. Her voice kept beating at him like a hammer. It made his head hurt. "I suppose we should have passed them by."

"It wouldn't have been your nature to pass them by," Promise broke in defiantly. "You're too good. You're the one who always wants to help people. You were right to go. You had to go because you are a doctor."

Ishtar Baynes unleashed a cackling laugh. "Help people! He just wanted to show off. Well, look what it brung him! Busted glasses, and everybody's laughing at him. He can't see to show off now. He can't see to play doctor. God showed *him* a thing or two."

She laughed in a screech of pleasure.

"I won't hear this!" Promise said. She turned her head with a jerk and leaned her forehead on Harry's shoulder. He said nothing. She looked up, saw his dejected, grieving abstraction. "You *are* a doctor, aren't you, Harry?"

Ishtar Baynes whooped with laughter.

"Yes," Harry said doggedly. "Yes, I am a doctor. Ask Mrs. Ruth. I am a doctor."

"I ain't going to leave you alone till you tell the truth!" Ishtar Baynes said. "You wait and see how I'm going to make you suffer till you tell the truth, Mr. Creekmore."

Four days passed. They were making good time now in spite of the steady ascent of their journey. The Wind River Mountains rose up blue and spectral against the horizon. "South Pass!" Shawnee Joe said. Some of his own gloomy silence was dispelled by the sight. "Maybe we're going to get down in the desert safe. Maybe the cholera ain't going to get any of us. By God, if it don't get us, I'll say a hundred and fifty Our Fathers when we get to San Francisco! I'll say so many Hail Marys the sweet Virgin will come and ask me to hush up so she can get some sleep!"

Adam laughed. The triumph of getting across South Pass, going over the Continental Divide, might be enough to bring the old man back to himself. If they could make it to Salt Lake City, they could force Jason to stop over for the winter. With the Mormons. Whether he liked it or not.

"I want to see Jason arguing away with Brigham Young about marriage," the old man said with great satisfaction. "That will be a spelling bee. Who knows! Jason might like the idea if he tried it. I always thought it'd be pretty good to have a bunch of wives around the house."

And so they passed the water dipper around at night and ate their bacon and drank coffee and bundled themselves against the cold while the cheerful fire blazed in their midst, and they felt sound and strong.

Adam's spirits began slowly to lift. He did not understand himself, this alternation between terror and peace. He had endured haunting things, but they seldom haunted him once he had left them behind. He had learned things about himself he had never suspected. He had committed murder and adultery, and still he kept on living. His mind seemed to shut down the heat of his guilt in the way he had seen dampers on stoves shut the fire off. He went on doing the ordinary things that got them higher and higher along the way that led up to South Pass. He and Henry worked steadily together morning and evening, and Adam said, "Henry, by God! You're *already* a man! You do a man's work, and that's what makes a man!" And he delighted in the boy's shy smile of pleasure.

Adam was still troubled when he looked at Harry sitting by the fire at night. Harry baffled and beaten and peering blindly into the rosy flames while Promise sat like a frail and anguished guardian by his side. But he was not crushed by the smothering weight of guilt, hopelessness, and frustration he had felt at Independence Rock. Now the episode of the cholera was becoming only an accident, an incident that he

485

would tell stories about someday. And on these evenings, when he felt rested and strong and ready for anything, he convinced himself that they would find new glasses for Harry. Maybe in Salt Lake City. There had to be some Mormons with bad eyes. And so there would be Mormons who made eyeglasses. And if you could make eyeglasses, you could just multiply the recipe by four and make eyeglasses for Harry Creekmore. Harry would be all right again. Adam looked forward to that; he missed Harry's banter and gaiety. *I'll pay for it*, Adam thought. *I'll pay anything it costs to get him new glasses.* And having made that firm resolution, Adam told himself that everything was going to be all right now. Everything would be good again.

Then Rebecca got sick.

Her chamberpot reposed in her wagon in its customary place, set under the plank with a round hole cut in it. The chamberpot large and ornate porcelain, purple with bright yellow flowers (daisies, someone meant them to be) raised on its livid sides and brightly painted. Handcrafted somewhere back East on a potter's wheel, one of the ordinary relics of a lost home.

Rebecca was private about her bowels and her bladder. She used the pot in the daylight when no one was with her or else stealthily at night. When Samuel detected an unpleasant smell, he emptied the pot efficiently and quietly. When there was water he washed it out. When there was no water he dutifully scrubbed the interior with sand. No one watched when Samuel carried the chamberpot off from the trail to empty it discreetly, then to scrub it clean. The wagons did not pause in their lethargic progress. He caught up with them, marching in long, swift steps, sweating a little.

Afternoon with the road climbing steadily. The Sweetwater River reduced to a trickle, crossed one last time, then left behind. The air cool even with the sun still high. South Pass maybe ten miles away, the land empty, wind soft and grass waving. Sage growing in clumps.

Rebecca had used her chamberpot recently. Samuel had scrubbed it out in that final little trickling of the Sweetwater. The purple creation with its still yellow daisies was riding serenely on Samuel's wagon seat, airing out. And suddenly in the midst of the plodding calm, Rebecca was yelling for Samuel. His name again and again. The voice frantic, a screech of unbelief.

Samuel rushed inside, bending over her. She was white,

paralyzed with embarrassment and amazement, holding herself half out of the rocking chair, gripping the bent, wooden arms of the chair with both hands, aghast at herself. "Samuel! I need the *toilet* again!" A hiss of anger, terror, and humiliation. "My stomach is burning *up!*"

Samuel rushed for the pot. But too late. She messed in her clothes. She made tight, speechless little gestures to shoo her husband out again. Wanted to free herself in private from the fouled dress. And while she was wriggling out of the filthy sodden garment, moaning with the agony in her belly, she was hit once again with the diarrhea.

This time it was unbearable. Like being stabbed in her lower belly with a jagged, white-hot poker. Her bowels locked up on her, a balloon of gas swelled in her like a bomb. And the pain knocked her across the plank toilet seat, whimpering desperately like a dying dog, unable to move. And finally when she recovered just enough strength to speak, every syllable cost her torments. "Samuel? Samuel? Samuel?"

He rushed back in to help, his wide, dull face stricken with uncomprehending bewilderment.

The stink in the closed wagon was awful. He did not understand what was happening. He had never seen his wife naked before. But there she was, flung over the plank toilet on her knees. She might have been praying except that her fouled skirt was thrown up behind her, and her big, white buttocks was thrust up at him like some bizarre cannon, propped up by her knees. Excrement the color of watered milk drooled out of her, running down one of her thick, fatty thighs. Rebecca was utterly helpless, smitten, weeping with pain and humiliation, hysterical with fear, unable to move. Samuel worked at her desperately, clumsily. He wrenched the skirt off, pulling it over her head. Ignored her choking plea that he shut his eyes.

Samuel would not let anyone help him, not even Jason. No other man could see his wife naked. But Harry Creekmore could come in because he was a doctor and because he was blind.

"What about it, doctor?"

Harry gagged with the smell. "Laudanum," he muttered. "We have to give her laudanum. It's the only thing that does any good for the cholera." His voice was dull and flat.

"You give it to her!" Samuel began to sob. "Cholera! Cholera! Cholera!" He muttered the word again and again.

Outside the rest of them gathered around, heard Samuel

crying. The old man looked balefully at Adam. "It's cholera. I knowed it. White shit! White shit! That's the sure sign. She's got it, and he give it to her. Harry. It's your friend Harry Creekmore's fault."

"No," Adam said. "I'm the one. I was there, too. I made Harry help me bury all those dead people. It's my fault, not his."

"You only went with him because you wanted to save Miss Promise from going!" Ishtar Baynes crowed. She wanted her revenge on Harry. Not on Adam. "He was the one wanted to show off. Wanted to raise them folks from the dead. Thought he was God. It's his fault."

"If we hadn't buried the dead, we wouldn't of been there long enough to get it!" Adam shouted at her. He felt the tempest of human emotion rising against Harry. He could not understand why they did not blame *him*—Adam Cloud, the true felon, the real disrupter of every good thing!

"You got to bury the dead," the old man said solemnly. "Leave the dead up above ground, and you ain't no better than a dog."

"No! No!" Adam tried to reason with them. But he could not bring himself to explain that he had done it to humiliate Harry. Burying the dead not a sign of mercy; a sign of penalty.

"It's Mr. Creekmore's fault!" Ishtar Baynes shrieked. "He's give us all the cholera! It's his fault!"

Panic in the air like the dry smell in an old house just when you smell the smoke that means fire. Fear craving a scapegoat, somebody to destroy so that the rest of them might be saved. Harry a sacrificial lamb, and Ishtar Baynes the high priestess of vengeance.

Samuel got laudanum out of Harry's bag and poured it down Rebecca's throat. "It burns!" Rebecca whimpered piteously. "It burns like fire." They could hardly hear her voice because it was so faint.

"Drink it!" Samuel commanded. His eyes were red, and his face was fearful. "Dr. Creekmore says it will save your life. Drink it! Drink it!"

"I didn't say it would save her life," Harry said very softly. "I said it might save her life."

Rebecca drank. She slipped into unconsciousness. Her diarrhea stopped, and Samuel scrubbed her, cleaning her methodically and carefully. Tenderly. "It's working. She's going to be all right!" Samuel nearly cried with relief. He looked at

Harry. "By God, it's working. You are a doctor. Sure enough!"

"Maybe," Harry said, his voice toneless. "Maybe. We'll see."

The sun burned down. The clouds floated peacefully overhead, scarcely moving. All the world locked in a thrall of beauty. The wind rustling in the sage, bending and unbending.

Samuel sat away the hours by Rebecca's side. Harry sat with him, not speaking. Waiting. It was hot inside. Around three o'clock, Samuel came out. He walked stiffly from sitting so long, and he was worried and gloomy. "She's still asleep. But now she's burning up with fever." His voice was slow, hoarse, perplexed.

"We'll make compresses," Jessica said. She was sharp with Samuel. "You've got to let Ruth and me take care of her now. I cooled Promise's head many a time when she was young, with a fever."

Adam thought of Jessica, alone in a little house in a strange place, disgraced, abandoned, tending to a sick child. He had said scarcely a word to Jessica since he had buried the dead at Independence Rock. She had not come to be with him. Something broken between them.

The old man looked at her and shook his head. He was very stern: "You better be careful, ma'am. You'll be getting the cholera yourself."

Ruth spoke up. "Well, I'm not going to get any cholera. I've already had my fight with death. If losing an arm didn't kill me, I don't reckon I'm going to die with cholera."

The old man opened his mouth to speak to her and then shut it silently. He went out in the sunshine, and sat down with a jug of his precious whiskey. It was the first time anybody had seen him drinking whiskey in the open daylight. Adam went looking for him after a while and found him staidly drunk, his legs crossed before him, the jug between his legs, resigned.

"This here is good whiskey," the old man said in a thick voice. "If I die of the cholera, this whiskey is going to go to waste. Some goddamned Indian's going to get it." He tipped the jug up and drank.

Adam was frightened. "What's wrong with you? You can't just give up!"

"I can damn well give up if I want to," the old man said.

"You can't!" Adam cried.

"It ain't right to go on pretending. We ain't going to make it. Leastways I ain't going to make it. We got bad luck riding with us. Maybe just age."

Adam had nothing to say. He sat down with the old man, and the two of them sat without speaking. The old man kept drinking just enough to stay on the edge of drunkenness that is just short of oblivion.

Around twilight the old man said: "I never should of left Missouri. I could be a good farmer back there now. With my own little place. Have sons and grandsons to look after me in my old age. Money in the bank. Little pink granddaughters to dandy on my knees. Go to church on Sundays and to town on Saturdays, whittle and talk with my friends, joke and gossip and such like. I had fun while it lasted with my squaws and my wilderness, while the trapping was good ... While they was something to get for my plews. I used to look at the Oregon country and see the woods, the spruce trees and the larches and the maples for as far as you could see some places, and I heard the rivers running over the rocks, and I seen waterfalls like you ain't never dreamed about, waterfalls you could hear for miles like thunder in the bowels of the earth. And I thought to myself, *Lordy, this country can't never run out!* But it did, Adam! Damned if I know how it happened, but that big country just run out and left me dry!"

The old man pulled his ancient beaver hat down over his eyes and went on tipping the jug up whenever the easeful drunkenness seemed to be slipping away. Adam thought that down there somewhere in the dark of a hat brim, the old man might be crying.

"Listen, you done the right thing," Adam said. "Coming out here. I seen people living like you say you want to. Living back home. Doing the same thing all their lives. It ain't no good. This is better. You done right."

Adam felt himself close to tears. He cast a glance up to the naked rocks that marked the crests of the Wind River Mountains. High up there a sheen of snow hung on the granite against the blue sky, snow that had defiantly hung on under all the assaulting of the summer sun. Now the summer was slipping away. The snow had won its contest with the heat, and at this hour with the sun dropping off to the west, out of sight now behind the mountains, the snow was red like blood, and the wind blowing down out of the pass was very cold.

At suppertime Rebecca came out of the laudanum coma

and began to vomit. She lay parched, now strangely cold, under a wool blanket pulled over her as she lay on the bunk, a monument of obese flesh scarcely veiled. Samuel came out again, shaking his head and weeping. Ruth and Jessica went back in to be with her. It took two. One to hold her forehead and the other to hold the pail to catch the vomit. Harry came out and Promise led him to a wagon tongue so he could sit down. He was weary and silent. He put his black bag between his slender legs. He looked off into the lavender dark of a nearly blind, twilight world. Promise sat by him and held his hand. Nobody spoke to them. He had brought cholera to them. He had to cure Rebecca, and he had done all he knew to do. If she died, he would be an outlaw.

Inside the wagon Ruth bent low to speak to Rebecca during a moment of calm. "How are you feeling now, Rebecca? How are you, honey?"

A bare motion, a flickering of eyelids, and then a feeble whisper. "I'm just fine. They ain't nothing wrong with me. Nothing at all. Just a little dyspepsia. I'll be all right."

Her eyes fluttered open then, and she stared into Jessica's face, a face white in the whale-oil lamp, shadowed, firm, beautiful with composure. The vision had the effect of black magic on Rebecca. Her own sallow face with its mottled cheeks, its fatty shapelessness, grew tight with hatred. She tried to raise herself off the bunk. "You! Get out of here, you! It's *your* fault! You *Jonah!*" And with that biblical allusion to sanctify her hatred, Rebecca leered up at Jessica, eyes popping with the strain.

Jessica spoke coldly in regal calm: "I only want to help you, Rebecca!"

Rebecca's hatred fueled her will. She croaked, "I don't need *your* kind of help! I don't need nothing *you* got to give me. You was the one that filled Jason's foolish head with notions about going West."

"I did no such thing." Jessica spoke in a serene tranquillity.

"He didn't never mention going West till he married you! We all know that. You put a hex on him! You put a curse on all of us. Get out! Get out!" Her whisper was frantic and terrible. And outside Samuel heard it, heard the urgency in his wife's hatred. He came in and stooped over them, a huge form hulking under the low arching canvas cover in the evil and heavy air.

"You better get out of here, Mrs. Jessica," he said with just

491

a hint of menace in his voice. "You're just making her worse."

"Yes, get her out of here, the hussy!" Rebecca hissed, and big tears formed in the sides of her yellow eyes and rolled down her temples.

"Rebecca Jennings!" Ruth said, weeping herself now with sorrow and indignation. "Don't speak evil of good folks now in the hour of your death!"

"I ain't going to die. I'm fine. Just fine. King Jesus is coming back to get me before I die. He promised me. The Lord God ain't going to let me die. I'm going to be caught up to meet the Lord in the air." Her voice, faint and whining, dwindled almost to nothing.

Ruth was irrepressible, solemn, brave. "It is my bounden duty as a Christian to tell you that you are going to die, and you should not meet your Maker with hatred in your heart, Rebecca."

"I don't hate nobody! I don't hate nobody! She's a whore. That's what the trouble is. Mrs. Baynes told me what I always knowed. Jason married a whore. Samuel's mamma said she was a lewd woman. Samuel's mamma said she married Jason for his money."

"For his money!" Ruth uttered a dry, iron chuckle of absurdity. "Rebecca, you poor, foolish thing! Don't you know Samuel's mamma hated all of us! She said bad things about you, Rebecca. Cruel things. You know she did. God have mercy on her poor soul!"

"No! No! She loved me better than any of you. Her and me was like sisters!"

"No!" Ruth said firmly, quietly, with a terrible resolution. "It was not like that. She said you was like a cow. She told you to your face that you smelled bad. She said you was too familiar with that preacher. What was his name?"

"Get out! Get out! Both of you! Get out!"

Ruth doggedly shook her head. Righteousness demanding some meaningless vindication in the last hour, demanding confession. Jessica stood stock-still, proud, unflinching, looking at Ruth. Ruth the prophet, declaring justice. "I ain't going to leave as long as you need me. Jessica ain't going to leave neither. I love Jessica. I want her with me to help me when you die, Rebecca."

"I ain't going to die. I don't need you. I don't need nobody but Samuel and the Lord. Get out! The Lord's coming. He's going to damn you for persecuting me. Get out."

"Maybe you better leave," Samuel said. Very worried, in torments of fear and uncertainty, looking down at this wife he adored.

"No! We're staying right here!" Ruth was granite.

Rebecca passed into an insane delirium. There were moments in the long night when she emerged from her raving like a piece of flotsam swept to the surface of a black sea by a blacker current out of the depths. "This is Ironton, ain't it, Samuel? You ain't been lying to me all these weeks, have you, Samuel?"

Samuel shook his head slowly. "No, I ain't been lying to you, Rebecca."

Rebecca began to cry. A feeble snuffling. "You're mean to me. You always was mean to me, Samuel!"

Ruth spoke up harshly from where she sat at the head of the bed. "That ain't so, Rebecca! You know it ain't so! Samuel's been good as gold to you. He loves you more than you deserve!"

"He don't! He don't!"

"I do, honey. You know I do. Oh, I love you with all my heart!" Samuel was disconsolate.

"No, you hate me. I know. I'm a poor, persecuted woman! But I got the last laugh, husband. You know our baby loved *me!* He didn't love you!"

"That ain't true, Rebecca. You know it ain't true!" Samuel was close to tears.

"No!" she whispered with all the burning spite that a feeble whisper could bear. "He just pretended to love you. But he told me . . . He told me how he really felt, Samuel! He said to me again and again, 'Mamma, I just despise daddy! He's stupid, mamma! So *stupid!*'"

Ruth broke in again, outeaged, out of breath with revulsion at what she was hearing. "Rebecca Jennings, with God as my witness, that is a damnable lie! You know it is a damnable lie!"

But Rebecca went weakly on as if Ruth had not spoken. "'My friends laugh at him!' That's what he said, Samuel. 'And I'm ashamed of him!' Them was his very words, Samuel!"

"No, Rebecca. No!" Samuel put his head in his big, brown hands and wept.

"Rebecca Jennings! How can you go meet God with a lie like that on your lips!" Ruth's strong voice broke in pleading and horror. Rebecca paid no attention. Her entire life had come down to this point of fire. All those years compacted into a flaming dot intended to burn a hole through her husband's heart and to punish him for not serving her with the devotion she deserved.

"We let you be happy, Samuel. But I was the only one he loved. He pretended to love you just because I made him lay his hand on the Bible and swear."

"Hush, Rebecca. Hush!"

"He ran away because of you, Samuel! He wrote to me and explained it. I never showed you the letter."

"No, Rebecca. He's dead. He's dead."

*"I don't want to die, Samuel. Don't let me die."*

"You ain't going to die, Rebecca. Oh, honey, you ain't going to die!"

*"At least not out here. I don't want to die out here. If I have to die, take me back to Ironton. Let me die with my friends!"*

In the darkest hour of the night, sometime after two in the morning, Rebecca died.

The two women who had sat by her bed got up to cleanse her and to prepare her for burial. Samuel came heavily down into the gloomy dark fitfully illuminated by the campfire, his heart broken, his head downcast.

"Is she . . ." Jason began, unable to finish the question.

Samuel, equally unable to form the single word of the answer, could only nod.

"Dead!" Ishtar Baynes shrieked. She was squatting by the fire, drinking black coffee out of a tin mug. She had not volunteered to do anything to help because vomit made her sick. "She's dead! She's dead! Oh, the poor, dear woman! She was the sweetest woman I ever knowed! She was like a mamma to me. Knowing her has meant the world to me!" Her voice was loud and frantic, and yet she did not rise from her squatting, and her agitation did not make her spill a single drop of her coffee, and when she was done with crying out, she went back to drinking her brew and cried out again only when she took her nose out of the cup to take a breath.

Jason, dazed and weary, shook his head. "I promised we would all make it to California . . ." He could not finish his thought.

"I loved her," Samuel said. He was sobbing. "I tried and tried to prove to her that I loved her, and she wouldn't never believe me, Jason. And it's too late now. It's too late."

"Oh, Mr. Jennings," Ishtar Baynes cried. "She's in heaven

now with Jesus and all the holy angels. She sees everything you do. She knows everything you think now. And you can still prove you love her. I'll show you a way. I swear she'll be satisfied then."

Adam could not bear it. He went silently to Jason's wagon and took out a spade. He set off to the edge of the firelight to dig a grave.

As he went, he heard Ishtar Baynes turn on poor Harry Creekmore. Harry sat blankly on the wagon tongue, like a sightless statue carved out of soap, his coat unbuttoned, his world a blur of hopeless confusion. Promise sat next to him, her face white in the lamplight, frozen in fear and grief.

"You didn't save her, Mr. Creekmore!" Ishtar Baynes crowed. "All your fancy talk about being a doctor, and you couldn't save that poor, dear woman. Well, it's like I said. You ain't no doctor. You'll tell the truth before I get through with you, Mr. Creekmore. It won't be long now."

Harry looked blindly in her direction. He pulled what dignity he could summon from the shadows and spoke to her with restrained calm. "No doctor can save everybody, Mrs. Baynes. We all die. Even doctors die."

She leered at him. "But you ain't no doctor at all, Mr. Creekmore. A real doctor could of saved her!"

Harry shook his head dully and murmured, "I am a doctor, Mrs. Baynes. I saved Mrs. Ruth's life. I proved I was a doctor when I saved her life."

As if to support his claim by the evidence of her body, Ruth came down out of Samuel's wagon and went over to speak to Asa. She seemed strong and substantial and serene in the mysterious firelight, her motherly body a fortress against evil, the stump of her arm somehow a sign of the price she had paid the powers of darkness to ransom all the rest of them. With Ruth there Adam thought he could feel the demons of night flutter away.

He decided to go beyond the firelight, to get far away from all of them. He could not disguise his own feelings to himself and was afraid he might speak them to the others. If anyone had to die, he was glad it had to be Rebecca. She got what she deserved. Now if Mrs. Baynes would only die, he would dig her grave with jubilation. He would spade the dirt in on top of her with the ecstasy of Pentecost. Proof of justice in the universe.

*God, kill Mrs. Baynes, and I will repent, and I will believe in you!* His prayer was more fervent than any prayer he had ever prayed in his life before.

At dawn, when he had dug the grave, he came tramping back into camp to be with the rest of them. He was worn out with his toil. He was sweating so profusely that all his clothes were sodden, and he was giddy with sleeplessness and fatigue. He had never felt so unsteady. The chill morning wind of the high country ripped through his clothing and made his teeth chatter, and he cast a longing gaze toward the whitening east with its promise of day and heat.

It was Henry who rushed to meet him, a small gray form moving against the immense grayness of the lightening earth. And when Adam saw the helplessness and the terror together in Henry's face, he knew what was wrong even before the boy could whisper that Ruth was sick.

# 55

---

*O they tell me of a land where no storm clouds rise,*
*O they tell me of a land far away!*
*O they tell me of a land far beyond the skies.*
*O they tell me of the unclouded day . . .*

So they sang in slow, mournful cadences rising and falling in the entryway to South Pass under the glowing and peaceful sun. And Ruth was sick in Jason's wagon, with Jessica and Promise to watch over her. Ishtar Baynes did not sing, professing herself to be too broken up over Rebecca's death, standing with her head artfully downcast and her hand over her eyes to veil nonexistent tears. Adam thought that he read a look of cunning and triumph there. The men sang strongly, in quavering rhythms, loudly, desperately. But the wind carried the cry of their frail assurance away, so that at the remove of twenty yards their sound was thin and plaintive and the words so feeble that they could not be understood.

Jessica tended Ruth, tended her fiercely, spat at Asa like a cat, told him to go to the devil when he ordered her out of the wagon. And Asa backed away before her fury and went out muttering. His eyes cold and hostile. He would not let Ruth have laudanum because laudanum had not saved Rebecca. Harry said it was the only hope. Jessica got into Harry's black bag, fetched the laudanum, and gave it to Ruth in a dose that made her sink into a heavy sleep. As Harry predicted, the diarrhea and the vomiting stopped, but her skin remained pallid and dry, and she passed into a chill so that even her breath seemed cold.

Harry stood helplessly outside, having done all he knew to do. He wanted to assume the proper manner of a doctor seeing a difficult case through, believing almost unconsciously that if he could look like a doctor, Ruth might live. But without his glasses to give him a bearing on the world, he did not even know how to pose. He only succeeded in looking helpless and unsure of himself.

The rest of them stood or sat around in lassitude and foreboding, hardly speaking to one another. There was not a tree in sight. The sun was intensely hot at noon except when a big, soft cloud passed between it and the earth, and then the air turned uncomfortably cool. Clifford Baynes, surfacing again to be somebody rather than something drifting along with them, worried about the cholera. He whimpered, self-pitying and frightened and imagining symptoms in himself, until his wife told him to hush up—the first authoritative thing she had said to him since Scott's Bluff. And he looked at her, swallowed, and hushed, his attempt at rebellion against his wife ended in ignominy.

It was eerie to Adam how the cholera that killed others seemed to restore Ishtar Baynes to strength. While everyone else was struck into confusion by the plague, she reasserted herself, and nobody was up to resisting her. Clifford Baynes looked around, found no friends, and after a while rolled himself into the shade under Samuel's wagon and fell asleep.

Henry went in and sat by his mother for long periods of time, holding her hand. She gave no notice of his presence, and he made no sound. When he emerged, he came silently to be with Adam.

Adam was touched by Henry but did not know what to say to him and so said little. The boy was struck still by that watchful reserve that will come to strong children before a disaster that they cannot comprehend. He did not go to his father, and Asa did not seek him. Asa paced in the open air and brooded and looked with silently burning hatred at

Harry. Adam knew that if Ruth died, Asa would try to do something to Harry. But it seemed hardly worth considering.

*I can take care of Harry.* Asa was a coward. Adam would destroy him if he tried anything.

Jessica sat by Ruth and tenderly washed her face with a rag dipped in a pail. Ruth was in such a deep coma now that she could not swallow. Jessica was sweating hard; her blond hair was stringy and disheveled. From time to time she had to come out to breathe so she would not faint, and when Adam saw her he thought of how strong she looked. But he saw also the age in her face, and he was troubled. Sometimes he was angry with himself, for in the midst of this calamity he thought not of the cholera but of how he had made love to Jessica. And he was not warmed and comforted by what he had done or even guilty, only puzzled. They had so little to say to each other now; they seemed to have passed without quite knowing it into different worlds.

Jason climbed up inside the wagon once and looked at Ruth locked in her dry chill, her mouth agape and her breath swift and shallow. He came out again, muttering something none of them could understand.

The light was intense. Nothing but the unquiet wind making the bright sage, dry green and burnished yellow, dance hypnotically in the brilliant sunlight, enough to make you dizzy. The pungent smell of turpentine in the sage made the air sharp and clean-smelling. The slow motion of the day itself, turning in dreamlike languor, was like eternity wound up in a watchspring.

And Mrs. Baynes strutted around, speaking to first one of them and then to another, to Jason, to Asa, in long, head-nodding monologues to Samuel, going in to the wagon where Ruth lay, coming out again, glaring up at the sun, looking at Harry Creekmore in vulturous expectation and triumph.

The old man squatted in the sunshine with Adam. He held his swollen hands extended before him into the heat of the day. He could scarcely bend his fingers at all. They were like red sausages thrust out from his puffy hands. Every slight motion of his arms and legs caused him pain. He turned very stiffly to Adam and said, "Adam, we got to kill that woman."

Adam looked at him with a start. "Mrs. Baynes?"

"Yep. I can't get my fingers around the trigger of a gun. You got to do it yourself."

Adam's heart beat hard; his mouth went dry. "I didn't

think you was afraid of her. I didn't think you was afraid of none of these folks."

"That was before the cholera. I didn't know we was going to get cholera. I didn't know that there doctor friend of yourn was going to be a fool. I didn't know this was going to happen to me in August this year." He held his puffy hands out and looked at them as if he had never seen a sight like them before.

"Just . . . kill her?" Adam had thought of killing her. But it had been a fantasy.

"One bullet," the old man said earnestly. "You got a pistol right there. Take her tonight like an old horse and shoot her in the head."

Adam pondered. He felt apathetic, unable to raise himself to do anything that took will. "The law . . . ," he murmured and did not know how to end his thought.

"There ain't no law out here but what you decide it is. You're the law. You go kill her. Tonight."

Adam got up and walked off in a daze. He tried to summon up his resolution to kill her. He remembered the knifing intensity of his prayer that she should die. He looked up into the serene clouds and wondered if God grinned up there in a little celestial joke.

*You prayed that she would die, Adam Cloud! Very well! Kill her yourself and believe in me! I grant you the authority.*

Adam felt the solid weight of the pistol in his belt. He put his hand down to the butt of the gun and stroked it as if to transfer its strength into himself. He began preparing his mind. He imagined what it would be to put the gun up against her head. He squeezed his trigger finger.

He reasoned with himself. *Things are just about to get out of hand! Rebecca's dead. Maybe Ruth's going to die. Samuel's dangerous now. A barrel of gunpowder. Mrs. Baynes whispering into his ear ever five minutes. Trying to throw a spark down. Asa an enemy from the beginning. If I kill that woman, I can handle them. Things will settle down.*

He tried to inspire himself with the details of the murder. He supposed she would flee when she knew he was going to kill her. People would be screaming at him to stop. Jessica. Promise. They would see her die. Messy. Well, then, he would sneak up on her in her sleep. Blow her brains out. Terrible to think of shooting anyone asleep. Cowardly. Something wrong with it anyway he turned it. The more he thought about it, the more impossible everything became.

He pondered these austere thoughts until sunset, striving to get a grip on himself, to make himself do the deed. He had killed before; he could kill again.

But he could not make himself do it.

*Why couldn't she of been one of them Indians?*

Then at twilight his mind was removed from Ishtar Baynes because Ruth died.

It was up to Adam to dig another grave. His mind was numb. *I should of dug this one in the daylight.*

He tried to figure all the things Ruth's death meant. He tried to grieve. His head swam backwards to a thick reservoir of horror somewhere in the dark of his consciousness. Something was about to break, to crush him to death. He threw himself into his digging.

He was thankful to be away from the rest of them. Out of that fire of emotion now blazing through the camp. Ruth's death stunned them. Asa shed hot, hysterical tears and cursed Harry. Adam wondered if Asa had loved his wife at all. What seemed to grieve him was a general despair for himself and his prospects, in this world that had turned against not just his daughter and his wife but against him. It was young Henry whose sorrow was most intense and least complicated. His mother was dead. He knelt by the body, his head on her breast. He held her hand, and he wept with a broken heart.

Ishtar Baynes shrieked at Harry in a litany of conquest. "What about things now, *Mr.* Creekmore? You didn't save Ruth after all, Mr. Creekmore. You ain't no doctor! Ruth's dead, Mr. Creekmore! Ruth's dead!"

Harry had no answer left to give. Ruth had been his proof to himself that he was a doctor. He sat cross-legged in the grass with downcast eyes and bowed head, his hands lightly clasped in front of him. Promise sat beside him, looking at Ishtar Baynes now with terror, feeling that the walls were down at last and that she and Harry were both helpless before the fury of this woman's assaulting evil.

Adam shunned the camp and dug the grave, because Harry's humiliation after Ruth's death was too much to bear. Nothing on earth could have saved Ruth or Rebecca, Adam told himself. Still, Ruth's death broke a net of confidence that had held them all to Harry. Ishtar Baynes cut the net, piling detail on detail about their meeting on the road to Nashville, Harry's head-feeling there, and people listened to her because nobody could say anything. Ruth's death smothered their words. And Ruth herself, the sign of Harry's triumph in the world, his authority, was dead.

Adam dug thoughtlessly, plunging the spade down, taking it up full of dark earth, flinging the dirt away from him into the night, digging in again. *Ruth will lie here forever.* A man become a machine. Tireless. Wanting not to think. *Right here. Ruth.* He was sweating. He did not care. When he heard the rifle shot explode back in the camp, he jumped up in alarm like a man awakened from a deep sleep. He heard the sounds of turmoil; he very distinctly heard Ishtar Baynes scream. He paused to prime his pistol. Then he raced back to camp.

He found demonic confusion, magnified and made lurid by the violent dancing of the fire. Samuel stood holding the old man off the gound, the way a large and clumsy child might clutch a small rag doll against his body. The look on Shawnee Joe's face was so empty and so indistinct in the shadows that Adam's first thought was that he was dead. Asa was standing a little apart holding a rifle, looking at the old man in a daze. Ishtar Baynes sat only half-detached from the darkness, her face as pale as a corpse, her head flung back in terror and astonishment. She was breathing like a bellows; her husband had fled into the dark.

Jason was speaking in a loud, almost hysterical voice, expostulating with the old man. And Jason was holding a Bowie knife shining dully in one hand, so that Adam's second thought after believing that the old man was dead was that Jason was about to kill him. So he came into the camp on a dead run, flourishing the revolver, pointing it at Jason, yelling, "Don't you hurt Joe!"

Jason turned around like a man in a trance and dropped the knife. Samuel released the old man. Asa threw the rifle down. And the old man came staggering toward Adam, holding out those swollen, rheumatic hands, his red eyes imploring Adam to do something. But it was Ishtar Baynes who explained it all.

"That old fool tried to shoot me!" Her voice a screech of outrage and fury in the night.

The old man muttered: "I did, Adam. I tried to kill her. But I couldn't hold the gun. Shoot her now, Adam. Right this minute. You've got the gun in your hand. Kill her!"

Adam, still holding the pistol, turned slowly toward Ishtar Baynes, his mind struggling to absorb what had happened. Her face was frozen in his direction. He caught a glimpse of Jessica out of the corner of his eye. She was standing in the shadow of Jason's wagon, where Ruth's corpse still lay in the hammock. Jessica's face seemed unusually pale in the uncertain light, and yet she was poised and perfectly composed, and like some impossible telegraph her mind seemed to be saying to him, *Kill her.*

Some surge of resolution must have rushed into his face. Ishtar Baynes cried out anew, "My God! Now *he's* going to kill me! Oh, God! Oh, *God!*" She screamed, her head thrown back like a stricken turkey's, and her bloodcurdling gobble of horror resounded and resounded into the black night, pulsating toward the snowy crests of the Wind River Mountains standing still and silent high above them and carrying to infinity beyond.

It was perhaps that heart-rending female scream of the most abject terror that stayed his hand. For he simply could not squeeze the trigger on his pistol, and after holding it foolishly for a moment and staring with even greater foolishness and confusion toward the yowling form of Ishtar Baynes, Adam said in disgust, "My God! You're all crazy!" With that he put the gun back in his belt. His hand was trembling. *I scared her good. That's enough! She won't bother us after a scare like that.* Self-justification for his weakness. A surge of relief in him that he did not have to kill her.

"You fool!" the old man said in disgust. 'I thought I'd taught you better than that. You ain't nothing but a fool. You ain't learned nothing. I was wrong. You ain't no good for this country. You're nothing but a coward. You ain't no good for nothing."

And with that outraged malediction and rejection hanging in the night air like gunsmoke, the old man whirled away and went stumbling off to his tent to find his jug.

They buried Ruth in the dawning, before the sun was hot, their eyes awash with grief, with terror, with dull astonishment, confounded with their defeat. Her death was like the hidden ending to a book. They had arrived at the last page, her arm mended, her strength restored, happiness for everyone with good in triumph and evil in defeat and all conflict resolved. Then they had turned that last page in peaceful idleness and discovered disaster and rout written in the last paragraph. Her death made all life a chaos. Things did not work out.

Things just happened.

Ruth was wrapped in a blanket. She was no longer Ruth but a lumpy, bulky shape discernible as vaguely human but

502

unnatural and otherworldly in its long, still rigidity. The blanket of coarse brown wool had been on her bed, Asa's bed, in Ohio, where they had lived with her flowers in the dooryard and the scent of sweet roses rising in the warm spring air to permeate the house and give it the clean fragrance of a garden. In that blanket she was buried, and there were no roses here to put on her grave, not even any wildflowers. And there was no organ to send her to rest in a swelling anthem of sound. Only the frail, discordant voices of a remnant unbravely singing to the wind:

> *Ye fleeting charms of earth, farewell,*
> *Your springs of joy are dry;*
> *My soul now seeks another home,*
> *A brighter home on high.*
> *I'm a long time trav'ling here below,*
> *I'm a long time trav'ling away from home;*
> *I'm a long time trav'ling here below*
> *To lay this body down.*

Farewell to Ruth! Ruth the warm and lovely, mother of them all, strong and hopeful. Ruth an oblong package, wrapped in that wretched-looking blanket, and laid in the black earth. Adam's hands were as stiff as flatirons when he took up the spade and began to shovel the dirt back again, the clods showering down on that shapeless thing, shutting it away from the sun, away from flowers, forever, leaving Ruth to lie still in a grave that would be unmarked and soon forgotten.

"There's a curse on us, Jason!" Asa speaking, his voice first a sob, then tight and thin under the high pressure of his lust for vengeance.

"No," Jason said dully. "There isn't such a thing, Asa. No curse. My God, this is the nineteenth century!"

"Yes! Yes, there is! Just look around, brother. Call it what you want. But to me it's a curse."

They squatted together in the black shade of a wagon. The two graves were scars in the waving sage. The morning sun poured over the earth, and heat waves rolled up from the long sweep of the upland plains. Jason stared at the graves.

"You promised to get us to California!" Asa said. His voice was a hiss, a whisper of zeal and condemnation. "We ain't got to California, Jason. My Rachael . . . dead! Rebecca.

503

And now Ruth! My God, Jason, *Ruth!*" His voice broke, Asa near to panic. He had depended on Ruth's firm solidity more than anybody could know. "How do you explain it, brother? If it ain't no curse, tell me what it is."

"I don't know. I don't know." Jason's words were flat, drained of all energy, comatose, full of phlegm. Jason beaten.

"Most folks make it through to California without no trouble," Asa said, his voice boring in like a needle-sharp awl in soft leather, turning, turning, remorselessly twisting in Jason's hide. "For most folks, this here's just a lark going cross country. They camp out, sing songs, enjoy the scenery, meet folks like themselves, get there safe and settle down. But look at us, Jason. We've been cursed, and if we're under a curse, they must be a reason for it. Who's guilty, Jason? You tell me who if it's not you!"

Jason looked up, his face bleak, terrible, and baffled. Very slowly, fearfully, he shook his head. "It's not my fault," he whispered. "I swear to God! It's not my fault!"

Asa looked narrowly at him. Jason's defensive cringing, almost imperceptible to anyone else, was visible to a brother. "Now think, Jason. Think! You're the captain! If something's gone wrong, it must be something you done. Sometime you done something that brought this on us. Think what it was." Asa's face, twitching with malice, burned with knowledge. Jason had done something to bring the curse upon them all.

Asa stared at him, his mind working in heavy calculation. Then he looked knowingly out into the sun at Jessica. She sat, shading Henry with her body, stroking his blond head. She wore a long blue dress of cotton, and it had faded with the journey and was blue like the morning sky. Henry sobbed on her shoulder; she held him tenderly.

"Somebody's guilty, Jason," Asa said, his voice more firm now. Flat with conviction and a terrible resolution. "You're the captain. You're the one that's got to punish the guilty one."

Jason was thinking of New Haven. Of the house on Orange Street with the light falling into the night under the great elm trees. Of failing everything at Yale. Of whoredom and corruption, lust and ambition. He knew Asa was accusing him. He turned on his brother: "I am not guilty of anything. Now leave me alone!"

"*Somebody* is guilty, Jason." The voice drilling at him. "Somebody brought this on us. You must know who it is, Jason. You can't deny it any longer."

Jason felt like a small animal driven into a corner. "*I* have not done anything to deserve this, brother." Jason lumbered awkwardly, hastily, to his feet and walked out into the sunlight. Heat smacked him like a flail. How could it be so hot now, when it was so cold in the night? Jason baffled, feeling something inside him snap like a tight, wet rope suddenly breaking under too much of a load.

Asa followed him, relentless and unmerciful. "I didn't say *you* did anything, Jason. Not exactly. I'm talking about that woman you married! She's the cause of all our trouble! Nothing ain't gone right since you married her, Jason. First, mamma died. Then Rachael. Then Rebecca. Now . . . Ruth!" The mention of his wife's name in all this tension made Asa dissolve in tears. But still he pursued his brother, the two of them tramping over the sage, throwing black shadows.

They came to Jessica, to Henry, stopped, stood over them. Asa looked down with blazing, tear-filled eyes. "She's the guilty one, Jason. She's the one that's the cause of everything."

"Asa, what are you talking about?" Jessica defended herself with awful dignity. Little Henry pressed against her, his face pushed into her soft bosom, his neck bent in an attitude of uncomprehending and helpless childish fear. Jessica had both arms around him, holding him close.

Asa seemed to see his son for the first time in hours.

"You get *away* from her!" Asa lunged at them, seized Henry by the arm, jerked him up, and flung him away. Henry went staggering into the brilliant sunshine. Jessica started after him. But Asa grabbed her by the wrist and jerked her cruelly back so that her head snapped. He screamed insults at her. Samuel came out, stood by, arms folded, impassive and still and waiting. Adam, coming over from yoking the oxen, saw Samuel and felt a chill in his spine. *He's convinced, too. He believes she is our curse.*

Adam moved swiftly, seeing Jason was not going to help his wife. He grabbed Asa by the hair from behind and jerked him back so sharply that Asa's neck popped. And with Asa's head twisted back like that, Adam slapped him with an open hand so hard across the face that Asa went tumbling in the grass like a brittle sack of reeds.

"You leave her *alone!*" Adam cried.

The old man came out of his tent and hobbled over to Adam with his head wisely cocked. "All right. Remember what I told you. Back in Westport. You got to kill him now.

Go ahead and do it!" A voice quiet, like conscience, cold and merciless, speaking slowly and firmly.

Asa lay back in the grass, his hand to his face in astonishment and shock where Adam had hit him. Asa afraid now. Adam delighted to see the anger knocked out of him, replaced by naked terror. Samuel impassive and waiting. He would follow Adam's lead still, because of the bond forged between them back in Missouri. And the old man crouched there in the sun like the prince of darkness saying again, "Go ahead, Adam. Kill him. Right now."

"No!" Adam said, annoyed, frustrated, tired of being pushed around by everybody—Asa, the old man, this whole mad crowd. Beaten by the sun, by disease and death, and by the dull conviction in his heart that *he* was the Jonah, responsible for all the evil that had fallen on them. *He* had made Harry stay to bury the dead at Independence Rock. *He* had asserted his pride by taking Rachael over the river. And *he* had killed those two ragged Indians so far, far away, whose vengeful spirits no doubt pursued them across this great and tremendous land. He was sick and tired of the person he was. He longed to vanish like a wisp of cloud absorbed in the great, still light. Why didn't somebody blame him so he could die?

He muttered: "No, I won't kill him this time. No. But by God, Asa! You touch Mrs. Jessica again, and I *will* kill you. I will chop your head off!" A gruesome threat to hide Adam's weakness. Adam spent. He turned away.

"You won't have the chance to kill him again," the old man said, raising his insistent voice as if he could not believe the foolishness he was witnessing. "He will kill you first chance he gets now. It's you or him!"

Adam ignored him and went back to yoking the oxen. No one to help him. All of them struck to helpless apathy for a few moments, their energies suspended. He did all their work now; and they expected him to do it. He was weary, dizzy, and everything seemed unreal. His vision swam in the sunlight, and the heat made his head throb.

Jessica stood for a moment, livid, angry, and utterly silent. She rubbed her wrist where Asa had hurt her; she looked haughtily and contemptuously down at him as if to say, *I cannot be bothered by the likes of you, Asa Jennings. You are scum. Riffraff.* And she went to console Henry.

She got the boy to his feet. He had ceased to cry. He was still with a terrible and watchful calm in his young face. Vigilant brown eyes sought his father out. Silently measured the man who cowered in the grass, dumbly holding his face where Adam had hit him.

It was Ishtar Baynes who first recovered her voice. She had come out to watch like a bird perched on a pole. Her voice was shrill as she called after Adam; her words carried like shot. "You can bully us around, Mr. Adam, because you got a gun. And you're stronger than most of us. But what Mr. Asa says is the truth. Mrs. Jessica there! She started it all by making us throw out them pretty things way back down the road. She upset things. We was going along fine up till then. But she had her way, and you had your way because you two was in it together. Wanting to puff yourself up. Treat everybody else like you was better than they was. And I know why you and her has been so thick, Mr. Adam. You've been carrying on with her like she was your whore. So you're going to take up for her. Ain't it so, Mr. Adam? You got to take up for your whore!"

Adam whirled around! So Ishtar Baynes knew! He stood gaping at her for a moment. How? The secret knowledge of her kind. Adam stood looking at her across that space tormented by the brilliant sunshine, and for just an instant he felt naked in front of the world.

But all at once he recovered himself, and a joy of victory flooded up in him. By God! Now was the time to let the thing out! Adam would confess and let them all be damned. Take Harry, Promise, Jessica, the old man, and tell the rest of them to go to hell. Take Henry, too. A last vengeful deprivation for evil Asa! Damn them all!

He started walking purposefully toward Ishtar Baynes. With every step strength seemed to pour up into him from the earth he trampled underfoot. He was ready to admit it all with a ringing laugh and a dare. What could anybody do about it? Nothing. He felt giddy with triumph, and as he marched toward her, he actually saw Ishtar Baynes lose her smile and begin to retreat.

He was opening his mouth to rob Ishtar Baynes of her moment by bragging of what he had done when suddenly Jessica spoke, her voice burning with indignation.

"If you have one shred of proof for anything you are saying, Mrs. Baynes, I would like to know what it is!"

"Proof!" Ishtar Baynes screamed. "I don't need *proof*, you hussy! I can tell by the look in your eyes when you look at him. I can tell by the way he takes your clothes off with his

507

eyes when he looks at you. I seen you two walking in the dark, in the middle of the night, when you ought to of been in bed with your husband. That there's proof enough for me. *I know what folks do in the dark!*"

Again Adam opened his mouth to speak. He was five feet from Ishtar Baynes now. She was treading backwards, hardly knowing that she was in retreat. And Adam was grinning, the grin of a lion. He was ready to make Jason squirm. *Yes, Jason, I did what you can't do. I made love to your wife. And I'm going to take her away from you now. This morning. I love her, Jason. And she loves me.*

That was what he was going to say. But his mind tripped on the thought, *She loves me.* Did she love him? She had never once said so. And now something in Jessica's tone made him pause. For less than a second he hesitated.

Jessica broke in, speaking earnestly to her husband, red-faced and indignant. "This horrid woman is an evil and filthy liar, husband. I hope you take her for exactly what she is. You *know* what she is!" Each syllable the heavy, rhythmic beating of a sledgehammer pounding ice.

Jason was dumbfounded. He threw a terrible glance at her. He had never even imagined that she could be unfaithful to him. His voice broke, and he looked at the ground. His nether lip trembled ridiculously, like a hurt child's. "Jessica . . . Wife! Please, God!" He willed with all his force to lift his eyes and look at her directly. "Tell me the truth! Is there anything to what this woman says? Is it true?" He looked at Adam. Adam was looking with foolish astonishment at Jessica's hard face.

"There is not one word of truth in it!" she said. "I stand here with Almighty God as my witness. I have not touched Adam Cloud, and Adam Cloud has not touched me!" Her adamantine voice would have cut steel.

Now Adam Cloud was confounded. *My God! She's the best liar of all!* The incredible thought was a burning coal in the cool fabric of his brain, an appalling knowledge for a man to have of a woman. He was angry with her. With himself. This was the time to tell the truth! Jump up on a wagon seat and make a ballad out of their sin! Grab Ishtar Baynes by her lank hair and scream the finest details of their copulation into her ear. Tell her how good it had been. Mock Jason . . . Ride off then, like the wind.

But Adam could not tell the truth because Jessica was determined to lie. And Adam did not understand. She could not love Jason! Jason was old, a man with a face gone to crumbling stone, gray, haggard, spent. A simpler reason than love for a husband. A woman who had made one catastrophic mistake in life could not admit to another. How would Promise feel if she knew . . .

*It don't matter! We'll fix everything up. Get the girl and Harry to California! Let them do what they want, then. If they don't never want to see us again, it's all right with me.*

But it was not all right with Jessica.

Samuel spoke in a mutter. Vaguely stubborn and accusing. "I come out one night. When you was asleep, Jason. The night I was sick. Adam was supposed to be out here alone, on watch. And I seen them together." He looked at Adam longingly. "I don't think Adam would do nothing wrong. I don't know about her."

"Did you see us do anything wrong, Samuel?" Jessica's brassy eyes flashed at him.

Samuel spoke doggedly, shaking his head in negation. "No, ma'am. But I seen you together, and you wasn't supposed to be together."

"See there, Mr. Jennings!" Ishtar Baynes, pushing her advantage with a shriek of pleasure.

Jessica ignored her. "I told you what happened," she said, assuming a calm so natural and so grand that she might have been giving an order for groceries in the market. "I could not sleep. I did not want to disturb my husband. I took a walk. I talked awhile with Adam because I felt safer with him. Did you want me to go out by myself and let the Indians steal me?" An aloof sniffing of scorn, akin to laughter.

"A likely story!" Ishtar Baynes cried, like a witch dancing before Satan. "Look at her! You can *tell* she's lying!"

But to Adam the most dreadful thing of all was that he could look at Jessica and swear in his heart that she was telling the truth, that not a one of his wild and passionate memories of her flesh, her naked heat, was any more than a dream or worse—a figment of the wicked imagination generated by his terrible lust. He felt himself losing his hold on what was real.

"Disprove my story if you can!" Jessica said, her blue eyes flashing.

"I *know* she's lying!" Ishtar Baynes shrieked.

"No, we don't know that," Jason said dully, shaking his head. "I must believe my own wife. I cannot doubt my own wife."

"The safest rule in life is to doubt all women, whether they are wives or not," Clifford Baynes said.

Jason obviously did doubt, for he was the sort who thought the worst whenever it was suggested to him with authority. He searched for some support. Anything to hold him up in this terrible moment. He turned to where Harry sat silently on the ground. Promise held Harry by one arm, both her arms wrapped around his, and her head lay against his shoulder, and her long, dark hair tumbled down the back of his filthy coat that would never be white again.

"What about it, Dr. Creekmore?" Jason said weakly. "You're a medical man, a professional man. What do you think about this?"

It was a beseeching, confused cry for help. Somehow Jason's imploring, cowed voice pushed Harry at last beyond the outer limits of his restraint. He looked blankly up in the direction of Jason's voice, which in its very abjection and weakness had become unbearable.

"I can't tell you anything, Mr. Jennings. I'm not a doctor. Mrs. Baynes is right. I'm just a pretender. Everything I told you about being a doctor was a lie. I'm sorry. Now leave me alone."

For a moment Adam thought the tumult bursting around him must be the heavens crumbling like glass before the crack of doom and the blast of the awful trumpet. But he understood soon enough that the shrill clangor in his ears was the shrieking ecstasy of Ishtar Baynes, vindicated at last.

There was only one thing to do. Get them moving. Adam did it.

In spite of the gleeful caterwauling of Ishtar Baynes. In spite of the dead look in Promise's silent face. In spite of Jason's stunned murmuring. In spite of the scalding hostility percolating around them now like water boiling up out of a cauldron in the dark earth.

Adam and Henry got the oxen yoked and hitched. They got the mules packed. Adam helped the old man up on his riding mule. He got Harry and Promise to walk ahead of the wagons, apart from everybody else. He yelled the Jennings brothers into motion, cursing them for delay, suddenly pausing to clap Samuel on the back and to laugh as if they had been the best of friends. And in the midst of everything, Samuel smiled and looked pleased. And they got the oxen going up the long saddle between the mountains, to South Pass.

510

So they were moving, and Adam was thinking. He rode ahead of the rest of them where he could behold the unsullied high country without seeing the tiny figures of humans, wagons, and stock inching along behind him. And he made plans.

When all of them had settled down, they would have to split up. Maybe at the next settlement, Fort Bridger, up ahead. Maybe before then. Adam would make the division he thought best. Take his people on with the four mules. Would Jessica come with him now? Henry? He was too weary, too drained, to worry about questions like these. He would tell them what he thought, and they could do what they wanted. But he knew that he was going on. With Harry. He would force Harry Creekmore to come.

Jason stumbled along by his oxen like a man in a daze. Arcadia was dead. When Harry proved to be a charlatan, Arcadia dissolved like candy melting in the sun. Harry's belief had sustained Jason. Now Jason was nothing but an old fool making a pointless journey to the West, where there was no gold left, where all the dreams had turned to lead. Jason thought Harry had duped him, swindled him, not seeing that Harry had deceived himself, feeling only his own irrevocable loss and sickening humiliation.

Adam could see the outlines of what Jason felt. Far from mocking him, Adam thought he was pitiful. And somehow the dream of California that had seemed absurd as long as Jason believed in it, now became for Adam something grand and beautiful when Jason rejected it. *He was right about a lot of things!* The thought hard and sad.

The sun burned on Adam's head. His eyes ached when he saw the sharpness of the granite mountains, the heat waves pulsating upwards from the green and yellow sage. He shut his eyes and tried to think about California. His father. The sea ... The hound barked. Adam looked at him. The dog loped ahead, the only completely happy creature in sight, sniffing in joy at some scent. Long tail waving like a standard. *I've got to give that dog a name!*

He shut his eyes against the light. *God, the sun ... Why isn't it cool up here? Cold last night. So high. Ought to be cool.* His head burned with the light. His stomach was beginning to feel uneasy with the heavy rising and falling of the mule beneath him. The reek of sweat from the mule's back was stifling. *It stinks! Can't get away from it.*

He did not let them stop for nooning. Nobody really hungry. The oxen restored by the long wait for human death. *People go down; animals go up.* Empty thought. His head filled with empty thoughts. *If we stop, we'll all bunch up together, and we'll start yelling at each other again. Get this day over with. Forget it. Make the pass by nightfall. Start down on other side. Water running into the Pacific.*

Something decisive and sweet about the prospect of getting over the Continental Divide by the end of this evil day. A new birth. The East finally left behind for good. *Poor Ruth!*

Adam opened his eyes and looked at the blue mountains. The fields of snow on the jagged crests made him more dizzy. His face was hot. *Snow would feel so good.* His head light. *Snow.* So far away. Everything far away. *We're going so slow. It's a hundred miles to the top of the pass. A million miles to California.*

The ache in his head began to throb. *My belly aches.* His mother had a tonic. Something thick and heavy with a sharp smell and a burning taste. Big black letters on the yellow label. "Good for Upset Stomach." Adam remembered. *Dr. Cardwell's Indian Elixir.* Why did all tonics come from Indians? *Should of brought some with me.* Harry Creekmore. *Nashville. He was going to be mayor of Nashville. Then President.* Foolishness. He glanced up at the sun, turning in the saddle, feeling his stomach cry out in protest at that slight movement.

*Christ! I got to shit!*

The urgency of his need threw him into panic. Bowels full of gas. Shit straining at the gates. He turned the mule aside. Tried to find some sheltering declivity in the earth. Some hiding outcrop of stone. Anything to conceal his embarrassment. *Something up ahead.* His head roared. No time to wait. He forgot about shame.

He slid off the mule, bent double now with the pain in his guts. It was coming. Down in the tall sage. How good it was to see the sage come up around him. Relief. Down with his pants. Just in time. The shit burst out of him like something pent-up behind a breaking dam. A foul, evil stink. Strange and awful to have come from himself.

*What's going on?*

He was very dizzy now. Hitched his pants back up. Stood. The world swimming around him. The Wind River Mountains floated above his head. *I never knew mountains could float.* His stomach heaved. *Feel better if . . . Get it out!* He remembered how tenderly his mother . . . She held his head

512

while he vomited. Guilt about his mother. *I did not love her enough.* Nobody here to care for him. *Ah!* Vomit burst from his mouth, splashed with a heavy, steamy noise into the grass. *No one to help . . . Help!* A silent scream.

His head was pounding so hard that he did not know how it remained fixed to his body. Sight cut at his brain. He squeezed his eyes shut. His knees trembling, giving way. He felt the grassy earth coming up to meet him. He was shitting again. In his pants. He fell headlong. The earth seemed so cool. The grass gentle. His face burned. But then he was peaceful and mildly surprised that he did not care how much he fouled himself. *Nothing matters!* It was a revelation. He had never known such peace.

Far off in the dreamy back of his mind, a thought soft with mystery blew against him. *I have the cholera. I am going to die.* With all his remaining force he rolled over so he could see the brightness of the sky above him, so he would not die in the dark. He tried to make something terrible out of death so that he might prepare himself to meet the unknown. But he could not be afraid. Nothing seemed important but to recline happily in the grass, under that splendid, hot sunshine where everything seemed so big and so peaceful, where sky was so much more important than earth. Lying without any striving at all in the still vastness of yellow sand, in an open oven, being translated into light.

# 56

Delirium was bliss to Adam Cloud. He was only very dimly aware of Shawnee Joe croaking just over his head, "Now you'll see, Adam Cloud! Now you'll see! I was right! You should of killed her!"

But the old man's voice seemed remote and entranced, far off down a valley somewhere, resounding in gentle coves where cattle grazed in lush, green grass and billowing trees made still reflections in pools of bright water.

He felt Samuel's strong arms picking him up. Arms with

muscles in them like steel balls. He felt himself letting his bowels go again, a spurt of liquid. He did not care. His body was somebody else's concern now. Someone was taking off his befouled clothing. He was naked. Shameful! He wanted to laugh at the thought of shame. But he had no energy to laugh. Someone was washing him with cool water. Washing him gently everywhere with a cloth, saying something in worried consolation that he could not understand. It was so far away. Jessica's voice. The gentle touch of her hands. Soft and cool.

"Look at the woman! Seeing his nekkedness! Shame! shame! I told you, Mr. Jennings!" Ishtar Baynes. Victory on victory. The woman drunk with her triumphs. But to Adam her cry was like the very distant cawing of a crow in the remote depths of a cool forest.

He did not care about anything. He was laid in the bunk where Rebecca had died. The almighty sun came flooding through the tawny canvas cover and cast a tan shade over everything. He lay with his eyes peacefully shut in the tan gloom, and he thought, *How beautiful it all is!*

"He's cold, cold as ice!" A hand laid firmly on his brow. The voice of Promise, sick with fear, frantic and breaking. And Harry—good Harry Creekmore, Adam's beloved friend—murmuring something to her. Adam yearned to raise himself up, to tell them they were wrong to worry, to comfort them. *Don't fret!* He felt no pain. No discomfort. Only a floating serenity. He wanted to tell them that death had always been the worst thing he could imagine. But it was not bad. They should not be afraid. For him or for themselves.

But he had no strength to speak. And it was so much sweeter to shut his eyes and to drift aimlessly than it was to do anything else. Better than thinking. His detachment more blissful than anything else he had ever known.

"He's going to die!" The amazed cry of Ishtar Baynes. Like a mean child finding much more than she had expected under her tree at Christmas time. She was now in command. Nothing left to restrain her. With Adam dead, no one could keep her from her revenge. But Adam did not care anymore. He only wished that Ishtar Baynes might find the peace to meet death.

He had no idea of time. He passed into deep sleep and dreamed. He awoke sometimes to night and sometimes to day, and sometimes he heard loud voices muted by his isolation in himself, and sometimes he heard weeping, and sometimes there was only the blessed silence and the wind whipping lazily at the canvas top of the wagon. A curtain within himself parted briefly, revealed scenes on the outside, closed again, leaving him in the velvet dark.

Promise was sitting beside him, crying. "They won't let mamma stay with you anymore. They dragged her off. Swallow!" He swallowed because she seemed to want him to swallow so badly, and he wanted her to be peaceful. His throat was dry.

He wandered on wings to the highest mountains, where the snow was, and he sailed over the jagged peaks like a great bird on the wind, untouched by a single hard splinter of rock, and he saw the earth spread out before him for a thousand miles.

"Come outside with us, Mr. Creekmore. You got some debts to pay. You stay here, Miss Promise. Ain't nobody mad at you. You've been took in like the rest of us. You just keep out of the way!"

"No, no! You can't take him. You can't ... Adam, they're taking Harry away! Adam, please God! *Adam, get up! Please get up!*"

"Your friend Adam ain't going to help you none, Miss Promise. He's dying. Come along, Mr. Creekmore. You're the one we want to talk to."

"I'm coming, my good man. Please take your very dirty paw off my arm. I can't see how dirty it is, but I can feel your filth! Promise, now listen to me. I am going outside. You must stay here. They are not going to hurt you. You are safe here. They have promised me you would be safe if you stay here!"

"What have they done with mamma?" The girl hysterical.

"I don't know. Please, stay here! Adam needs you. Adam is your only hope. Stay here."

"Oh, Harry, I love you! I love you! I don't care what you are! I love you!"

"He's a serpent! That's what he is."

"I love you, too, my dear one. And if you love me, you must stay here. You must take care of Adam. Adam will take care of you."

Adam, lying in his bunk, stuporous and still, thought: *Harry's doing that real good. Ain't no actor in England or none of them far-off places that's better than our Harry Creekmore.*

But down deep in himself, Adam's bliss was disturbed.

515

When Asa led Harry away, Promise stayed behind and knelt down beside him, her arms around his neck, her hair against his face. She was pleading with him to get up, and he could feel her tears on his neck, and he wanted to get up to please her. But he could not. He tried to speak, and all that emerged from him was a long and penetrating groan.

Some sort of trial was afloat. He heard Ishtar Baynes shouting accusations, heard a thin murmur of masculine voices in assent, heard Harry laughing. Poor, blind Harry being condemned for his sins against them all. And Adam wanted to rouse himself and confess his own guilt. *I deserve to be punished. I made Harry stay and help bury the dead. The time we stayed there was what gave us the cholera. My fault. And I don't mind dying.* Yet all his efforts came to only an extended sigh, and Promise put her arms around him and wept as though they were now alone against the world.

*Good for me to die! It shows there is justice. I am guilty for the cholera. I deserve to die because I brought the plague.* He thought of how good the world was, how orderly in its justice, and his peace came back to him.

So he drifted for a long time with nothing happening, a dark and peaceful silence caressing him like the warm breath of a woman in love and at peace. Time so long that there was no time, and he slept like a child conscious of its sleeping, enwrapped in cool, damp clouds, swaying with the gentle rocking of the universe.

He saw Ruth's flowers growing in California, fields and fields of them running down to the blue sea in colors so bright that they dazzled his eyes. Ruth was moving serenely along the rows in a huge, blue sunbonnet, her face hidden to the sun and to him, bending sometimes to pluck a weed. And Adam Cloud was following her, his heart light, laughing easily. He said to her finally with immense unburdening, "God almighty, Mrs. Ruth! You know I had the strangest dream! It was a nightmare while I was dreaming it. But now it's all over, and it's right funny. I dreamt you was dead of the cholera on the way here and never did have no pretty flowers in California!"

"No flowers in California! Why, Mr. Adam, that was a crazy dream sure enough!" She turned her broad back on him, folded her two hands serenely together and looked out with pride on her acres of blossoms, and she laughed with pleasure.

*Adam! Adam! The old man's taken sick. He can't walk!*

516

*He can't stand up. Mrs. Baynes told Samuel to lay him out in the sun, Adam. And Samuel did it. There's nobody to take care of him. He's going to die.*

Promise, terrorized by a world of unimaginable horror now unfolding on her like black wings in the sunny reaches of South Pass. And Adam could do nothing but murmur words of consolation she could not understand.

His mind stuck restlessly for a while on the old man. He tried to tell Promise, "It's not so bad to die." But the thought troubled him, and deep inside him among the shadows he felt a stirring of guilt and rebellion. *It ain't right to want to die.* He could not bear the conflict, and so he left it and went laboring back to Ruth.

Ruth was telling him again a story she had recounted before, on the trail. It was a funny story, and Adam laughed. For the first time this Ruth of his vision turned and looked at him and her face under the big sunbonnet was a fleshless skull, with staring, empty sockets for eyes, and she slowly vanished quite away, and the flowers vanished with her, leaving the world dim and tan again. *Death is horrible.* The rebellious thought disturbed his peace. He fought against it. Death and corruption ... But in the corruption, the flowers bloomed again. The peace came back, and his body turned warm and numb. His mind was empty.

*They're arguing what to do with my Harry, Adam. Henry's run off. He's taken the mules with him, Adam. That little boy. Out there by himself. What does it mean? The old man's unconscious in the sun. Samuel won't let anybody go near him, Adam. Samuel! Can you imagine? He was always so good.*

Promise laughed. She was hysterical with fear and bewilderment. She hardly knew where she was.

Adam struggled to reach her. But he could not, and his mind descended to darkness. Was it Promise, whispering in frenzy at his ear? Or was it only the wind blowing down from the pass up there above them somewhere? He thought he felt his hound licking his face. The faithful hound! But he was too weak to turn his head. Could not open his eyes. His lids like steel bands. And anyway, he did not care for anything out there in the world where the voices and the wind spoke softly. Nothing mattered.

He was with his father again in Bourbon County, a single long and heavy rifle between them. Winter. They had been hungry. The great oaks and the tremendous chestnuts, bare of

517

leaves, their gaunt, dark branches reaching like imploring hands to the bleak gray sky. Air sharp and cold, and his father was speaking in a low, patient voice:

*You find a place where the deer cross, Adam. Then you just lie there, and you wait. You wait and wait. You can't go looking for the deer. He'll hear your footsteps in the leaves. You got to make yourself real still and not think of nothing but the deer and your shot. Don't think about the cold. You be the cold, and it won't bother you none because then it'll be like your feet or your arms, and you won't feel it special. And when you shoot, you aim just a little in front of him. Because some way you can't figure out, he's going to know about that shot just the second before you shoot, and he's bound to bolt like a streak of blue lightning.*

And suddenly, materializing out of the wintry afternoon, the deer came, an enormous stag, great, arching antlers proudly probing the air, his long muzzle black on the end, raised in stately detection, the stag not walking but parading, sniffing, knowing something was not right but not figuring it out yet. They were hungry for meat! That thought blazed in Adam's head when he looked at the stag. And what Adam always remembered was that his father did not snatch the rifle away to take the shot himself but let him fire, and Adam's shot was just the way his father said it should be, and the deer fell with a crash in the cold woodland, falling in the same smooth, uninterrupted motion with which he leaped, a surge into blackness, and his strong flesh was meat for their table for weeks.

*He's dead, Adam. The old man's dead. Can't you get up, Adam? They're going to drag his body off. They're not even going to bury him. They've tied mamma up in Jason's wagon. I'm scared, Adam! Oh, I'm so scared!*

He heard loud voices bursting like bombs in the fiery sunshine outside. And Harry Creekmore, the old Harry miraculously restored, shouting in his ringing, happy voice: "You're *still* a whore, Mrs. Baynes! Don't you see? It doesn't matter if I'm a doctor or not! *You are still a whore!* And you are a cuckold, Mr. Baynes. You ought to grow horns in that foolish head of yours! A cuckold with a thousand men who had a dime to spare!" And Harry Creekmore laughed, a wise, bold man laughing at a party where he stood with a brandy glass in his hand and the authority of wealth and worldliness in his voice.

"Sir!" Clifford Baynes said in hopeless, choking outrage.

518

Harry still laughing. The shadows of his vision transformed into a broad stage where he could play any role. Now he was the superior Georgia planter addressing knaves. "Just imagine, my dear fellow . . ."

"I am not a fellow! I am a professor of Latin!"

"Enough, my dear fellow! Enough. A man your age, reputedly a professor, telling young urchins with wealthy parents how to live! And you married yourself a washerwoman and you were just too innocent to know that she was a used-up old whore! I vow, Mr. Baynes! That is the funniest thing I ever heard of! You're a perfect fool, Mr. Baynes!"

"Sir!" Clifford Baynes was close to tears. Harry laughed again, never gayer in his life, never more superior.

"It's a lie! It's a lie! I'm as pure as the virgin snow!" Ishtar Baynes was shrieking in that shrill, bitter tone that belied all her words.

Harry laughed on. "You may have been snow once, Mrs. Baynes. But lots of folks have gone sledding on your hills!"

Jason's voice—numb, solemn, lethal. The dreamer of dreams whose illusions were gone. "But, Mr. Creekmore, the question of this woman is of no account. What we are talking about is that *you* are guilty of destroying a noble experiment by *pretending*. The hope of a nation! The hope of all humanity! Gone! Why did you do it? You pretended to be a doctor. Pretended to be able to help those people who contaminated us. *You pretended to believe in me!*" Jason's voice broke on this final, infinite indecency.

"I thought you needed me, Jason. You're not man enough to stand up by yourself. Somebody has to prop you up."

"You lied to me all along. You deliberately lied to me. You looked me straight in the eye and lied."

"You draw lies like honey draws flies, Jason. Lying is all I could do with you." Harry laughed again, hugely enjoying this burst of honesty and his drama. "And I tell you the truth, Jason," he said with a sigh of immense satisfaction and in his tone of maddening and unassailable superiority, "by the time I was done, my dreams were a lot better than yours. You had tin dreams, Jason. I dipped them in gold and made them worth something."

"It was the noblest dream ever dreamed by man," Jason whimpered.

"Sure it was!" Mrs. Baynes shrieked. "I still believe in you, Mr. Jennings! I still believe!"

"God bless you, Mrs. Baynes," Jason said in a trembling voice. "Oh, God bless you."

Harry laughed again. "You see, Jason. People just have to lie to you."

They had sat Harry down on a box to be judged. To be sentenced. He sat there easily, and though he could not see, he could feel their furious eyes on him, and the finality of hatred and revenge in their voices gave him no doubt about his fate. Pushed to the extremity, Harry discovered bravery. And he spread his long legs nonchalantly before him and ran his hand thoughtfully down his long, blond beard and looked out into the blur of brilliant colors that swayed together and gave him solace as they had done in his lost and remembered childhood.

"I tell you what I think is the noblest dream in the world, Jason. A big white house with a picket fence around it and a green lawn and a wife and children and the same thing over and over again every day for as long as anybody can see in the future. You're never going to do better than that. If you want something else, my friend, it's because something's missing in you, Jason. Maybe for you it's because you're a dull bore, and you know it. Even if you did go to Yale."

Harry laughed again at the mention of Yale in his infuriatingly offhand and superior way, as if all the passion of Jason Jennings driving them across the plains had been no more than a clown's act to take up time before the real show.

Jason stared at him in cold silence and turned away. His last hesitation about Harry gone now. Ishtar Baynes shouted again and again. "It ain't too late. We'll go build our Arcadia yet. People will come to us. Don't you worry, Mr. Jennings. Long as you got me, you got somebody to believe in you. And I ain't never going to stop believing in you!"

"She doesn't make you as happy as I did, does she, Jason?" Harry laughed. The old Harry Creekmore. Free of the world.

Ishtar Baynes made her final summation. "Now he has got to be punished, Mr. Jennings. That is the first law of things. Criminals have got to be punished. What kind of world is it when criminals get away with murder? It's like spitting in the face of God!"

"Yes," Jason said. "Yes."

"He killed Rebecca, Samuel!" Ishtar Baynes cried. "You remember that. Pretending he was a doctor made him go fool around with them folks that had the cholera. And he brung

heir death back, and he killed Rebecca. Just like he'd put a
gun up to her poor, sweet head and pulled the trigger."

Harry laughed yet again. "No matter what you do to me,
I'm still better than you are, Mrs. Baynes. You're still a
whore. And in my world—where I grew up—we wouldn't let
your kind come in to sweep our floors. Our slaves were better
than you." He laughed and thought of that vast and invisible
audience out there, admiring the dash and daring with which
he played out his heroic part. He did not think he would
leave a dry eye in the house.

# 57

Adam drifted on clouds of delirium to memories of his father's silences. The long silences of those ruminative evenings
when Joel Cloud sat pondering the fire, thinking and worrying about bright gold in California and not only about gold
but about the passing away of something he could not put
into words even as he felt it going, for he was not a wordy
man. But something being lost forever that he could feel with
all his heavy heart.

The silences were troubling to Adam Cloud, but then he
knew that his father was troubled, too, and that he groped
about in a lonely and maybe terrifying world of his own,
where no one else could go. But they were benign silences for
all their mystery. Sometimes Adam felt compelled to speak,
to say something—anything—to keep his father from going
away completely into the dreamy fantasies of his mind, where
he might never wish to leave.

And in those moments when the boy spoke like somebody
desperately throwing a rope out to a man drifting away in a
black river of dreams, Adam never found anything but a shy
grin of wakening and surprise, for his father came back and
gave his boy the welcome of a man not naturally demonstrative, for whom the smallest gestures meant something profound.

To Adam that shy grin of awakening always meant love.

And never once was there a change in his father's face from something natural and defenseless to something contrived and guarded, intended to hide himself and make an impression which, like armor, would keep the world at bay. There was never anything false or self-protective about Joel Cloud, and Adam loved the man for his simplicity.

Now out here and dying, Adam thought that he possessed his father's love just as if the two of them had found each other in California! He did not have to seek Joel Cloud anymore.

"Adam, you have to swallow the water. You have to live! Please, Adam. Please, God! Swallow." Promise pleading with him. He could not open his eyes, but he felt the trickle of water in his mouth, and he swallowed.

How strange it was that cholera had come to Bourbon County and had missed him, had waited to strike him down here in the midst of this empty and ghostly land. Adam Cloud thought of heaven, where there would be no memory of earth, no memory of anything, no names at all, where even God had no name and no memory. And there would be perfect silence, like the benign silence of his father on those long nights, but this would be the silence of the universe itself, and that silence would be his rest forever.

He heard the sound of Jessica screaming! A bizarre sound for someone so habitually cool and restrained. But she was clearly screaming in terror. He heard running feet, a rain of blows muffled by a soft body, and the screaming stopped, and he heard Jason's voice, angry, bitter, and out of breath, out of patience, furiously cursing his wife. In the middle distance he heard Promise screaming and Asa crying out something in terrible wrath, and the girl stopped screaming and fell to sobbing, choking on her sobs, her weeping a strangled sound of broken grief and utter horror, and in a moment she was back in the wagon with Adam. Asa spoke nearby, angrily, like a thunderclap in Adam's ear. The no-name hound growled fiercely and barked, and Asa cursed the dog, but the dog went on snarling, and Asa departed grumbling.

*Adam, they're going to hang me, my friend. At long last, they have decided. Isn't it strange? They blame me for everything. I never thought I'd die like this! What would my father say to have a son hanged? Well, now! I just hate to die so dirty! I can imagine dying well enough if they'd just let me have a hot bath first. But Mrs. Baynes says they have to have their revenge right now, Adam. Poor thing! She thinks hang-*

*ng me will restore her long-departed virginity! Well, they*
*have granted me one last request. They let me say my last*
*words to you, Adam. I don't suppose you can even hear me.*
*But if you can, remember what you swore! If you get well,*
*remember! My last words, Adam! My last request on earth.*
*Take care of Promise! My God!*

Adam felt a frenzy creeping into his consciousness. He tried to pull himself out of the bunk where he lay because the relics of his willpower were telling him to come to Harry's rescue. But his body, exhausted of all strength except the bare force to live, would not obey the command of his brain. He could not even keep his eyes open.

He did see Harry's anguished face swim briefly in his vision. A dizzying spectacle of white fringed by a rich blond beard and long blond hair falling in waves. And using all his strength and all his will, he rolled himself over and gaped out the open back of the wagon, saw Jason's wagon with its long wooden tongue, empty of the oxen, propped up high, and he saw huge Samuel lifting something dark against the sun, saw the sun shining on a yellow rope looped around the top of the wagon tongue, a rope that ran shortly down to a silhouette of a human form, and very dimly he perceived that the form was Harry and that Samuel was lifting him up to let him go and that as Samuel stepped away, the rope held Harry against the hard and awful sky, and Harry's long legs encased still in the filthy white pants that were the last badge of his respectability went kicking, kicking, kicking, and Adam could not look anymore.

But in the darkness of his soul he heard a howl of joy from the throat of Ishtar Baynes.

*Call me a whore!*

He heard Promise shrieking in hysteria, and his mind floated away again because he could not bear the world. Now he yearned with all his heart to die.

But Adam Cloud did not die. The miracle or maybe the simple perversity of cholera. It seemed to him that weeks and weeks passed, though Promise told him later that only six days went by between the time he took sick and the morning he came weakly to himself again.

He awoke in a flooding sweat that was like being drenched in a vat. He thought that he was lying in his own excrement. The idea was uncomfortable; he was ashamed. He tried to sink again into sleep. For his sleep had been so good that he did not want to wake up. When he lay sleeping it seemed that the things that had happened had all been a dream. And now he lay tentatively musing over the thought that everything might have been real after all. He was not sure he had the strength to go on living if things were real.

But he lay on blankets that were not fouled, and he was clean. The air blowing into the wagon was cool. Almost cold, though the sunlight came down through the canvas. And as he unsteadily opened his eyes and hoisted himself to a sitting position, he found that the effort did not make him dizzy, and the terrible pain in his bowels was gone. He was still so feeble that he could hardly move. Looking down at his arms and hands, he saw with dismay that they had withered; they were like the bones of a skeleton covered with dewlaps of sallow skin, and he was afraid for his vanity, for he could imagine that his face looked old.

He looked out through the open back of the wagon and saw that Jason's wagon was gone. He saw the yellow sage grass, saw it waving in the wind, saw the sky, saw that a familiar world had come back. He had to lie down again because he lacked the strength to keep sitting. Very softly and feebly he whispered, "Is anybody there?"

In answer he felt his hound licking him wetly in the mouth. He turned his head and tried to fend the dog off. In just a moment he heard Promise gently shooing the hound away, and she was drying his face carefully with a cloth.

Adam looked up at her. The face that looked down at him was so drawn, so emaciated, so horribly old, that it didn't seem like Promise. "Are you all right?" he whispered.

She could only nod; her eyes filled up with tears at the effort of communication.

"Where are the others?"

She shook her head, either to express ignorance or to make a sign that she could not speak. In a little while she went away and came back with some gruel that she fed him with a spoon. It was hot, so he knew there must be fire. Looking over her shoulder as she bent to feed him, Adam saw Henry squatting just behind her, bare-footed, peering at him with those intense, brown, thoughtful eyes.

"Henry!" Adam whispered. "I dreamed ... I thought you had gone!"

"I come back," the boy said. "I followed the rest of them over the pass, and when I was sure they was going on, I come back."

"The others have gone."

"They've all gone except us. Three days now."

"They took Jessica?"

"They taken her off with them. In the wagon that belonged to Uncle Jason. She was tied up. They taken all the oxen, too."

At the mention of her mother's name, Promise began to sob openly. Still not speaking, seemingly caught in a prodigious bewilderment. Henry reached out and stroked her long dark hair as though she had been the child and he the adult. She got up and went out, crying softly, and Henry solemnly watched her go, then moved over to a box and sat down. He looked calmly at Adam.

"She's pretty broke up. Don't say nothing all day long. Just sits. Or walks around and cries. She ain't spoke two words to me since I come back."

"Poor thing!" Adam felt tears in his own eyes. And in his heart there stirred a powerful rumination of guilt. He had wanted to die. Perhaps if he had not wanted to die, he might have roused himself. The fact that he had wanted to die so badly now seemed to him like a vague and monstrous betrayal. Something to be hidden; he hoped Henry would never know.

Henry sat, leaning forward on his sturdy knees, his brown hands folded in front of him. A very adult gesture of resignation, incongruous and touching in a child. *He won't never be a child again. He's growed up all at once.* He wore coarse, drab overalls, straps hitched over his shoulders and a shirt his mother had made him, badly worn now, with torn, short sleeves. His long blond hair, bleached nearly white by the sun, was slightly wavy; it came down to his neck. Adam looked at him, saw that he was beautiful, and remembered how Ruth had loved him.

"They've been Indians over the pass. No white folks. Some kind of Indian meeting going on back down there toward Fort Laramie. They don't come close when I holler that we got cholera here. They can understand what cholera means, I reckon. Cholera and whiskey. I reckon all the Indians can understand cholera and whiskey. Them two words." Henry spoke in toneless inflections, talking to make talk, not expecting that his words meant anything.

"Well, at least we're not bothered with Indians," Adam said. Making talk, avoiding the dark fringe of the thing so close to both of them.

Finally, after a long interval of silence Henry spoke very softly. "They hung Mr. Creekmore."

Adam felt the tears come again. "I thought they did. It was like a dream." His voice broke.

"I seen it!" Henry's voice painfully matter-of-fact, something you did not want to hear in a child his age. Children should not know things like that happened in the world. "I hid off in the sage grass and seen the whole thing. Wasn't nothing I could do. Daddy and Uncle Samuel—and Mrs. Baynes. Mr. Baynes, he got sick. I don't mean from the cholera. He got sick when he found out they was really going to do it. Uncle Jason read something out of the Bible while they held Mr. Creekmore."

The silence again. Adam heard the wind pick up, make the torn canvas on the wagon ripple, die again. Henry resumed, his voice lower still.

"Mr. Creekmore laughed at Uncle Jason. He laughed like he was at a party. They hung him off the end of the wagon tongue."

Silence again. Adam lay there with his eyes shut. He felt the hot tears trickle out of his eyes and roll slowly down his temples.

"They run off without even burying him. Cut him down and left him lying in the grass and hitched up the oxen and ran off. Mr. Jason, he was whipping the oxen like he wanted to drive 'em into hell. Miss Promise, she throwed herself on Mr. Creekmore, but he was dead. He was all bloody in the nose and the mouth."

Adam could say nothing. He felt a terrible wrath rise in him, and with the wrath strength came back. He would live now; he would live to take his revenge.

"I buried him," Henry said.

Adam was astonished and opened his eyes.

"Wasn't nobody else to do it," Henry said softly. He looked down at his bare feet. "I buried him over yonder. I dug the grave as deep as I could. It taken me all night long."

Adam's voice quavered. "You're a good boy, Henry."

"I didn't have nothing but a blanket to wrap him in. Like we buried mamma." Adam expected that Henry must cry. But the child did not falter. He kept on talking calmly, quietly, telling the way things had been, as if getting them out in the open would settle something. Finish the horror. Expose it to the sun so it would evaporate and be clean again.

"Harry wanted a coffin," Adam said, letting his eyes rest

on the blond wood of the overhead hoops of the wagon as if their strength would strengthen him. They were so still against the rippling canvas of the top.

"I didn't have nothing to make a coffin with. And I was afraid daddy might come back. I wanted to get Mr. Creekmore in the ground soon as I could. I thought I might have to run off again, with Miss Promise this time." Henry spoke slowly, his words carefully measured out but not hesitant.

Adam ruminated briefly over what the boy was telling him. That if the Jennings brothers and the Bayneses had returned, he would have abandoned Adam to them. Henry speaking factually. Adam understood. Agreed.

"You didn't want to go with your daddy." It was Adam who hesitated.

"No." Henry's big eyes met Adam's, and Adam thought the boy's mouth might have trembled.

Silence again. The wind. Adam moved slightly. Heard the rustle of his body on the blankets. After a while Henry said, "I couldn't think of no words to say over the grave neither."

"It's all right. You done what you could."

"It's better to have the words. It ain't a real funeral without the words."

Adam felt a lump in his throat, felt the hot tears coming again. He shut his eyes. He fought against crying. Did not sob. But the tears came out just the same.

"I brung the mules back," Henry said. "I hid out with them till everybody else had gone."

"You done good, Henry! Lord! You done as good as could be done."

"I taken your rifles and your pistol, too, Mr. Adam. And the little keg of gunpowder and some of that other stuff. Food and such. I didn't figure you was strong enough to use the guns. But I didn't want them other folks to steal them."

"Henry, you thought of everything."

The boy sternly shook his head in negation. "No, I didn't think how to shoot them guns. I had the pistol when I sneaked in to watch them hang Mr. Creekmore. I come up real close and laid in the grass and pointed it at daddy and pulled the trigger. But it didn't go off. It just went pop."

Adam lay there with the tears streaming down his face, his eyes shut, and he thought a long time about what Henry was saying. There was nothing adequate he could say in response.

527

So he fixed on a trivial thing. "It has to be primed. I should of taught you."

They were quiet again.

"I buried Mr. McMoultrie, too. They just left him out there and let him die in the sun. Mrs. Baynes wanted it that way."

"Did he have the cholera?"

"Nope. I think he just give up. I don't know."

Adam took a deep breath and could hardly speak. He still felt his tremendous guilt, and the thing was mingled with absurdity. He remembered the old man back in Westport Landing, how tough he was, how insanely he had died. And all because Adam Cloud had begged him to join a bunch of silly fanatics who were going West to look for the kingdom of heaven! *If it hadn't been for me, he'd be in California now. Warm and alive.* The old man's fate and how easily it might have been avoided made a shape that loomed so terribly in Adam's mind that finally he could not comprehend it.

*All hands shall be feeble, and all knees shall be weak as water. They shall also gird themselves with sackcloth, and horror shall cover them; and shame shall be upon all faces, and baldness upon all their heads . . .*

Finally he took a deep breath, and his words came out tight and constrained, like sharp things cutting his tender throat. "Don't worry, Henry. We'll get them someday. The world ain't big enough to hide them. I'll find that woman, and I'll tear her skin off her body, a patch at a time. I'll take her teeth out one at a time with a hammer."

Henry shook his head gravely. "I just hope we don't never run into any of them folks again."

Adam lay there with his eyes shut. "You wait and see," he said hoarsely. "We'll find them."

"I ain't never going to look," Henry said. The finality in his voice made him seem like an old man, very wise, and Adam thought of how the voice of Shawnee Joe always seemed to be in command of events.

"And they took Mrs. Jessica?"

"They tied her up and put her in the wagon. Uncle Jason, he beat her up something awful. He said she didn't love him. He said she'd made all the trouble by making him throw stuff out way back there. If she hadn't done it, we wouldn't of been on the river the day we was when Rachael was drowneded, and we wouldn't of been coming through the pass back there at Scott's Bluff when the storm hit us and made the wagon wreck and hurt mamma. And if we hadn't been held back all that time, we'd of been on by Independence Rock before them folks come down with the cholera, and we wouldn't never of caught it."

Henry traced the net out to the last square of logic, and Adam heard him and thought of Jessica and longed for her and their lost times together. His anger was making him sick again. Poor Jessica! Where was she? He felt terror at her helplessness. Perhaps her fate was finally worse than Harry's. But even then he could not believe that he would never see her again.

Days passed. Thought suspended. Every moment ageless, and in an ageless world time wheels on itself with no reference to anything, and no one thinks the hours pass swiftly or slowly or go by at all. Time is nothing.

Henry and Promise took care of chores, cooked when they were hungry. At night Promise slept in one of the bunks in the wagon, next to Adam, and sometimes in the still deep of very early morning he could hear her crying in her sleep. Henry took one of the rifles and the faithful hound and slept out among the mules. The rifle was much taller than he was. But Adam taught him how to prime it and shoot it, touched by Henry's determined and quiet effort to be a man, to protect the stock and themselves.

Promise fed him until he could sit up long enough to feed himself. He was a sack of bones. His skin was a dead yellow and hung on him in long folds. When he tried to walk the first time, he nearly collapsed and had to lie back down again. The slight effort cost him hours of exhaustion. He was afraid he might never get his strength back, and he lay on his bed in panic and helplessness. But he decided that his fear was a good sign. When he had been truly close to death, he had not been afraid. Finally he tried to walk again, and this time he managed a few steps, and he kept trying, and every time it was just a little easier.

He knew that cholera came back sometimes. And when it did there was no hope left. People who relapsed always died.

Adam lived for days close to the borders of life, feeble, hoping for nothing, looking out at the towering mountains and up at the blue sky through the rear of the wagon, thinking with a devouring loneliness how it might all dissolve, for he might yet die. But then he passed an intangible point, and he knew he was going to get well.

Henry came bursting into the wagon early one morning shouting, "Mr. Adam, looky here!"

Adam jumped up with a start, his heart pounding. He thought some terrible danger had fallen on them. Ishtar Baynes come back. But the boy's face was suffused with wonder and delight. "It's a cow, coming to see us!"

"A cow!"

Adam did not understand. He got carefully up, emerged from the wagon and looked. There, coming down the pass with her tremendous milk-swollen udder flopping ponderously from side to side as she walked, was a large black-and-white spotted cow. From time to time she stretched her neck and bawled. Adam recognized the demand. And in that way so common to him, he knew a surge of joy after his long darkness.

A cow! Abandoned or strayed God knows where. Come on them like manna in the desert. Adam led her up gently, saying, "Sa, bossy, sa!" He put his hand up to the large hipbone on her right, and she moved her hind leg obediently back on his side, and he took the water pail and stooped and planted his head against that hollow place in a cow's belly where the milker's head was supposed to fit. He laid hold of her big red tits, and white, foamy jets of milk went spurting down into the bucket. The frothy smell that rose up from the milk reminded him powerfully of home. But more, it reminded him of the sweet, orderly regularity of the good life.

They drank the frothy milk warm, and it was sweet and good to the taste. Adam scratched the cow behind the ears and under her neck and led her out to graze. He felt peaceful with the cow. He felt the strength in himself. He decided that it was time for them to be going now.

It was cool in the evenings. Truly cold. Adam knew it must be September already. The moon was growing again, and when the moon had been full the last time, it was August 11. Adam noticed these things in the way of farmers from time immemorial. He knew that the moon would be full again around September 10. And he knew that they would not make it to California this year.

All the haste for nothing.

His money belt was gone. He spoke softly to Promise. "Did . . . Did Mrs. Baynes take my money?" The girl nodded and tried to speak but could not. Adam put his arms around her tenderly, and she came to him and laid her head on his shoulder like a badly stricken child. He consoled her, felt her helplessness, and wondered if she would ever speak again.

Day after day she had stared out from the wagon into the relentless bright days marching over the mountains. She seemed hypnotized by the passage of light and dark, suspended in a state of numb shock, unwilling or unable to speak a word. Her stillness was only broken when she walked out into the sun to stand over Harry's quiet grave. Then she wept silently until Henry came and led her gently away.

On the day they found the cow, Adam decided they would leave. The mules had no collars. No way to hitch them up to pull the wagon. So they abandoned it and packed the mules with what provisions they could carry. They would cross the pass and find some place to winter, and in the spring they would go on to California.

"Seems funny," Adam said, musing to Henry. "Harry and me. We stopped to help you folks fix a wagon. Now we don't have none of the wagons left. If we'da knowed back then what was going to happen, we could of left all the wagons behind, put our stuff on muleback and ox-back, and we'd of been in California a month ago."

His mind filled up with what might have been, and he could not bear it.

*I should of told them on that first day, when I got back with the wheel. Harry ain't no doctor. He's just fooling. He don't know what's real and what's not.*

Two or three easy sentences. And everything would have been different.

He saw himself as the peg around which terrible events had revolved. He went back again and again to that moment in St. Louis when he refused to give up his father's money to buy them passage up the river on the steamboat. It was so vivid that he could almost shut his eyes and step through a transparent veil to that moment and make right in an instant all the things that had gone wrong since that day.

*Why, yes. I'll be glad to pay the fare for everybody.*

One sentence. A different train of events. So many lives saved.

*It was all my fault!*

In tramping moodily around in the tall grass, something caught his eye. A reflection of dull black in the morning sun, half-buried in the yellow sage. He bent and picked it up. It was Jason's diary, abandoned either because Jason had cast it away or because it had fallen by accident from the wagon in Jason's flight from this place.

The diary was a thick ledgerbook made for the balancing of accounts paid and receivable. The heavy pages were rumpled and stained with dew and rain, and the cover was swollen to the bursting in places. On the frontispiece, Jason's name was boldly inscribed in heavy, black ink. Below the name, set in quotation marks and written with even larger and more flowing characters, was the single word meant for an address: "Arcadia."

Adam turned with idle curiosity to the book itself to see what Jason had been writing night after night when he toiled so studiously at his journal. Written again and again and again was a simple message Jason had inscribed to himself: "I am good! I am good! I am good! I am good!" At times the word "good" was underlined. Sometimes it was underlined twice. Nearly always it was followed by an exclamation point. Page after page the same sentence was repeated, sometimes neatly, sometimes scarcely more than a rapid and furious scrawl. The handwriting degenerated as it marched through the book, becoming less and less legible. Finally, about two-thirds of the way, the diary was concluded with a single sentence. "Nothing is any good at all." That thought was expressed in a nearly impossible scratching with the steel pen, and after it only the white pages remained, lined in black, with blue printing clear at the top of each page: "Paid Out        Received."

Adam turned through the book again and again, as if it might tell him something else. But in vain. He looked around to see that no one had observed him pick the thing up. Then he put it down again carefully and buried it in the thick grass and left it to rot back into the earth like all dead things.

He glanced up at the peaceful sky and took a deep breath. The air was cool, even at this hour of the day. It was time to be going.

# 58

Much later on—years and years later—Adam managed to ask Promise the question that had always haunted him.

The night when they were happiest together. They were eating their first dinner after the birth of their son. Adam called him "our first-born" then, not knowing that he was both first and last. He still expected other sons to fill the big house and to anoint his heart. Slow start, long run, somebody said. And the baby asleep upstairs in his crib, watched by a diligent nurse, was the beginning of something new. Yet another beginning for Adam Cloud.

Promise was happy, too, and her eyes, so often veiled, met his directly and merrily over the candlelight, and the unhealthy lines in her face were smoothed out by her pleasure and by the soft dimness. They talked, and they laughed. Moments when they laughed together were rare. Adam had never been so happy.

He was the one to suggest that they name their son Harry Creekmore Cloud—the first time that name had been mentioned between them in years. Promise only nodded her head, for she still could not speak when his name was uttered. So the name was duly inscribed, and they were happy and shared something more fully than they usually shared things.

But while they laughed, like a ghost arriving enshrouded in the midst of their banquet, the thought of Harry's forgotten grave came to him, a grave somewhere back up there in South Pass with the wind blowing over it. He thought of the lonely stars shining coldly down, and his old guilt came back. Why had he survived when so many had died?

He thought sometimes that he ought to feel guilt for marrying Promise. He had made love to her mother. There was a taboo against incest. So people said. And there were moments when Adam was puzzled about why he felt none. A rational, dispassionate, and almost grateful wondering, for the truth was that he could not imagine what else he could have done.

And so his marriage to Promise presented him with no more guilt than the necessity to breathe or to eat. The guilt that gnawed at him was something else. Why had he lived so long? He knew there was no necessity to survival, for people had died. Harry had died.

So all at once Adam Cloud blurted out his perplexing question. "Promise, why didn't they kill us ... you and me ... back then?"

It was the first time they had ever talked of those days in South Pass. Her face clouded, and the tiny lines above her fine nose deepened. Her smile died amid the dark strands of her long hair that fell on each side of her face. Adam was nearly frantic lest he had shattered the precious moment, and for just a wink he thought she would lapse again into her habitual still silence and rise from the table without a word and in remote abstraction gather her long dress around her and go sweeping up to her bedroom, leaving him troubled and alone.

"I've always wanted to know," he said softly, insistently, holding her in her chair by his voice. "Please . . ."

She looked down at the clean linen tablecloth, stuff like Harry's ancient suit, and she fingered it with her pale and delicate hands and frowned in a daze as though that horrible scene in the hot sunlight long ago were being mysteriously reenacted on the white fabric. She stared at those images for a while with entranced and terrible fascination, and then she looked gravely up at him, and their eyes met in a solemn touch across the candlelight.

"They said we were innocent," she said very quietly. "We had not done anything wrong. Samuel said that. He would not let them kill us." And then she paused, looking at him with a steady and terrible interrogation. "They *were* right, weren't they?"

Adam understood then that Promise had nourished a secret question of her own over the years. Again he felt the burden of her mother's bold lie, come just in time to save his life. For if he had confessed his guilt with Jessica as he had wanted to do, the cholera would have attacked him as it did, and when he was helpless, they would have killed him. In one of those infinitesimal specks of time that can compress so much memory, he recalled Jessica, lying in the long, cool grass beneath him, her breath in his face, and the distant blue lightning silently flickering across the great sky.

Adam felt those memories pass, like the ghost of the light-

534

ning itself, and he looked steadfastly at his wife and said very softly, very firmly: "We *were* innocent. *You* were innocent, God knows . . . And so was I."

"Mamma said you were innocent. That there had been nothing sinful between you. Mrs. Baynes said mamma was lying. Mrs. Baynes wanted to kill you both. Like they did Harry. But Jason said they had no evidence to do that. And that if you were guilty, the cholera would kill you."

Adam laughed bitterly. "And why did he think the cholera killed Ruth? Why did it kill Rebecca?"

"He said they didn't believe. They were like the Israelites in the wilderness. God would not let them cross over into the Promised Land."

Adam shook his head. The old, frustrated anger came boiling up in him so that he could hardly talk. "Dear God in heaven!" he mumbled.

"Asa wanted to . . . to violate me. Then I would not be innocent anymore, you see. I would not be a virgin, and they could kill me. But Jason would not let him. He said they would expose me—and you—the way the Greeks used to expose their babies. And if I lived, it would be because God had decided I should live. And you, Adam. And if we died, it was because God had decided we should die."

They sat looking at each other for a long time. The candles were topped by still points of light, and Adam thought of the white snow topping the peaks of the Wind River Mountains.

"Well, we lived," he said finally. "We both lived." He made an unsuccessful effort to laugh. "I guess that proves something, doesn't it?"

There was a long, strained silence, and in its thrall Adam could hear the indistinct voice of a servant speaking in the kitchen. Echo of laughter. He had an impulse to confess to Promise the truth, that he and Jessica had been lovers. In the truth he thought there might be a faint chance of getting to his wife, finding some point of compassion where they could love each other truly and banish the vague futility that had dogged her ever since he married her in fulfillment of his vow to Harry Creekmore.

But he knew that she would recoil from him and be more remote than she had been, and he could not bear that. So he let the moment pass away and kept his silence and maintained his lie. He wondered then with a mad sense of frustration what had happened to Jessica and where she might be.

*She is probably dead!*

"I love you!" he said almost frantically across the table, his voice so full of his sudden emotion that he thought it must burst, and he reached for Promise desperately with his eyes. "I love you more than you can ever know."

She smiled sweetly at him and reached for his hand with her pale, thin one. "You have been so good to me," she said softly. "Nobody could be better to a wife than you are to me."

Her hand was cold in his, and her smile made all her delicate features look dreamy and serene. Adam's heart turned to marble in his chest. A tombstone. For never in those, rare, emotional times when he cracked with his feeling and declared his love for her, never once did she look back at his helpless and yearning face and say to him, "And I love you, too, Adam."

Like himself, she had made her own vows to Harry Creekmore, long before.

# 59

At the time, moving over South Pass in the September sunshine, Adam consoled himself with fantasies of vengeance.

He would spend his life seeking Ishtar Baynes. The rest of them, too, but especially her. And when he found them, he would rescue Jessica, and then he would kill them all one by one. He would shoot Samuel with a rifle, mercifully through the head, like an old horse. He would shoot Jason in the same cool spirit. A bullet, too, for Clifford Baynes. Perhaps a bullet in the mouth, the place where his rodent teeth stuck out, shoving his thin lips forward in that perpetual attitude of inquiring greed and hunger. Break those teeth to smithereens with a large bullet. Cherish the horror in his fearful little eyes when the gun was put up to his mouth.

Asa? Adam would kill him more slowly. Tie him up by his wrists to a stout branch on an oak tree. Scalp him alive. Build a slow fire under his naked body, just hot enough to keep him screaming. Leave him roasting there until he died. At the last, a pitcher of cool water in sight so he could beg for it. *I will sit there and drink water while he looks down at me and cries for a sip. And I will laugh at him and throw the water on the ground.*

And Ishtar Baynes. When Asa was dead, Adam would turn to her . . .

They put into Jim Bridger's fort for the winter. Jim Bridger. "Old Gabe." Trapper, farmer, scout. Guide, spinner of yarns, mysterious failure. Discoverer of the Great Salt Lake. Now he was the owner and operator with old Lewis Vasquez of a "fort," hardly worthy of the name. It was called a fort because it had a palisade. A squalid, ramshackle collection of mud-daubed log cabins within a stockade that looked ready to topple when the wind leaned on it.

Jim Bridger.

A legend before he was fifty years old. Knew the West the way the tongue knows the teeth. But he had located his trading fort just far enough off the main line of the overland trail so that most of the emigration passed him by to the north, and wealth bypassed him, too.

"We don't have no money," Adam said. "It was all stole. We was friends of Shawnee Joe McMoultrie. He said he knowed you."

"Ain't nobody got no money," Jim Bridger said, scratching himself with an expression of prodigious melancholy. He was a lanky, deeply tanned man with perpetually baffled gray eyes. But he did laugh when he talked. And when he spun yarns, his eyes gleamed with distant places, and his voice took on a hushed, reverent intonation as if to say, "Listen to me! What I'm telling you! It's the most wonderful thing to me because I seen it, and hearing's good. But seeing's better."

He looked with speculative interest at Adam. "You knowed ole Shawnee Joe, eh? Where was it you knowed him?"

"On the trail. I had the cholera. I reckon he had it, too. Something. He died of it."

Jim Bridger shook his head. "I never figured something like the cholera would get him. I thought he'd be taken off by the Blackfeet." He made a ticking noise with his tongue and looked very sad. "But folks die all kinds of ways, don't they?"

"We got our own food, and we got a milk cow. We just need a roof over our heads. I'll work for what you give us."

"It's all right," Jim Bridger said with a sigh of forlorn resignation. "You going to California?"

"Yep. My daddy's in California. He'll take care of us when we get there."

"He find gold in California?" Jim Bridger's pale eyes flashed enviously. Two pearls of interest.

"Nope, I don't reckon. I don't know. He wrote me a letter. He didn't say nothing about gold."

"Where's he at?"

"Somewheres around Sacramento. I don't know just exactly where."

"Well, you can stay, I reckon. I'll be right glad for company."

So the long winter passed. The snows piled up, and the winds came. Winds howling like nothing Adam had ever heard before. The cabins were drafty and cold away from the fire, and so there was nothing to do for days at a time but to huddle by the great mud fireplace in the main building while Jim Bridger talked.

Slowly Adam learned an astonishing fact. Men and women and even children arrive at a compromise with the horrors they have known. At least most do. He learned to treat horror like a collection of pictures kept locked up in a steel strongbox in his head, something that had happened, something fixed in memory, lying there dully gleaming like a razor in the grass, but inert. What could you do about the past? Finally nothing but lock it away. Not exactly forget about it. You could not forget. But you did not have to pore over it all the time.

You still had to do the ordinary things once the horror was gone. Eat. Forage for feed for the stock. You had to journey to where the dark spruce trees covered the snowy hills and there chop wood for fire and bring the wood back. You had to sleep. You had to fend off nightmares and get up in the morning and tramp out to the latrine. You had to keep warm, and sometimes you even had to speculate about the future.

And if the past came on you sometimes like a vertigo, dizzy and sickening, you still had to keep waiting for winter to break, for spring to come, so you could get on the way again. To make the journey that had to be continued just because you had unaccountably started it and survived it thus far and must pursue it to the end because the only other choice was to die.

He worried sometimes about how he would find his father. Increasingly he was certain that either he would not find the man at all or else that he would find him and that Joel Cloud would not want to see him.

So he tried to make some plans for what he would do when Joel Cloud turned them away. But here his thoughts collided with an icy and gloomy mystery. He did not know what he would do in the face of this final rejection.

His heart was dead except in those moments when he writhed in his fantasies of bloody vengeance. And as the listless months fell off like frozen leaves in a wind, even his vengeful imaginings became uninteresting to him. They were in their own way like the soft illusions Jason had nourished of Arcadia. They were unreal and worthless except as a narcotic for the soul. And Adam languished finally without any feeling at all.

Promise was silent, doing everything mechanically. Sometimes she cried out in her sleep, and Adam would jump up from his bed and cross the icy cabin floor to call her name softly. Invariably Henry jumped up, too. He and Adam stood shivering together in the freezing dark and waited until her breathing became even again, and then they crept back to their own sleep. She remained silent and withdrawn, seeming to sleep with her eyes open, suspended in a trance during all the long days. Slowly Adam understood that she would never truly recover from all that had happened.

Almost miraculously, spring came as usual after the hard winter. The snow melted, the wind lost its teeth, and the sun marched higher in the sky; in the valleys the grass turned green. Time to go again. Adam loaded their mules and they said their goodbyes and moved on.

# 60

So they came down to Sacramento in May of 1852, and that was the first month Adam Cloud spent in California, the golden shore.

Sacramento was as unreal to him as if he had just topped a bleak mountain and seen jasper walls rising in milky splendor before him and golden streets gleaming endlessly ahead of him, heard a fanfare of trumpets and a booming voice welcoming him to the heavenly city.

It was not physical beauty that entranced him, though the blooming spectacle of the valley where Sacramento lay did take his breath away. No, he must admit that this was not heaven but California and that California was of the earth, earthy. Sacramento! A motley collection of ramshackle frame houses cut from new wood, sometimes green when it was used for building and now warped. Some buildings whitewashed. Most unadorned by any paint at all. Some mere shacks that stood amid muck, a couple of log cabins. A few very strong, tasteless new buildings of brick rising frumpily from the general mass. And here and there Adam saw a swampy little yard where some brave woman was coaxing flowers to grow.

He thought of Ruth and wondered where her garden would have been. And in the swirl of the town Ruth seemed unreal to him. An image of the mind strangely remembered.

The city reeked of horseshit, and horses went tramping up and down, their big heads cocked in the bridles, pulling wagons that creaked and bounced and clattered, and there were brown oxen moving along, and brown mules and black mules, even a cow or two tramping through the streets, as Adam's cow did, with flopping udders and an occasional moo of soft complaint.

Men swarmed everywhere. A city ninety-five percent male. Men in long coats that looked hot in the warm afternoon sun but testified, in some way known only to the wearers, to some standing in the world. Men like Adam Cloud in rough, homespun shirts without cuffs or collars, with sweat widening darkly under galluses or across broad shoulders. Men in black woolen hats. Men with no hats but with long hair unskillfully cropped. Men with rags tied around their foreheads, still unaccustomed to the California sun. Men in tall boots in every shape of novelty and every state of decrepitude. Men passing, repassing, looking withdrawn, often grim, and sometimes rowdy. A lively tension everywhere. And Adam thought that all these men—including himself now—were measuring themselves against all the rest. He knew they were here to make good.

They looked fit for making good, these men. Adam sup-

540

posed that the long journey across the country had cut out the weak. He pondered the effect of breeding men by passing them through the harsh prairies and the high mountains, the great, continental filter of disease and struggle that strained out the dregs and drained a new race of men through the Sierra Nevada into California.

And in spite of all the hardship and the horror, the sickness and the death and the shattering of dreams and maybe of faith itself, Adam Cloud was proud of himself, proud of Henry, proud of Promise, because they had been the ones who made it. They had the right to walk the thronged streets of Sacramento simply because they were there. A place in the world created by their long march and by the elemental fact that they were still alive.

He thought back over those who had stayed behind, too fearful or too dull to move. Adam was better than all of them, and the pride that swelled in his heart was something wonderful to him, and it made Sacramento beautiful in spite of everything there that was ugly.

There were saloons. Coarse women in the saloons dealing cards and throwing dice. Music pouring out the doorways of the saloons into the crowded streets—an enchantment and an excitement that made Adam's head throb. People lived close to something final in California, out beyond all the cautious lines anybody had ever thought to tie around life. But sometimes they remembered the old restraints, the ancient orders. When Adam led the mule bearing Promise through the streets, men looked up to her. Heads turned as she passed, and one foolish, poor-looking old man with a nap of curly white hair took off his old blue cap and put it over his heart as she went by.

Sacramento surged and steamed with life, and excitement thrilled in its veins, throbbing with the combined hopes and energies of that special tribe of humankind that had made it all the way. Californians all. And riding down the earthen street, leading three mules plodding behind the one he rode—with a young woman, a boy, and a mooing milk cow—Adam Cloud knew that he had come to the right place and that for the rest of his days, California would be home.

The problem was to find Joel Cloud in Sacramento.

Adam did the only thing he knew. He dismounted and started asking people on the street, leaving Henry to guard the stock and take care of Promise. It embarrassed him to

541

speak to total strangers. "Excuse me, mister. But do you know somebody named Joel Cloud? Tall feller? Black hair? Blue eyes? About forty? You ever hear tell of a man named Joel Cloud? From Tennessee?"

Men shook their heads. After a day Adam thought it might be hopeless. But he went back a second day and a third, making a grid of the streets now, going up first one and down the next, and in the hot afternoon he came on a man in drab denim who looked at him with a cocked head and in a flash of dim recognition repeated the name. "Cloud? Hell, boy, I don't reckon I know if that's his last name or not. But they's a feller named Joel that runs a mail service for the mines. I reckon he's the only honest man in California!"

Adam was directed to a little building behind a livery stable on a dusty side street that smelled of garbage. He went there with a furiously beating heart, the no-name hound loping happily along beside him. He peeked in the glassless window and saw his father standing there, bent in conversation with a youth about Adam's age. Joel Cloud, stoop-shouldered as he had always been, heavier, older, his hair cut more neatly than Adam had ever seen it, and most astonishing of all, a pair of steel-rimmed spectacles perched on his thin nose.

The young man to whom Joel Cloud spoke was sitting with a frown of concentration at a shabby little desk made out of weathered planks. The desk had papers on it, and some wooden crates were stacked in a corner, and in his father's long, stern face, Adam saw the painful bewilderment that Joel Cloud had always experienced when he was presented with the mysteries of writing. And all the gloomy doubts that had been packed up in him like folded darkness suddenly rolled away, a burden he had carried on his back across the plains, now cut loose from him forever.

The no-name hound was less hesitant than Adam. Under the table sprawled old Luke, the paternal canine that had accompanied the paternal Cloud across the continent. The no-name hound rushed in, Luke jumped up, and the two dogs sniffed at each other and wagged their long hounds' tails. Joel Cloud was just beginning to absorb this odd reunion of familiar dogs, understanding who the newcomer was, when Adam walked in and said, "Pa."

The two of them stood looking at each other for what seemed a thousand years. Adam noticed that there was gray in his father's black hair. But in his father's face—a lined face, always shy, always embarrassed by emotion, always gentle—Adam saw every sign of love pass in a way that perhaps the two men alone understood out of all the world. Adam had big tears standing in his eyes, and Joel Cloud had tears in his eyes, too.

But they were men, not able to sob in the presence of one another, and they did not. They did not throw themselves into an embrace. Such displays of feeling were not their way. But in their very reserve and silence there was something that bound them uniquely to each other. Adam felt a great peace. He knew that his long journey had come to a good end.

"Did your mamma come with you?" Joel Cloud said at last, peering apprehensively around Adam and into the sunny street.

"She's dead. She died last year. I've been a year on the road."

"A year!"

"I had some troubles."

Joel Cloud nodded solemnly. He was too honest to pretend grief for a wife Adam knew he had not loved. He said nothing for a while, absorbing Adam, the news of death, puzzled by the suddenness of this reunion. Finally he murmured, "I knowed you couldn't of got my letter to you. I just sent it off last month. Lord, Adam! It's like a miracle of God! It's so good to see you again. Three years! I didn't think it was going to take that long when I left. You've growed!"

"Did you?"

"Did I what?"

"Really send me a letter, asking me to come?"

Joel Cloud laughed. The good, old laughter, shy and quiet. "Sure I did, Adam. I got Fonze here to write it. Didn't I, Fonze?"

The young man who had been at the table was standing, grinning, friendly and embarrassed. He put out a hand. "He sure did. I'm Fonze Ratledge, Adam. I'm right proud to make your acquaintance. Your daddy ain't done nothing but talk about you since I've knowed him."

Adam could not say anything. He looked at Fonze and squeezed his big hand, and he knew almost with a start that he was back in that limited, clear, good world where men told the truth naturally, spontaneously, without even imagining that the truth was anything special or dangerous.

"I've got a living now, Adam. A good living," Joel Cloud

543

was saying. He put his hands on his hips and arched his back. He was very proud.

"Did you find gold?"

"Well, not gold like you think. I didn't dig nothing out of the ground but dirt. But I found out folks will pay you the gold they find if they think they can trust you when they need things done. Trust! That's worth a lot of gold out here. I've got a freight business now, Adam. Freight and mail. It's a good business."

The men were silent again, grinning foolishly, appraising each other after their long separation, liking what they saw.

"You've got so big, Adam! I'd of knowed you anywheres. But you sure ain't no boy like you was when I left. You must of growed half a foot since I seed you last. You're much a man."

"You've got big, too, pa."

Joel Cloud laughed and patted his stomach. "I'm getting *fat!*"

"Nah, you ain't. You just filled out."

They hesitated once again, not knowing what they should be saying to each other after all this time. Joel Cloud looked more muscular, stronger and more confident. Adam thought of how far they had both come, how hard their journey had been, how much time had passed. He asked the question he had to ask just because it was in him, to make his father's answer a seal of sorts.

"Pa, was it worth it? Are you glad you come? Did you get some stories to tell?"

Joel Cloud grinned in his own shy way and scratched his head. "Now that you're safe and sound, Adam, it's worth all it took to come. Stories? Well, I reckon I got some stories to tell. But I ain't got time. It's hard out here. But it's real good, too. They's something always going on, and they's something abuilding all the time. I feel like we're right on top of something big out here, big and new and full of glory. Sure, boy. I'm glad I come."

Adam felt the tears rise again, and he was thankful when his father turned around.

"Adam can read, Fonze. Just like you. Fonze is real educated, Adam. He's my chief clerk. I've seen Fonze read books."

"I ain't read nothing but the Bible," Adam said.

Fonze grinned in amiable superiority. "Well, that's a start, I reckon. I sure am glad to meet a man that's educated. I fig-

544

ure it this way, Adam. The world depends on us educated men."

"I sure do depend on Fonze, and that's a fact," Joel Cloud said.

Adam smiled. He liked Fonze Ratledge.

"Listen, Adam," Joel Cloud said suddenly as though an idea had just struck him. "We need us a rider to take a load of stuff out to the goldfields north of here a piece. My other boys is all out. You reckon you could ride for us? You reckon you could find the way?"

"I got two folks with me," Adam said. "A woman and a boy. They've had a hard time. I'll tell you about it. You got somewheres they can put up?"

"Sure, they can put up with me if they ain't particular. I got me a house now. It ain't nothing fancy, but it's better than a cabin. Right now I need me a rider I can trust to get out of here this very afternoon. You reckon you could do that for me, Adam?"

Adam laughed. His father's face was so earnest that Adam realized the dreamer in Joel Cloud was gone forever, swept away by the flood of important things that needed to be done to make money this very minute. It made Adam a little sad to think of how different his father had become. And so he laughed in the way people will laugh at the unexpected in those they know well and love much.

Joel Cloud was surprised at the laughter and frowned in puzzlement. It did not seem to occur to the father that the son might want to sit down with him, recapture the lost events of three years apart. Joel Cloud was in a new world—California. He had an immediate problem, and now he had a reliable man to solve it. His son.

Adam shrugged and grinned softly and shook his head in peaceful acceptance of the common things. He was washed by an immense feeling of thanksgiving that he was alive. "Sure, pa. You put my folks up at your place and tell me where I'll need be going."

And that afternoon Adam started up to the minefields, to a settlement called Downieville, leading four pack mules laden with mail and goods for men digging the future out of the good earth.

And so that was the way Adam Cloud came to find his father in California, to end a long journey by making one that was not so long, and that is the way a new life began for him in a new land.

545

# 61

And Adam Cloud made good in California. He had a knack for making good, for surviving, and he discovered in California a knack for managing things.

Two weeks after he arrived he could sit down at the plank desk in his father's office and spread the rudimentary maps of California before him, and he could plot the roads and the towns and see in a glance just where their express company ought to be hauling goods to make the most profit, just what goods ought to be hauled, what prices they ought to charge. He could look at men and tell what they were inside, and he hired good drivers.

And one slight advantage piled up on other slight advantages, accumulated first in prosperity and then, within a decade, in wealth.

"I tell you, Adam, you were born with something," Joel Cloud said, marveling. "It's magic. And if we'd stayed back there, back in Bourbonville, we'd never of knowed what you can do. You don't owe me much, I reckon. But you owe me that. I left."

Adam laughed, pleased at the compliment, and more pleased that it was true. He was born to make good in California. And Joel Cloud had done the first deed; he had been restless, and he had been bold.

He and his father never referred to Bourbon County as home.

It was all hard work, and Adam abandoned himself to it the way his father had done. There were always things to do—deals to be made, competitors to be studied, underbid, sometimes helped, sometimes absorbed, limits to be set. "I reckon I learned one thing," Adam said. "You don't want to do too much. You don't want to try to be God. Pride goes before destruction." It was the only Scripture ever on his lips. And restrained by its caution, Cloud & Cloud moved with de-

546

liberate and circumspect power into a steady expansion that gradually made their name a power in the West.

In time the harsh memories of the journey across the continent passed into the back of Adam's mind and lay nearly forgotten among the shrouded things that he put there and did not often think about.

The years passed, and there were times when Adam Cloud glanced up at a calendar in late August when Sacramento steamed like a pot, and a chill went through him, and he shuddered, not just at the memory of those days when they were stalled in South Pass but at the swift falling of that fiery experience into the cool, remote, and mysterious realm, as broad and bottomless as a dark sea, where time goes. It seemed to him at first that he might have to endure it all again. And it was a puzzle to him that nothing ever came back and that intense experiences, glory, horror, and the petty details of ordinary life, dwindled alike to become fragments of color, smell, and disconnected sound, all fading, fading.

There were moments—especially in his later years when he moved to San Francisco—when he would walk out onto the terrace with his coffee very early in the morning, and in a way unpredictable and overwhelming the mingling of dawning air and fresh wind off the sea and the pale sky overhead combined with the strong smell of coffee to bring back those mornings on the plains so powerfully that he was nearly crushed with memory.

Then it seemed that he could shut his eyes and hear in the sea wind the creaking of the harness leather, the unsteady drone of waking voices, the rumbling complaint of the old man, and he thought he could open his eyes quickly and look toward the Pacific and see in the morning haze Jessica's lithe form bending over a ghostly fire, smell the bacon in the pan, hear its frying.

But the strange moment of that lost presence passed away as swiftly as it came. The sun continued rising out of the East, and the mist over the sea dissolved, and the solid world remained the same, and Adam walked back into the house, shaken and perplexed, to resume the life he had found in California.

At first he put advertisements in newspapers inquiring about Jessica. "Reward for information concerning Jessica Jennings, white woman, tall, blond, about thirty-five, blue eyes, last seen in the late summer of 1851 in South Pass, heading for California."

For a while he ran the ads in papers in Sacramento and in San Francisco, and then in other papers, every month. After a year he began to doubt that they would ever bring her to light again. But he continued posting them on the last day of August and on the day before Christmas. In time he looked on the little enclaves of type as flowers to be laid at Jessica's grave, and he placed them and paid for them without any hope at all that he would ever hear from them.

Henry grew up, and Cloud & Cloud sent him off to medical school in the East, to Philadelphia. Adam missed him while he was gone and was relieved and pleased when he came back and settled down to practice in San Francisco. And then he was alarmed with the years to see that Henry had not only grown up but that he began to grow old. Adam, seeing Henry in middle-aged and portly medical dignity, balding, could shut his eyes and remember him in the green meadow by the road on that afternoon long ago in Missouri. A blond, sober child, grave and vigilant even then.

*If I'd told the truth, Harry would of lived, and I never would of knowed what became of Henry. God knows what would of happened to him.*

They talked often through the years, Henry coming to sit on Sunday afternoons. They would look out over the white surf of the beach far below them to the vast, blue sea beyond, and they would talk about what was in the newspapers or what had happened to them both during the week, about who was sick, and who had died, about politics and scandal.

In the good days, before Promise died, she used to come out onto the veranda wrapped in a shawl against the cool sea wind, emerging not only from the house but from her own stillness. When Henry came, Promise could laugh and be merry. Henry was so serious that he made people laugh without trying. Adam knew that Promise remembered Henry as the last person on earth to do a service for Harry Creekmore.

Only one time in all those years did they ever speak of the journey that had brought them together. It was after Promise had died, and Adam was left alone. Henry went to Chicago to a medical conference on contagious diseases and came back and sat one Sunday afternoon with Adam, looking very preoccupied and even more solemn than Henry usually looked.

"What's eating you anyway?" Adam said.

548

"Well, I learned a real funny thing about cholera at that meeting I went to, Adam."

"Cholera!" The word made Adam shiver. "Ain't nothing funny about the cholera."

"No, I mean funny *peculiar,* Adam."

"I don't want to hear nothing about the cholera."

"All right." Henry shifted uneasily in his chair and was silent. Far out to sea a small white sail shone on the blue water.

Adam sat still, his mind in turmoil. "What was it you learned?"

Henry cleared his throat and pulled a finger around his collar. "Well, you remember when we come on those people with the cholera? At Independence Rock?"

"Do I remember? Of course I remember. What about it?"

"Well, we always thought they gave us the cholera."

Adam waited through a maddening silence. Henry cleared his throat.

"Well, it might not be so. I mean, we don't know exactly. But it just might not be so."

Adam looked queerly at him to see if sober Henry had suddenly indulged himself in a very bad joke. In some way he could not explain, he was angry and afraid. Not at Henry. At something dark, flapping its wings as though aroused from a long sleeping in his heart.

Henry spoke in a rush to get it over with. "Adam, they don't think you get the cholera by touching people that have it. Doctors treat it all the time now, and they don't get it if they're careful. You have to boil water to drink when you're around cholera, and you have to be sure you don't eat anything raw that might have grown in contaminated soil. But if you take those precautions, you are not going to get the cholera. It's infectious, Adam. It isn't contagious."

Adam nearly wept with frustration. But he held onto his outward calm. Unrelated chunks out of the past began to fall together, crushing something he had built up in his mind. "The old man, he wanted us to drink coffee when we was in the flatlands."

Henry nodded, very gravely. Adam wished Henry would laugh sometimes. Break tension. Adam felt the tension like a thin wire around his throat, tightening.

"You see, he made the wrong deduction, Adam. But he had the right idea. You boil water to make coffee. That

549

makes the water safe. But we didn't drink coffee all the time. When did we stop drinking the coffee?"

Adam wrestled with his memory. "We drunk water in Ash Hollow. The springs. I remember the springs."

"Yes," Henry said thoughtfully. "And we passed the dipper around."

"But mostly it was up above Fort Laramie." Adam brushed his hand over his face, trying to clear something away. "The old man said it was all right to drink water coming down out of the mountains."

"And we drank the water with the tin dipper. You remember the dipper? Uncle Jason passed the water around in a tin dipper. He made a ceremony out of it. You remember that?" Henry looked very sad and wise.

Adam threw up his hands. "Oh, hell, Henry, I ain't no schoolboy. I don't follow you. Just get on with it."

Henry's face grew more somber, and his words came out softly and very carefully. "All right, Adam. Don't get mad. Ain't no sense in getting mad. Not after all these years. It doesn't matter now. I'm saying this Dr. Koch has figured out that cholera is not a contagious disease. It isn't carried through the air like smallpox or even the mumps or the measles. You have to eat something or drink something with the cholera germs in it, or you have to kiss somebody that's got the cholera. And that's how you get it."

"I don't see what that's got to do with it."

"When you and Harry came back to us, after you'd buried the dead, you went over to the river and washed yourselves up with lye soap. You even boiled your clothes because you said . . . I remember it was you that said you wanted to get the stink of death out of them. Do you remember that?"

"Yes, I remember."

"And you didn't eat anything over there. You didn't drink anything."

"I don't know. No, we didn't. We didn't eat anything. That man with the bacon . . . Or drink anything. We didn't drink anything but water out of the river."

"All right. All right. I'm saying if a doctor does that today, he can be in the middle of a cholera epidemic, Adam. And he's not going to get the cholera."

"Well, *we* sure got the cholera, goddammit!"

"All right. When you were burying those people, you might have wiped your mouth. Wiped the sweat out of your face. Something. Got the germs in you that way. But it isn't likely.

550

It's more likely we got it from somebody who was traveling with us."

Adam felt a chill surge up his spine, and the goosebumps came out on his arms. He was sitting in a Japan chair, and suddenly it became unbearably sharp and disagreeable. He got out of it and heavily paced the floor. "What do you mean? Who? Who was it?"

Henry shook his head hopelessly. "We'll never know that. But there are people who can carry disease germs around in their bodies—their mouths, their intestines, wherever. They don't get the disease themselves. Or if they do, it's a mild case. Doctors call them carriers. I figure we had somebody carrying the cholera along with us, all the while we were coming West. And then something triggered it off. We don't know what; we never can know that. Can't understand. But when ... Well, the dipper. Handing it from mouth to mouth. When we started drinking out of the dipper, the disease had a chance. It waited for a while. Then it got out, and it hit all those people who didn't have some kind of natural immunity to it."

Adam shook his head heavily. His entire conception of the past was breaking up: Harry had suffered because he lied. Guilt brings retribution. If he—Adam Cloud—had not been seized by arrogance, his yearning to humiliate Harry, then none of them would have got the cholera. Adam married Promise because he told himself he ought to be punished for what he had done. Something comforting to a universe where evil deeds were punished, even if you were the one who suffered. And now the growing conviction that he might not have been responsible for the cholera was not a comfort but a devouring darkness. He wished Henry would stop; but Henry was intent now, pursuing this abysmal line of thought as if he were on the trail of a difficult diagnosis.

"You remember when Uncle Samuel took sick that night?"

"Yes, yes, I remember." Adam impatient. And after all these years he could feel the blood rush to his face in shame. Samuel got up that night. Found him with Jessica out in the dark. *Where did Jessica go?*

"Well," Henry went inexorably on, "as I look back on it, I figure what Uncle Samuel had was a mild case of the cholera. It's hard to know . . . But it wasn't much of anything. A bellyache. So there must have been something in Jennings blood to fight it off. I didn't get it. Uncle Jason didn't get it." He paused for a very long time. "My father didn't get it."

551

After forty years it was still almost impossible for Henry to speak of his father.

Adam cleared his throat. "Several folks didn't get it if you remember," Adam said testily.

Henry nodded in that maddeningly sober way of his. "Well, I figure that somebody who didn't get it was carrying it and gave it to them that did come down with it. Uncle Jason, maybe. Maybe my father. Uncle Samuel. Maybe me. One of us that didn't get the sickness."

"I bet it was Mrs. Baynes."

"It could just as easy have been Aunt Jessica."

Adam wrestled with something too big for him to hold. "Henry, them folks at Independence Rock *did* have the cholera, dammit! We got it *after* we run into them!" Adam's blast was a cry for sense.

But Henry looked very professional and superior, armed with knowledge. Adam remembered the expression in Harry Creekmore. He supposed all doctors wore it as a badge. "Just coincidence, Adam. I don't think they gave it to us. You say that something happens just because it comes after something else, and you don't have science. You have superstition. This *is* the nineteenth century, Adam. We've left some notions behind."

"You're trying to tell me Harry Creekmore died because of a . . . a *coincidence!*"

"I guess so. Yes. I guess that's what I'm saying." Henry shook his head and pursed his lips and let his eyes drift out to sea. "But so what, Adam? People die in accidents all the time."

"No," Adam said. "It wasn't that way." He bit down on his jaw. But he knew Henry was right. He felt a blackness yawning beneath his feet.

*I just wish one time in my life things would be what they seem to be.* An old thought, and he was wandering alone in the infinite dunes. He and Henry talked of other things after that and never brought up the subject of cholera again.

But sometimes Adam brooded about his life. And sometimes in the deep of night he awoke with a start and looked at the clock ticking away beside his lonely bed, and he remembered Promise, and he resented her.

*She could have tried to love me!* He thought he had deserved her love for all he had sacrificed to her. And sometimes with her long in the grave, he was still angry with her for not giving him a chance, not pushing aside in her heart the figment of a Harry Creekmore who had never given her anything but dreams. In the daylight, he knew that love is never a bargain, mere promises exchanged and kept. He recalled his oath to Harry, and he was doggedly proud to have kept it faithfully, and it was only in the middle of the night that he sat up thinking of how different his life might have been if it had not been for Harry Creekmore.

Sometimes he thought involuntarily of Sylvia Roberts. And knew with a bitter and moody irony that the woman he did marry and serve devotedly never gave him half so much as Sylvia Roberts in her yellow cotton dress had given him at one meal on a bright Sunday in a mysterious springtime, long, very long ago.

But then Adam reflected that there must be a fatality to all the past, and you might as well resign yourself to it. It seemed that everything that had happened was fastened by unbreakable steel wire to everything else. Things had to be just the way they were. No use blaming anyone for them, for everyone was caught up in the same grinding machine, and everyone finally triumphed a little and suffered much. He thought of his mother and how proud she had been of her shabby porch and how she had died unloved.

*We are chips on the flood.* Jessica's thought. True.

Henry's revelation about the cholera, if it were true (and nobody could know for sure), somehow made the flood more dark and more terrible than before. And rising in the blackness was Adam's certainty that Jessica had been made of stronger stuff than Promise. Jessica could forget things, make a new life, live with the daily work. And if Jessica had survived . . .

Adam came to resent Promise even when she was still alive, for she was not as resilient, not as wise, not as bold, not as profound as the woman her mother had been. He never expressed the resentment. There would have been no use. It was just the way things fell out.

And Harry Creekmore, riding gallantly toward that ominous encampment of death-soaked, abandoned wagons at the base of Independence Rock was something inevitable. Even if they had not caught the cholera from that doomed encampment, people thought Harry was responsible. And what they thought was more important than the truth. Harry had ridden out there to be a man in the eyes of Promise, to act a part to stir her feelings, and he had died in that slowly swinging rope, an awful black against the soft blue sky, playing his role to the end so that she might remember him as a hero long after the curtain had fallen.

Well, it had worked out precisely the way Harry had intended, and he could be at rest back there in the forgotten and unmarked grave where he lay, underneath the wind blowing down out of South Pass. Harry had been remembered, and he had been adored. And the whole drama of Adam's life was changed by the role Harry insisted on playing. And what was there to do about it once it was all done? The dead could ensnare the living, but the living could do nothing to the dead, not even curse them.

So the play was finished. The audience had left the theatre. Adam sat alone on the stage, ruminating into the dark pit of empty seats.

Promise never responded to Adam in the night, and in all their years together he made love to her only rarely and always felt afterwards that he had done something vaguely wrong, not because he had loved her mother and violated the ancient taboo, but because he had violated another man's wife when that man loved her and she adored him. Always he felt unfulfilled and sad after it was over, and finally he left his wife alone.

Yet he was faithful to her because he loved her in his way, and he could not bear to be unfaithful to that love no matter how little she loved him in return. He assuaged the needs of his body by working very hard. He did have a son. A miracle, he thought it was. And he loved his boy. The boy loved him, and because he was born to be the kind of person he was, Adam Cloud did not let his occasional brooding and the sadness in the back of his mind convince him that life was in vain. His life seemed to define itself as a pattern of obligations, and he labored to meet them, to keep his responsibilities to the world in order, and to sustain those in his family and without who depended on him.

And when Promise lay dying, still not old but worn out by the invisible erosion within, she smiled with her eyes closed dreamily, her black hair spread like a delicate fan around her pale face and over the white of the pillow, and she murmured very softly, "Harry?"

Her son spoke to her hesitantly, bending over her, putting his hands gently on her thin, white shoulders. A beautiful boy, slender and with delicate features like herself, earnestly looking at her and saying, "Mamma? I'm here, mamma. Mamma?"

554

But he was not the Harry she called. Her eyes fluttered open in surprise and pleasure and looked beyond her boy, beyond the walls, beyond the limitations of time and space. "I knew you'd come!" she whispered. She shut her eyes in rapture and breathed deeply once and not again, not calling Adam's name. That single sentence spoken to the mystery around them was her last word, and Adam turned away and looked out to the broad sea and wondered with a sigh if Harry Creekmore and Promise knew that they were together at last.

From a successful express business Cloud & Cloud went rather naturally into railroading. The age of the long-distance wagon displaced by the age of steam, Cloud & Cloud liquidated, its assets vanishing into the steel treasure of the Central Pacific Railroad, empire of speed.

When old Leland Stanford died in 1893, Adam Cloud happened to be standing next to the grave, his head bare and his hat respectfully in his hand, when a newspaper photographer took a picture. The picture appeared the next day in one of the San Francisco newspapers. The caption identified Adam as "A friend to Senator Stanford for over forty years."

A few days later Adam was sitting in his office, staring out the large window over the bay, lamenting Leland Stanford, thinking within himself that perhaps it was time to retire. One of his secretaries came in wearing a queer look, mingled humility, curiosity, and scorn. "Mr. Cloud, sir ... There's a woman out here to see you ... A very dirty woman, sir."

"A woman?"

The discomfort in the male secretary's face was terrible. "Yessir. I tried to get rid of her. But she swears she knew you a long time ago. She says you'd want to see her."

Adam puzzled over the man's expression and over his announcement. "What's her name?"

"Baynes, Mr. Cloud. She said to tell you she was Mrs. Clifford Baynes."

"Ishtar Baynes!" Adam cried aloud and jumped up in such emotion that the secretary, a weak, thin young man named Harrison, turned pale.

"I'll tell her to go away," Harrison said, recoiling. "I couldn't imagine that you'd want to see anybody that looked like her. But ... She insisted I tell you, Mr. Cloud."

Adam was filled with fury, disbelief, and loathing. The name was a cry from a nightmare world. He fought to control himself. "No, no," he said with difficulty, his voice husky and strained to the breaking. "Show her in, Mr. Harrison. And you stay just outside the door, you hear? If I start to kill that woman, you come in here and stop me."

And so Adam was standing, breathing very hard and glowering over his large, mahogany desk, when the polished oaken door opened again, and a bent, gray form came hobbling in, holding her thin arms over her sunken chest as if to keep warm and looking around with the bright, inquisitive, and greedy eyes that he remembered so well.

"Well, now, Mr. Adam, it looks like you done right well for yourself." She had become creaky with age, her body badly misshapen, and Adam would not have known her had they passed on the street. She looked at him with a conniving, gap-toothed grin, her mouth soft and shapeless, her face splotched with age, and Adam could see that her fingers were so twisted and lumpy with arthritis that she could not completely unclench her hands. "I've worked right hard myself, but the world ain't a place for justice, Mr. Adam." She heaved a pitiful sigh. "I ain't got nothing like this to show for all *my* work." She looked around, out the large window to the sea, and her rheumy eyes measured it all—the draperies, the fine leather chair in which Adam sat, the porcelain vase of roses on his desk, the silver frame on the wall that held the portrait of Promise on the day that she had married Adam.

Mrs. Baynes hobbled over and peered up at the picture like a witch. "That's Miss Promise, ain't it? How is she?"

"She's dead, Mrs. Baynes." Adam was outraged at the decent normality of his tone, but he could not help himself.

"Oh, she is, is she? Too bad. Too bad." Mrs. Baynes made a ticking noise with her tongue. "Well, we all got to go sometime. I bet you gave her a rich funeral, Mr. Adam. Spent lots of money on her coffin."

"She's in a vault," Adam said. "Safe from the damp."

"How much did that frame there cost you, Mr. Adam? The one with her picture in it?"

"I don't remember."

"Ah, these rich folks that's got so much money they don't remember what they paid for something as nice-looking as that frame there!" She turned back to Adam, and her malicious little eyes searched him up and down. "Well, well, well! I never dreamed you and me would run into each other again, Mr. Adam. I seen your advertisement in the papers. But I figured back then you wouldn't give me nothing if I come in to see you. And then I seen that newspaper picture the other day with you standing by that Stanford feller's grave, and I figured we're all going to die someday. Ain't that what you figure, Mr. Adam?"

"I don't reckon it's so far away for either one of us, Mrs. Baynes." Adam furious at himself for being so cool and restrained. He wanted to jump on this old woman and beat her to death. But she held him entranced.

She sat down without being invited, sat with her twisted hands in her lap, and looked up at Adam with the contrived and falsely benign grin of an old aunt come home. "You've got old, Mr. Adam. Too bad. You was real good-looking when you was young. But God! How you've broke!"

"I always said that if I could find you, Mrs. Baynes, I'd kill you on the spot."

"Why, lordy, I don't see why you want to kill *me*, Mr. Adam! Lordy, lordy! What's done is done, ain't it? It's all water under the bridge, ain't it? Let bygones be bygones, I always say."

"Let bygones be bygones!" Adam repeated the words in a stupor. "After all you did!"

"I didn't do *nothing*, Mr. Adam! *Nothing!*"

Adam was nearly beside himself. "You *killed* Harry Creekmore!"

"Oh, tush, Mr. Adam! I didn't do no such thing. You think a poor, weak woman like me is going to kill somebody! It was Asa and . . . and what was his name—the big man?"

"Samuel. My God! You don't even remember!"

"Oh, I've been through a lot since then, Mr. Adam. You can't expect me to remember their names. And their brother? What was he called? The one with all the funny ideas?"

"Jason."

"Jason! That's it. Sure enough. You know, I was trying to think of his name just last year or maybe back before that. And I couldn't do it to save me."

"Dear God, Mrs. Baynes! Dear God! How could you forget!"

"Oh, my memory ain't as good as it used to be. Well, anyhow! It was the big man and, and Asa that killed your friend."

"Harry Creekmore."

"Well, I just watched. And it ain't no crime to watch a hanging, is it? Lordy, if it was, you'd have to put everybody in California in jail! Wasn't you here during the vigilante time, Mr. Adam?"

"Yes."

"Then you seen a lot of folks hanging on the streets. Well, those men that hanged your friend, they got what they deserved in the end. Believe me, Mr. Adam!"

"What do you mean?"

She looked at him with a sly and crafty grin. "Wouldn't you like to know?"

Adam leaned forward on his desk, bracing himself with his clenched fists. His knuckles were white. "Goddamn you, woman! You tell me what you know!"

She was impervious to fear. "Sure I will, Mr. Adam ... For a price."

Adam collapsed in his chair, the wind knocked out of him. His chest hurt. "A price?" He sounded weak and foolish to himself.

"A price, Mr. Adam. Like you say ever year in your advertisement in the newspapers. A reward. Here you are—a rich man. And I ain't got nothing. I've been a washerwoman for forty years. And I can't do nothing no more because of my hands. All I got left to my name is a little information. And it's up in my head where nobody but me can touch it. If you want to buy it, I'll sell it. But you ain't going to get nothing out of me for nothing."

She smirked. He resisted the impulse to leap over the desk and strangle her on the spot. He knew she had him in a trap.

"How much do you want?"

"It'll cost you plenty."

"How much?"

She looked spitefully around at the fine furnishings in his office and looked coldly back at him, took in her breath—and dared.

"It'll cost you one hundred dollars!" She pronounced the sum as if it were prodigious and with the finality of a last offer. Adam nearly laughed. But he contained himself.

With all the contempt at his command, he reached inside his coat and drew out his black leather wallet and removed two new, green fifty-dollar bills and flung them down on the desk. She snatched them up clumsily in her stiff hands and looked at him, knowing she should have asked for more.

"And now, Mrs. Baynes, if you do not tell me what I want to know, I shall call the police and have you thrown in jail!"

"You can't just throw me in jail for nothing! This is America." She tried to sound defiant.

"A man in my position can have a woman like you jailed any time he wants," Adam said calmly.

She hesitated, looking first at him and then at the green money clutched in her knotty hands. Her little pink tongue darted out and moistened her thin, dry lips. She leaned forward in the chair with a terrible eagerness. Adam thought once again that she resembled some evil predator bird searching a field for helpless mice. Finally she sat back and looked him coldly in the eye.

"I reckon the Indians kilt 'em. Good enough for 'em, if you ask me."

"Indians! What Indians?"

"Oh, I don't know what Indians. My God, Mr. Adam. I ain't never wanted to be no expert on Indians. All I know is we was riding along pretty as you please down the Humboldt River, and them Indians taken after us. It was that Asa's fault."

"Asa!"

"We was hungry. Real hungry. And we come on an Indian village at night when all them redskins was sleeping. These was not particular smart redskins, Mr. Adam. They didn't even have nobody keeping watch. And that Asa, he said we'd have to kill 'em to get something to eat. And him and his brothers, why they just waded in with knives and done it up good."

Adam felt truly sick now. "Jason, too?"

"Sure, him too. They just all moved in on them redskins and chopped them up like they was butchering hogs. Lordy, it was bloody! The big 'un . . ."

"Samuel . . ."

"Well, he had hisself a good time, he did. He kept laughing and laughing. I think he was crazy myself. He had blood up to his shoulders, and it was dripping off his hands, and he had it all over his clothes. I think he would of eat them redskin carcasses if the oldest one would of let him."

Adam pressed his hands to his face. Ishtar Baynes went on, apparently oblivious to his agony.

"Well, next day, some of the friends of them Indians that was kilt in their blankets, they got to chasing us. But Clifford and me, we taken the horses and rode on ahead and got away. But them three brothers, I never seen them again. I reckon the redskins got all three of 'em." She made a ticking noise with her tongue. "I think I heard that big 'un screaming bloody murder when they got to him. Lordy, it was awful!

559

You know how mean redskins are. They torture people when they catch 'em. They're just a bunch of savages if you ask me. The oldest one of them brothers, Jason? Well, he had one good idea. He said the redskins ought to be wiped off the face of the earth. Like the Canaanites in the Bible."

"Jesus Christ!" Adam whispered. "Oh, sweet Jesus Christ!"

"But let me tell you, Mr. Adam. Clifford and me, we knowed it wasn't none of our business about them redskins. We just kept kicking them horses, and I thank the good Lord in heaven above for His blessings. Me and Clifford got clean away."

Adam opened his eyes and looked at her, remembering a detail. "Horses? We didn't have any horses, Mrs. Baynes. Where'd you get horses?"

Ishtar Baynes leaned back in her chair and crowed with her ancient delight at knowing something nobody else knew. "Why, of *course* you didn't know nothin' about them horses, bless your heart! We got the horses for Mrs. *Jessica!*"

Adam stared at her, stricken and dumbfounded.

"You see, maybe two, three days after we left you folks, we run smack into some other Indians. They was on their way to ... or maybe they was coming back from some big meeting somewheres. Some big redskin congress, I reckon. I tell you, they was redskins all over the place. Millions and millions of 'em. I was scared out of my wits."

"Indians!" Adam said dully.

"Not the same ones that kilt them three brothers now, Mr. Adam. No, these here Indians I'm talking about was a long time before that. We wasn't even down in the desert yet when we run into *these* Indians."

"Oh, my God. My God." Adam murmured, his words barely audible.

"And the oldest one, Jason, he taken the notion to swap Mrs. Jessica for five horses."

Adam felt himself beginning to cry. Mrs. Baynes did not even notice.

"He sure was mad at her for being so beautiful and not loving him. Not believing in him. He said she'd cast a hex on him. If you ask me, he was mad for the wrong things, Mr. Adam! But I reckon you know about that!" She shot him a snide and knowing look under her thin brows and laughed obscenely with that limp and nearly toothless mouth. "Anyhow, that's what he done. Law, law! I never will forget how the poor woman begged and screamed and took on something

560

terrible when that Indian grabbed her and taken her off! It would of broke your heart to hear it." She chuckled involuntarily.

Adam glared at her, his eyes running with tears, and his look was so filled with hatred that Ishtar Baynes quickly changed her tone from exhilaration to abject pleading.

"I done my best to stop it, Mr. Adam. Believe me I did. I said, 'Mr. Jennings, it ain't Christian to do what you're doing.' But he had a heart made out of steel, that man did." She lowered her voice as if to take Adam into a special confidence. "Tell you the truth. I always did think that man was kind of crazy. Didn't you, Mr. Adam? Well, we did get five horses for her, and it turned out we needed them five horses. Clifford and me, we wouldn't never of got away without them five horses."

"Five horses." The tears were rolling down Adam's cheeks. He wiped at them clumsily with the sleeve of his coat.

"Me and Clifford, we had them horses up ahead when the redskins got to chasing us down along the Humboldt. And we had the food in bags that them brothers had stole from the ones they killed. And we just come on. The brothers, well, they was back with the oxen and that old wagon, and we didn't go back to see how they was doing. I mean, you can't blame us for that, can you, Mr. Adam? We had to save ourselves, didn't we? It's the first rule of life. Save yourself."

"Jessica loved cities," Adam said dully, stupidly. "She would have loved San Francisco. So much to do here. To see. She could have heard music."

Ishtar Baynes shook her head and showed no feeling but the rare pleasure at being the center of attention. "Well, we don't always get what we want in this old, cruel world, do we, Mr. Adam?"

Adam shook his head. Everything was a blur. He felt cold, very cold, and it was hard to breathe.

"I sure didn't get what I wanted," Mrs. Baynes went on with a moist sigh. "I never did have me no hat shoppe. Now I don't reckon I ever will have nothing."

Adam moved his lips, but no words would come out.

"I been in California ever since, Mr. Adam. I saw your advertisements and started to come to see you lots of times. But I was afraid you wouldn't want to see me. I just waited till I had to come."

"The Indians treat their women worse than slaves," Adam murmured.

She seemed not to hear him; perhaps his voice was too muddled and low. "Do you remember Clifford, Mr. Adam? Tell the truth, if he'd got what *he* deserved, he'd of got scalped hisself! After all I done for him, getting him out here safe and sound, you know what the lowdown rascal done when we got to California? He left me flat! I don't know what ever happened to him. Personally I hope he died a horrible death, lonesome and sick and calling for me, Mr. Adam. He deserted me cold. And it was all your Mr. Harry Creekmore's fault. That awful story he told on me. About me being a whore and all that. It set Clifford's mean little heart against me, the rat!"

"But it was true what Harry said, wasn't it, Mrs. Baynes?" Adam's voice was husky and immeasurably strained. "You were a whore!"

"Sure, I was a whore back before I met Clifford. What's a woman to do, Mr. Adam? It's a man's world. And a woman's got to use what the good Lord gives her to make a living the best way she can. But as long as Clifford didn't know nothing about it, it didn't hurt nothing, did it, Mr. Adam? It was all water under the bridge, and I'd come out of it alive. Let bygones be bygones, I always say. Mr. Creekmore done me wrong, Mr. Adam. He brought up the past when it ought to of laid buried. We ought to forget about the past."

"Mrs. Baynes, you stole my money! The money I was carrying out here for my daddy. That money belonged to him and me. It come from selling our place back in Tennessee. You walked off with years of hard work. Now whose fault was that, Mrs. Baynes?"

"Well, you was sick fit to die, Mr. Adam. And I didn't see no stores for you to spend your money in, not out there in the mountains where we left you. And I didn't see no banks for you to put it in. And I figured I had as good a right as anybody to it, way things was, Mr. Adam. If you'd of died, the first wild Indian that come along would of got your money. And what's a redskin going to do with money, Mr. Adam? You tell me that!"

"I didn't die."

"That's just a detail, Mr. Adam. You was supposed to die. You had the cholera. Folks die when they get the cholera. I thought you was going to do what you was supposed to do. You can't blame me if you up and lived."

Adam put his face in his hands and helplessly, blindly, shook his head. "My God, Mrs. Baynes! My God!" He

562

looked up at her, feeling whipped and sick. "What did you do with my money?"

"Well, now, that's the *real* tragic thing, Mr. Adam. Clifford, he stole it from me when he runned off! Used your money to get shut of me. Tell you the truth, Mr. Adam! They's been many a time I wisht I'd of left your nasty old money for some redskin to buy hisself a bunch of whiskey with. If Clifford hadn't got his dirty little paws on that money, he wouldn't of never had the nerve to run off and leave me behind. I'd have Clifford yet! *And I'd show him a thing or two!*"

"So you never did get your hat shop," Adam said dully.

The worn old woman that Ishtar Baynes had become shook her gray head mournfully, and Adam saw on her withered face a genuine expression of sorrow. "No I didn't, Mr. Adam. And let me tell you! California sure did miss a style leader when I didn't get my hat shoppe! I could of put this state on the map! Lordy, lordy! How the cruel world has abused me, Mr. Adam. And I don't deserve it! I'm just a poor, simple woman that ain't never meant no harm to nobody."

Adam gaped at her like a fool and felt giddy. The smell of the roses in the blue vase on his desk made him sick. Ishtar Baynes was here, in his power. Forty years before, he would have given his life for such a moment. Vengeance would have been honey in his mouth, gold in his hands.

But how did you take vengeance against an arthritic old woman more than four decades after her crimes? *My God,* Adam thought in a kind of terror, *how old is she?* What did you do when she did not even admit to any crimes? How did you strangle her for murder when the worst thing she could imagine about her life was that she had failed to win a hat shop in California? How could you even think of sweet revenge when she grinned gummily and breathed her foul breath on you and said with sugary sincerity, "Let bygones be bygones," as if she were gracefully willing to forgive you for your wrath against her ancient wrongs?

Adam Cloud did not know the answer to any of these questions.

He thought of Jessica. She must have died a long time ago.

He had to clear his head and clear this vile woman out of his office. Otherwise he would not choke her, but he would strangle for air in her presence. A final irony! Summoning all his strength, he got up and called out in a loud voice, "Mr. Harrison! Mr. Harrison! Come in here!"

Harrison appeared immediately, opening the door, white-faced, frightened.

"Get this woman out of here!" Adam croaked. "And if she ever sets foot in this office again, you call the police and have her thrown in jail for trespassing on railroad property!"

Harrison advanced in a clumsy rush to lay hold of Ishtar Baynes. But she was already getting painfully to her feet, looking bored with Adam's show. "My goodness, Mr. Adam," she said impatiently. "You don't have to raise such a commotion. Why do you think I'd be coming back here? I don't have nothing more to sell you." She gave him a cold look of contempt. And pushing Harrison aside like so much straw, she went hobbling out without looking back, and that is the last Adam Cloud ever saw of her.

*What kind of fucked-up world is it when you can't even get revenge against somebody like her!*

Well, it was funny when he thought about it. Funny in the way complete absurdity is funny. Harry Creekmore would have laughed about it if somebody could have told him the story.

So many had died. But Ishtar Baynes had survived. Adam sometimes felt guilty even yet because he had not perished. But to her, survival was all the vindication she required. She was alive; and so she had done no wrong. The Jennings brothers had been killed out of a misplaced courtliness lingering in the midst of their savagery. Adam could see it. They had sent her on ahead with her worthless and trembling husband, while they stood their ground as men were supposed to do to defend a woman against savages.

*Poor fools!*

Samuel screamed. Probably meant that he was scalped alive. Digger Indians in the valley of the Humboldt. The Diggers were scarcely men. They delighted in scalping their enemies alive, mutilating them, killing them slowly. Samuel's fate. Probably the fate of the others, too. There was something horrible in thinking of the big, simple man swarmed over by a crowd of yowling savages, much smaller than he, thirsting for his blood because he was big, as though he had been a moose or a buffalo. And the bizarre thing was that though Adam could imagine it all vividly, he could take no satisfaction from it. It was not justice for what they had done to Harry, to Jessica. Not even revenge. Just something that had happened. Death. Like sunrise or sunset. All three of them probably died without any thought that they were being punished for anything. Jason probably thinking until the very first gush of the hot blood in his slit throat that he would be spared by a miracle. To build his Arcadia.

Adam stood exhausted at the window in his office and looked out to the misty sea. Waves were rolling in long swells against the sandy beach and the wind was blowing lines of water across the waves, so that the pattern was crisscrossed and in such constant motion that he could not fix his tired eyes upon it.

## About the Author

Richard Marius is the author of two highly praised books—a novel, *The Coming of Rain,* and a biography, *Luther.* He is an editor of the Thomas More papers at Yale and a professor of history at the University of Tennessee. He lives in Knoxville with his wife and three children.